Ham Helsing

MONSTER HUNTER

ALSO BY RICH MOYER

HAM HELSING #1: VAMPIRE HUNTER

Ham Helsing

Monster Hunter

Rich Moyer

WITH COLOR BY **JOSH LEWIS**

CROWN BOOKS FOR YOUNG READERS
NEW YORK

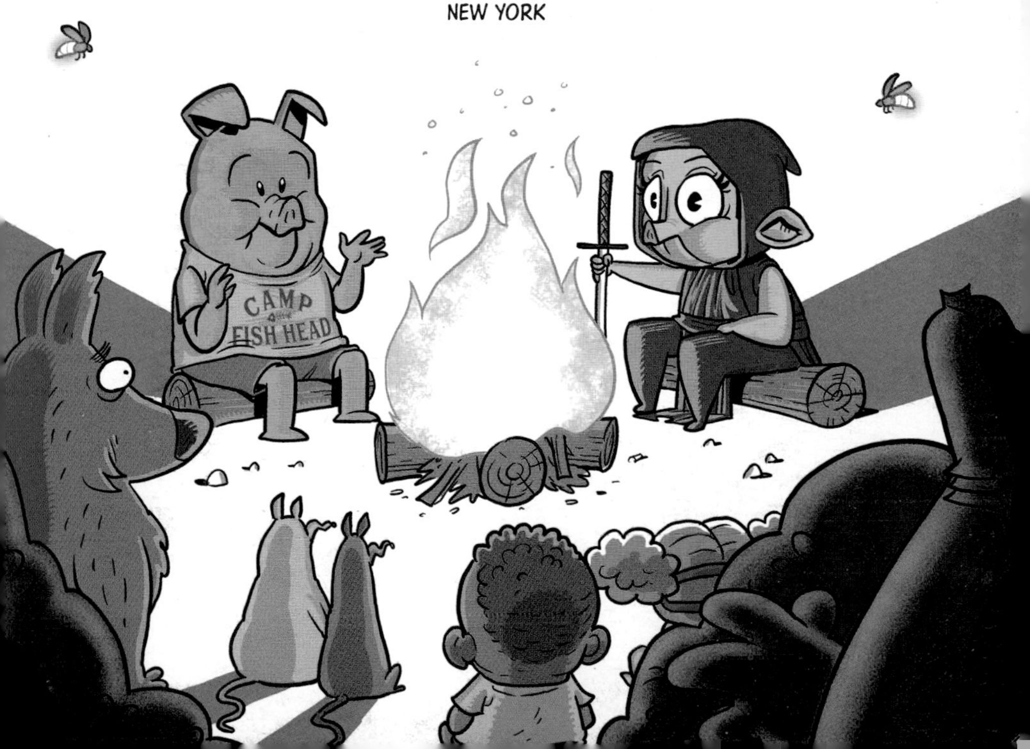
CAMP
FISH HEAD

This is a work of fiction. Names, characters, places, and incidents either are the product of the author's imagination or are used fictitiously. Any resemblance to actual persons, living or dead, events, or locales is entirely coincidental.

Visit us on the Web! rhcbooks.com
Educators and librarians, for a variety of teaching tools, visit us at RHTeachersLibrarians.com

Library of Congress Cataloging-in-Publication Data
Names: Moyer, Rich, author. | Lewis, Josh (Illustrator at Templar Books), colorist.
Title: Ham Helsing, monster hunter / Rich Moyer ; with color by Josh Lewis.
Description: First edition. | New York : Crown Books for Young Readers, [2022] | Series: Ham Helsing ; 2 | Audience: Ages 8–12 | Audience: Grades 4–6 | Summary: Ham Helsing and his crew are back to fight more monsters at mysterious Camp Fish Head Lake.
Identifiers: LCCN 2021043494 (print) | LCCN 2021043495 (ebook) | ISBN 978-0-593-30895-0 (hardback) | ISBN 978-0-593-30896-7 (library binding) | ISBN 978-0-593-30897-4 (ebook)
Subjects: CYAC: Graphic novels. | Pigs—Fiction. | Monsters—Fiction. | Humorous stories. | LCGFT: Funny animal comics. | Monster comics. | Graphic novels. Classification: LCC PZ7.7.M74 Haj 2022 (print) | LCC PZ7.7.M74 (ebook) | DDC 741.5/973—dc23

Cover design, logo, and inside color by Josh Lewis

MANUFACTURED IN CHINA
10 9 8 7 6 5 4 3 2 1
First Edition

Juno and Cleo. Sensitive,
smart, creative, and brave.

Seeing the world through
your eyes has been the joy
of my life.

If smiles were currency,
you'd have made me the
richest dad in the world.

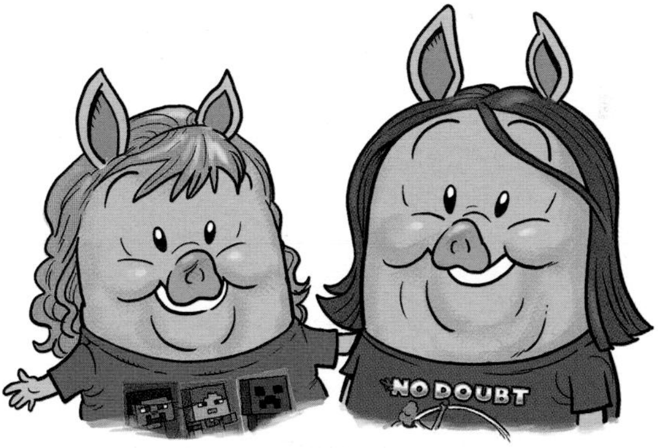
NO DOUBT

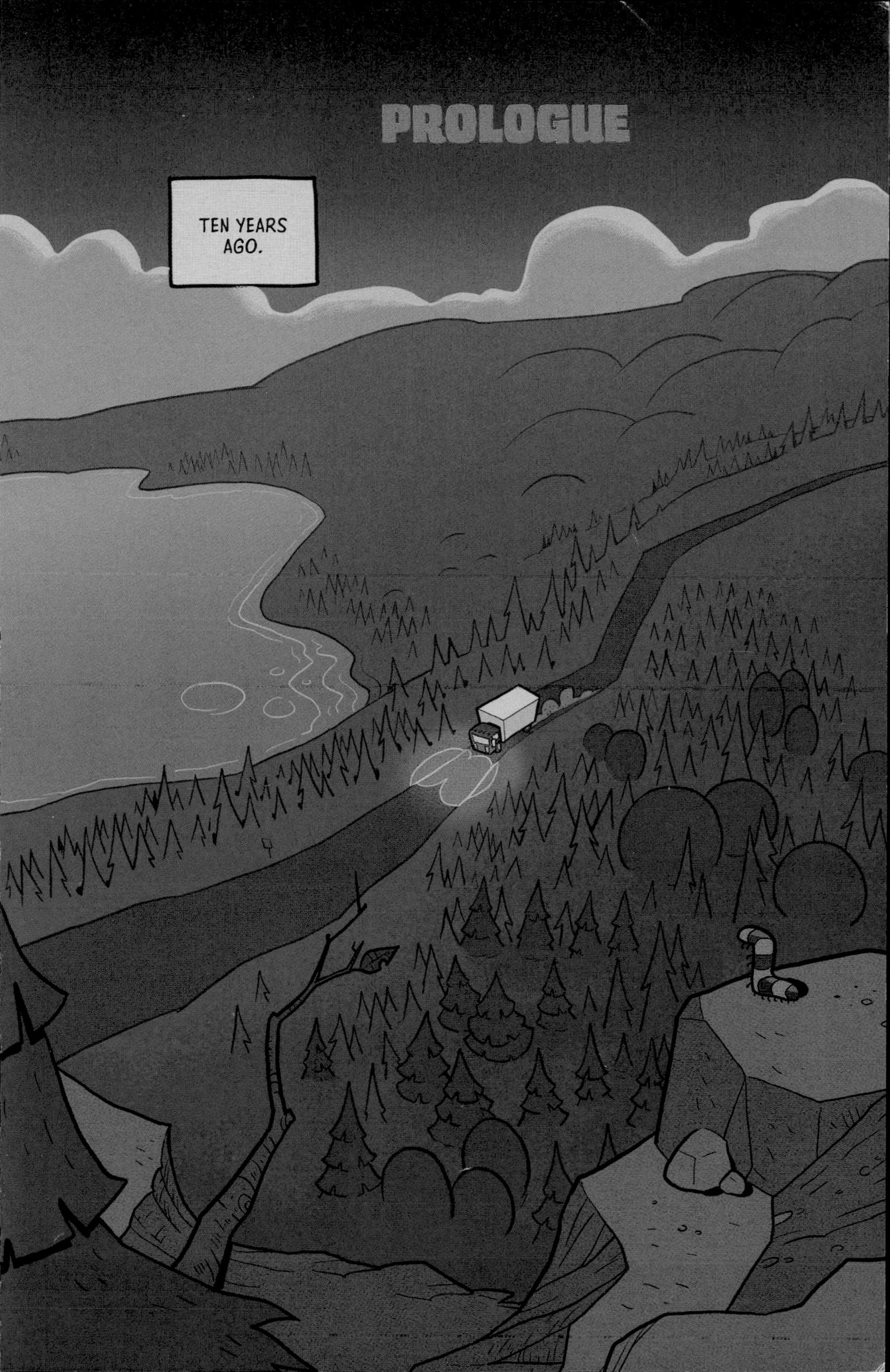
PROLOGUE
TEN YEARS AGO.

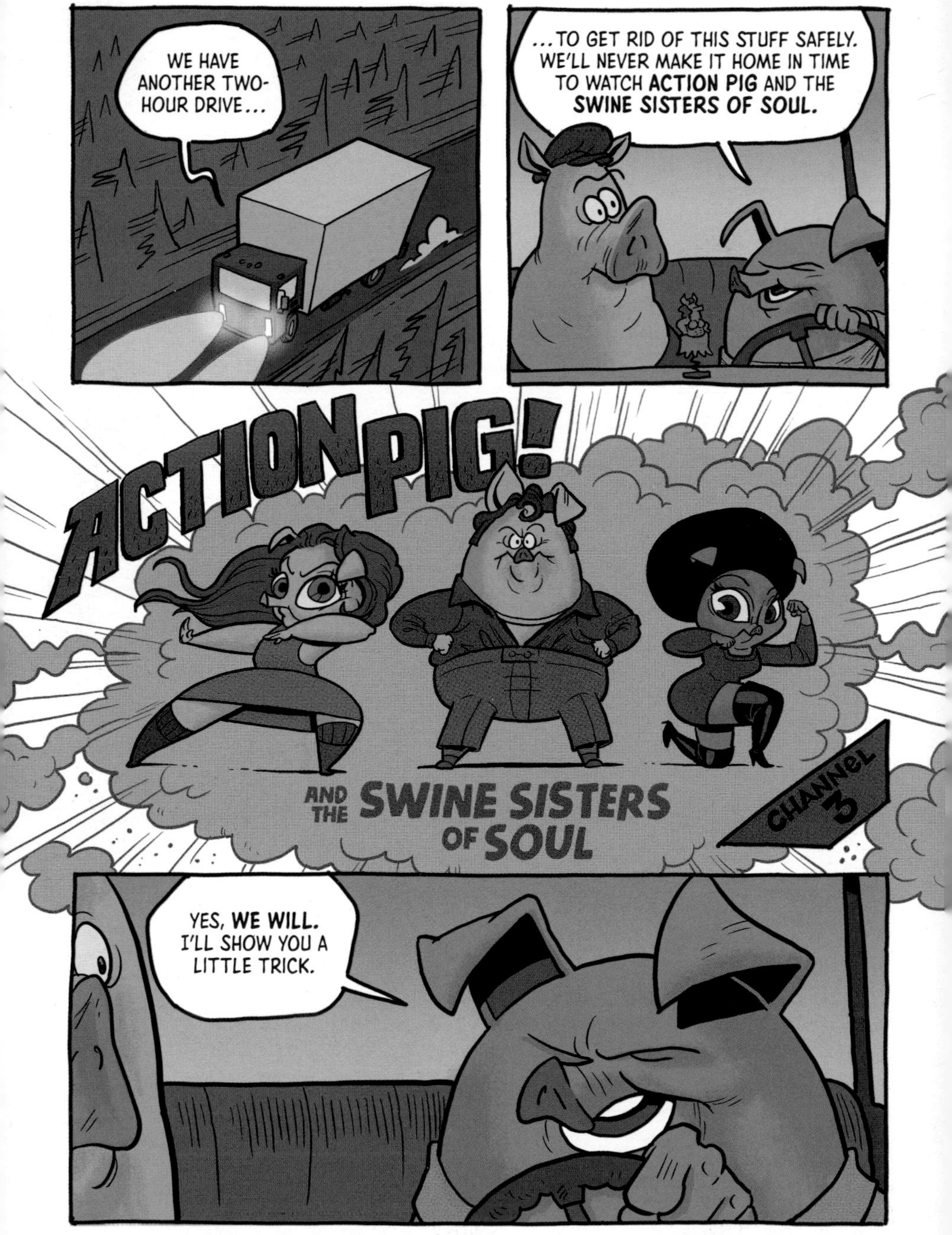
WE HAVE ANOTHER TWO-HOUR DRIVE...
...TO GET RID OF THIS STUFF SAFELY. WE'LL NEVER MAKE IT HOME IN TIME TO WATCH ACTION PIG AND THE SWINE SISTERS OF SOUL.
ACTION PIG!
AND THE SWINE SISTERS OF SOUL
CHANNEL 3
YES, WE WILL. I'LL SHOW YOU A LITTLE TRICK.

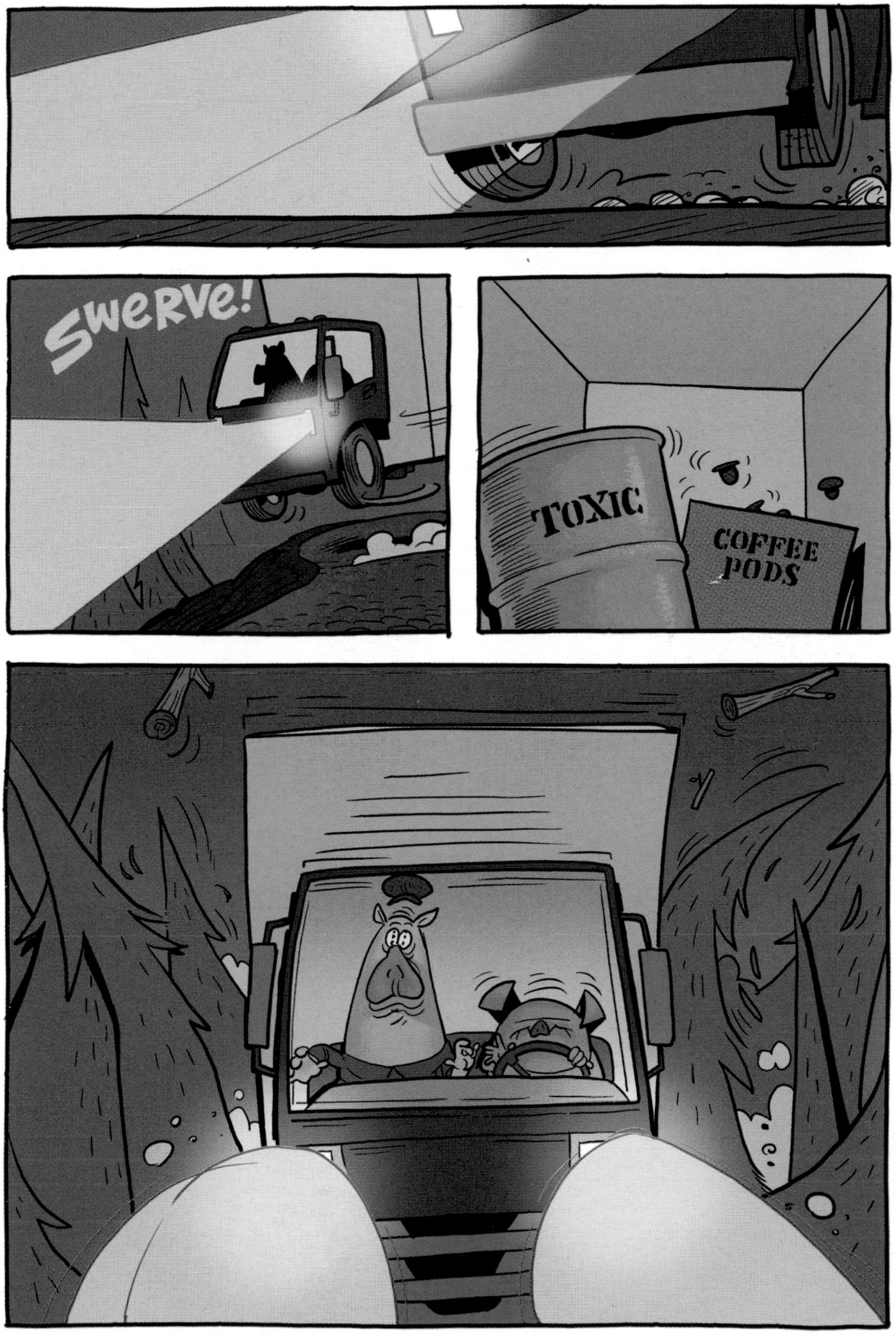
SWERVE!
TOXIC
COFFEE PODS

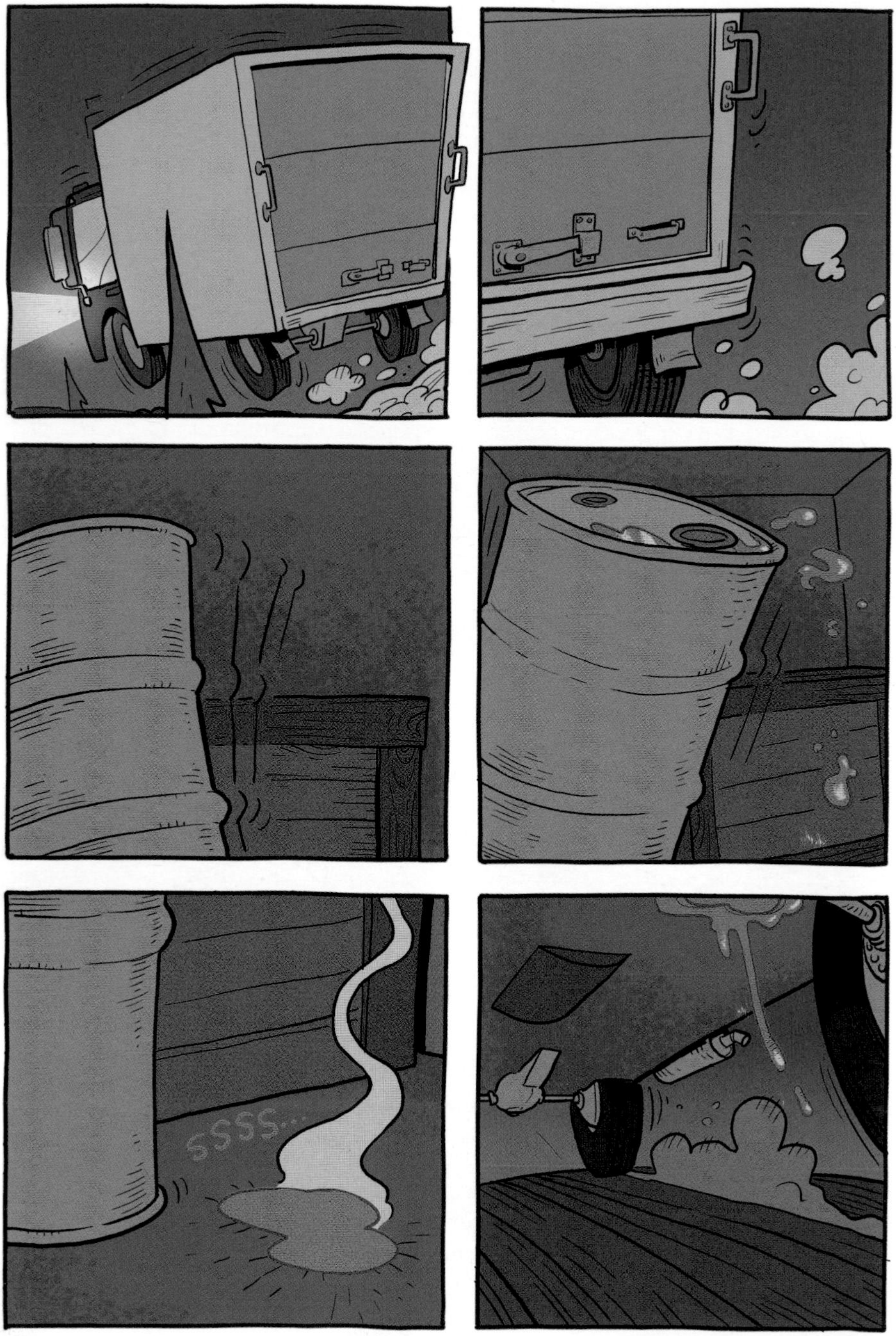
SSSS...

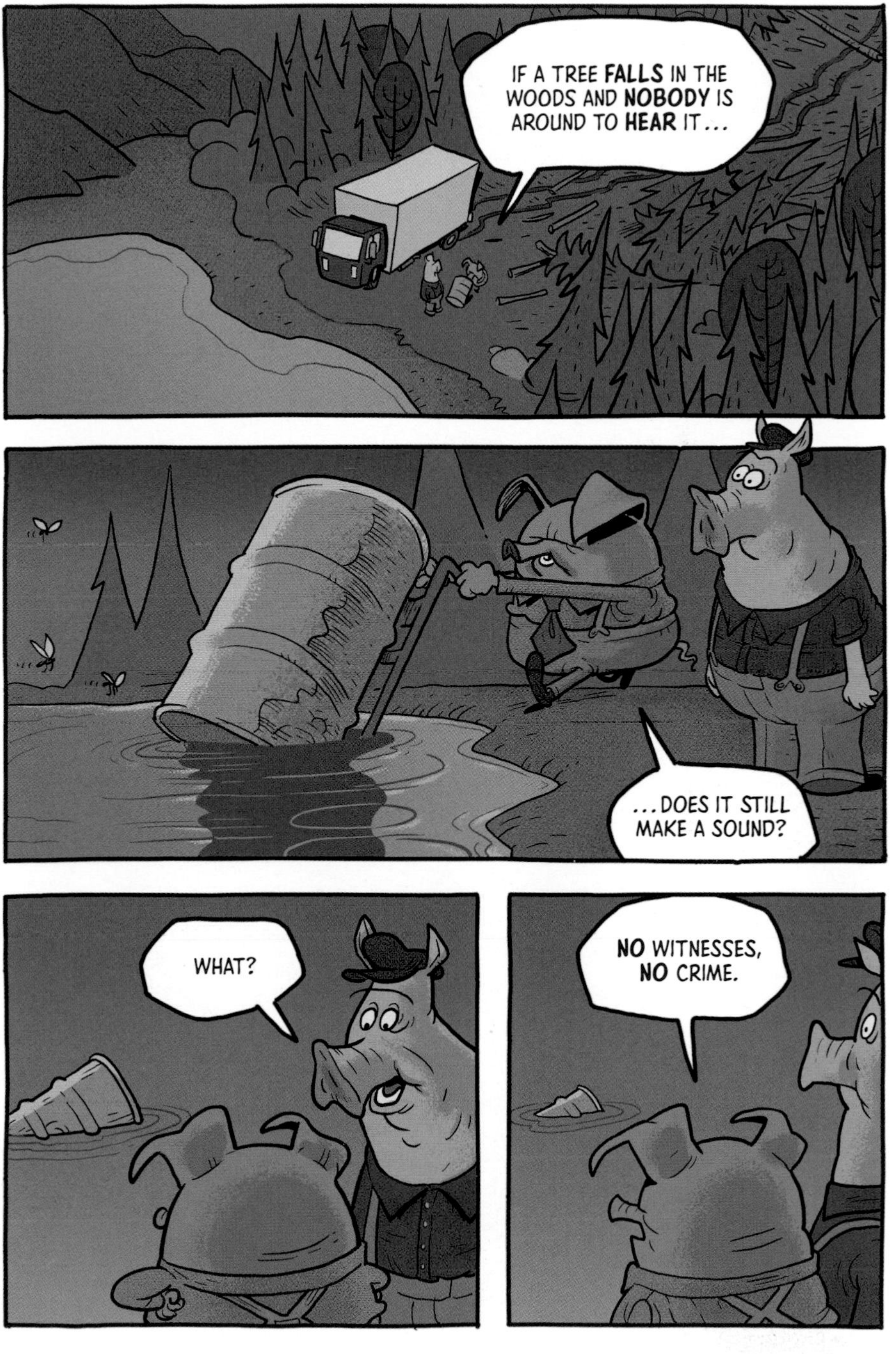
IF A TREE **FALLS** IN THE WOODS AND **NOBODY** IS AROUND TO **HEAR** IT...
...DOES IT STILL MAKE A SOUND?
WHAT?
NO WITNESSES, **NO** CRIME.

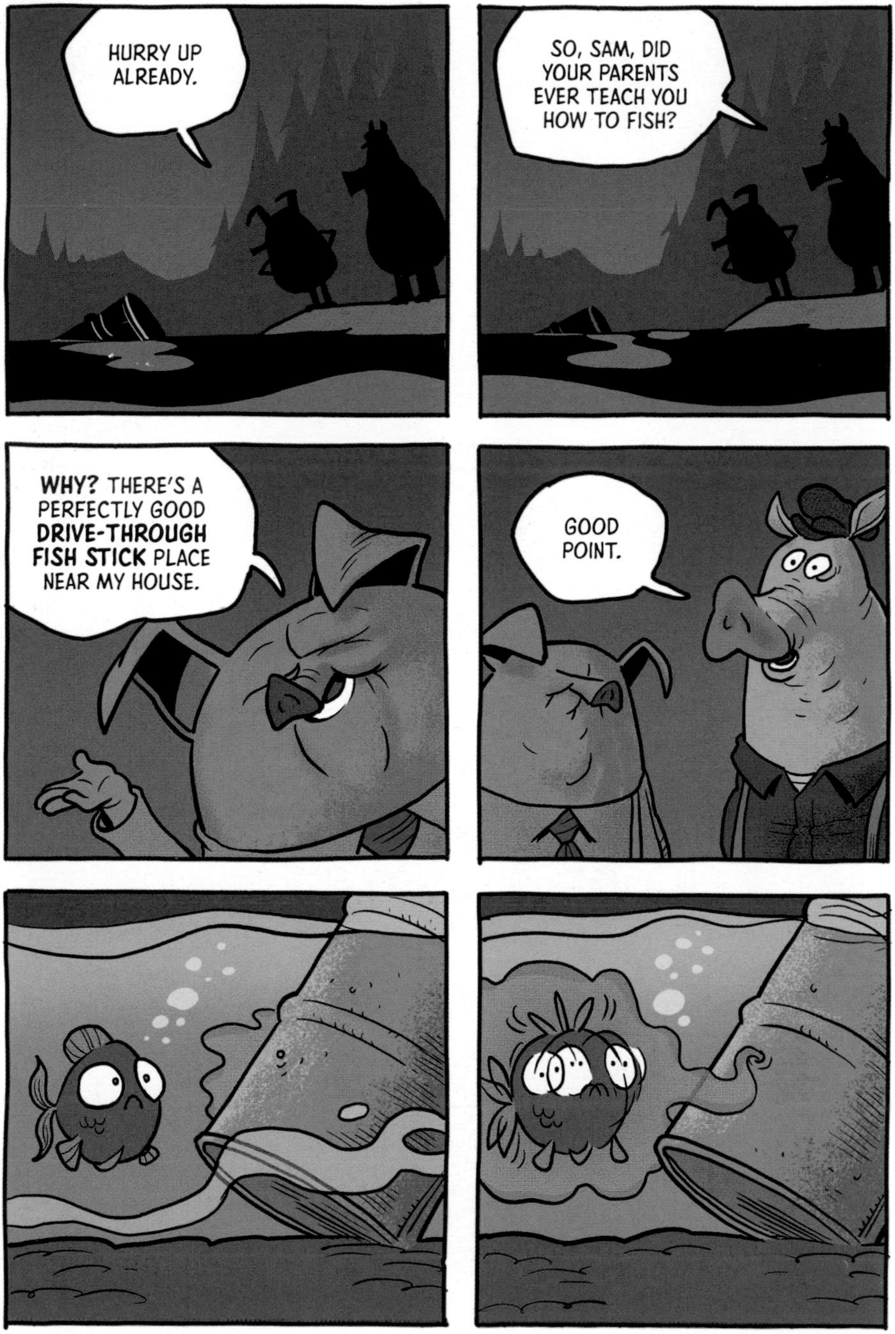
HURRY UP ALREADY.
SO, SAM, DID YOUR PARENTS EVER TEACH YOU HOW TO FISH?
WHY? THERE'S A PERFECTLY GOOD **DRIVE-THROUGH FISH STICK** PLACE NEAR MY HOUSE.
GOOD POINT.

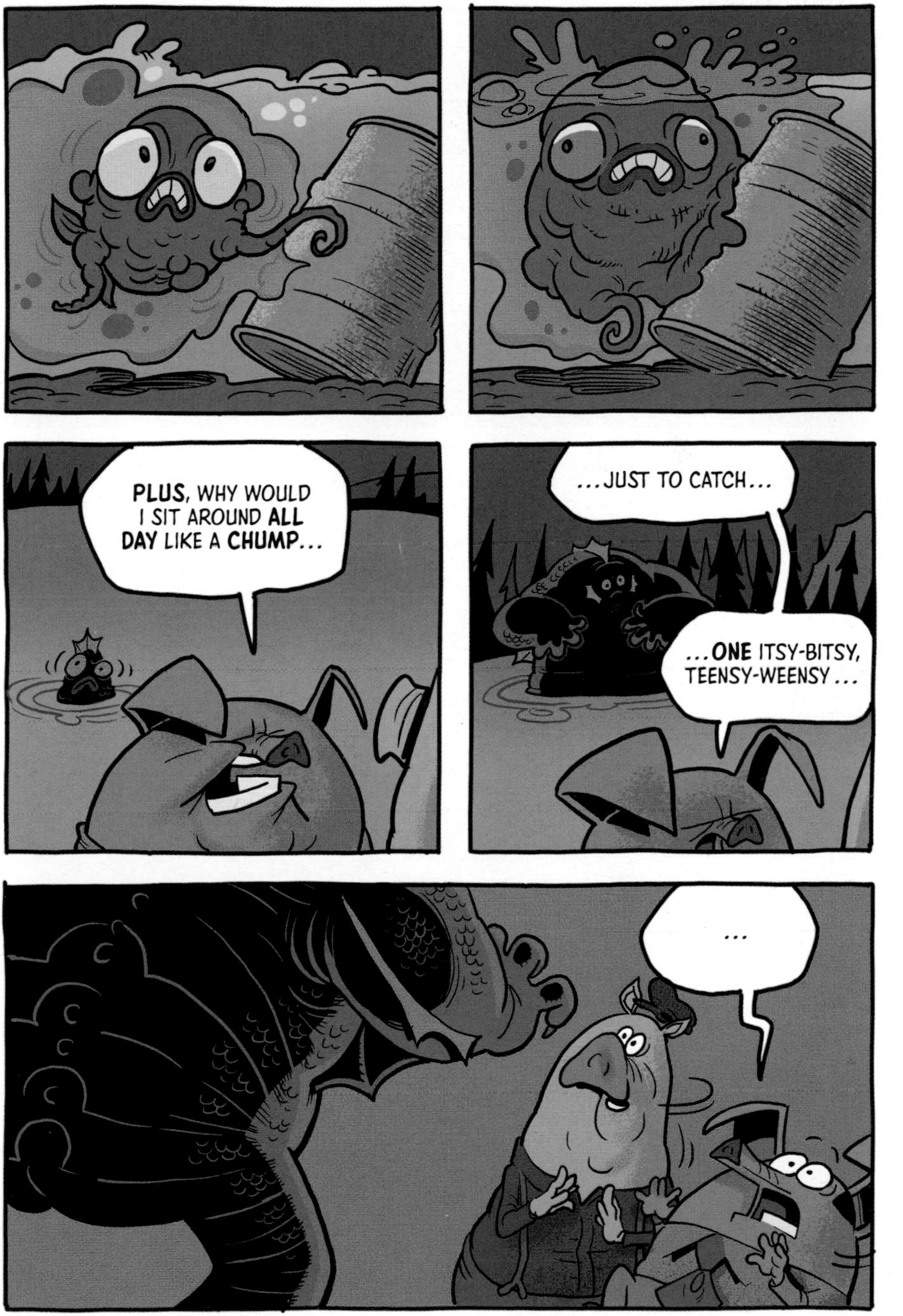
PLUS, WHY WOULD I SIT AROUND ALL DAY LIKE A CHUMP...
...JUST TO CATCH...
...ONE ITSY-BITSY, TEENSY-WEENSY...
...

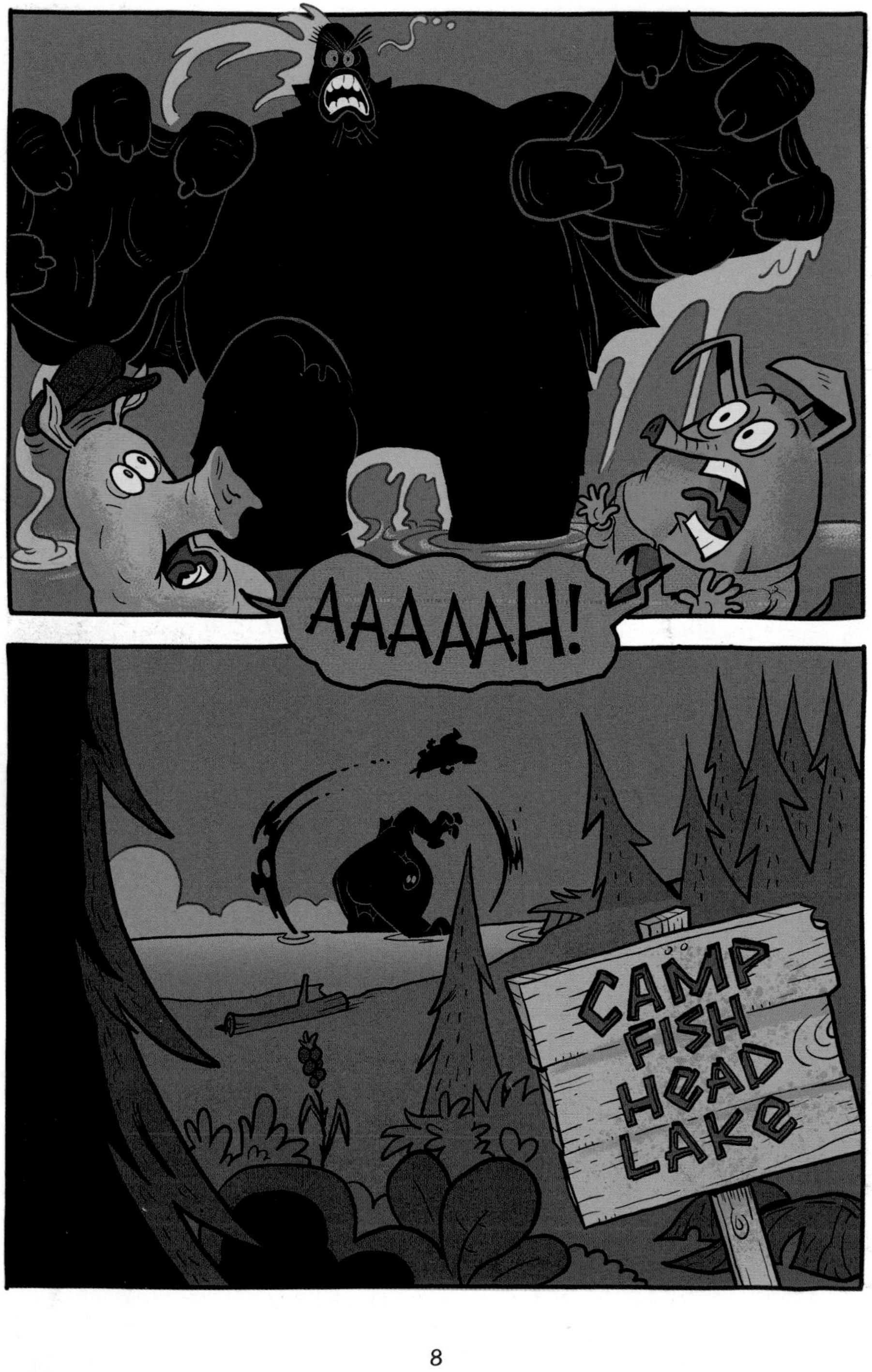
AAAAAH!
CAMP FISH HEAD LAKE

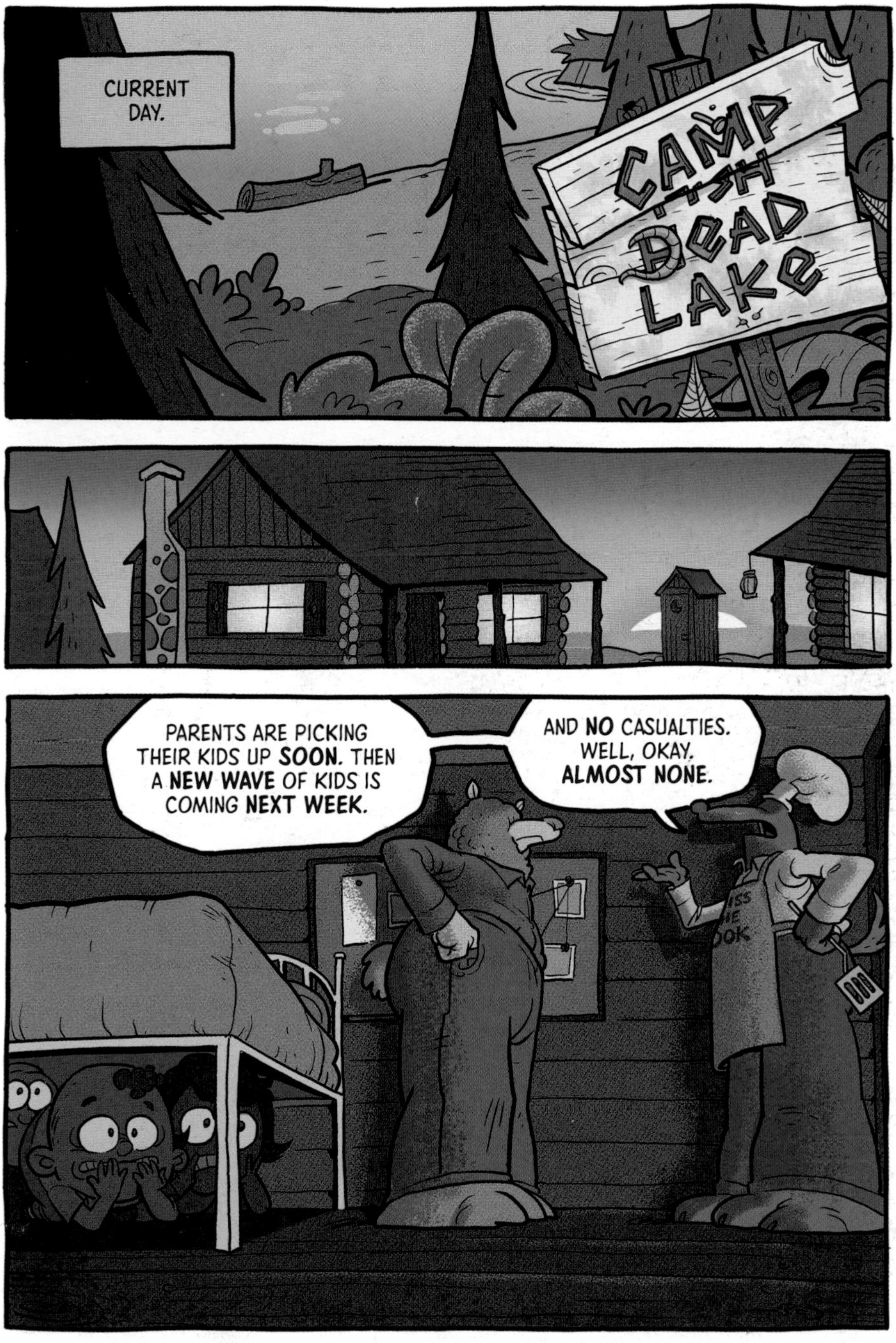
CURRENT DAY.
CAMP DEAD LAKE
PARENTS ARE PICKING THEIR KIDS UP SOON. THEN A NEW WAVE OF KIDS IS COMING NEXT WEEK.
AND NO CASUALTIES. WELL, OKAY. ALMOST NONE.

PUPPET THEATER
BLAH, BLAH, BLAH...
NO, STOP! AH! YOU'RE HURTING ME!
PUPPET THEATER
FLOP!

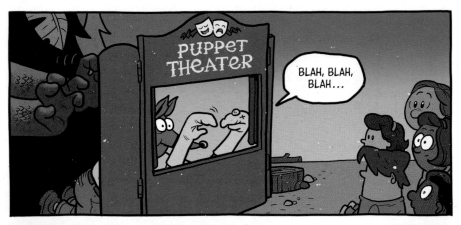

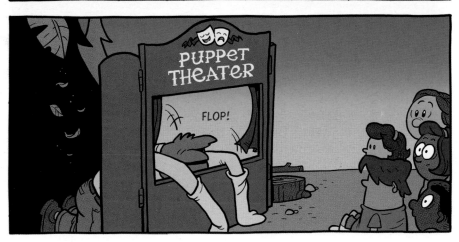

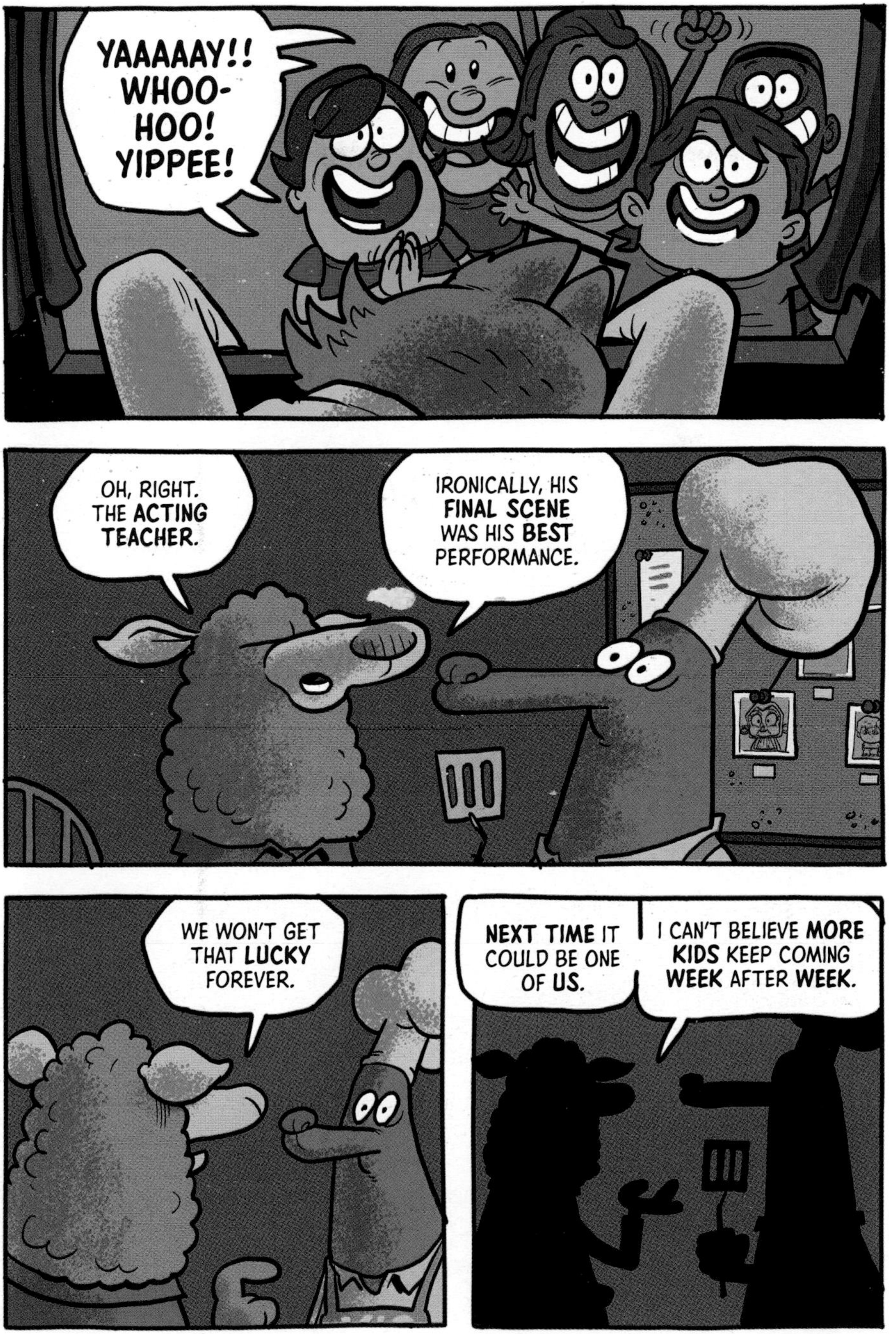
YAAAAAY!! WHOO-HOO! YIPPEE!
OH, RIGHT. THE ACTING TEACHER.
IRONICALLY, HIS FINAL SCENE WAS HIS BEST PERFORMANCE.
WE WON'T GET THAT LUCKY FOREVER.
NEXT TIME IT COULD BE ONE OF US.
I CAN'T BELIEVE MORE KIDS KEEP COMING WEEK AFTER WEEK.

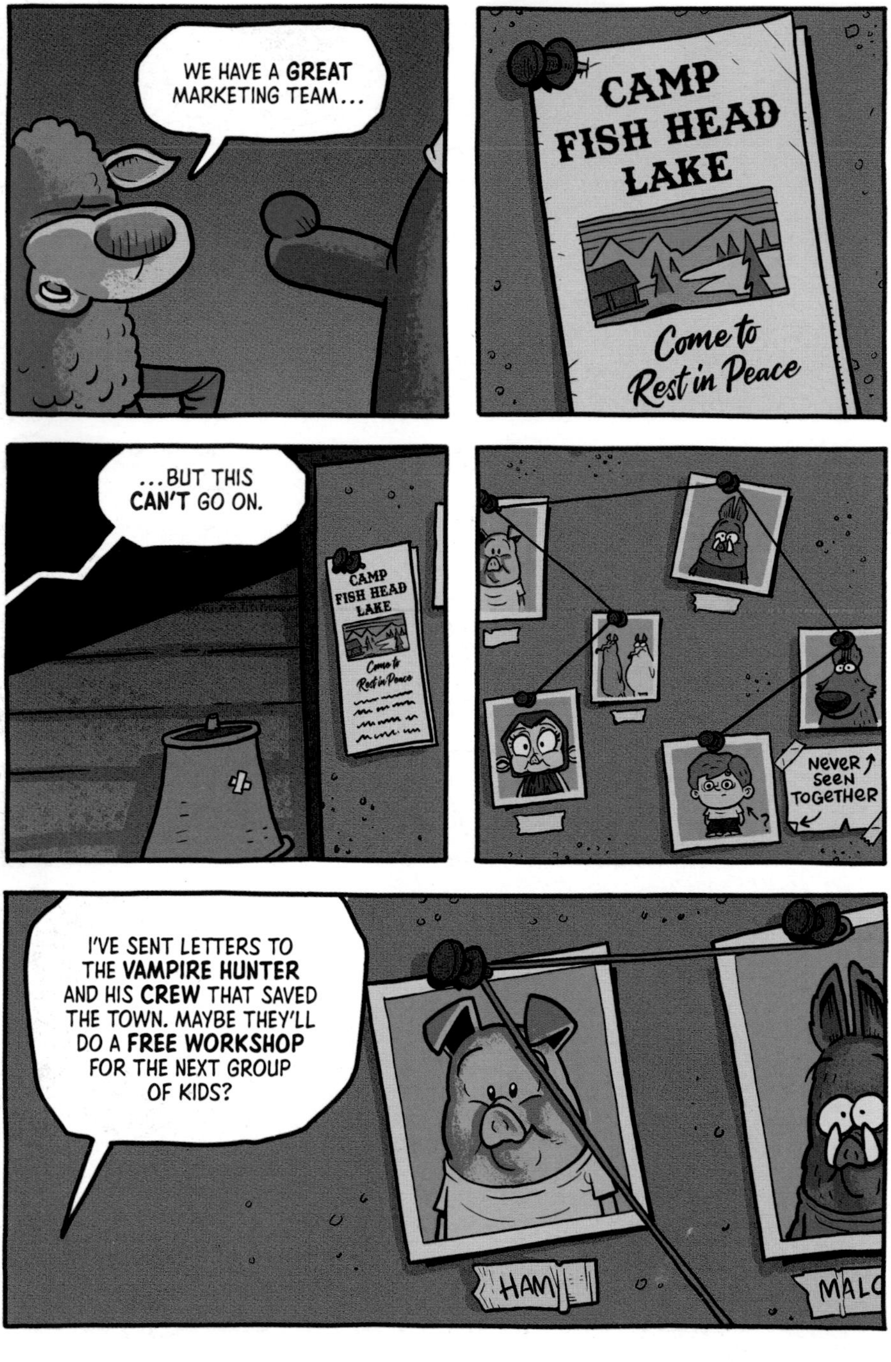
WE HAVE A **GREAT** MARKETING TEAM...
CAMP FISH HEAD LAKE
Come to Rest in Peace
...BUT THIS **CAN'T** GO ON.
CAMP FISH HEAD LAKE
Come to Rest in Peace
NEVER SEEN TOGETHER
I'VE SENT LETTERS TO THE **VAMPIRE HUNTER** AND HIS **CREW** THAT SAVED THE TOWN. MAYBE THEY'LL DO A **FREE WORKSHOP** FOR THE NEXT GROUP OF KIDS?
HAM

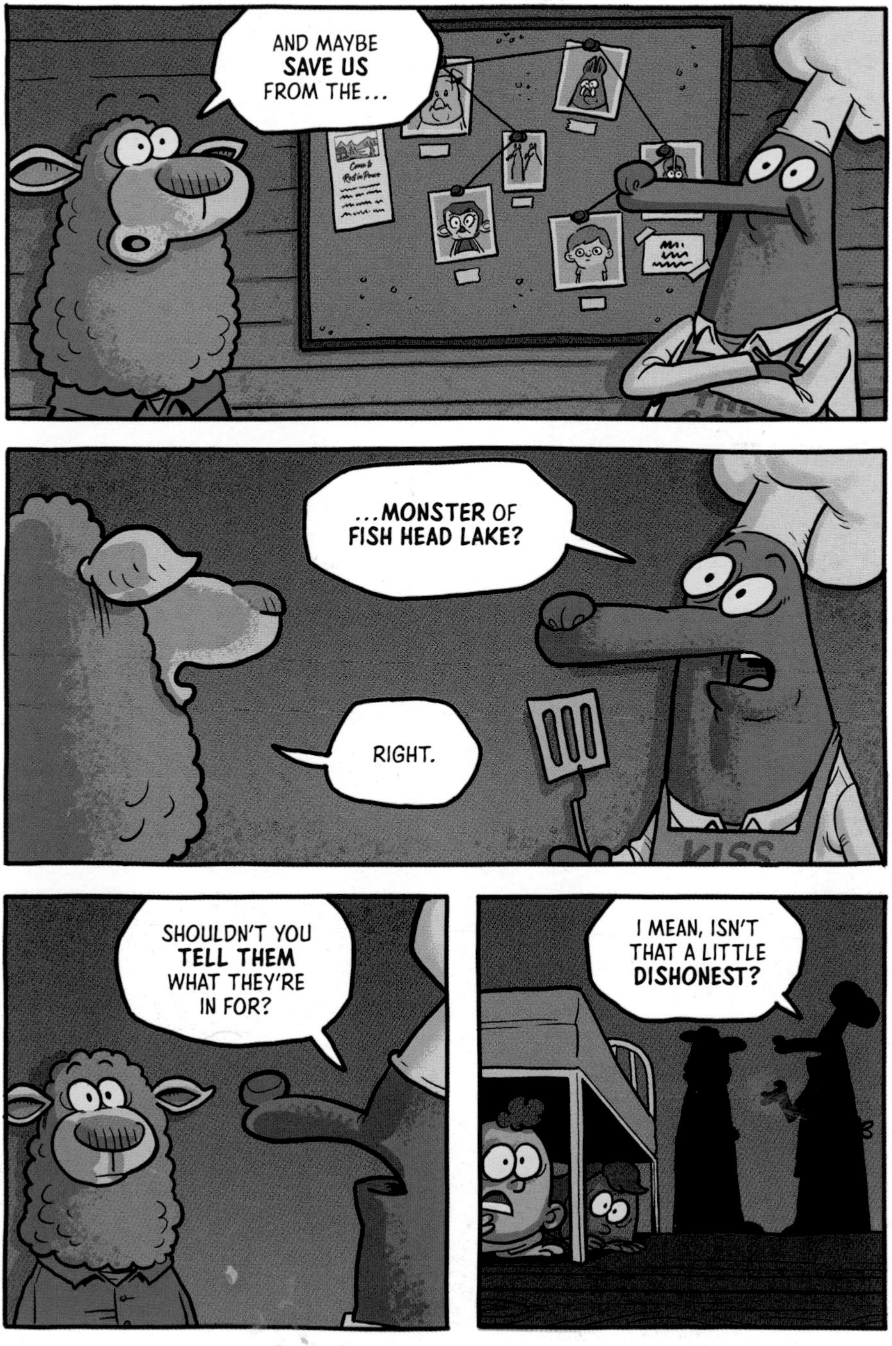
AND MAYBE SAVE US FROM THE...
...MONSTER OF FISH HEAD LAKE?
RIGHT.
SHOULDN'T YOU TELL THEM WHAT THEY'RE IN FOR?
I MEAN, ISN'T THAT A LITTLE DISHONEST?

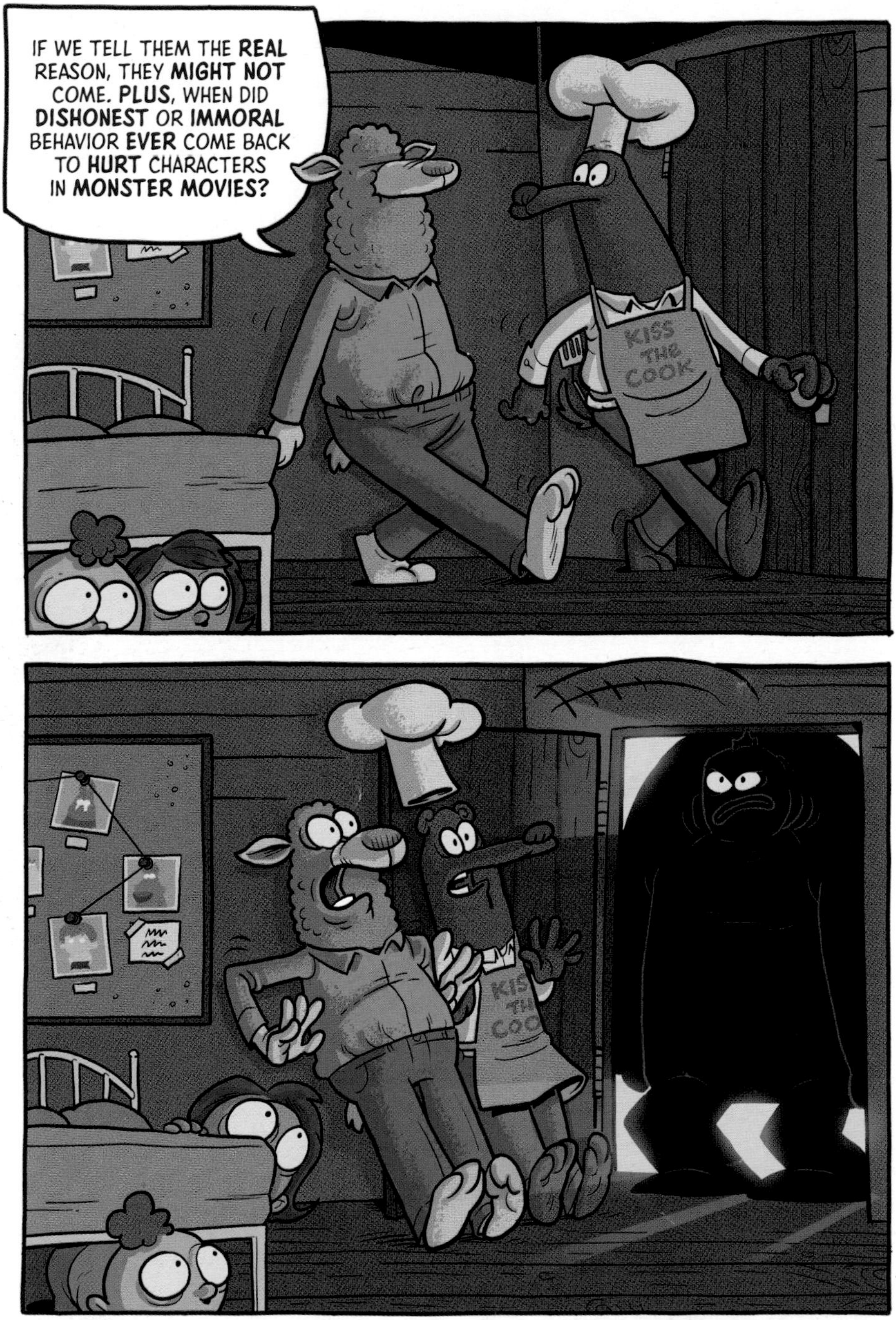
IF WE TELL THEM THE **REAL** REASON, THEY **MIGHT NOT** COME. **PLUS,** WHEN DID **DISHONEST** OR **IMMORAL** BEHAVIOR **EVER** COME BACK TO **HURT** CHARACTERS IN **MONSTER MOVIES?**
KISS THE COOK

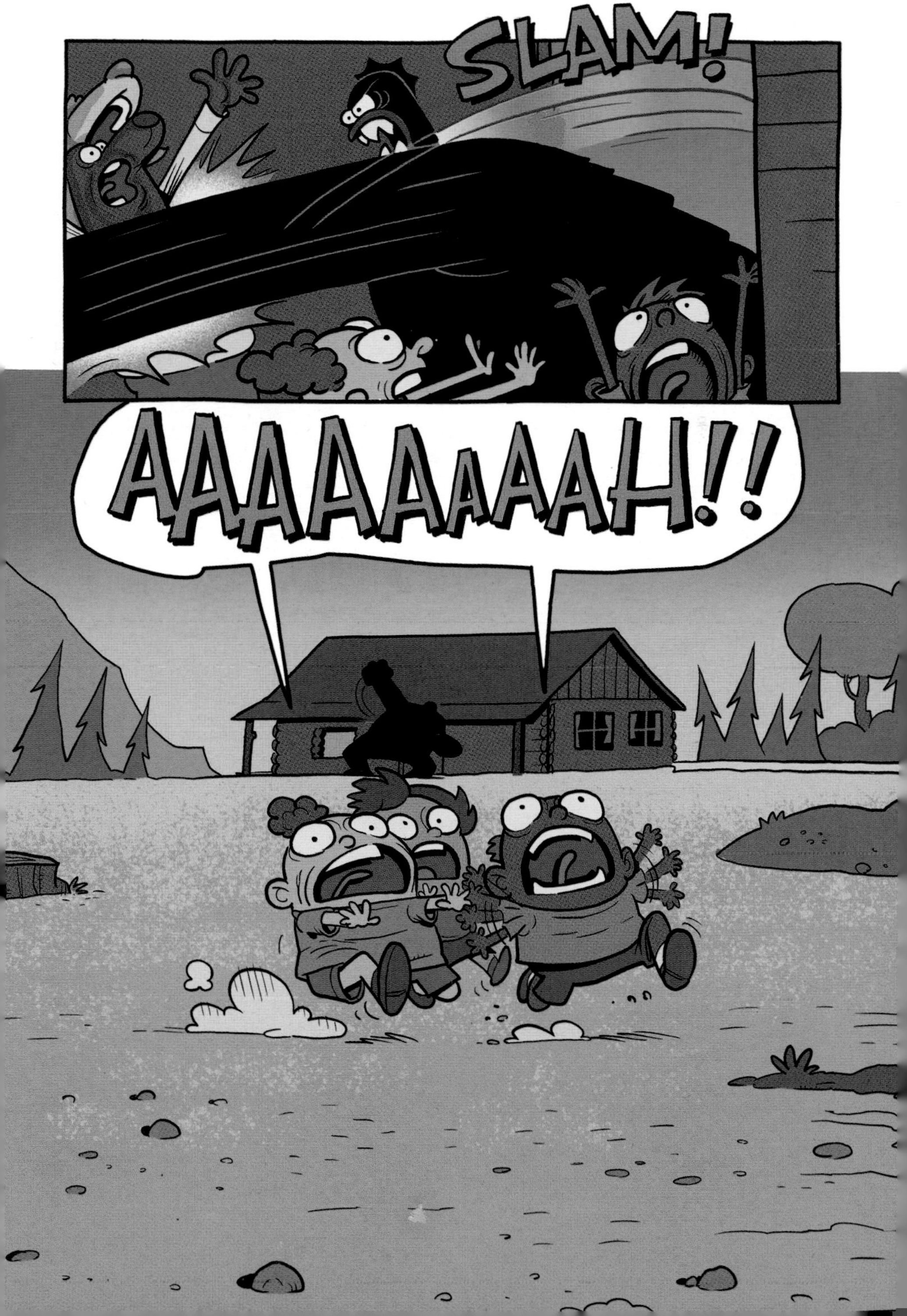
SLAM!
AAAAAAAAAH!!

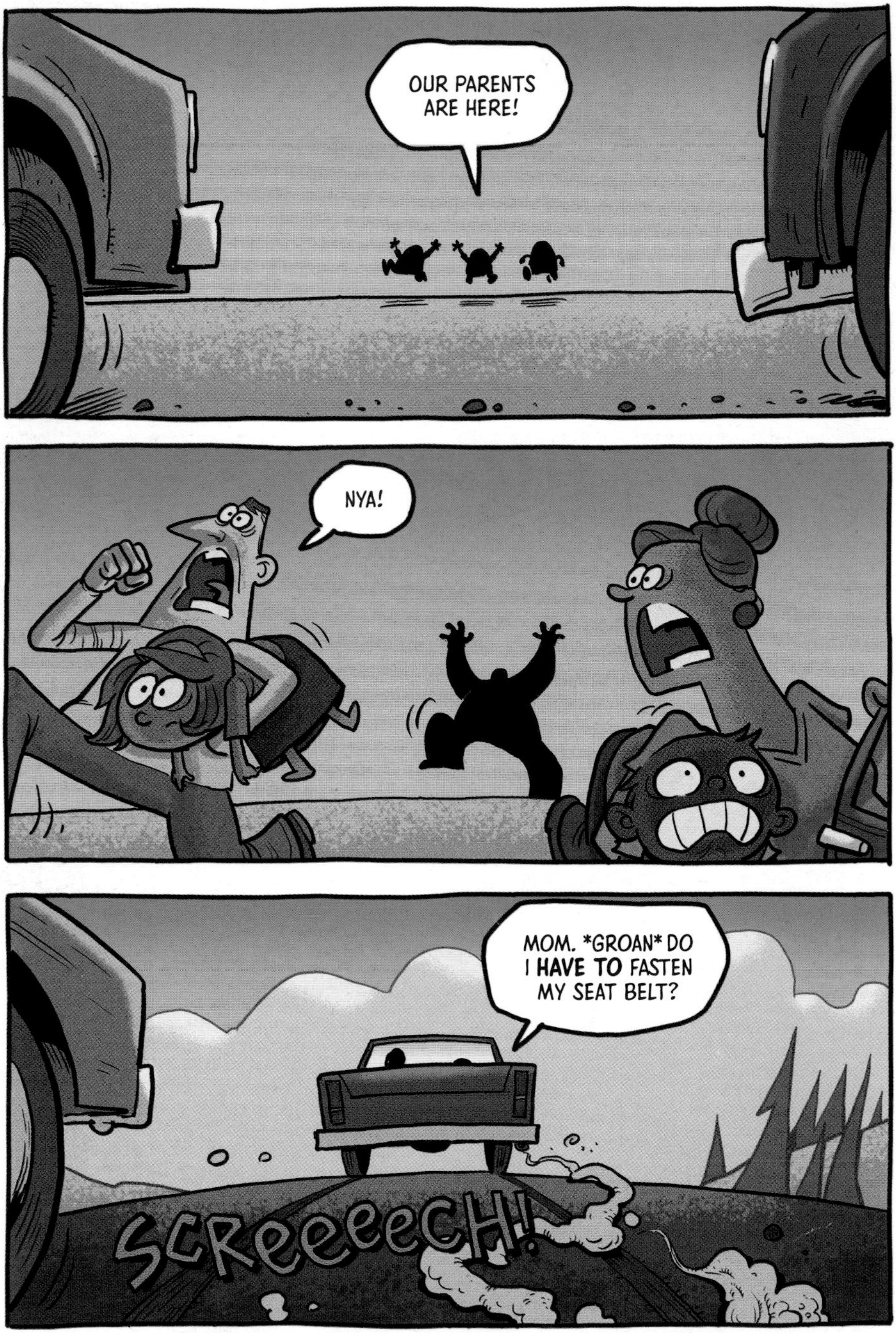
OUR PARENTS ARE HERE!
NYA!
MOM. *GROAN* DO I **HAVE TO** FASTEN MY SEAT BELT?
SCREEEECH!

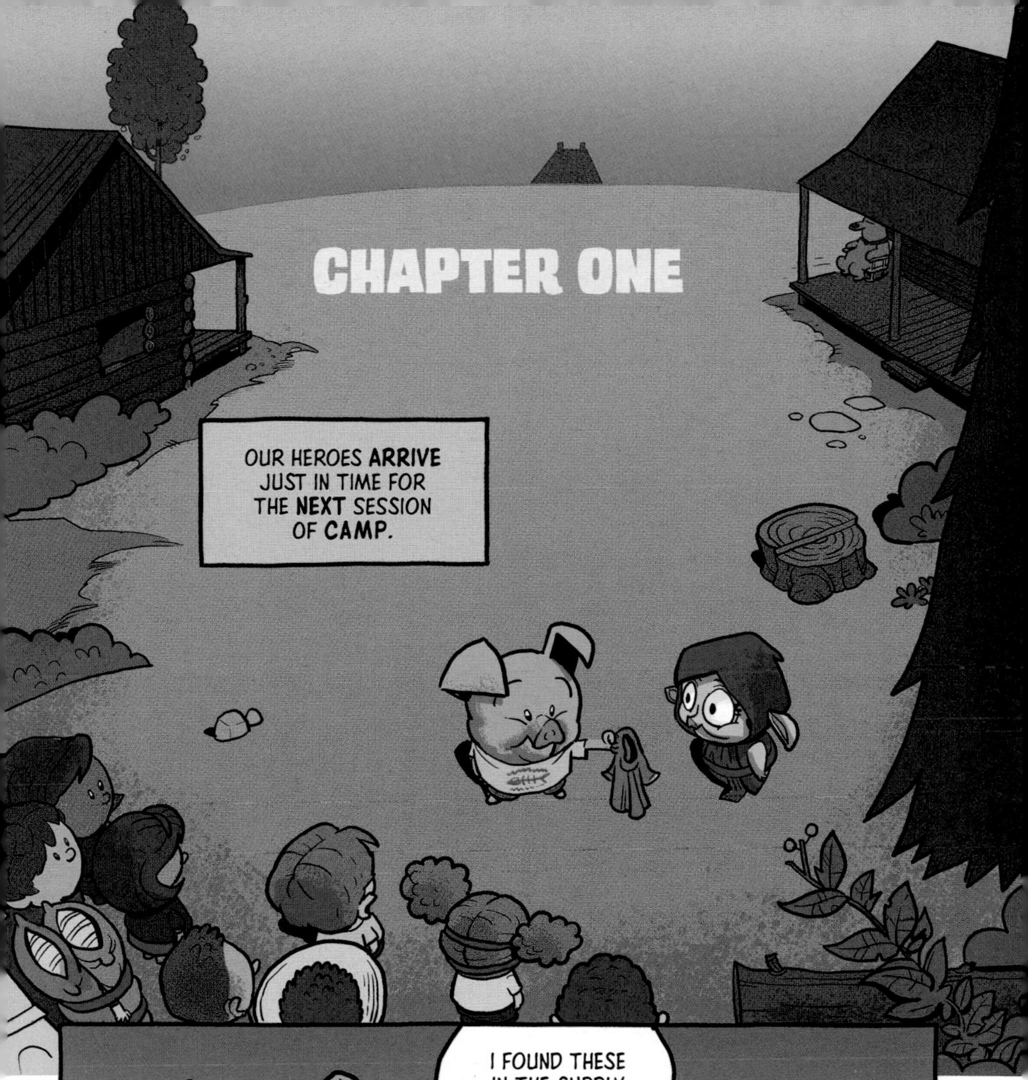
CHAPTER ONE
OUR HEROES ARRIVE JUST IN TIME FOR THE NEXT SESSION OF CAMP.

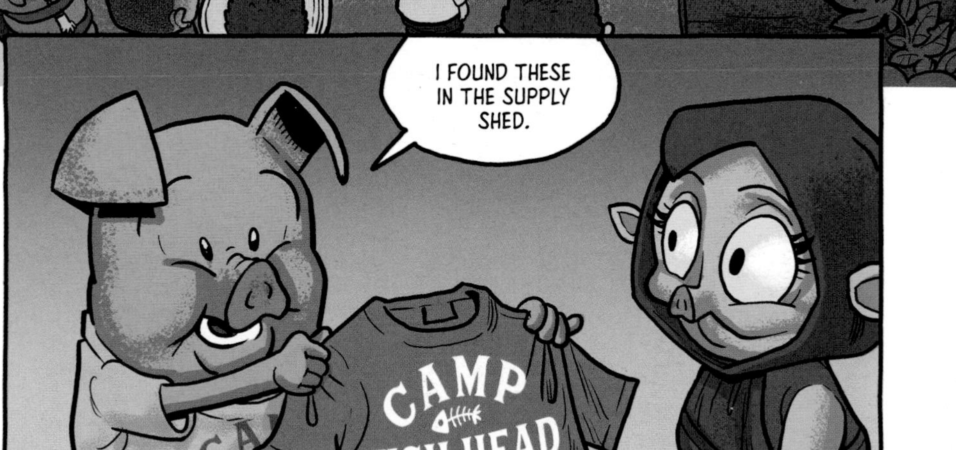
I FOUND THESE IN THE SUPPLY SHED.
CAMP
FISH HEAD

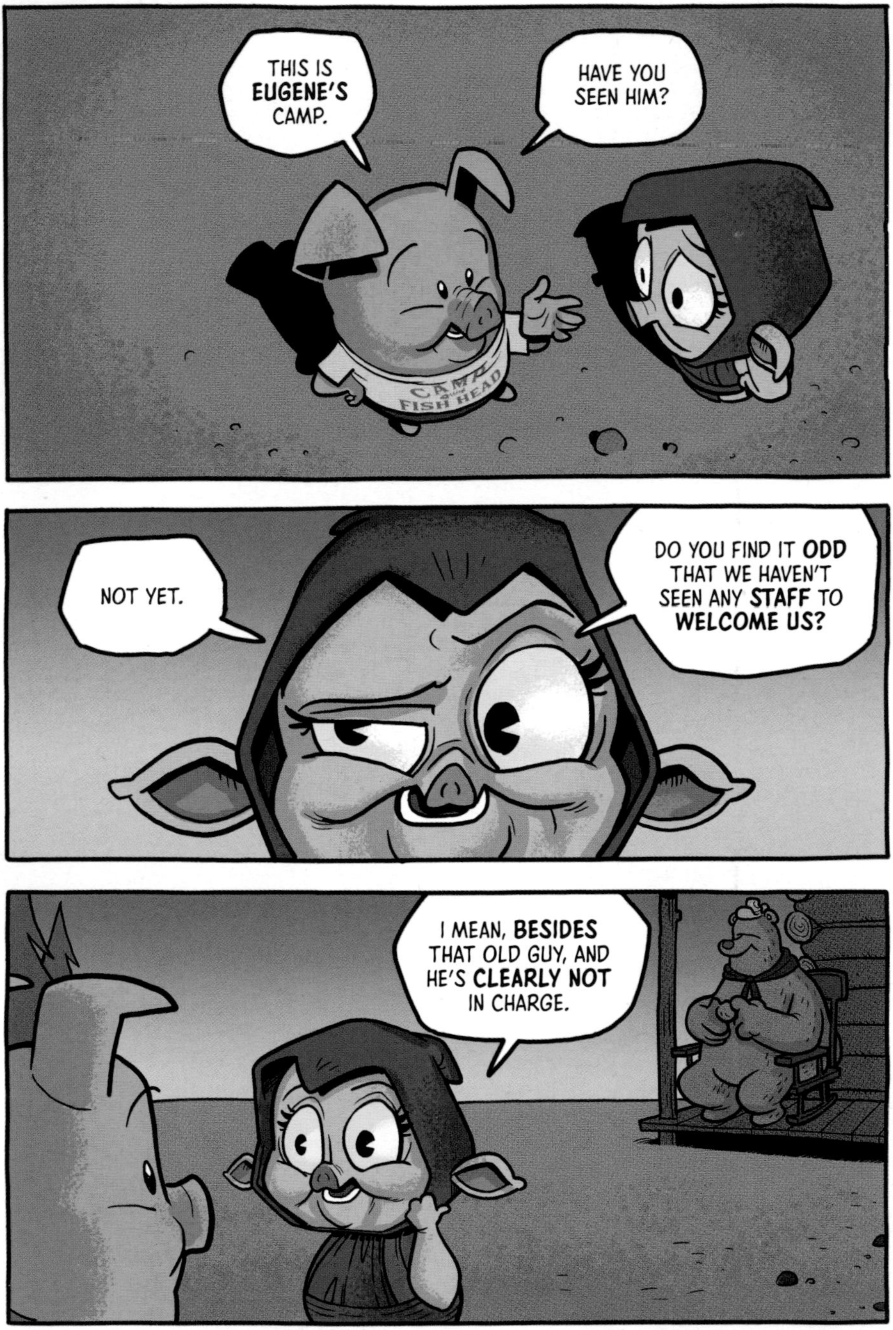
THIS IS **EUGENE'S** CAMP.
HAVE YOU SEEN HIM?
CAMP FISH HEAD
NOT YET.
DO YOU FIND IT **ODD** THAT WE HAVEN'T SEEN ANY **STAFF** TO **WELCOME US?**
I MEAN, **BESIDES** THAT OLD GUY, AND HE'S **CLEARLY NOT** IN CHARGE.

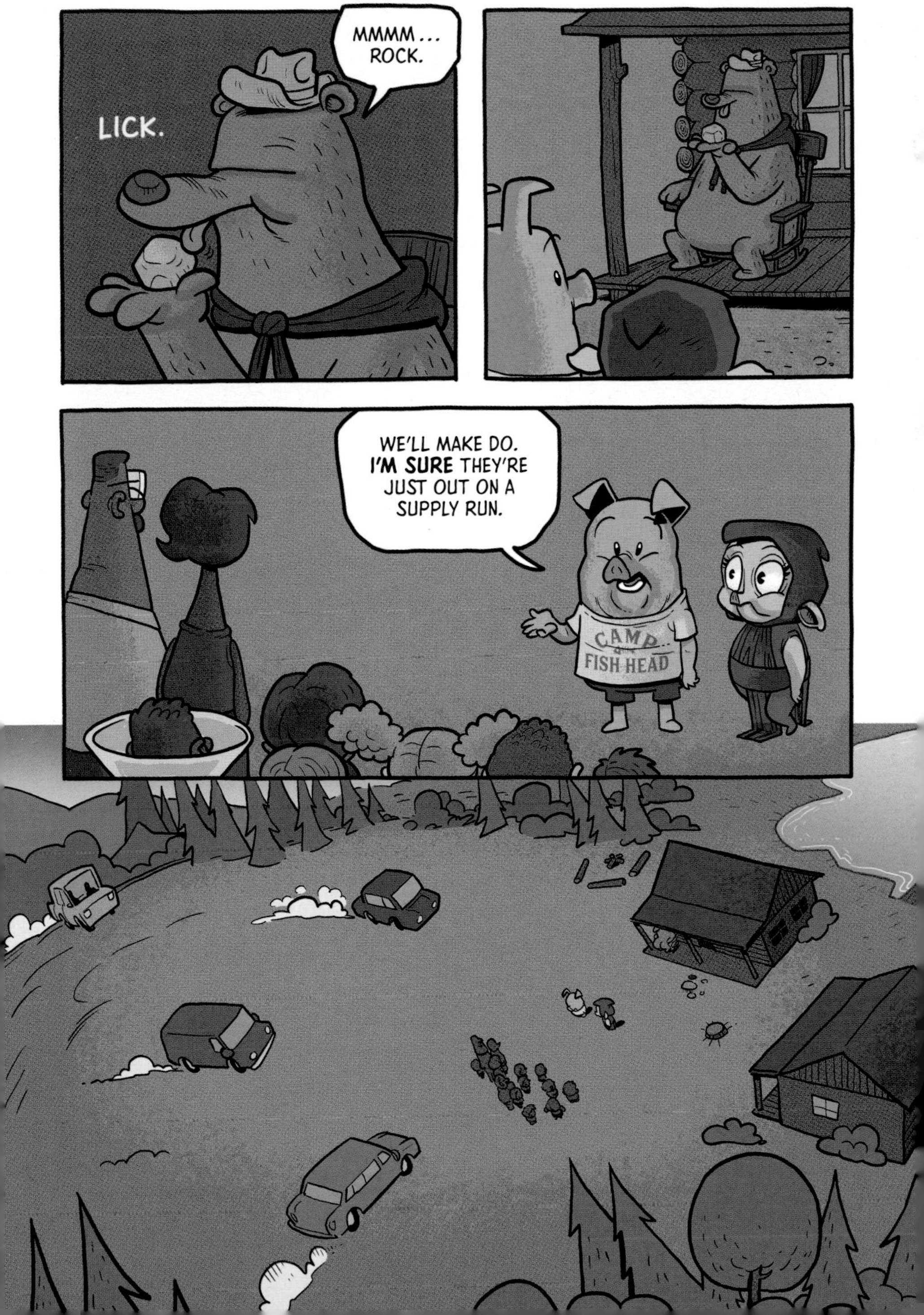
LICK.
MMMM... ROCK.
WE'LL MAKE DO. I'M SURE THEY'RE JUST OUT ON A SUPPLY RUN.
CAMP FISH HEAD

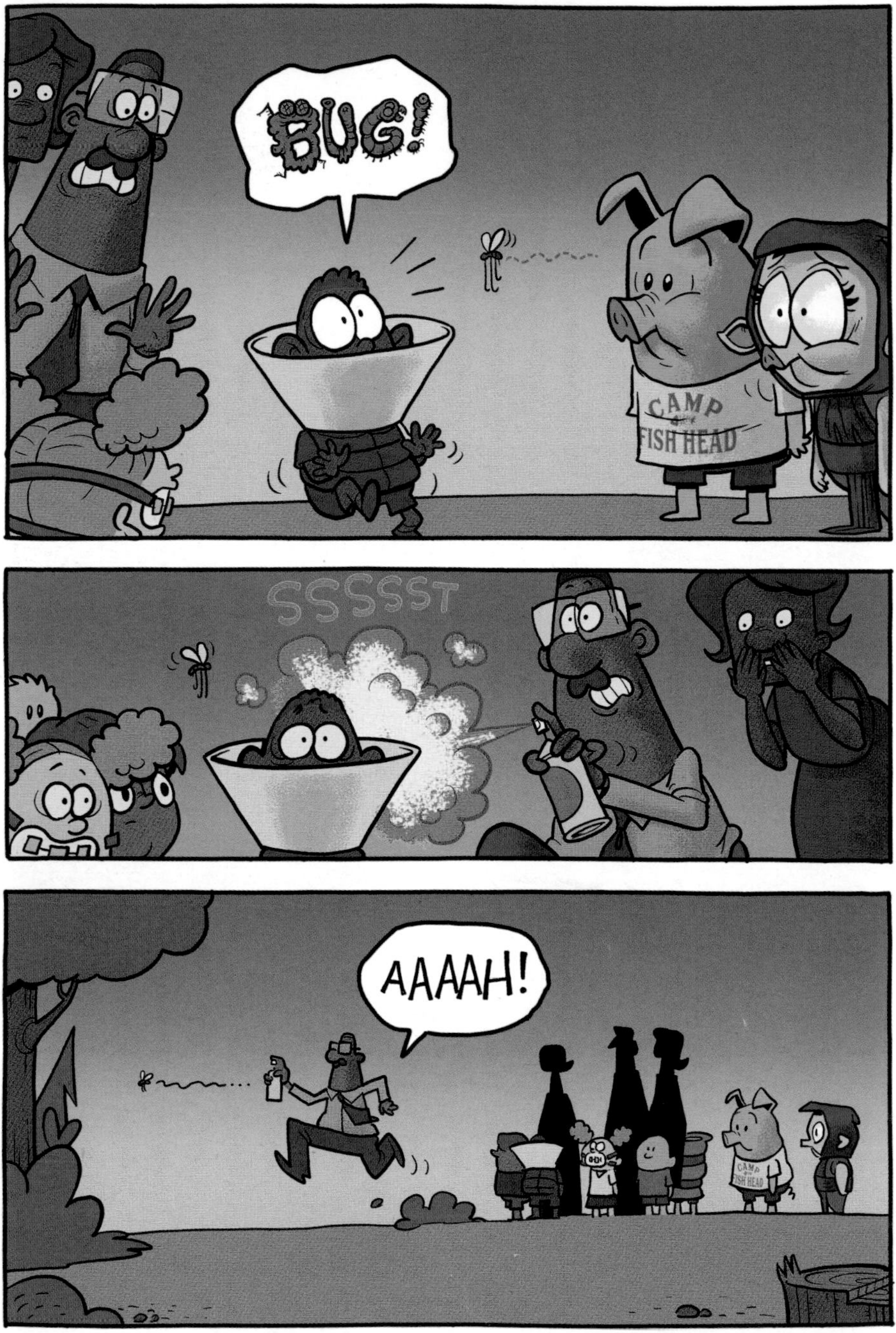
BUG!
CAMP FISH HEAD
SSSSST
AAAAH!
CAMP FISH HEAD

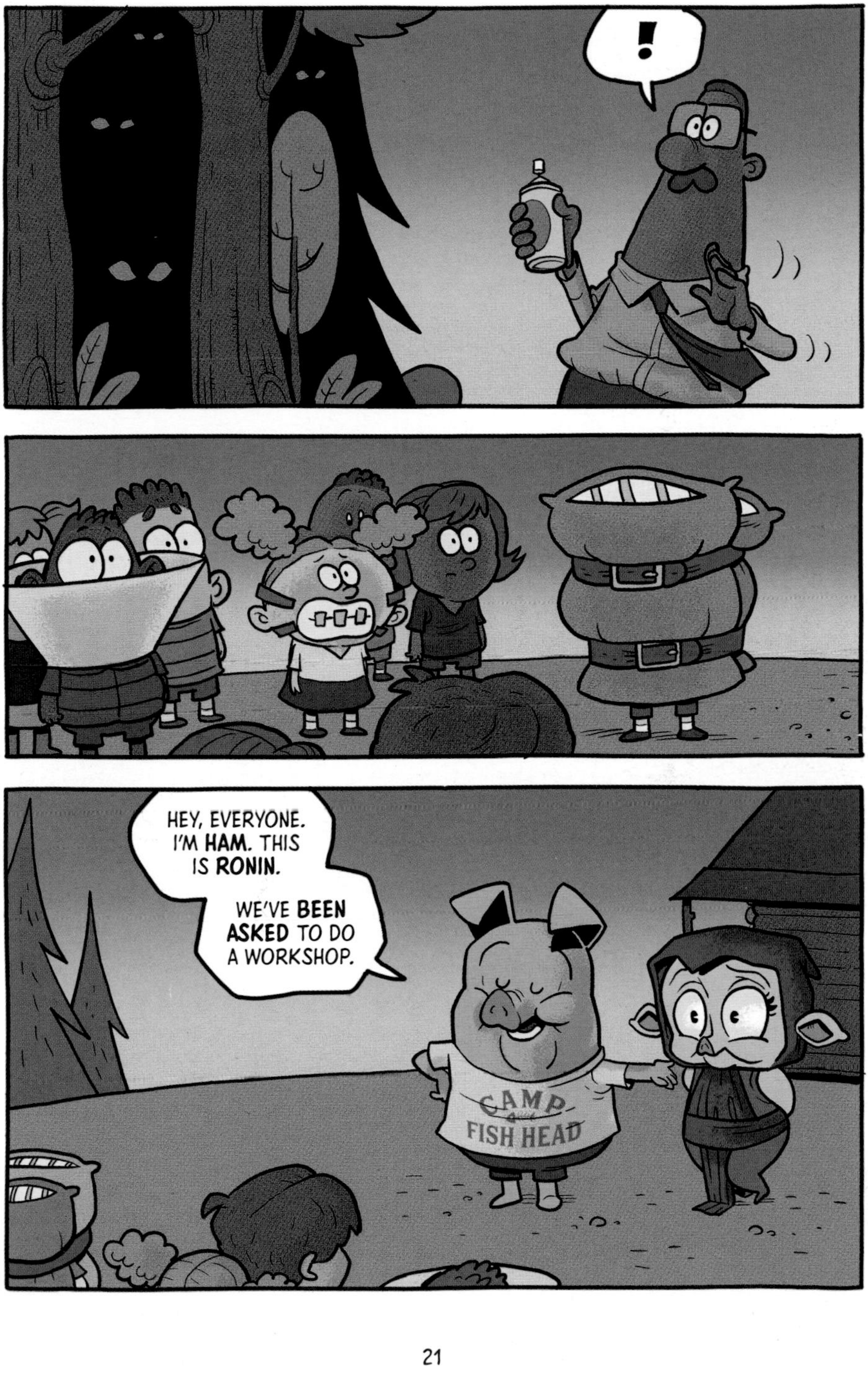
!
HEY, EVERYONE. I'M HAM. THIS IS RONIN.
WE'VE BEEN ASKED TO DO A WORKSHOP.
CAMP FISH HEAD

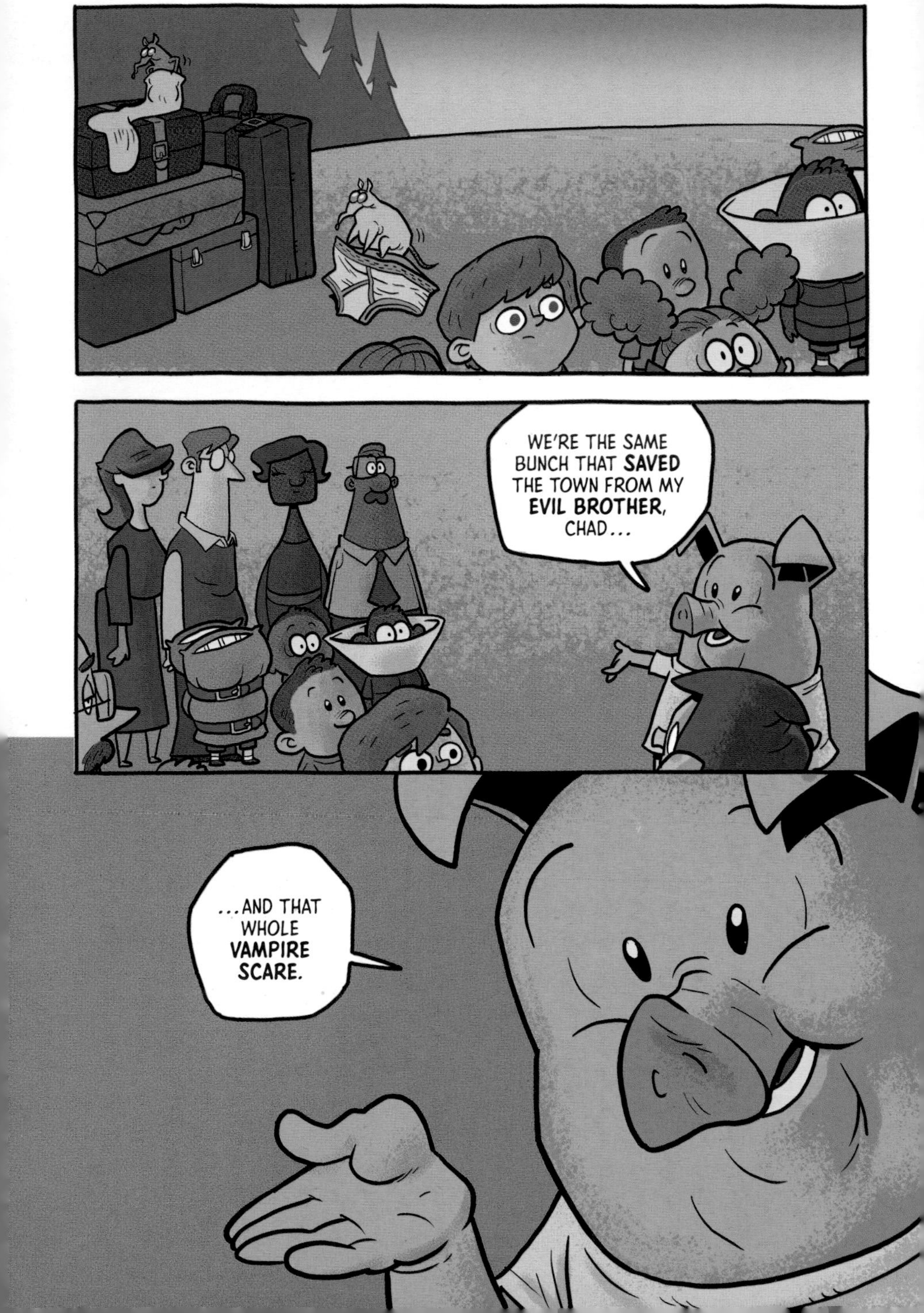
WE'RE THE SAME BUNCH THAT SAVED THE TOWN FROM MY EVIL BROTHER, CHAD...
...AND THAT WHOLE VAMPIRE SCARE.

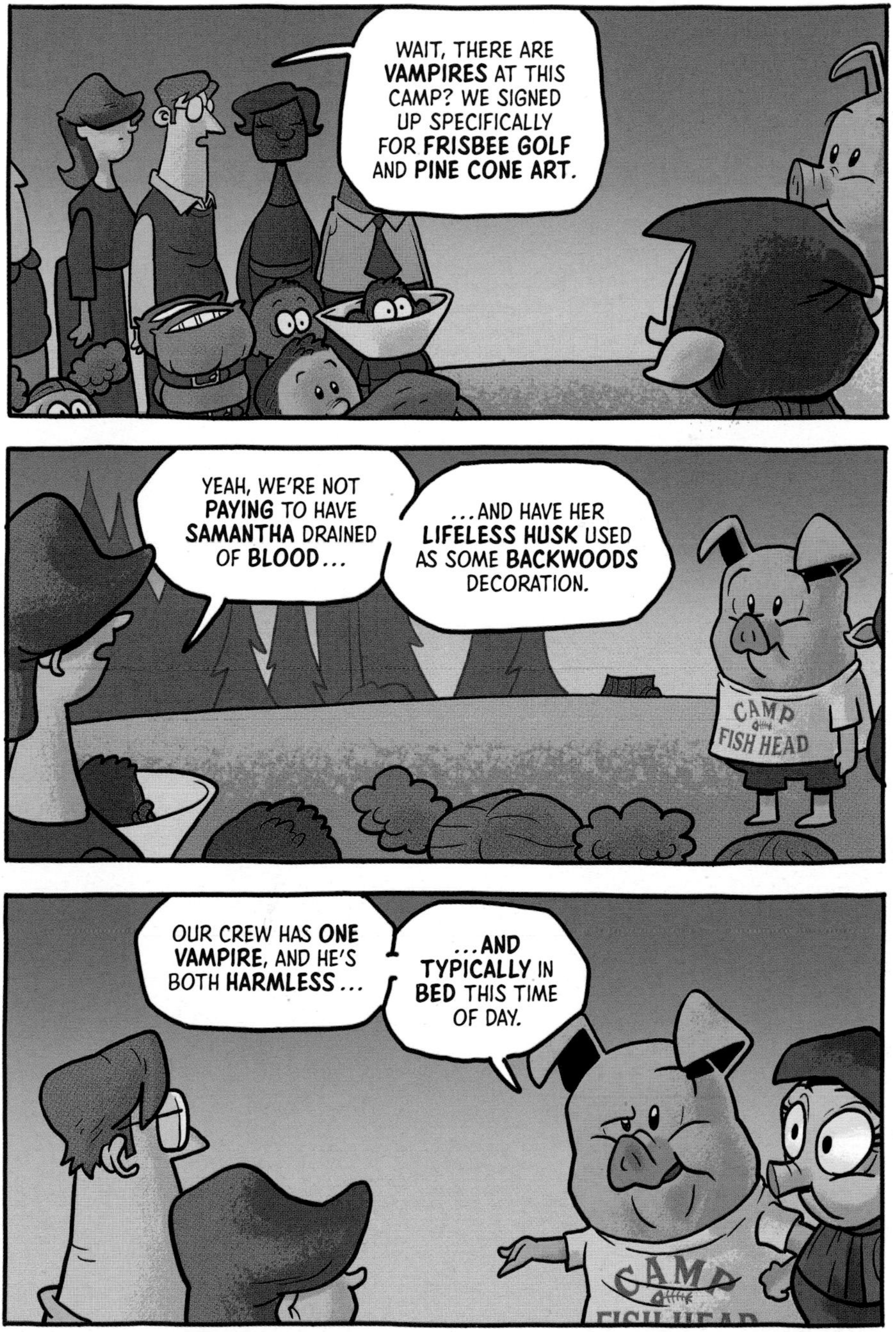
WAIT, THERE ARE VAMPIRES AT THIS CAMP? WE SIGNED UP SPECIFICALLY FOR FRISBEE GOLF AND PINE CONE ART.
YEAH, WE'RE NOT PAYING TO HAVE SAMANTHA DRAINED OF BLOOD...
...AND HAVE HER LIFELESS HUSK USED AS SOME BACKWOODS DECORATION.
CAMP FISH HEAD
OUR CREW HAS ONE VAMPIRE, AND HE'S BOTH HARMLESS...
...AND TYPICALLY IN BED THIS TIME OF DAY.

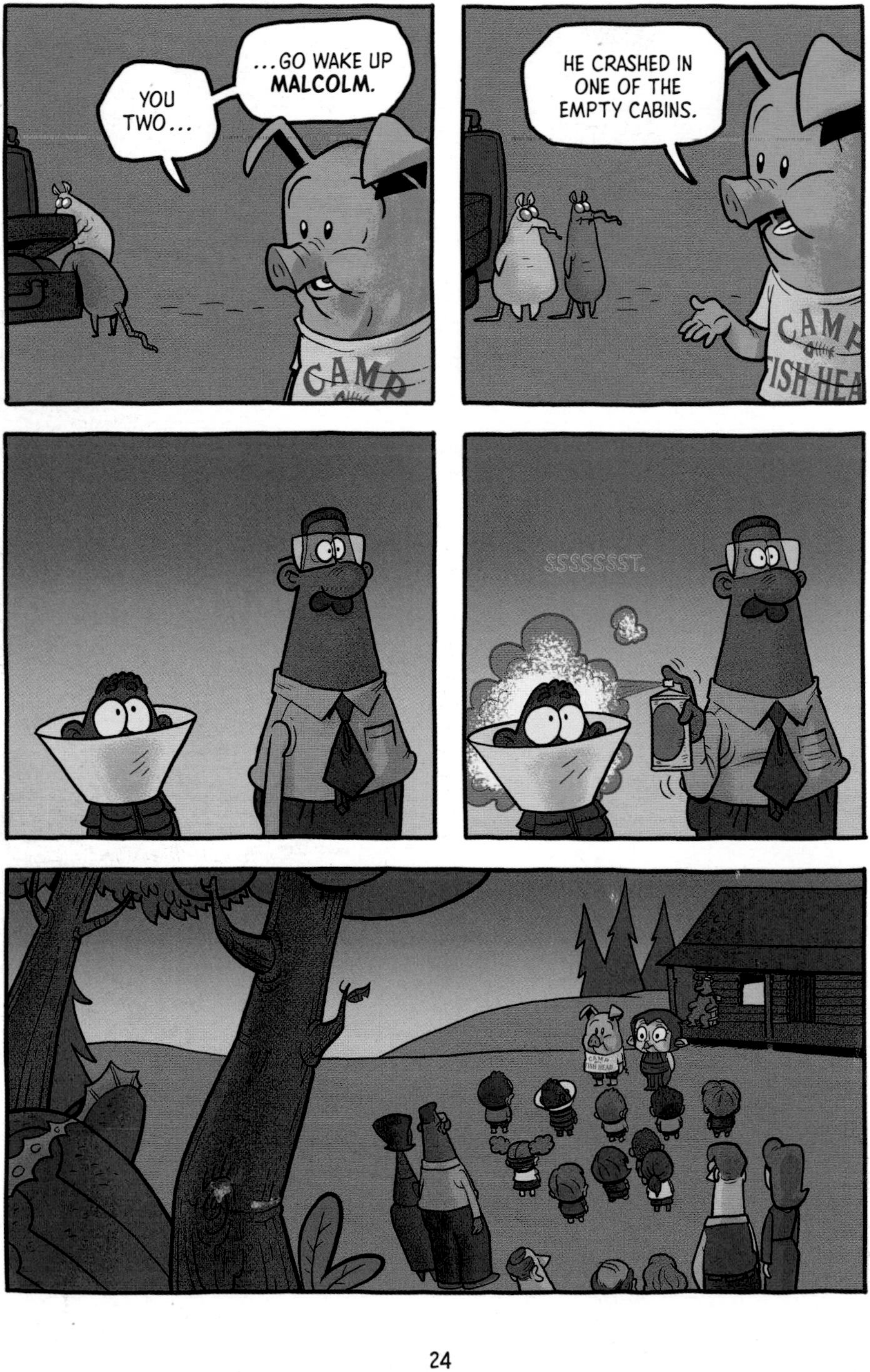
YOU TWO...
...GO WAKE UP MALCOLM.
HE CRASHED IN ONE OF THE EMPTY CABINS.
CAMP FISH HEAD
SSSSSSST.

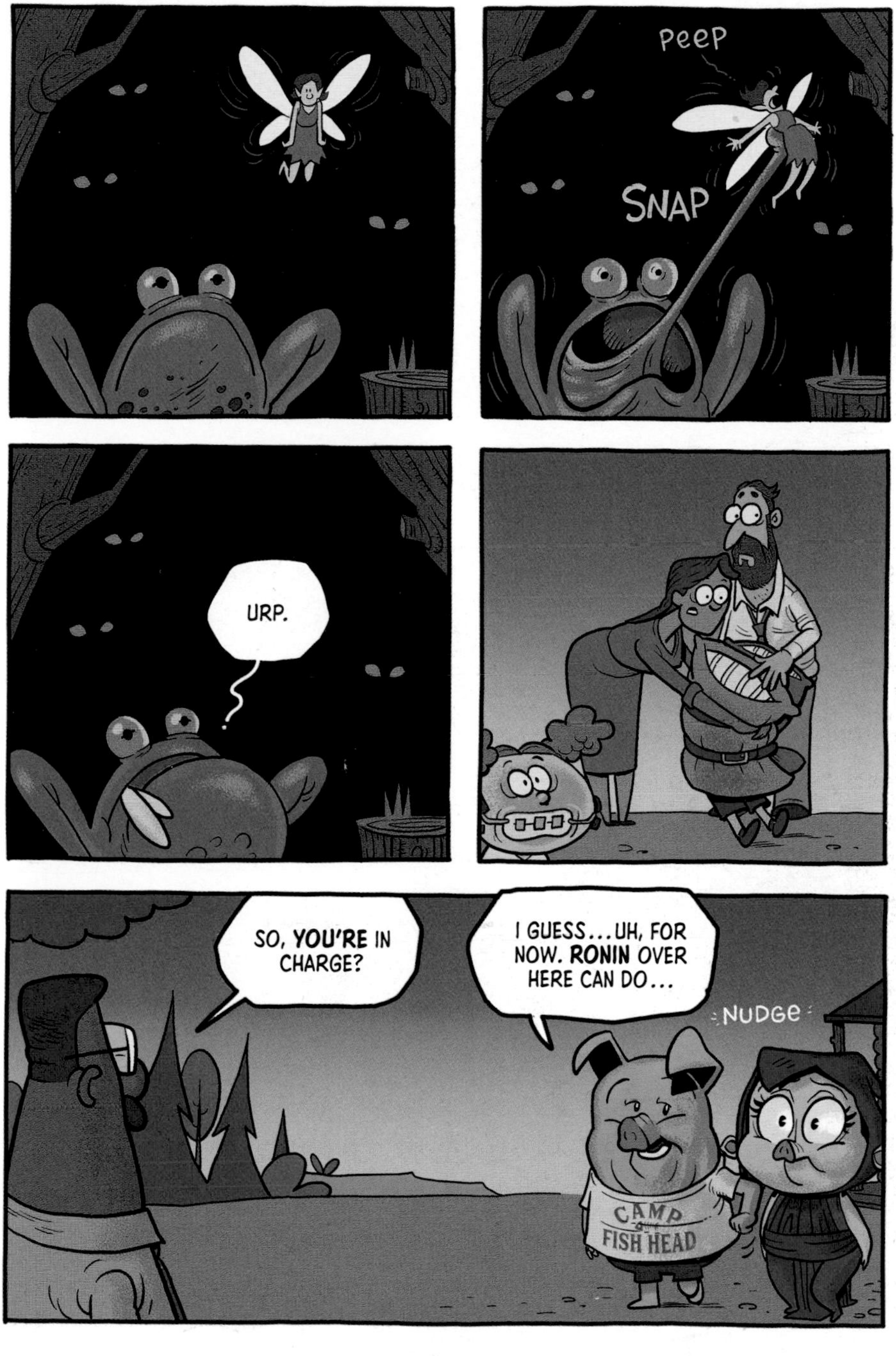
Peep
SNAP
URP.
SO, **YOU'RE** IN CHARGE?
I GUESS...UH, FOR NOW. **RONIN** OVER HERE CAN DO...
NUDGE
CAMP FISH HEAD

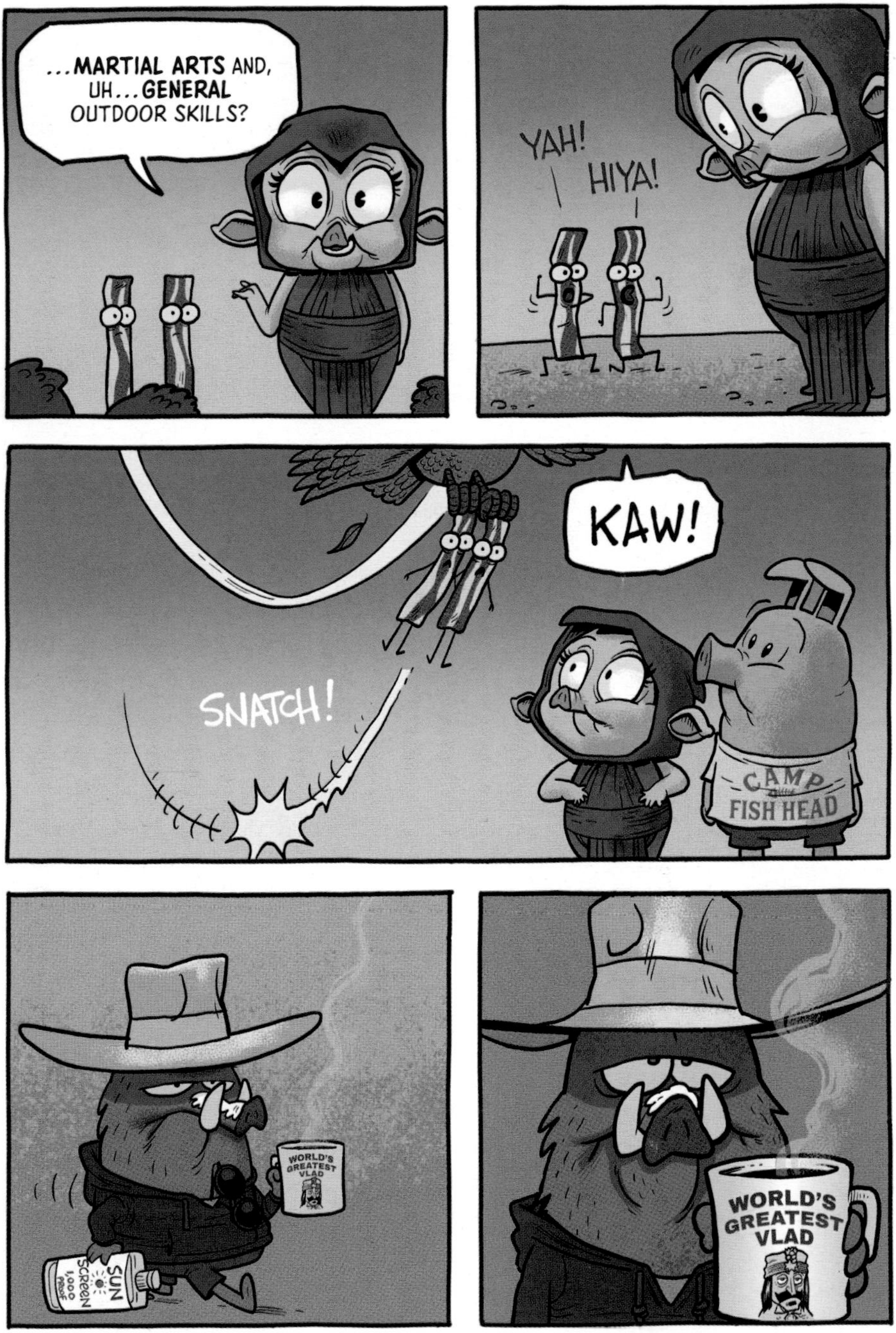
...MARTIAL ARTS AND, UH...GENERAL OUTDOOR SKILLS?
YAH!
HIYA!
KAW!
SNATCH!
CAMP FISH HEAD
WORLD'S GREATEST VLAD
SUN SCREEN 1,000 PROOF
WORLD'S GREATEST VLAD

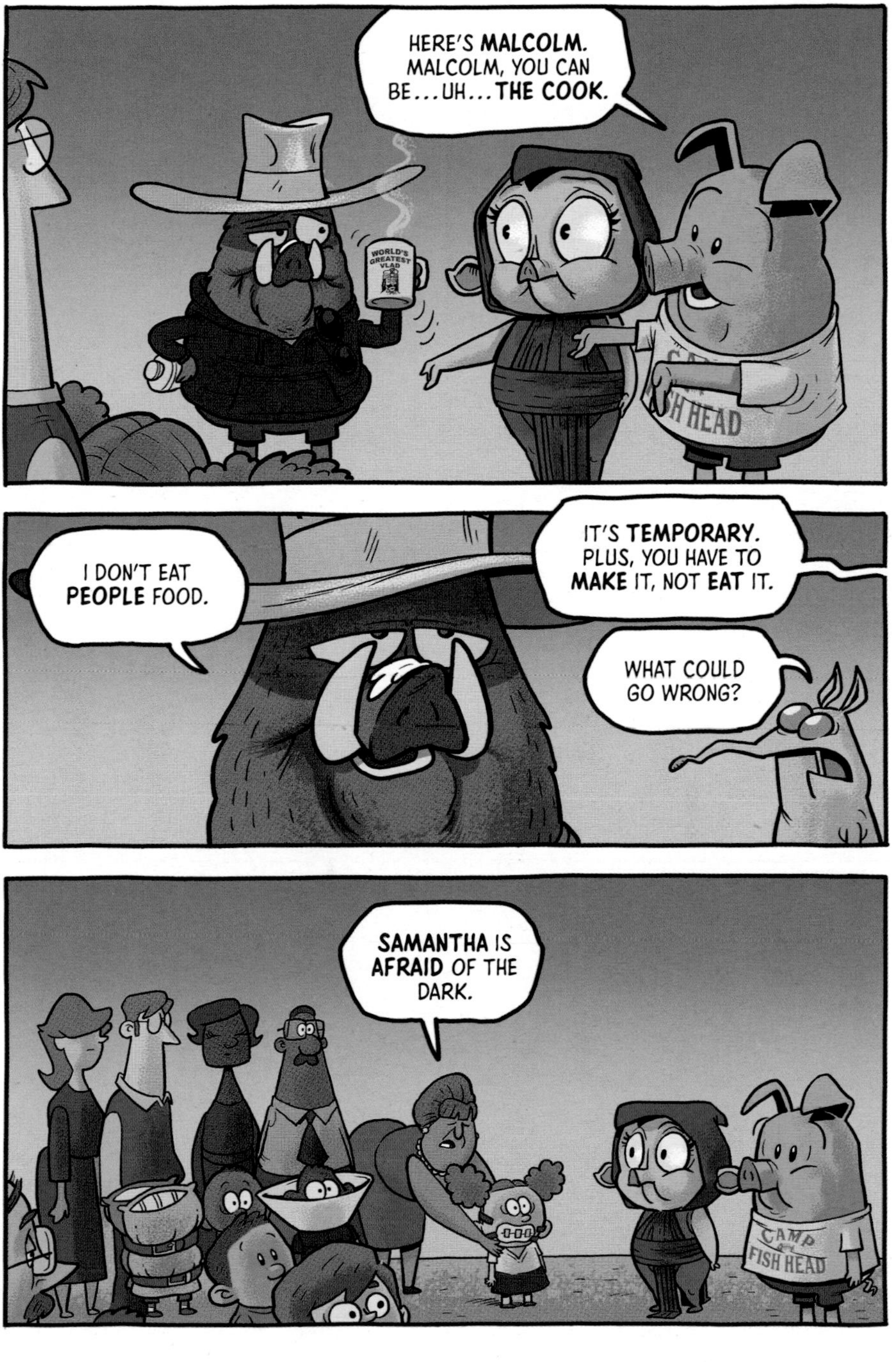
HERE'S **MALCOLM.** MALCOLM, YOU CAN BE...UH...**THE COOK.**
WORLD'S GREATEST VLAD
FISH HEAD
I DON'T EAT **PEOPLE** FOOD.
IT'S **TEMPORARY.** PLUS, YOU HAVE TO **MAKE** IT, NOT **EAT** IT.
WHAT COULD GO WRONG?
SAMANTHA IS **AFRAID** OF THE DARK.
CAMP FISH HEAD

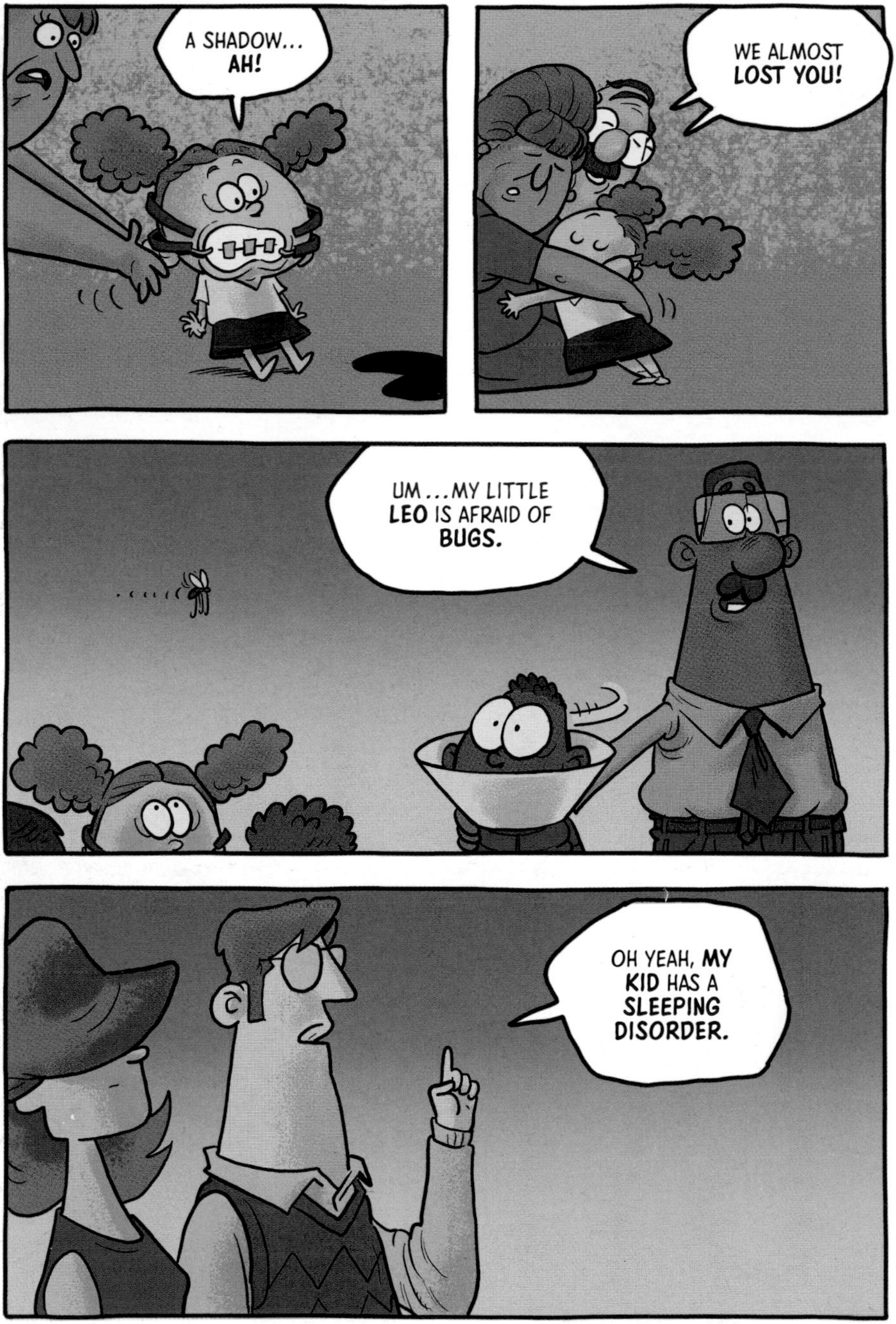
A SHADOW... AH!
WE ALMOST LOST YOU!
UM...MY LITTLE LEO IS AFRAID OF BUGS.
OH YEAH, MY KID HAS A SLEEPING DISORDER.

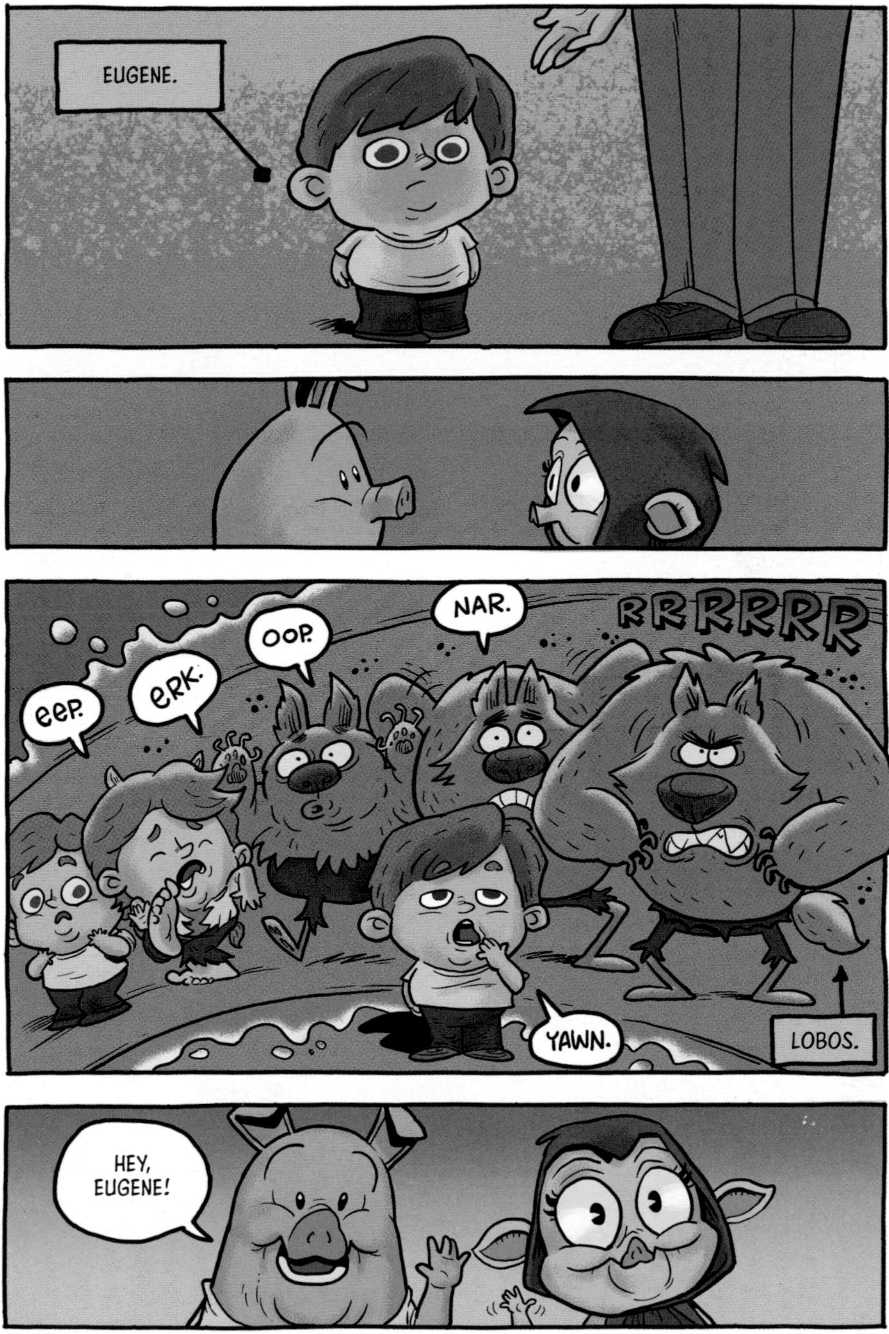
EUGENE.
EEP.
ERK.
OOP.
NAR.
RRRRRR
YAWN.
LOBOS.
HEY, EUGENE!

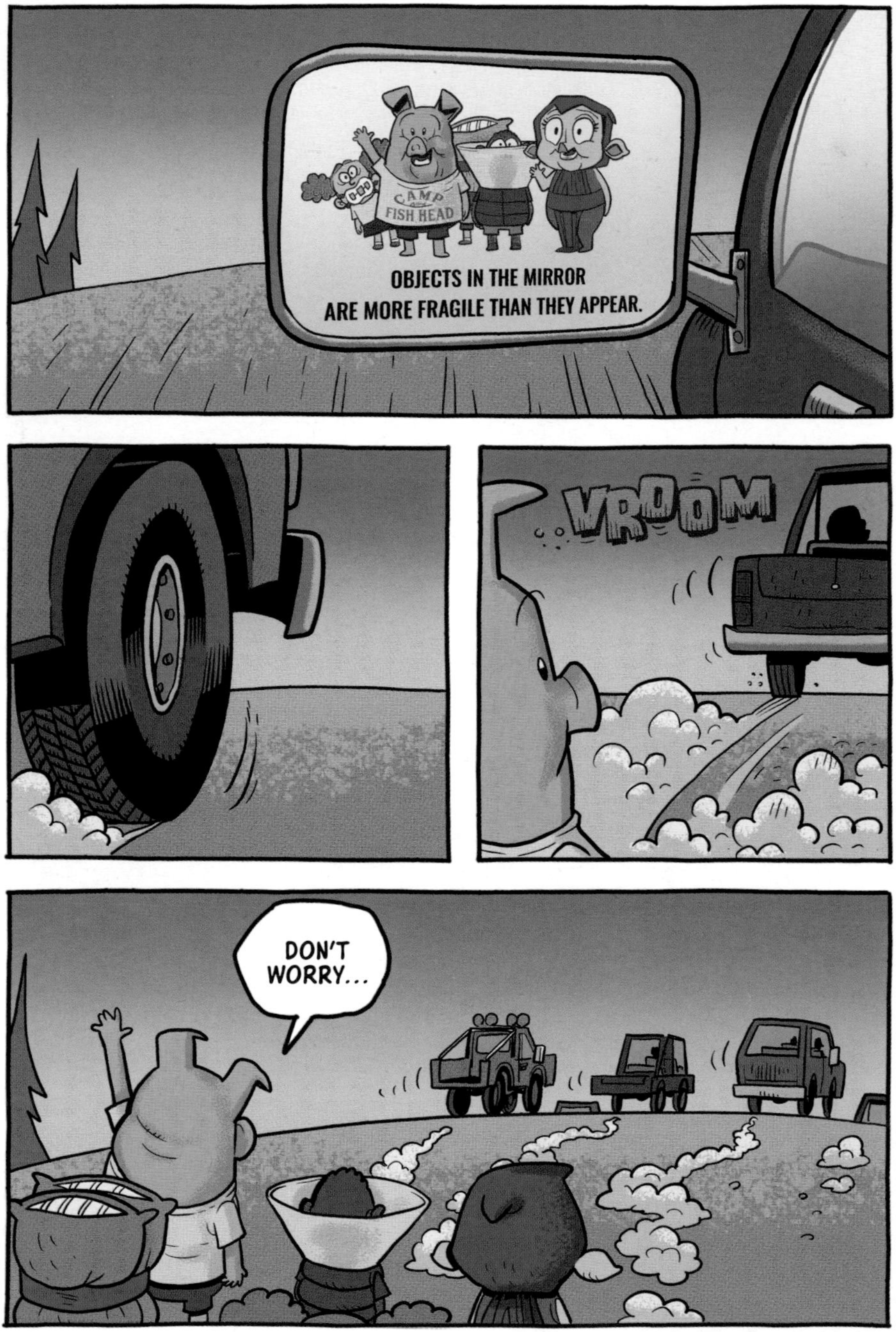
CAMP FISH HEAD
OBJECTS IN THE MIRROR ARE MORE FRAGILE THAN THEY APPEAR.
VROOM
DON'T WORRY...

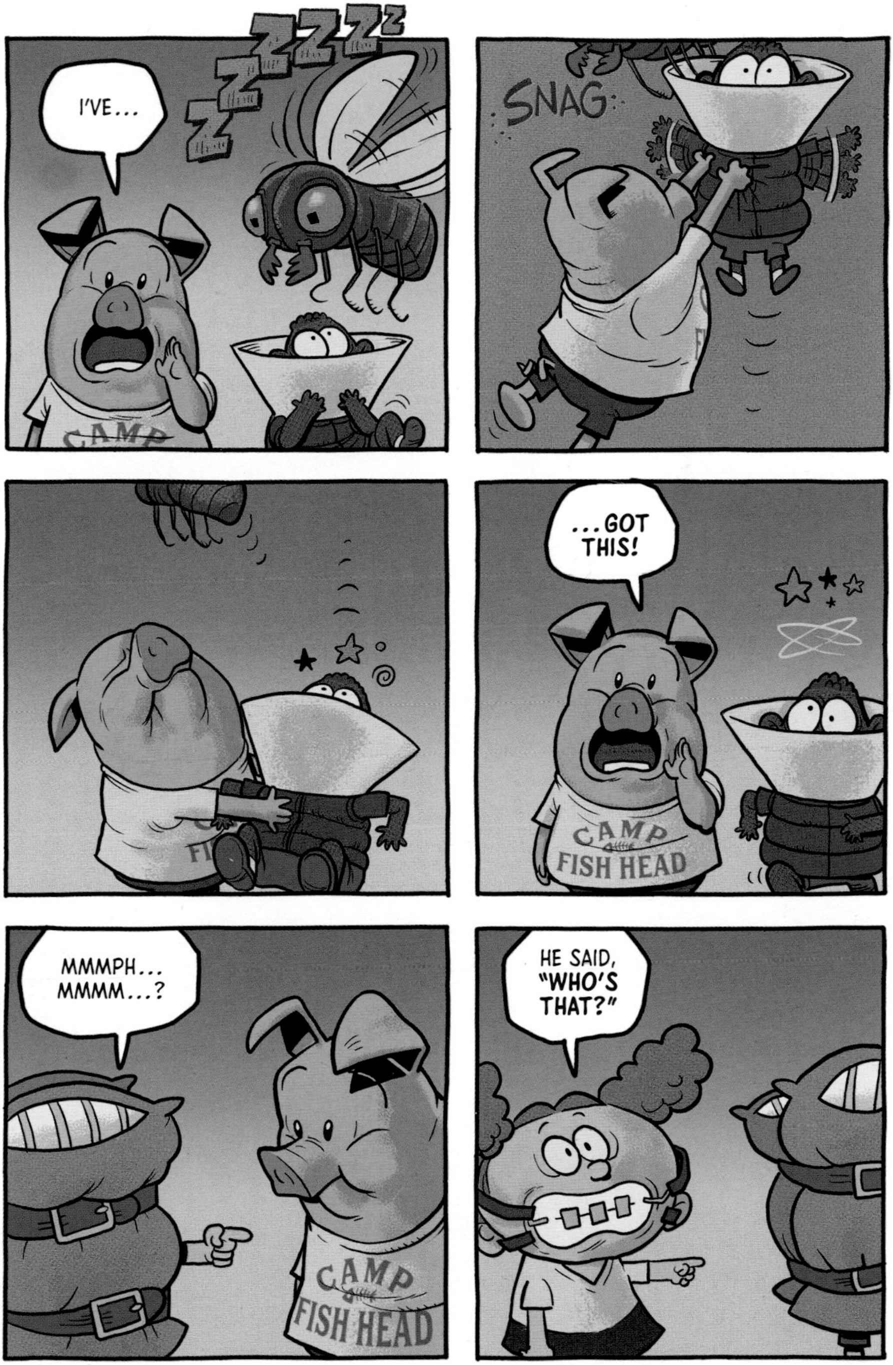
I'VE...
ZZZZZZ
SNAG
...GOT THIS!
CAMP FISH HEAD
MMMPH... MMMM...?
CAMP FISH HEAD
HE SAID, "WHO'S THAT?"

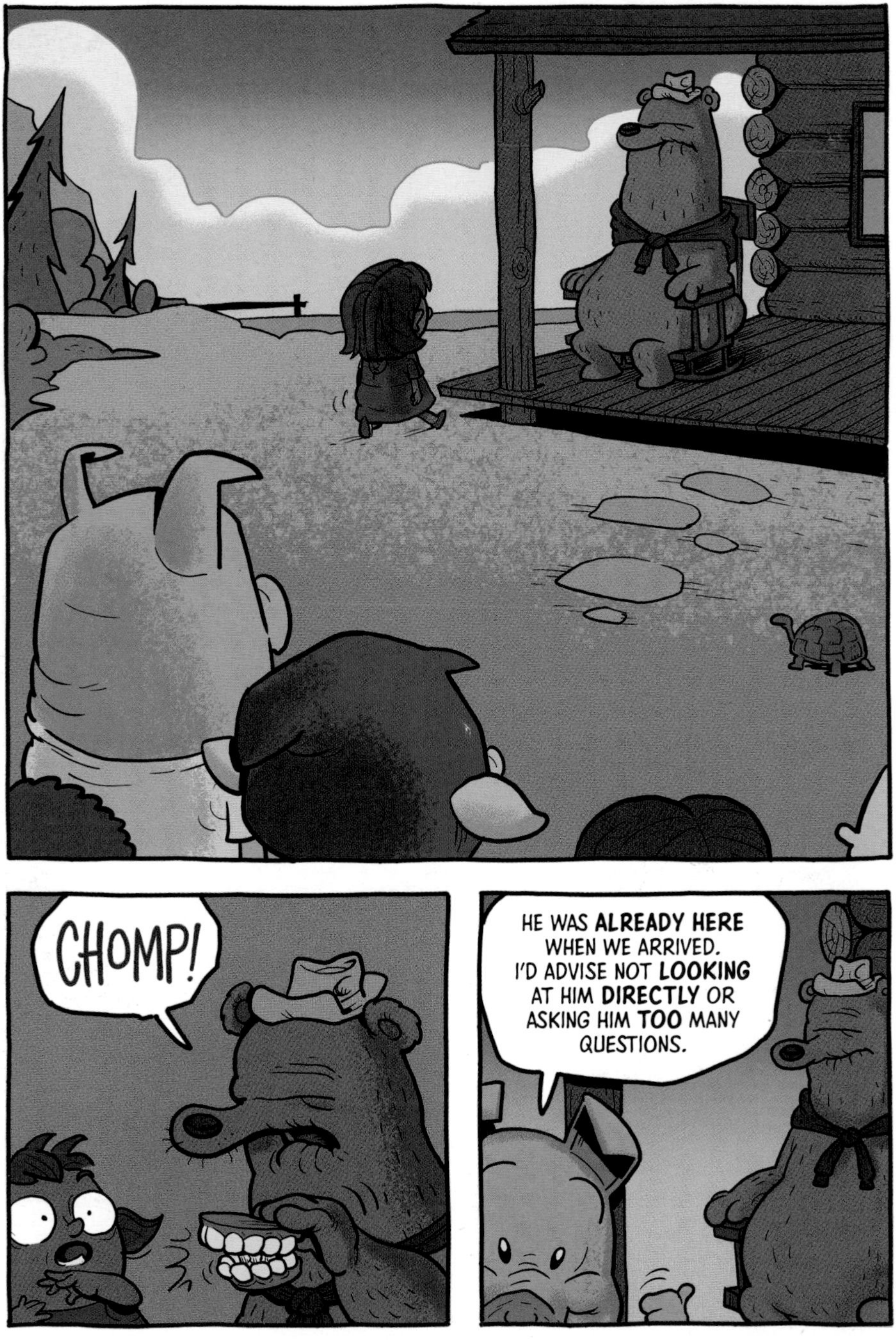
CHOMP!
HE WAS ALREADY HERE WHEN WE ARRIVED. I'D ADVISE NOT LOOKING AT HIM DIRECTLY OR ASKING HIM TOO MANY QUESTIONS.

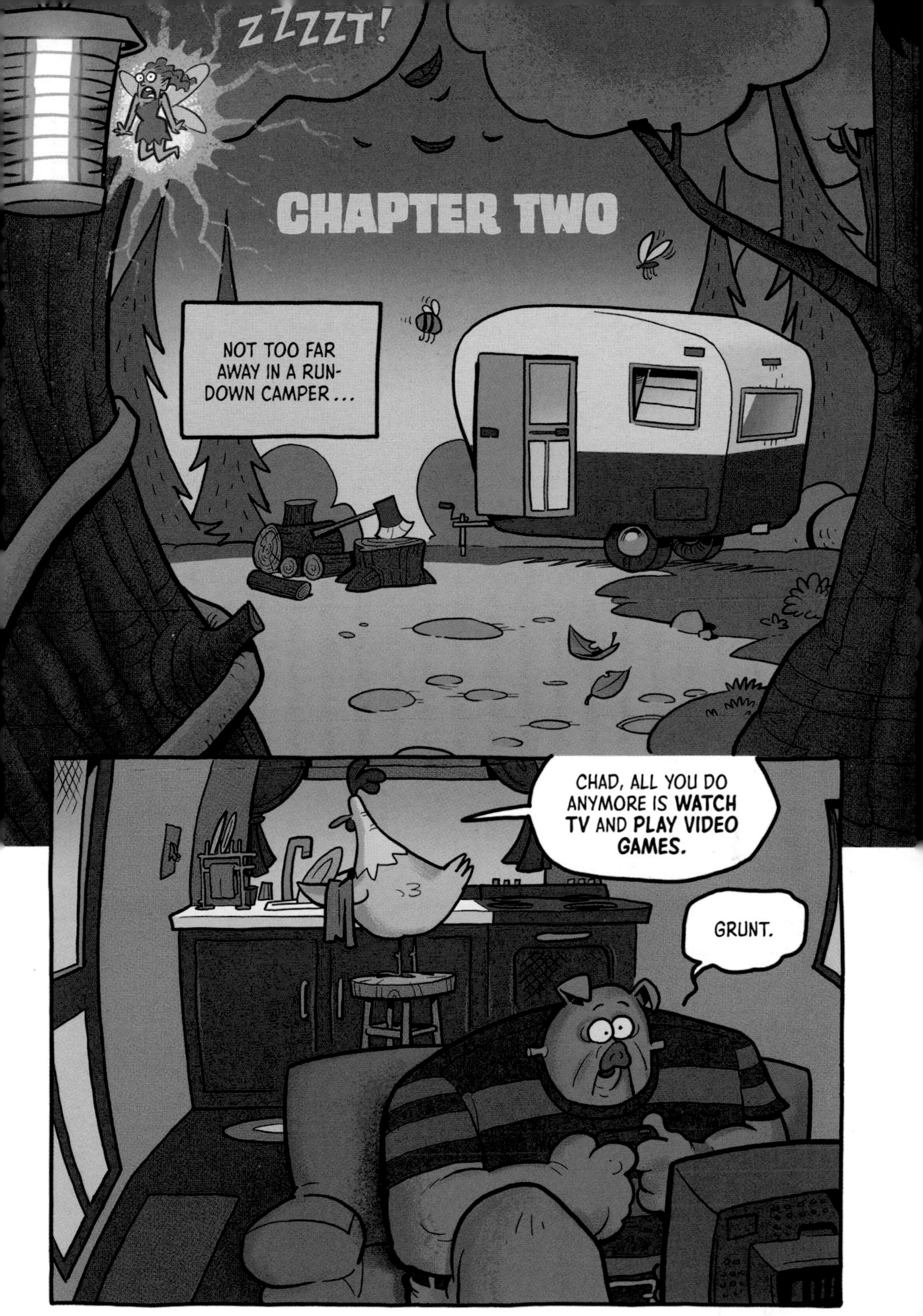
ZZZZT!
CHAPTER TWO
NOT TOO FAR AWAY IN A RUN-DOWN CAMPER...
CHAD, ALL YOU DO ANYMORE IS WATCH TV AND PLAY VIDEO GAMES.
GRUNT.

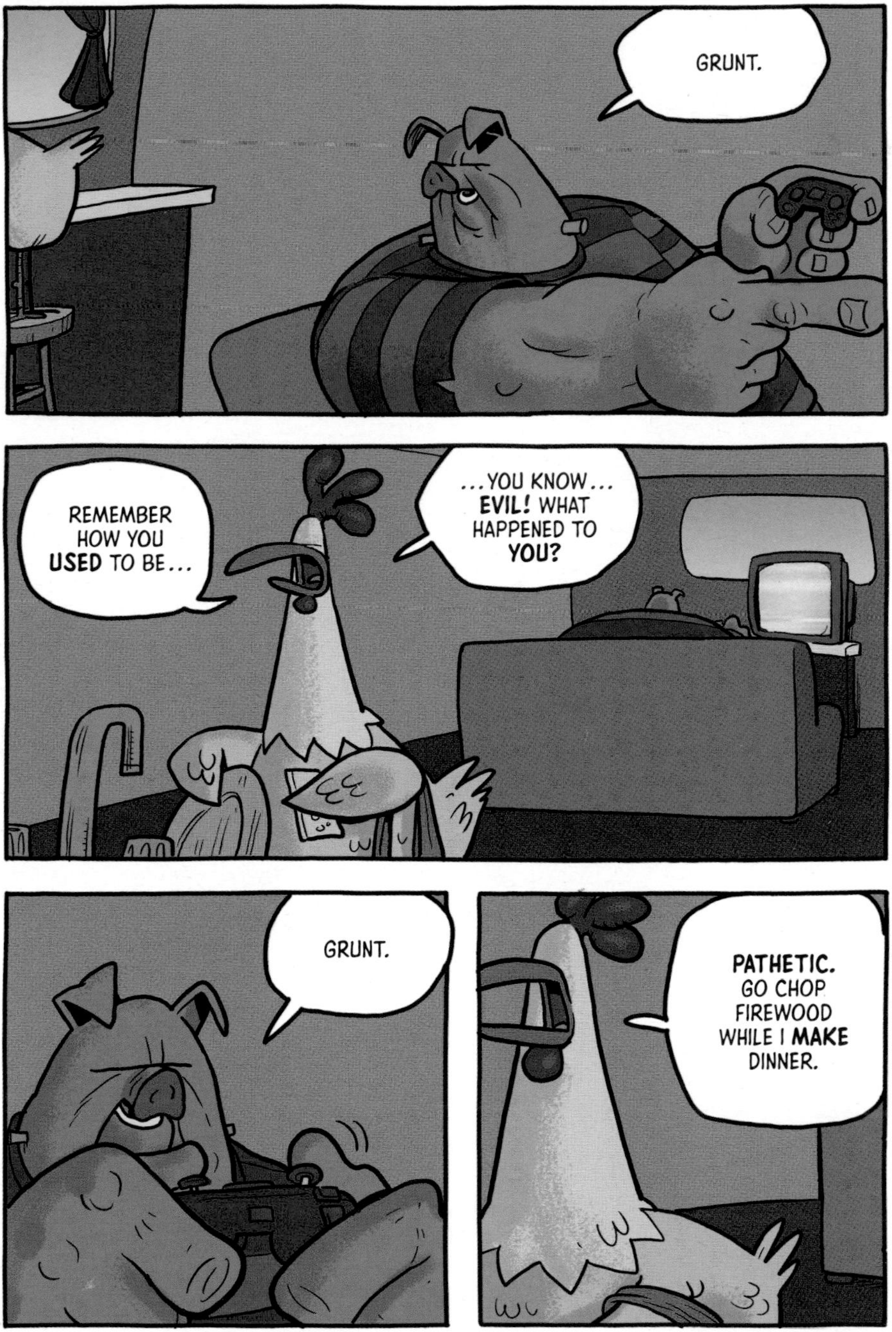
GRUNT.
REMEMBER HOW YOU **USED** TO BE...
...YOU KNOW... **EVIL!** WHAT HAPPENED TO **YOU?**
GRUNT.
PATHETIC. GO CHOP FIREWOOD WHILE I **MAKE** DINNER.

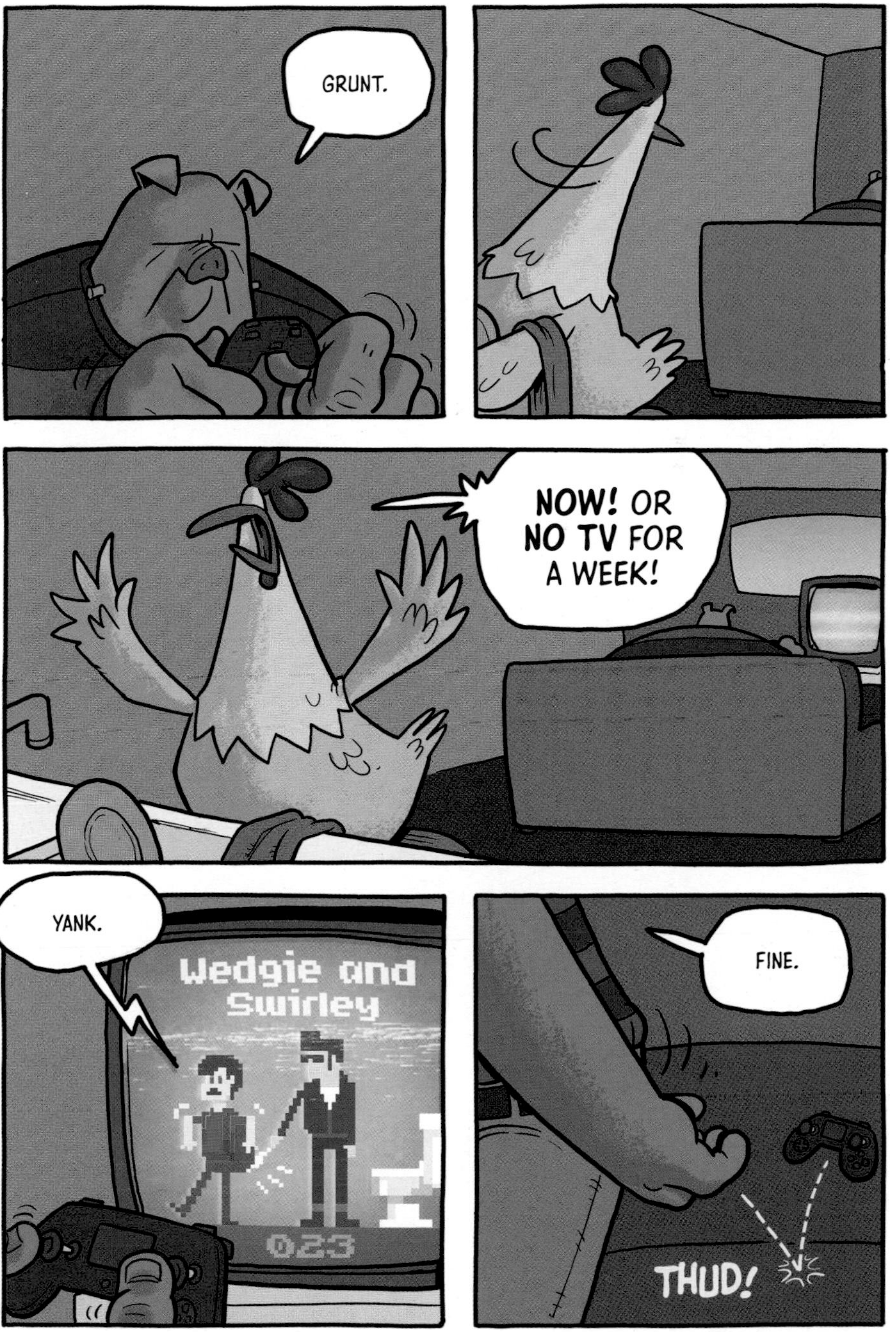
GRUNT.
NOW! OR NO TV FOR A WEEK!
YANK.
Wedgie and Swirley
023
FINE.
THUD!

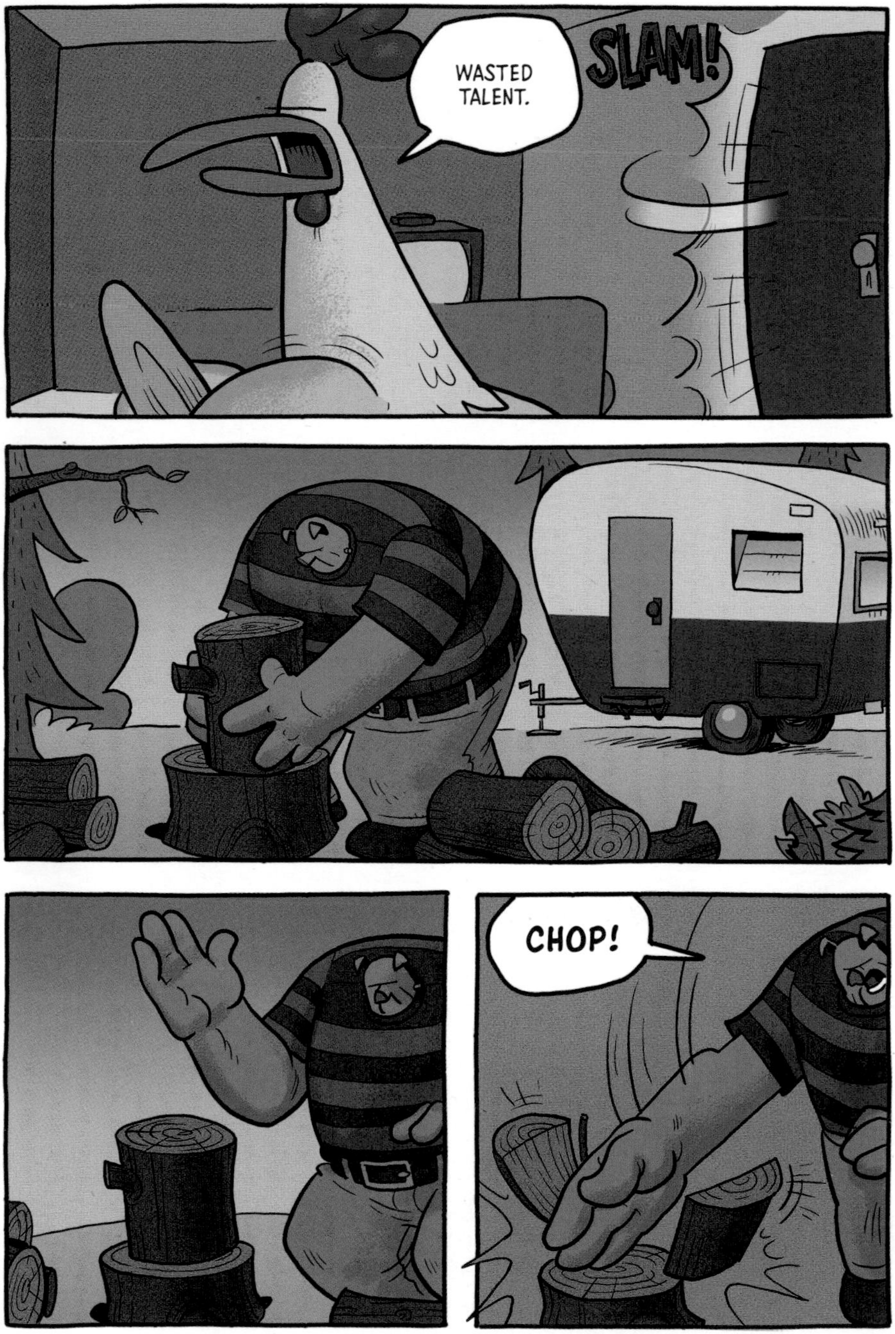
WASTED TALENT.
SLAM!
CHOP!

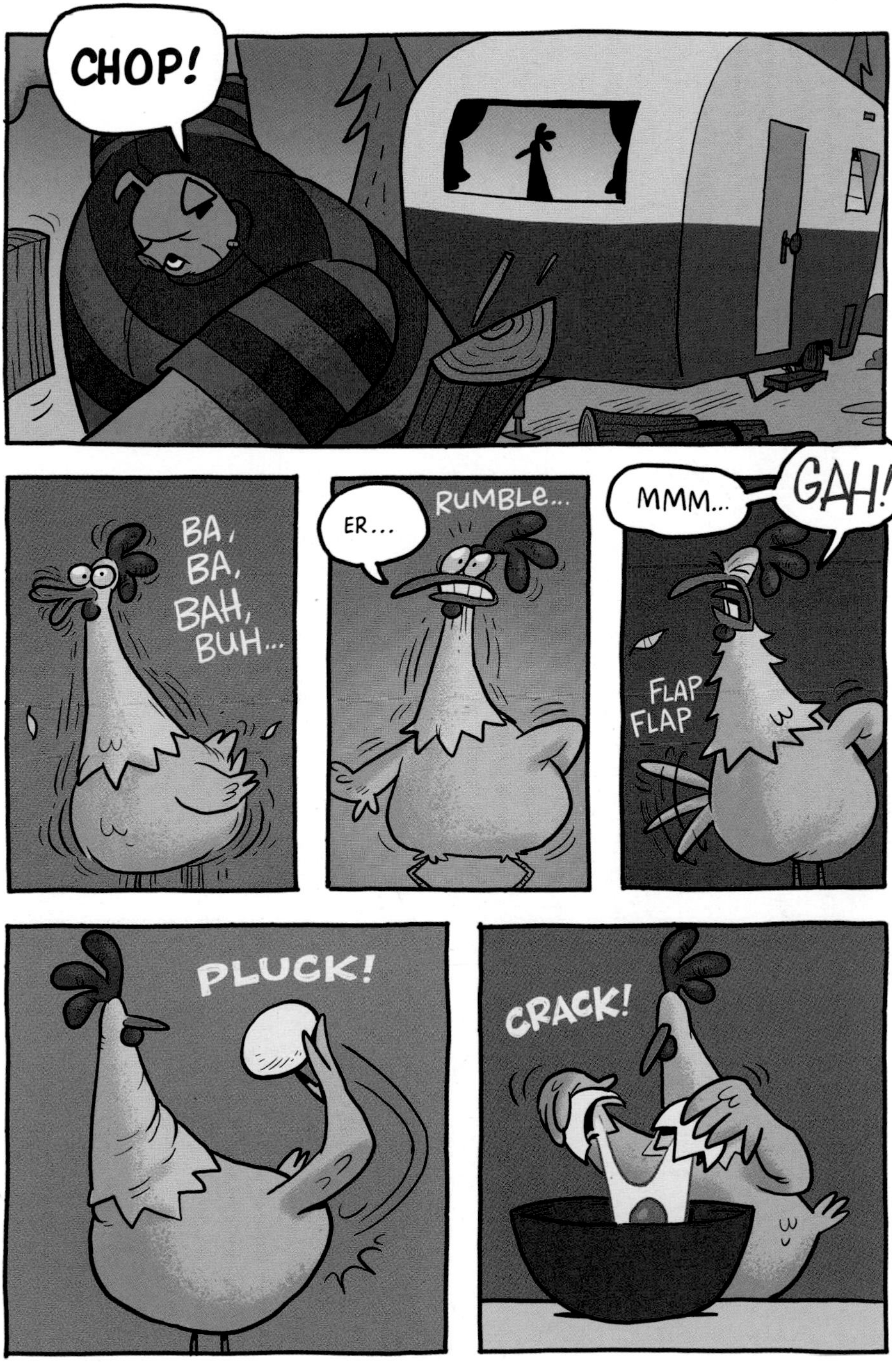
CHOP!
BA, BA, BAH, BUH...
ER...
RUMBLE...
MMM...
GAH!
FLAP FLAP
PLUCK!
CRACK!

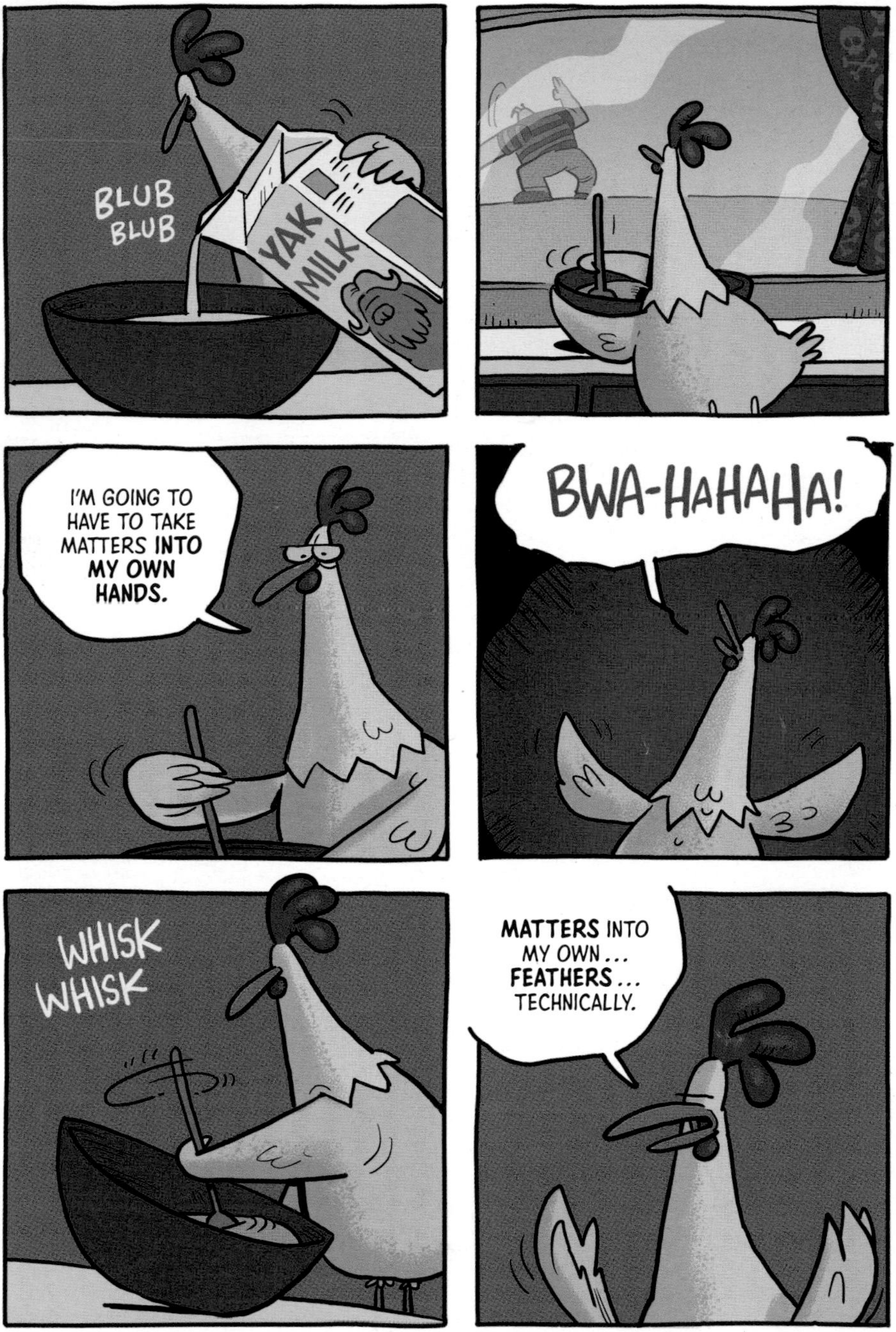
BLUB
BLUB
YAK MILK
I'M GOING TO HAVE TO TAKE MATTERS INTO MY OWN HANDS.
BWA-HAHAHA!
WHISK
WHISK
MATTERS INTO MY OWN... FEATHERS... TECHNICALLY.

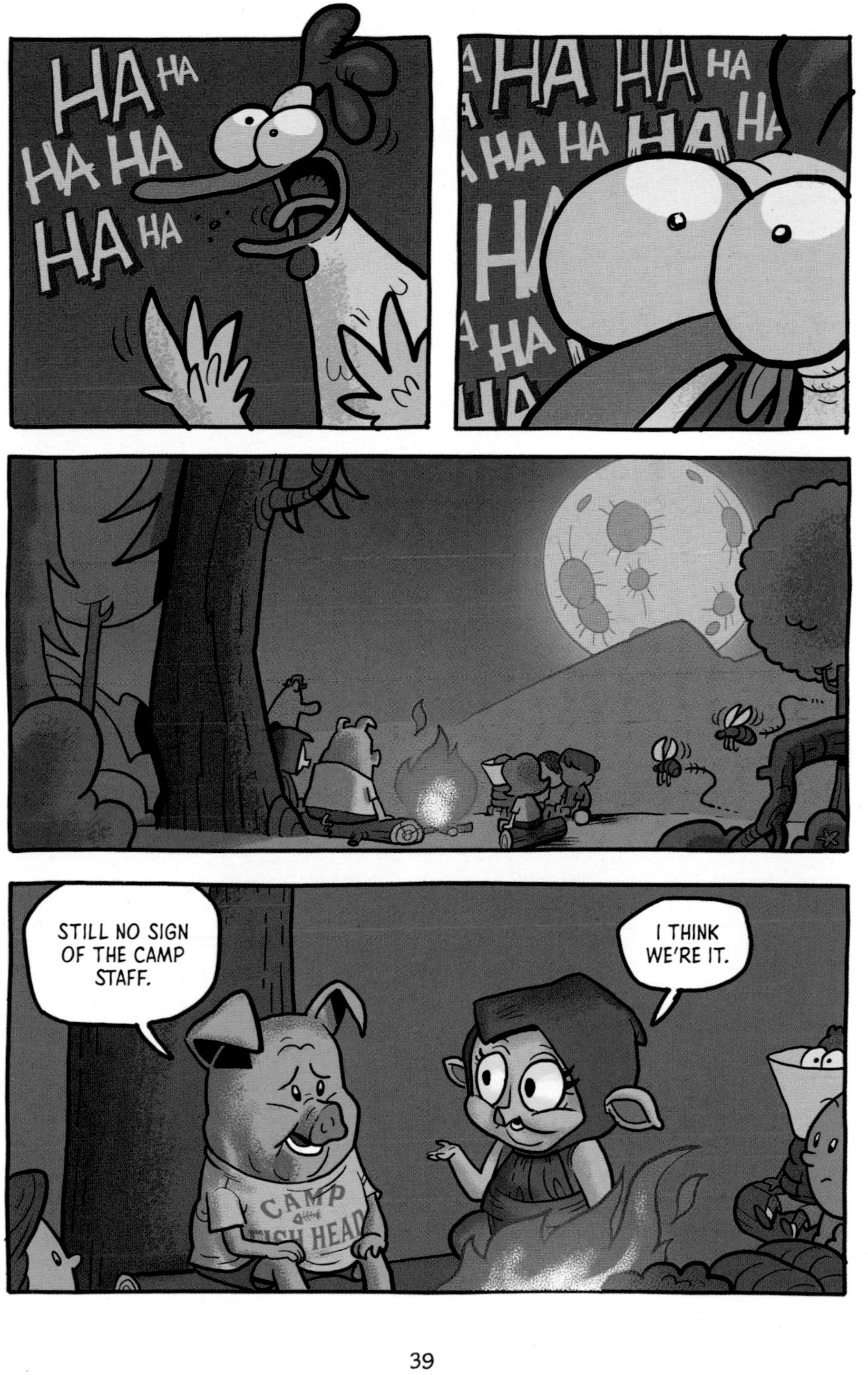
HA HA
HA HA
HA HA
HA HA HA HA
HA HA HA HA HA
HA
HA
STILL NO SIGN OF THE CAMP STAFF.
I THINK WE'RE IT.
CAMP FISH HEAD

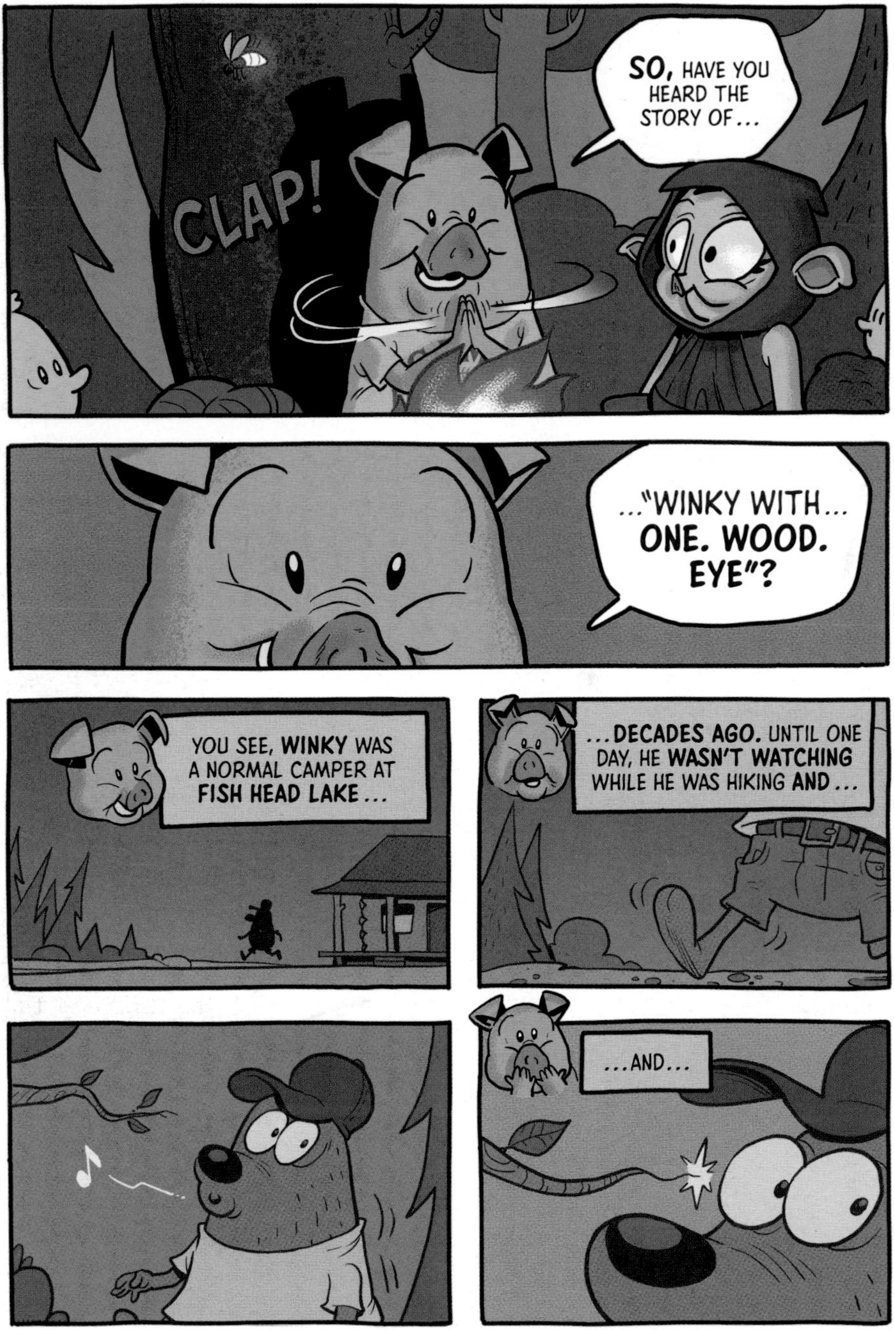
CLAP!
SO, HAVE YOU HEARD THE STORY OF...
..."WINKY WITH... ONE. WOOD. EYE"?
YOU SEE, WINKY WAS A NORMAL CAMPER AT FISH HEAD LAKE...
...DECADES AGO. UNTIL ONE DAY, HE WASN'T WATCHING WHILE HE WAS HIKING AND...
...AND...

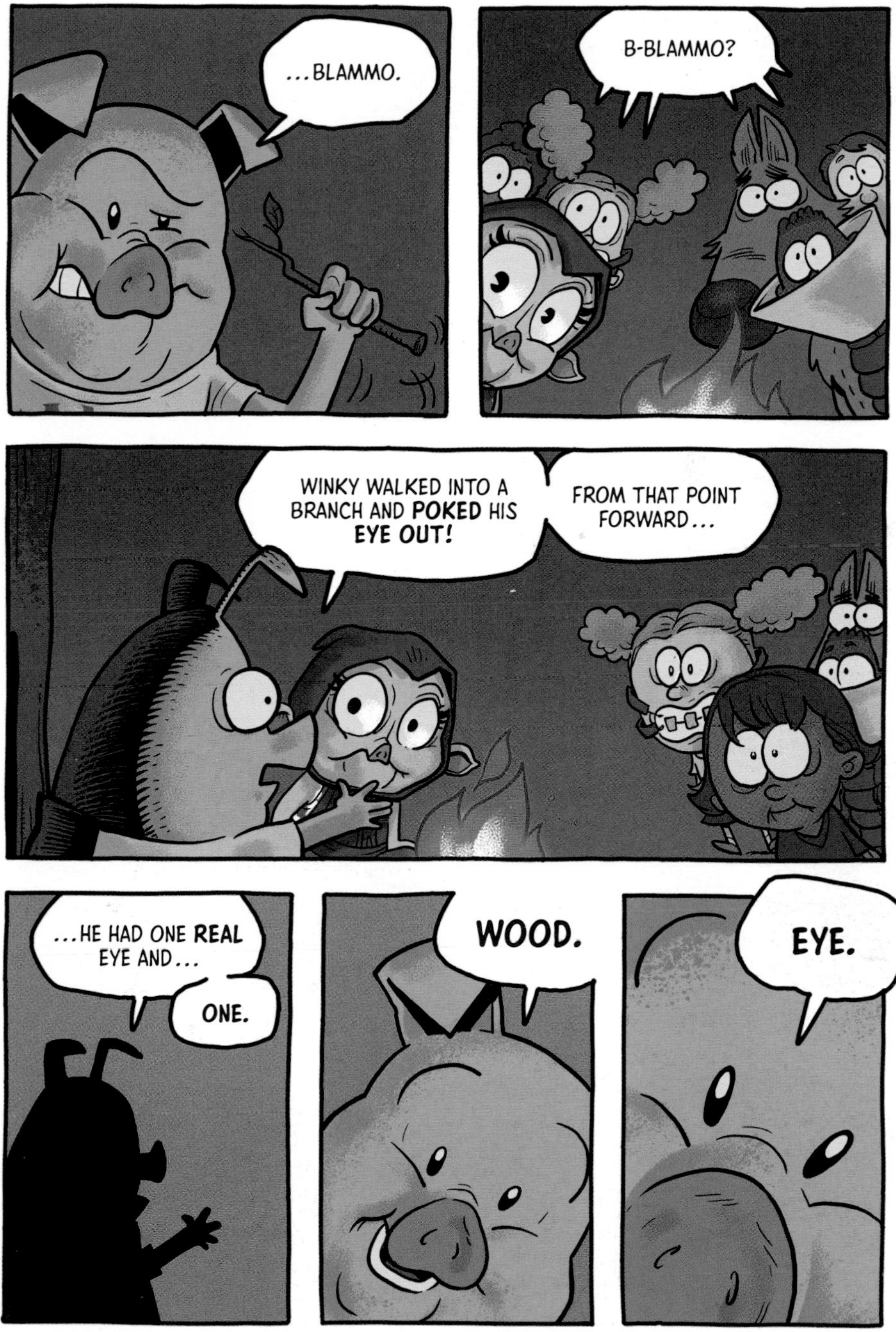
...BLAMMO.
B-BLAMMO?
WINKY WALKED INTO A BRANCH AND **POKED** HIS **EYE OUT!**
FROM THAT POINT FORWARD...
...HE HAD ONE **REAL** EYE AND...
ONE.
WOOD.
EYE.

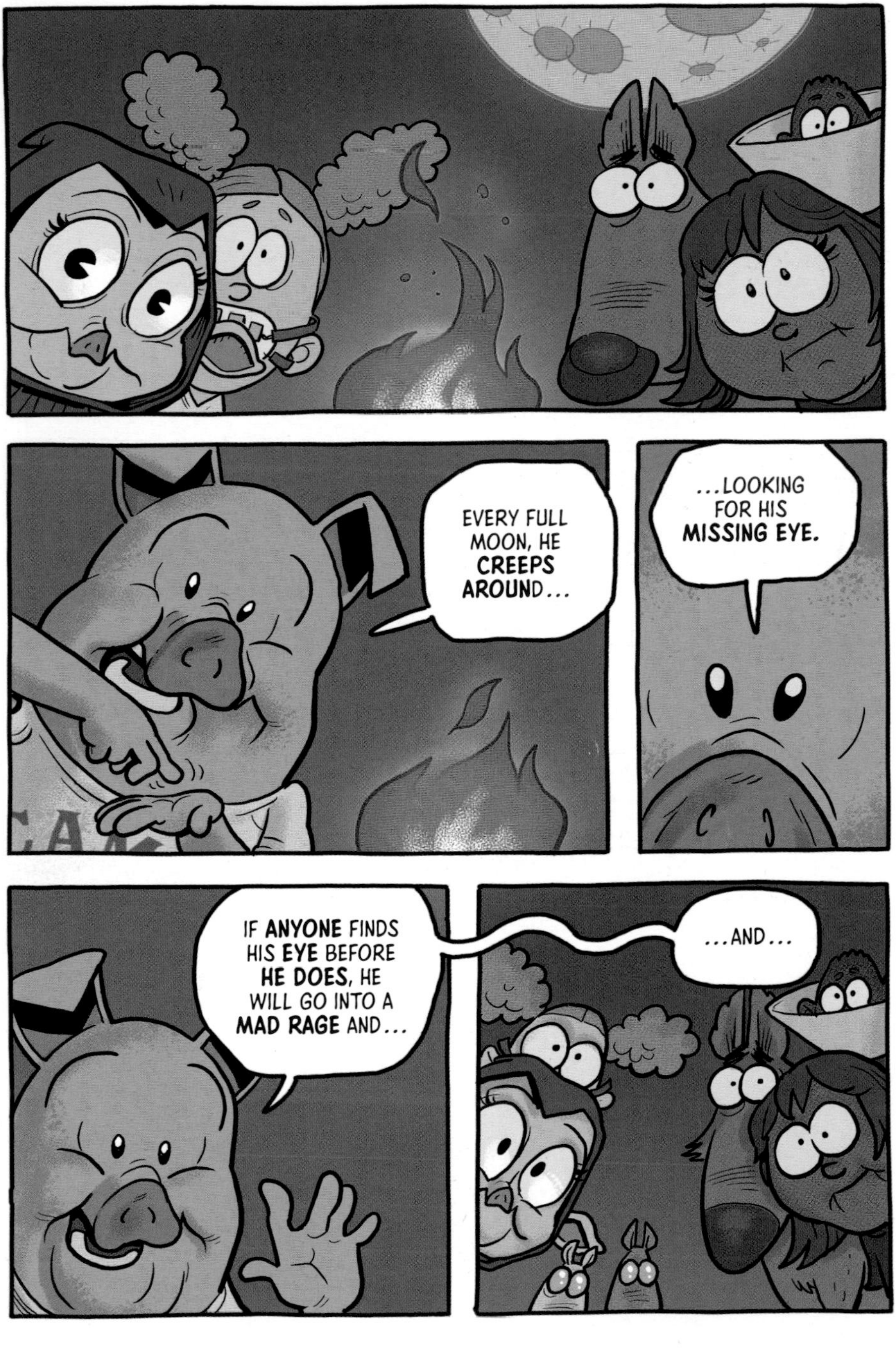
EVERY FULL MOON, HE CREEPS AROUND...
...LOOKING FOR HIS MISSING EYE.
IF ANYONE FINDS HIS EYE BEFORE HE DOES, HE WILL GO INTO A MAD RAGE AND...
...AND...

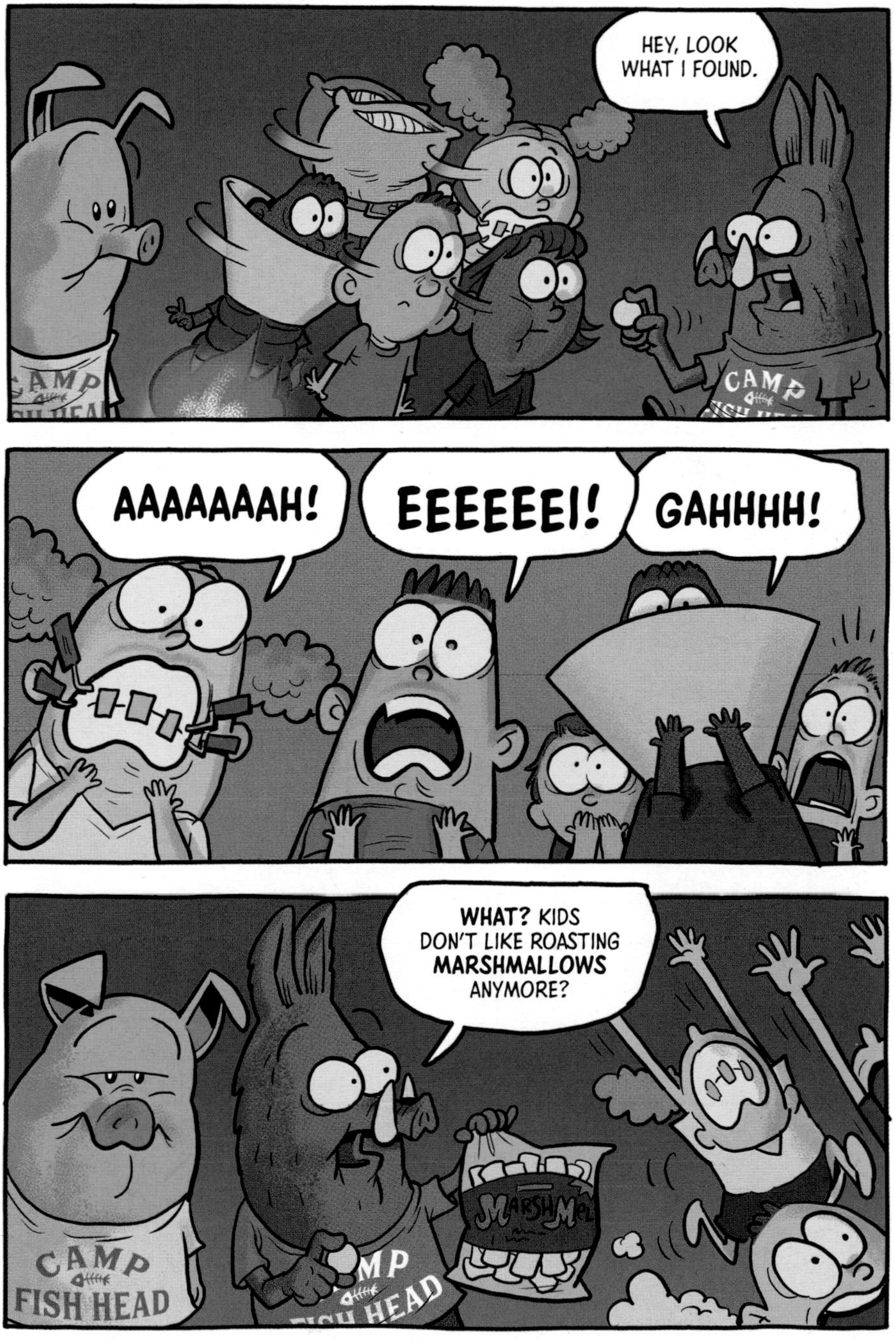
HEY, LOOK WHAT I FOUND.
CAMP FISH HEAD
AAAAAAAH!
EEEEEEI!
GAHHHH!
WHAT? KIDS DON'T LIKE ROASTING MARSHMALLOWS ANYMORE?
MARSHMEL
CAMP FISH HEAD
CAMP FISH HEAD

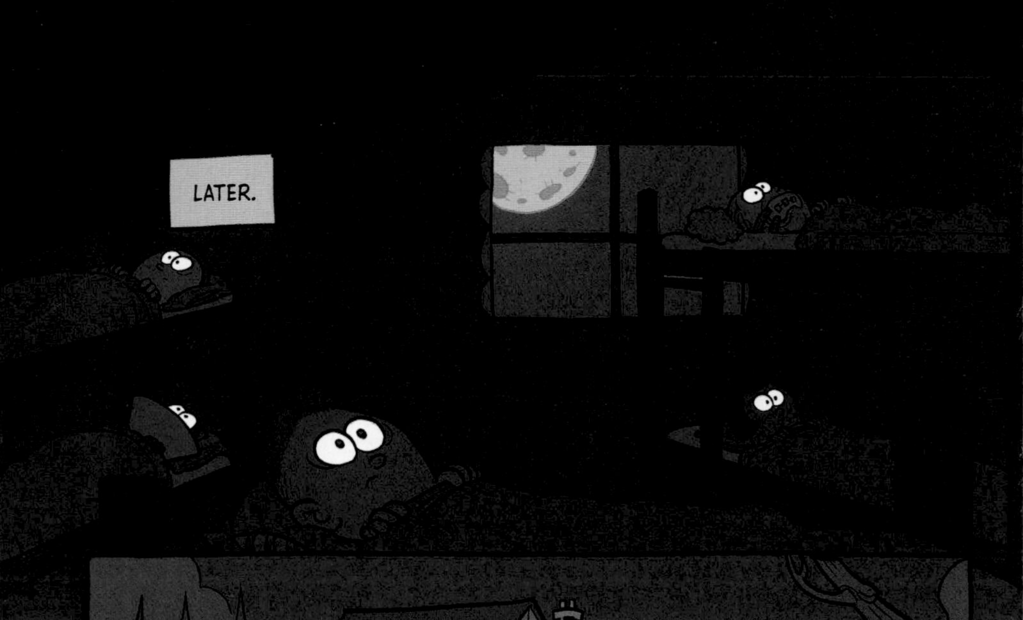
LATER.

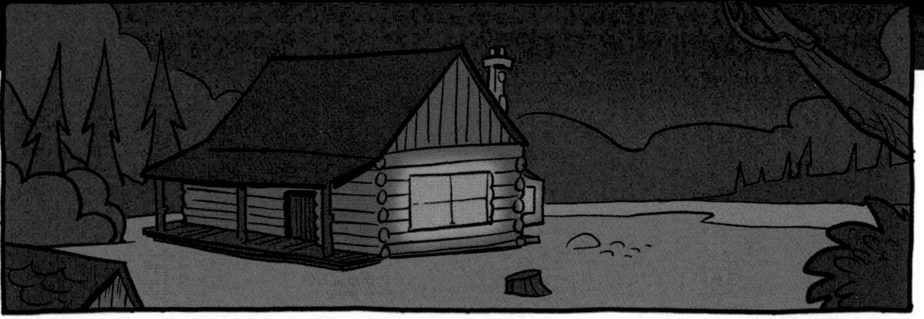

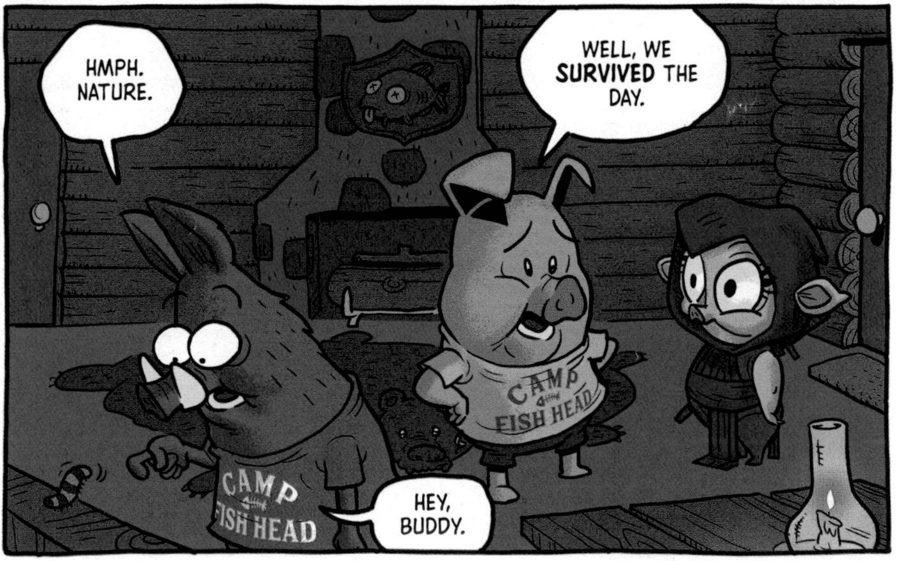
HMPH. NATURE.
WELL, WE **SURVIVED** THE DAY.
CAMP FISH HEAD
CAMP FISH HEAD
HEY, BUDDY.

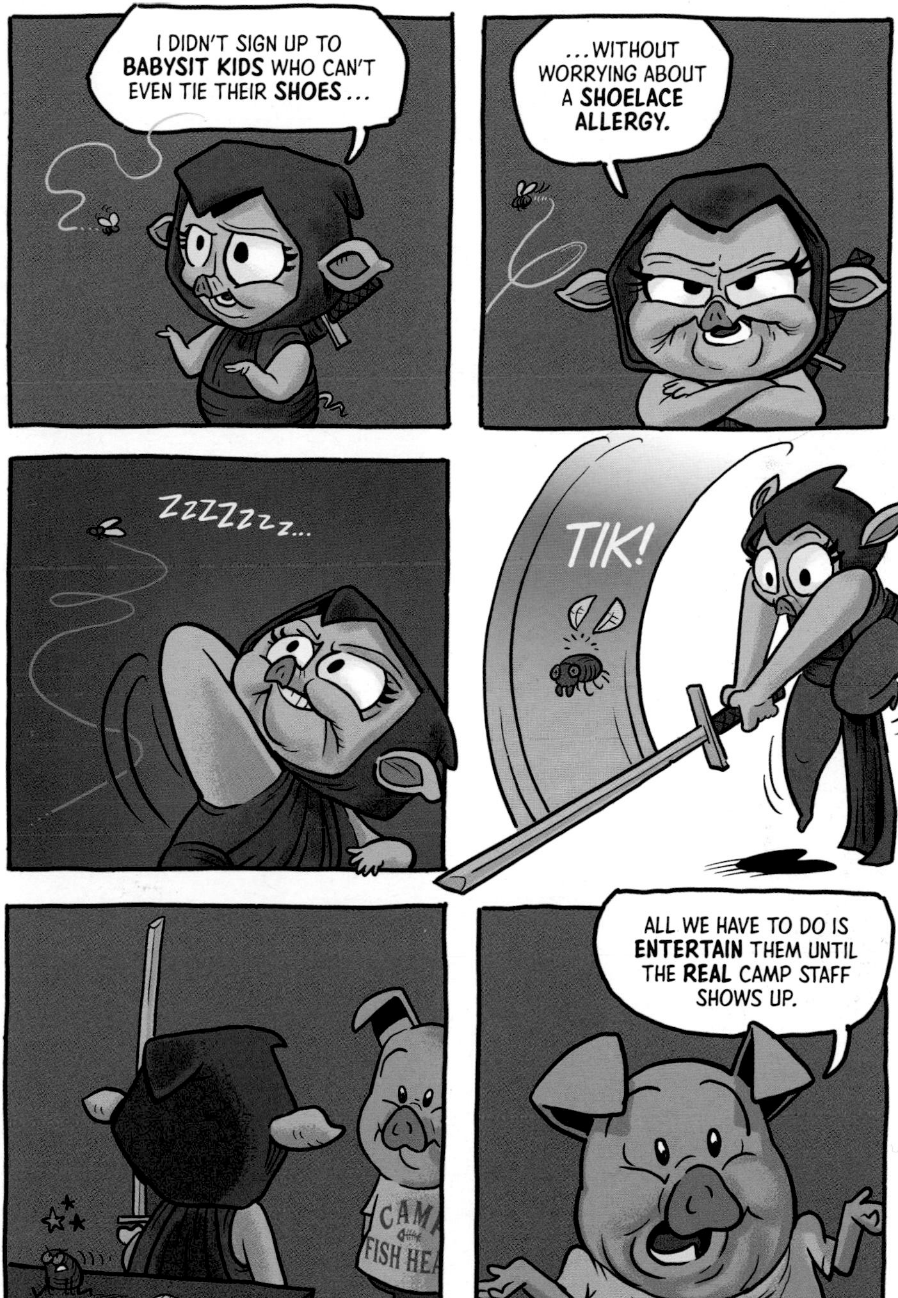
I DIDN'T SIGN UP TO BABYSIT KIDS WHO CAN'T EVEN TIE THEIR SHOES...
...WITHOUT WORRYING ABOUT A SHOELACE ALLERGY.
ZZZZZZZ...
TIK!
CAMP FISH HEA
ALL WE HAVE TO DO IS ENTERTAIN THEM UNTIL THE REAL CAMP STAFF SHOWS UP.

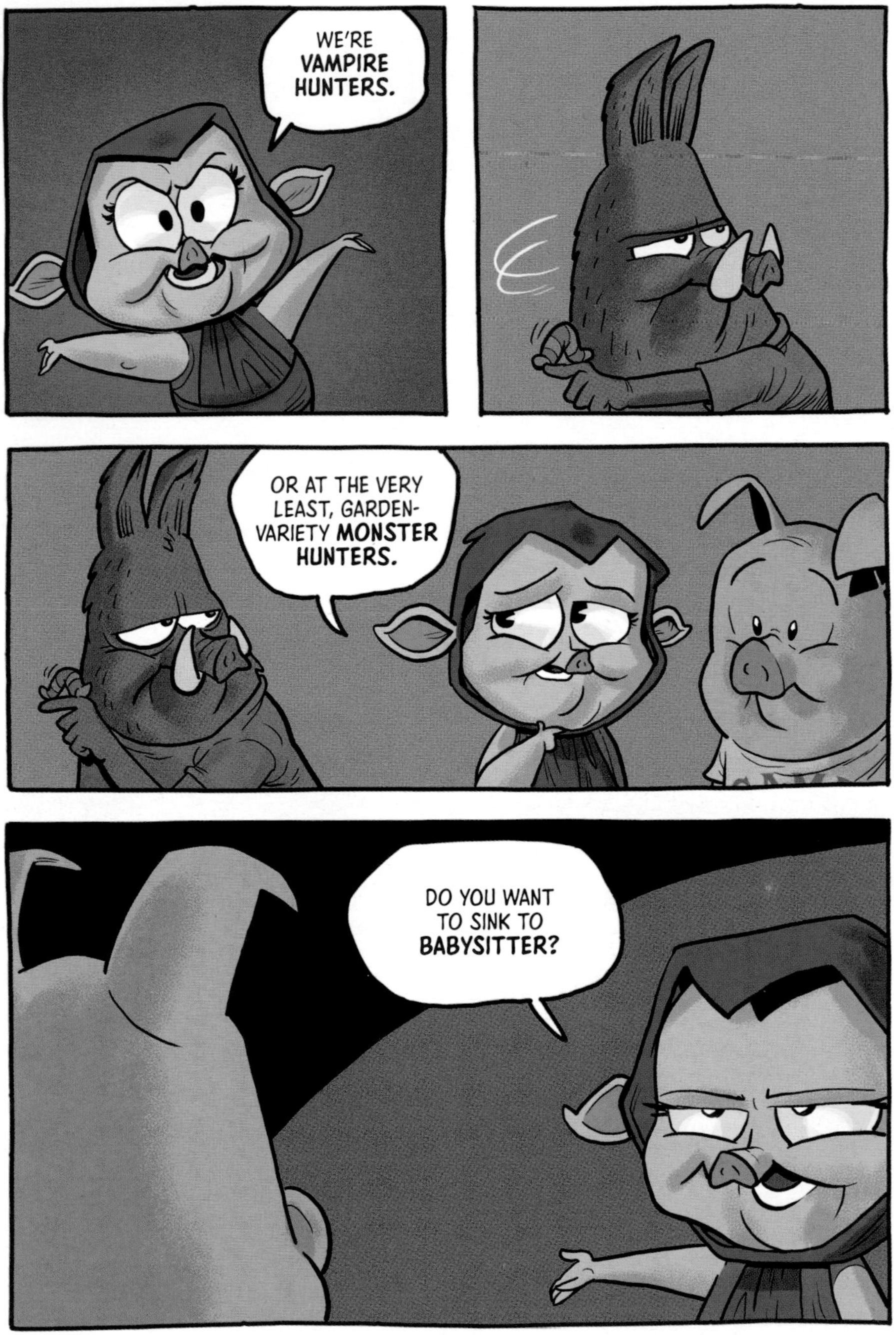
WE'RE VAMPIRE HUNTERS.
OR AT THE VERY LEAST, GARDEN-VARIETY MONSTER HUNTERS.
DO YOU WANT TO SINK TO BABYSITTER?

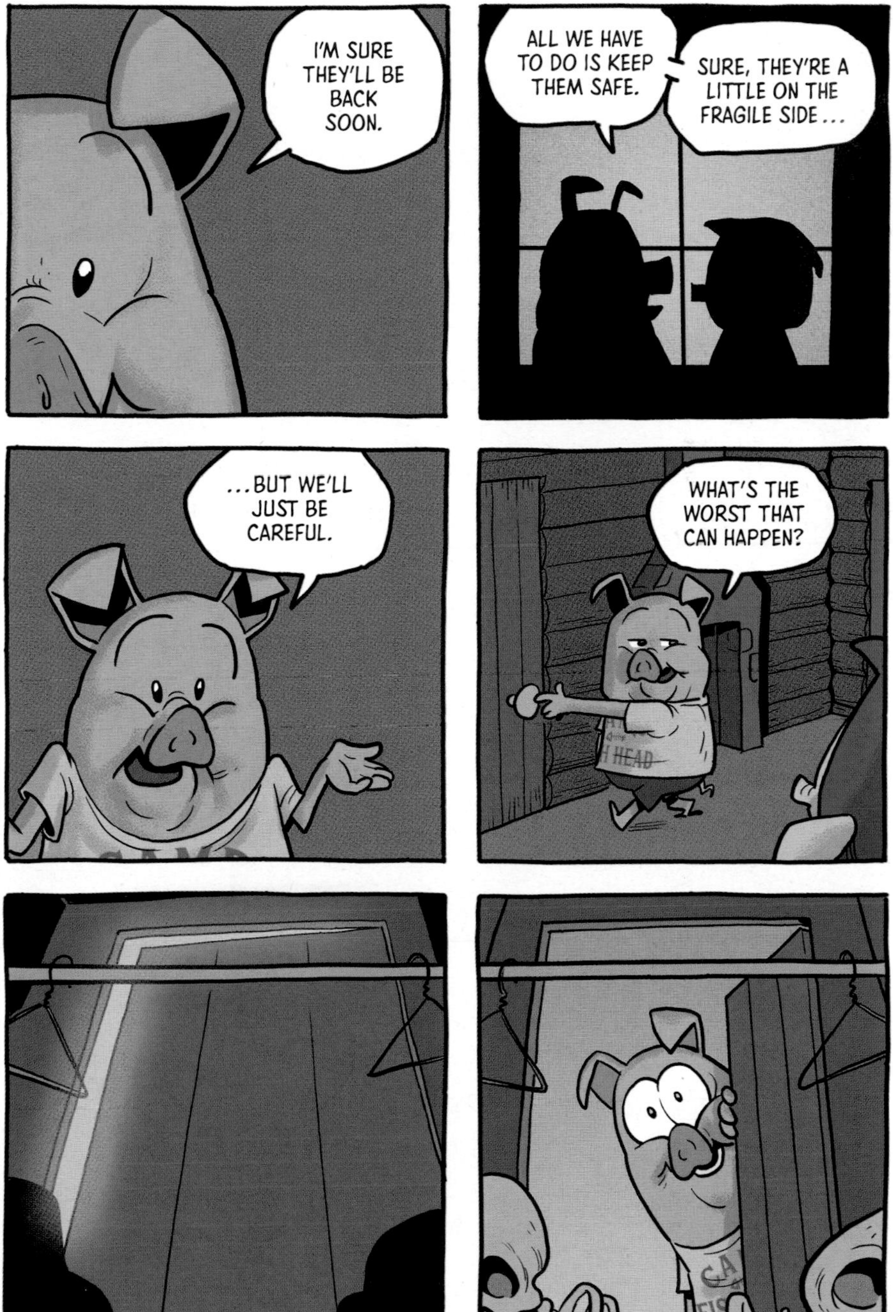
I'M SURE THEY'LL BE BACK SOON.
ALL WE HAVE TO DO IS KEEP THEM SAFE.
SURE, THEY'RE A LITTLE ON THE FRAGILE SIDE...
...BUT WE'LL JUST BE CAREFUL.
WHAT'S THE WORST THAT CAN HAPPEN?

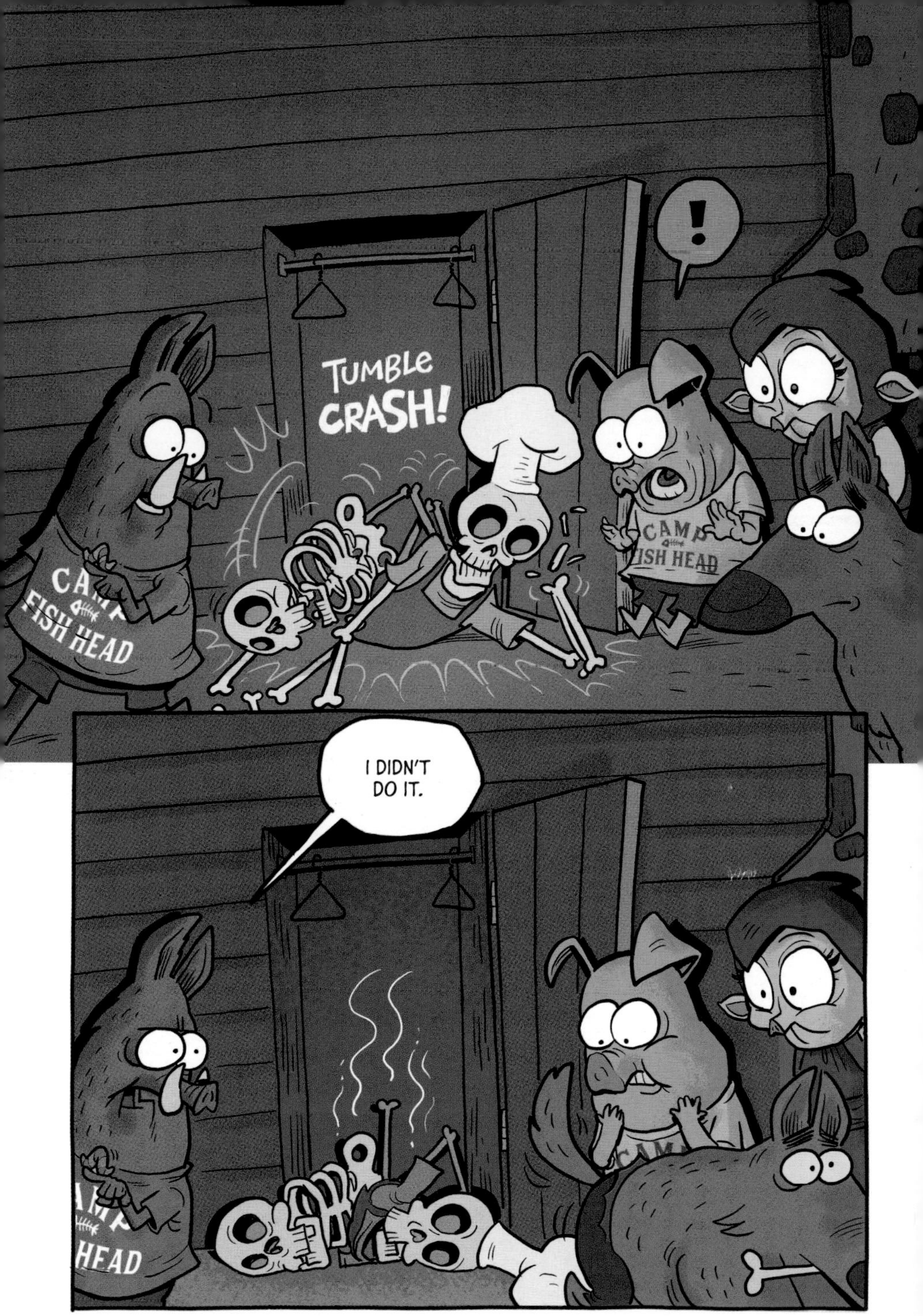
!
TUMBLE CRASH!
CAMP FISH HEAD
CAMP FISH HEAD
I DIDN'T DO IT.
HEAD

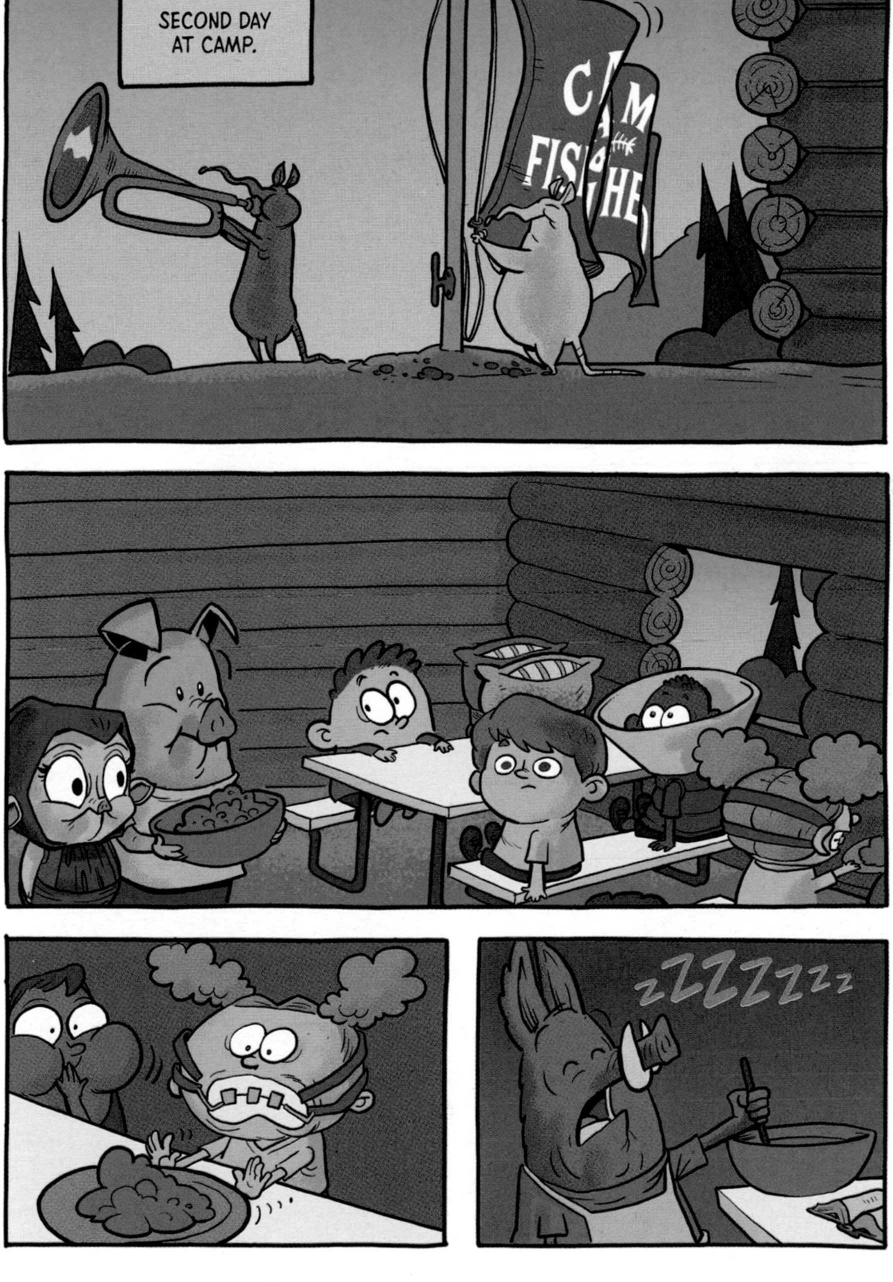
SECOND DAY AT CAMP.
zZZZZzzz

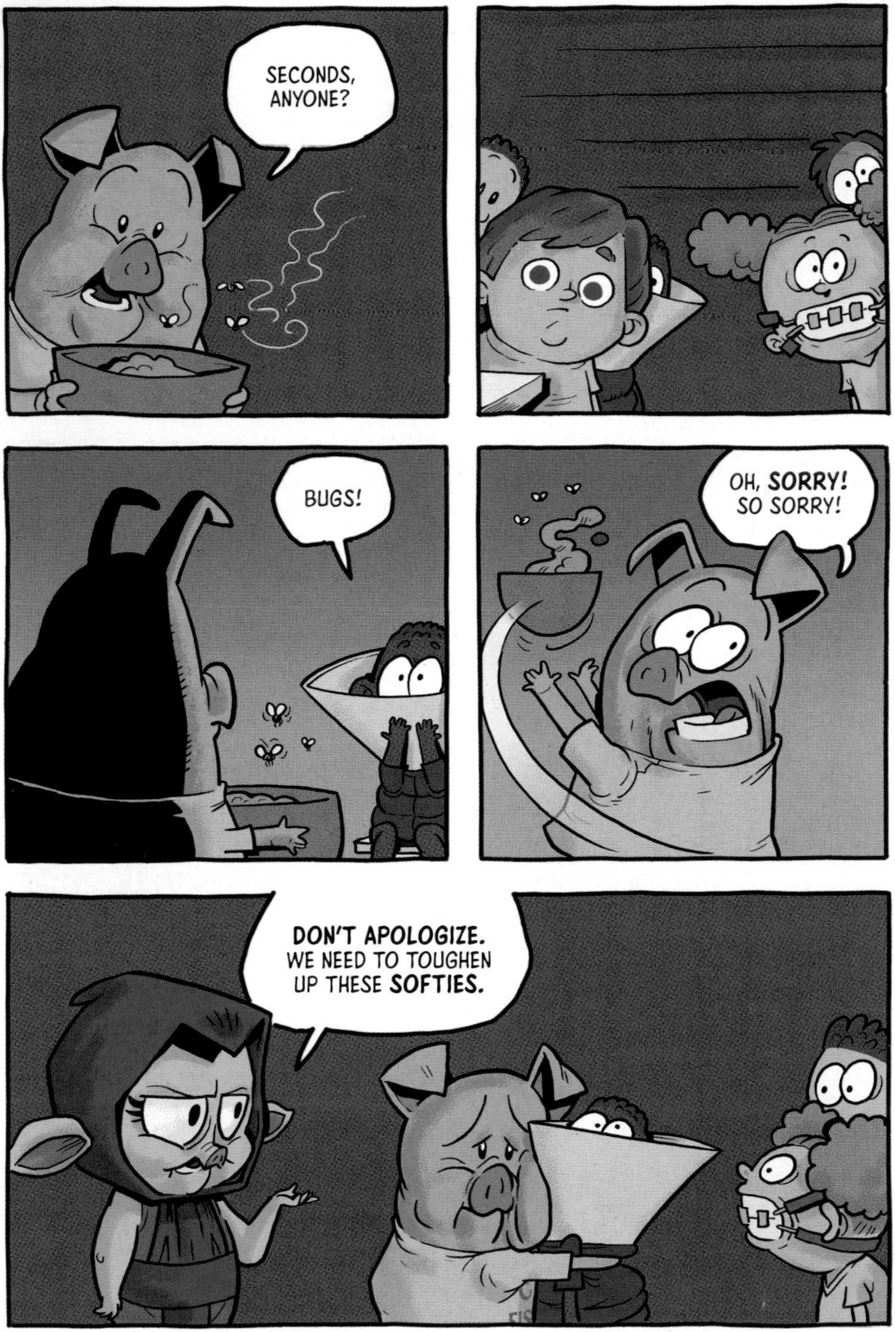
SECONDS, ANYONE?
BUGS!
OH, **SORRY!** SO SORRY!
DON'T APOLOGIZE. WE NEED TO TOUGHEN UP THESE **SOFTIES.**

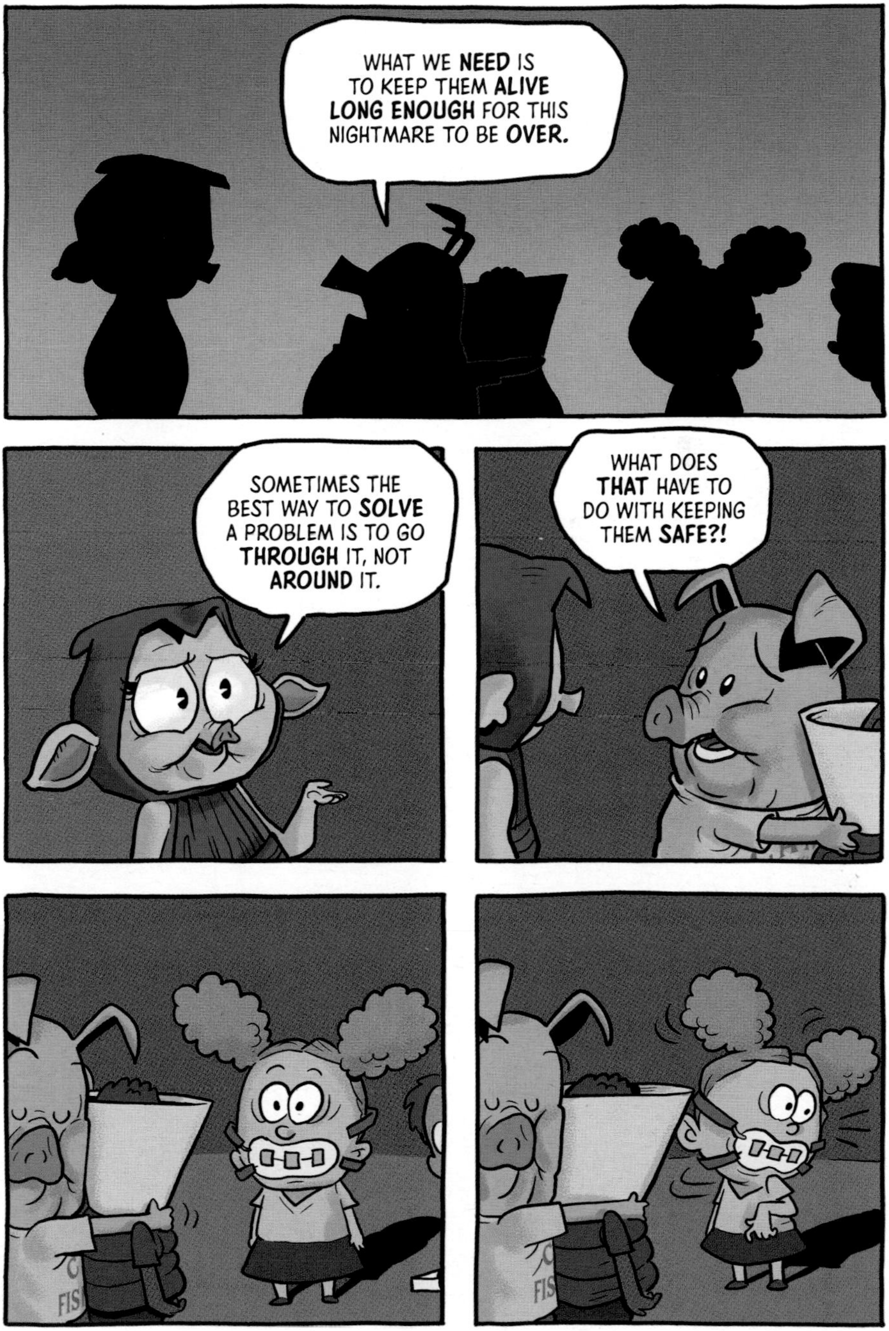
WHAT WE **NEED** IS TO KEEP THEM **ALIVE LONG ENOUGH** FOR THIS NIGHTMARE TO BE **OVER.**
SOMETIMES THE BEST WAY TO **SOLVE** A PROBLEM IS TO GO **THROUGH** IT, NOT **AROUND** IT.
WHAT DOES **THAT** HAVE TO DO WITH KEEPING THEM **SAFE?!**

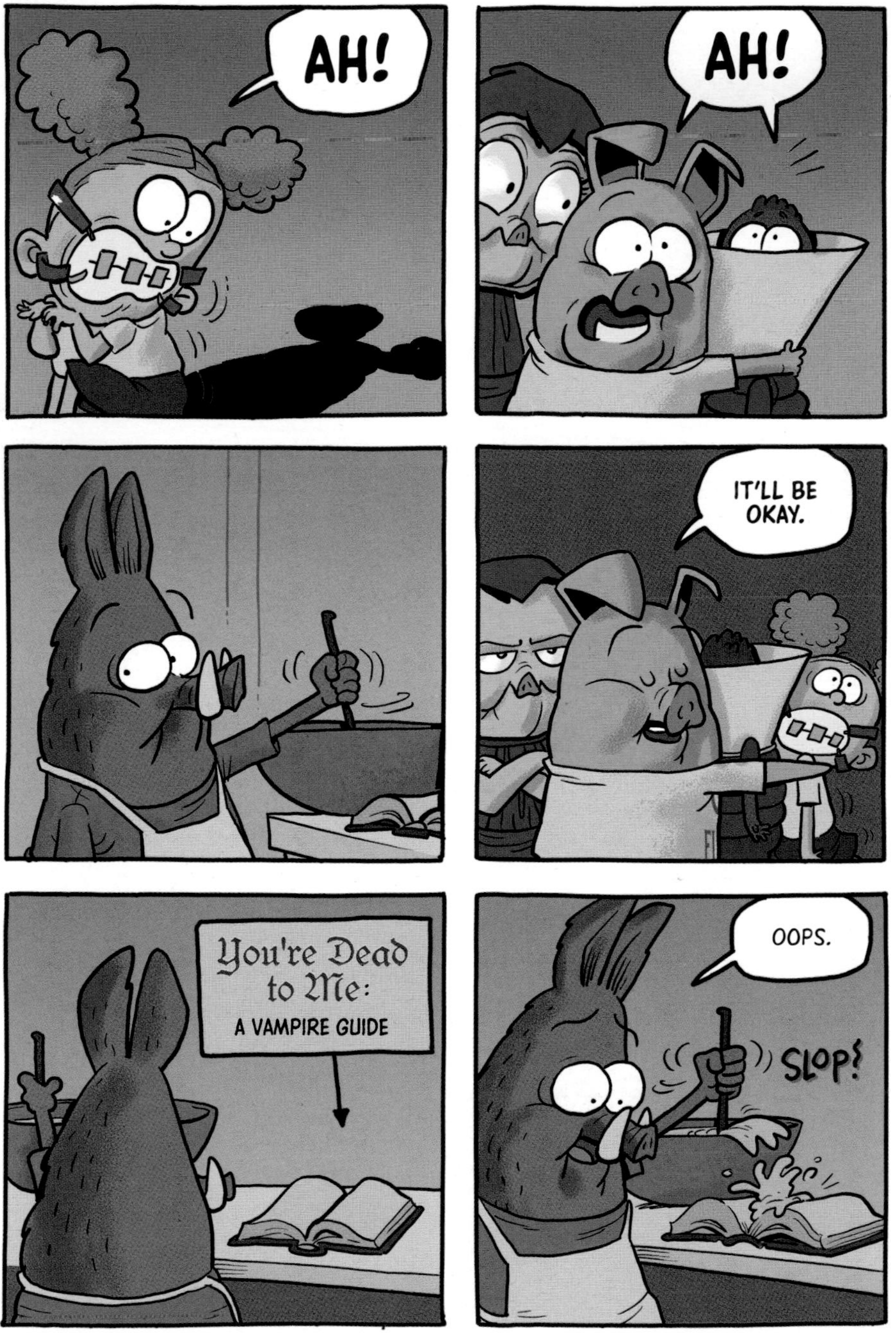
AH!
AH!
IT'LL BE OKAY.
You're Dead to Me: A VAMPIRE GUIDE
OOPS.
SLOP!

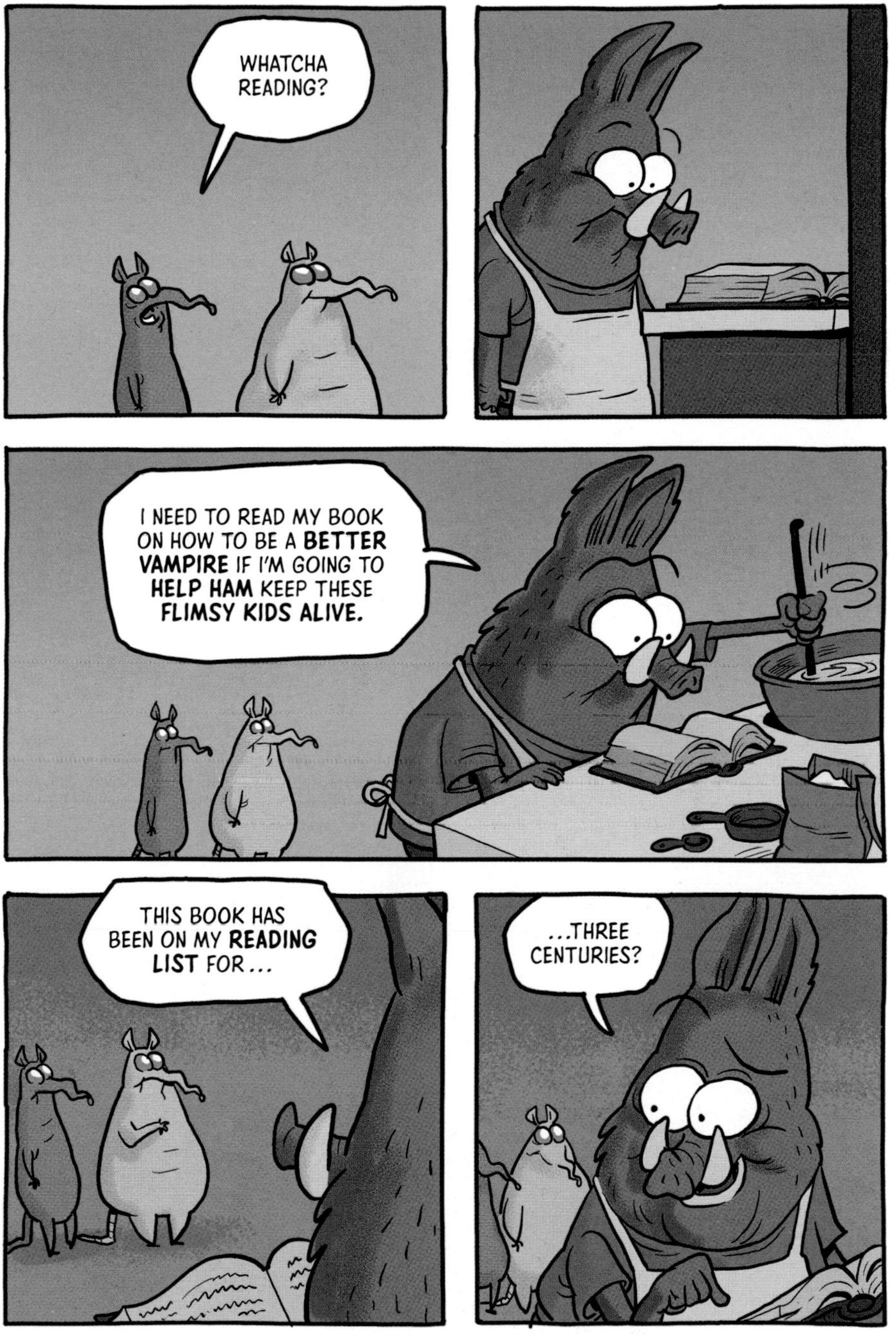
WHATCHA READING?
I NEED TO READ MY BOOK ON HOW TO BE A **BETTER VAMPIRE** IF I'M GOING TO **HELP HAM** KEEP THESE **FLIMSY KIDS ALIVE.**
THIS BOOK HAS BEEN ON MY **READING LIST** FOR...
...THREE CENTURIES?

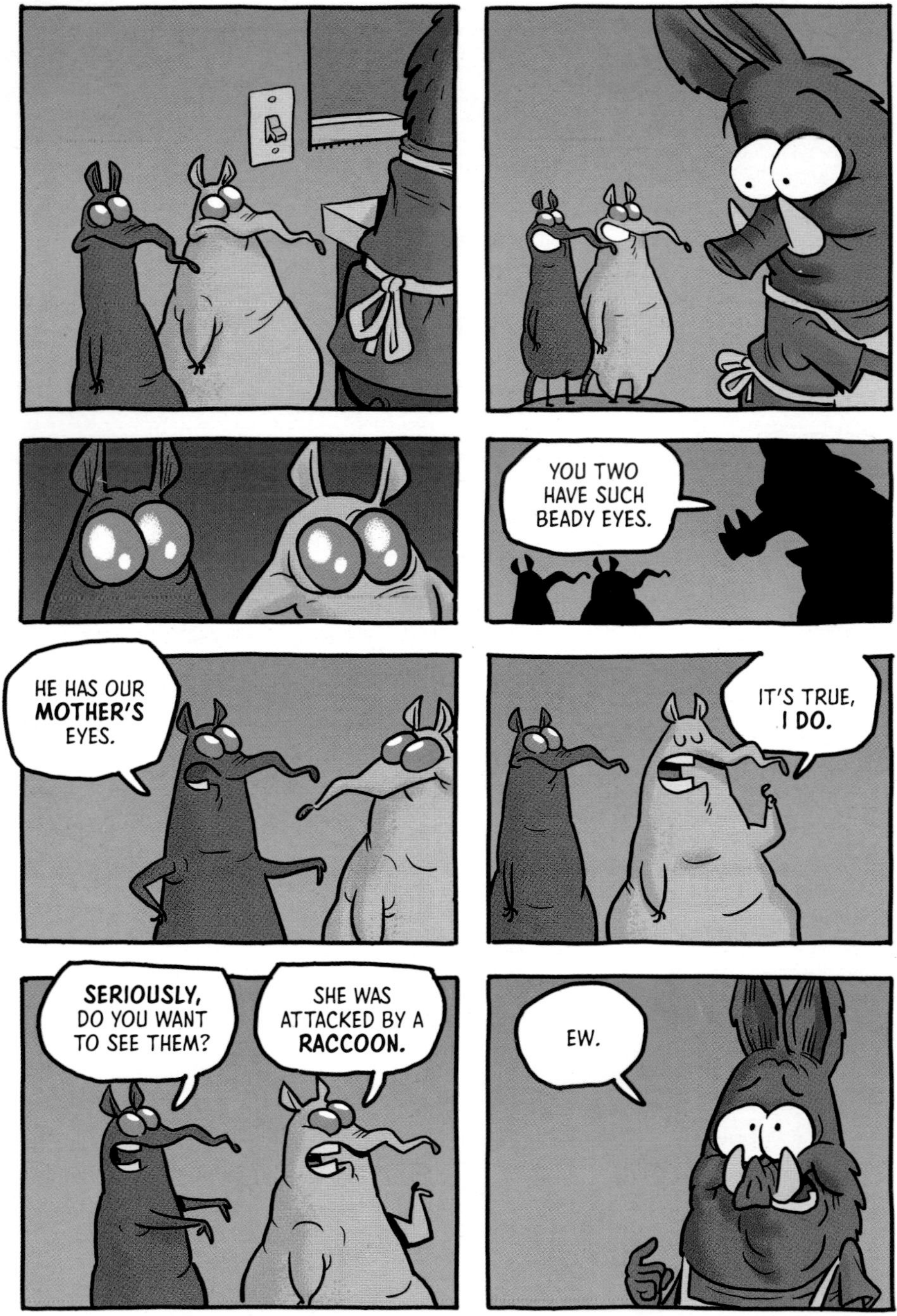
YOU TWO HAVE SUCH BEADY EYES.
HE HAS OUR **MOTHER'S** EYES.
IT'S TRUE, **I DO.**
SERIOUSLY, DO YOU WANT TO SEE THEM?
SHE WAS ATTACKED BY A **RACCOON.**
EW.

CLOP! CLOP!
CLOP! CLOP!

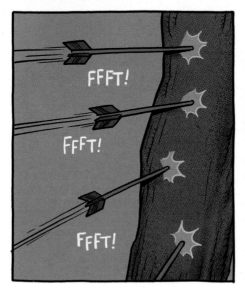

FFFT!

FFFT!

FFFT!

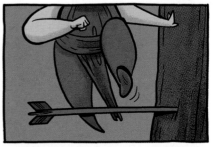

TWANG!

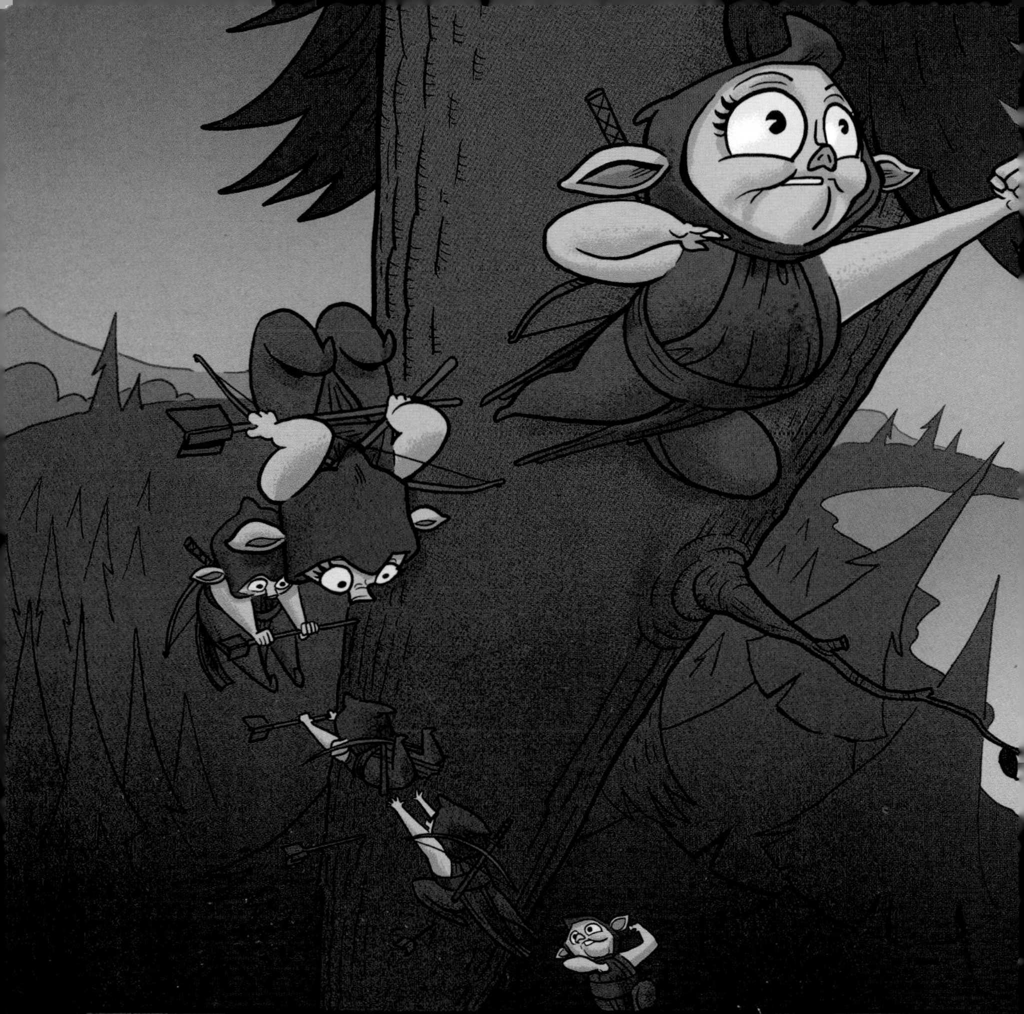

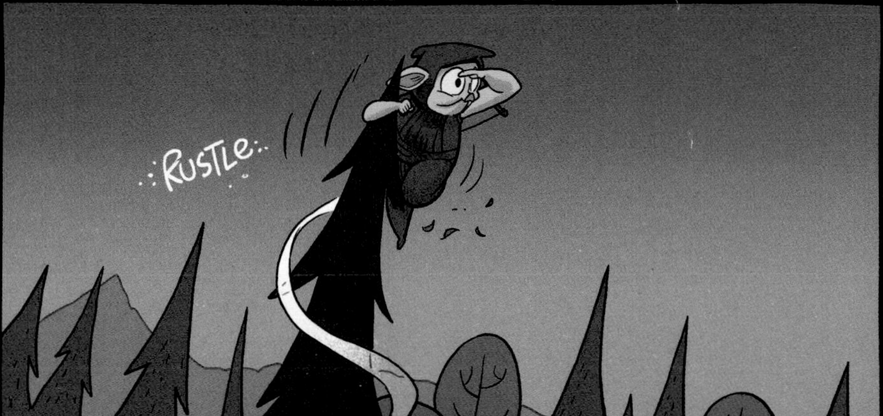
RUSTLE

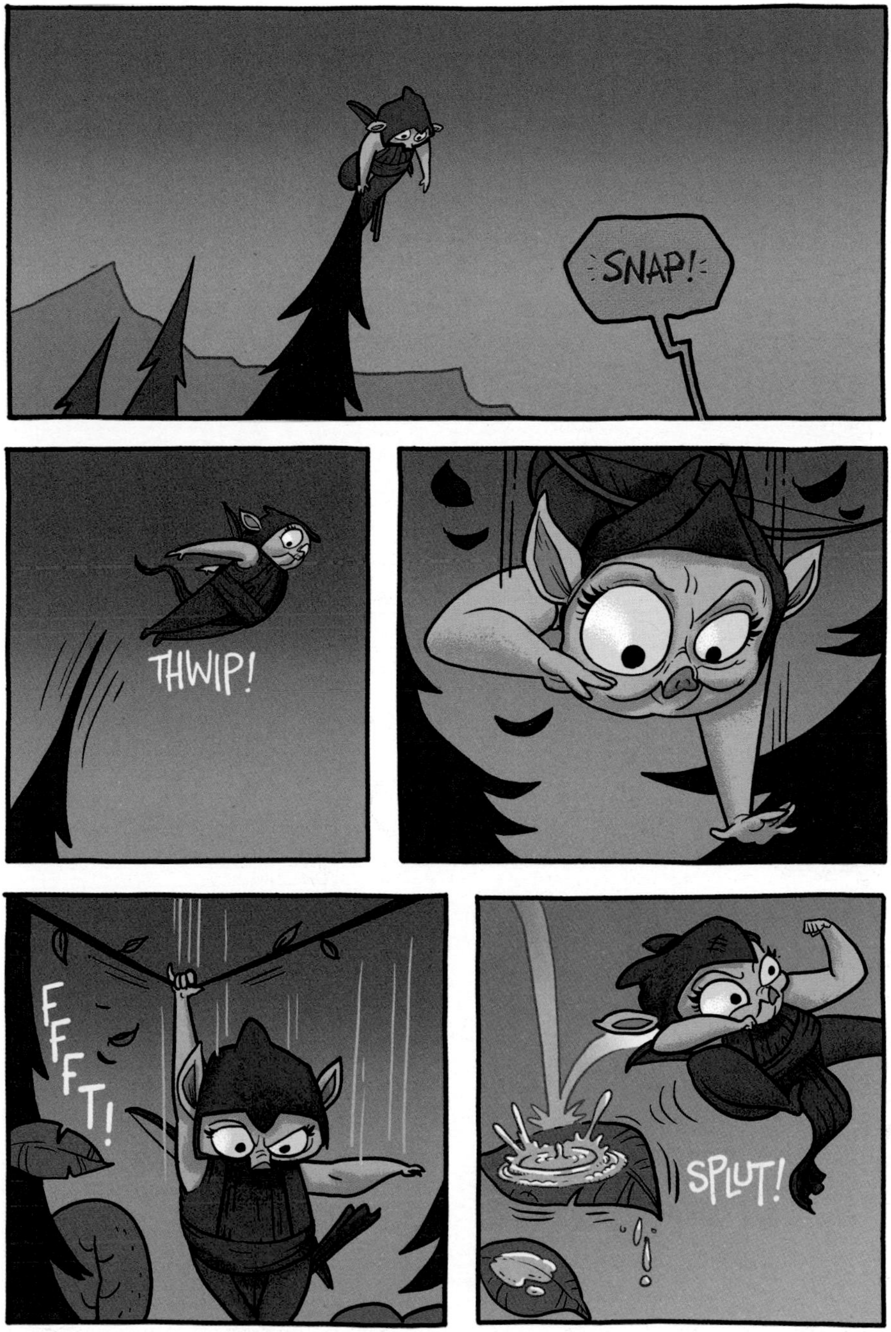
SNAP!
THWIP!
FFFFT!
SPLUT!

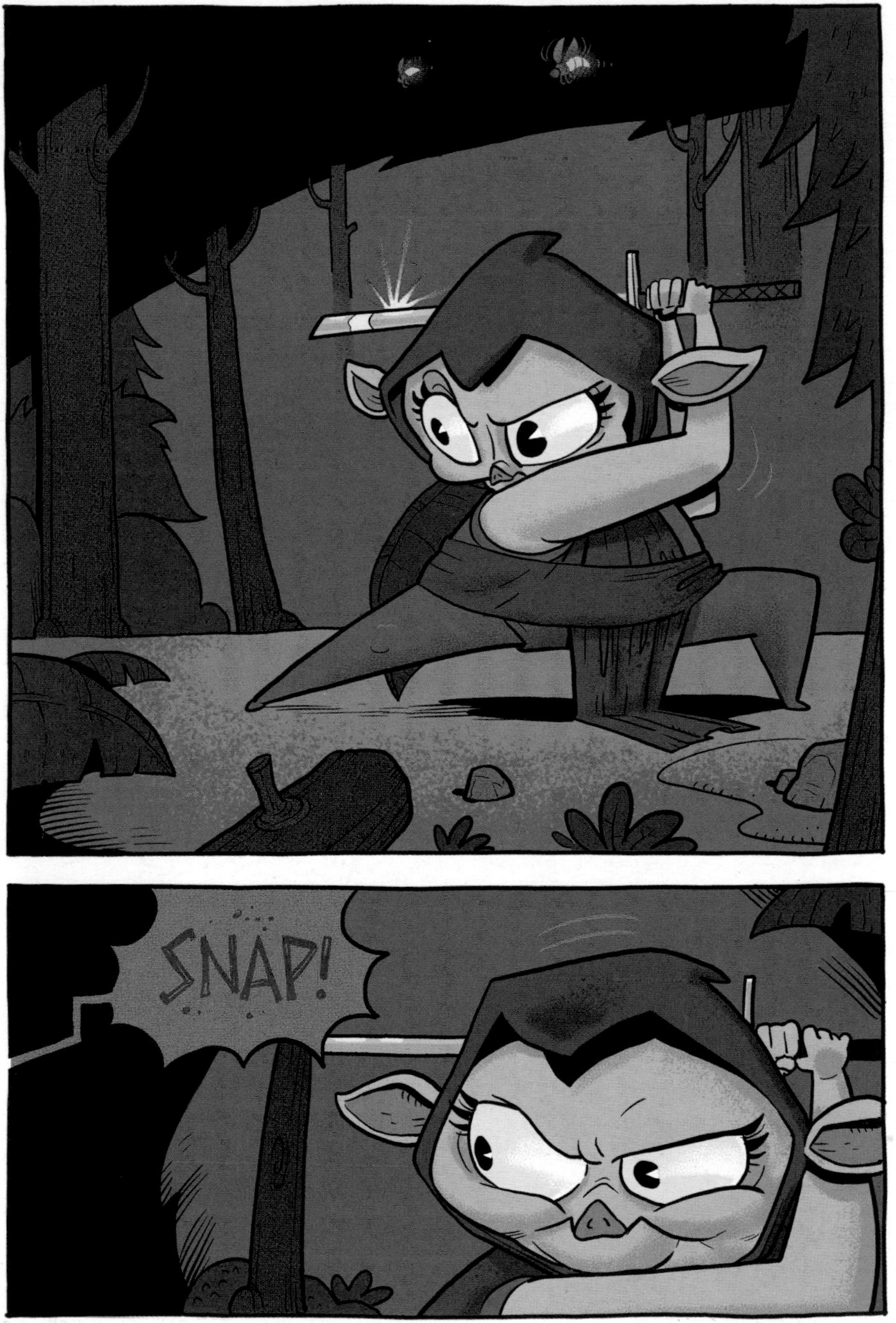
SNAP!

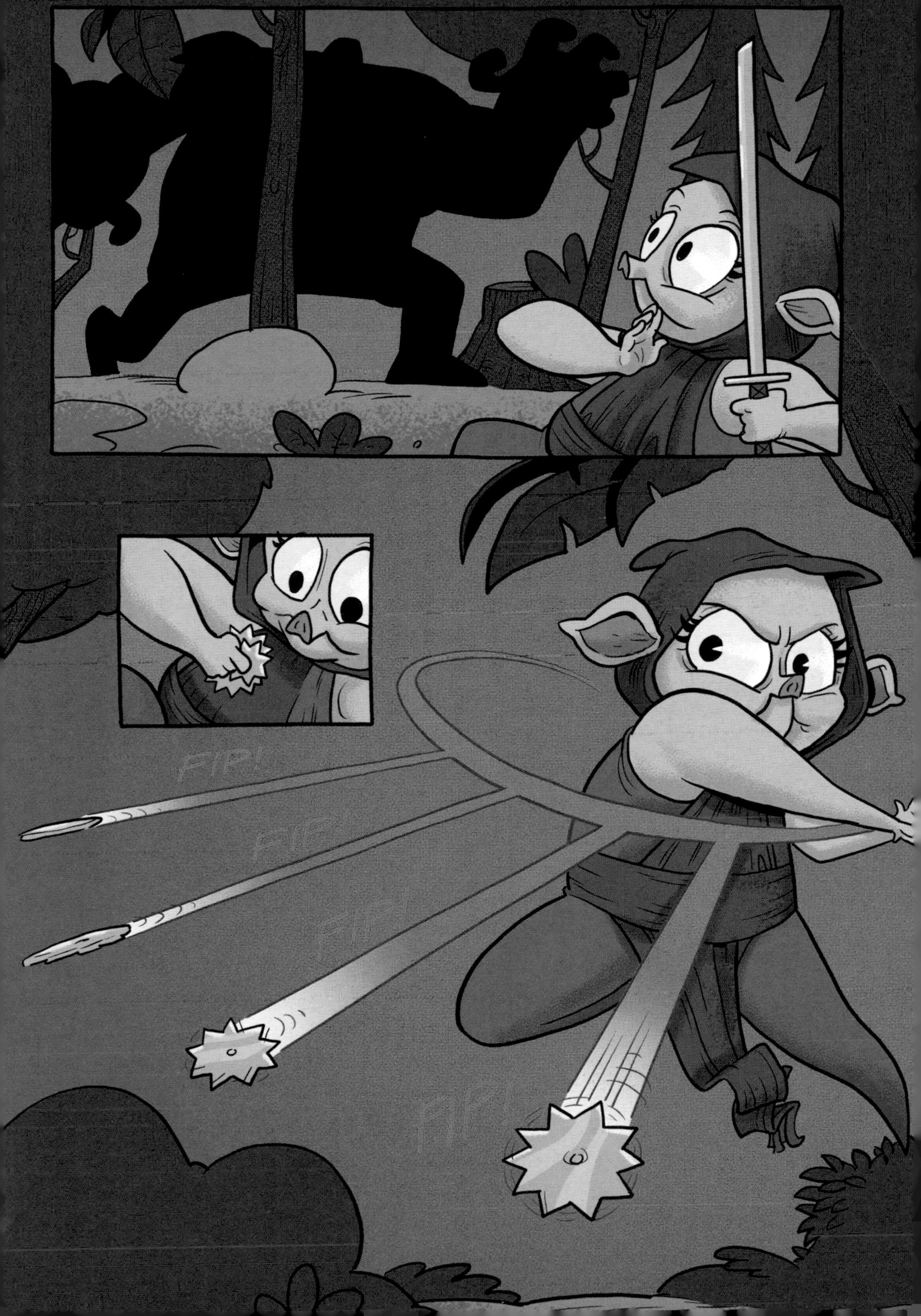
FIP!
FIP!
FIP!

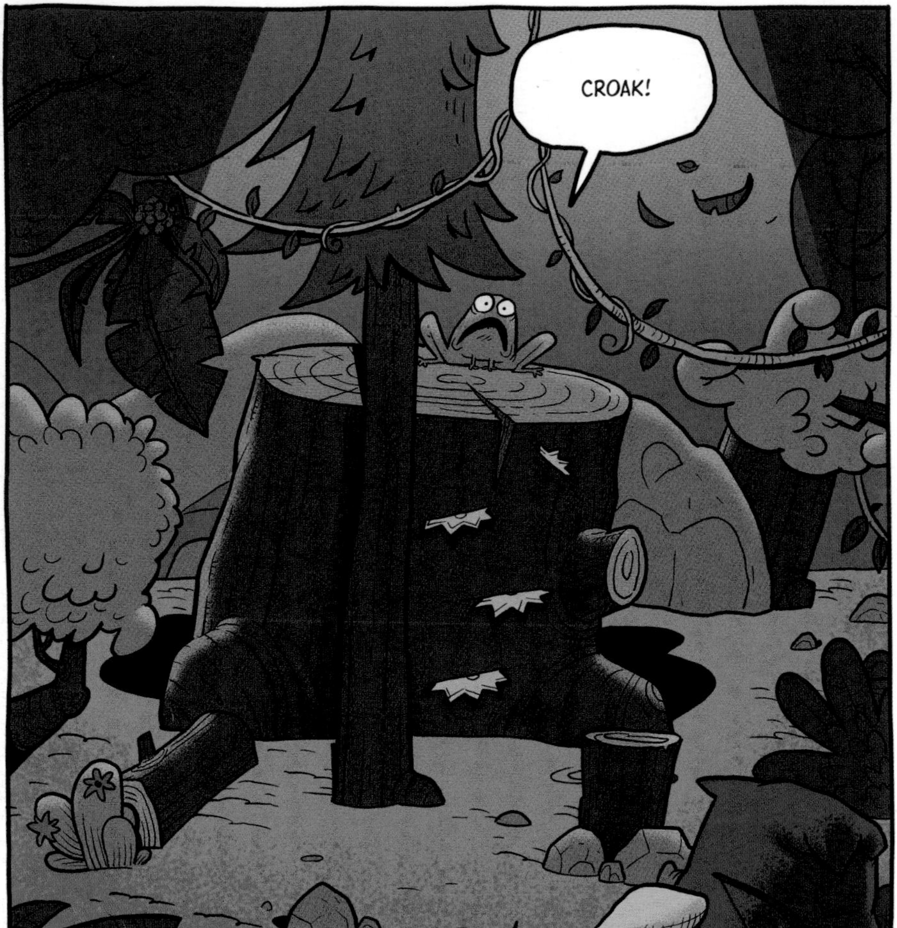
CROAK!

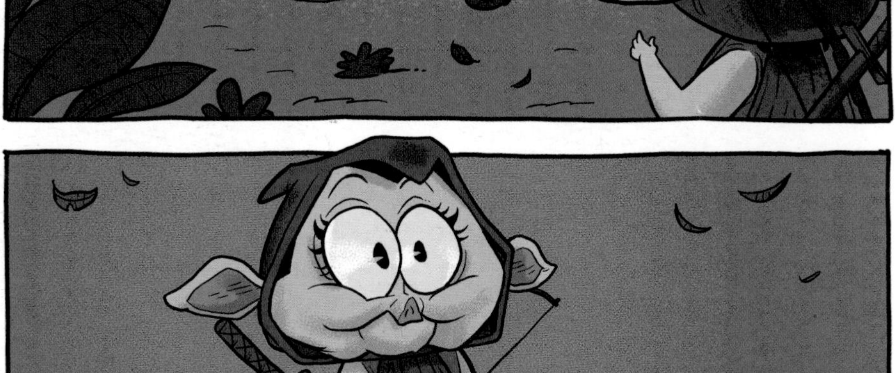

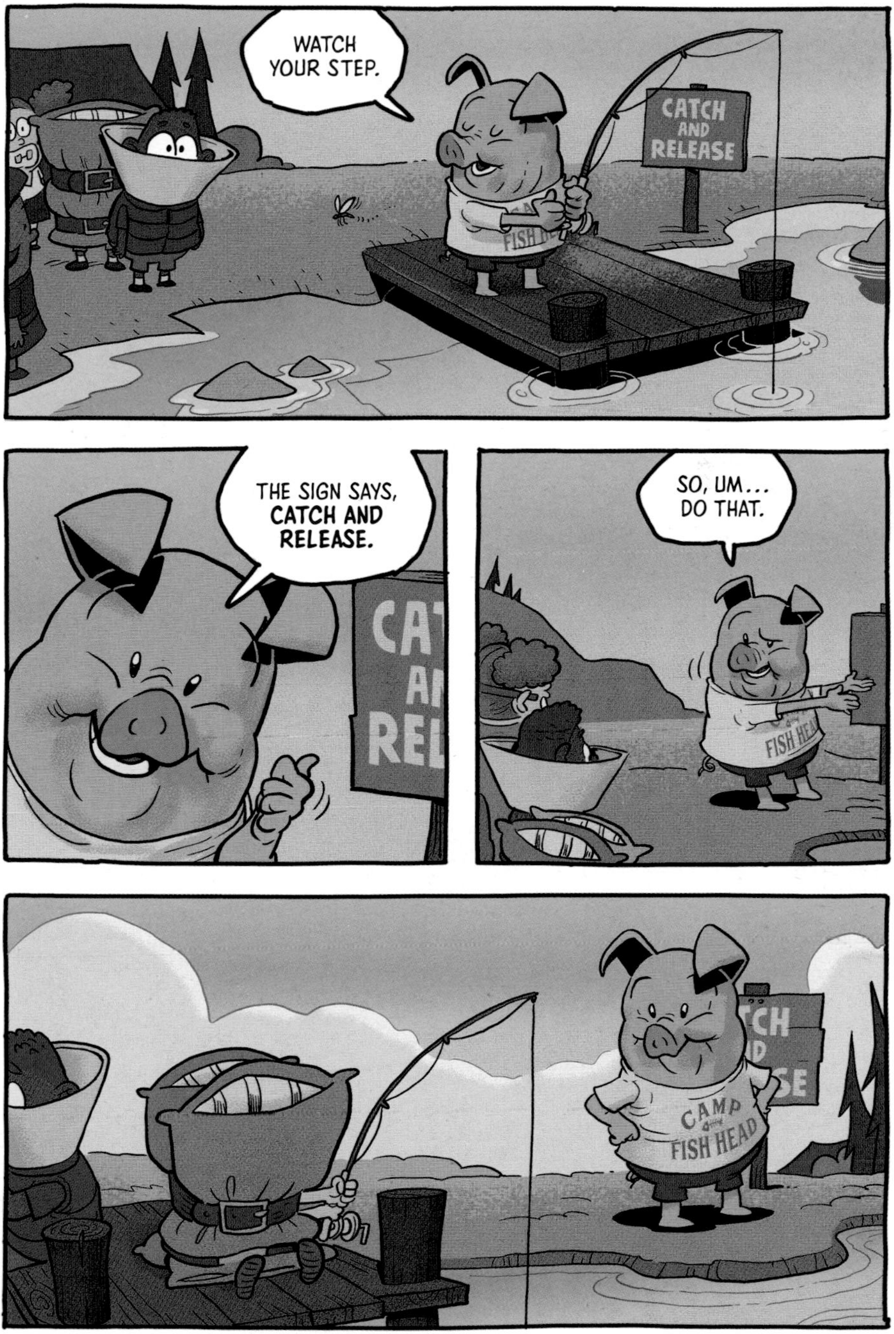
WATCH YOUR STEP.
CATCH AND RELEASE
FISH HEAD
THE SIGN SAYS, **CATCH AND RELEASE.**
SO, UM... DO THAT.
FISH HEAD
CAMP FISH HEAD

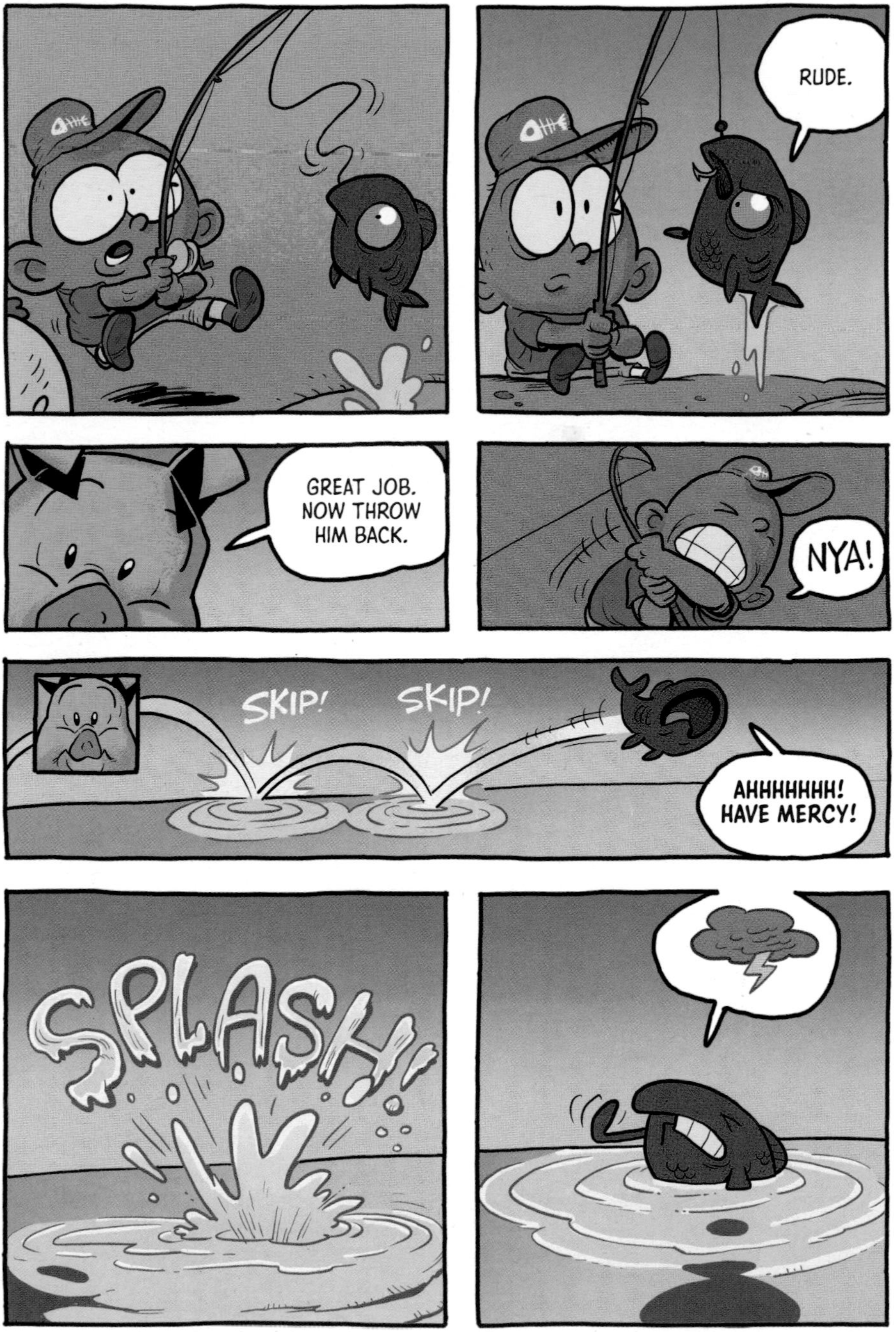
RUDE.
GREAT JOB. NOW THROW HIM BACK.
NYA!
SKIP!
SKIP!
AHHHHHHH! HAVE MERCY!
SPLASH!

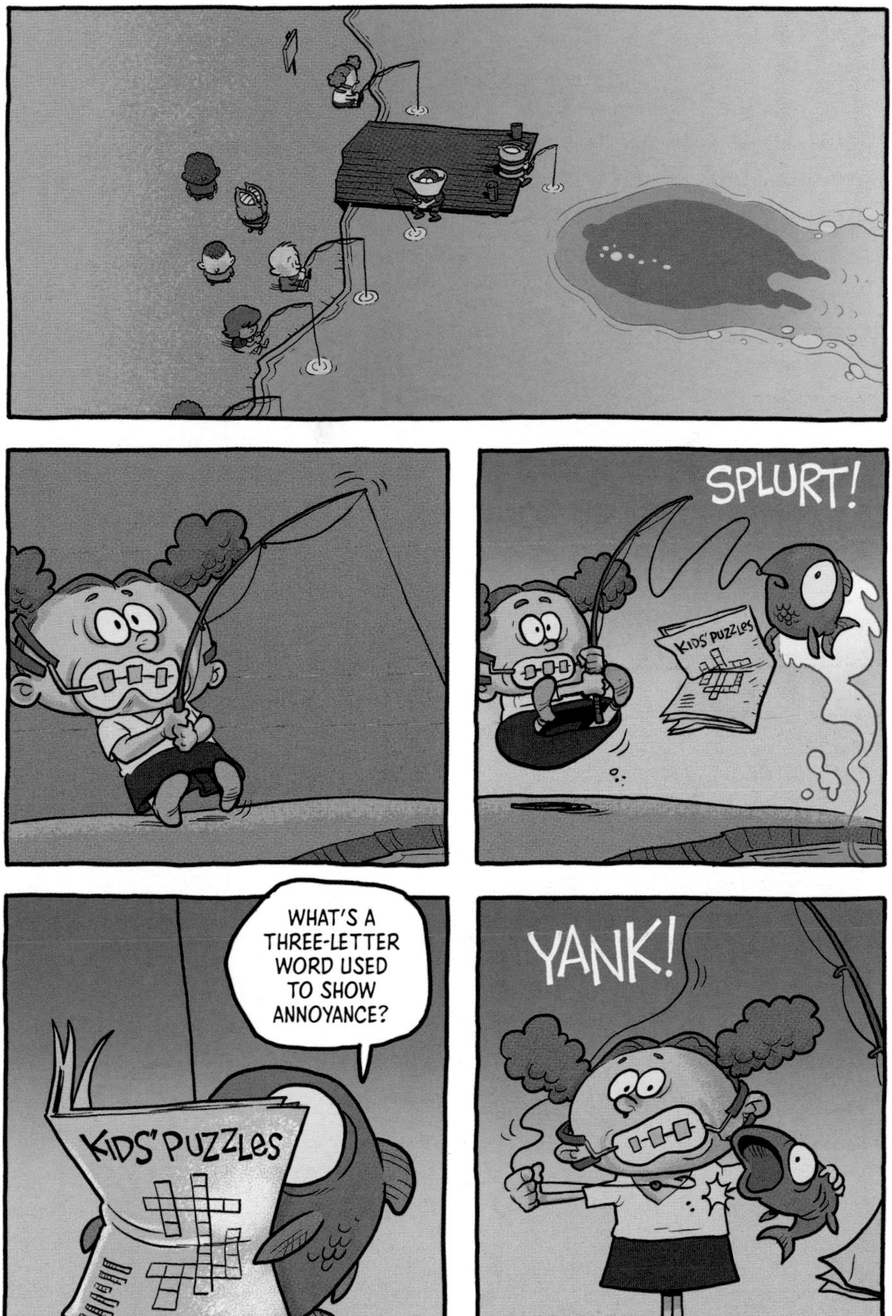
SPLURT!
KIDS' PUZZLES
KIDS' PUZZLES
WHAT'S A THREE-LETTER WORD USED TO SHOW ANNOYANCE?
YANK!

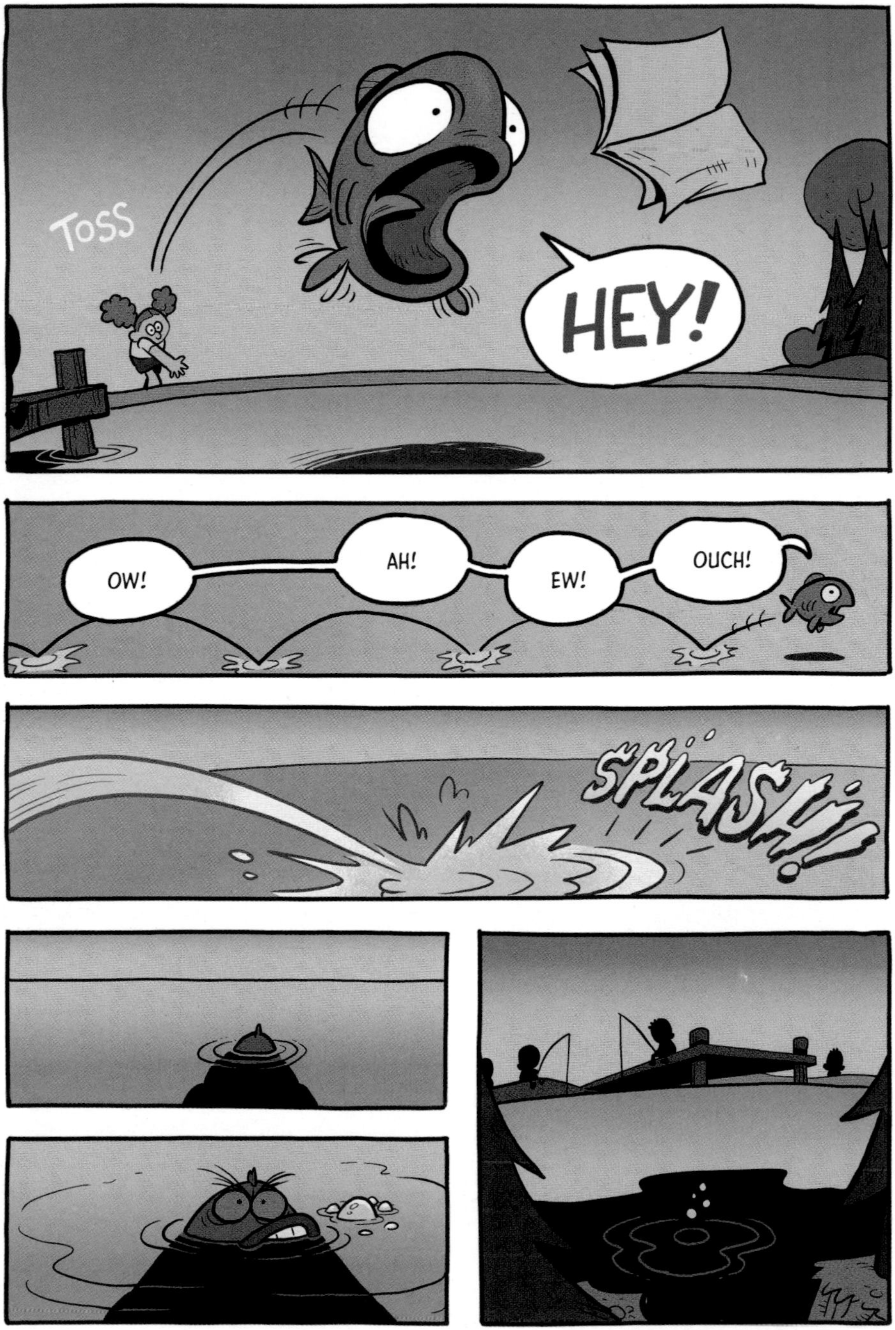
TOSS
HEY!
OW!
AH!
EW!
OUCH!
SPLASH!!

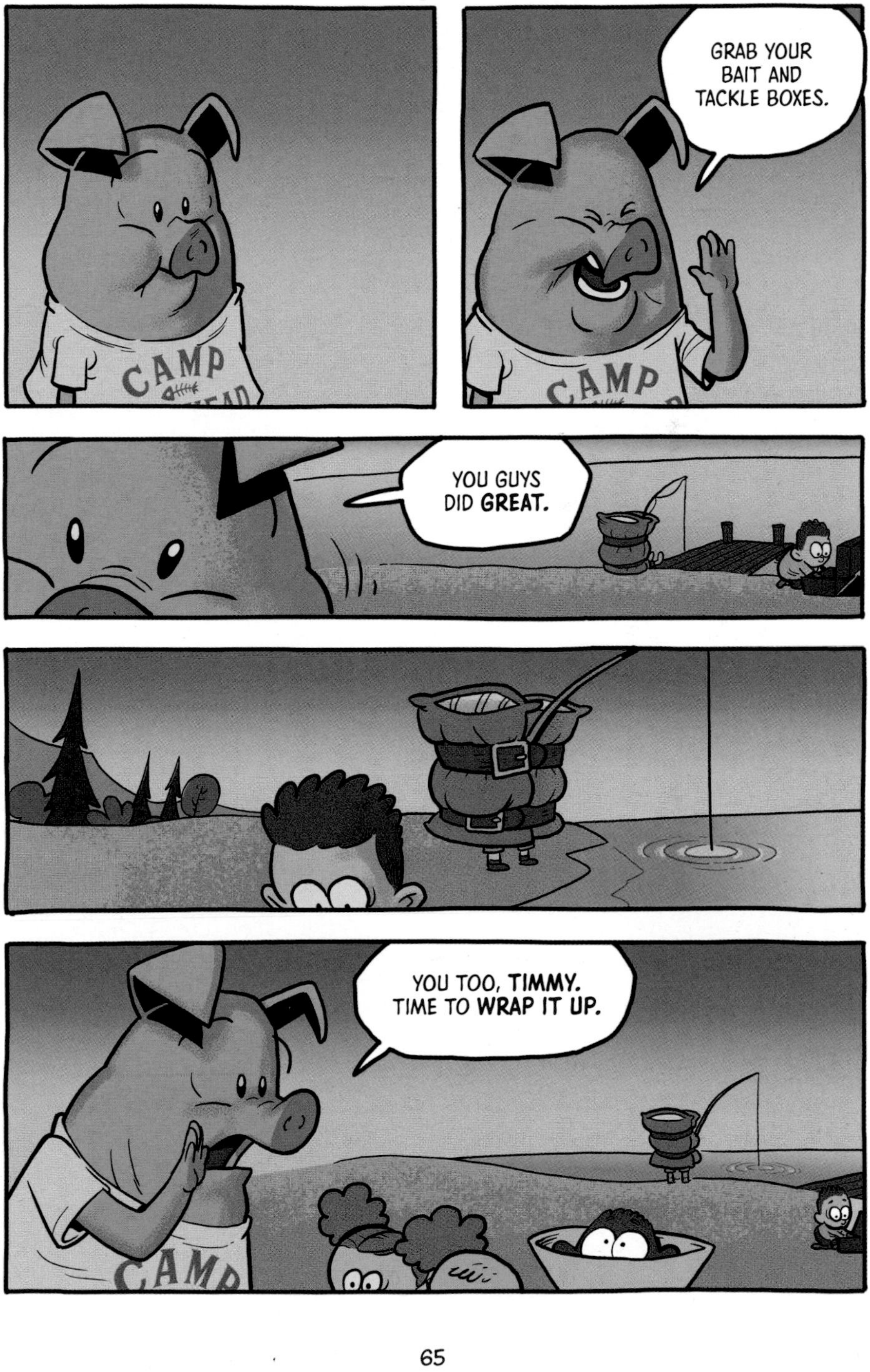
CAMP
GRAB YOUR BAIT AND TACKLE BOXES.
CAMP
YOU GUYS DID **GREAT.**
YOU TOO, **TIMMY.** TIME TO **WRAP IT UP.**
CAMP

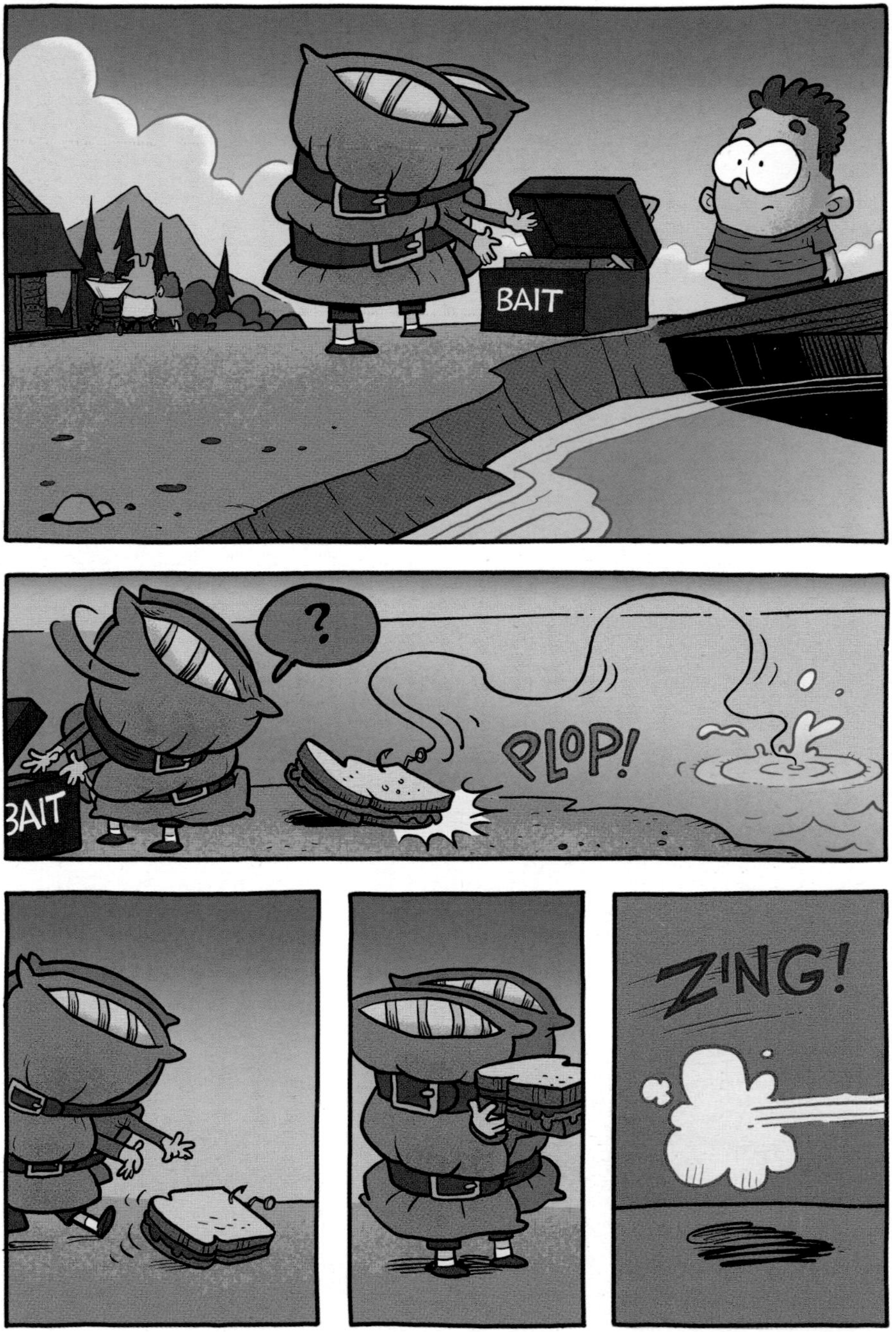
BAIT
?
PLOP!
BAIT
Z'NG!

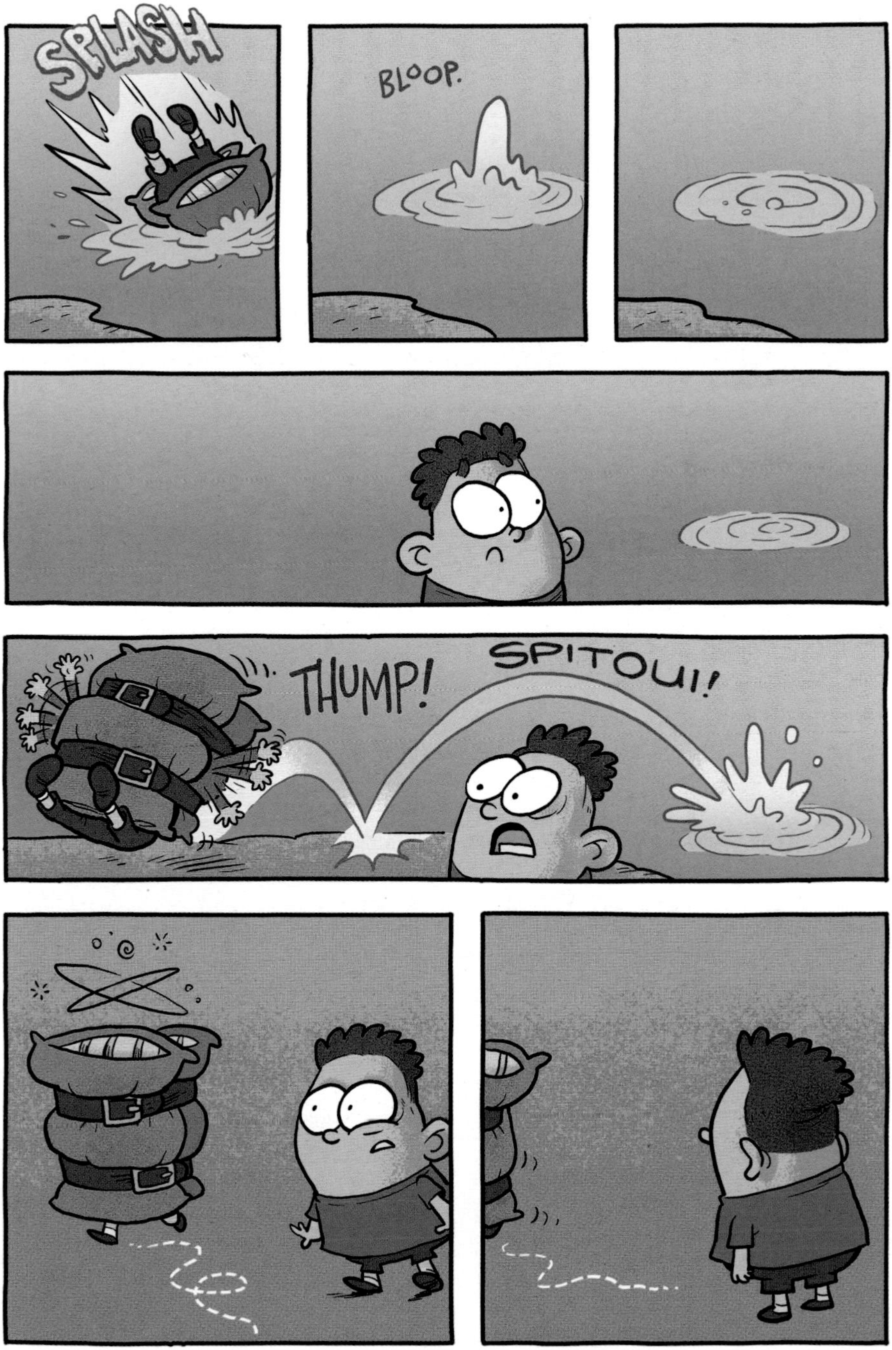
SPLASH
BLOOP.
THUMP!
SPITOUI!

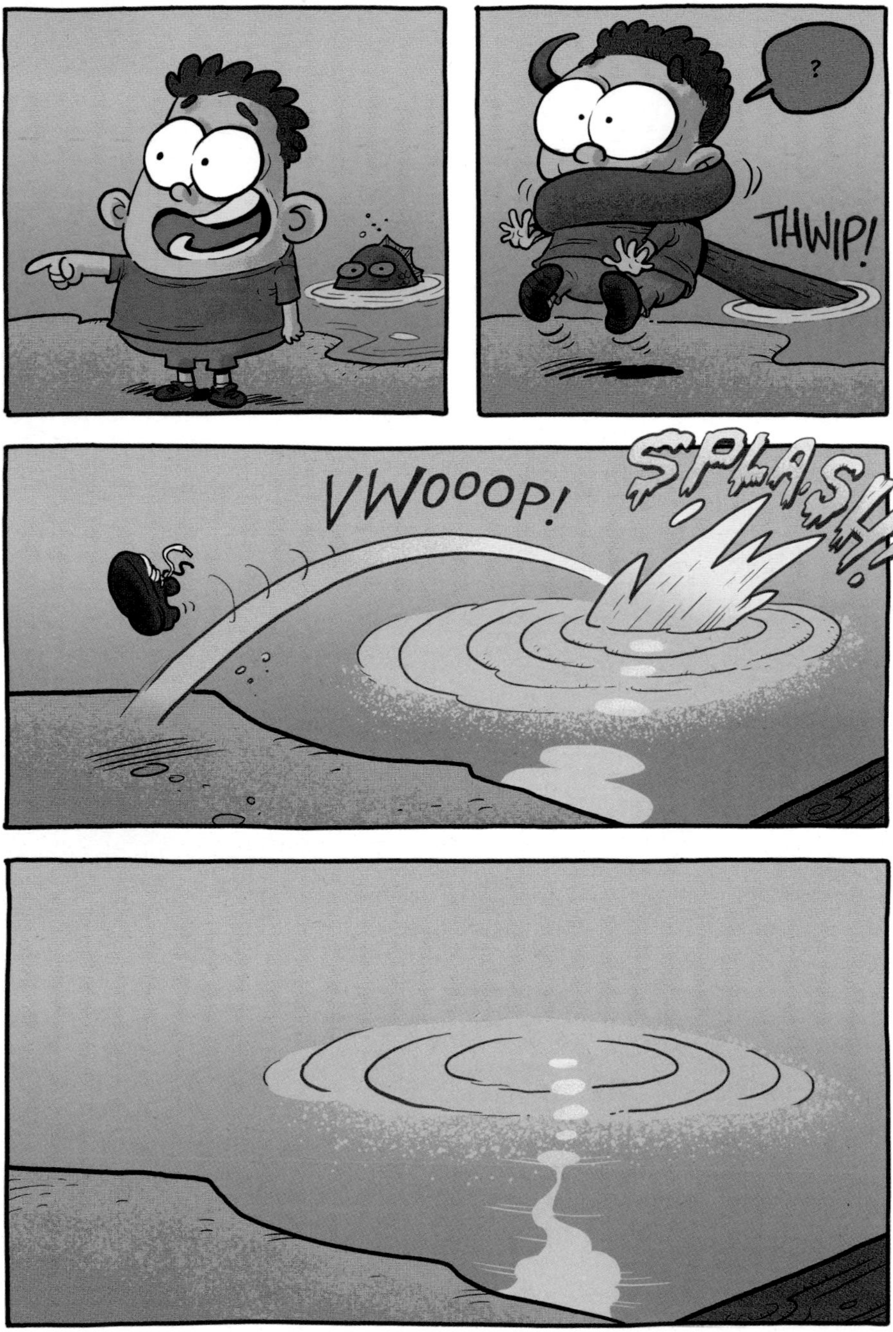
?
THWIP!
VWOOOP!
SPLASH!!

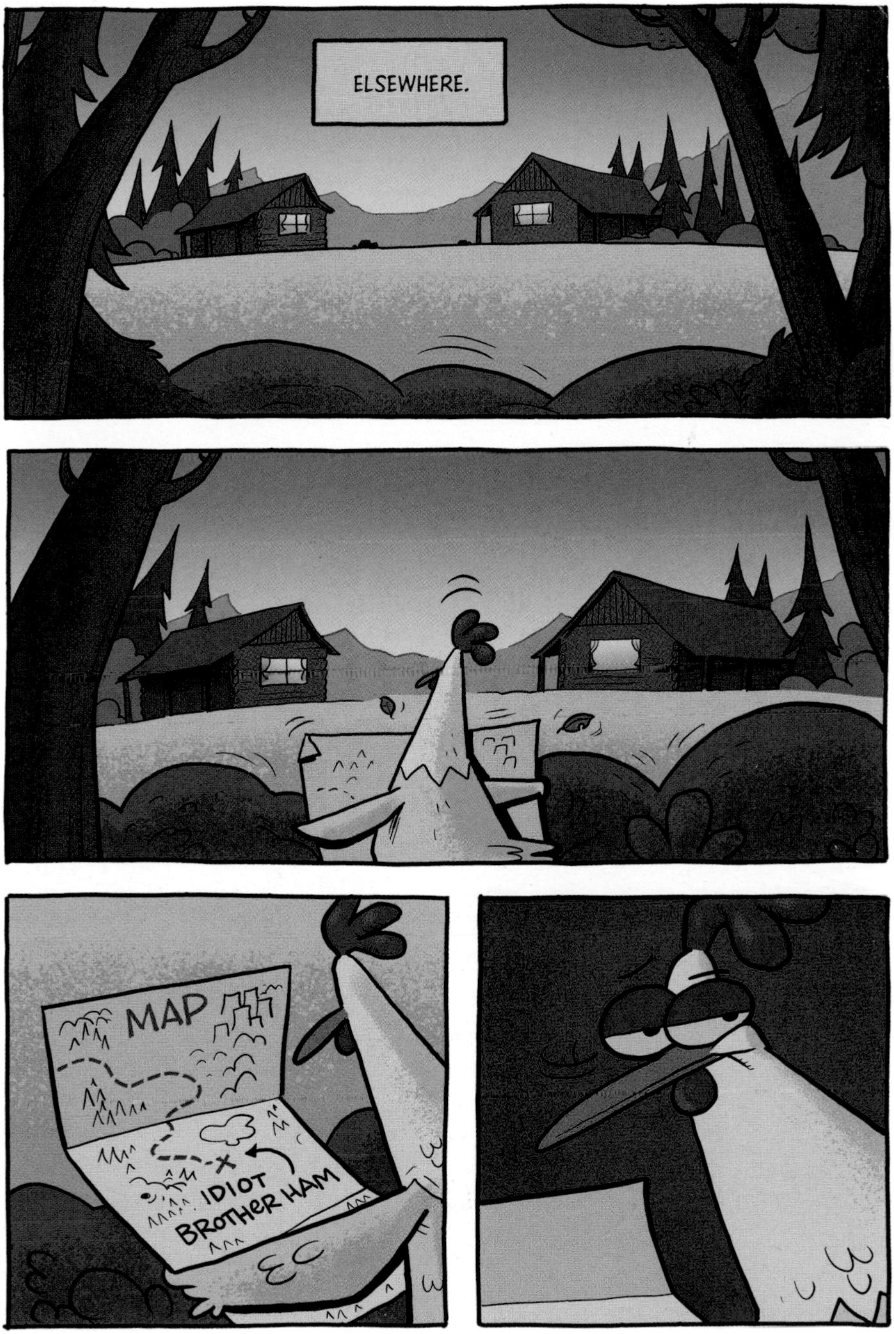
ELSEWHERE.
MAP
IDIOT BROTHER HAM

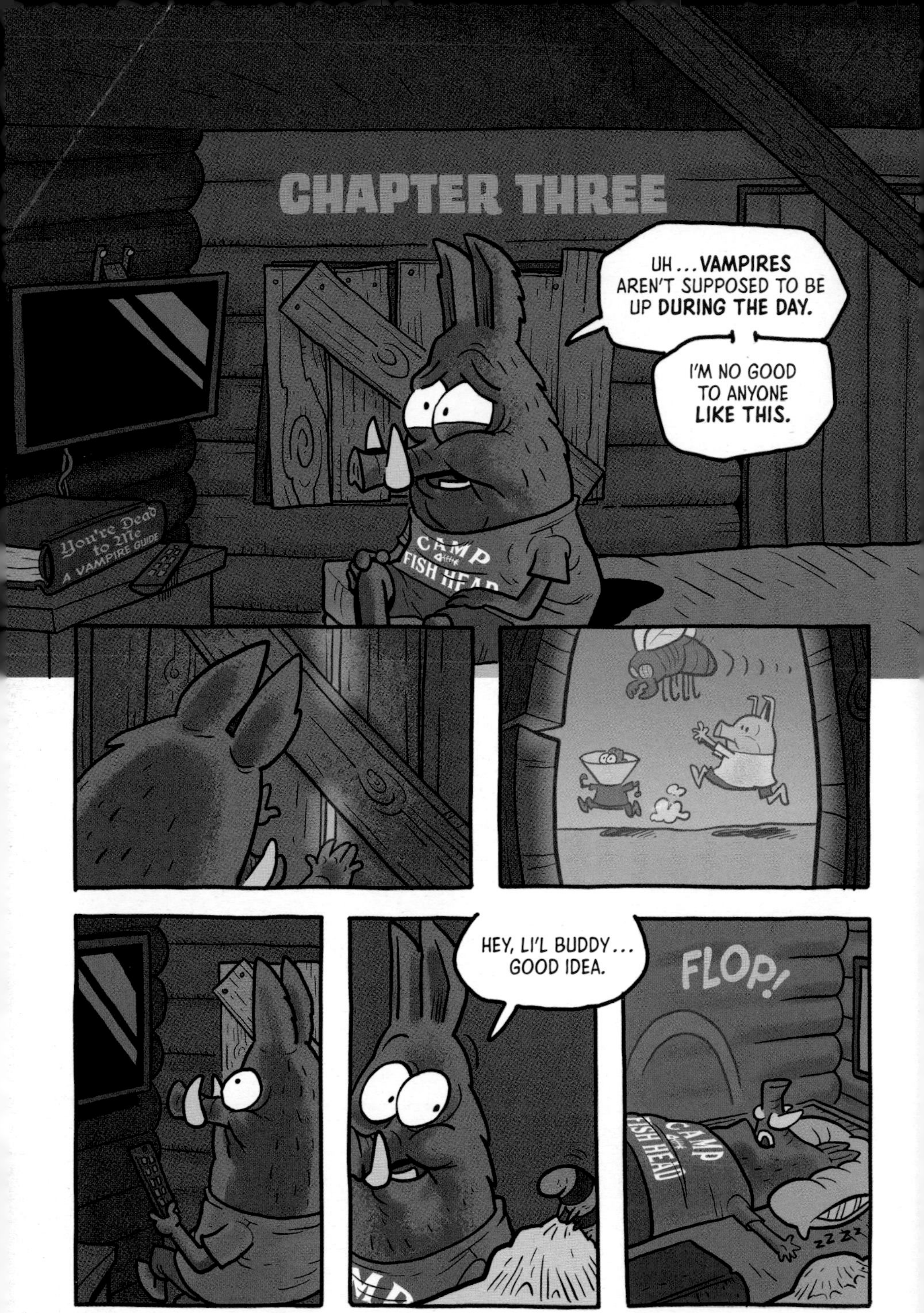
CHAPTER THREE
UH ... VAMPIRES AREN'T SUPPOSED TO BE UP DURING THE DAY.
I'M NO GOOD TO ANYONE LIKE THIS.
You're Dead to Me A VAMPIRE GUIDE
CAMP FISH HEAD
HEY, LI'L BUDDY ... GOOD IDEA.
FLOP!
CAMP FISH HEAD
ZZZZZ

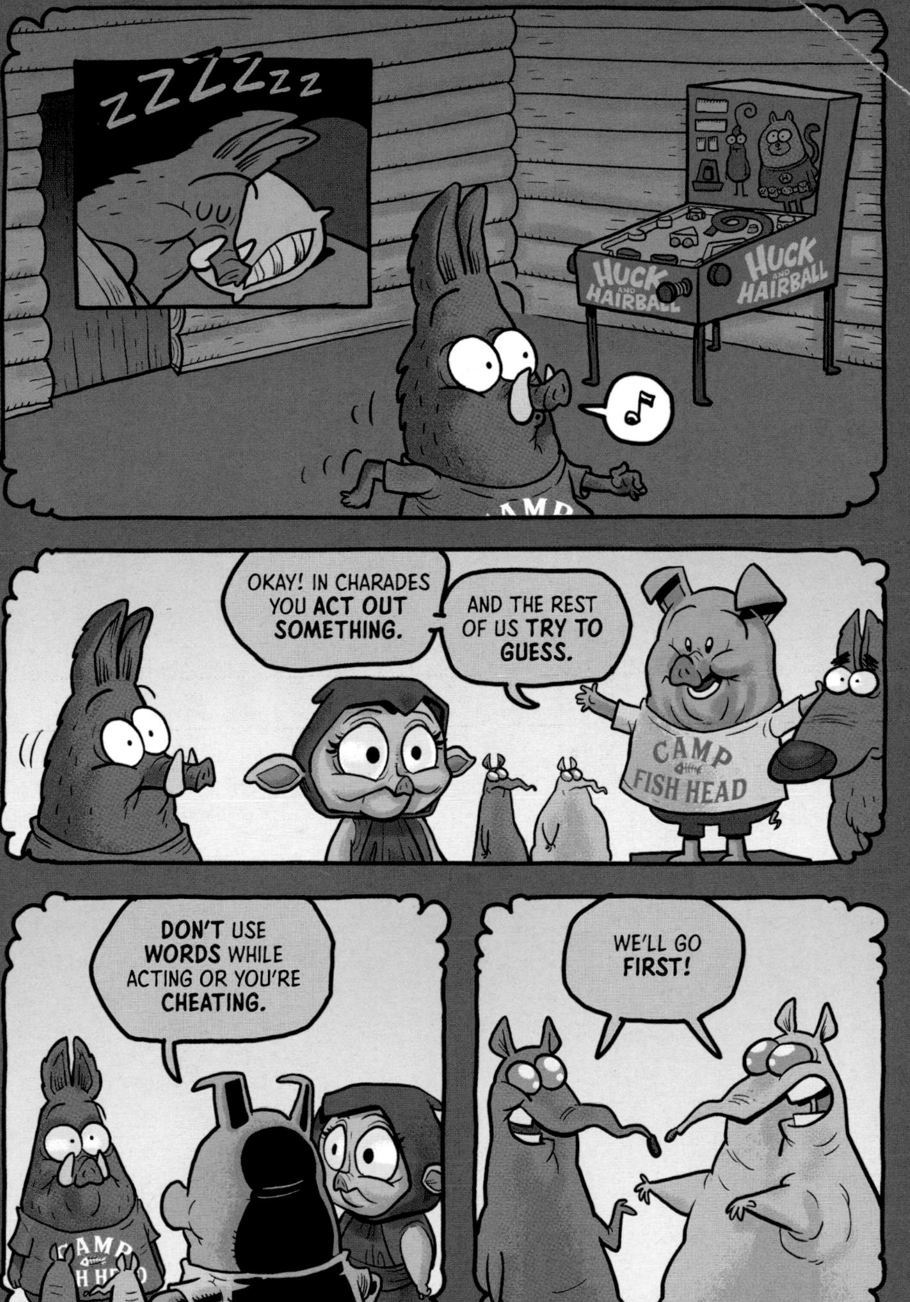
ZZZZZzz
HUCK AND HAIRBALL
HUCK AND HAIRBALL
OKAY! IN CHARADES YOU ACT OUT SOMETHING.
AND THE REST OF US TRY TO GUESS.
CAMP FISH HEAD
DON'T USE WORDS WHILE ACTING OR YOU'RE CHEATING.
WE'LL GO FIRST!

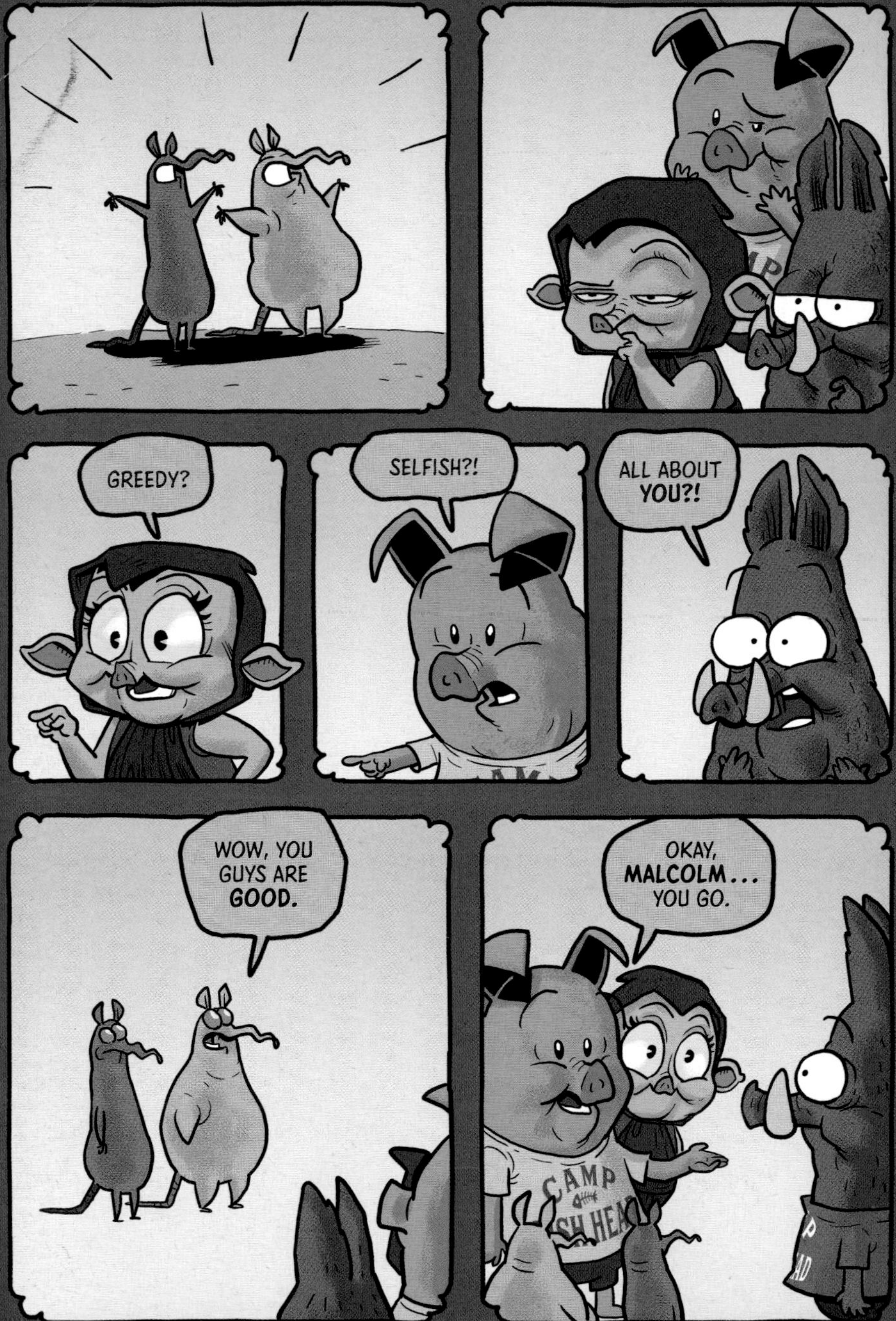
GREEDY?
SELFISH?!
ALL ABOUT YOU?!
WOW, YOU GUYS ARE GOOD.
OKAY, MALCOLM... YOU GO.
CAMP FISH HEAD

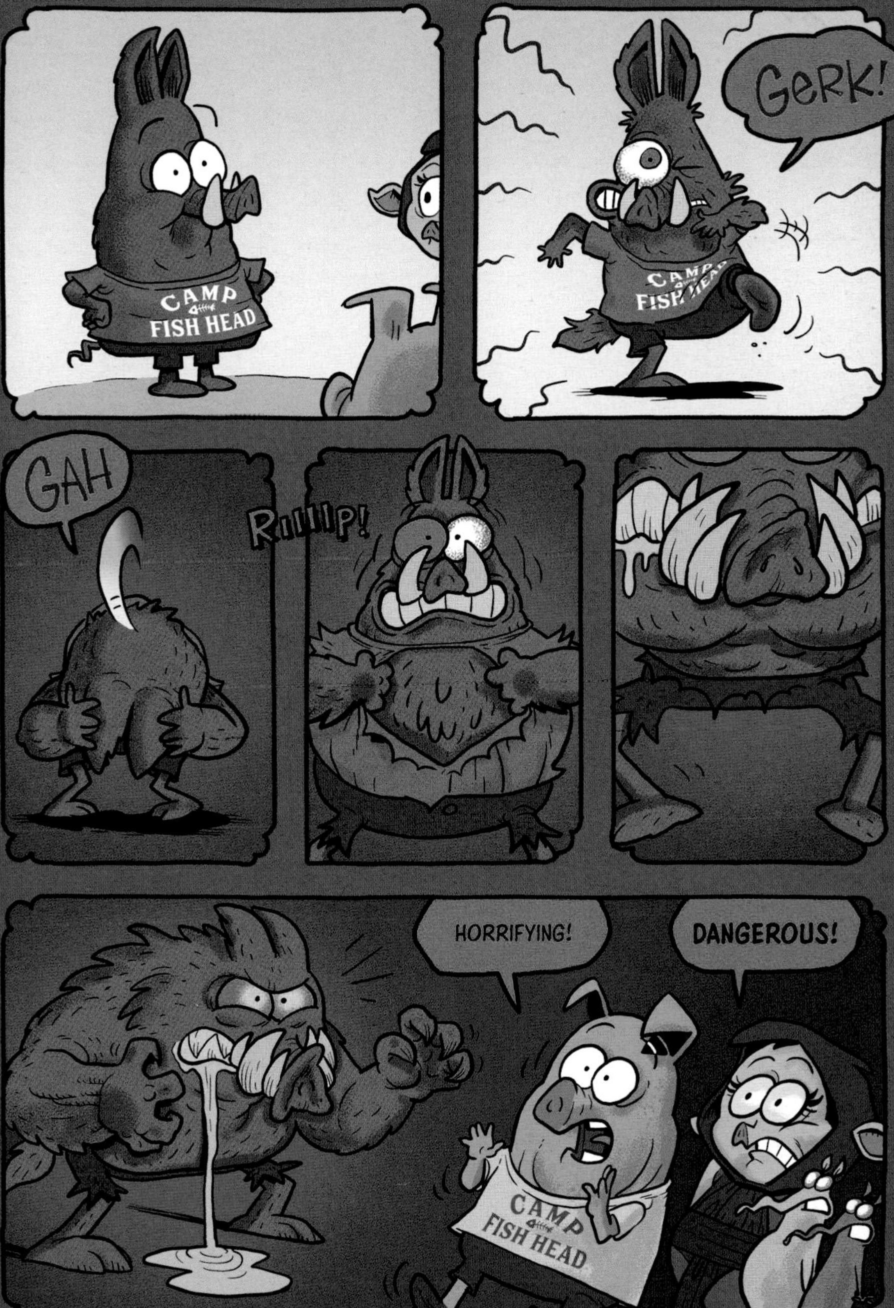
CAMP
FISH HEAD
Gerk!
CAMP
FISH HEAD
GAH
RiiiiP!
HORRIFYING!
DANGEROUS!
CAMP
FISH HEAD

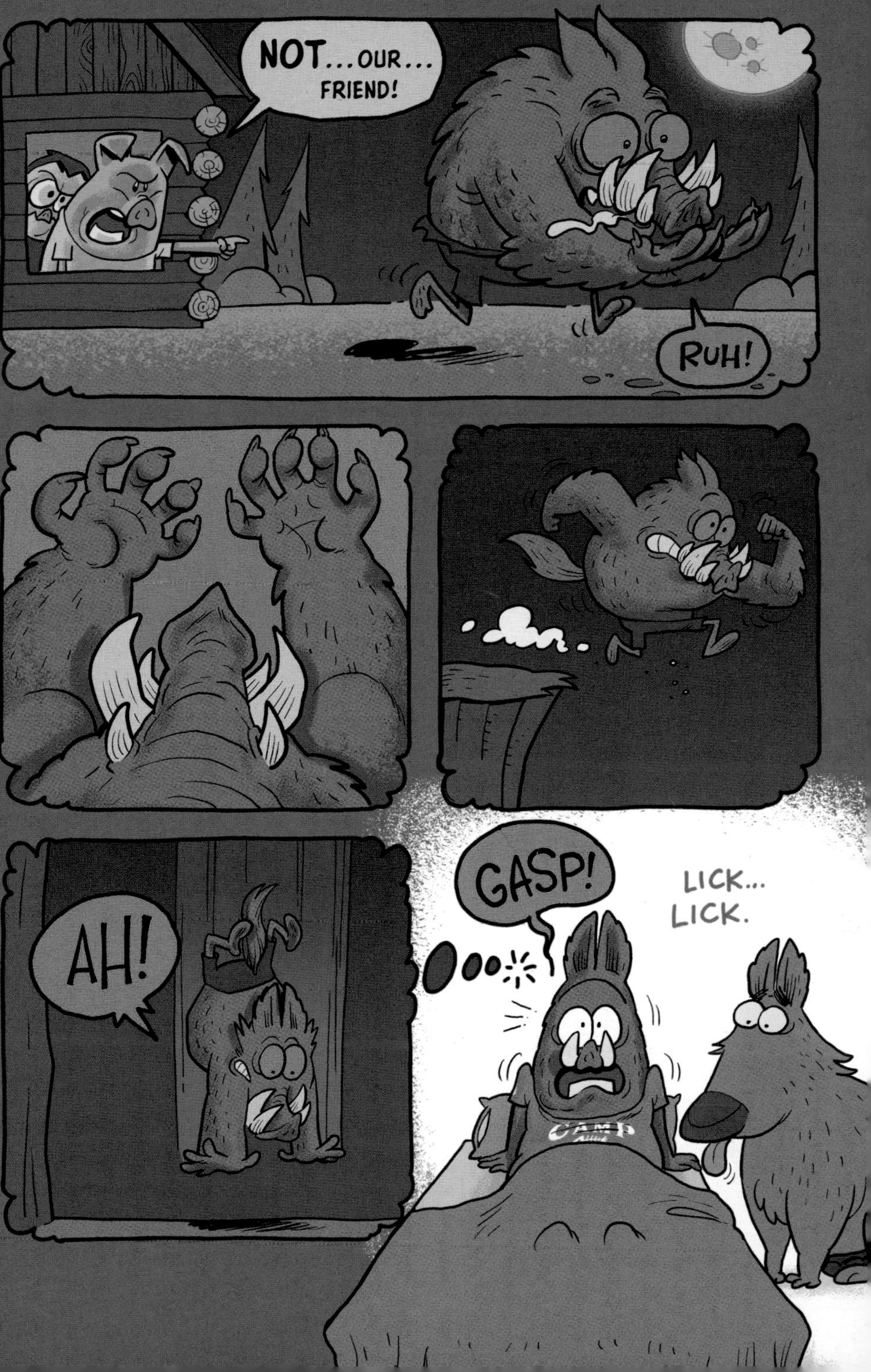
NOT...OUR...
FRIEND!
RUH!
AH!
GASP!
LICK...
LICK.
CAMP

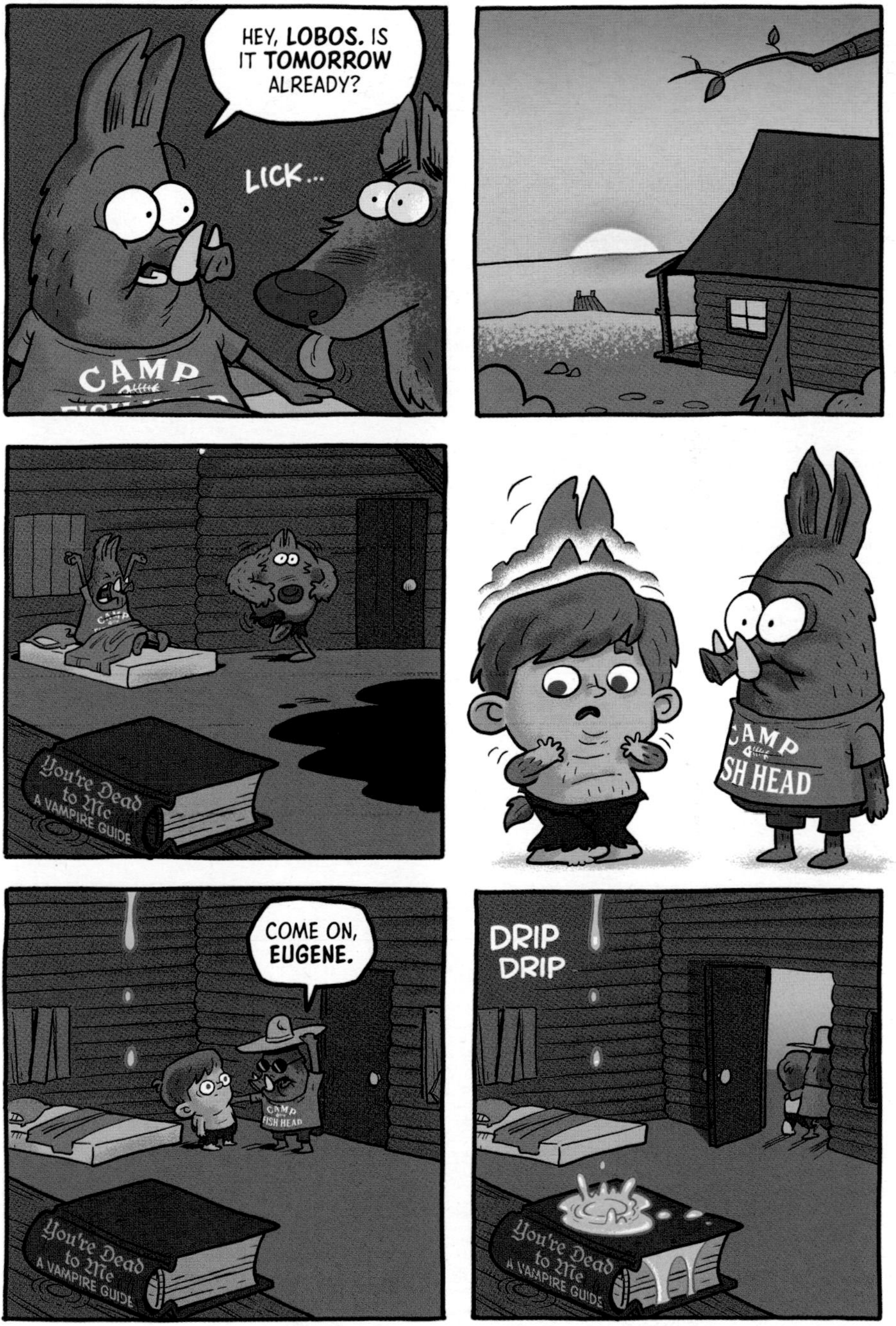
HEY, **LOBOS.** IS IT **TOMORROW** ALREADY?
LICK...
CAMP
You're Dead to Me
A VAMPIRE GUIDE
CAMP
SH HEAD
COME ON, **EUGENE.**
CAMP
FISH HEAD
You're Dead to Me
A VAMPIRE GUIDE
DRIP
DRIP
You're Dead to Me
A VAMPIRE GUIDE

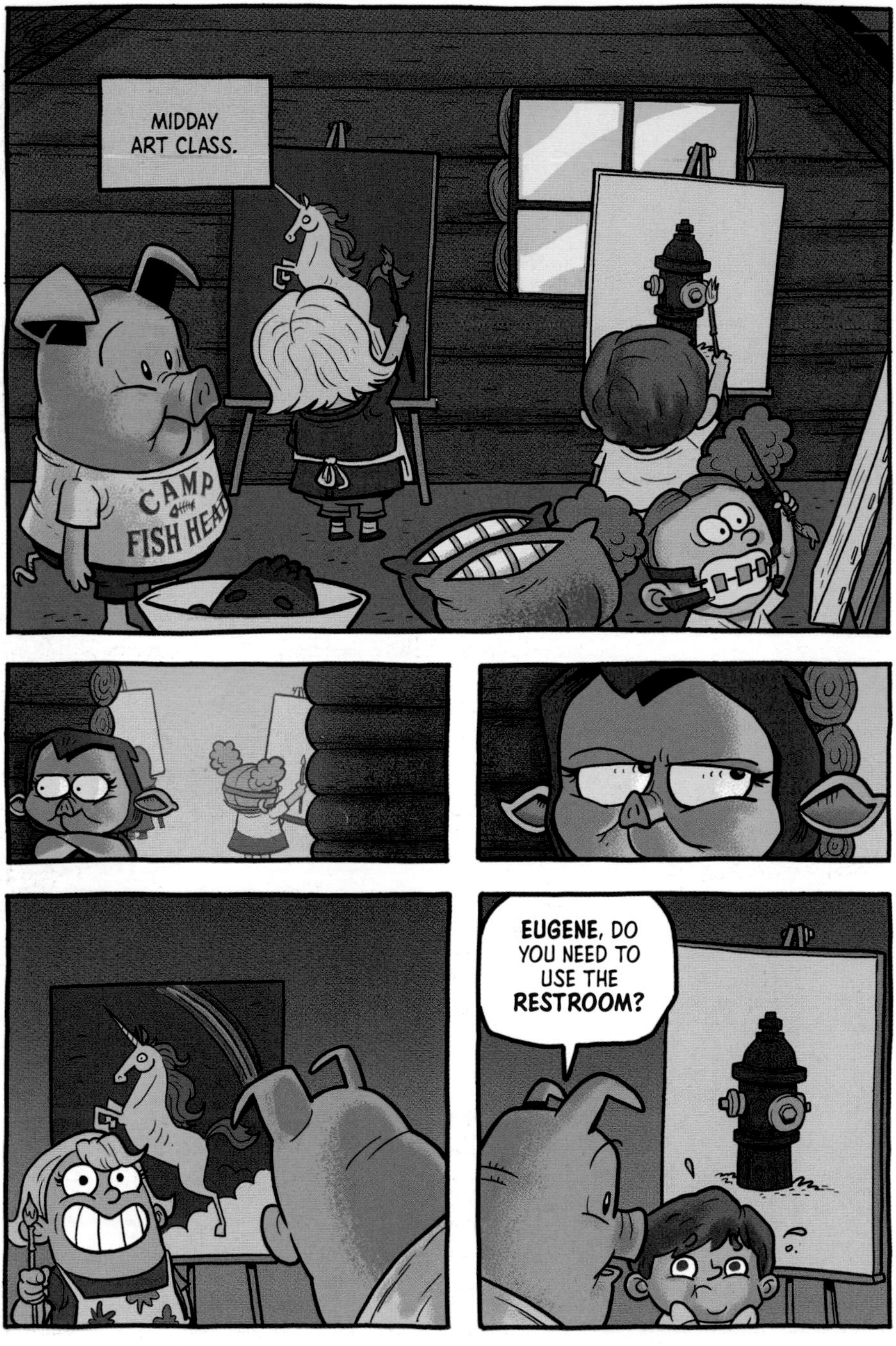
MIDDAY ART CLASS.
CAMP
FISH HEA
EUGENE, DO YOU NEED TO USE THE RESTROOM?

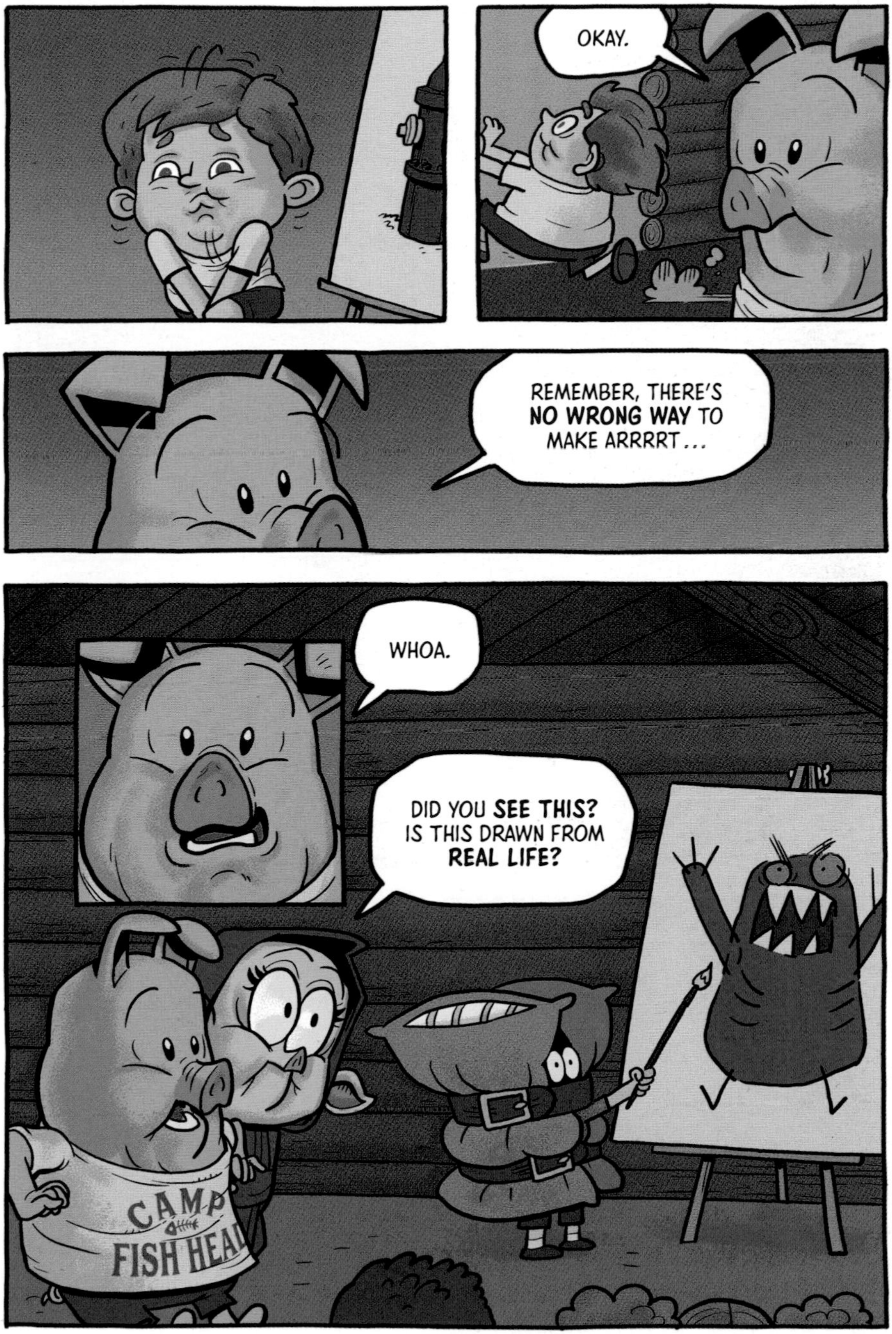
OKAY.
REMEMBER, THERE'S NO WRONG WAY TO MAKE ARRRRT...
WHOA.
DID YOU SEE THIS? IS THIS DRAWN FROM REAL LIFE?
CAMP FISH HEAD

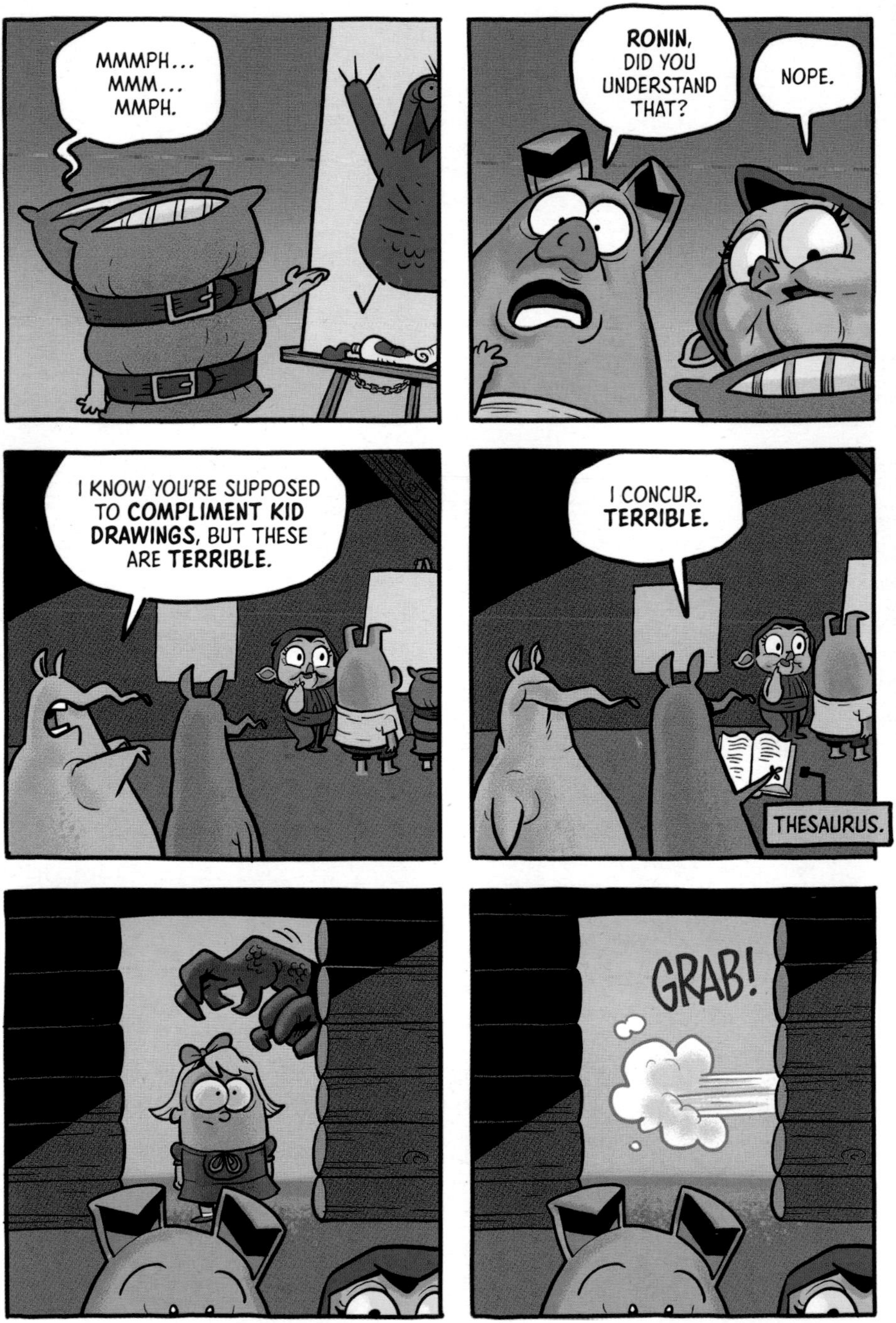
MMMPH... MMM... MMPH.
RONIN, DID YOU UNDERSTAND THAT?
NOPE.
I KNOW YOU'RE SUPPOSED TO COMPLIMENT KID DRAWINGS, BUT THESE ARE TERRIBLE.
I CONCUR. TERRIBLE.
THESAURUS.
GRAB!

CHAPTER FOUR

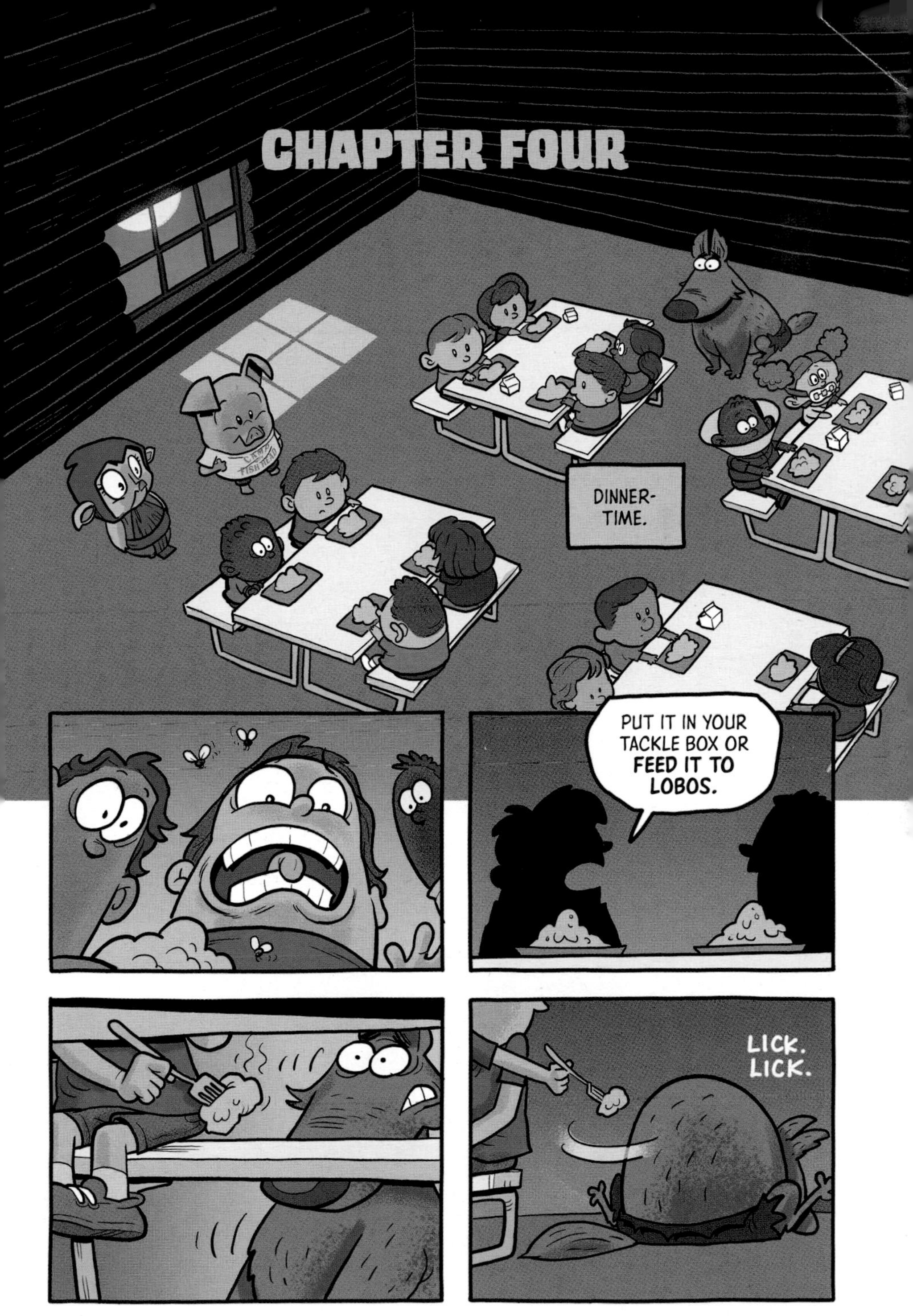

CAMP FISH HEAD
DINNER-TIME.
PUT IT IN YOUR TACKLE BOX OR FEED IT TO LOBOS.
LICK. LICK.

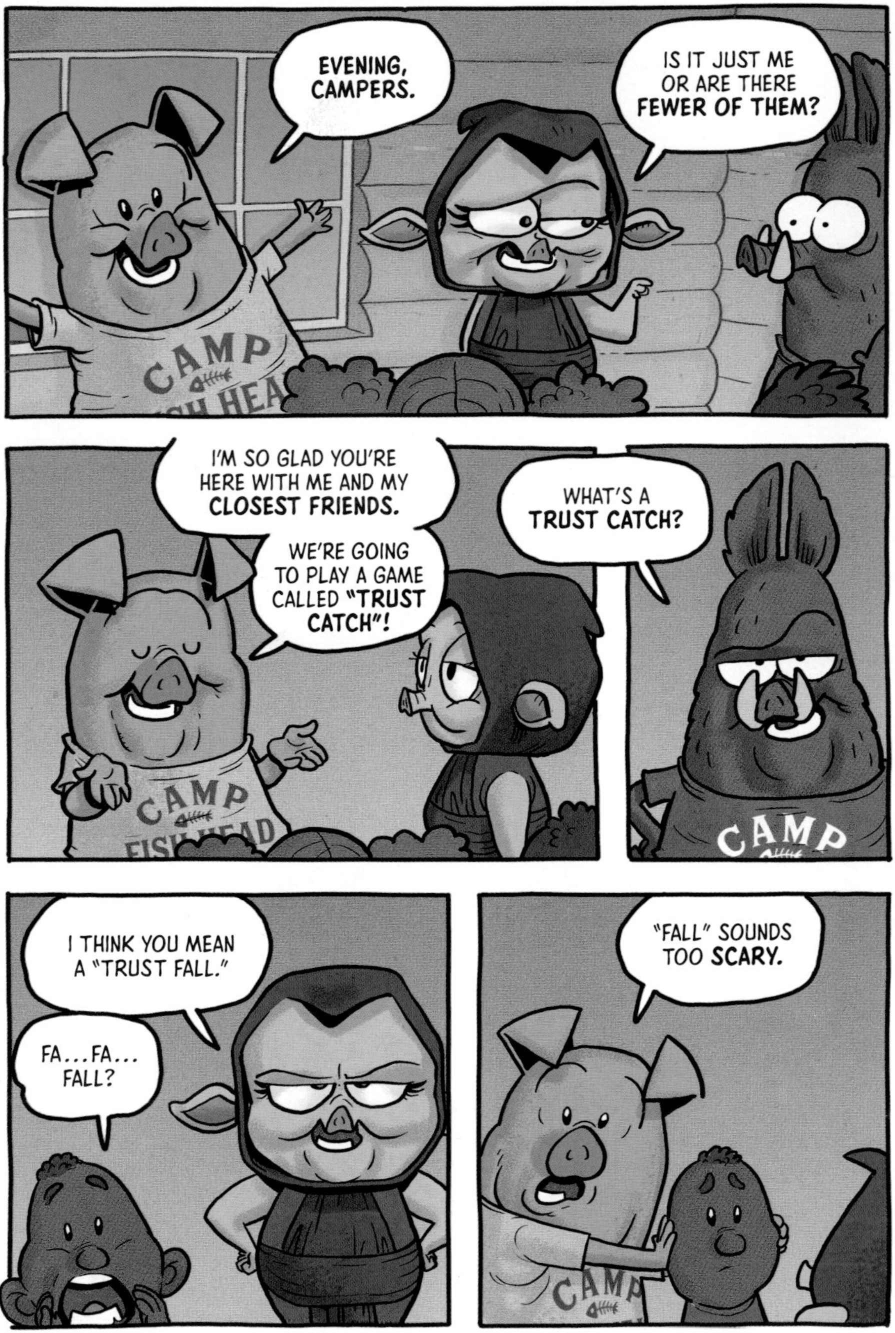
EVENING, CAMPERS.
IS IT JUST ME OR ARE THERE FEWER OF THEM?
CAMP FISH HEAD
I'M SO GLAD YOU'RE HERE WITH ME AND MY CLOSEST FRIENDS.
WE'RE GOING TO PLAY A GAME CALLED "TRUST CATCH"!
WHAT'S A TRUST CATCH?
CAMP FISH HEAD
CAMP
I THINK YOU MEAN A "TRUST FALL."
FA...FA... FALL?
"FALL" SOUNDS TOO SCARY.
CAMP

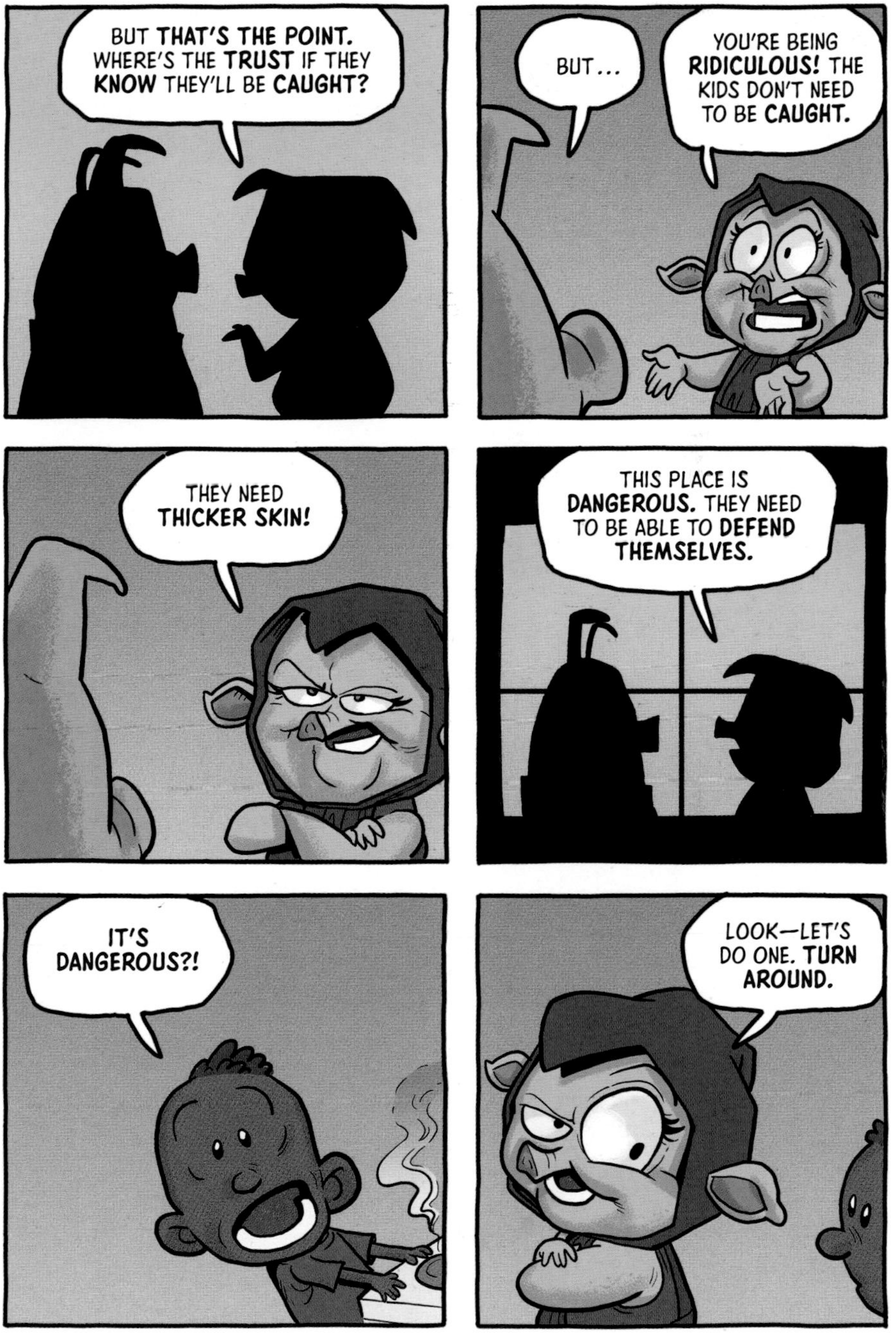
BUT **THAT'S THE POINT.** WHERE'S THE **TRUST** IF THEY **KNOW** THEY'LL BE **CAUGHT?**
BUT...
YOU'RE BEING **RIDICULOUS!** THE KIDS DON'T NEED TO BE **CAUGHT.**
THEY NEED **THICKER SKIN!**
THIS PLACE IS **DANGEROUS.** THEY NEED TO BE ABLE TO **DEFEND THEMSELVES.**
IT'S DANGEROUS?!
LOOK—LET'S DO ONE. **TURN AROUND.**

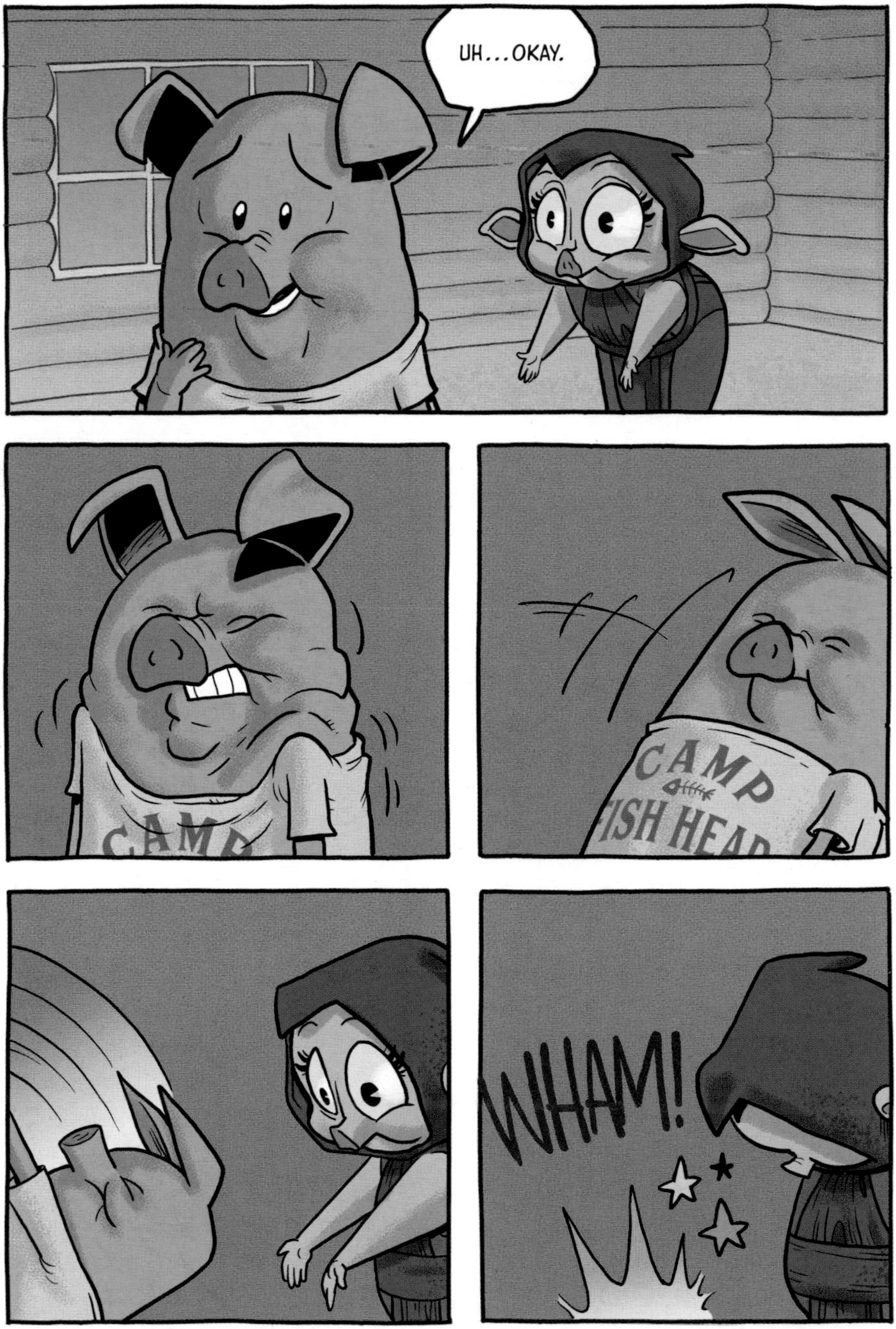
UH...OKAY.
CAMP
CAMP
FISH HEAD
WHAM!

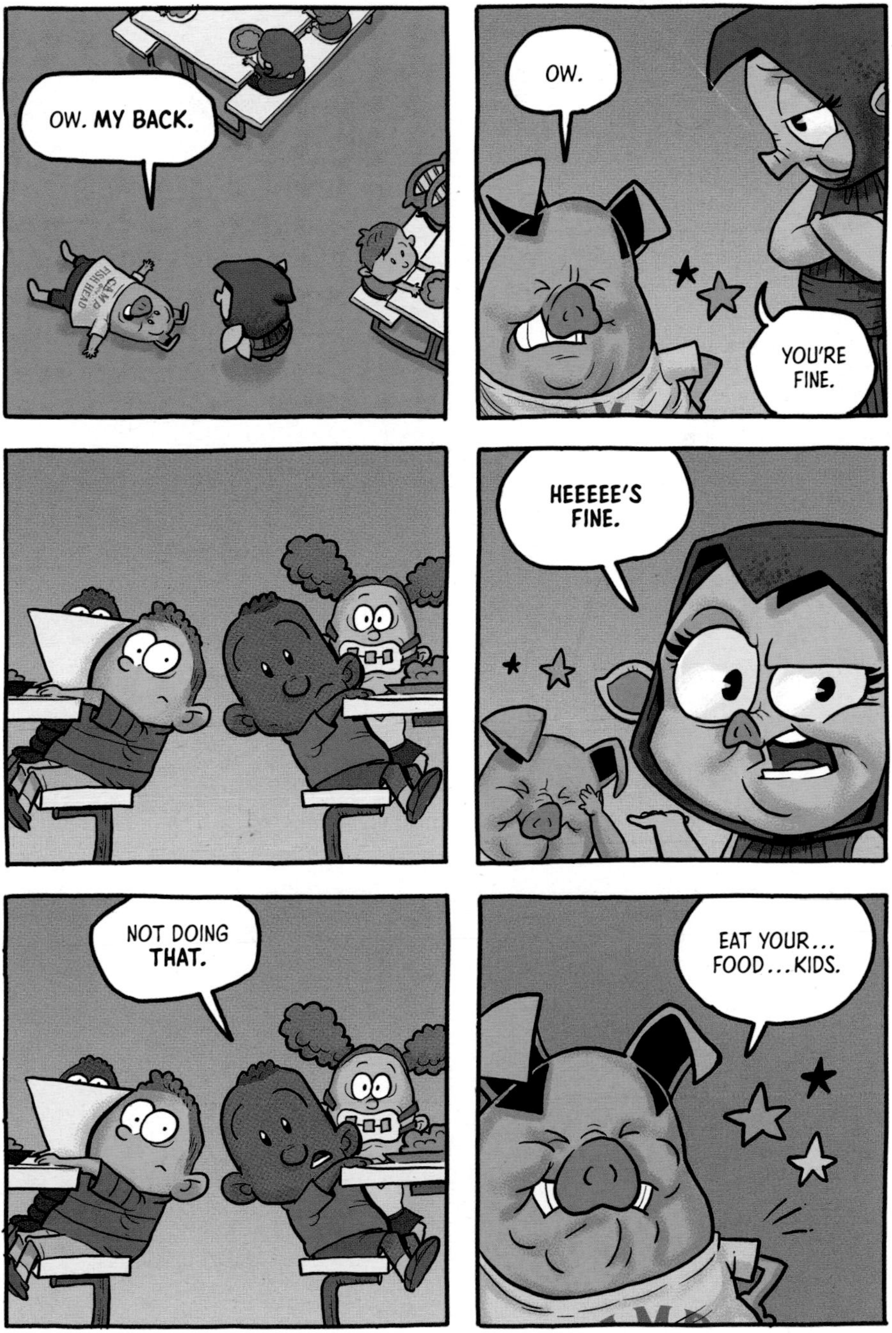
OW. MY BACK.
CAMP FISH HEAD
OW.
YOU'RE FINE.
HEEEEE'S FINE.
NOT DOING THAT.
EAT YOUR... FOOD...KIDS.

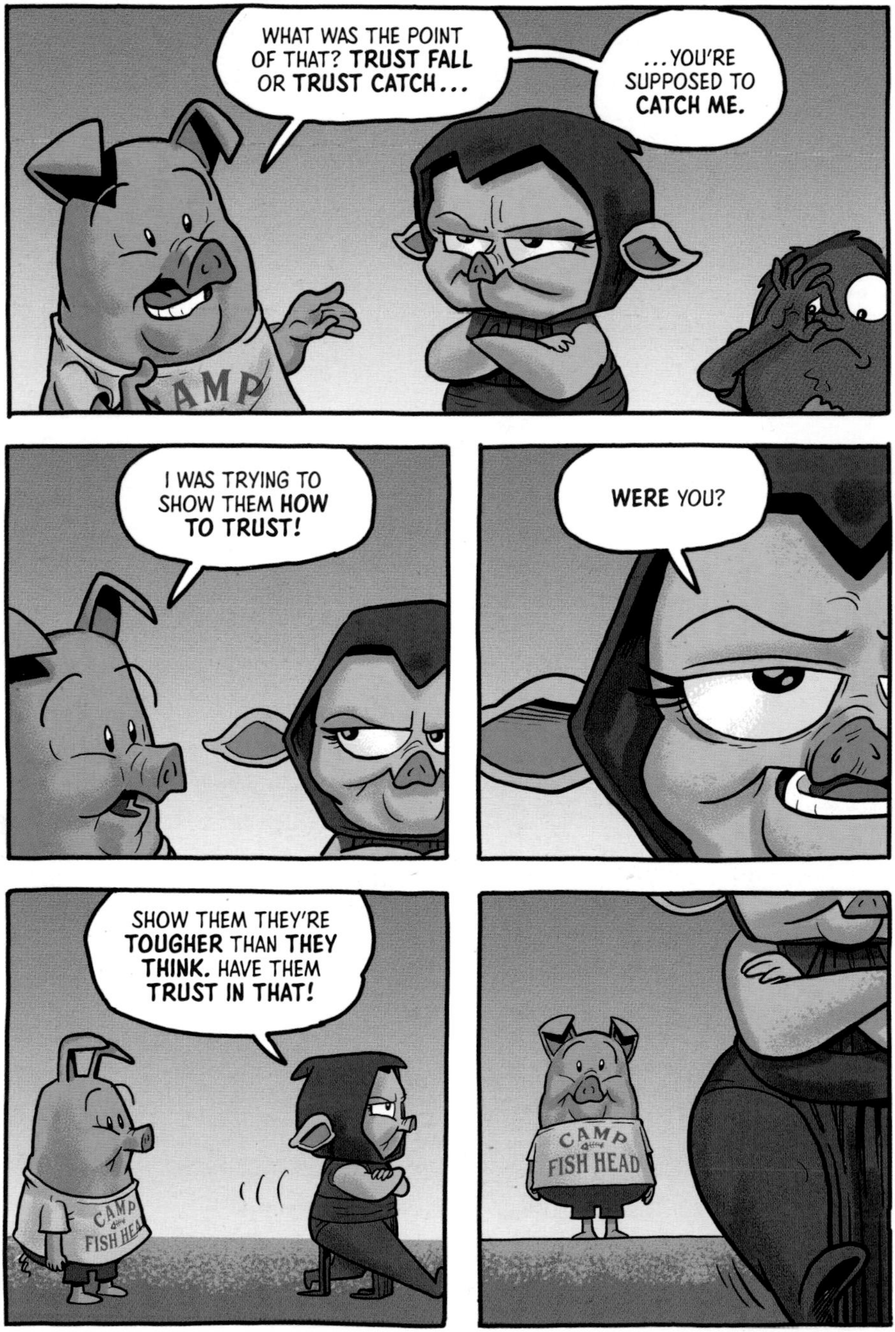
WHAT WAS THE POINT OF THAT? TRUST FALL OR TRUST CATCH...
...YOU'RE SUPPOSED TO CATCH ME.
CAMP
I WAS TRYING TO SHOW THEM HOW TO TRUST!
WERE YOU?
SHOW THEM THEY'RE TOUGHER THAN THEY THINK. HAVE THEM TRUST IN THAT!
CAMP FISH HEAD
CAMP FISH HEAD

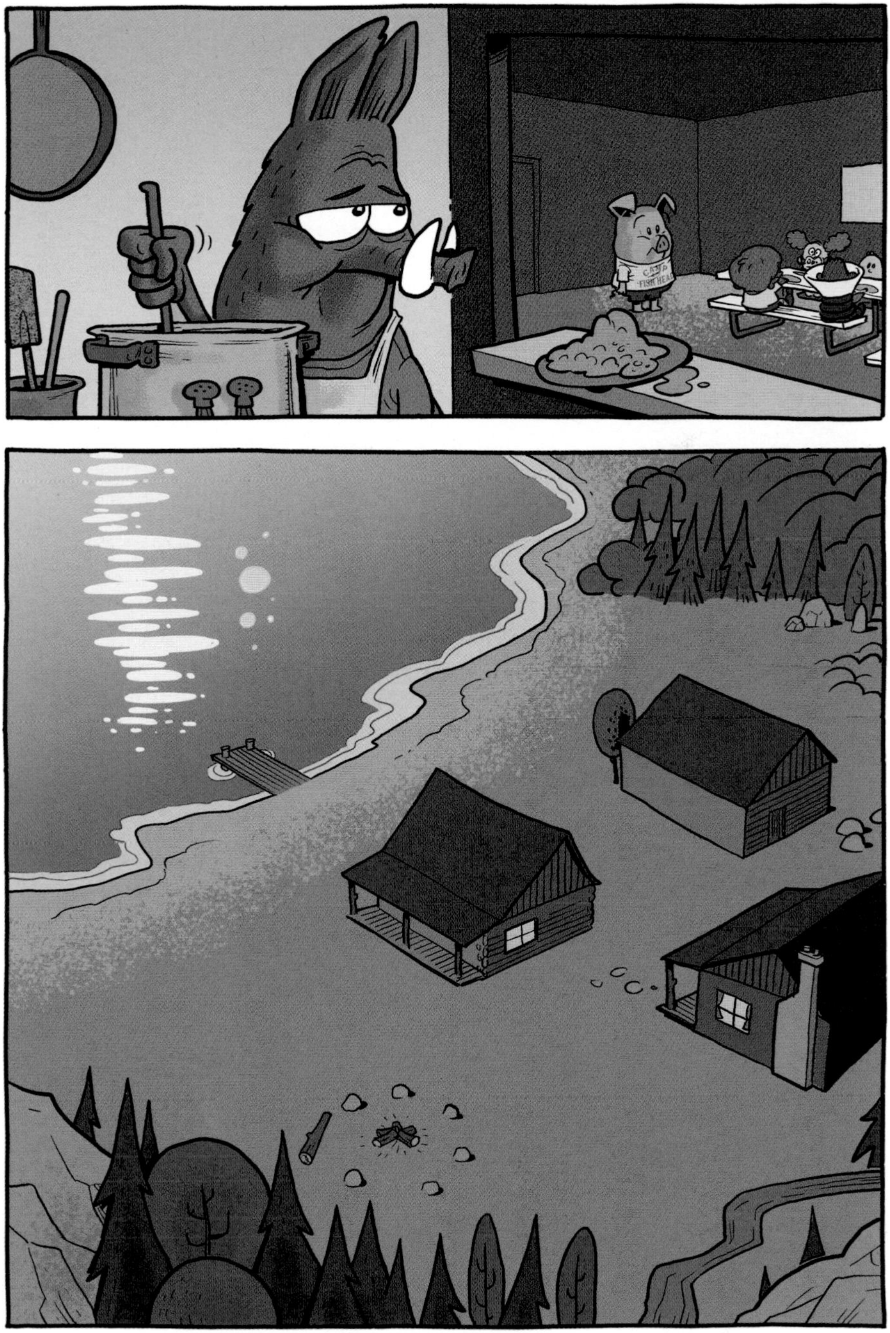
CAMP
FISH HEAD

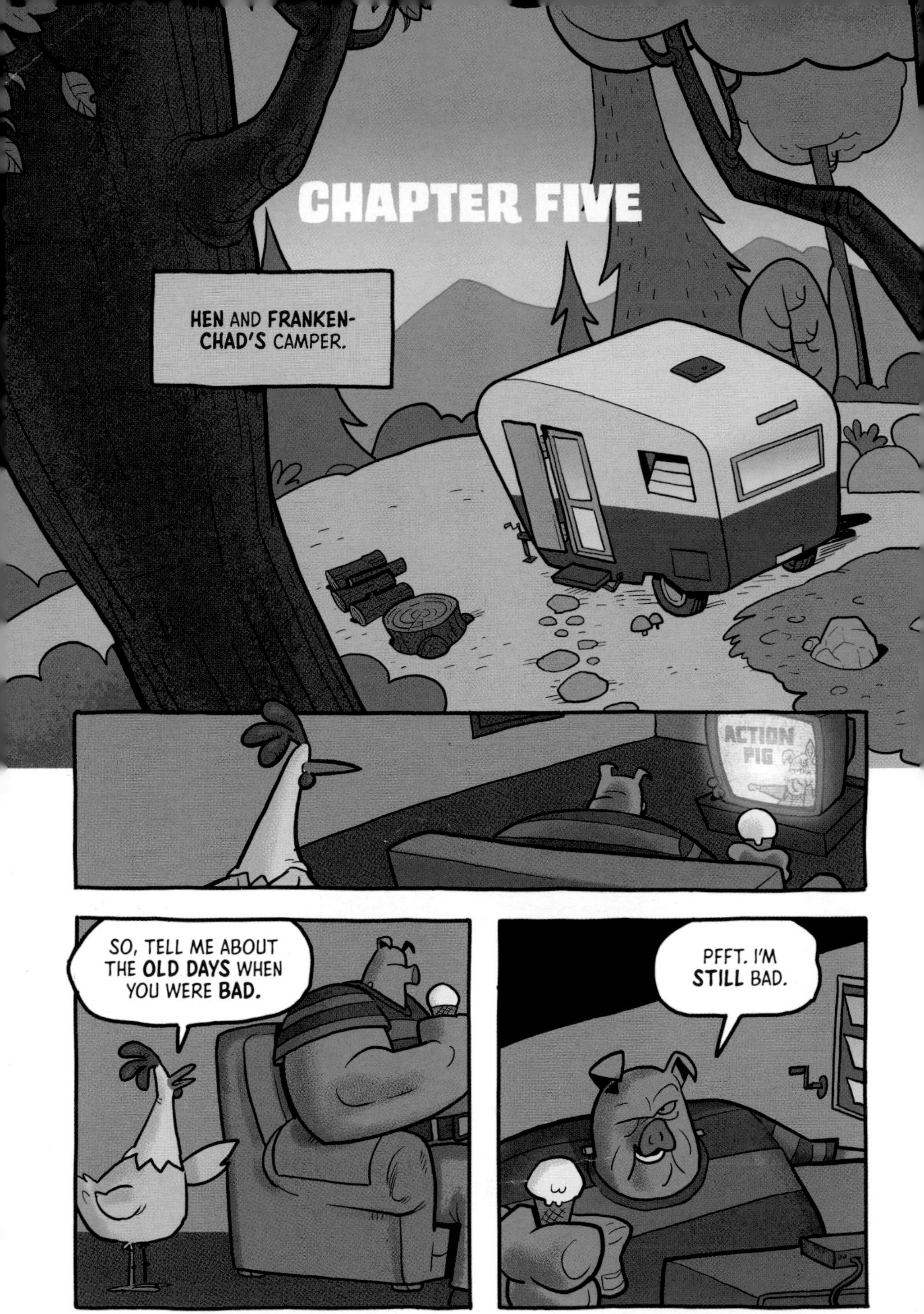
CHAPTER FIVE
HEN AND FRANKEN-CHAD'S CAMPER.
ACTION PIG
SO, TELL ME ABOUT THE OLD DAYS WHEN YOU WERE BAD.
PFFT. I'M STILL BAD.

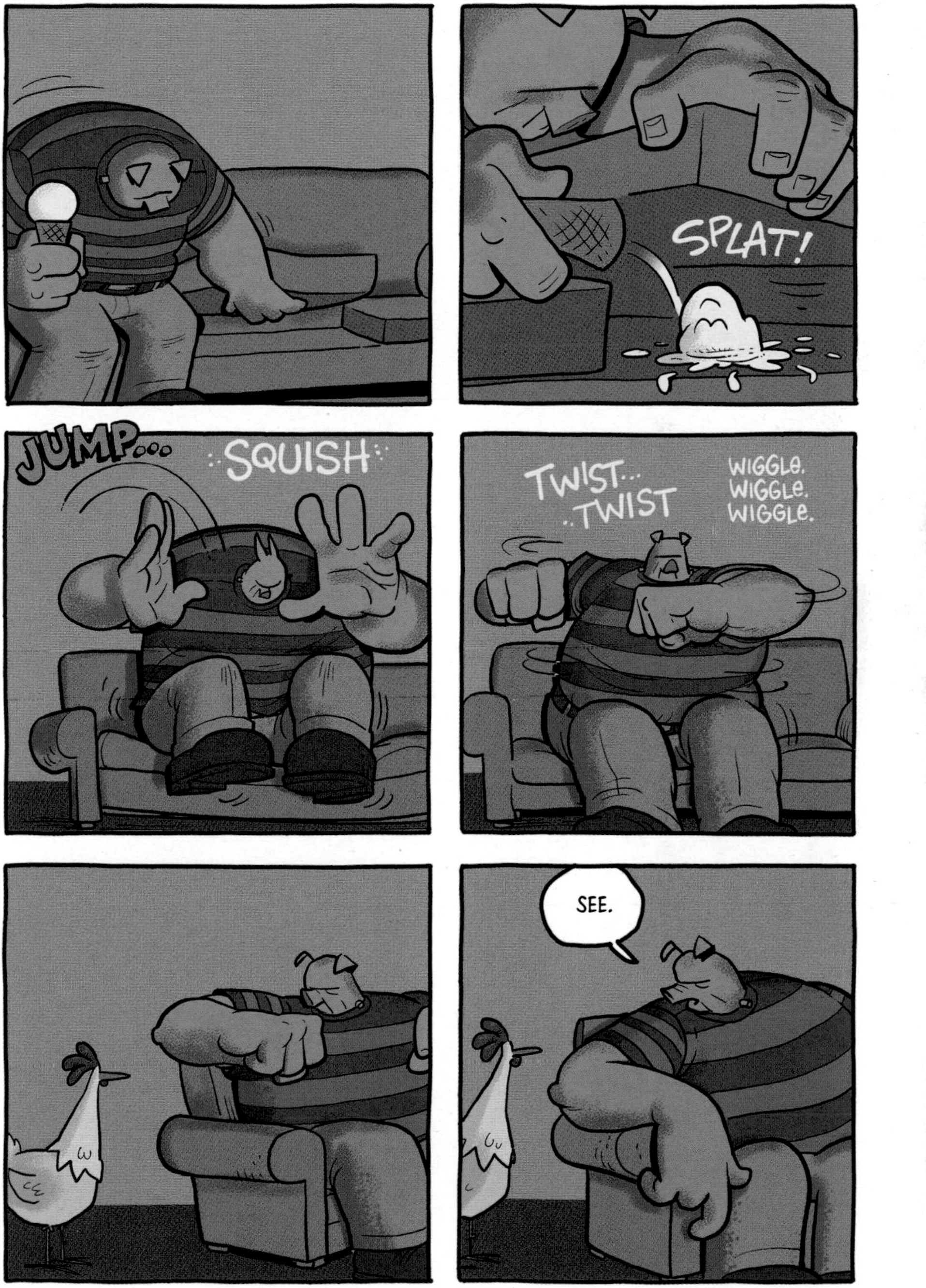
SPLAT!
JUMP...
SQUISH
TWIST...
..TWIST
WIGGLE.
WIGGLE.
WIGGLE.
SEE.

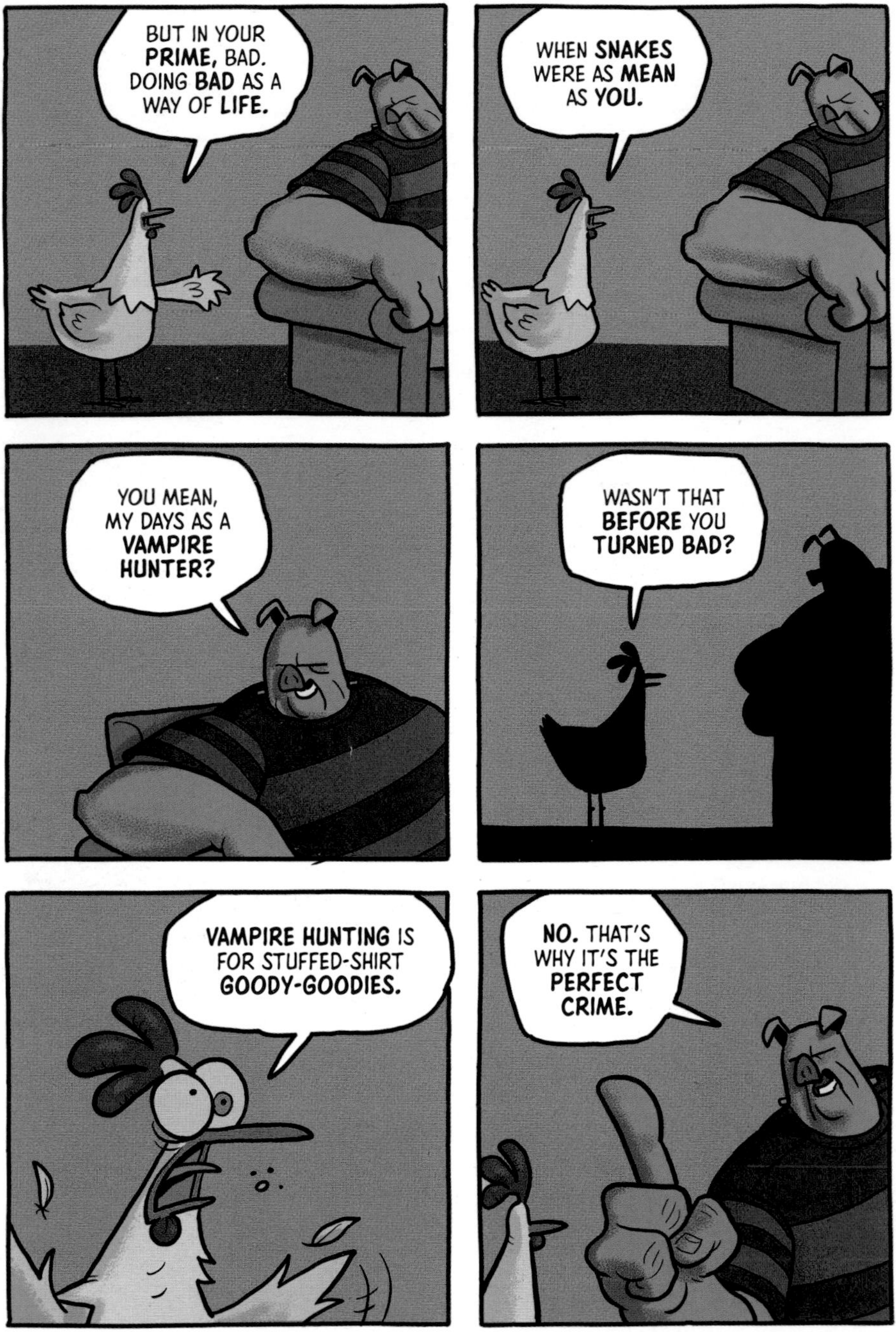
BUT IN YOUR PRIME, BAD. DOING BAD AS A WAY OF LIFE.
WHEN SNAKES WERE AS MEAN AS YOU.
YOU MEAN, MY DAYS AS A VAMPIRE HUNTER?
WASN'T THAT BEFORE YOU TURNED BAD?
VAMPIRE HUNTING IS FOR STUFFED-SHIRT GOODY-GOODIES.
NO. THAT'S WHY IT'S THE PERFECT CRIME.

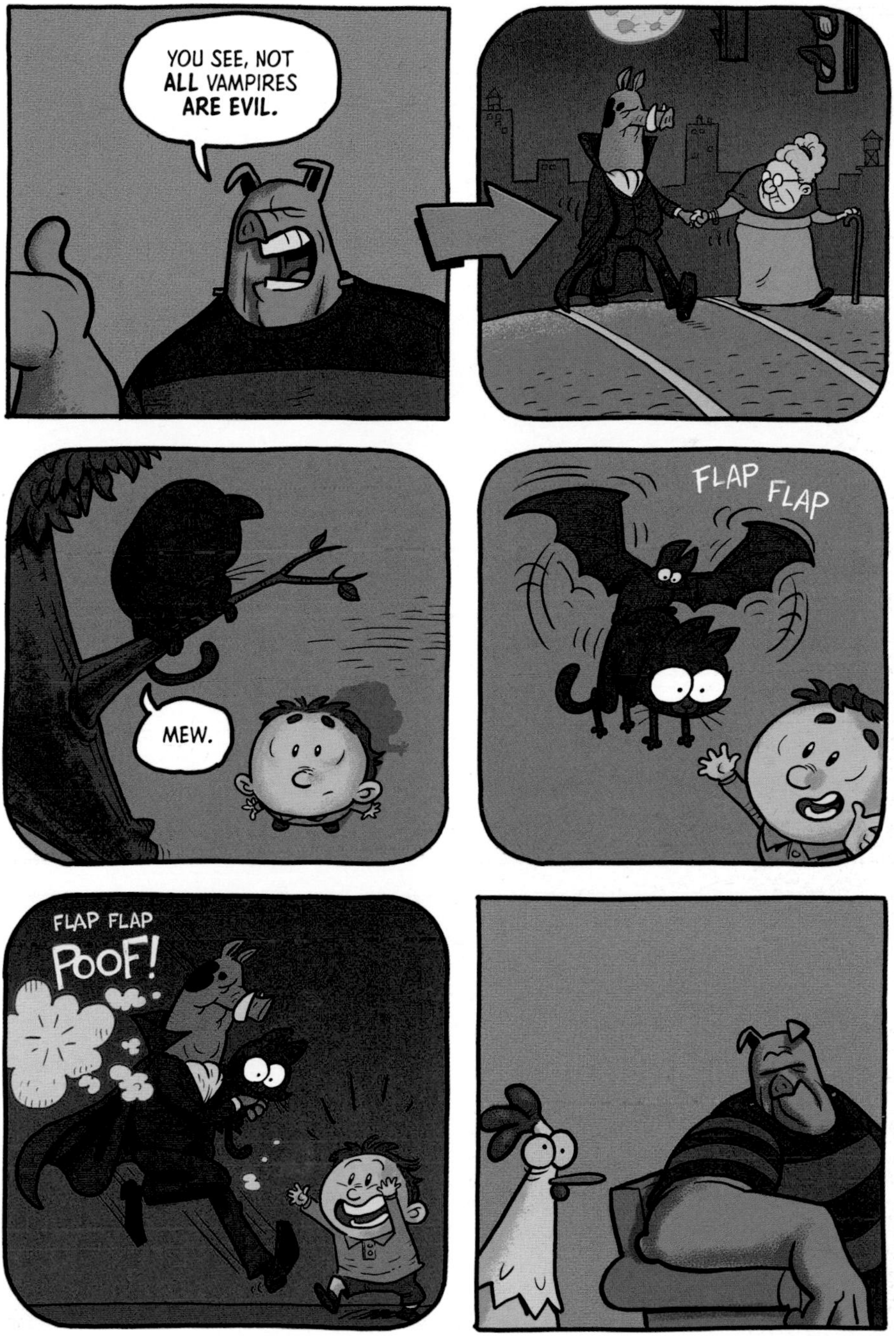
YOU SEE, NOT ALL VAMPIRES ARE EVIL.
MEW.
FLAP FLAP
FLAP FLAP
POOF!

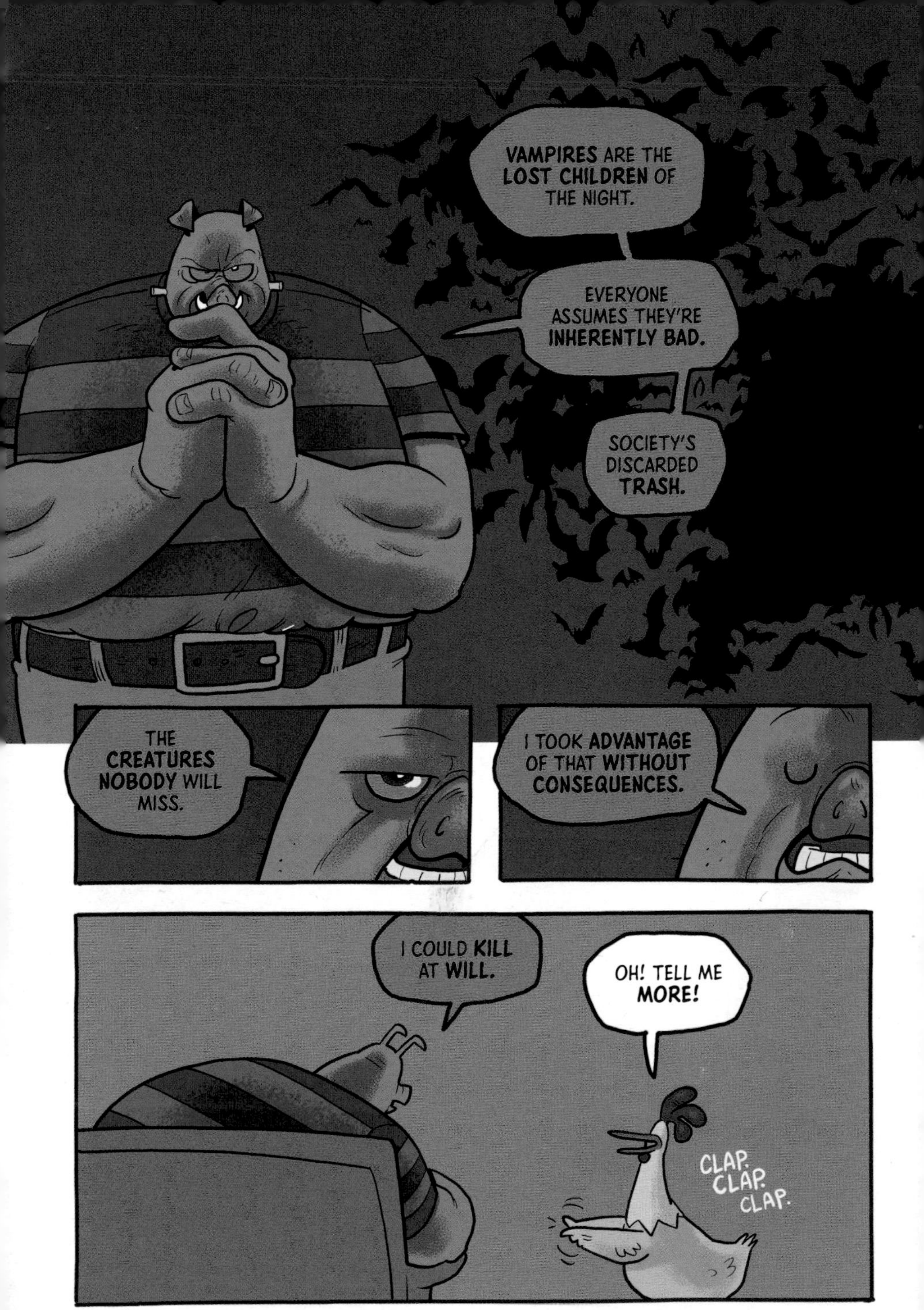
VAMPIRES ARE THE LOST CHILDREN OF THE NIGHT.
EVERYONE ASSUMES THEY'RE INHERENTLY BAD.
SOCIETY'S DISCARDED TRASH.
THE CREATURES NOBODY WILL MISS.
I TOOK ADVANTAGE OF THAT WITHOUT CONSEQUENCES.
I COULD KILL AT WILL.
OH! TELL ME MORE!
CLAP. CLAP. CLAP.

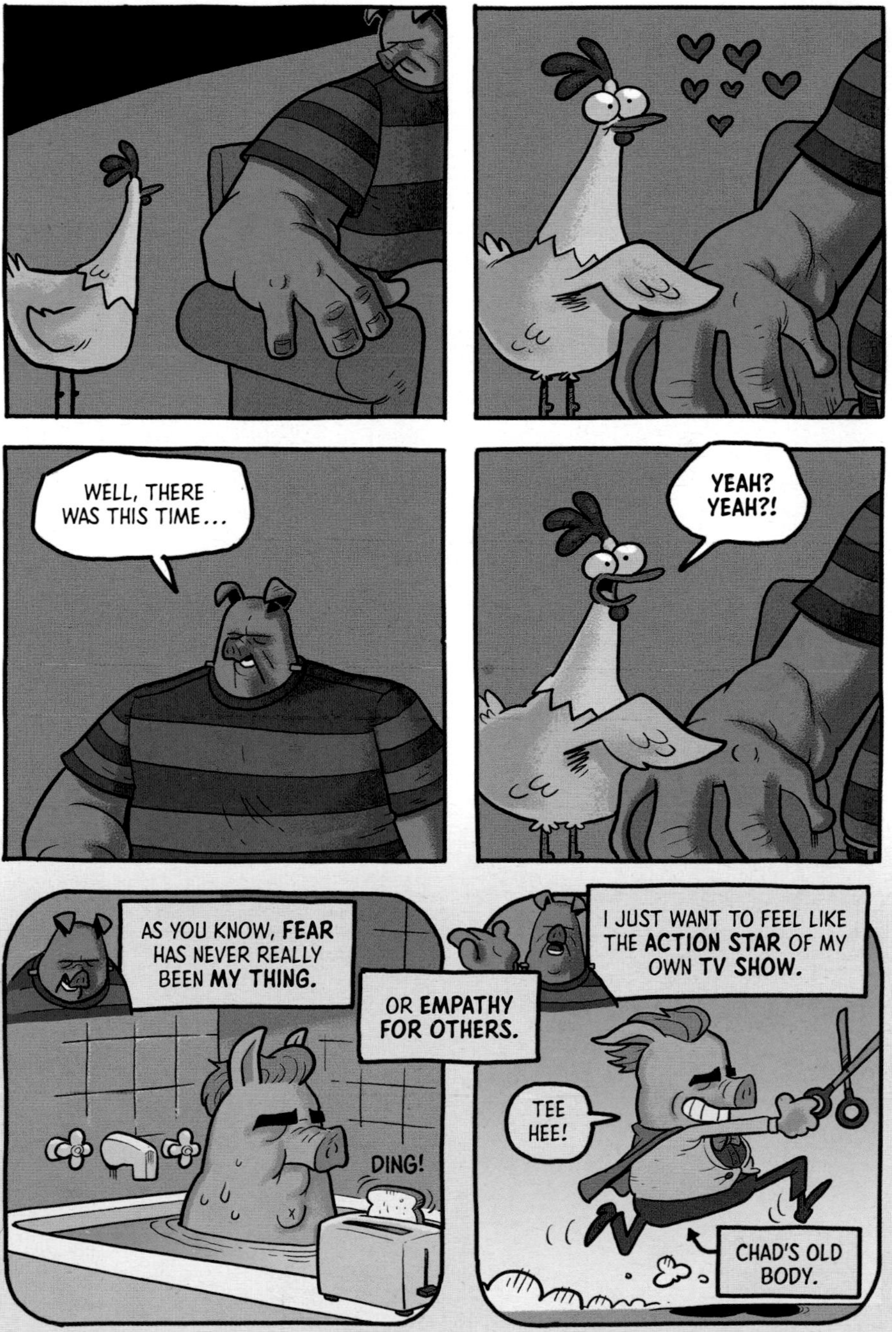

WELL, THERE WAS THIS TIME...
YEAH? YEAH?!
AS YOU KNOW, FEAR HAS NEVER REALLY BEEN MY THING.
OR EMPATHY FOR OTHERS.
DING!
I JUST WANT TO FEEL LIKE THE ACTION STAR OF MY OWN TV SHOW.
TEE HEE!
CHAD'S OLD BODY.

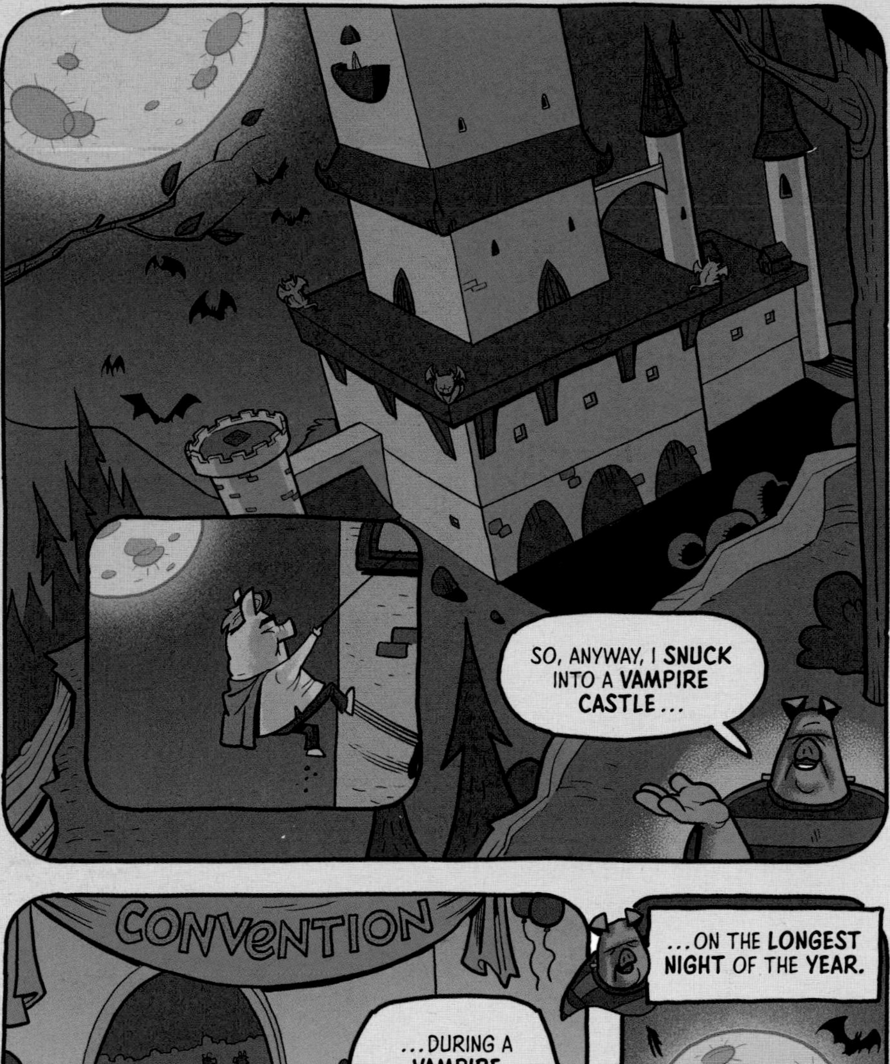
SO, ANYWAY, I SNUCK INTO A VAMPIRE CASTLE...

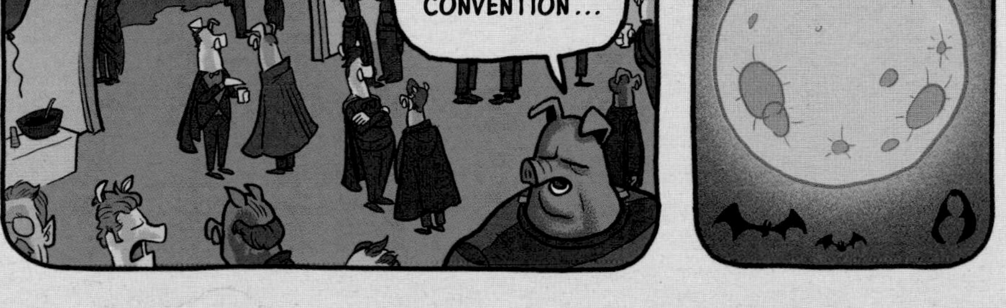
CONVENTION
...DURING A VAMPIRE CONVENTION...
...ON THE LONGEST NIGHT OF THE YEAR.

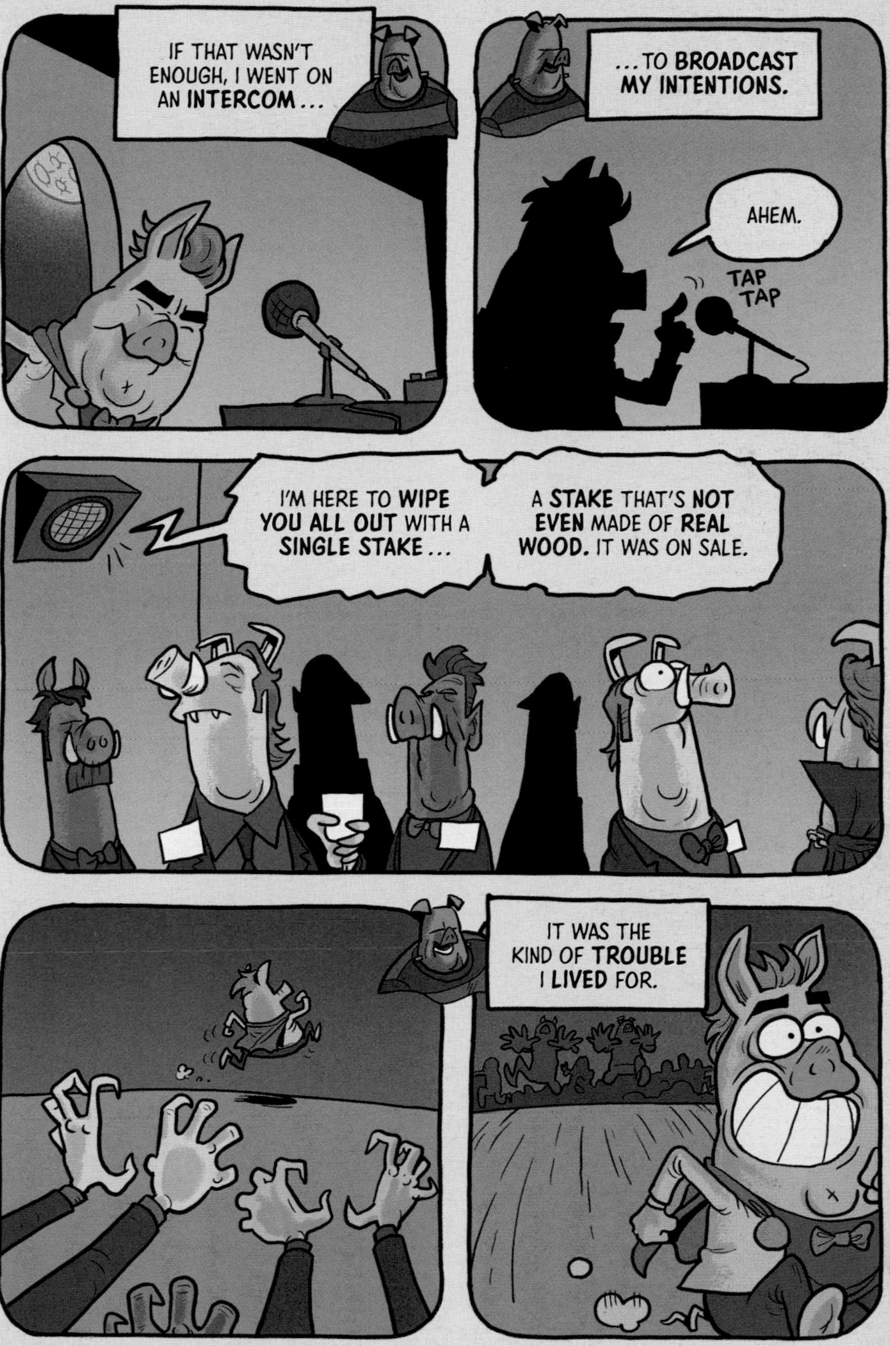
IF THAT WASN'T ENOUGH, I WENT ON AN INTERCOM...
...TO BROADCAST MY INTENTIONS.
AHEM.
TAP TAP
I'M HERE TO WIPE YOU ALL OUT WITH A SINGLE STAKE...
A STAKE THAT'S NOT EVEN MADE OF REAL WOOD. IT WAS ON SALE.
IT WAS THE KIND OF TROUBLE I LIVED FOR.

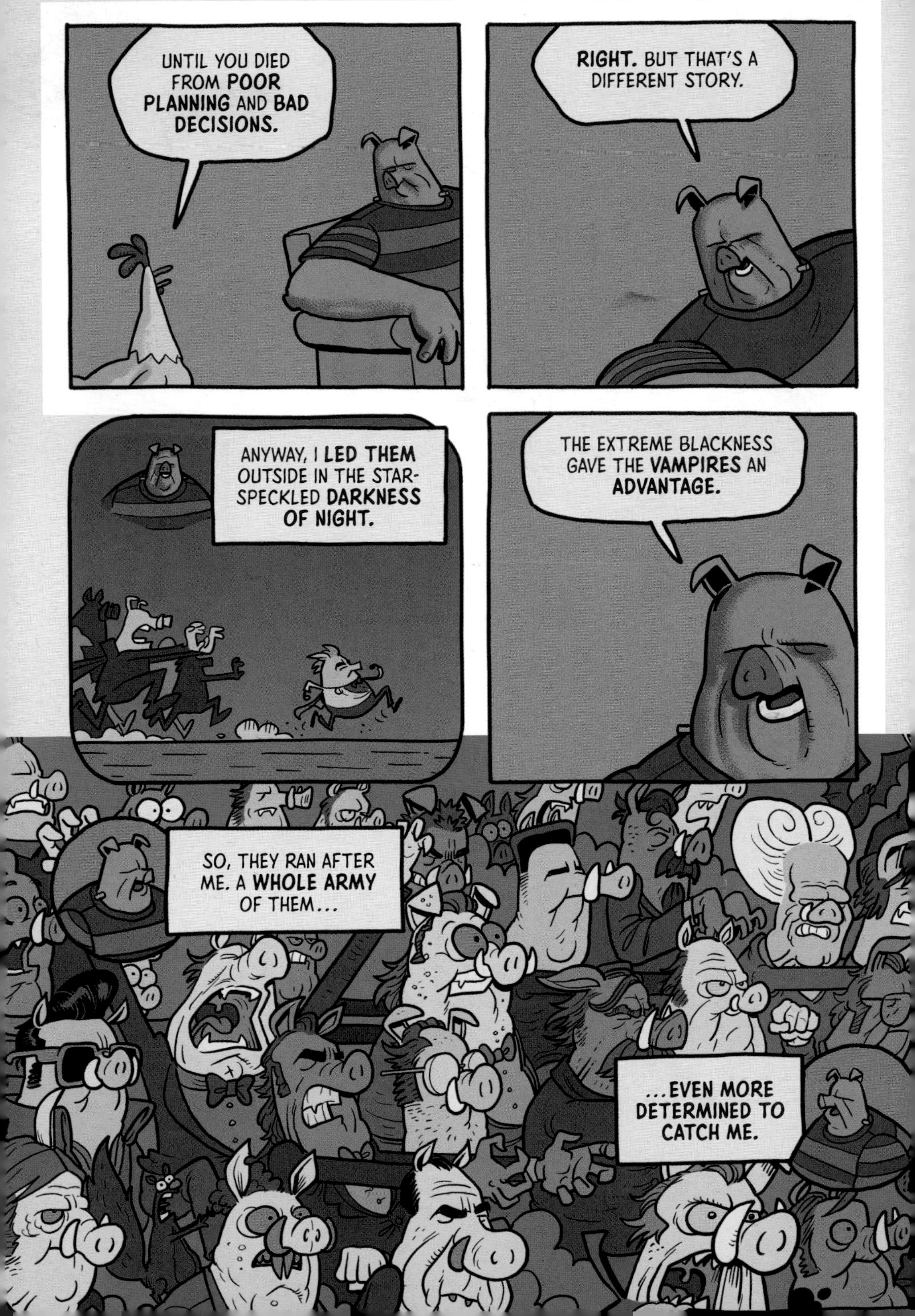
UNTIL YOU DIED FROM POOR PLANNING AND BAD DECISIONS.
RIGHT. BUT THAT'S A DIFFERENT STORY.
ANYWAY, I LED THEM OUTSIDE IN THE STAR-SPECKLED DARKNESS OF NIGHT.
THE EXTREME BLACKNESS GAVE THE VAMPIRES AN ADVANTAGE.
SO, THEY RAN AFTER ME. A WHOLE ARMY OF THEM...
...EVEN MORE DETERMINED TO CATCH ME.

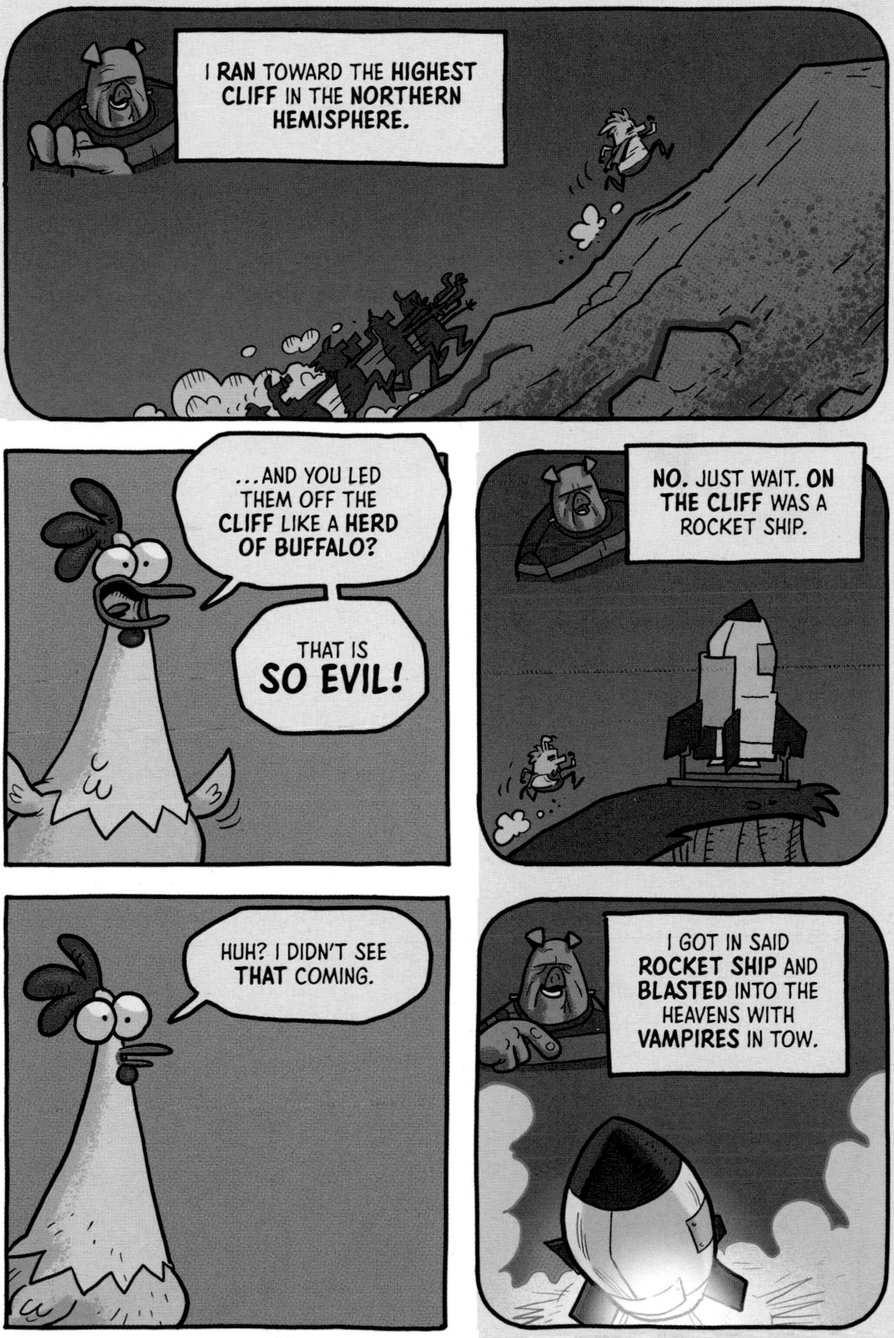
I RAN TOWARD THE HIGHEST CLIFF IN THE NORTHERN HEMISPHERE.
...AND YOU LED THEM OFF THE CLIFF LIKE A HERD OF BUFFALO?
THAT IS SO EVIL!
NO. JUST WAIT. ON THE CLIFF WAS A ROCKET SHIP.
HUH? I DIDN'T SEE THAT COMING.
I GOT IN SAID ROCKET SHIP AND BLASTED INTO THE HEAVENS WITH VAMPIRES IN TOW.

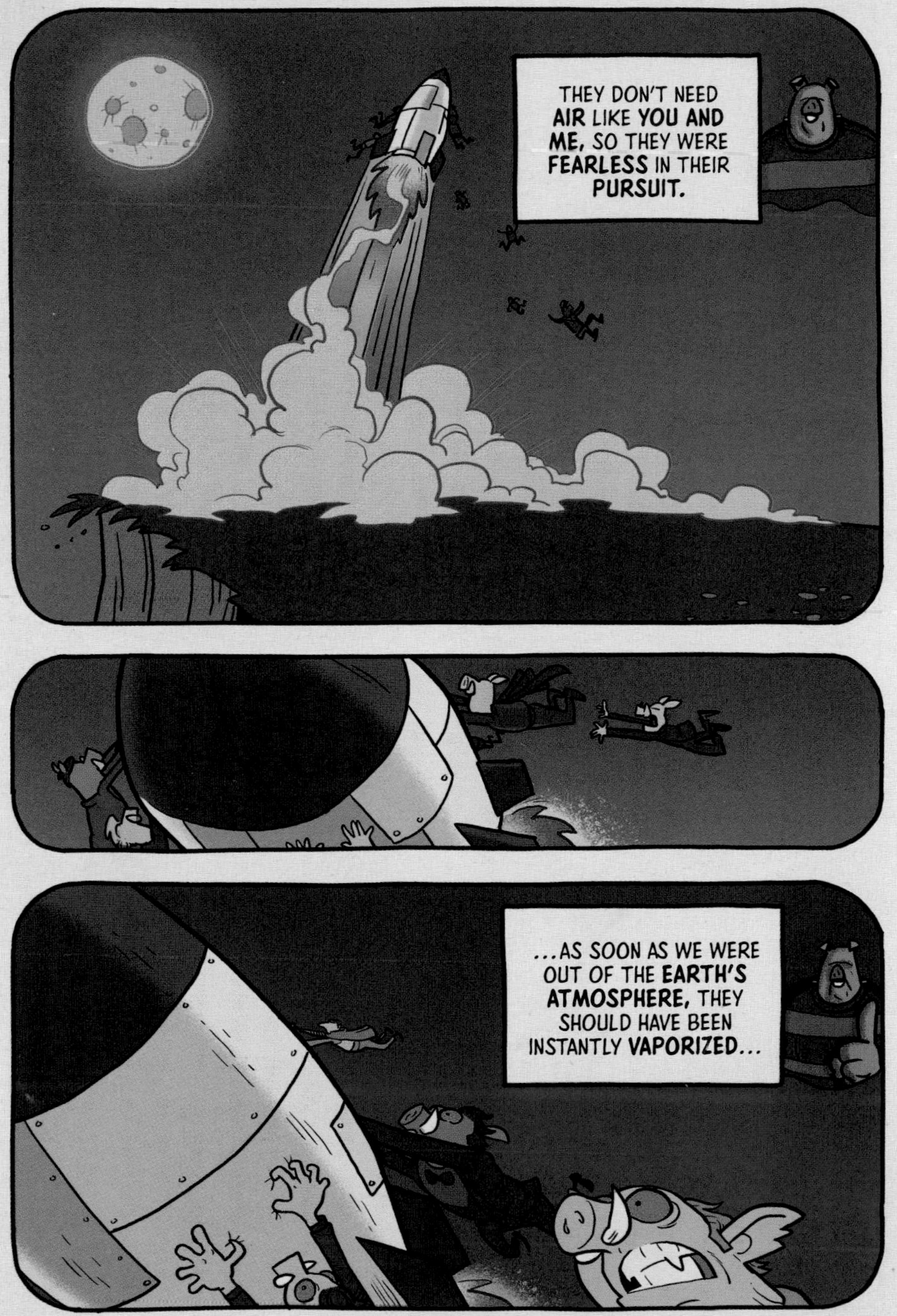
THEY DON'T NEED AIR LIKE YOU AND ME, SO THEY WERE FEARLESS IN THEIR PURSUIT.
...AS SOON AS WE WERE OUT OF THE EARTH'S ATMOSPHERE, THEY SHOULD HAVE BEEN INSTANTLY VAPORIZED...

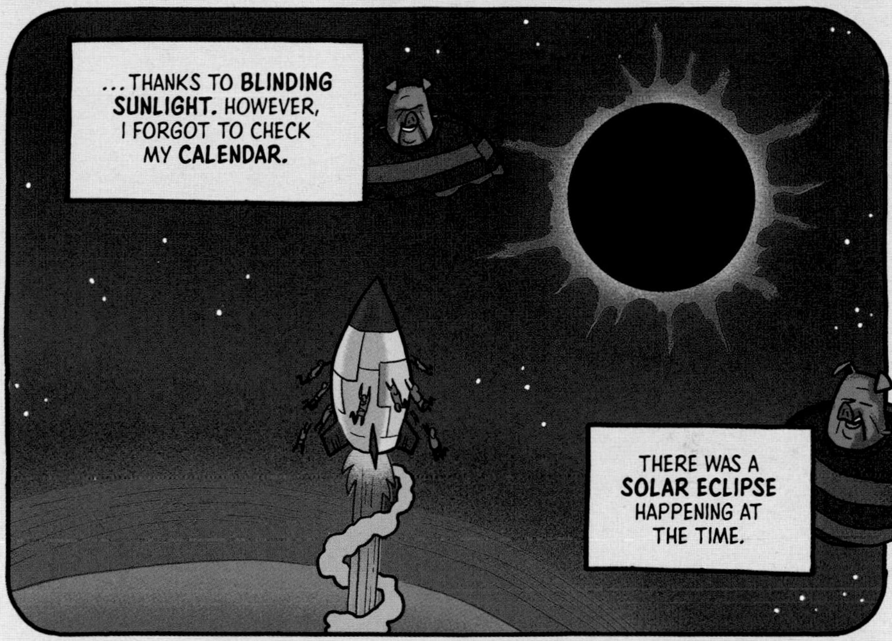
...THANKS TO BLINDING SUNLIGHT. HOWEVER, I FORGOT TO CHECK MY CALENDAR.
THERE WAS A SOLAR ECLIPSE HAPPENING AT THE TIME.

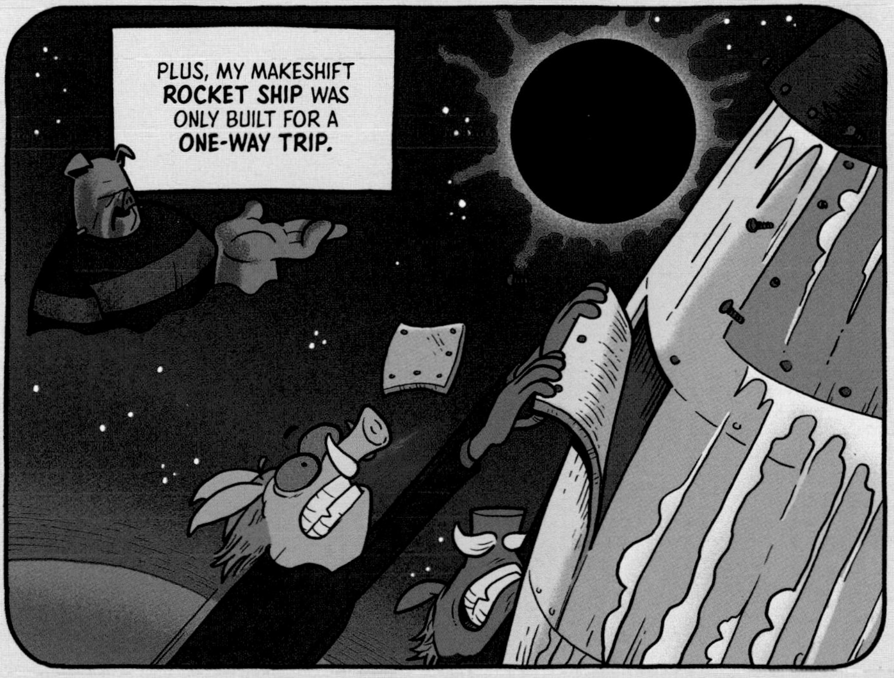
PLUS, MY MAKESHIFT ROCKET SHIP WAS ONLY BUILT FOR A ONE-WAY TRIP.

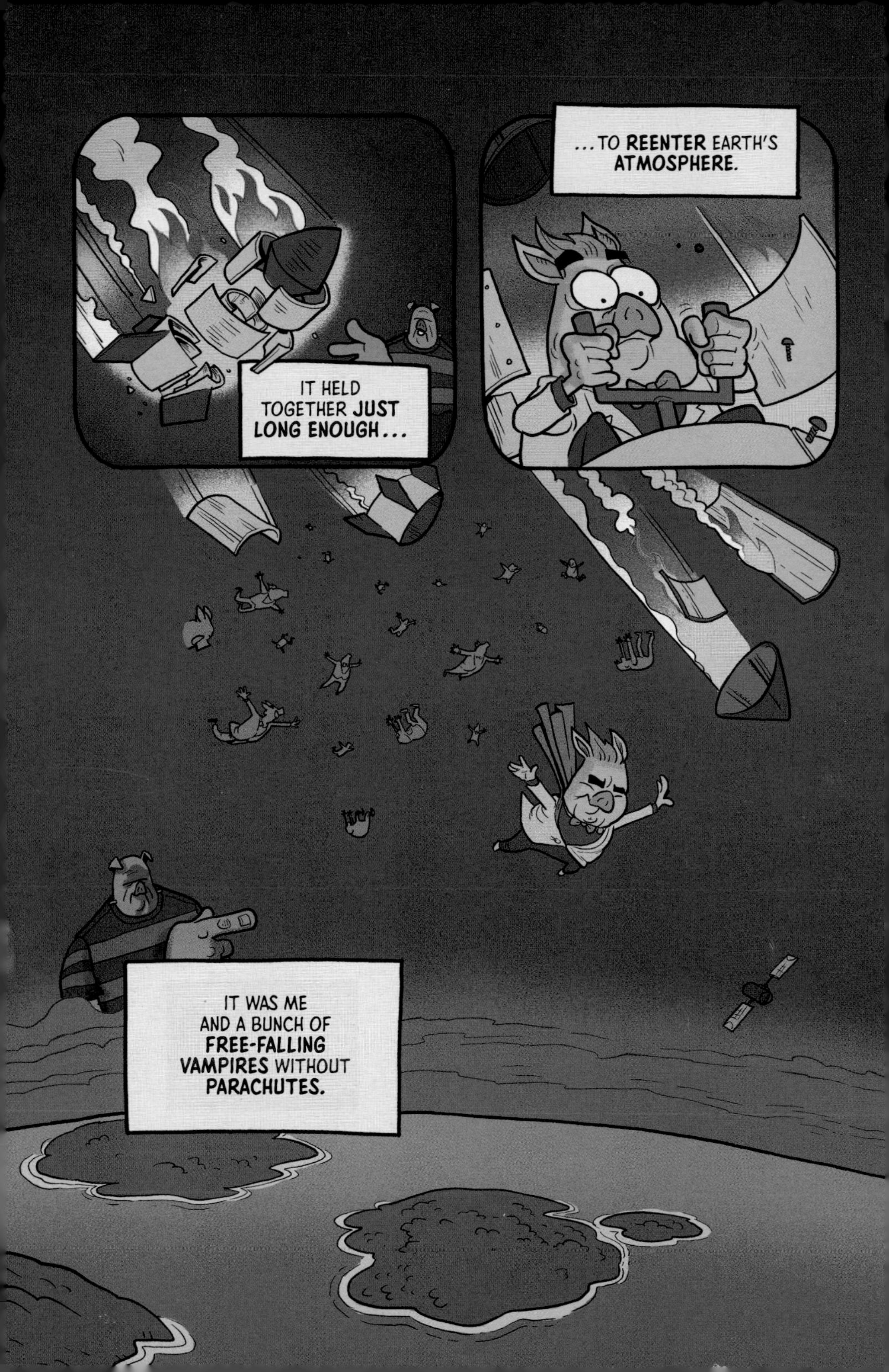
IT HELD TOGETHER JUST LONG ENOUGH...
...TO REENTER EARTH'S ATMOSPHERE.
IT WAS ME AND A BUNCH OF FREE-FALLING VAMPIRES WITHOUT PARACHUTES.

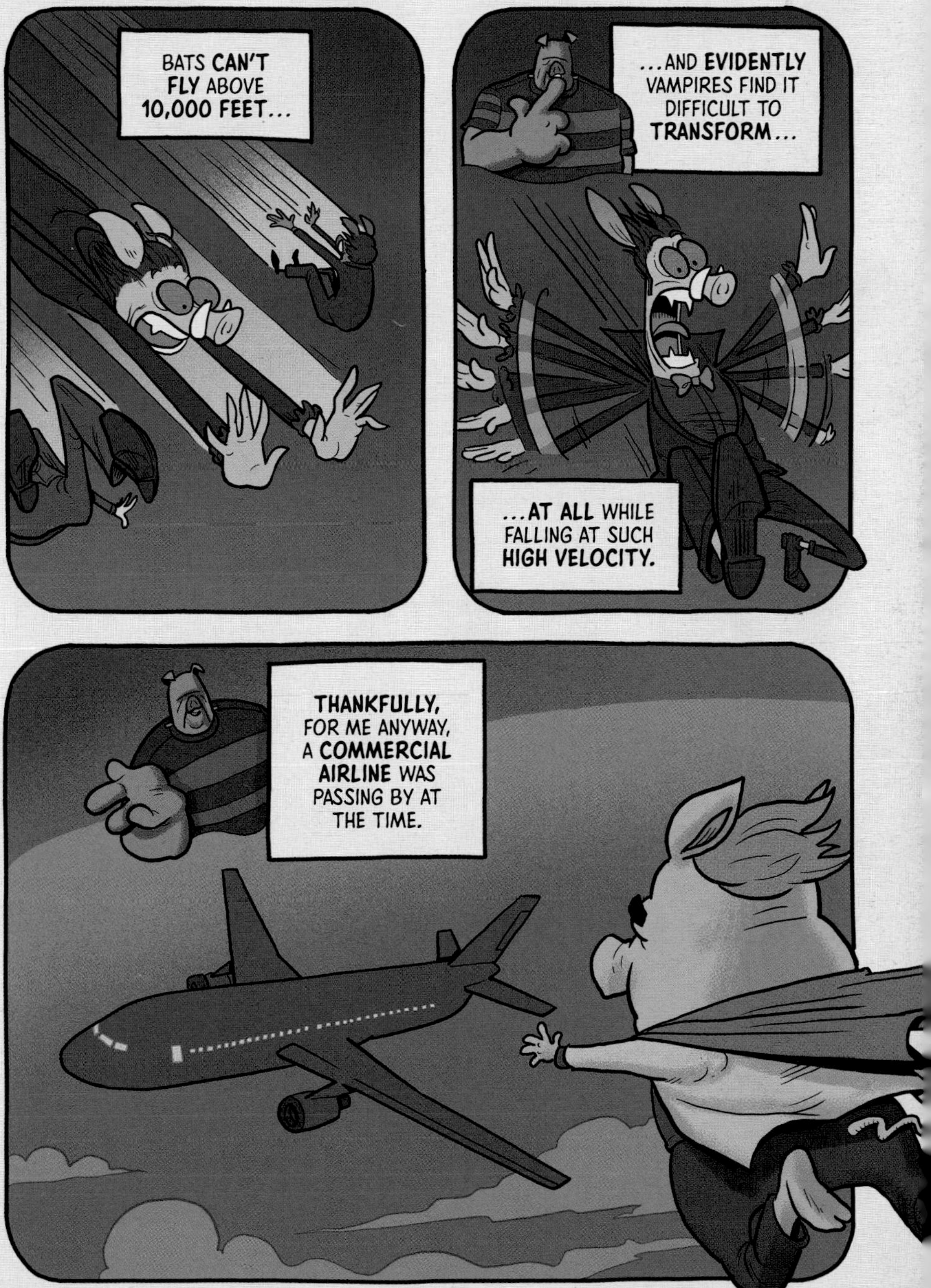

BATS CAN'T FLY ABOVE 10,000 FEET...
...AND EVIDENTLY VAMPIRES FIND IT DIFFICULT TO TRANSFORM...
...AT ALL WHILE FALLING AT SUCH HIGH VELOCITY.
THANKFULLY, FOR ME ANYWAY, A COMMERCIAL AIRLINE WAS PASSING BY AT THE TIME.

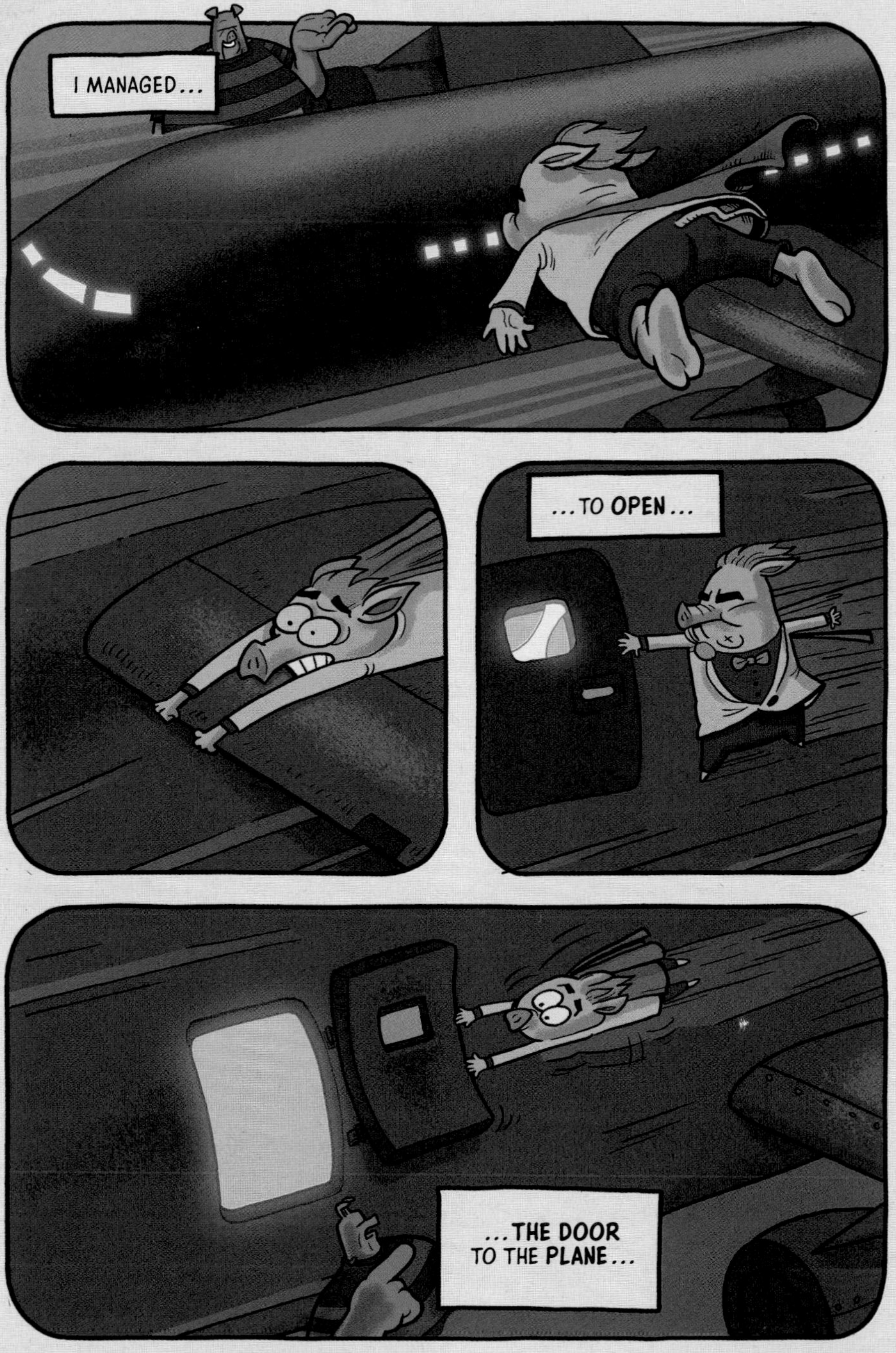
I MANAGED...
...TO OPEN...
...THE DOOR
TO THE PLANE...

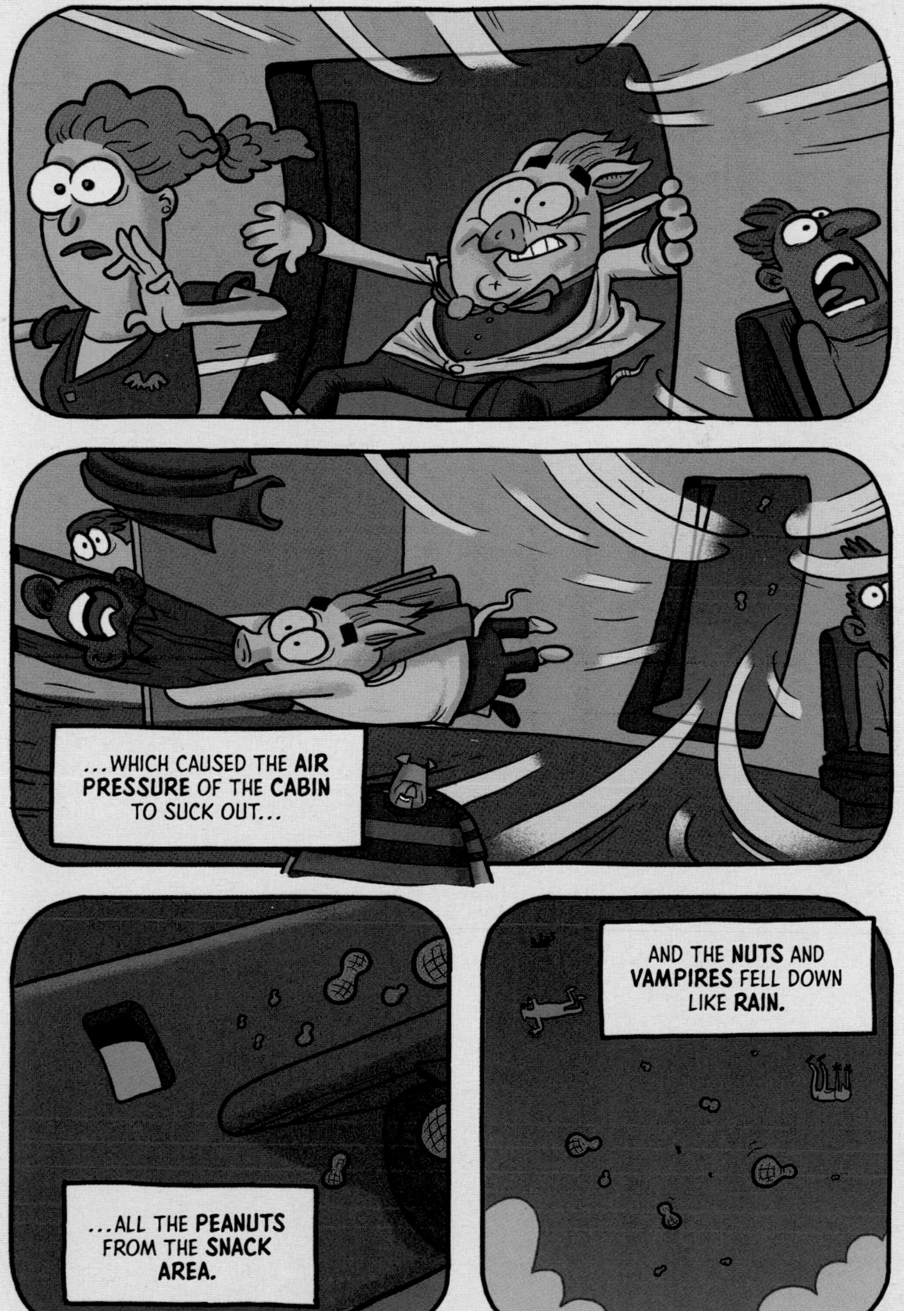
...WHICH CAUSED THE AIR PRESSURE OF THE CABIN TO SUCK OUT...
...ALL THE PEANUTS FROM THE SNACK AREA.
AND THE NUTS AND VAMPIRES FELL DOWN LIKE RAIN.

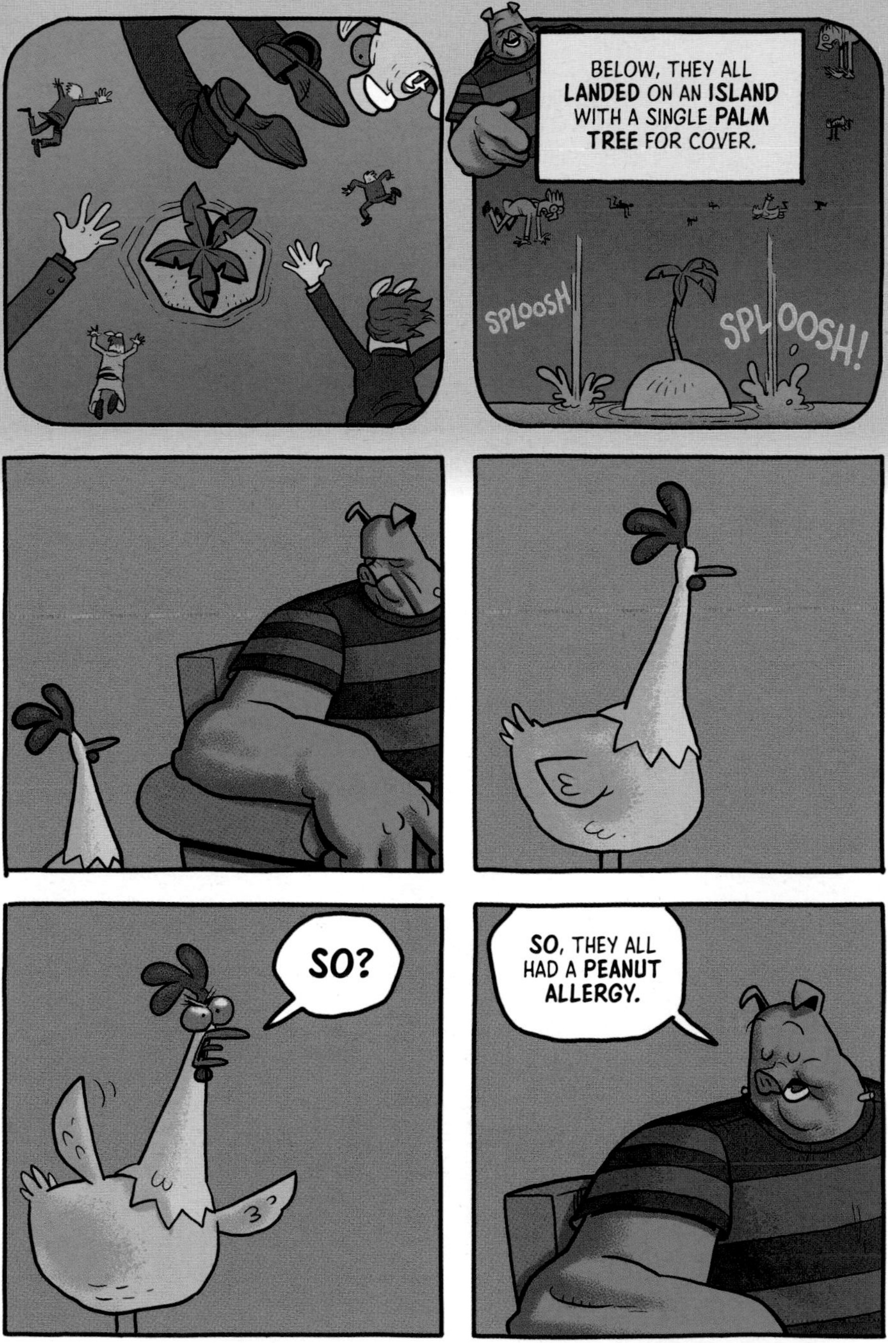
BELOW, THEY ALL LANDED ON AN ISLAND WITH A SINGLE PALM TREE FOR COVER.
SPLOOSH
SPLOOSH!
SO?
SO, THEY ALL HAD A PEANUT ALLERGY.

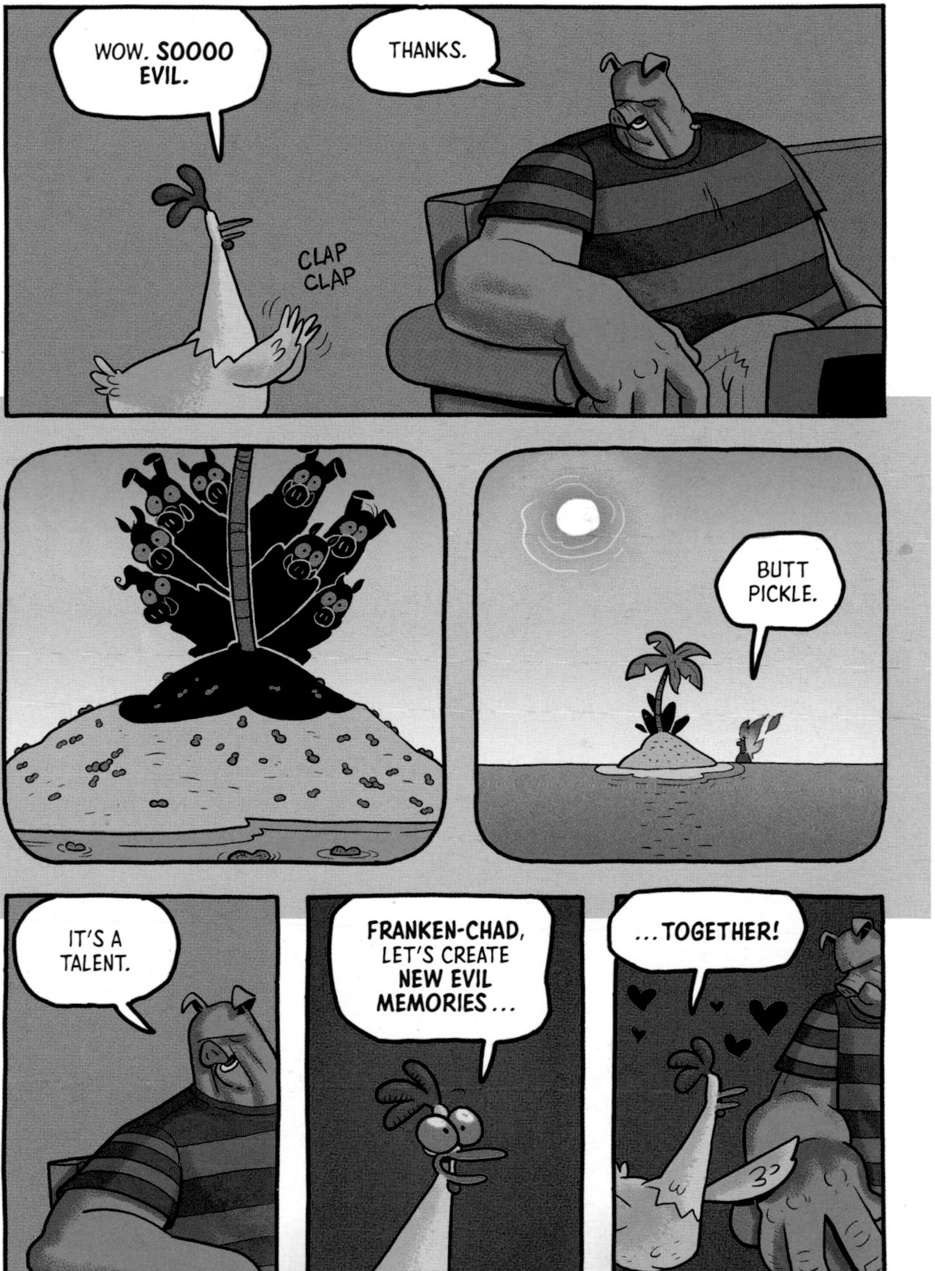
WOW. SOOOO EVIL.
THANKS.
CLAP CLAP
BUTT PICKLE.
IT'S A TALENT.
FRANKEN-CHAD, LET'S CREATE NEW EVIL MEMORIES...
...TOGETHER!

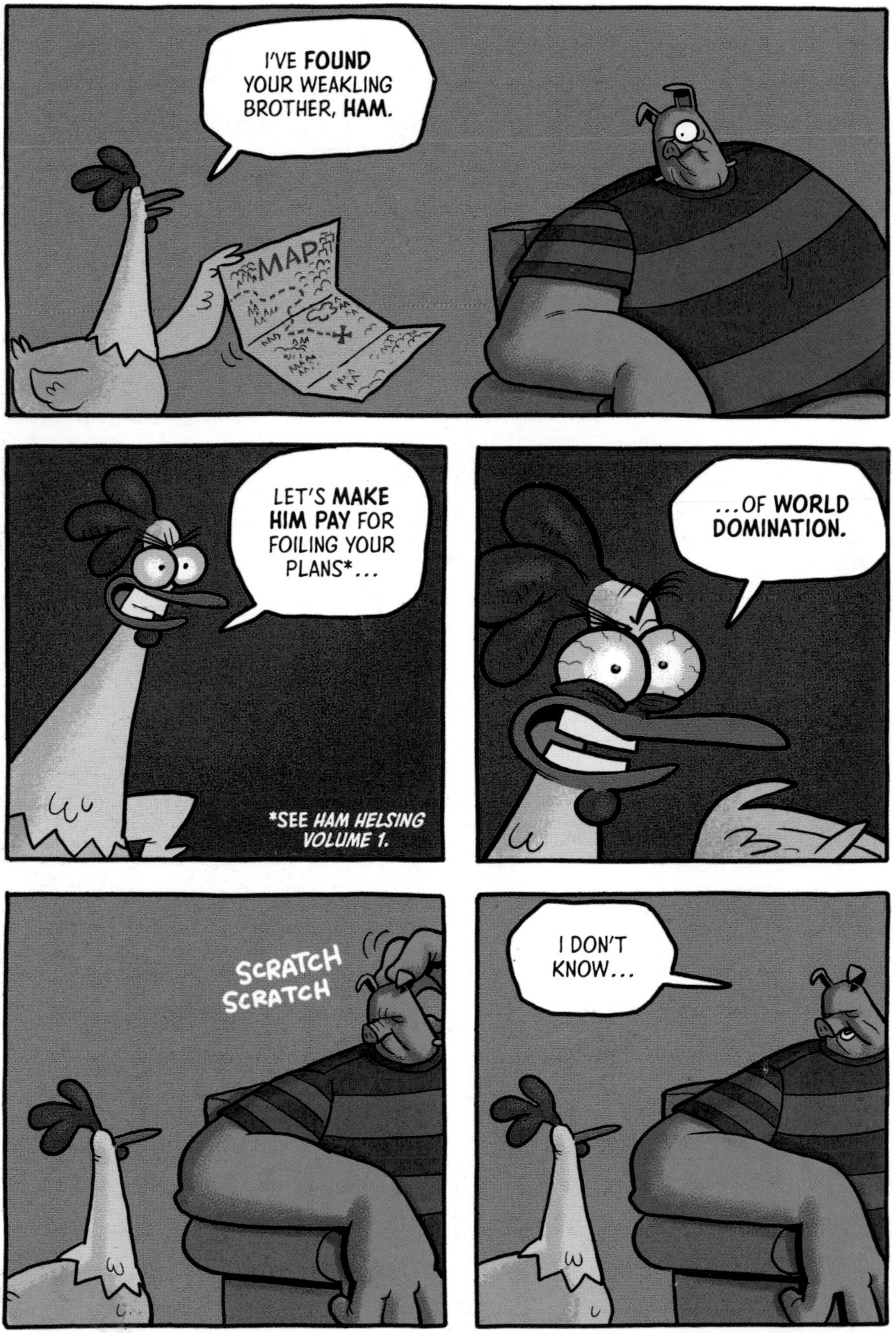
I'VE FOUND YOUR WEAKLING BROTHER, HAM.
MAP
LET'S MAKE HIM PAY FOR FOILING YOUR PLANS*...
*SEE HAM HELSING VOLUME 1.
...OF WORLD DOMINATION.
SCRATCH SCRATCH
I DON'T KNOW...

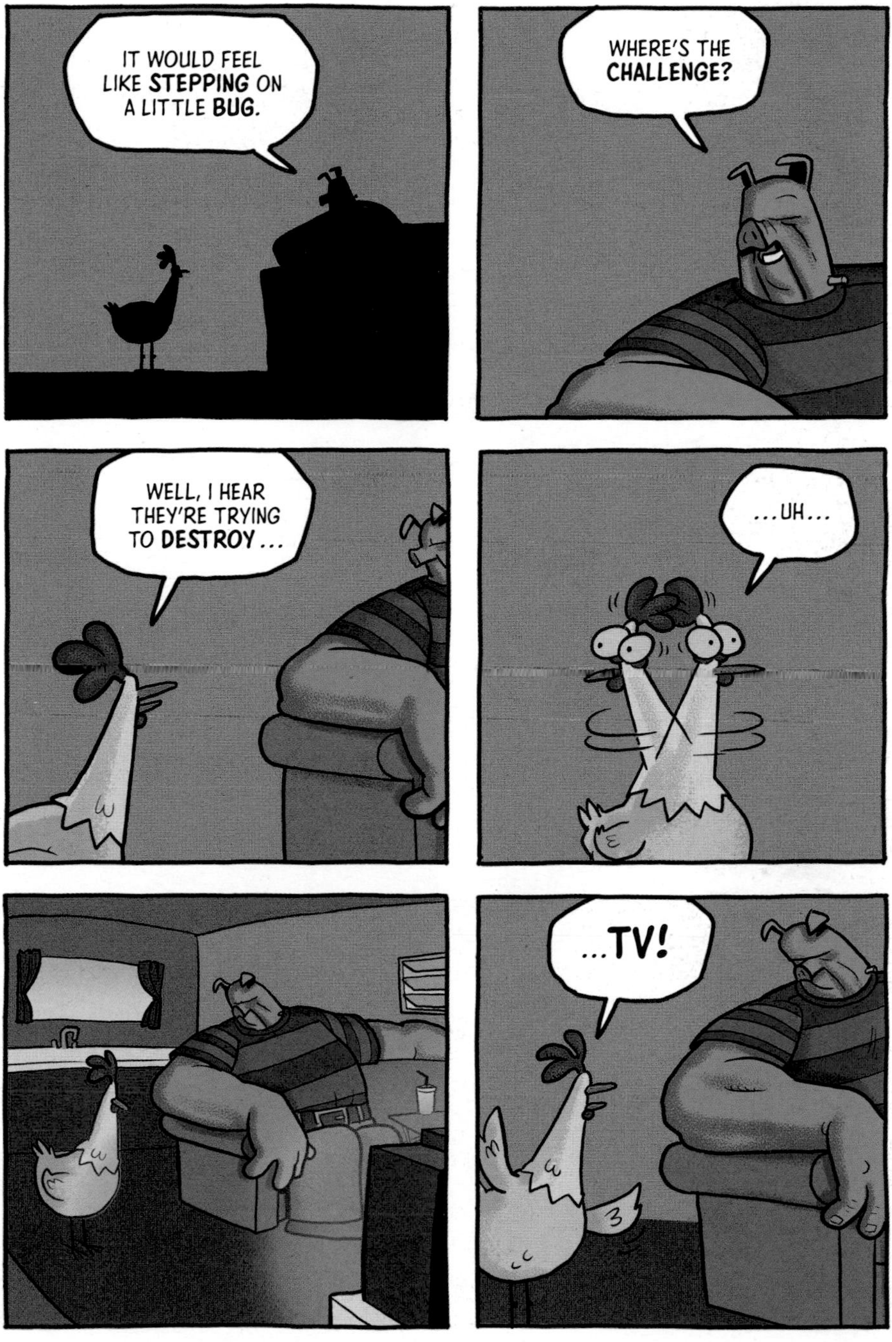
IT WOULD FEEL LIKE **STEPPING** ON A LITTLE **BUG.**
WHERE'S THE **CHALLENGE?**
WELL, I HEAR THEY'RE TRYING TO **DESTROY**...
...UH...
...**TV!**

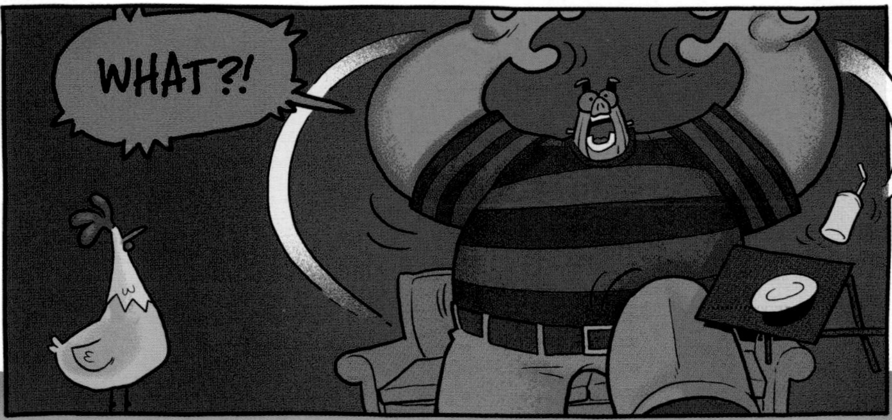
WHAT?!

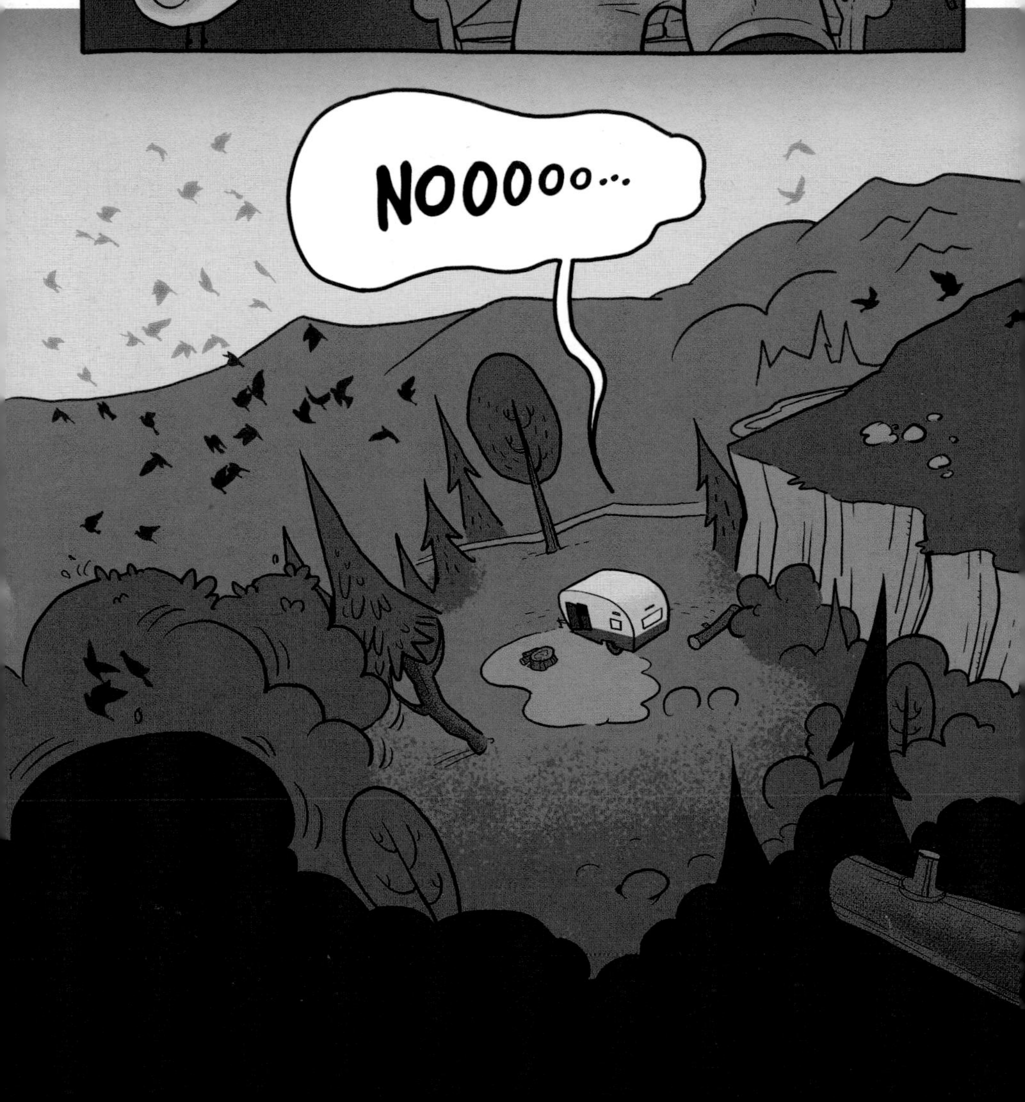
NOOOoo...

CHAPTER SIX

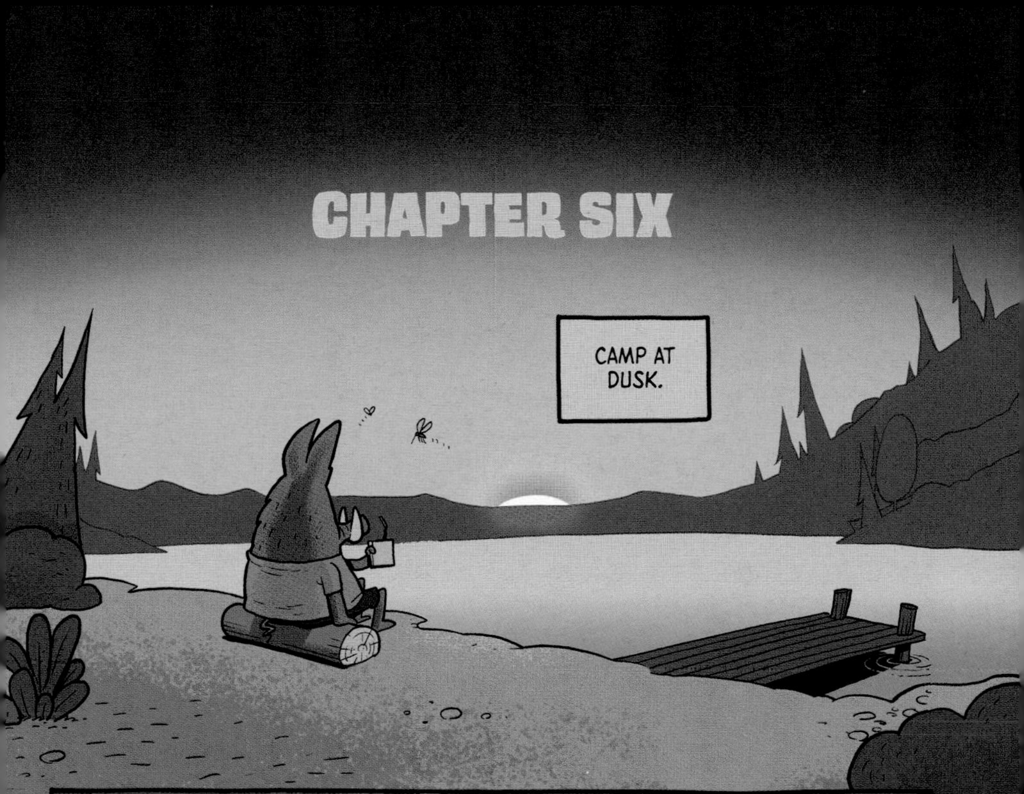
CAMP AT
DUSK.

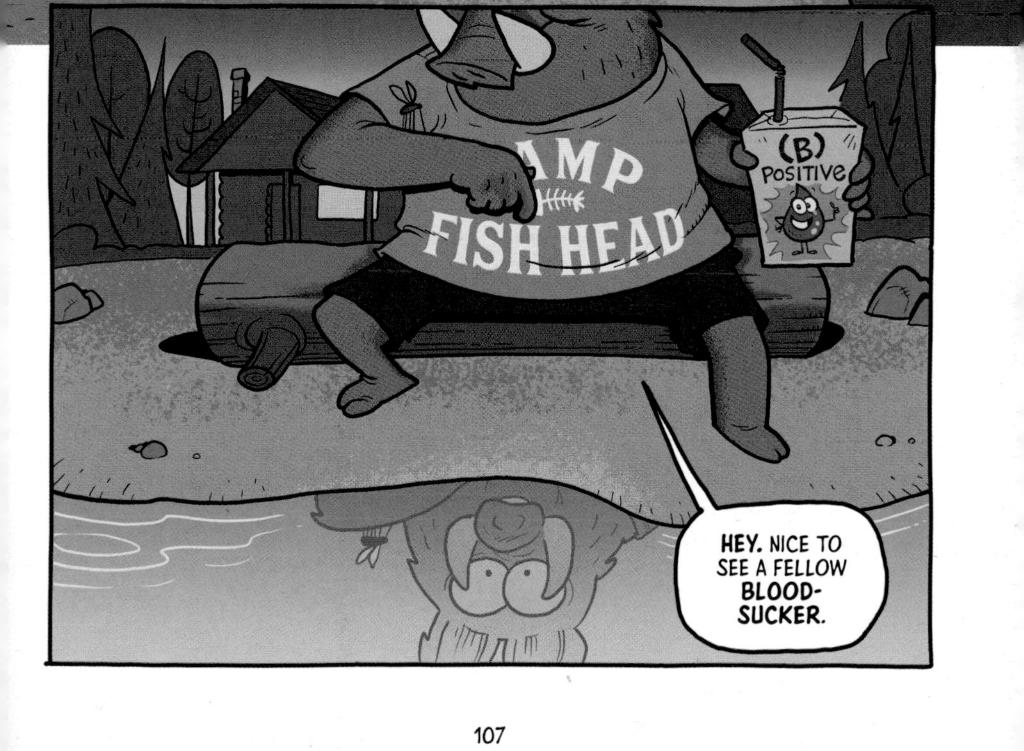
CAMP
FISH HEAD
(B)
Positive
HEY. NICE TO
SEE A FELLOW
BLOOD-
SUCKER.

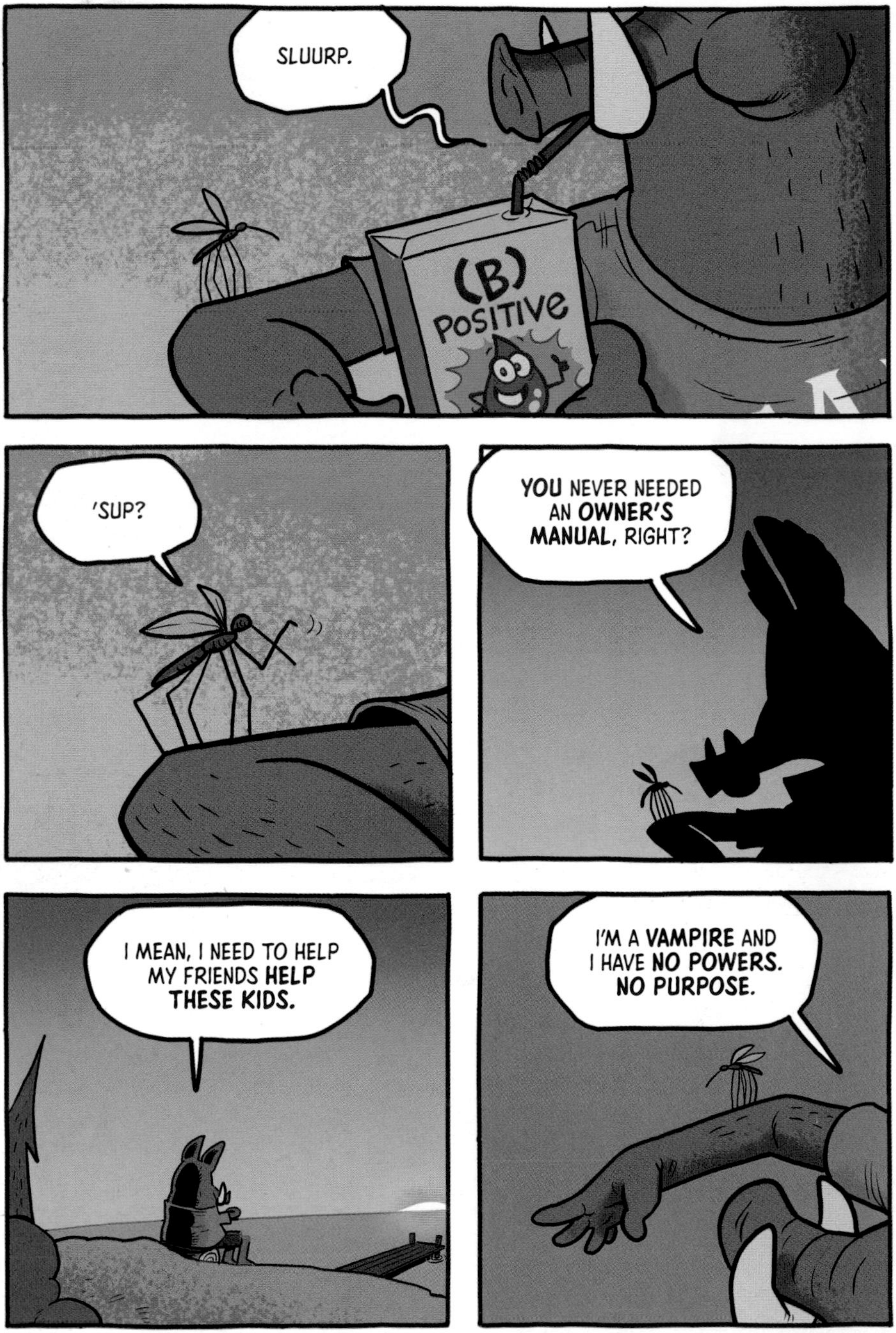
SLUURP.
(B) POSITIVE
'SUP?
YOU NEVER NEEDED AN OWNER'S MANUAL, RIGHT?
I MEAN, I NEED TO HELP MY FRIENDS HELP THESE KIDS.
I'M A VAMPIRE AND I HAVE NO POWERS. NO PURPOSE.

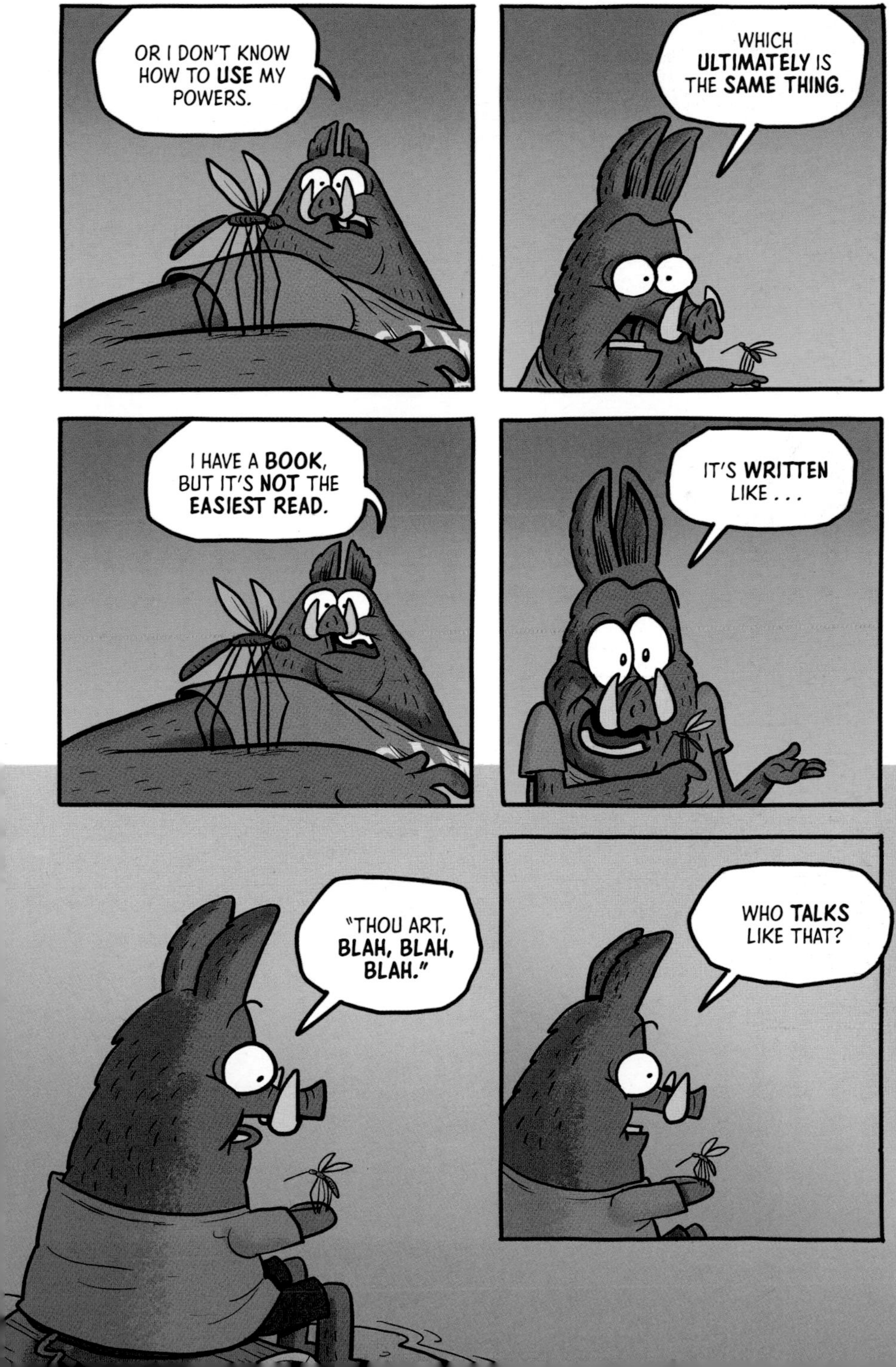
OR I DON'T KNOW HOW TO USE MY POWERS.
WHICH ULTIMATELY IS THE SAME THING.
I HAVE A BOOK, BUT IT'S NOT THE EASIEST READ.
IT'S WRITTEN LIKE . . .
"THOU ART, BLAH, BLAH, BLAH."
WHO TALKS LIKE THAT?

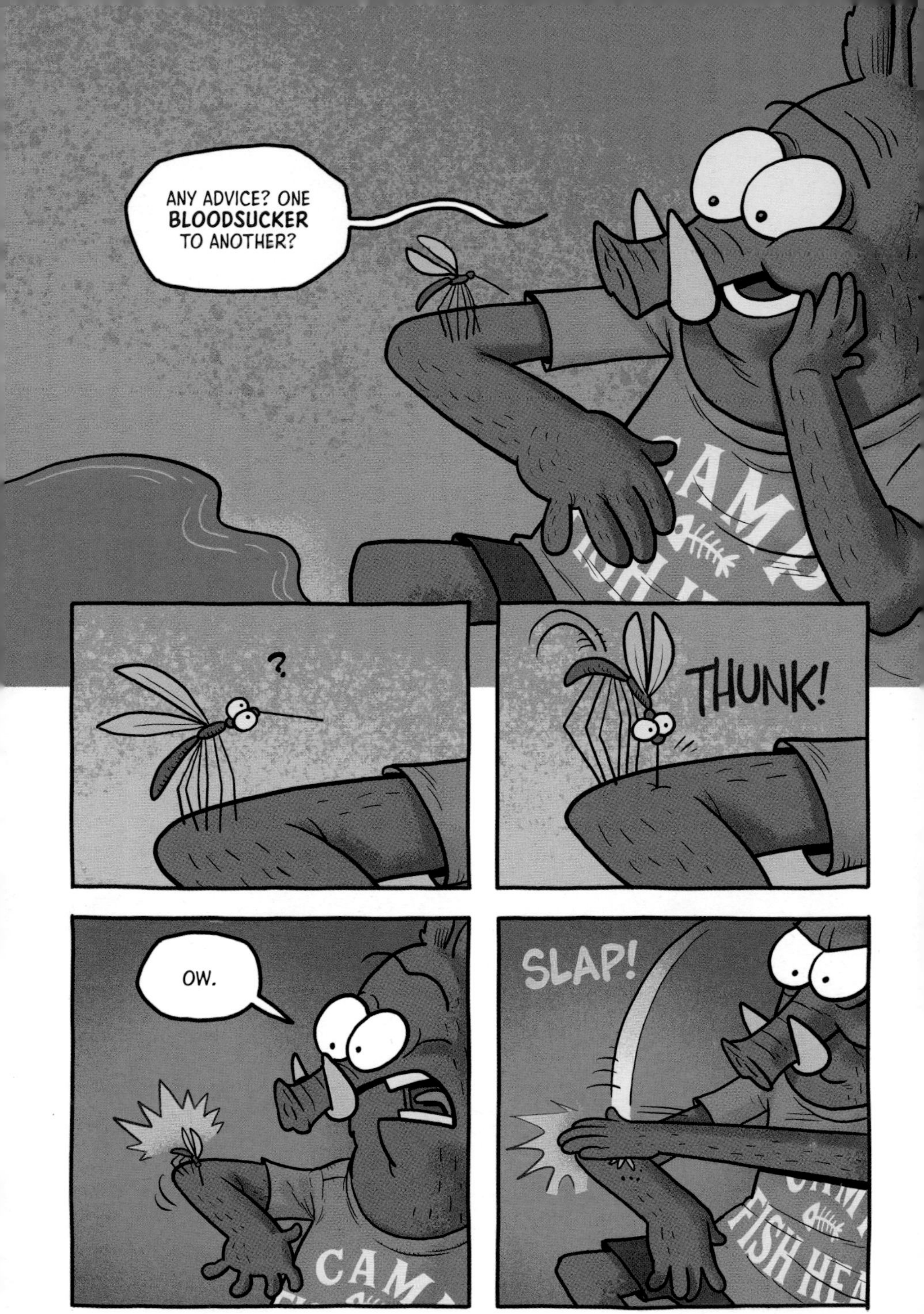
ANY ADVICE? ONE **BLOODSUCKER** TO ANOTHER?
?
THUNK!
OW.
SLAP!

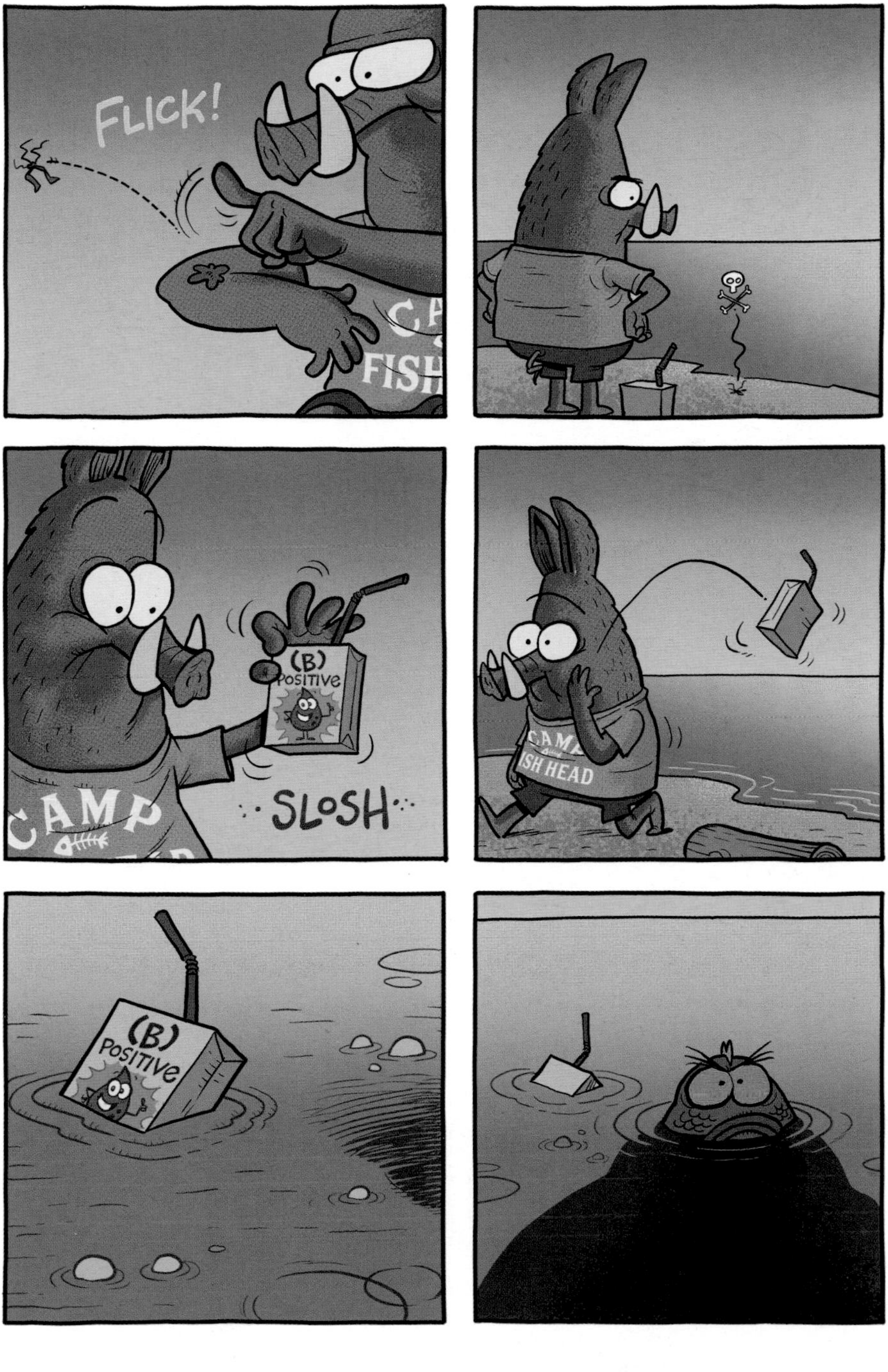
FLICK!
CAMP FISH
CAMP
SLOSH
(B) POSITIVE
CAMP FISH HEAD
(B) POSITIVE

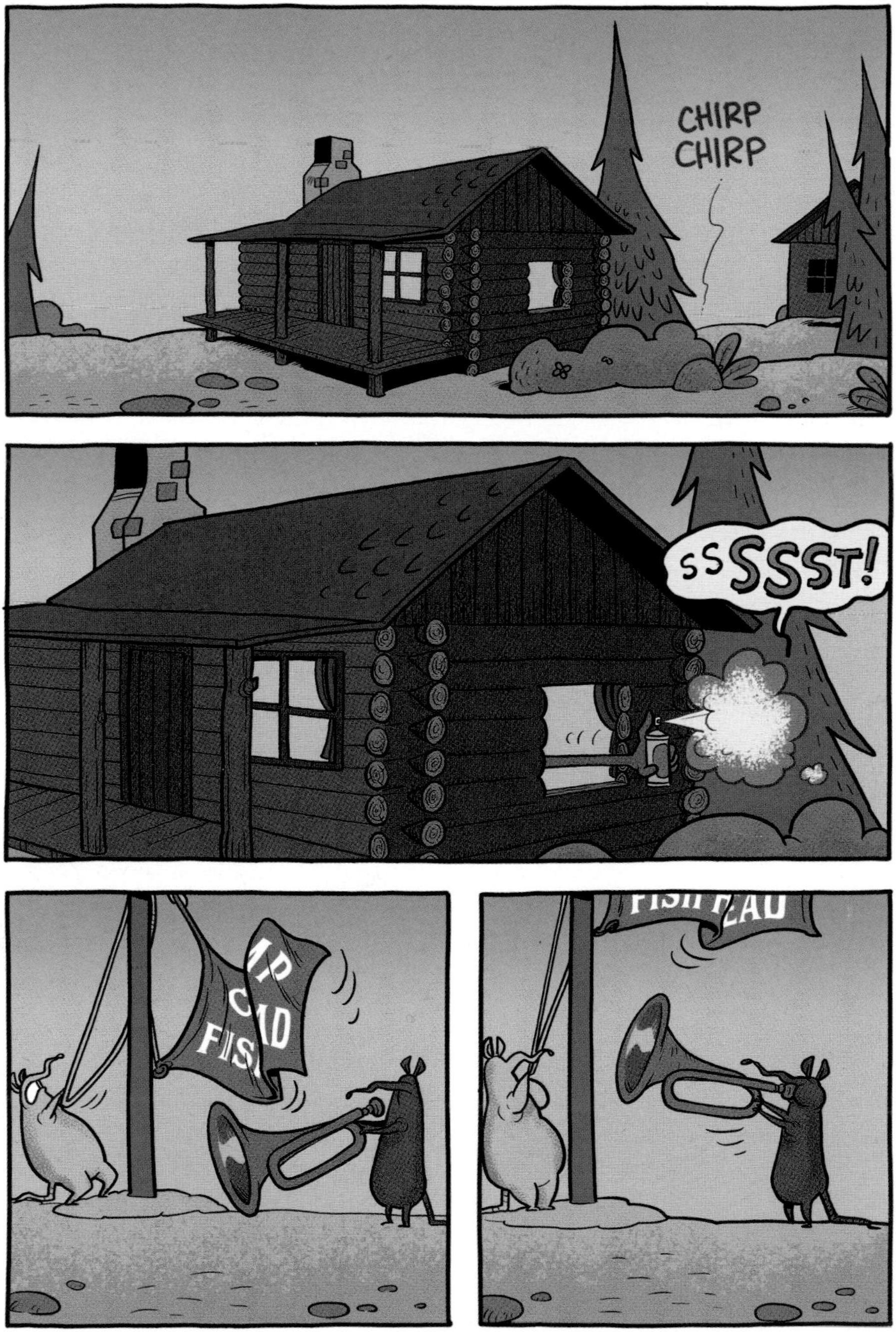
CHIRP
CHIRP
ssSSST!

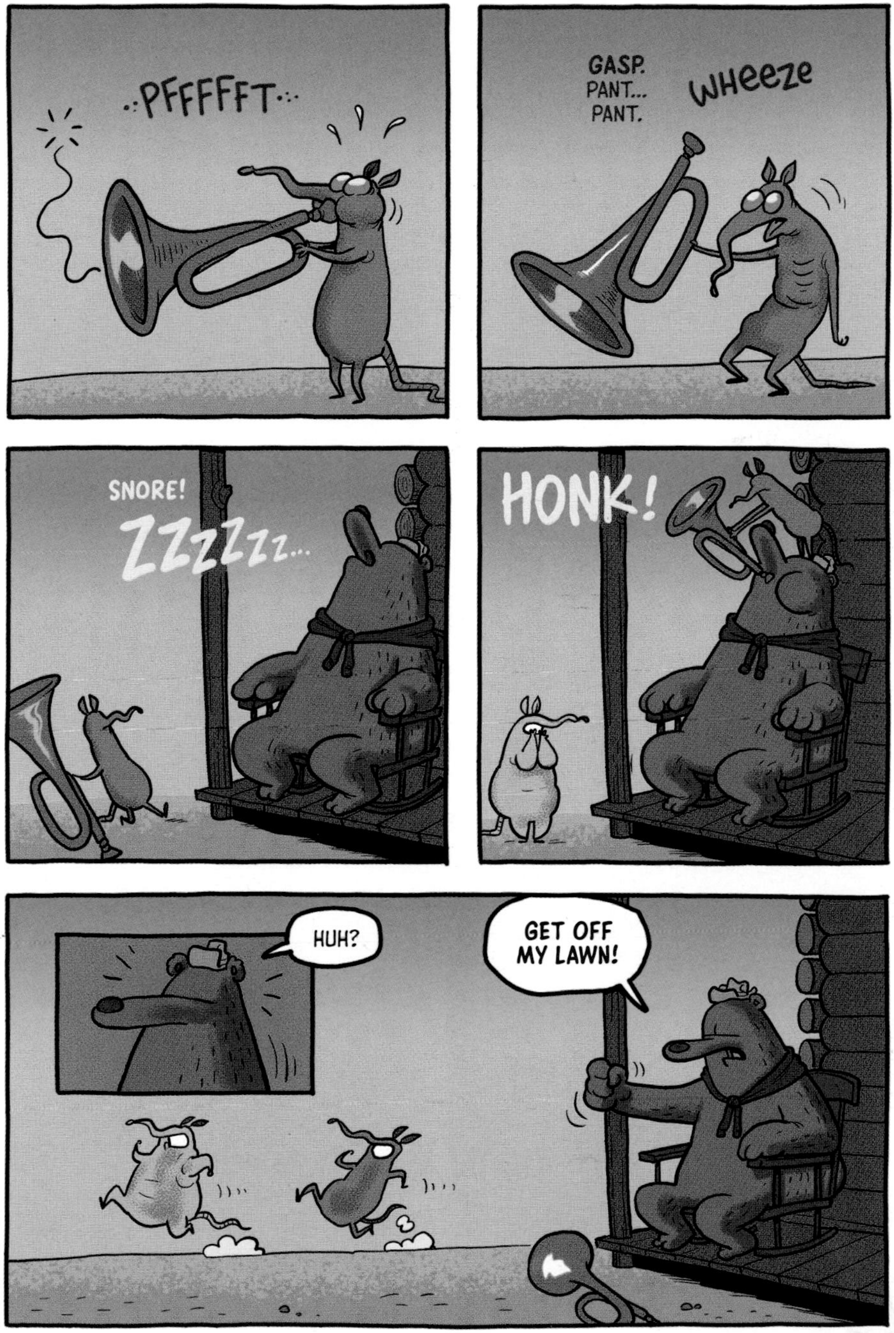
PFFFFFT
GASP.
PANT...
PANT.
WHEEZE
SNORE!
ZZZZZZ...
HONK!
HUH?
GET OFF
MY LAWN!

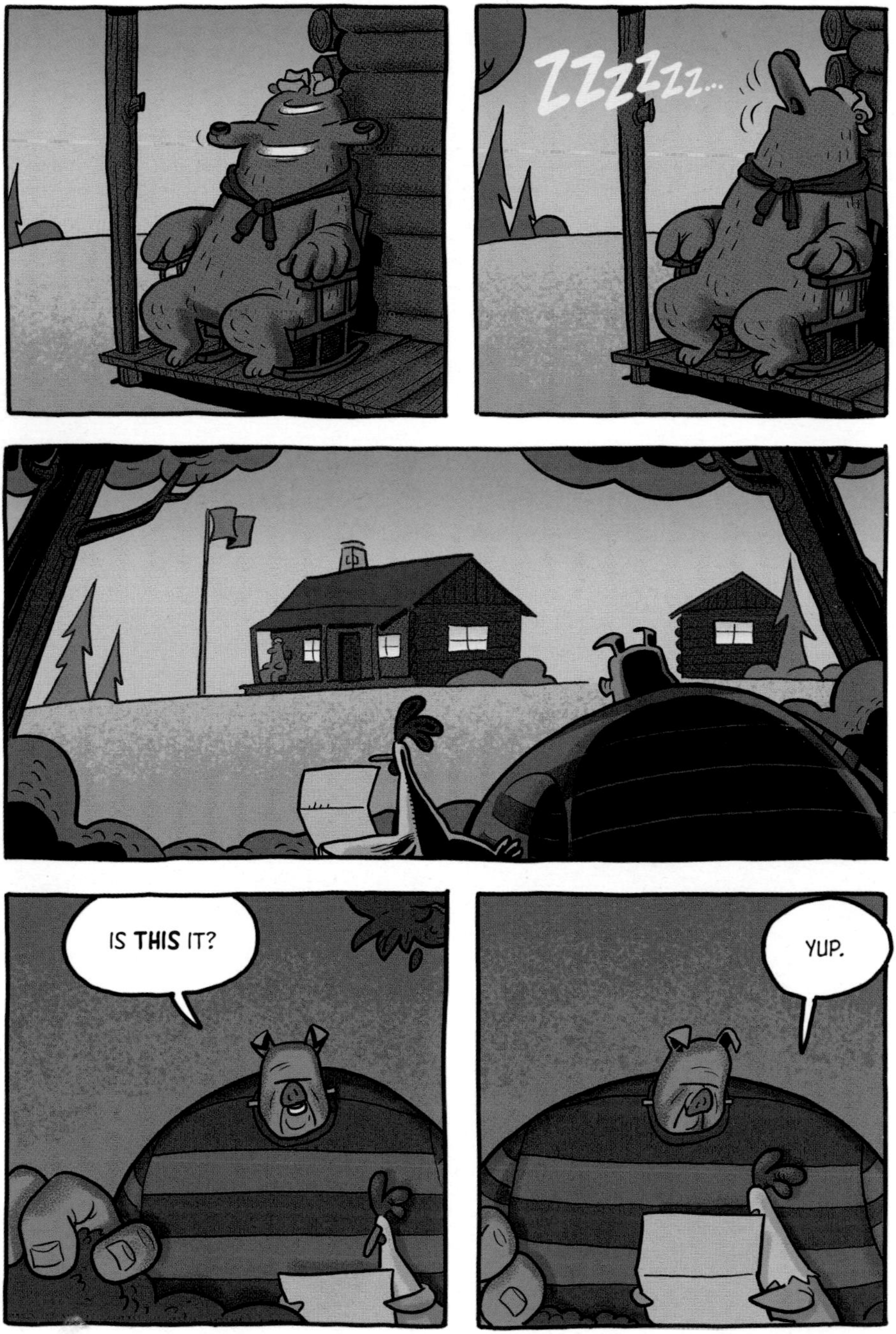
ZZZzzz...
IS THIS IT?
YUP.

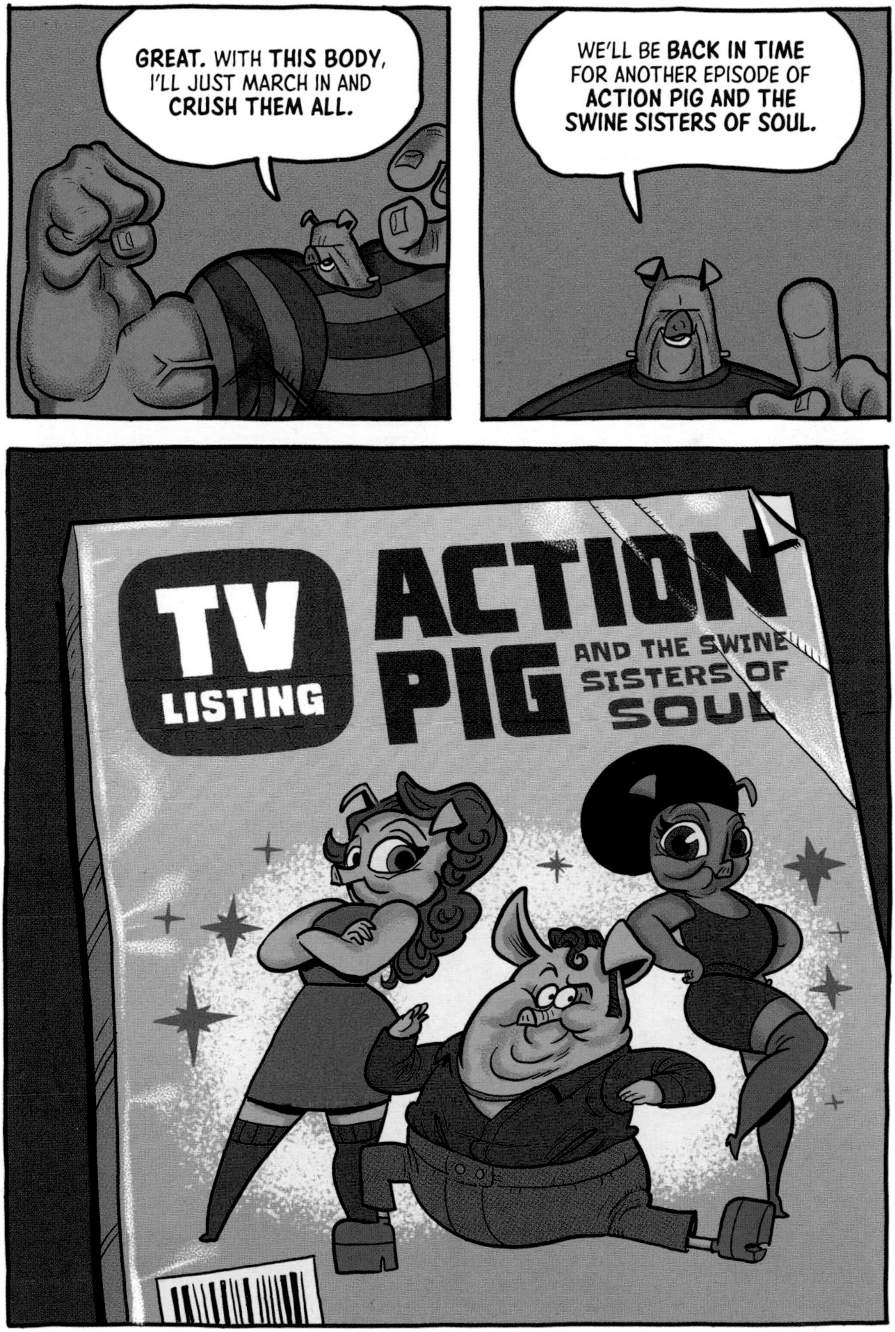
GREAT. WITH THIS BODY, I'LL JUST MARCH IN AND CRUSH THEM ALL.
WE'LL BE BACK IN TIME FOR ANOTHER EPISODE OF ACTION PIG AND THE SWINE SISTERS OF SOUL.
TV LISTING
ACTION PIG AND THE SWINE SISTERS OF SOUL

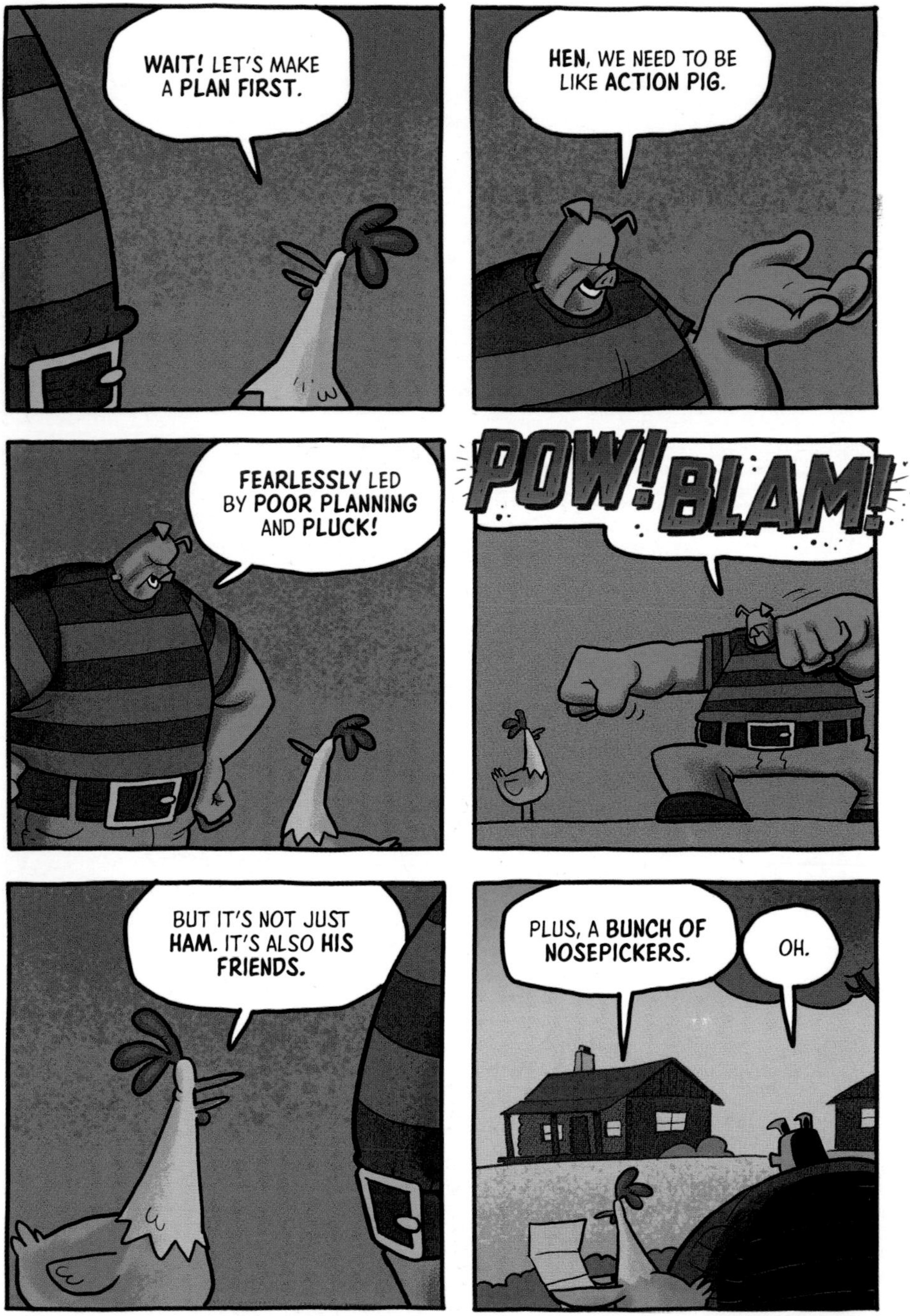
WAIT! LET'S MAKE A PLAN FIRST.
HEN, WE NEED TO BE LIKE ACTION PIG.
FEARLESSLY LED BY POOR PLANNING AND PLUCK!
POW! BLAM!
BUT IT'S NOT JUST HAM. IT'S ALSO HIS FRIENDS.
PLUS, A BUNCH OF NOSEPICKERS.
OH.

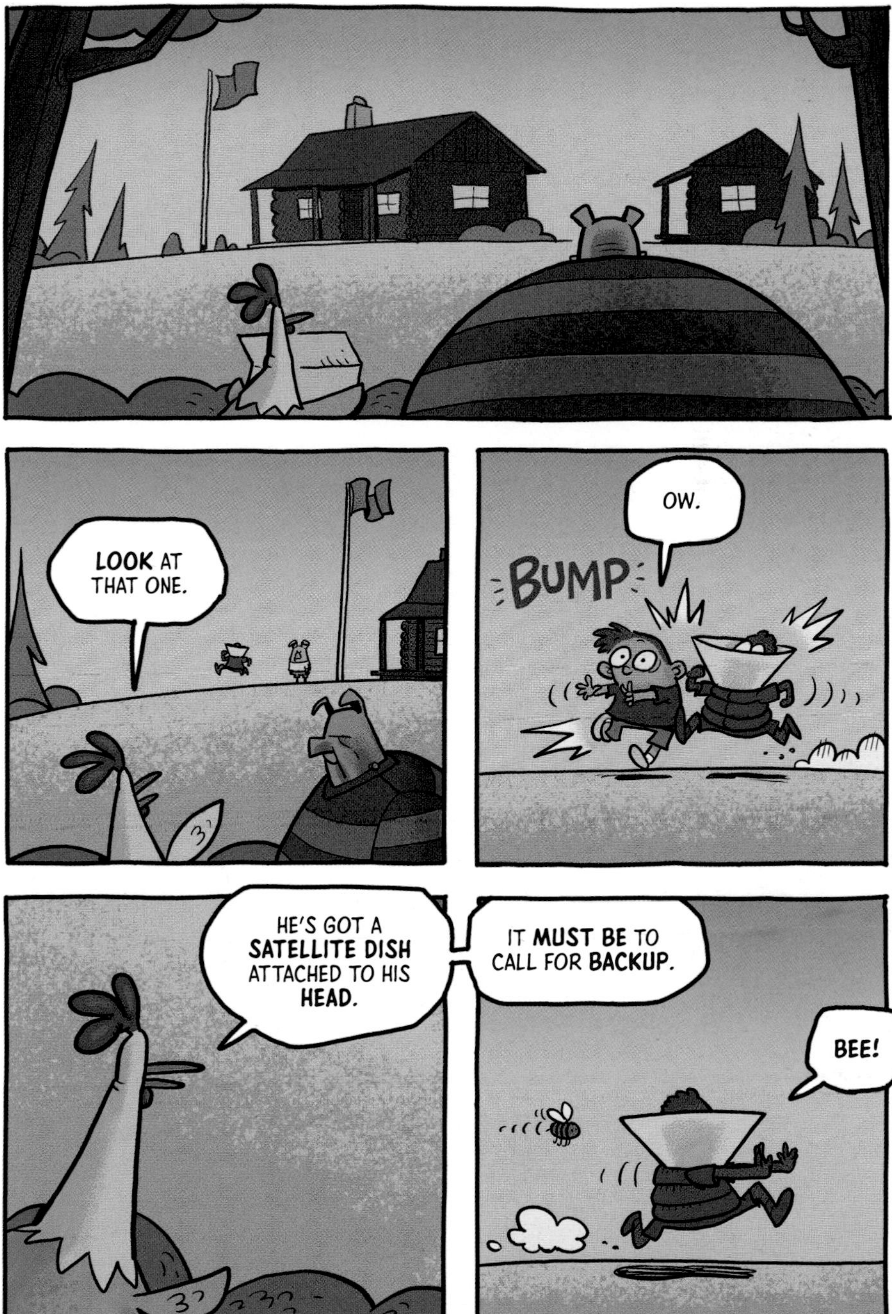
LOOK AT THAT ONE.
BUMP
OW.
HE'S GOT A SATELLITE DISH ATTACHED TO HIS HEAD.
IT MUST BE TO CALL FOR BACKUP.
BEE!

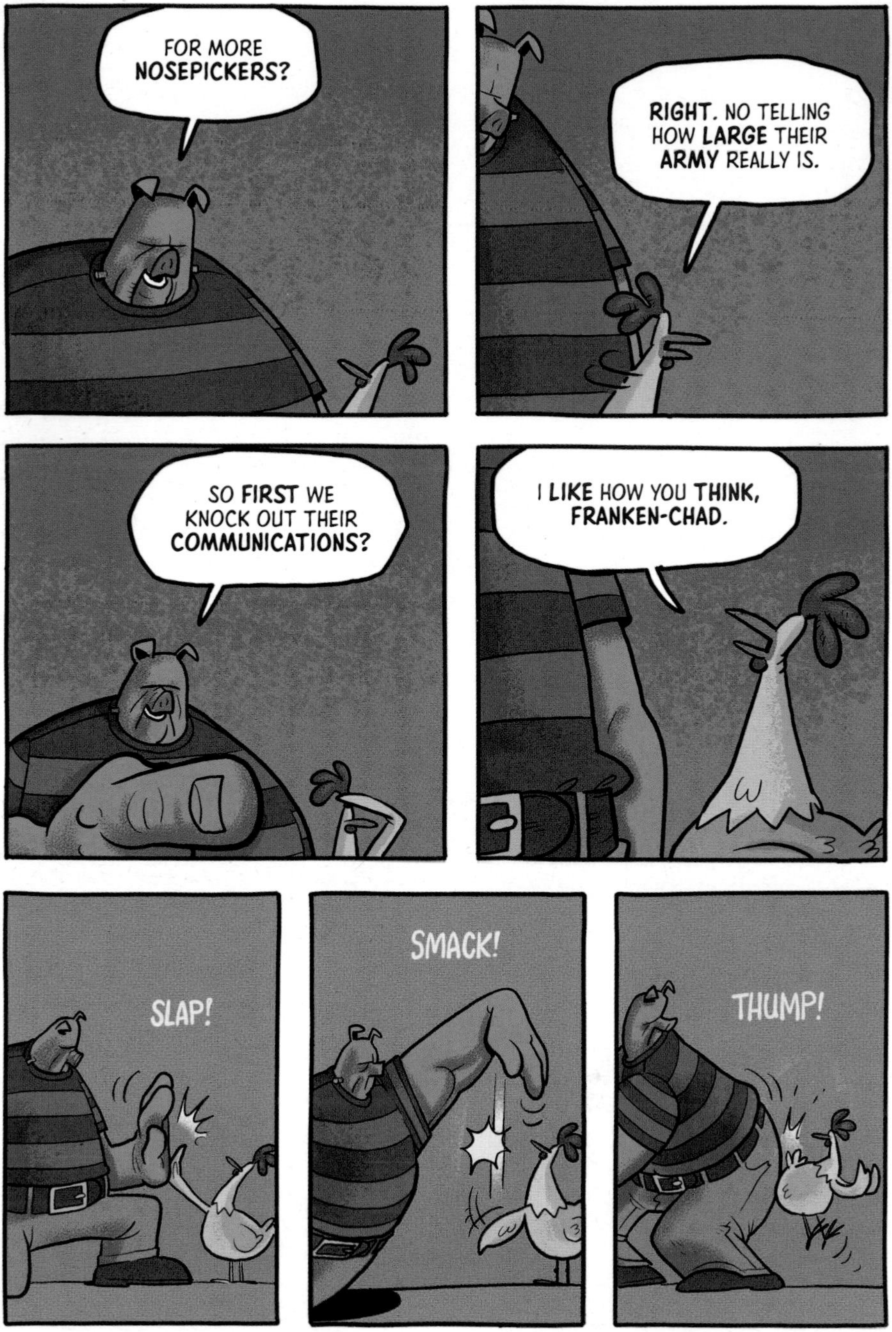
FOR MORE NOSEPICKERS?
RIGHT. NO TELLING HOW LARGE THEIR ARMY REALLY IS.
SO FIRST WE KNOCK OUT THEIR COMMUNICATIONS?
I LIKE HOW YOU THINK, FRANKEN-CHAD.
SLAP!
SMACK!
THUMP!

CHAPTER SEVEN

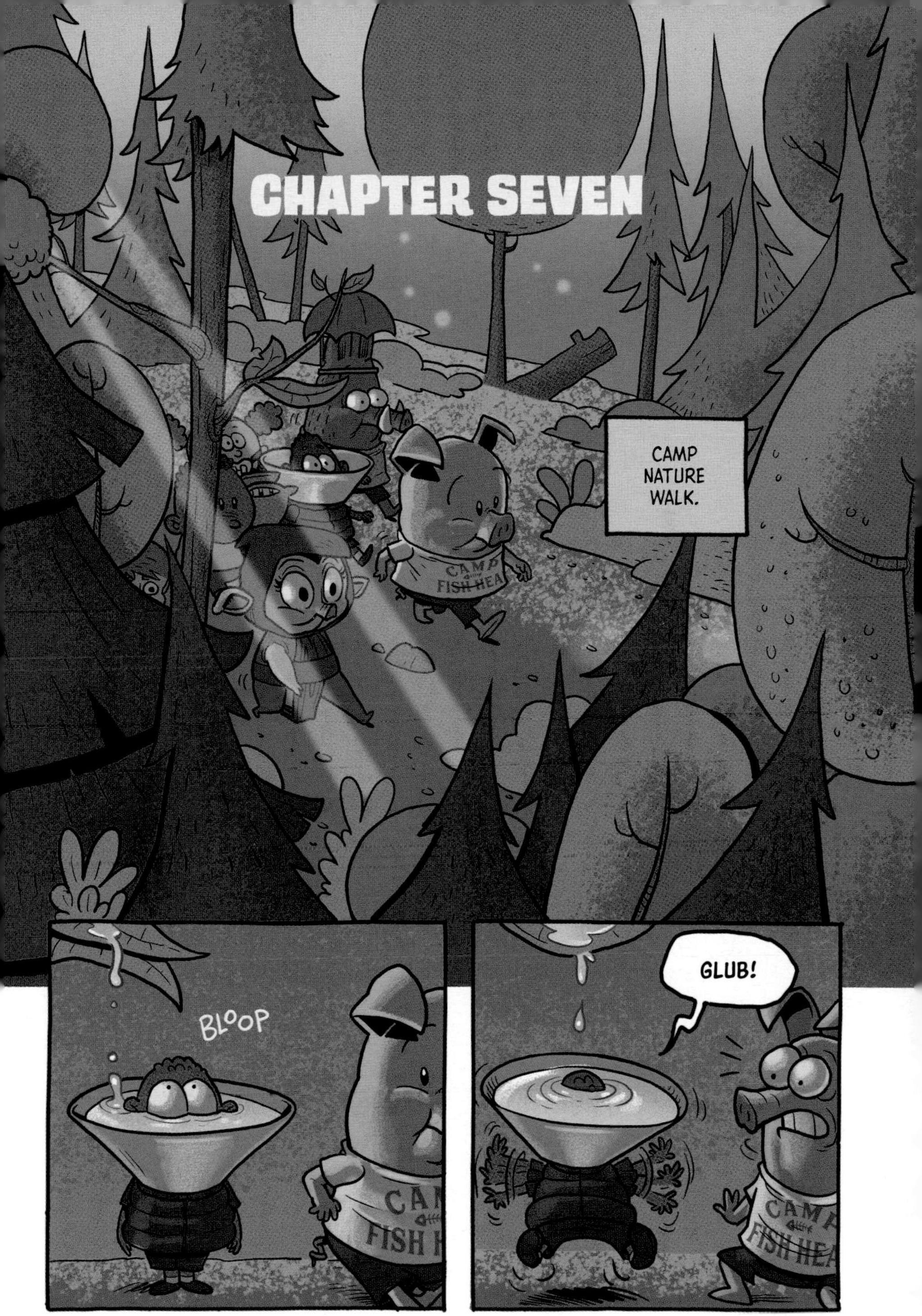
CAMP NATURE WALK.
CAMP FISH HEA
BLOOP
CAMP FISH HEA
GLUB!
CAMP FISH HEA

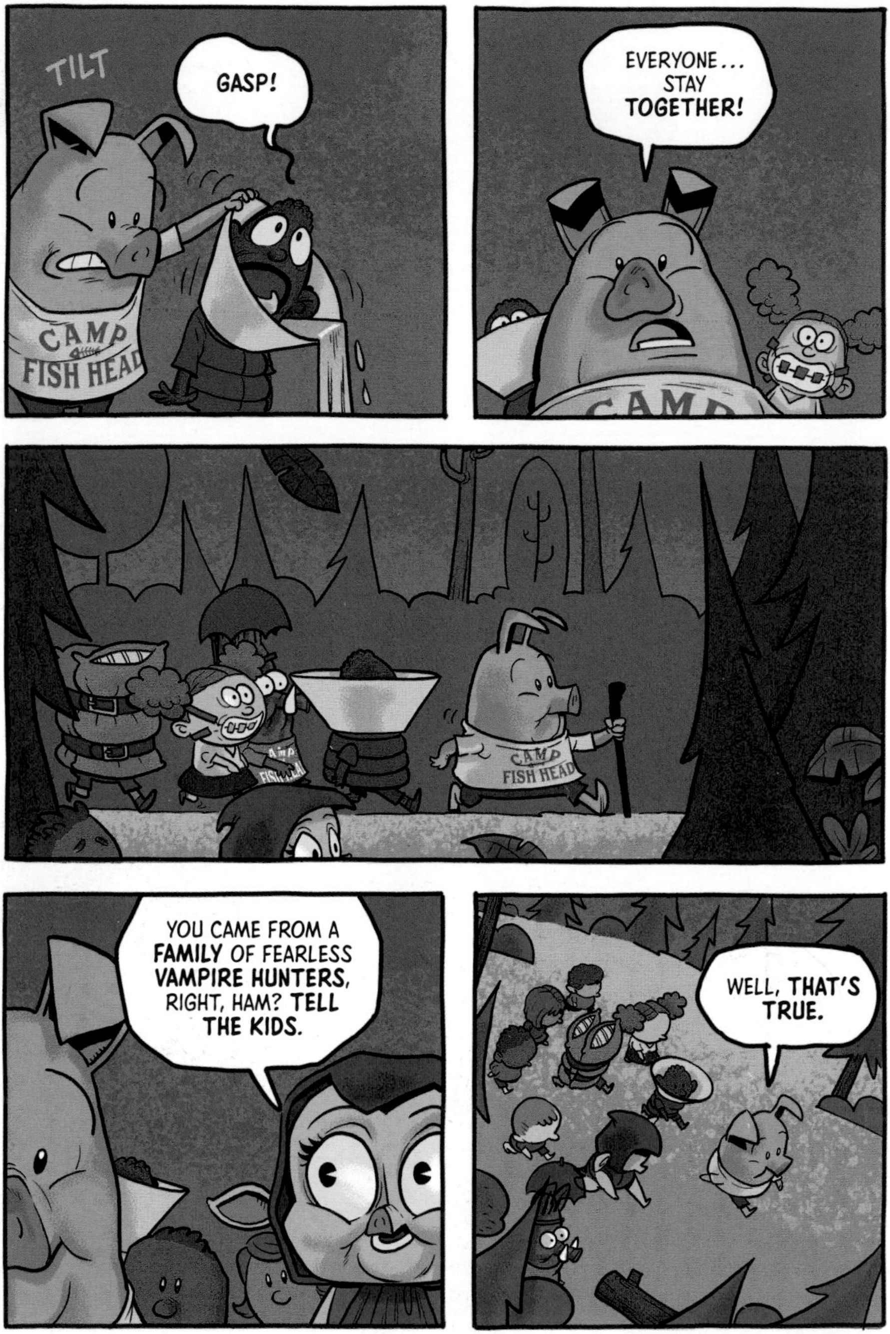
TILT
GASP!
CAMP FISH HEAD
EVERYONE... STAY TOGETHER!
CAMP FISH HEAD
YOU CAME FROM A FAMILY OF FEARLESS VAMPIRE HUNTERS, RIGHT, HAM? TELL THE KIDS.
WELL, THAT'S TRUE.

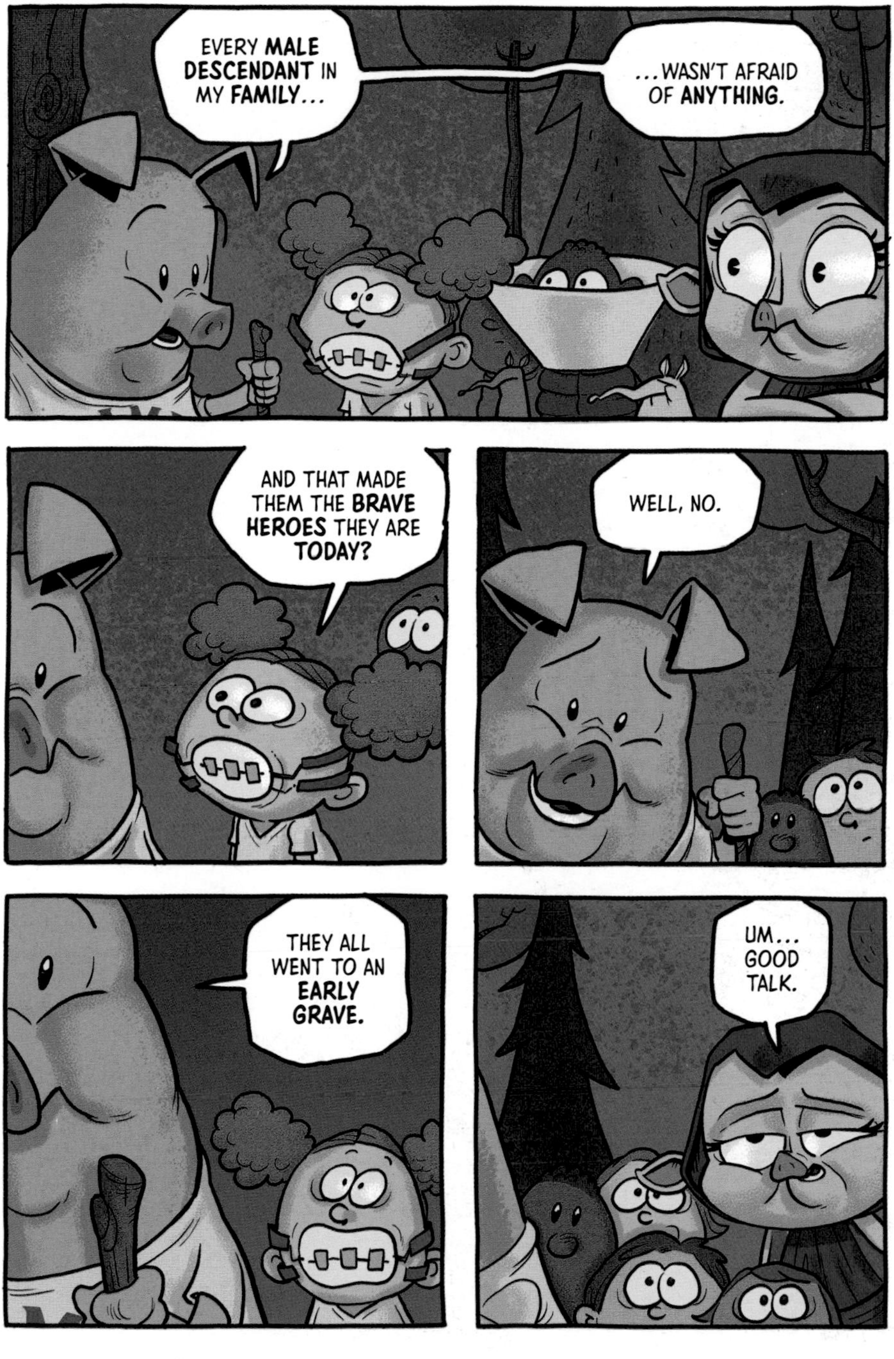
EVERY MALE DESCENDANT IN MY FAMILY...
...WASN'T AFRAID OF ANYTHING.
AND THAT MADE THEM THE BRAVE HEROES THEY ARE TODAY?
WELL, NO.
THEY ALL WENT TO AN EARLY GRAVE.
UM... GOOD TALK.

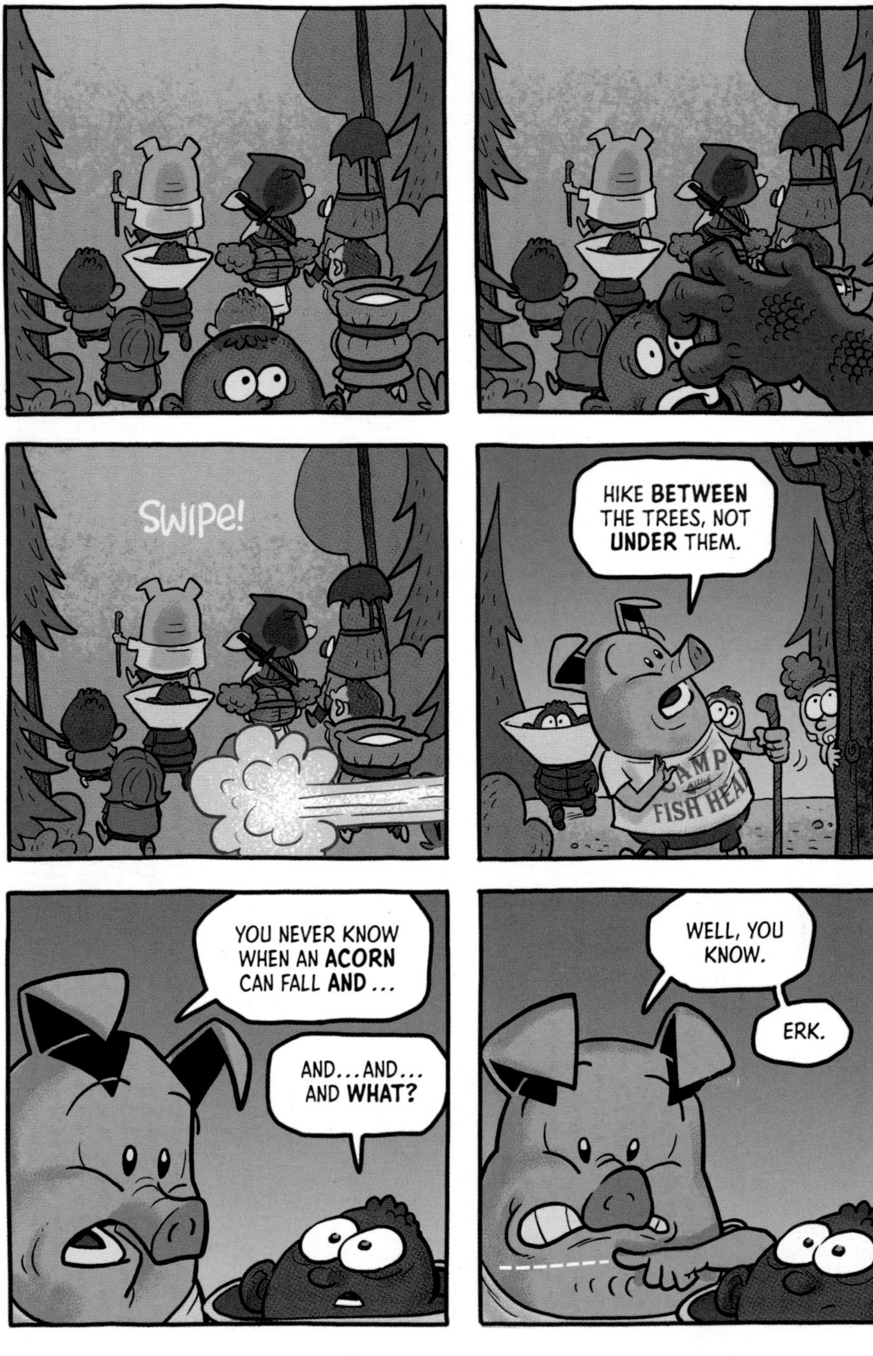
SWIPE!
HIKE BETWEEN THE TREES, NOT UNDER THEM.
CAMP FISH HEAD
YOU NEVER KNOW WHEN AN ACORN CAN FALL AND ...
AND...AND... AND WHAT?
WELL, YOU KNOW.
ERK.

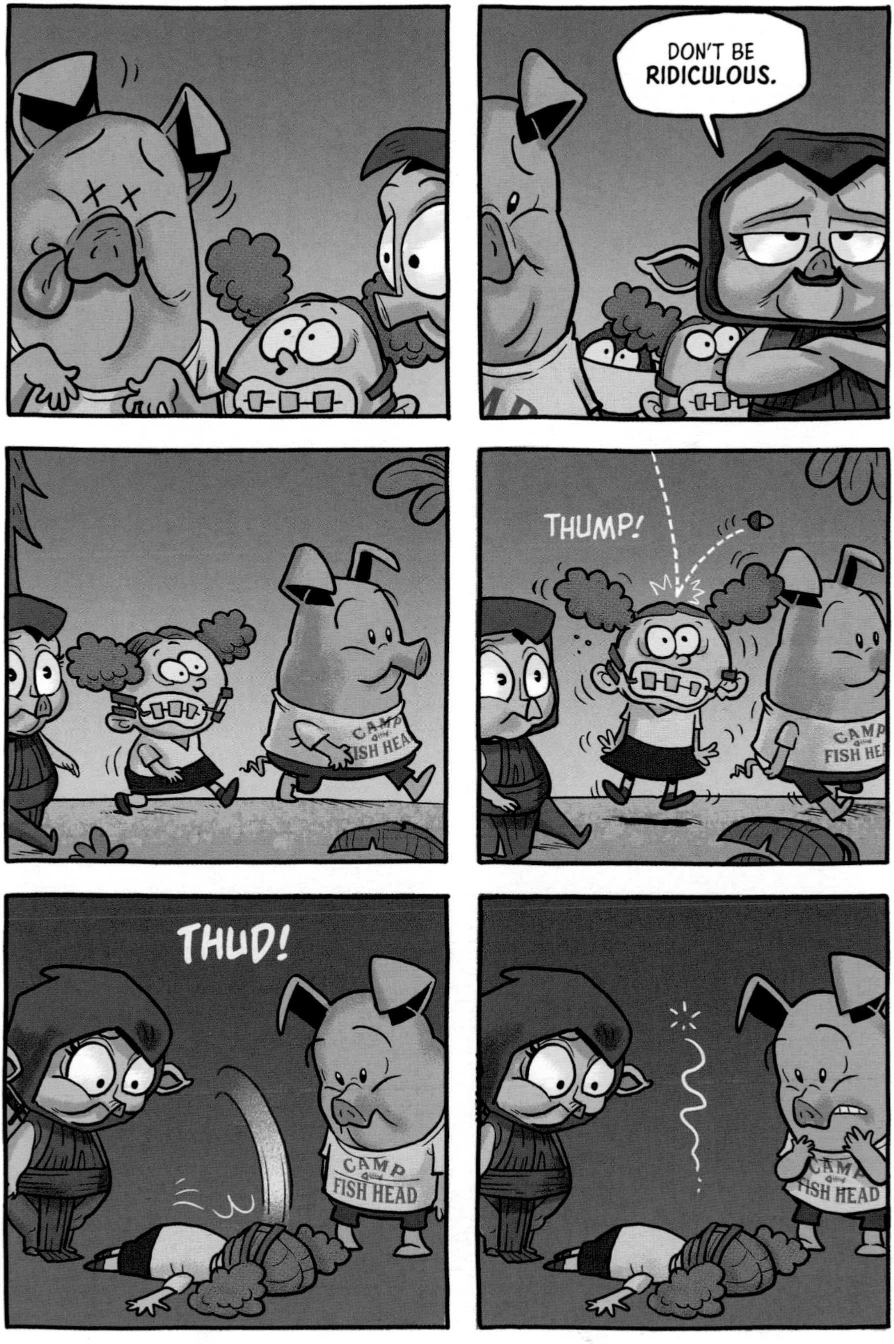
DON'T BE RIDICULOUS.
CAMP FISH HEAD
THUMP!
CAMP FISH HEAD
THUD!
CAMP FISH HEAD
CAMP FISH HEAD

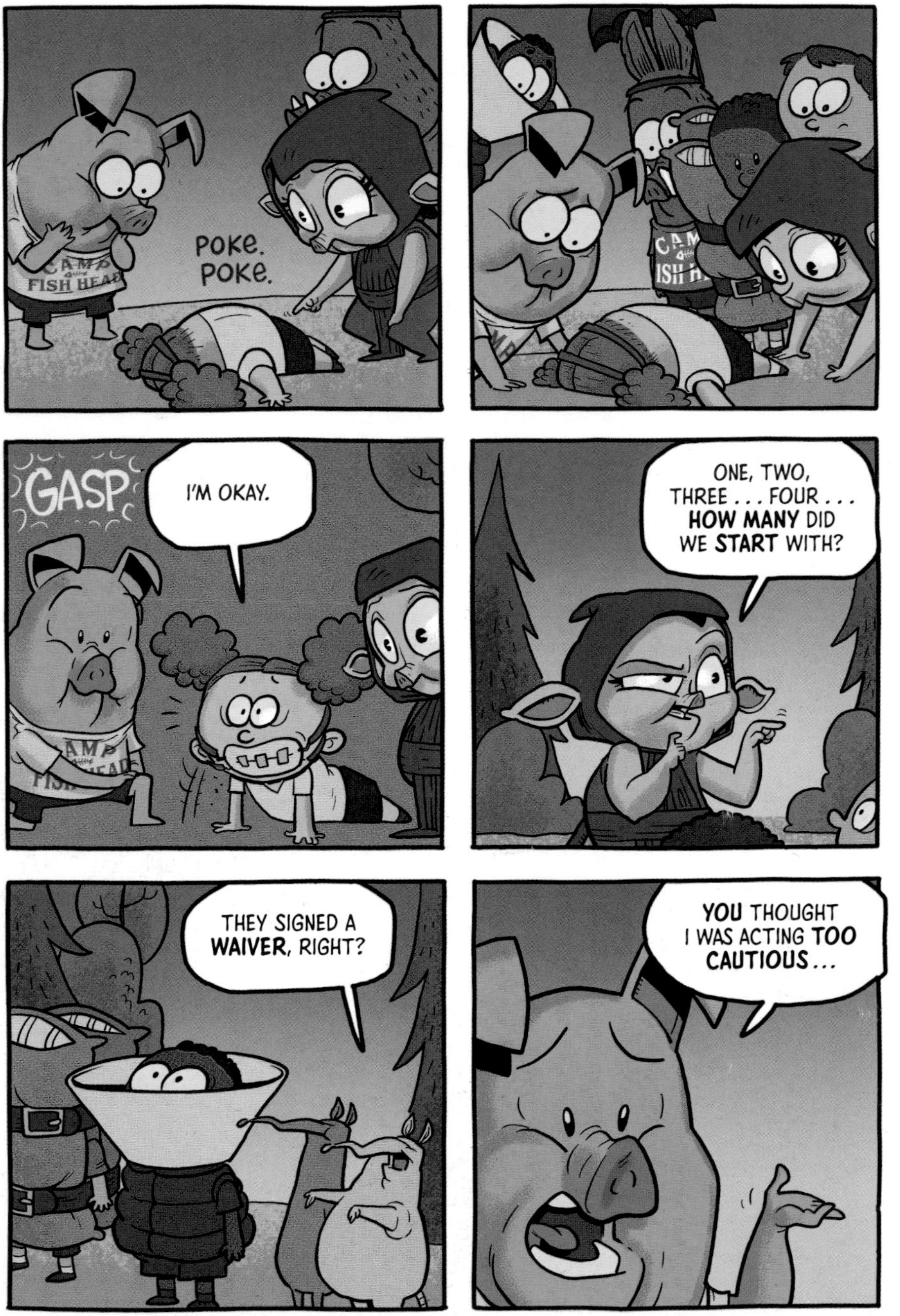
CAMP FISH HEAD
POKE. POKE.
CAMP FISH HEAD
GASP
I'M OKAY.
CAMP FISH HEAD
ONE, TWO, THREE . . . FOUR . . . **HOW MANY** DID WE **START** WITH?
THEY SIGNED A **WAIVER**, RIGHT?
YOU THOUGHT I WAS ACTING **TOO CAUTIOUS** . . .

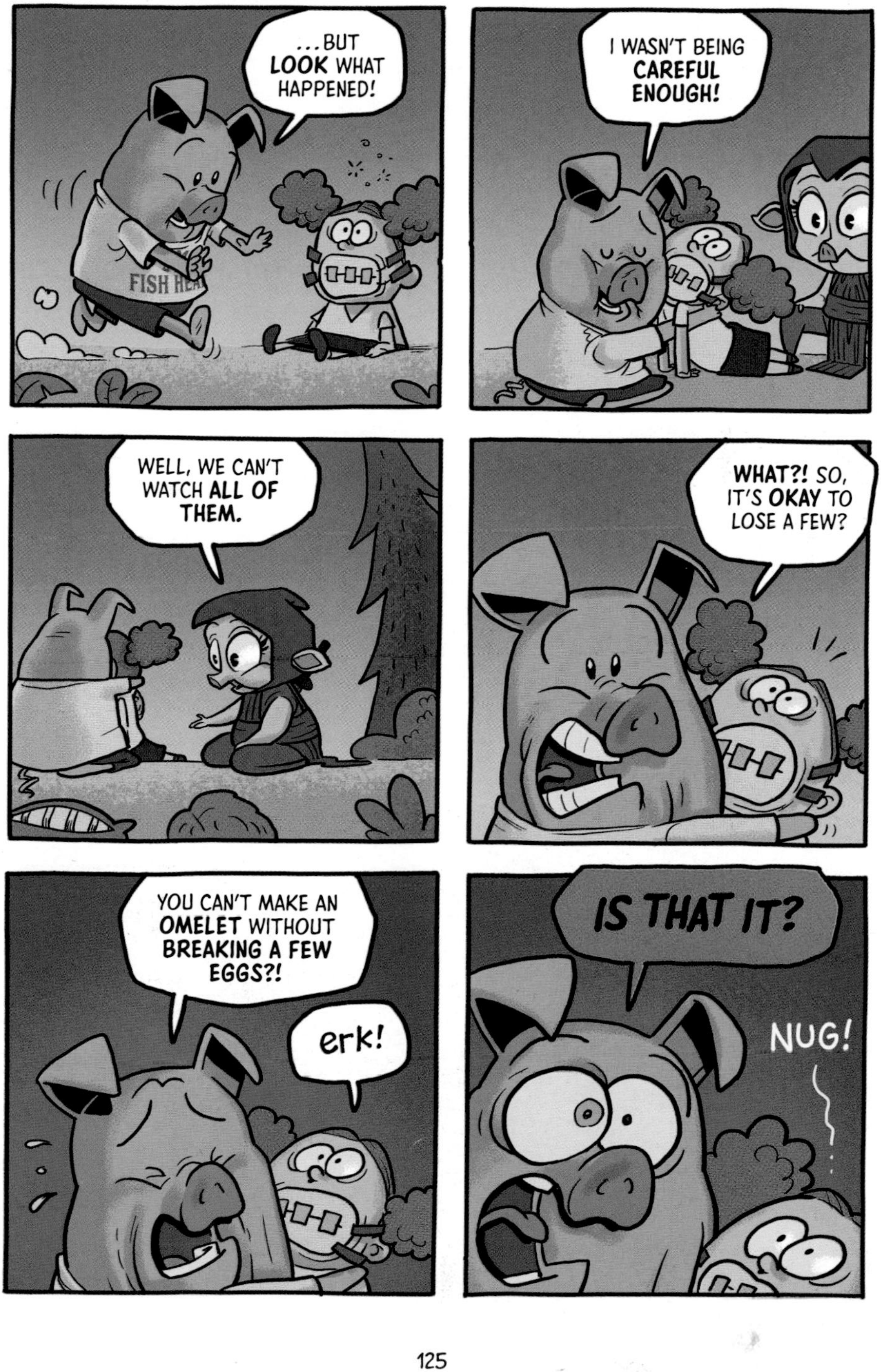
...BUT LOOK WHAT HAPPENED!
FISH HEA
I WASN'T BEING CAREFUL ENOUGH!
WELL, WE CAN'T WATCH ALL OF THEM.
WHAT?! SO, IT'S OKAY TO LOSE A FEW?
YOU CAN'T MAKE AN OMELET WITHOUT BREAKING A FEW EGGS?!
erk!
IS THAT IT?
NUG!

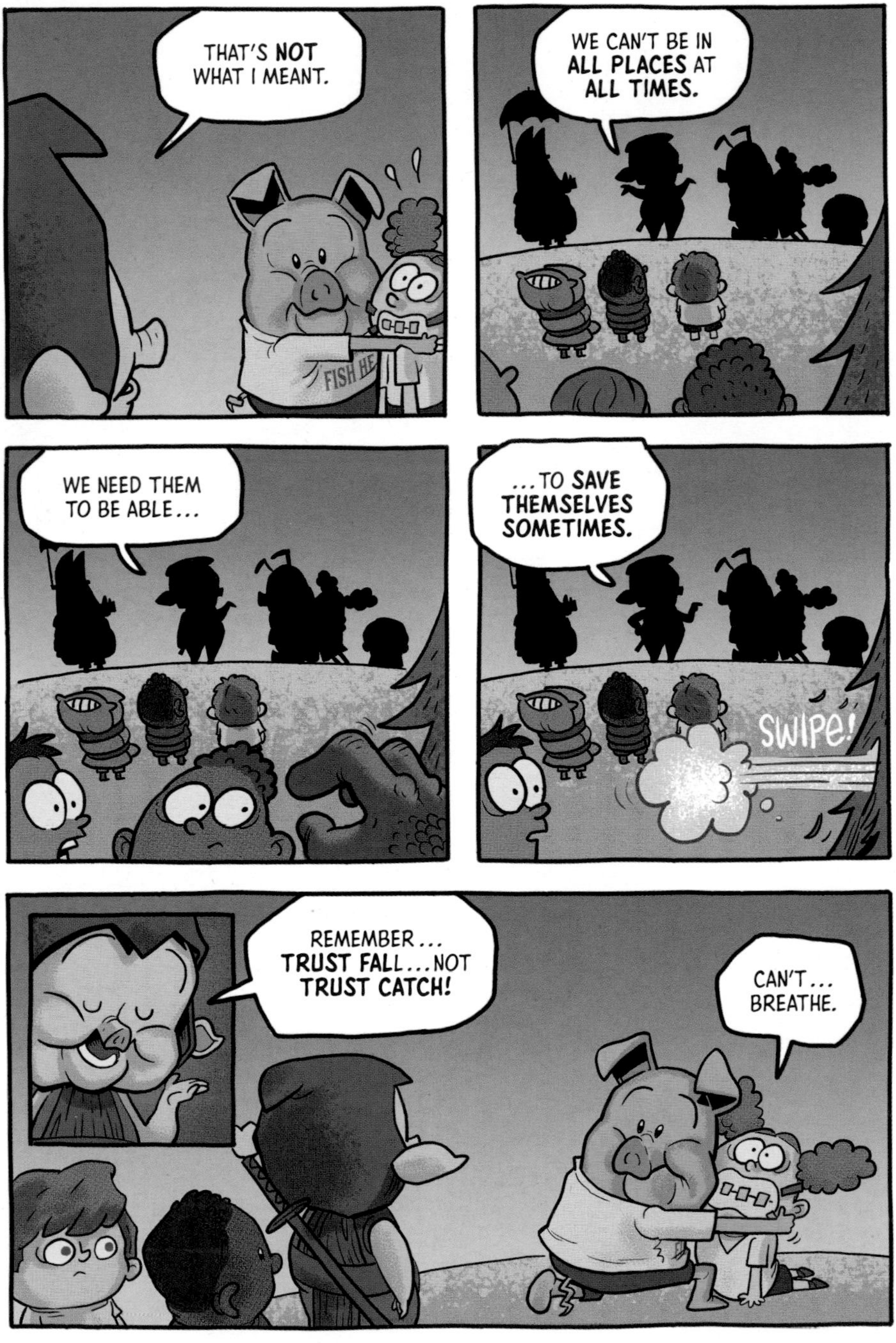
THAT'S NOT WHAT I MEANT.
FISH HE
WE CAN'T BE IN ALL PLACES AT ALL TIMES.
WE NEED THEM TO BE ABLE...
...TO SAVE THEMSELVES SOMETIMES.
SWIPE!
REMEMBER... TRUST FALL...NOT TRUST CATCH!
CAN'T... BREATHE.

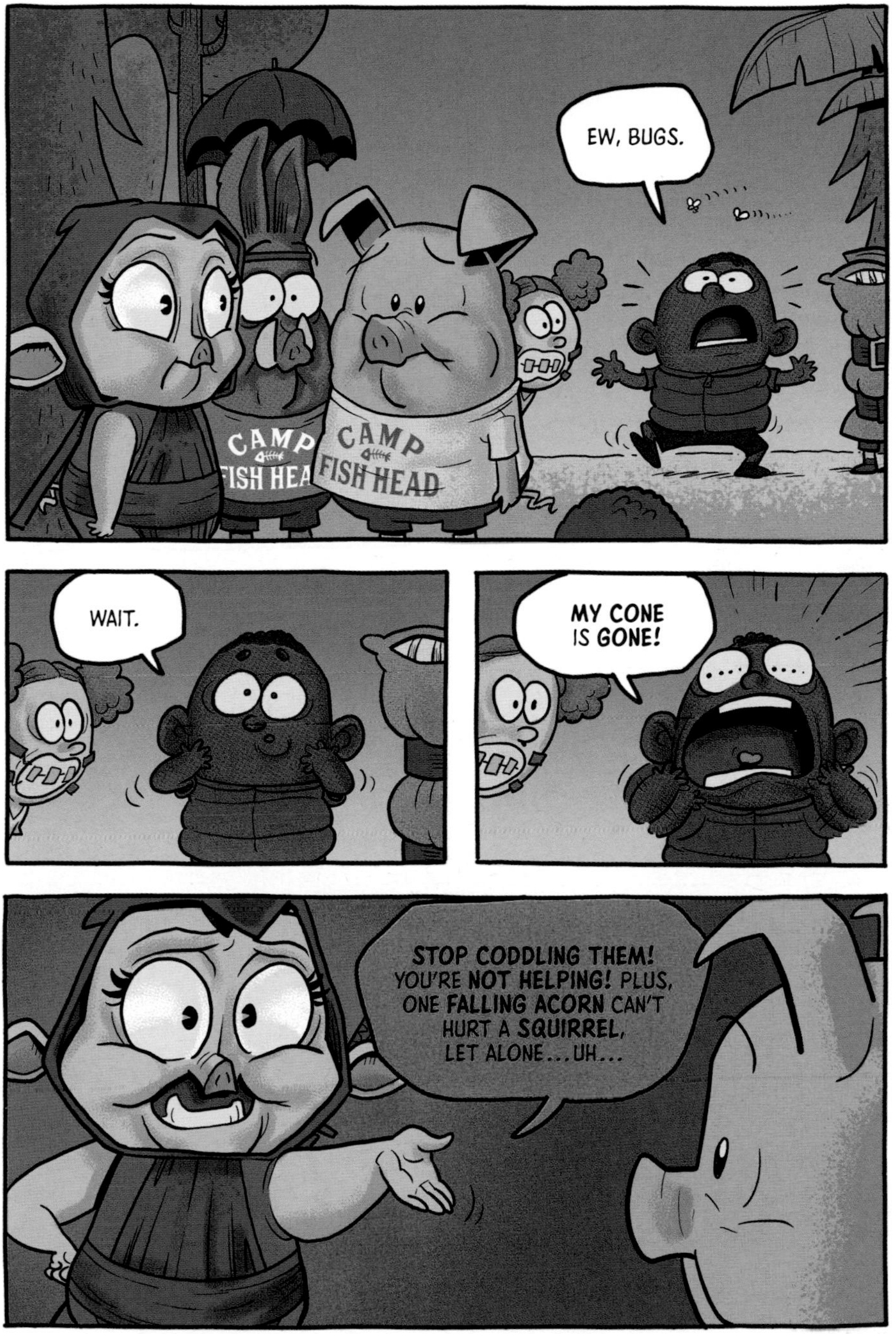
EW, BUGS.
CAMP FISH HEAD
CAMP FISH HEAD
WAIT.
MY CONE IS GONE!
STOP CODDLING THEM! YOU'RE NOT HELPING! PLUS, ONE FALLING ACORN CAN'T HURT A SQUIRREL, LET ALONE...UH...

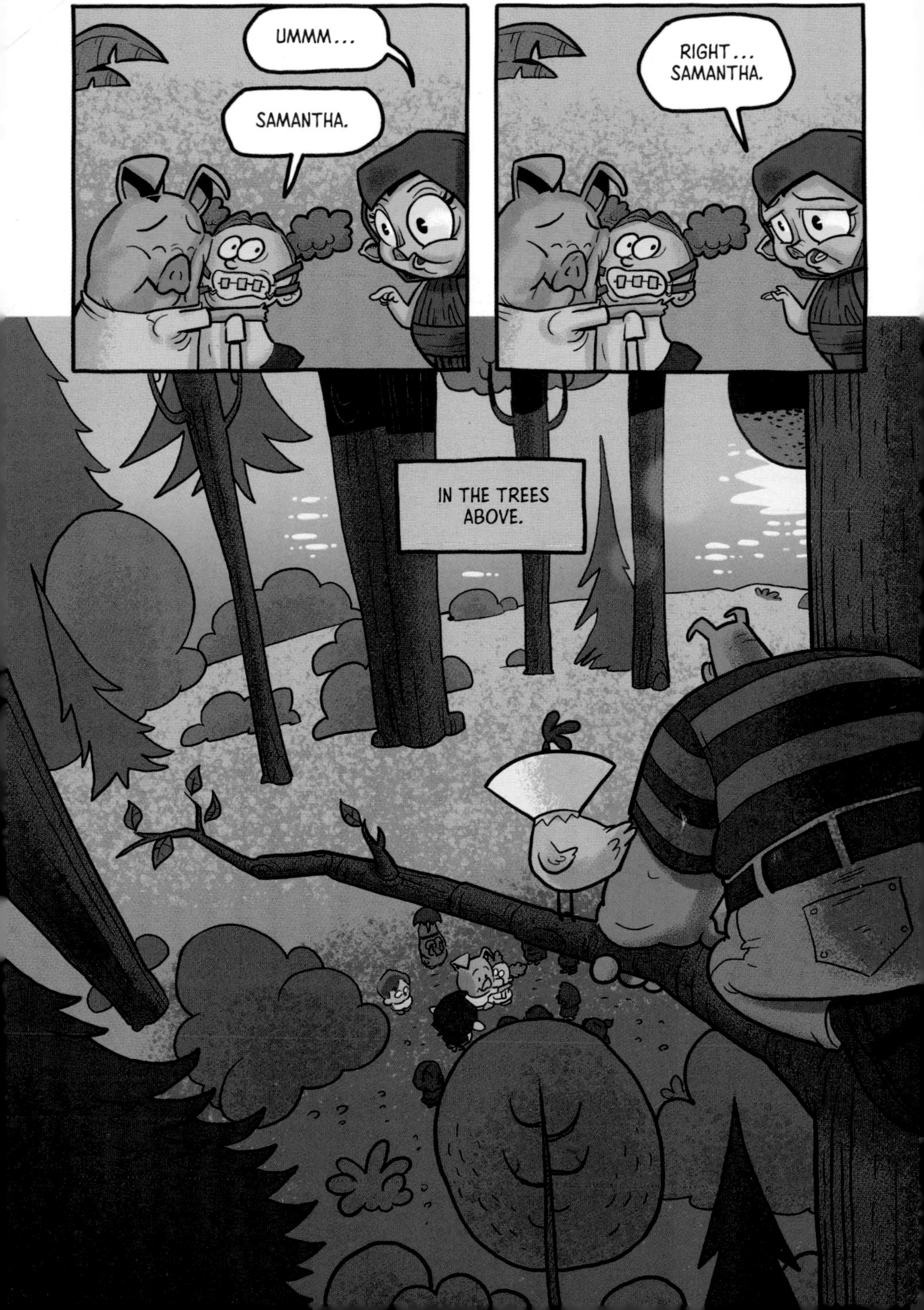
UMMM...
SAMANTHA.
RIGHT... SAMANTHA.
IN THE TREES ABOVE.

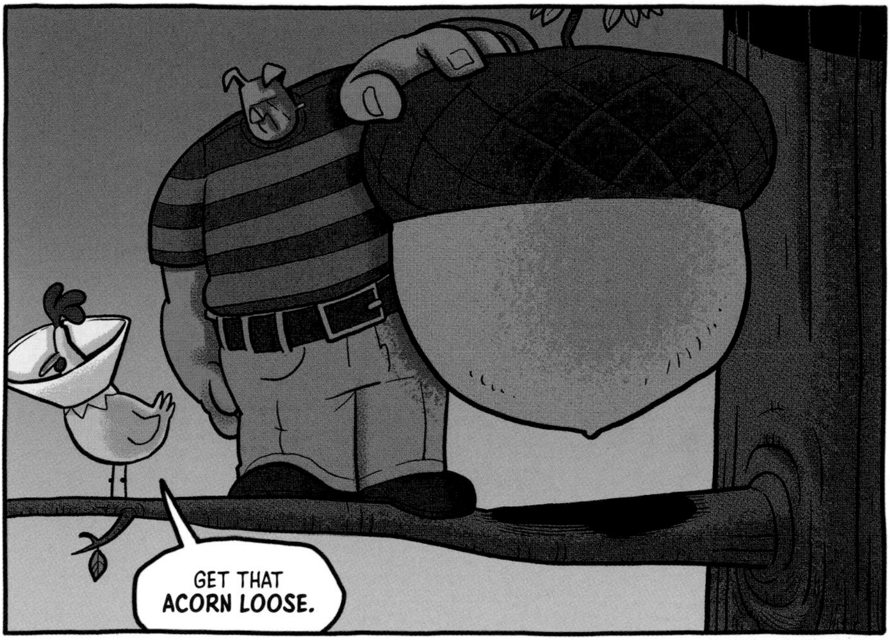
GET THAT ACORN LOOSE.

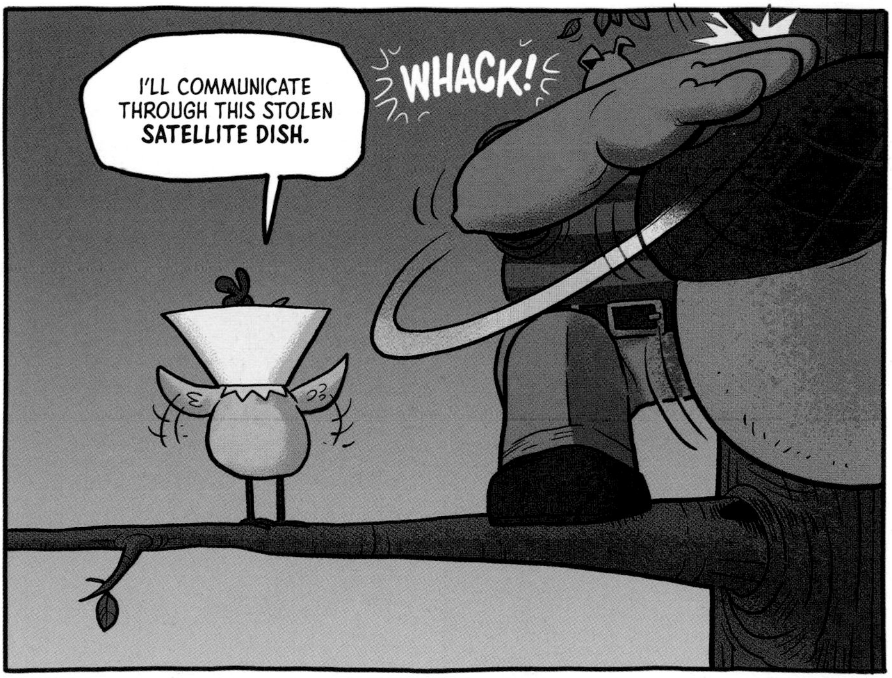
I'LL COMMUNICATE THROUGH THIS STOLEN SATELLITE DISH.
WHACK!

HUMANS. NO NEED TO SEND MORE NOSEPICKERS. WE'RE FINE. SO RELAXED.
RATTLE RATTLE
DON'T NEED HELP. PLEASE STAY AWAY. OVER.
SNAP!
HELLO? BRAVO. ECHO.

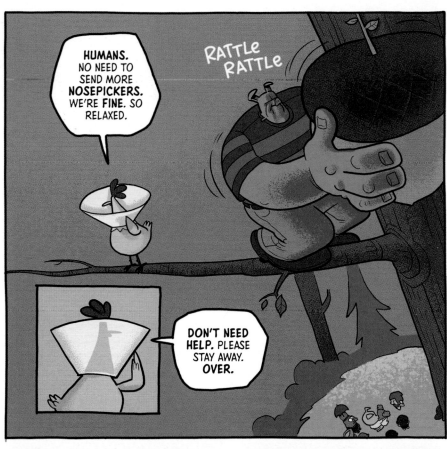

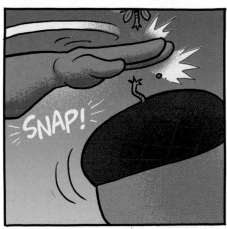

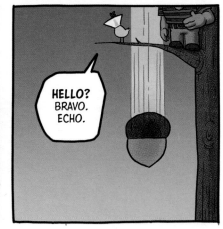

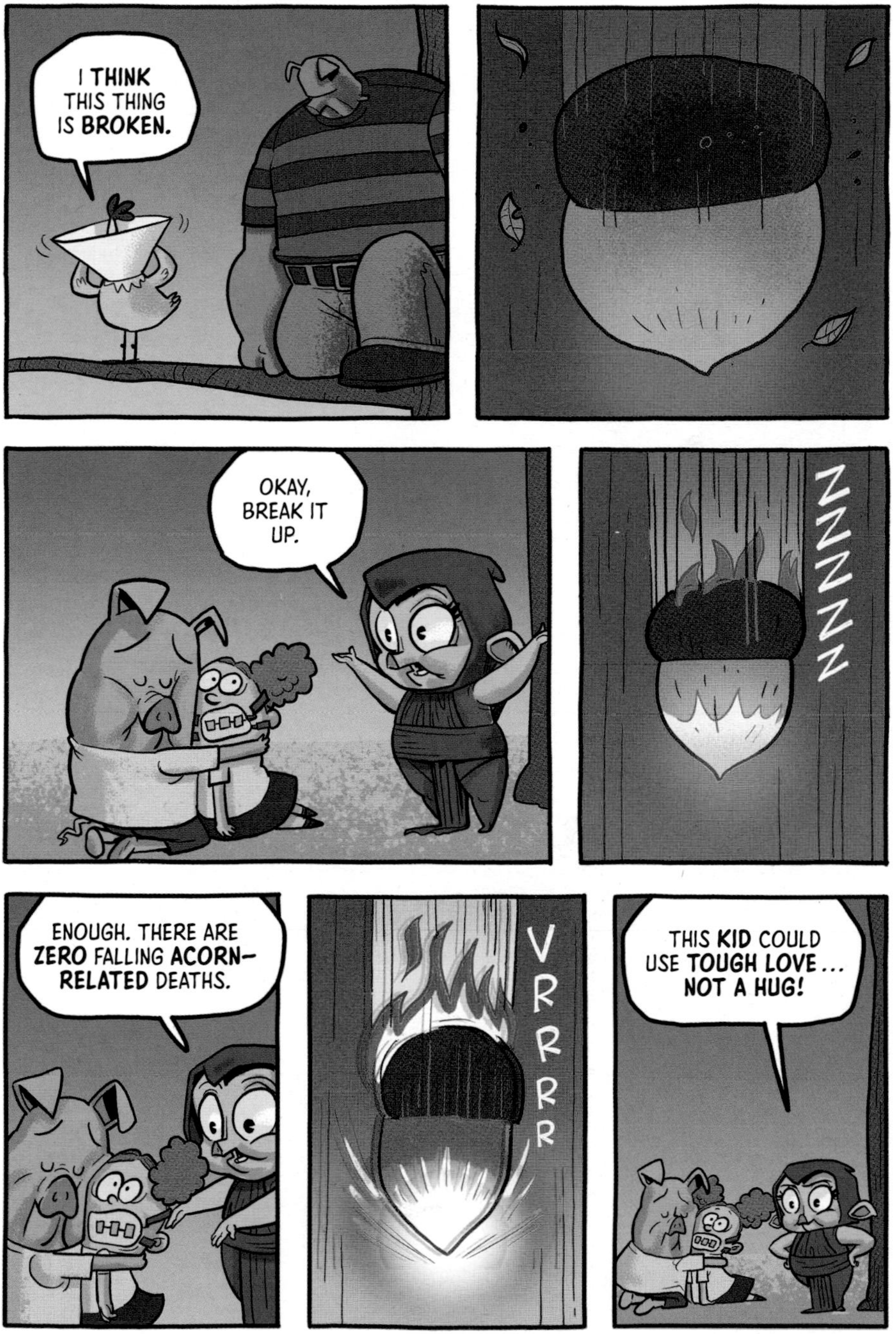
I THINK THIS THING IS BROKEN.
OKAY, BREAK IT UP.
ZZZZZ
ENOUGH. THERE ARE ZERO FALLING ACORN-RELATED DEATHS.
VRRRR
THIS KID COULD USE TOUGH LOVE... NOT A HUG!

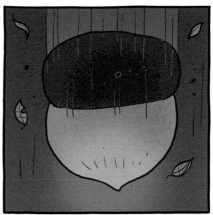

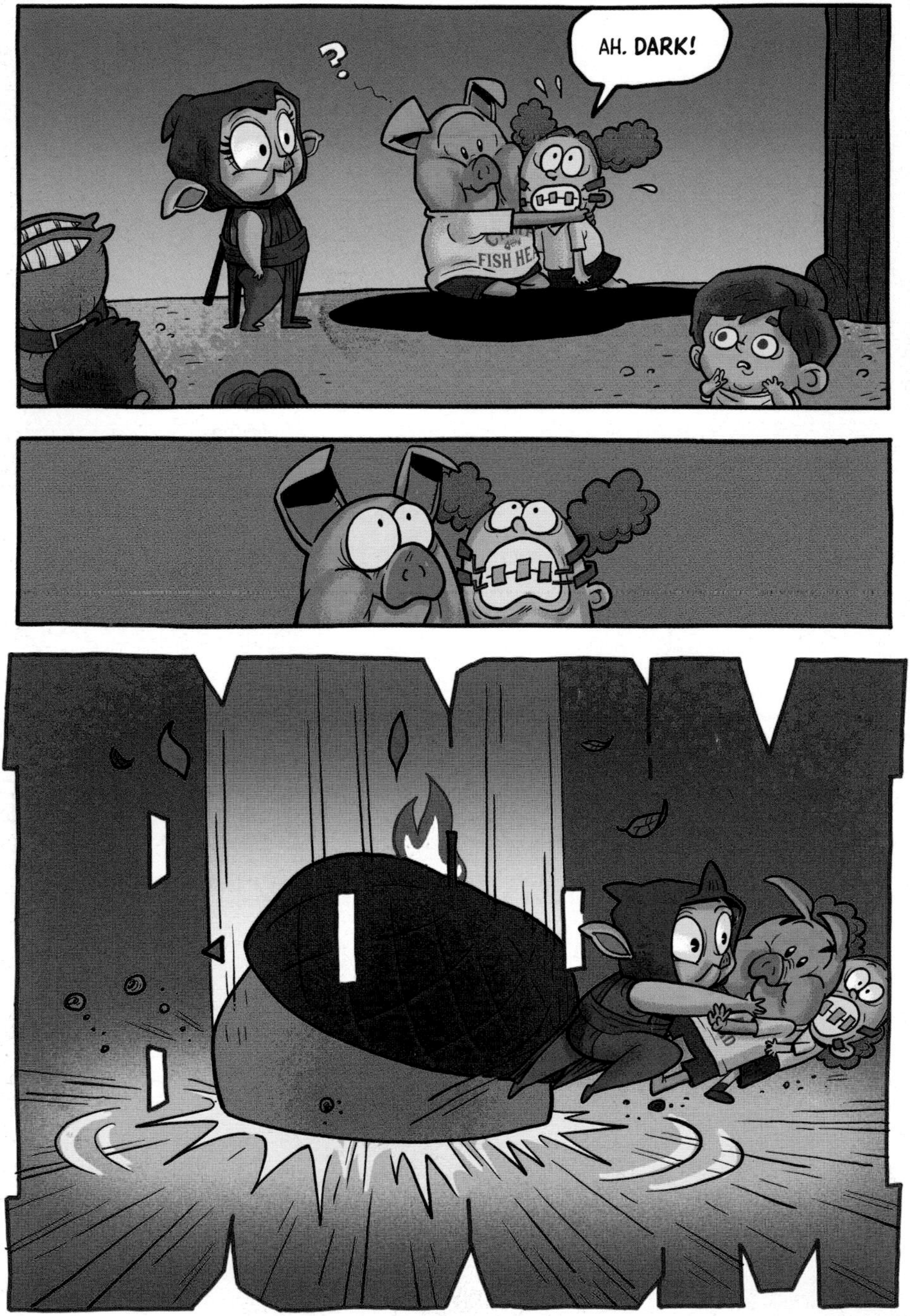
?
AH. DARK!
FISH HEA
BOOM

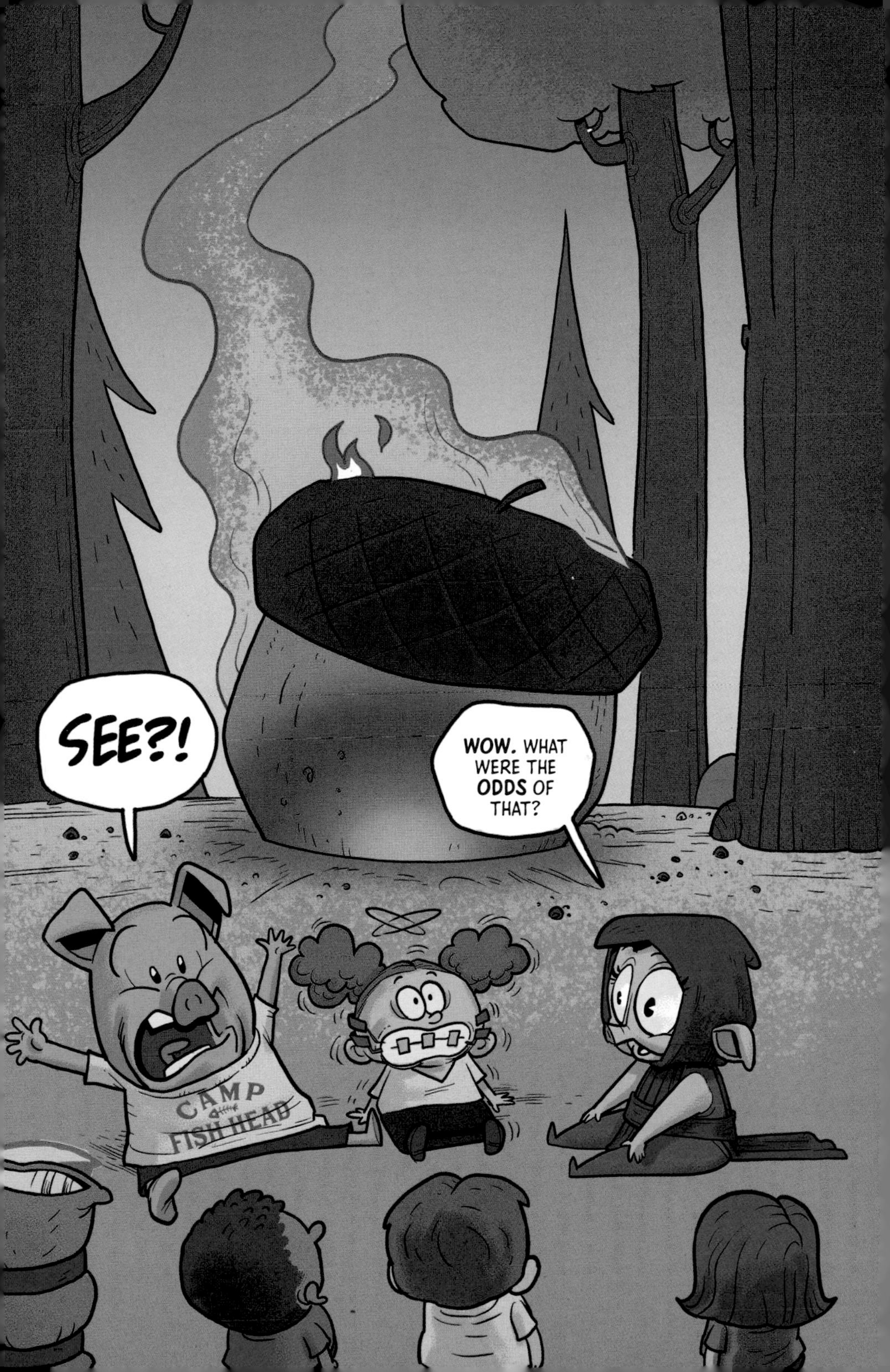
SEE?!
WOW. WHAT WERE THE ODDS OF THAT?
CAMP FISH HEAD

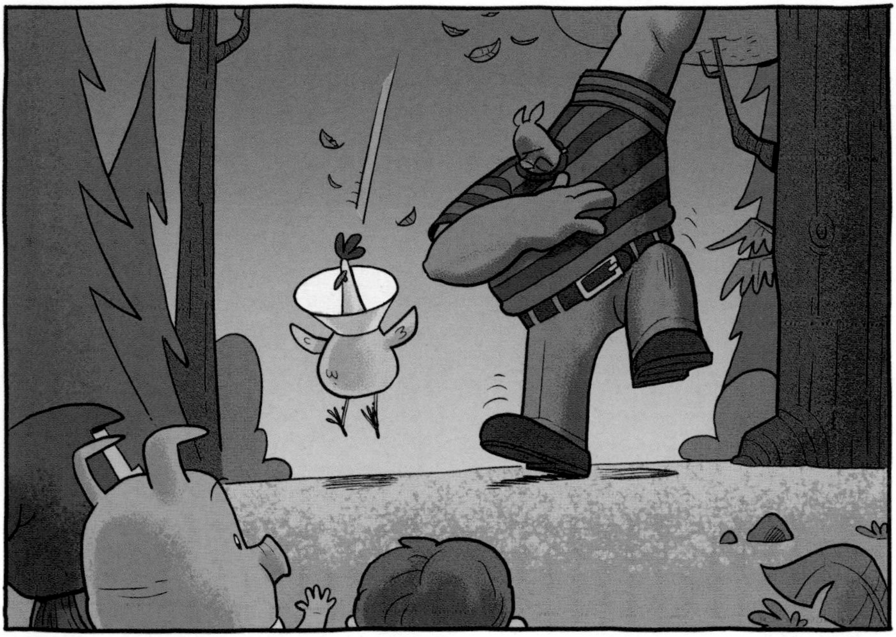

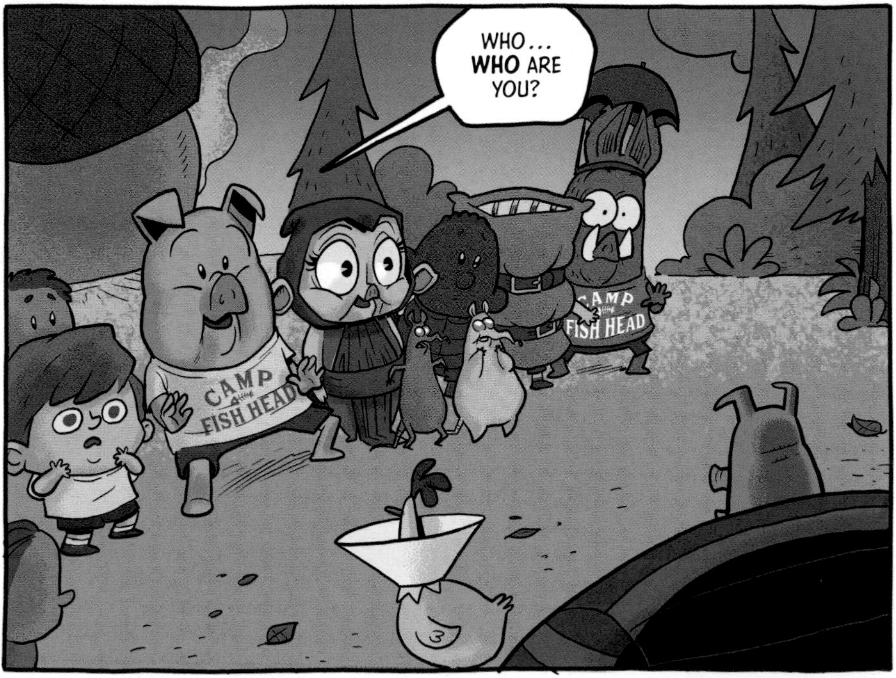
WHO... **WHO** ARE YOU?
CAMP FISH HEAD
CAMP FISH HEAD

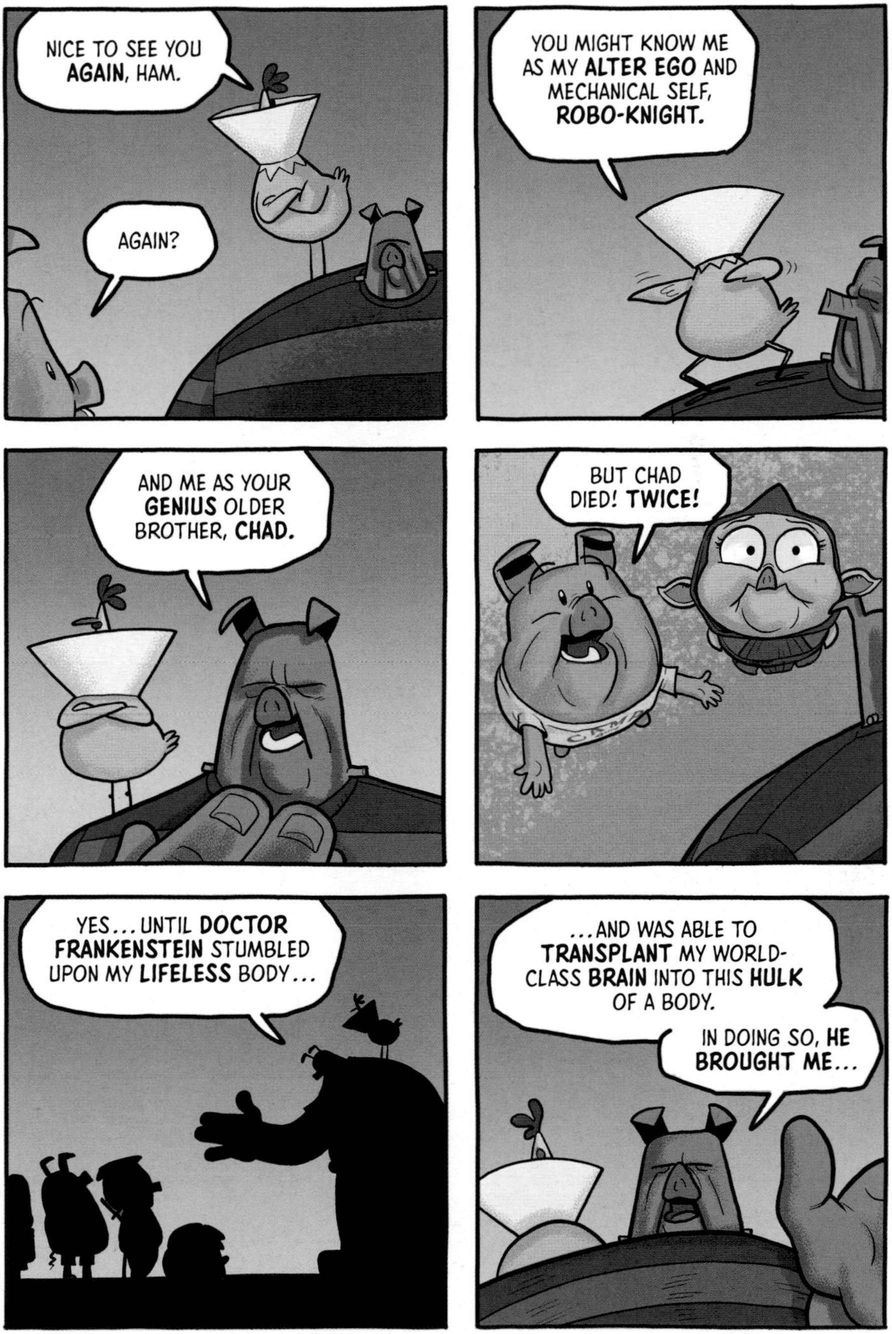
NICE TO SEE YOU **AGAIN**, HAM.
AGAIN?
YOU MIGHT KNOW ME AS MY **ALTER EGO** AND MECHANICAL SELF, **ROBO-KNIGHT.**
AND ME AS YOUR **GENIUS** OLDER BROTHER, **CHAD.**
BUT CHAD DIED! **TWICE!**
YES... UNTIL **DOCTOR FRANKENSTEIN** STUMBLED UPON MY **LIFELESS** BODY...
...AND WAS ABLE TO **TRANSPLANT** MY WORLD-CLASS **BRAIN** INTO THIS **HULK** OF A BODY.
IN DOING SO, **HE BROUGHT ME...**

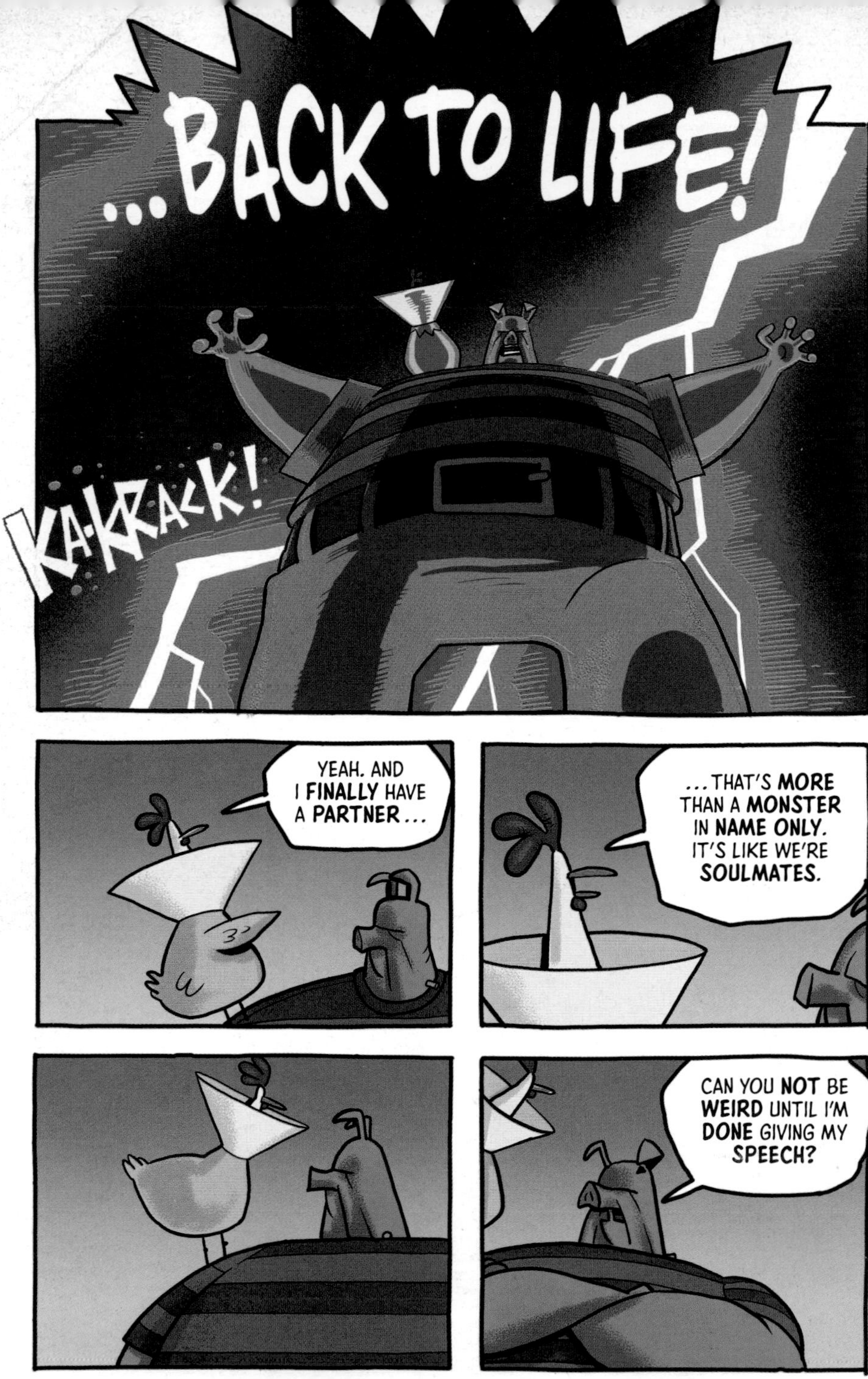
...BACK TO LIFE!
KA-KRACK!
YEAH. AND I FINALLY HAVE A PARTNER...
...THAT'S MORE THAN A MONSTER IN NAME ONLY. IT'S LIKE WE'RE SOULMATES.
CAN YOU NOT BE WEIRD UNTIL I'M DONE GIVING MY SPEECH?

CHAPTER EIGHT

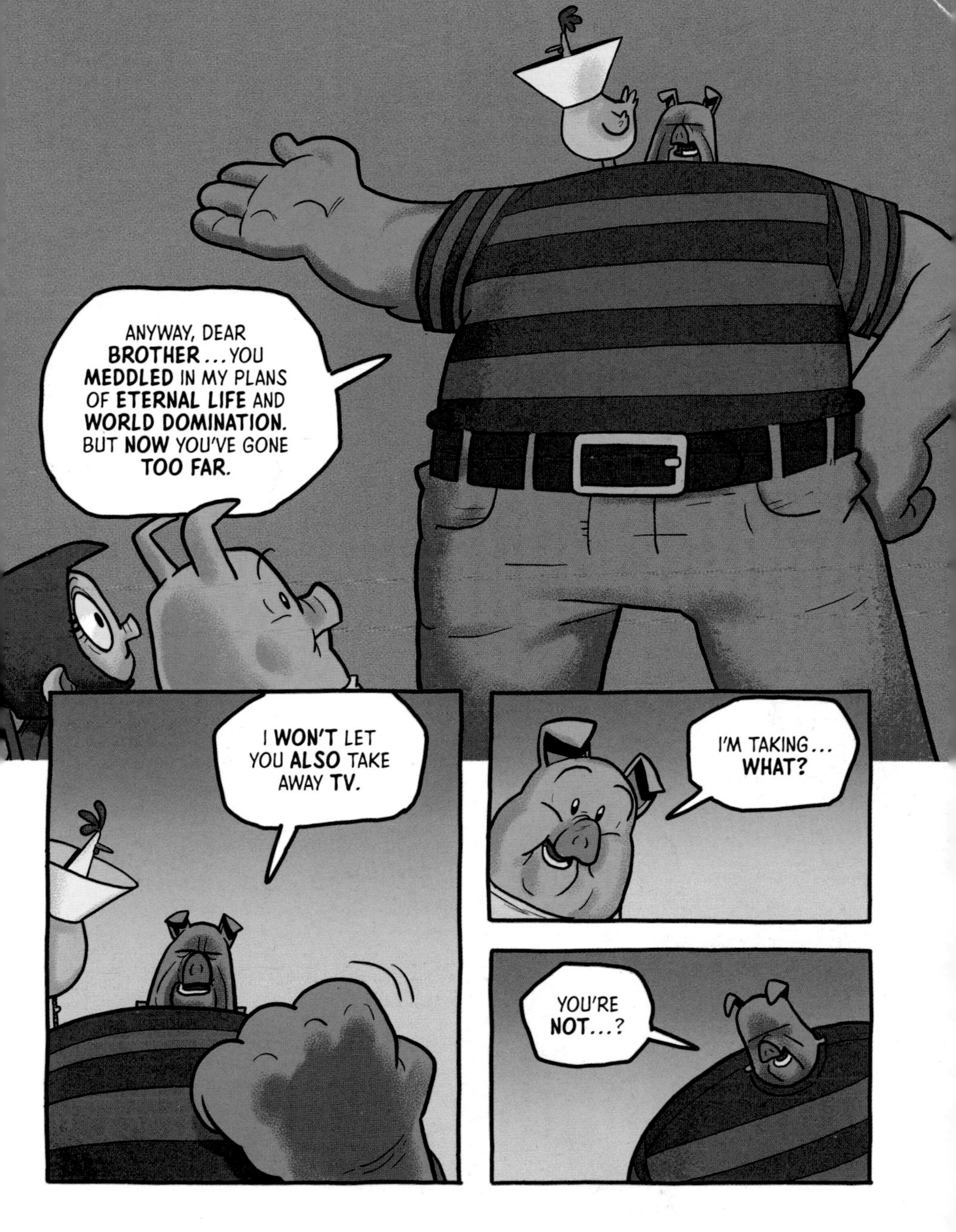
ANYWAY, DEAR BROTHER...YOU MEDDLED IN MY PLANS OF ETERNAL LIFE AND WORLD DOMINATION. BUT NOW YOU'VE GONE TOO FAR.
I WON'T LET YOU ALSO TAKE AWAY TV.
I'M TAKING... WHAT?
YOU'RE NOT...?

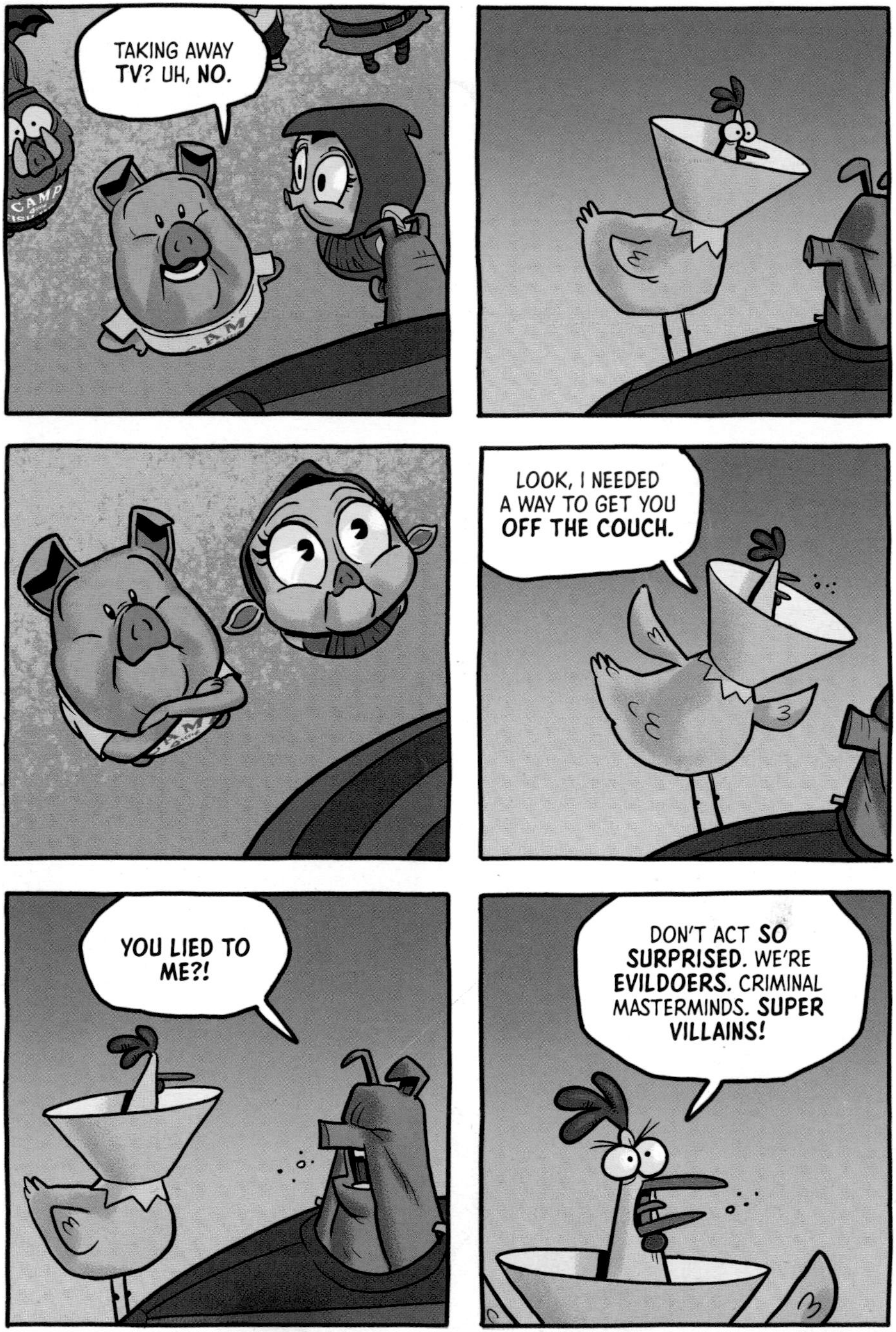
TAKING AWAY TV? UH, NO.
LOOK, I NEEDED A WAY TO GET YOU OFF THE COUCH.
YOU LIED TO ME?!
DON'T ACT SO SURPRISED. WE'RE EVILDOERS. CRIMINAL MASTERMINDS. SUPER VILLAINS!

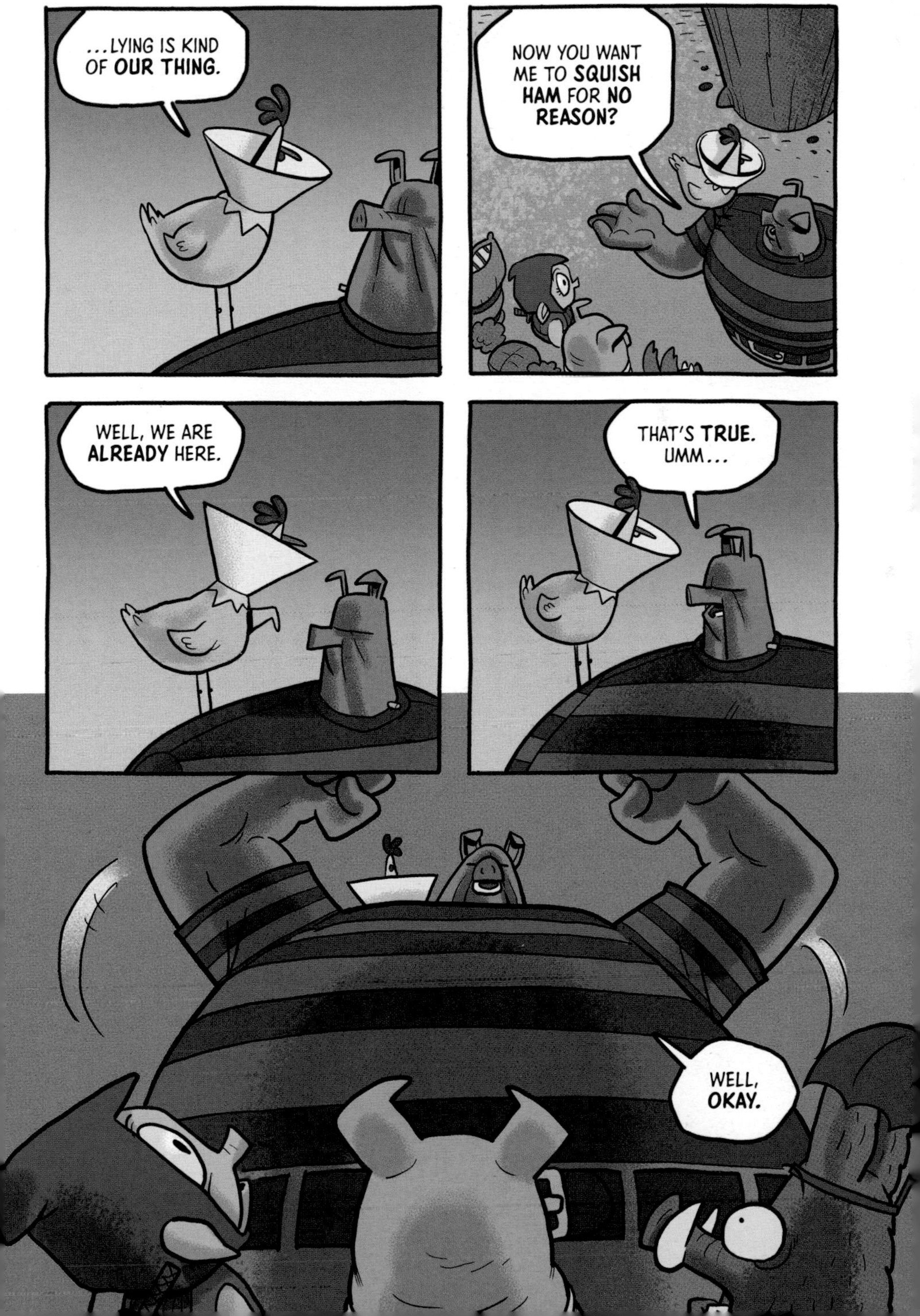
...LYING IS KIND OF OUR THING.
NOW YOU WANT ME TO SQUISH HAM FOR NO REASON?
WELL, WE ARE ALREADY HERE.
THAT'S TRUE. UMM...
WELL, OKAY.

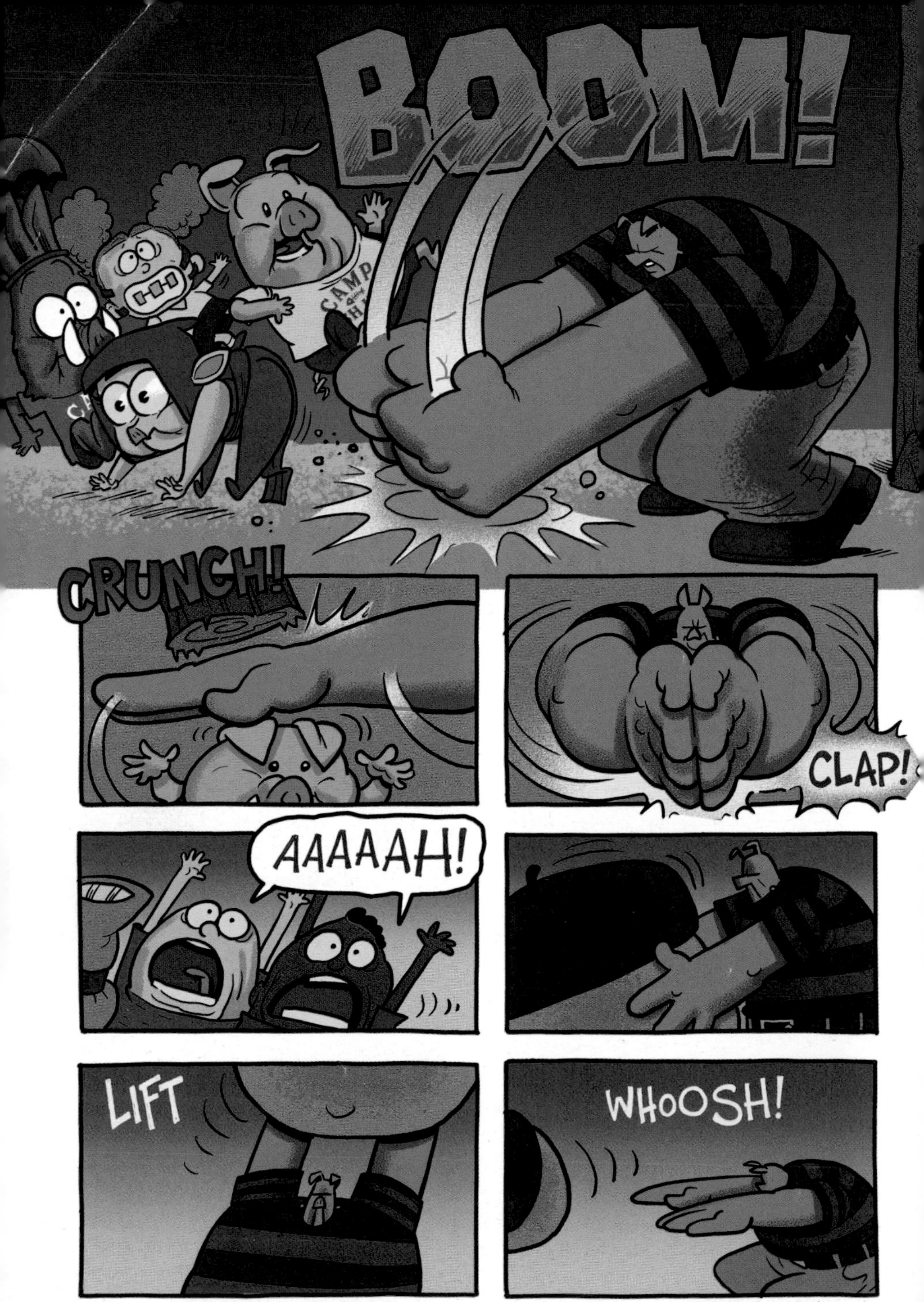
BOOM!
CRUNCH!
CLAP!
AAAAAH!
LIFT
WHOOSH!

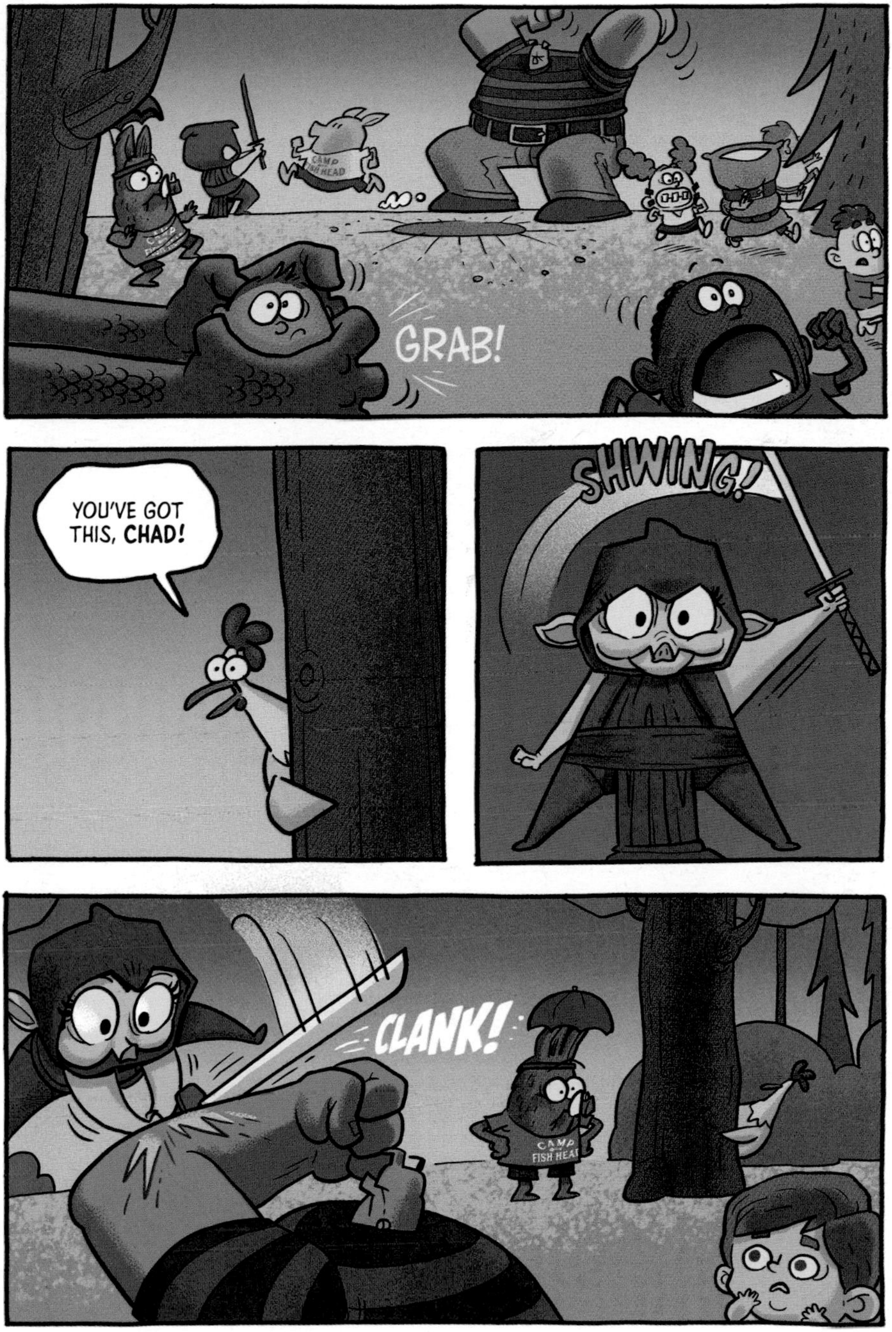
GRAB!
YOU'VE GOT THIS, **CHAD!**
SHWING!
CLANK!

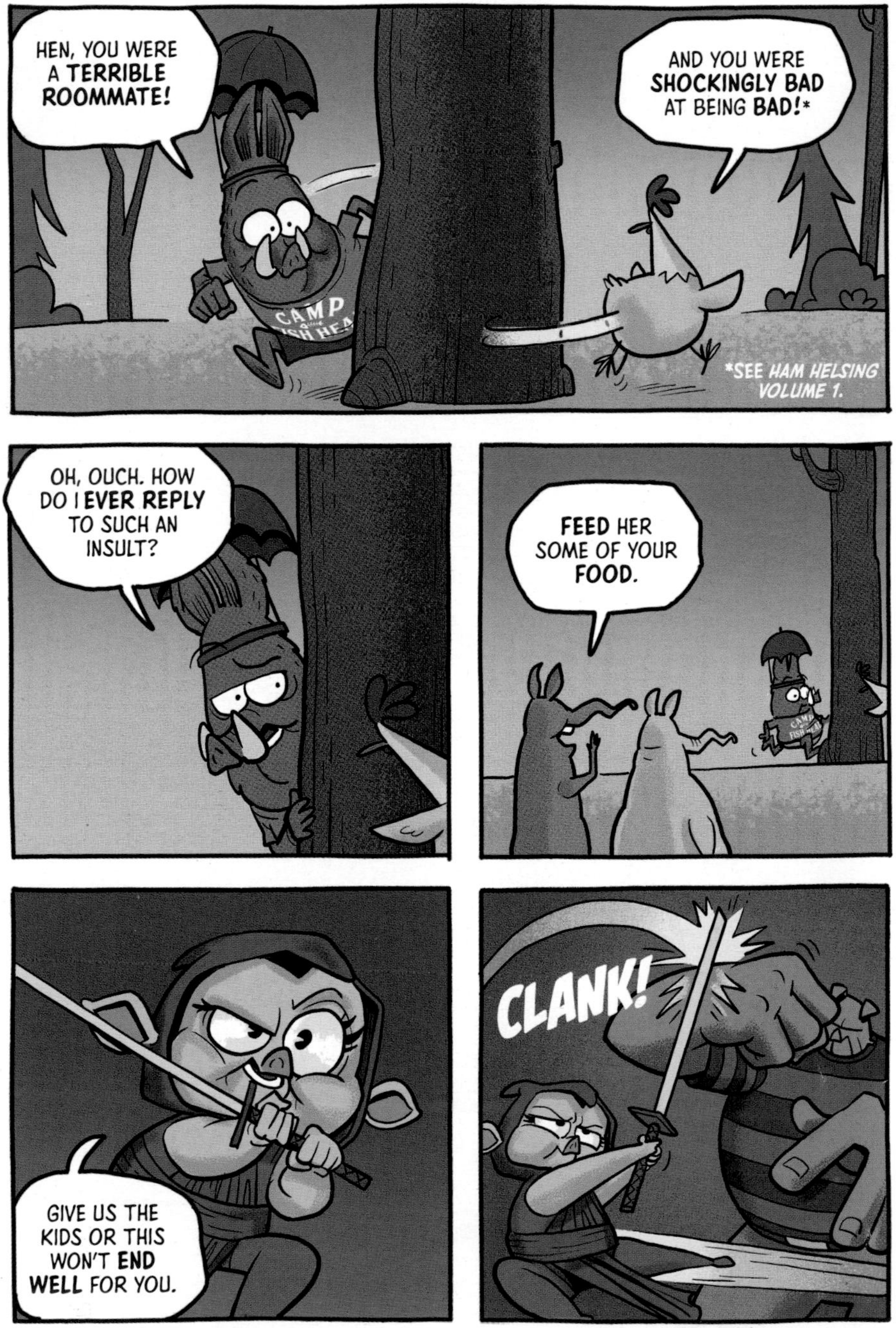
HEN, YOU WERE A TERRIBLE ROOMMATE!
AND YOU WERE SHOCKINGLY BAD AT BEING BAD!*
CAMP FISH HEA
*SEE HAM HELSING VOLUME 1.
OH, OUCH. HOW DO I EVER REPLY TO SUCH AN INSULT?
FEED HER SOME OF YOUR FOOD.
GIVE US THE KIDS OR THIS WON'T END WELL FOR YOU.
CLANK!

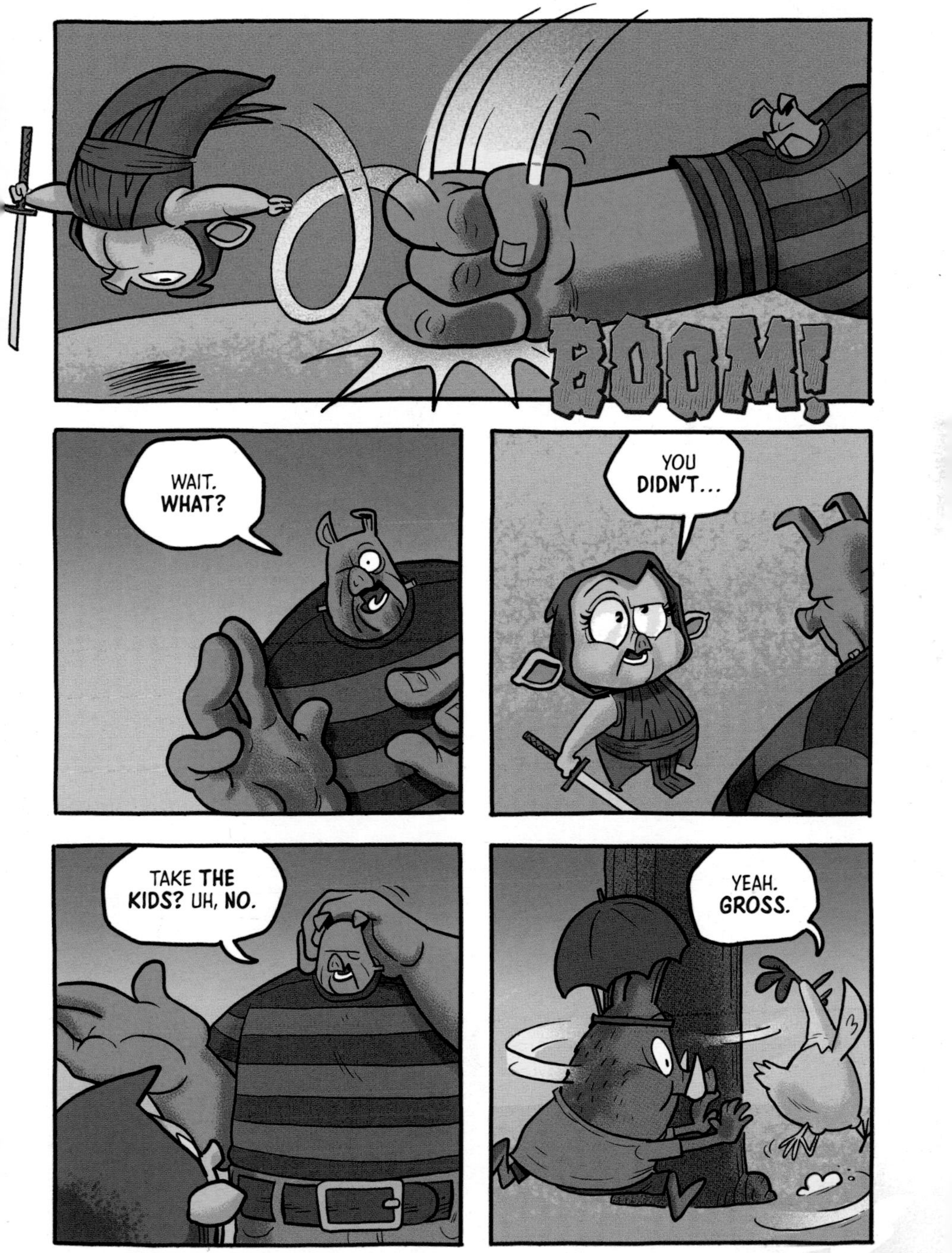
BOOM!
WAIT. WHAT?
YOU DIDN'T...
TAKE THE KIDS? UH, NO.
YEAH. GROSS.

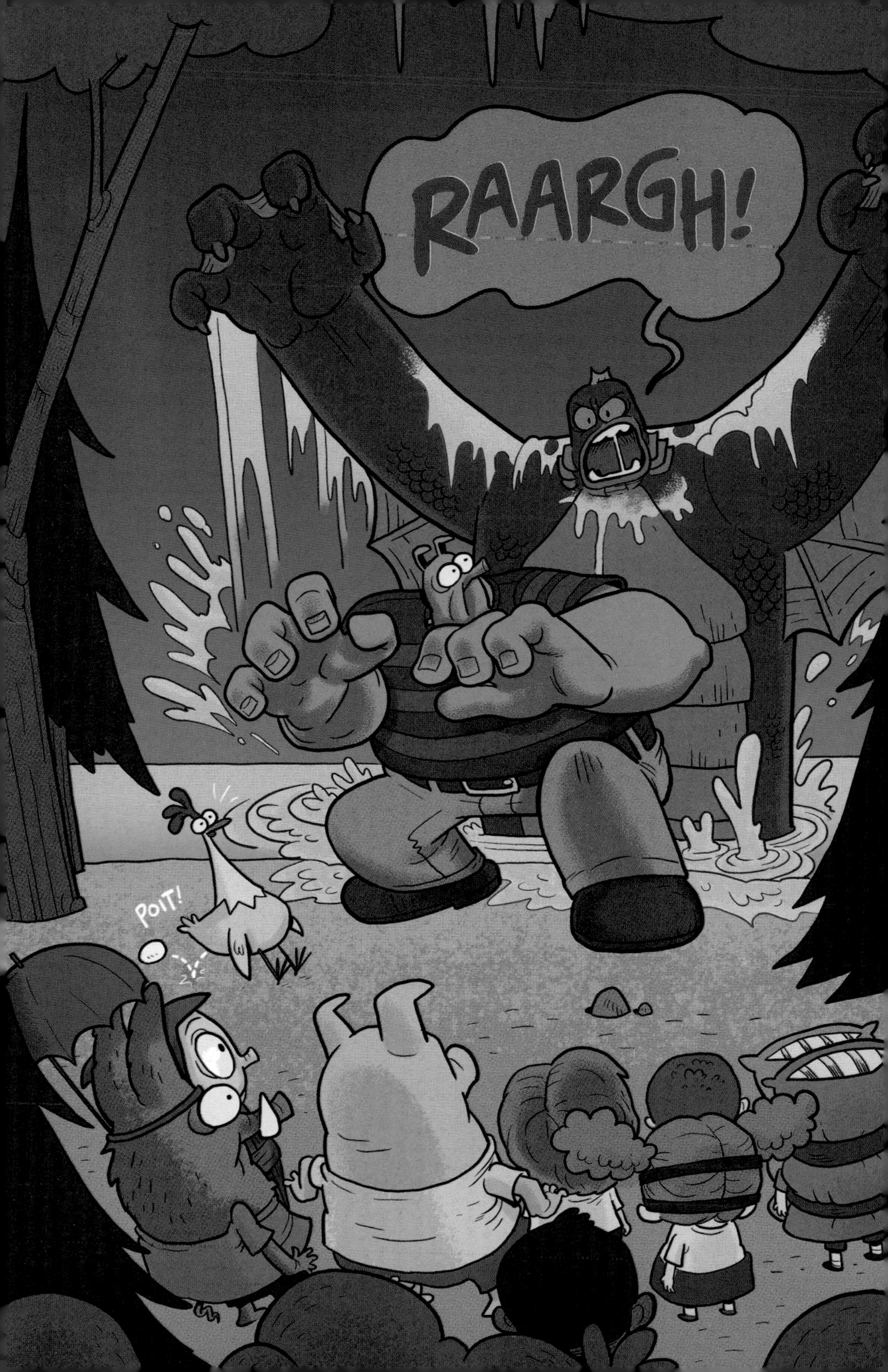
RAARGH!
POIT!

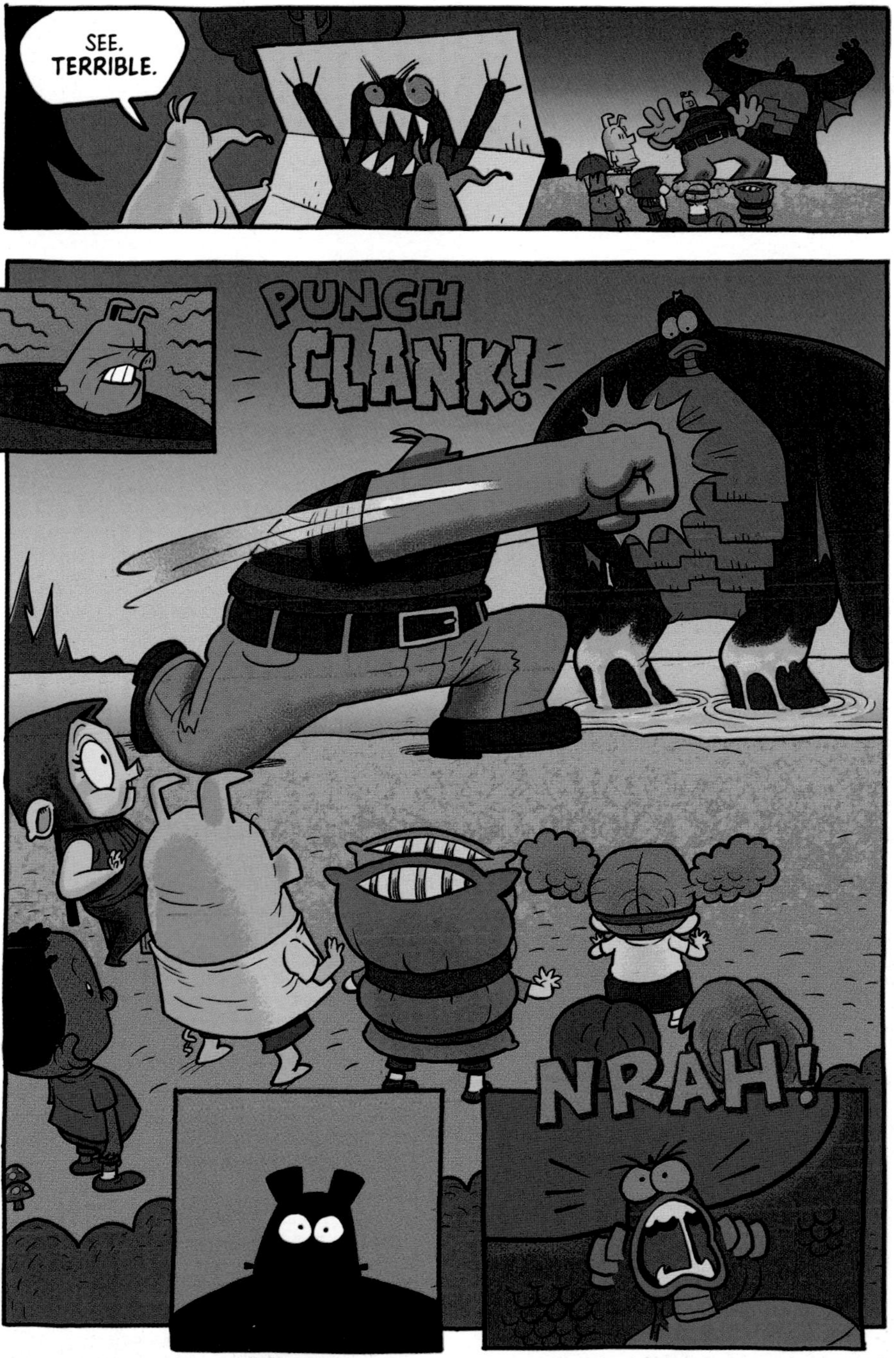
SEE. TERRIBLE.
PUNCH
CLANK!
NRAH!

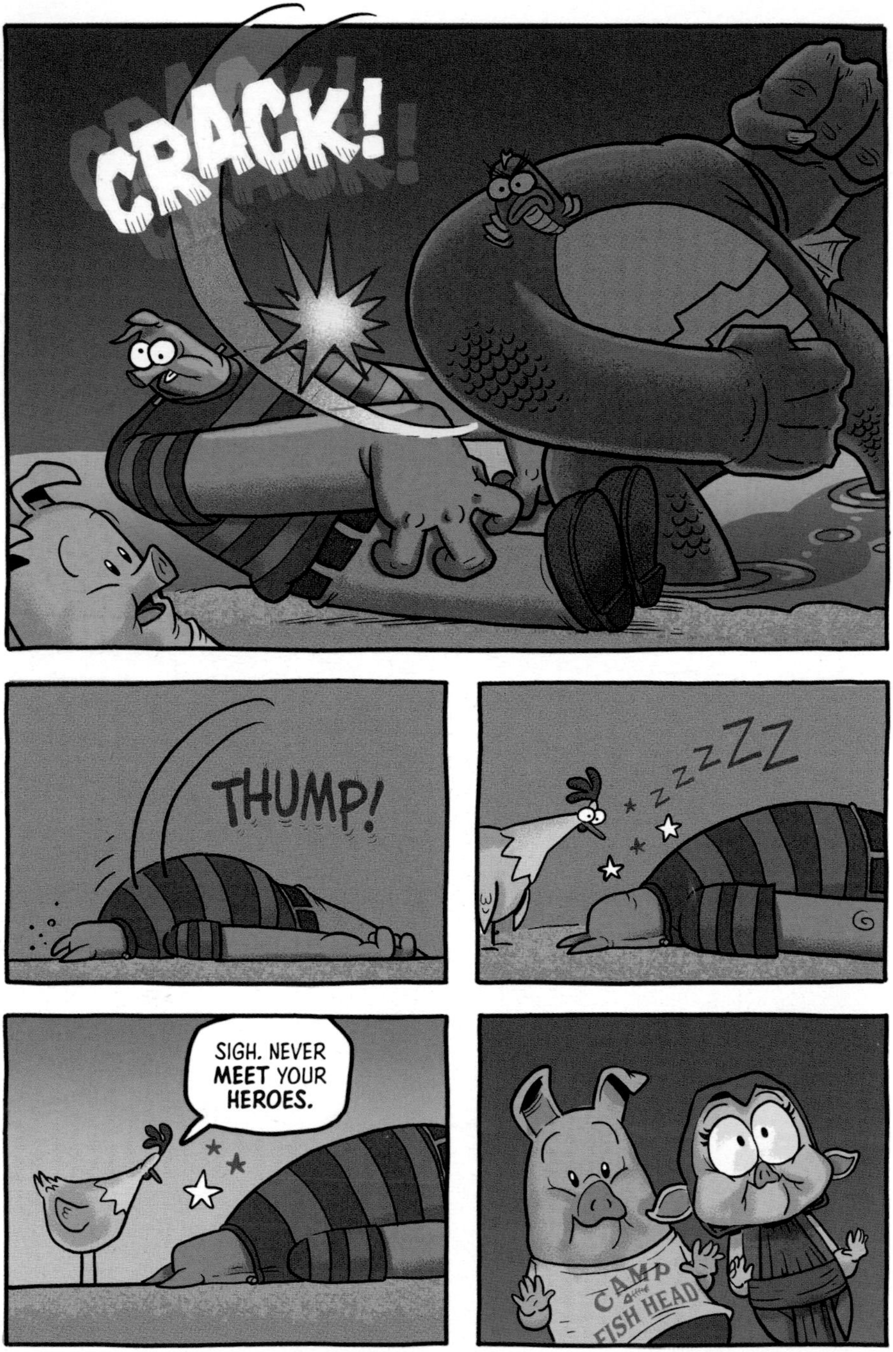
CRACK!
THUMP!
zzzzZZ
SIGH. NEVER MEET YOUR HEROES.
CAMP FISH HEAD

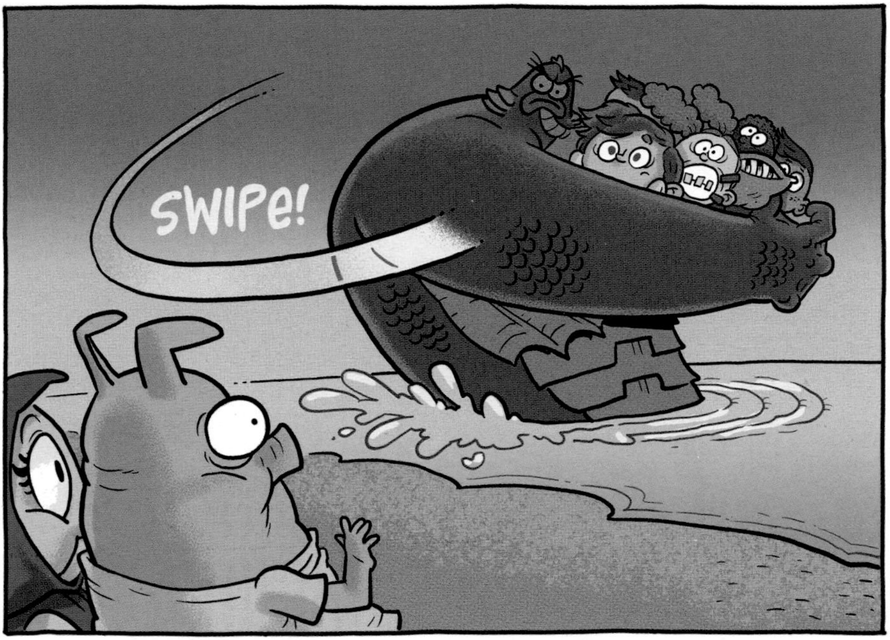
SWIPE!

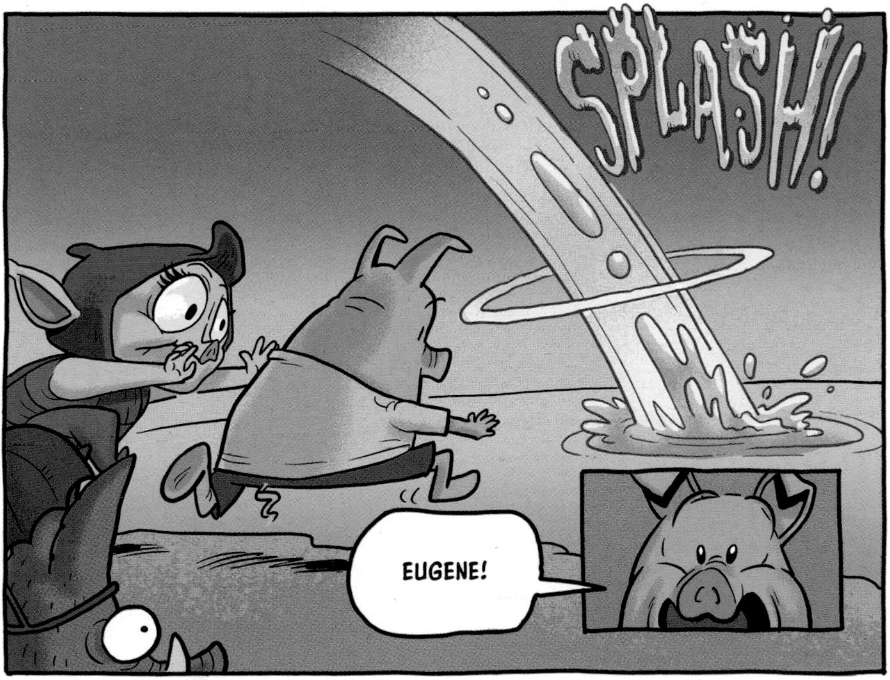
SPLASH!
EUGENE!

CHAPTER NINE

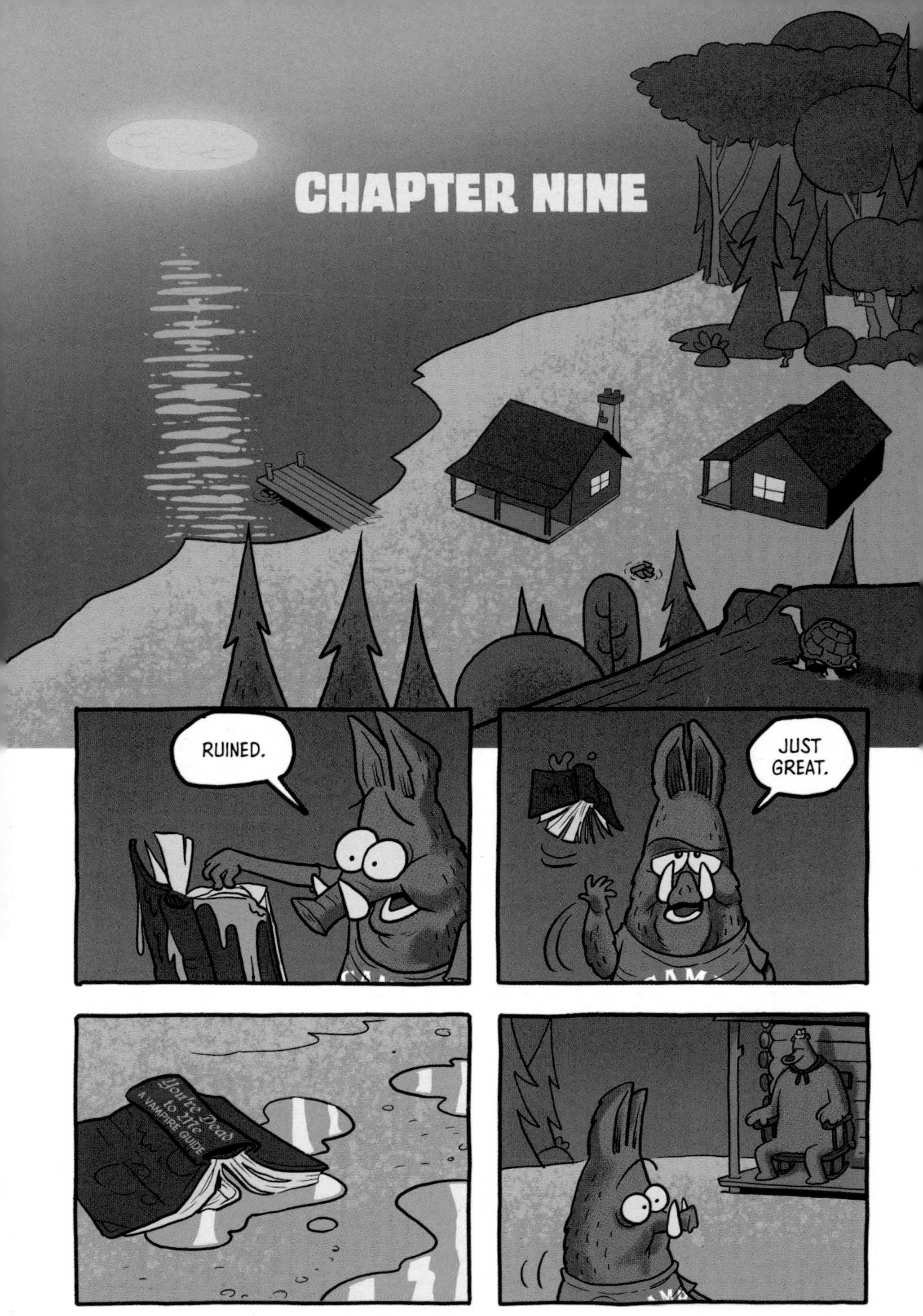
RUINED.
JUST GREAT.
You're Dead to Me
A VAMPIRE GUIDE

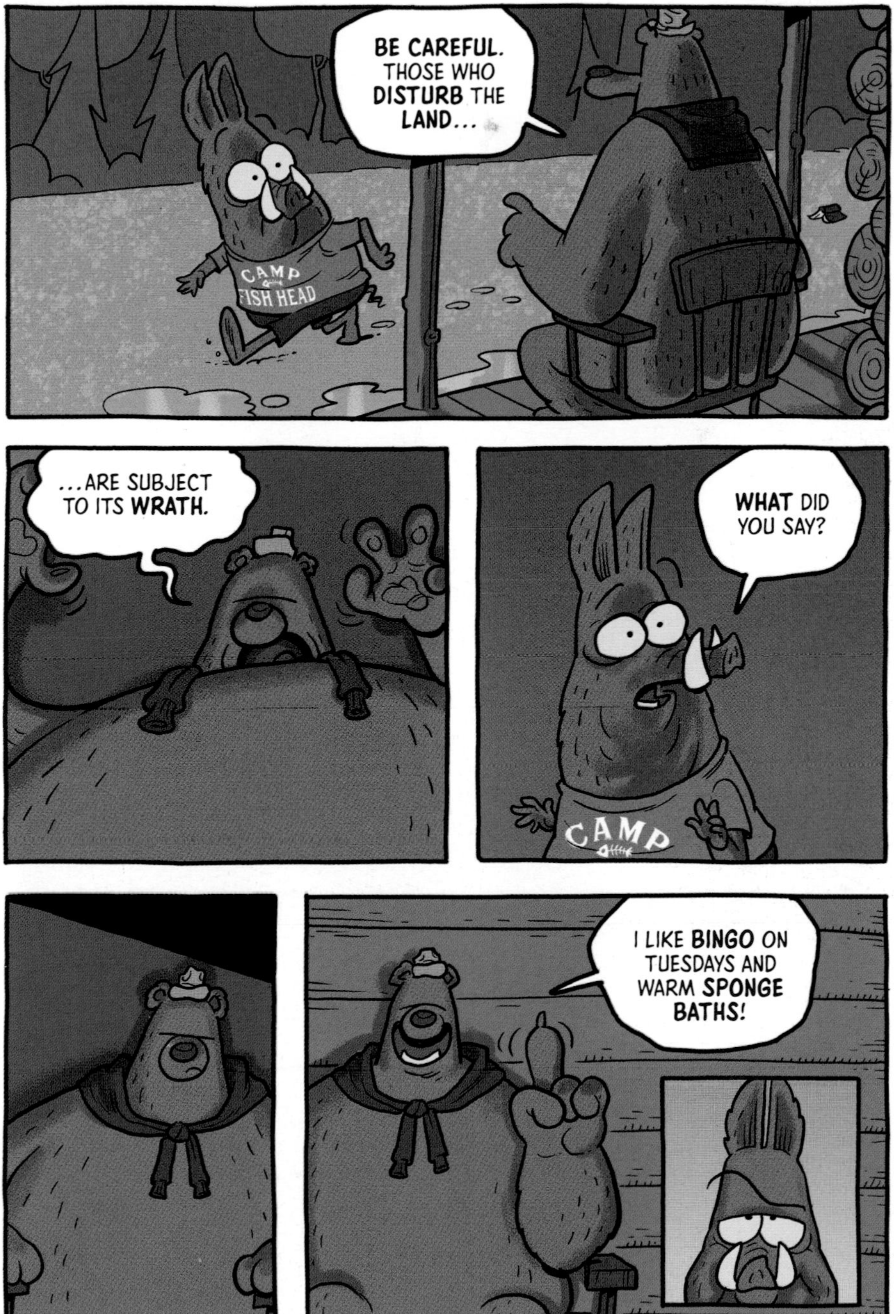
BE CAREFUL. THOSE WHO DISTURB THE LAND...
CAMP FISH HEAD
...ARE SUBJECT TO ITS WRATH.
WHAT DID YOU SAY?
CAMP
I LIKE BINGO ON TUESDAYS AND WARM SPONGE BATHS!

WHAT DO WE DO **NOW?**
CAMP FISH HEAD
CAMP FISH HEAD

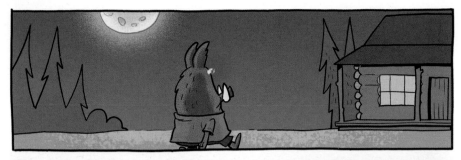

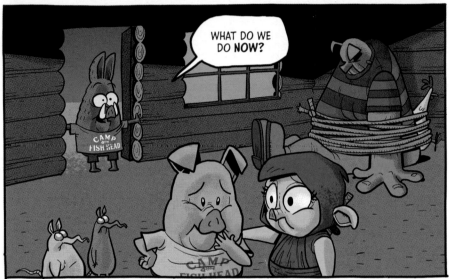

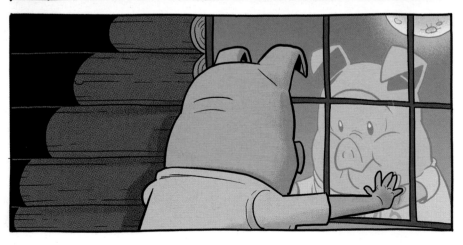

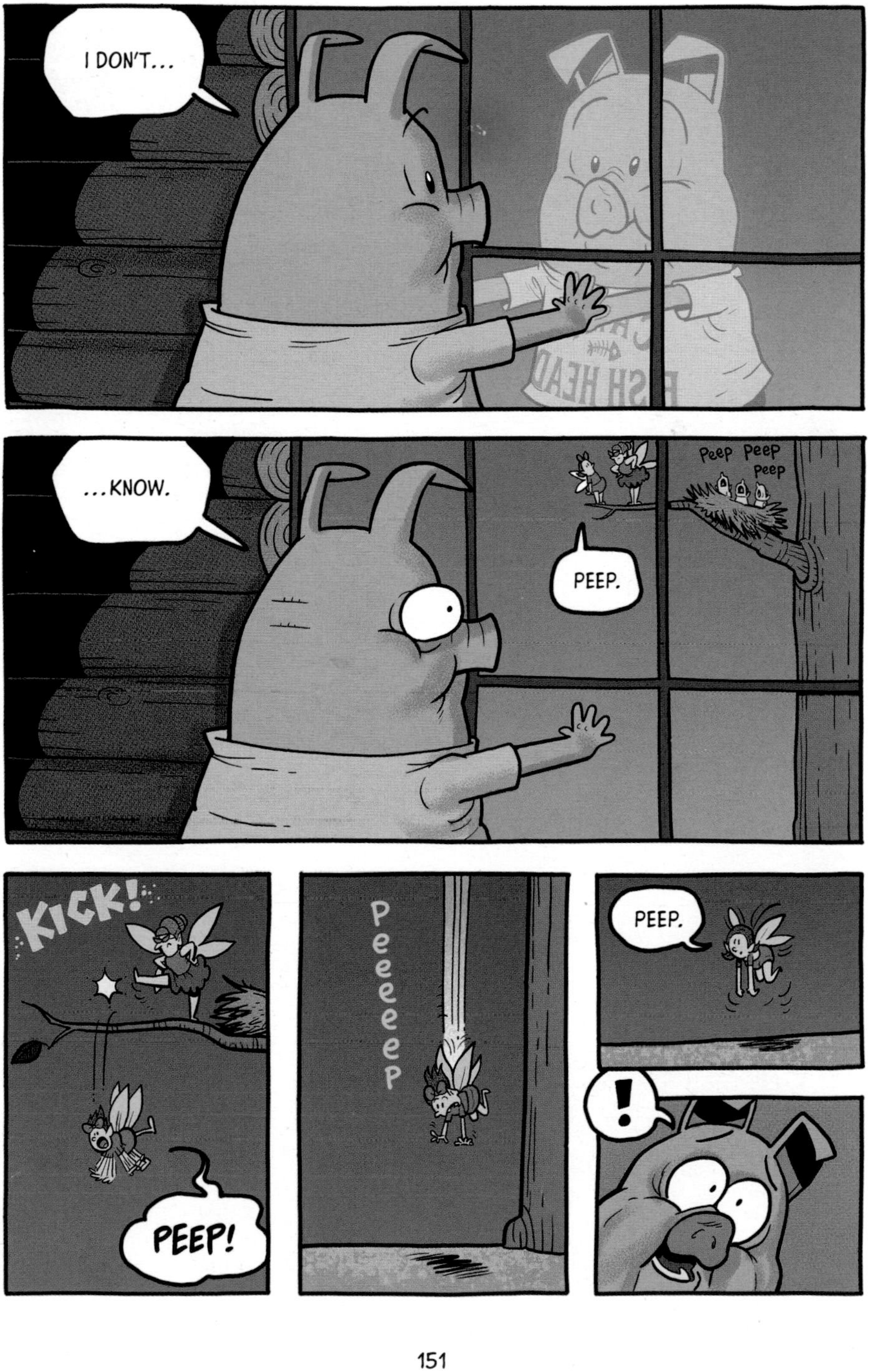
I DON'T...
...KNOW.
Peep Peep
peep
PEEP.
KICK!
PEEP!
Peeeeep
PEEP.
!

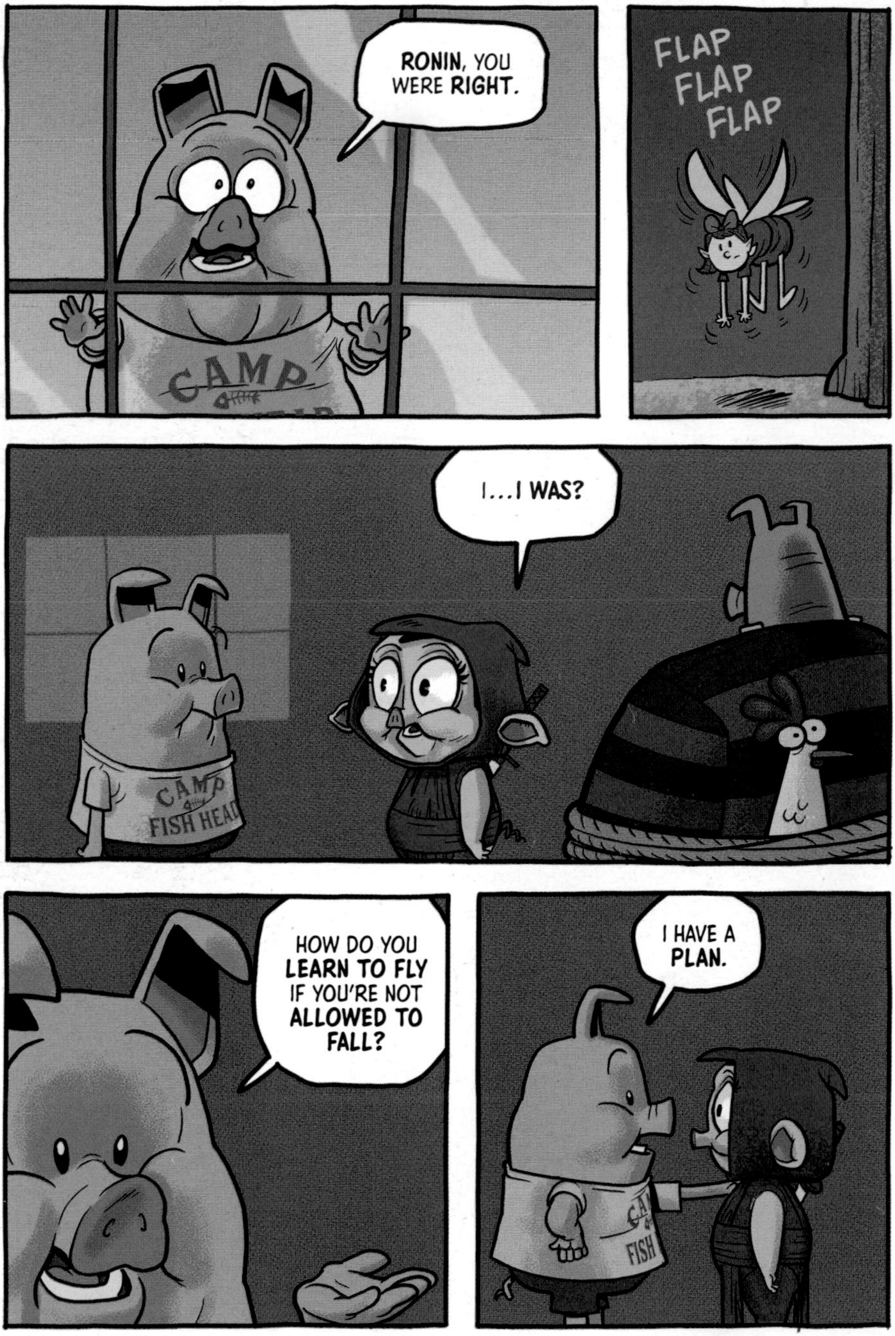
RONIN, YOU WERE RIGHT.
CAMP
FLAP FLAP FLAP
I...I WAS?
CAMP FISH HEAD
HOW DO YOU LEARN TO FLY IF YOU'RE NOT ALLOWED TO FALL?
I HAVE A PLAN.

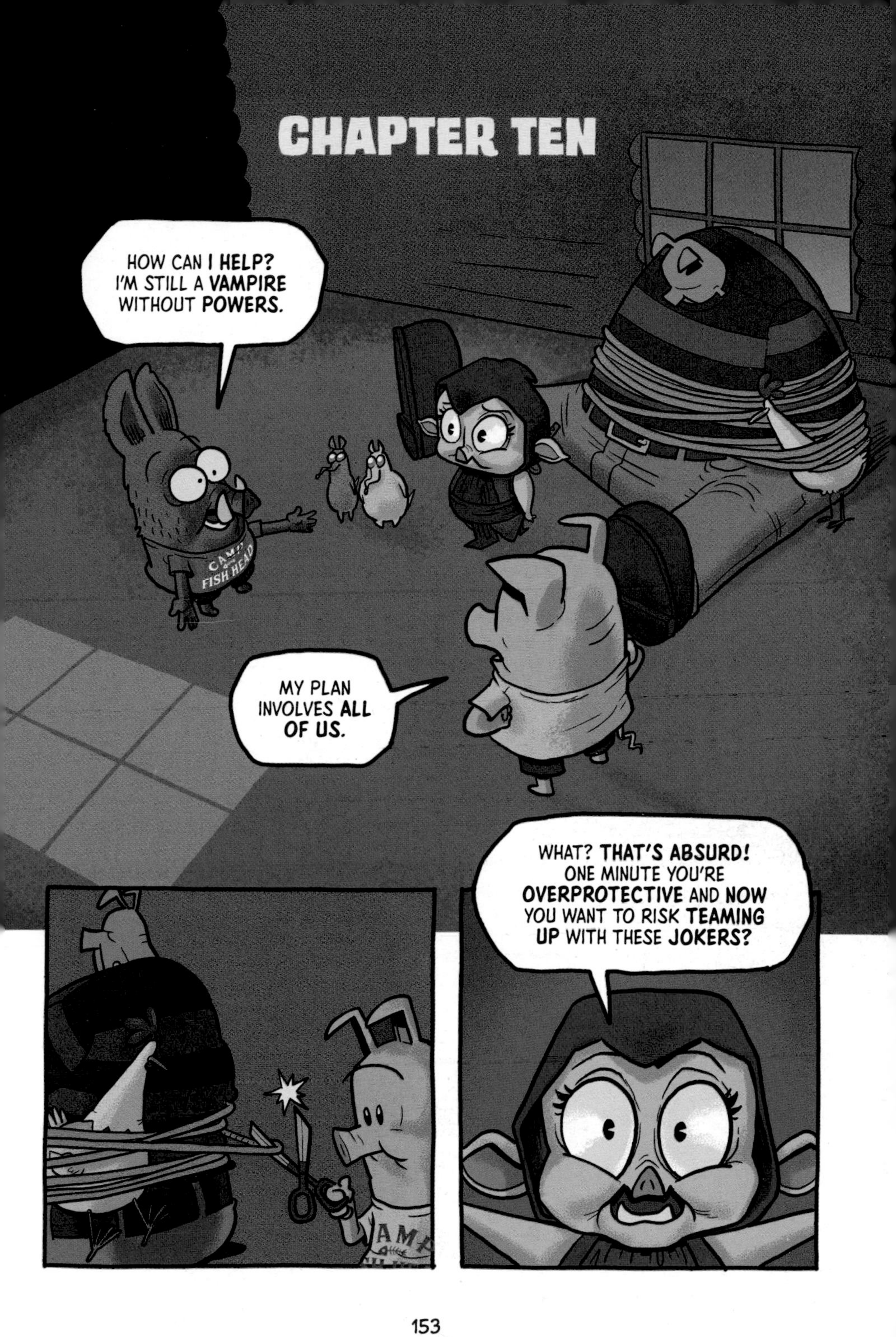
CHAPTER TEN
HOW CAN I HELP? I'M STILL A VAMPIRE WITHOUT POWERS.
CAMP FISH HEAD
MY PLAN INVOLVES ALL OF US.
WHAT? THAT'S ABSURD! ONE MINUTE YOU'RE OVERPROTECTIVE AND NOW YOU WANT TO RISK TEAMING UP WITH THESE JOKERS?

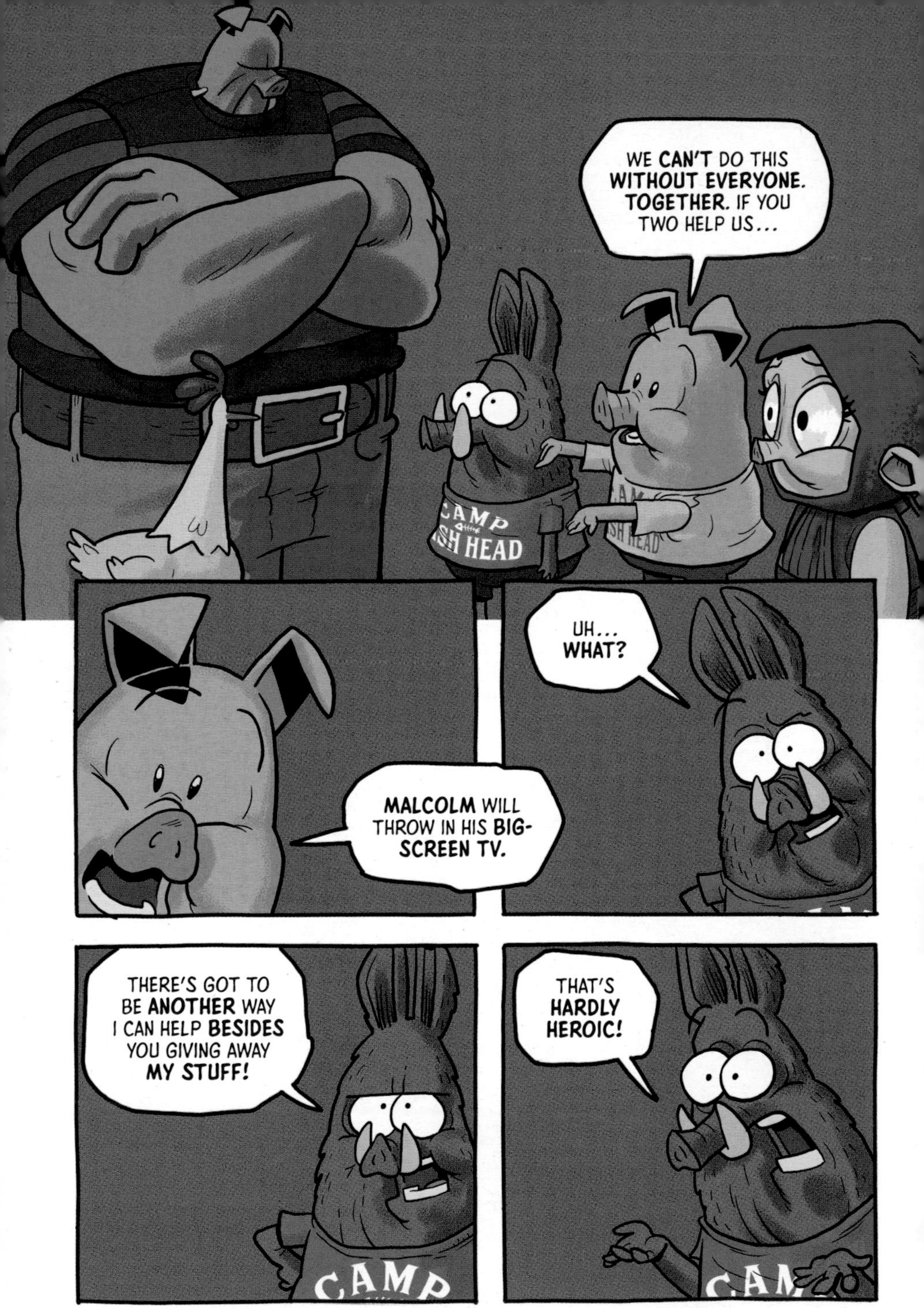
WE **CAN'T** DO THIS **WITHOUT EVERYONE. TOGETHER.** IF YOU TWO HELP US...
CAMP FISH HEAD
MALCOLM WILL THROW IN HIS **BIG-SCREEN TV.**
UH... **WHAT?**
THERE'S GOT TO BE **ANOTHER** WAY I CAN HELP **BESIDES** YOU GIVING AWAY **MY STUFF!**
THAT'S **HARDLY HEROIC!**

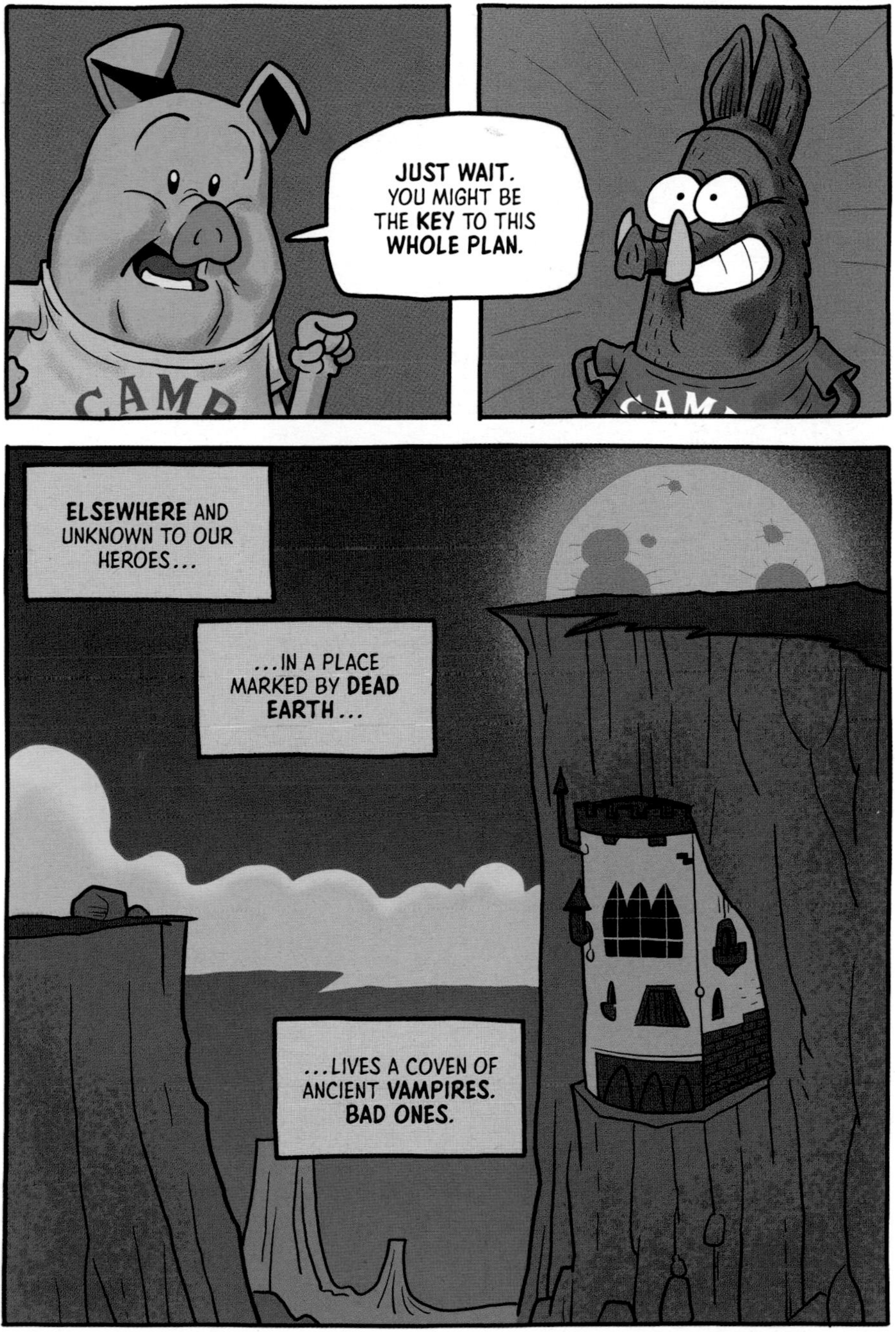
JUST WAIT. YOU MIGHT BE THE KEY TO THIS WHOLE PLAN.
CAMP
CAMP
ELSEWHERE AND UNKNOWN TO OUR HEROES...
...IN A PLACE MARKED BY DEAD EARTH...
...LIVES A COVEN OF ANCIENT VAMPIRES. BAD ONES.

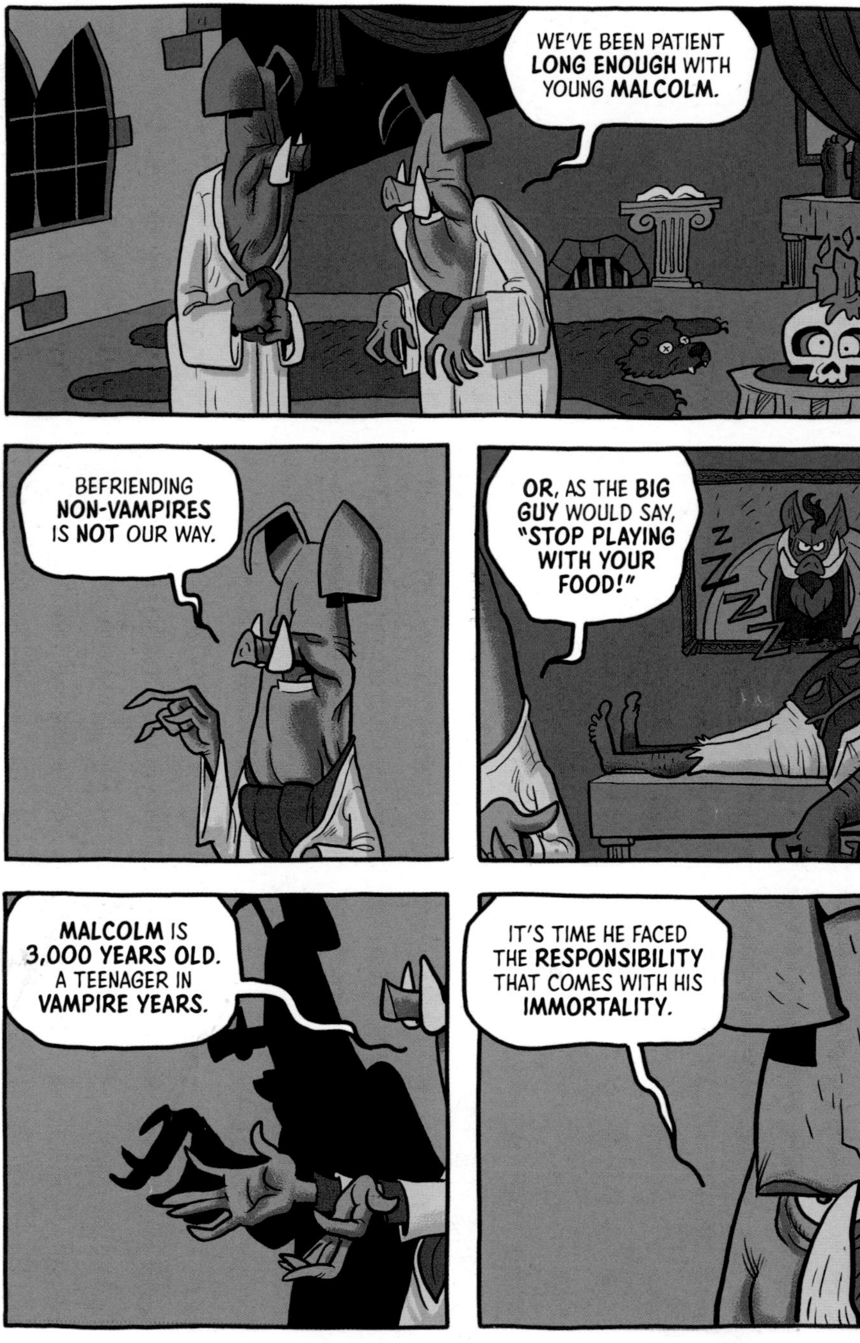
WE'VE BEEN PATIENT LONG ENOUGH WITH YOUNG MALCOLM.
BEFRIENDING NON-VAMPIRES IS NOT OUR WAY.
OR, AS THE BIG GUY WOULD SAY, "STOP PLAYING WITH YOUR FOOD!"
Z Z Z Z
MALCOLM IS 3,000 YEARS OLD. A TEENAGER IN VAMPIRE YEARS.
IT'S TIME HE FACED THE RESPONSIBILITY THAT COMES WITH HIS IMMORTALITY.

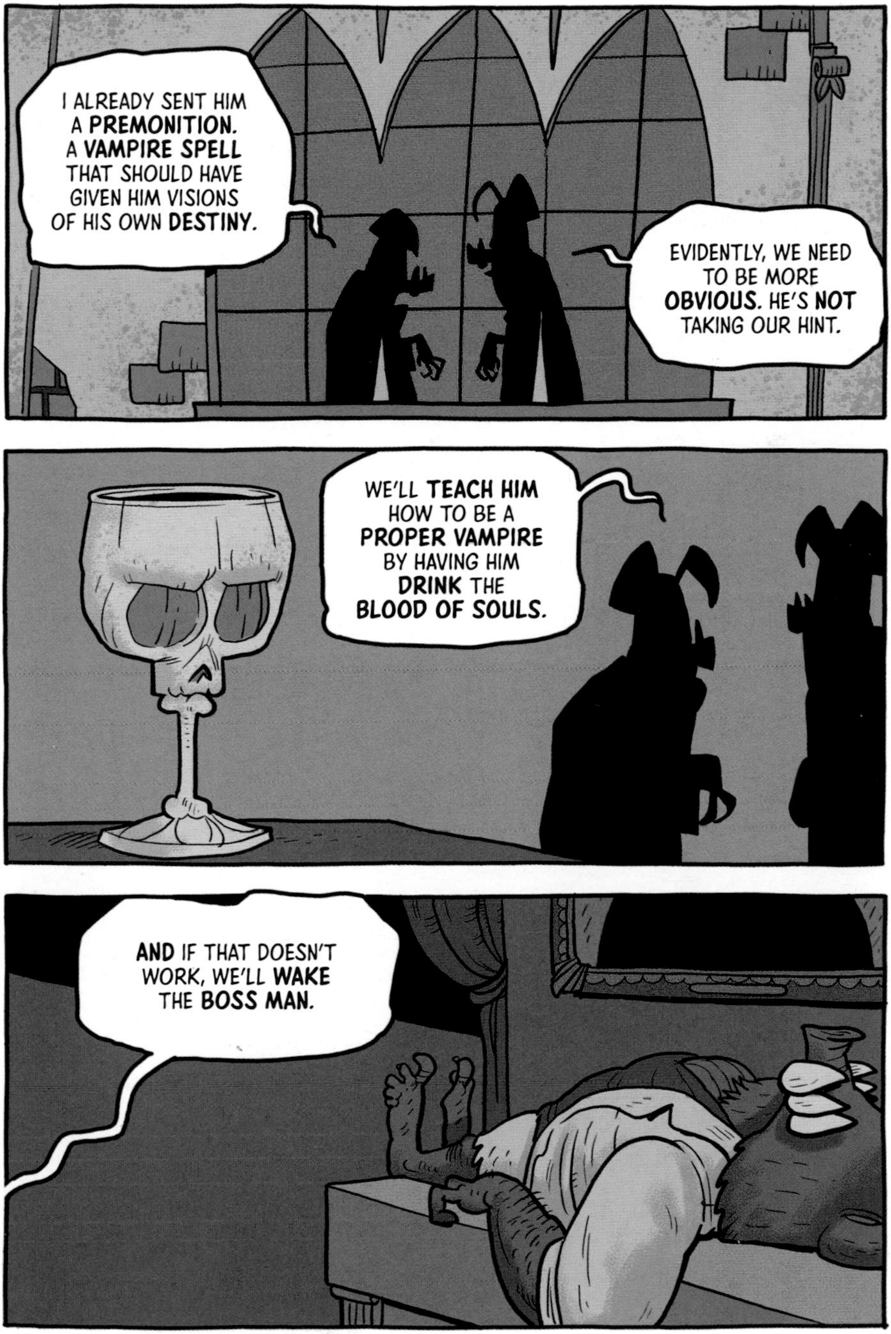
I ALREADY SENT HIM A **PREMONITION.** A **VAMPIRE SPELL** THAT SHOULD HAVE GIVEN HIM VISIONS OF HIS OWN **DESTINY.**
EVIDENTLY, WE NEED TO BE MORE **OBVIOUS.** HE'S **NOT** TAKING OUR HINT.
WE'LL **TEACH HIM** HOW TO BE A **PROPER VAMPIRE** BY HAVING HIM **DRINK** THE **BLOOD OF SOULS.**
AND IF THAT DOESN'T WORK, WE'LL **WAKE** THE **BOSS MAN.**

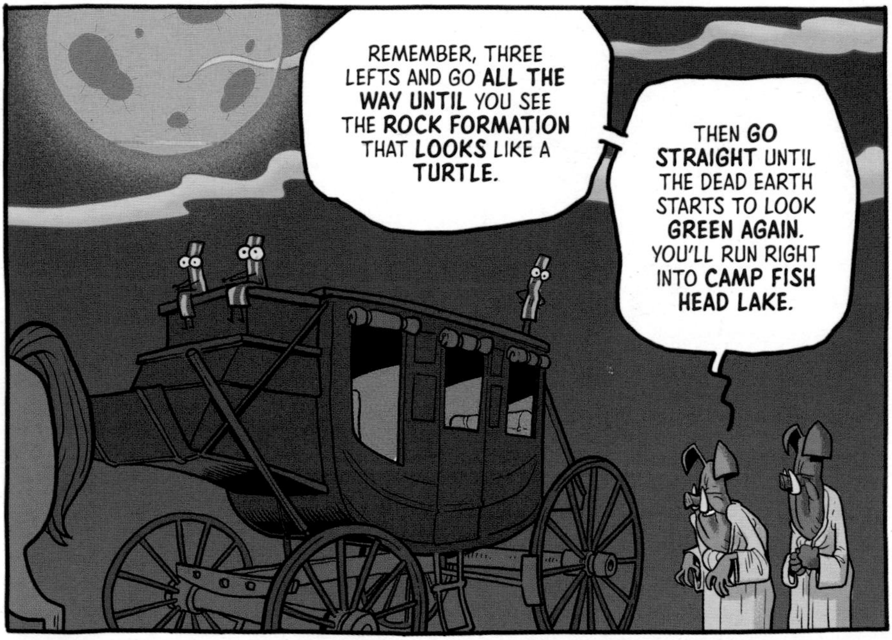
REMEMBER, THREE LEFTS AND GO ALL THE WAY UNTIL YOU SEE THE ROCK FORMATION THAT LOOKS LIKE A TURTLE.
THEN GO STRAIGHT UNTIL THE DEAD EARTH STARTS TO LOOK GREEN AGAIN. YOU'LL RUN RIGHT INTO CAMP FISH HEAD LAKE.

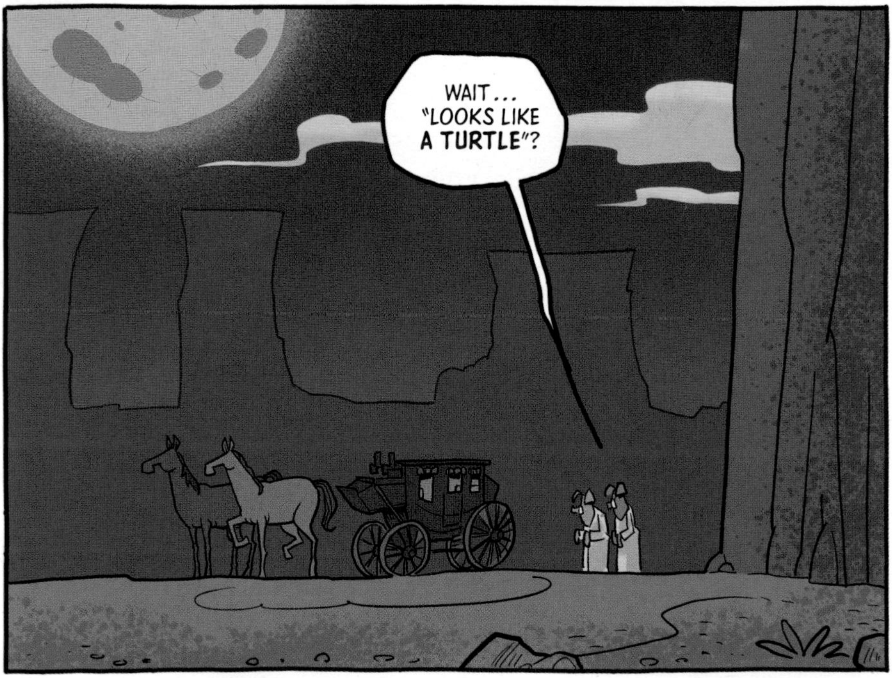
WAIT... "LOOKS LIKE A TURTLE"?

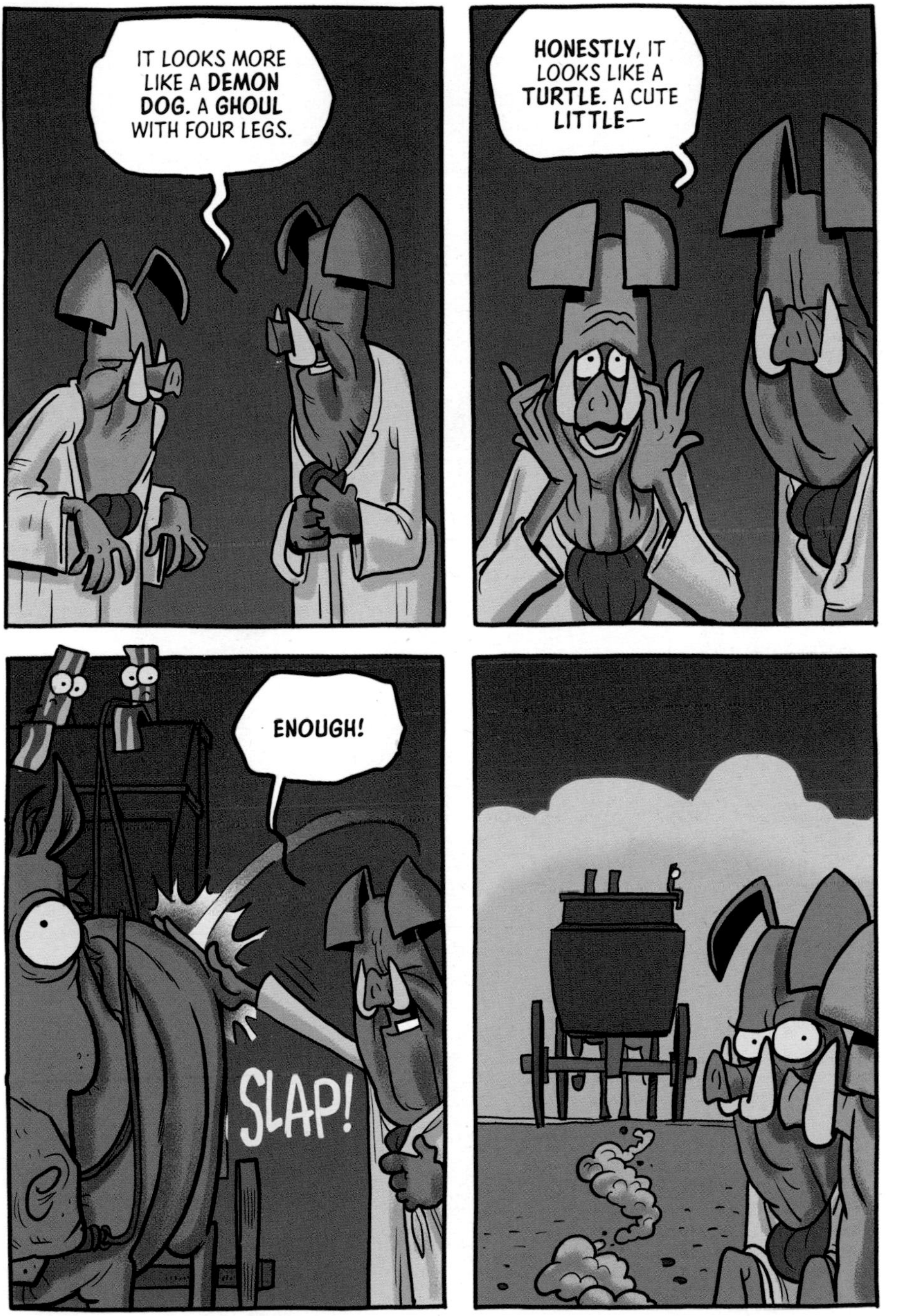
IT LOOKS MORE LIKE A **DEMON DOG.** A **GHOUL** WITH FOUR LEGS.
HONESTLY, IT LOOKS LIKE A **TURTLE.** A CUTE **LITTLE—**
ENOUGH!
SLAP!

CHAPTER ELEVEN

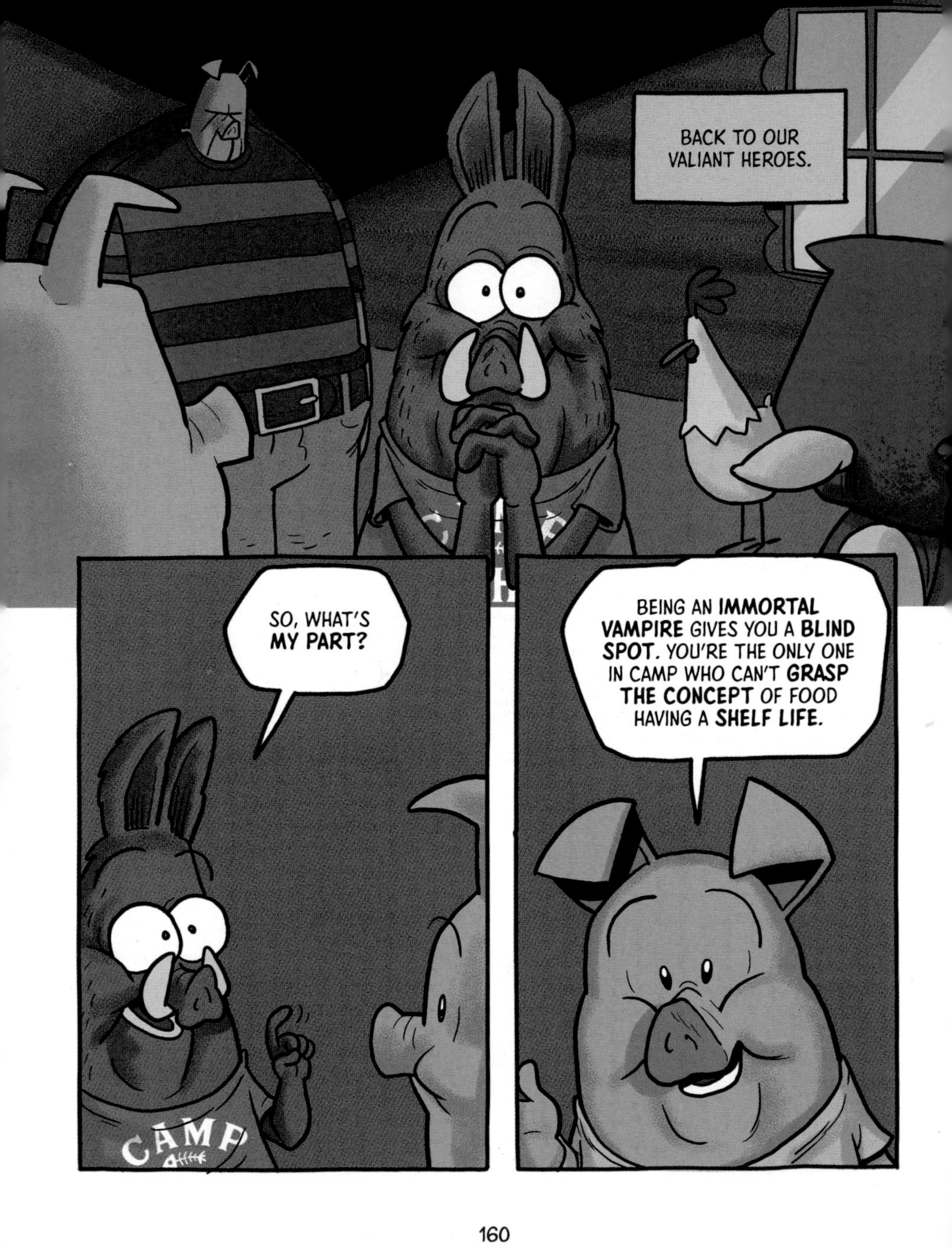
BACK TO OUR VALIANT HEROES.
SO, WHAT'S **MY PART?**
BEING AN **IMMORTAL VAMPIRE** GIVES YOU A **BLIND SPOT**. YOU'RE THE ONLY ONE IN CAMP WHO CAN'T **GRASP THE CONCEPT** OF FOOD HAVING A **SHELF LIFE**.
CAMP

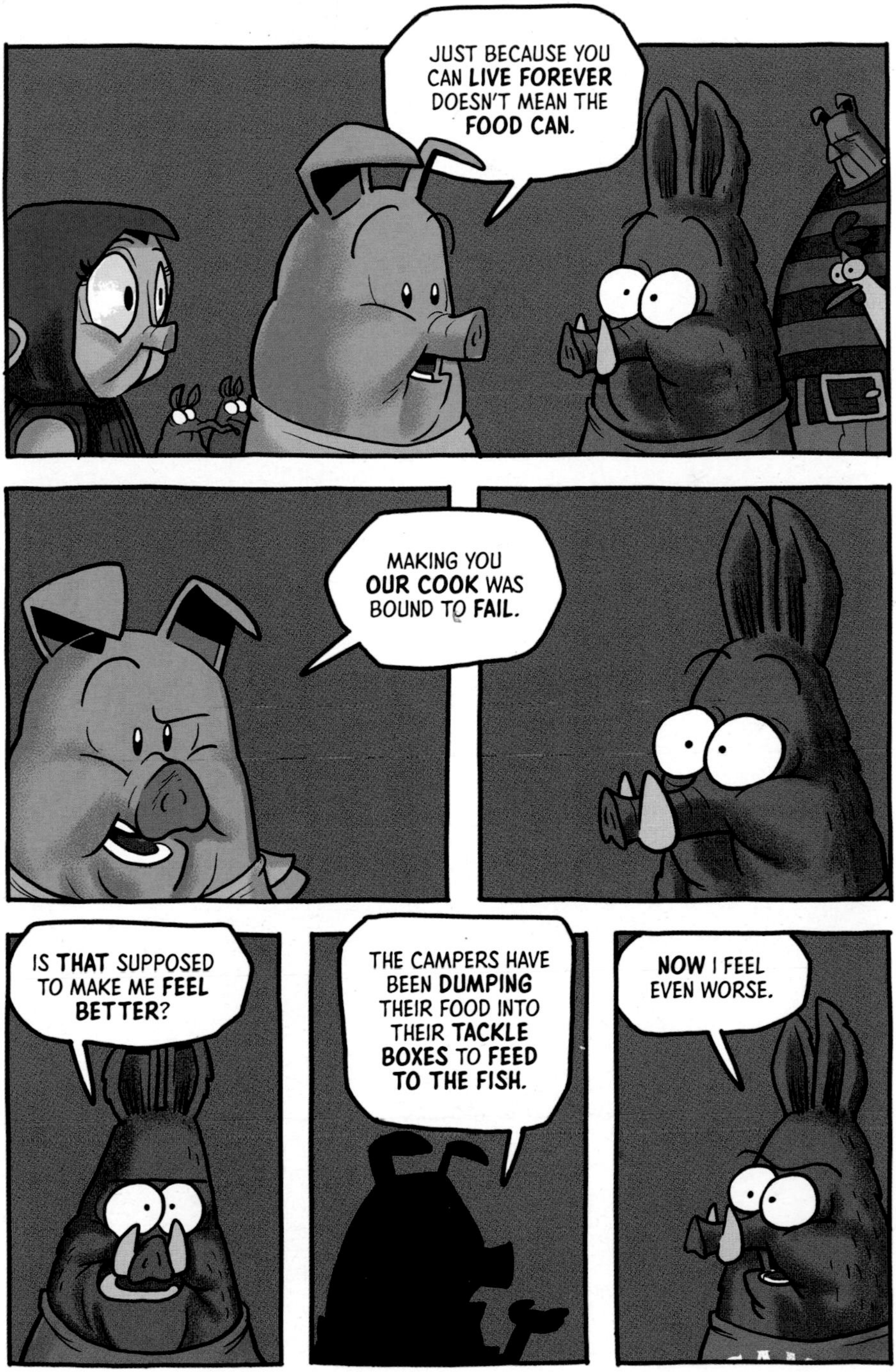
JUST BECAUSE YOU CAN LIVE FOREVER DOESN'T MEAN THE FOOD CAN.
MAKING YOU OUR COOK WAS BOUND TO FAIL.
IS THAT SUPPOSED TO MAKE ME FEEL BETTER?
THE CAMPERS HAVE BEEN DUMPING THEIR FOOD INTO THEIR TACKLE BOXES TO FEED TO THE FISH.
NOW I FEEL EVEN WORSE.

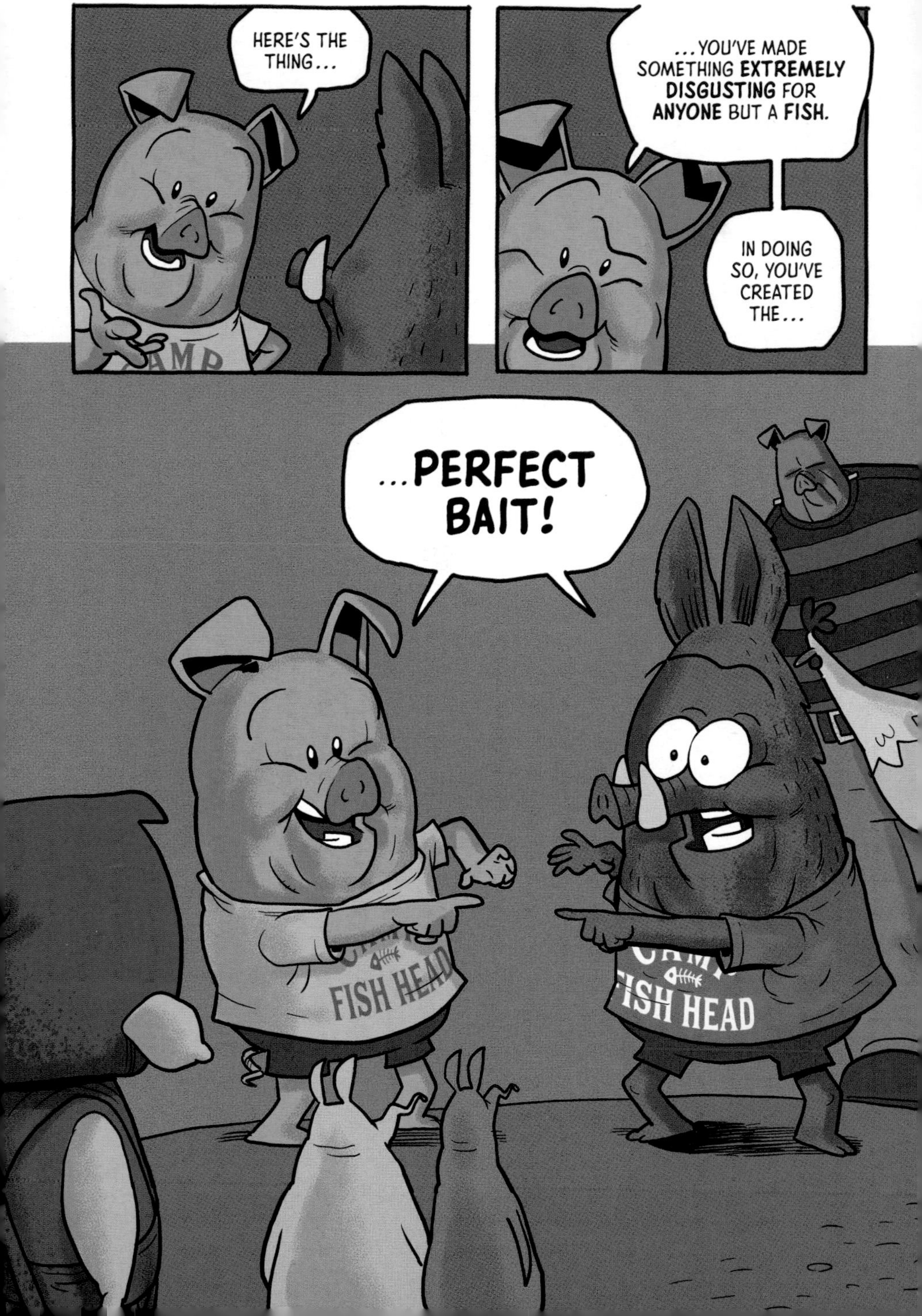
HERE'S THE THING...
...YOU'VE MADE SOMETHING **EXTREMELY DISGUSTING** FOR **ANYONE** BUT A **FISH.**
IN DOING SO, YOU'VE CREATED THE...
...**PERFECT BAIT!**
FISH HEAD
FISH HEAD

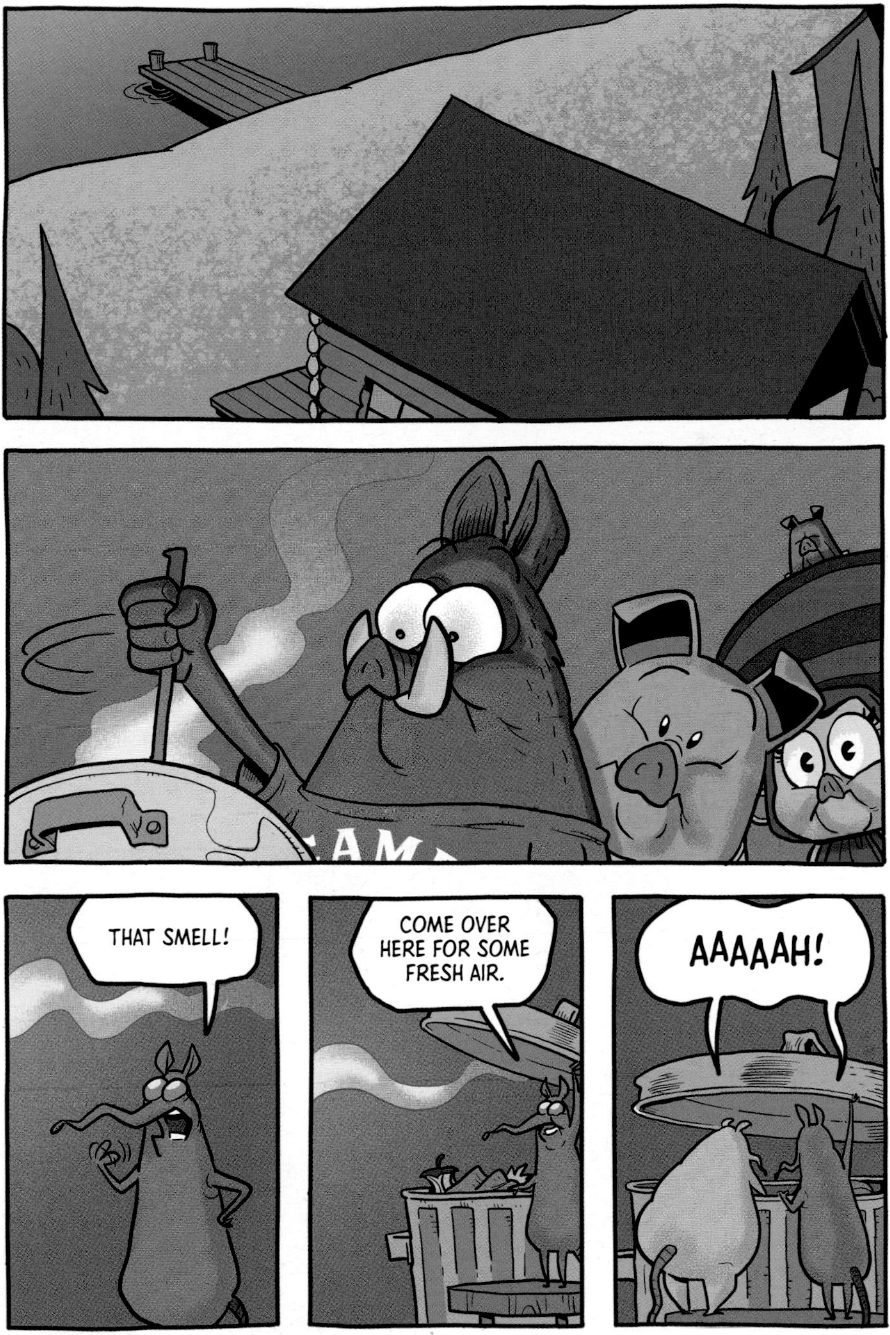

THAT SMELL!
COME OVER HERE FOR SOME FRESH AIR.
AAAAAH!

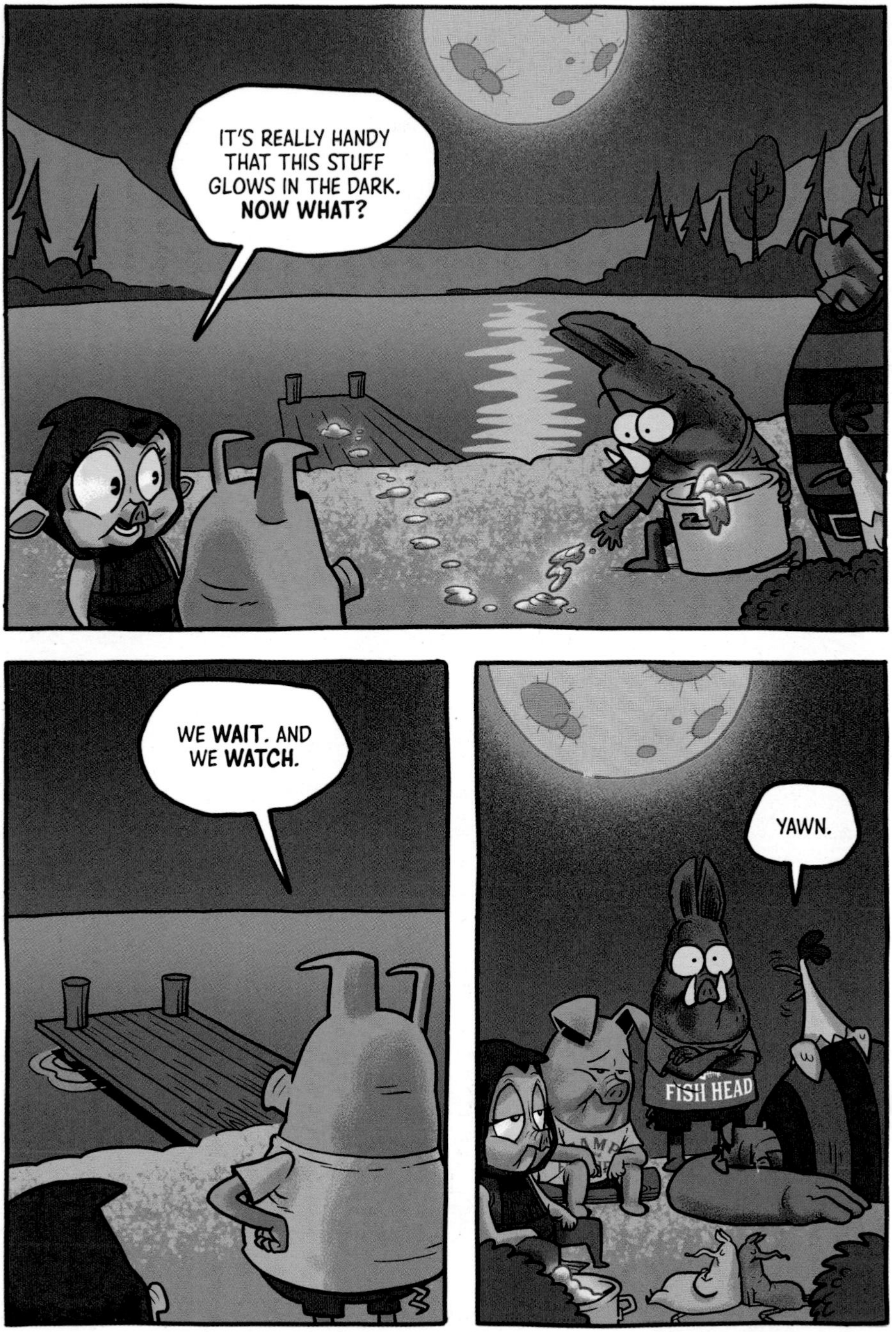
IT'S REALLY HANDY THAT THIS STUFF GLOWS IN THE DARK. **NOW WHAT?**
WE **WAIT**. AND WE **WATCH**.
YAWN.
FISH HEAD

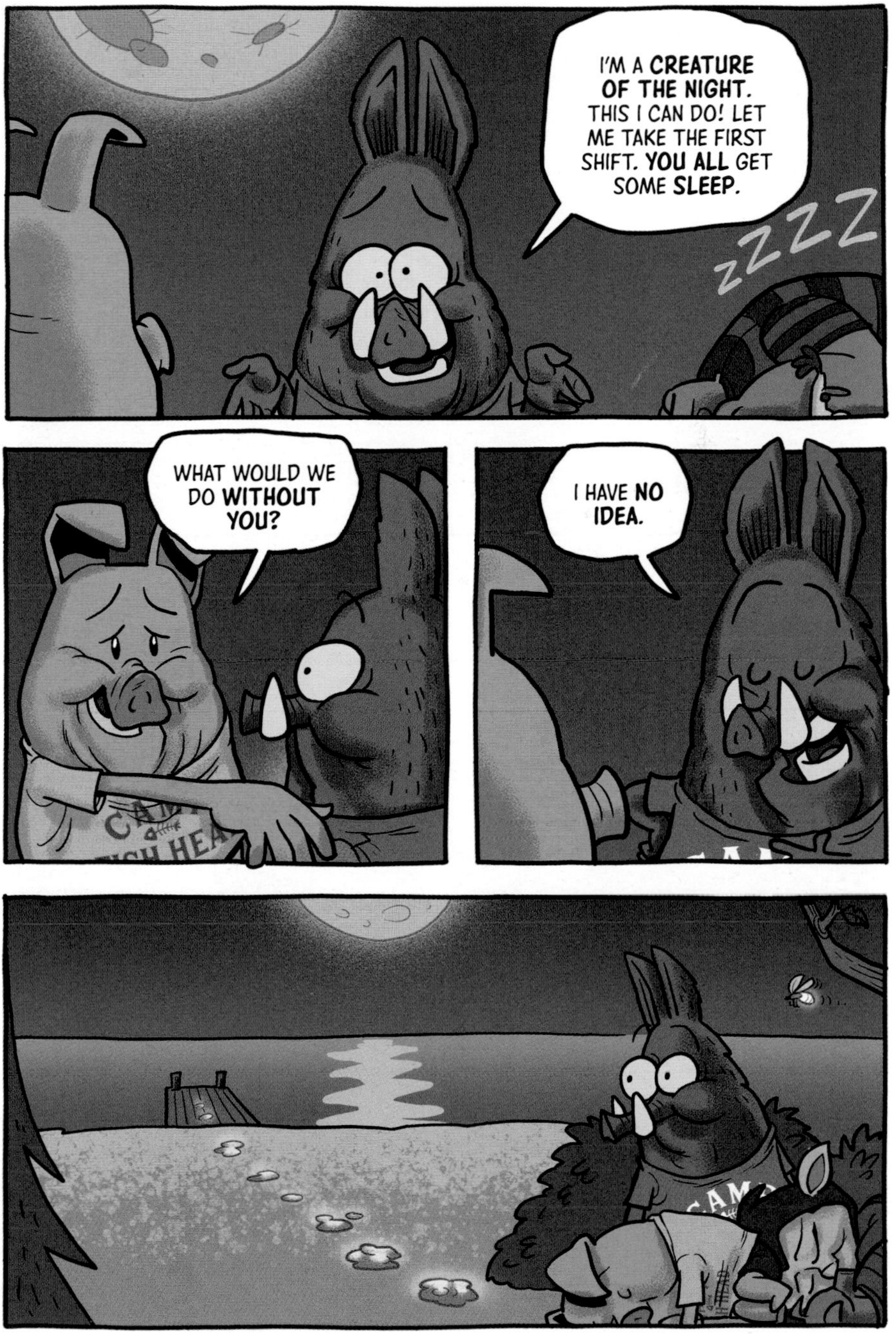
I'M A **CREATURE OF THE NIGHT.** THIS I CAN DO! LET ME TAKE THE FIRST SHIFT. **YOU ALL** GET SOME **SLEEP.**
zZZZ
WHAT WOULD WE DO **WITHOUT YOU?**
I HAVE **NO IDEA.**

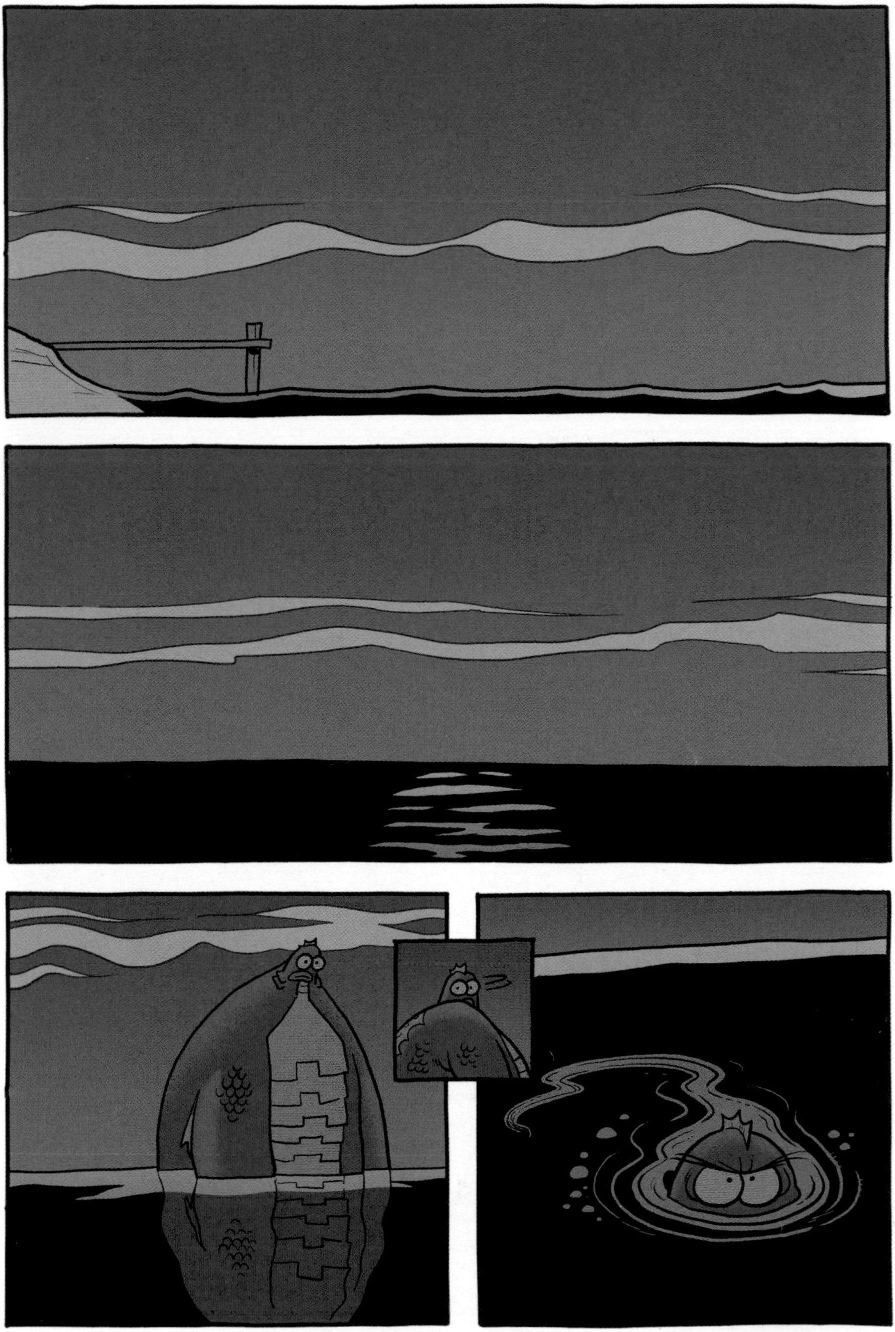

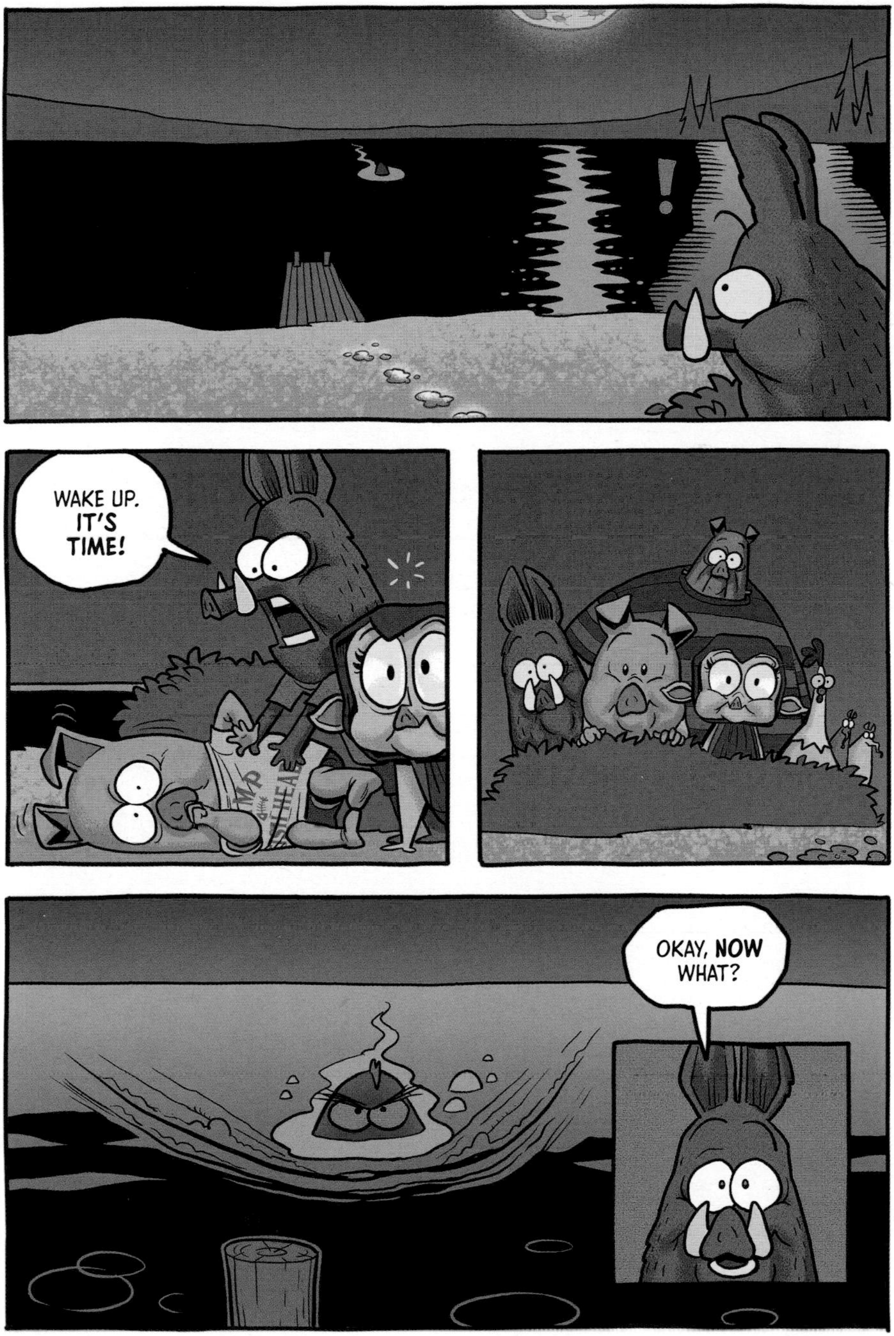
!
WAKE UP. IT'S TIME!
OKAY, NOW WHAT?

TOGETHER WE'LL OVERPOWER HIM.
PASS.
I LIKE A GOOD FIGHT, BUT HOW DO YOU KNOW WE CAN BEAT IT?
IT PUNCHED OUT CHAD IN TWO SECONDS FLAT.
UM... OPTIMISM?

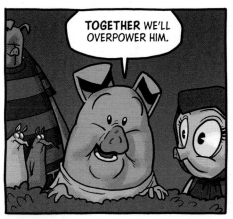

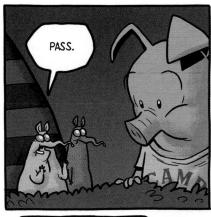

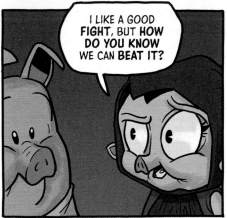

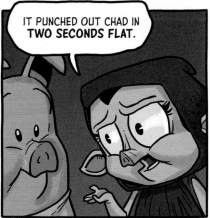

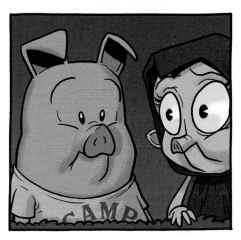

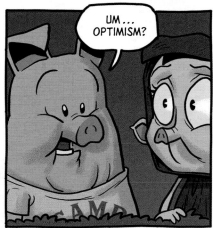

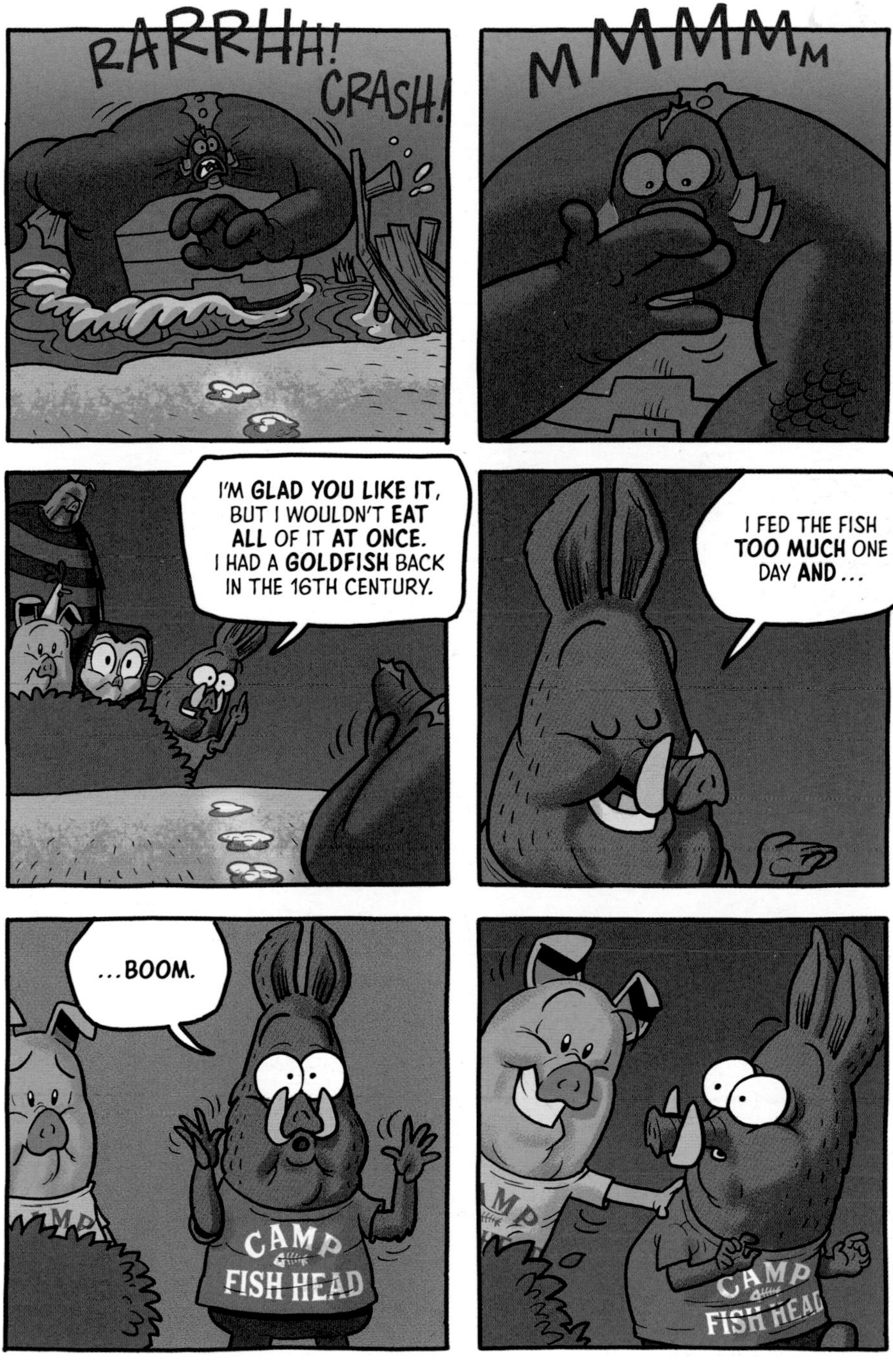
RARRHH!
CRASH!
MMMMMm
I'M GLAD YOU LIKE IT, BUT I WOULDN'T EAT ALL OF IT AT ONCE. I HAD A GOLDFISH BACK IN THE 16TH CENTURY.
I FED THE FISH TOO MUCH ONE DAY AND...
...BOOM.
CAMP FISH HEAD
CAMP FISH HEAD

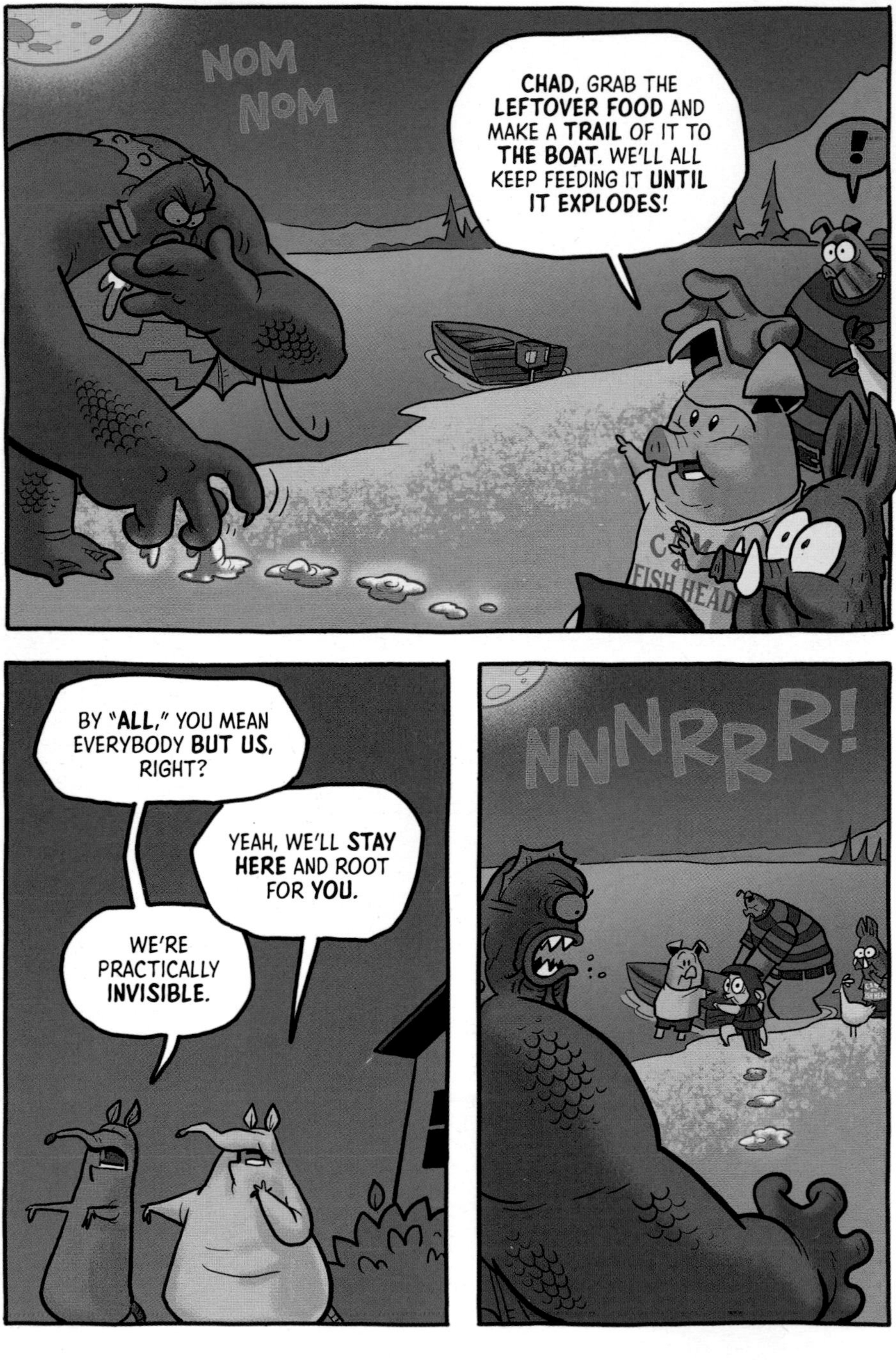
NOM NOM
CHAD, GRAB THE LEFTOVER FOOD AND MAKE A TRAIL OF IT TO THE BOAT. WE'LL ALL KEEP FEEDING IT UNTIL IT EXPLODES!
!
CAMP FISH HEAD
BY "ALL," YOU MEAN EVERYBODY BUT US, RIGHT?
YEAH, WE'LL STAY HERE AND ROOT FOR YOU.
WE'RE PRACTICALLY INVISIBLE.
NNNRRR!

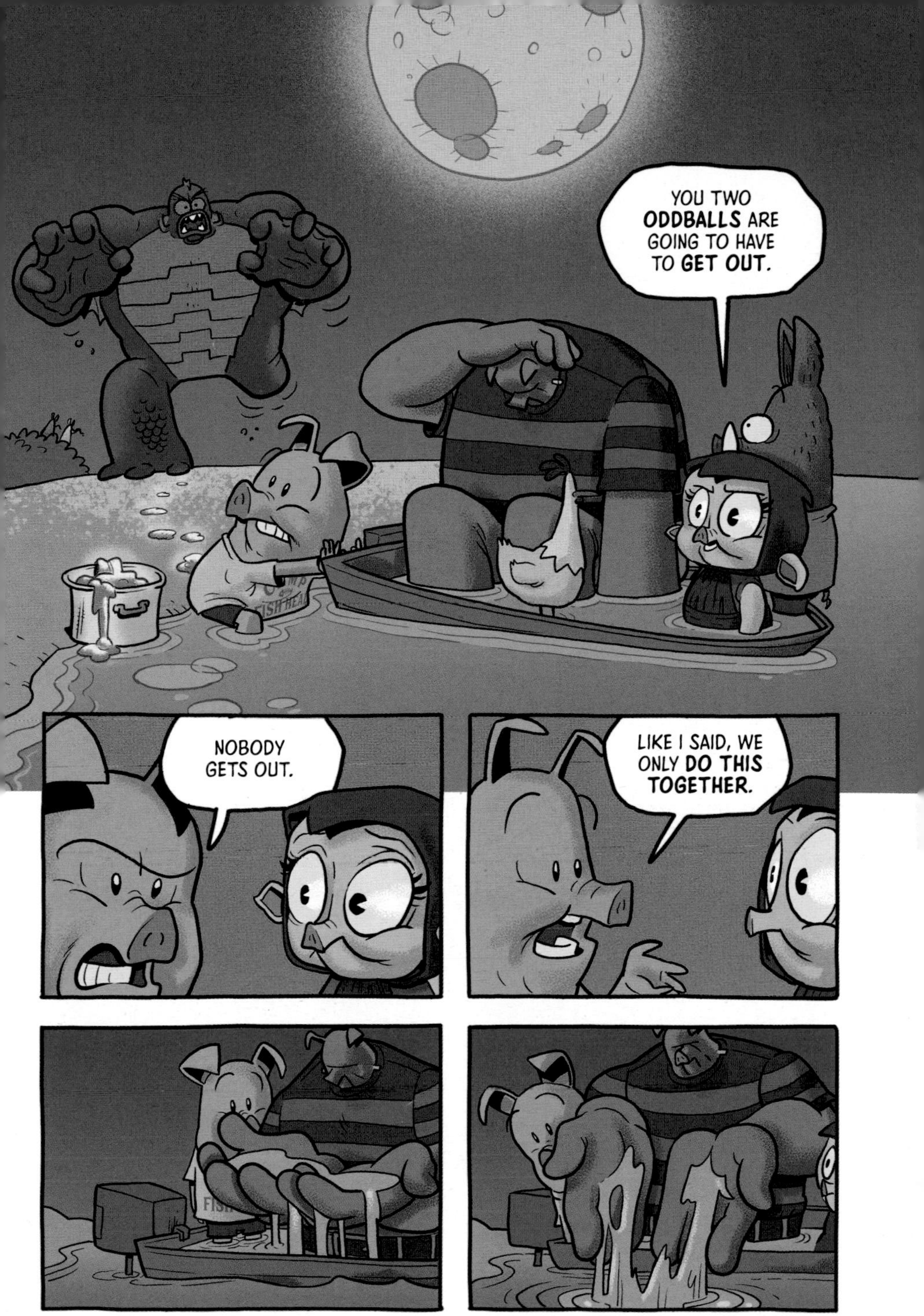
YOU TWO ODDBALLS ARE GOING TO HAVE TO GET OUT.
NOBODY GETS OUT.
LIKE I SAID, WE ONLY DO THIS TOGETHER.

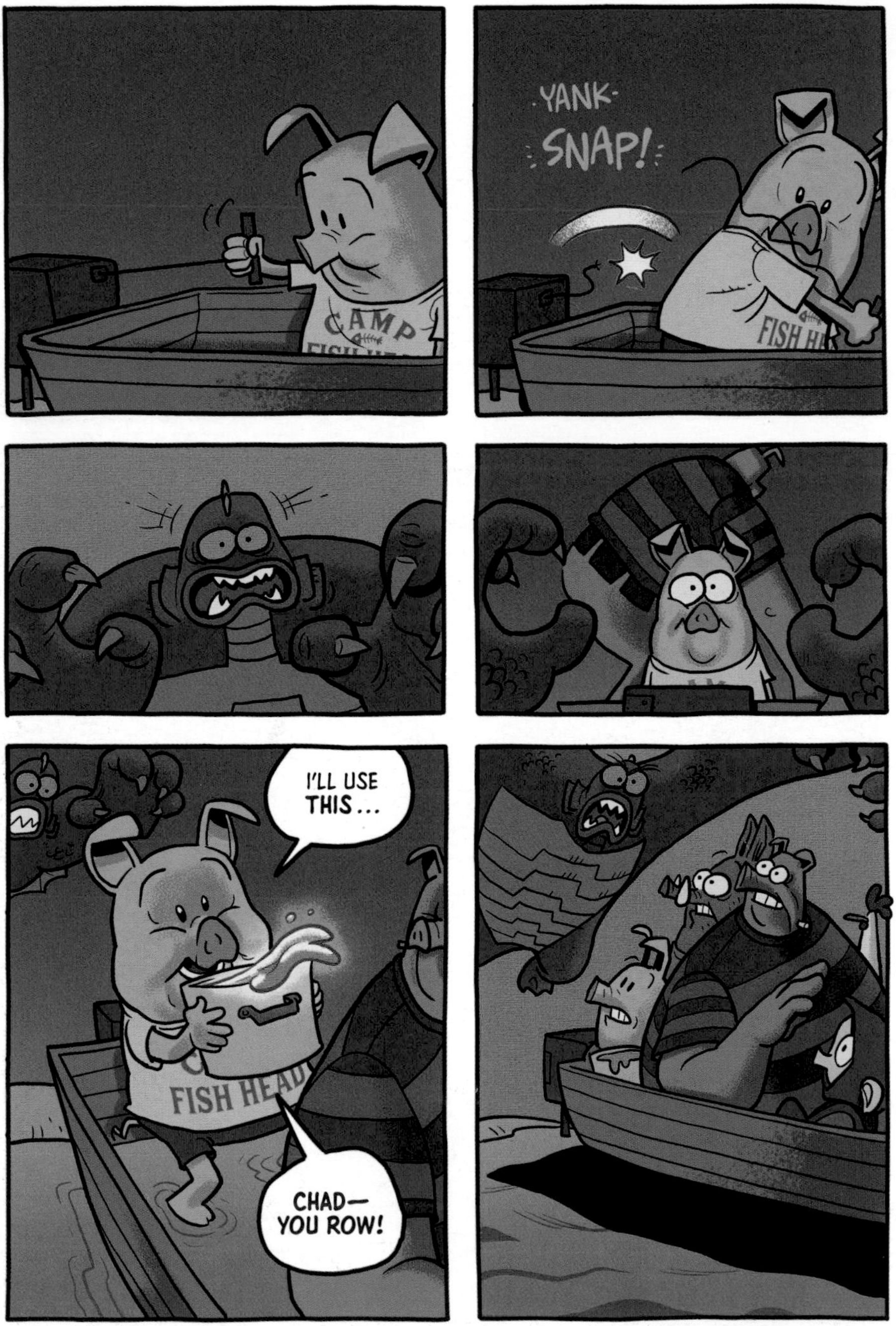
YANK
SNAP!
I'LL USE THIS...
CHAD— YOU ROW!

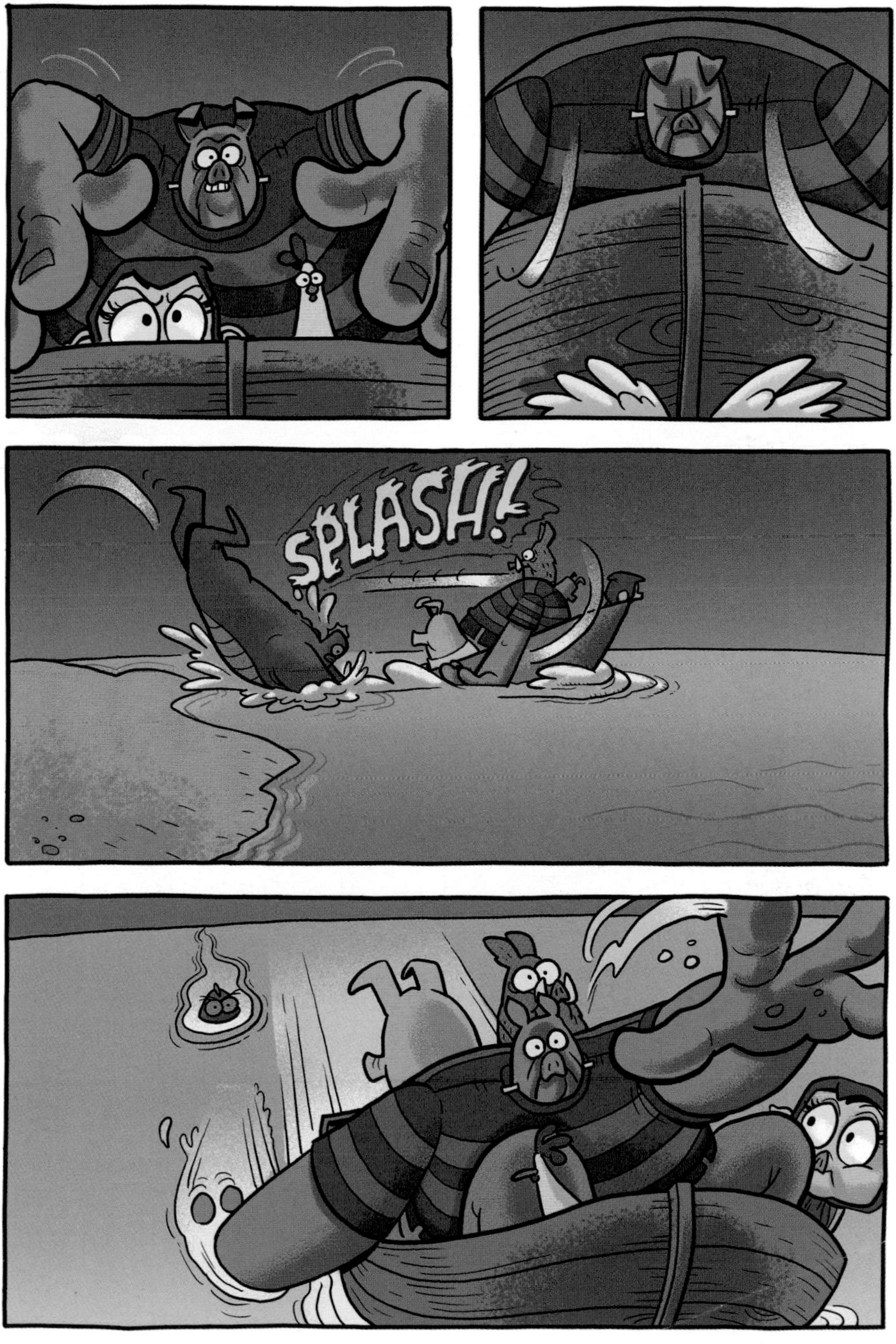
SPLASH!

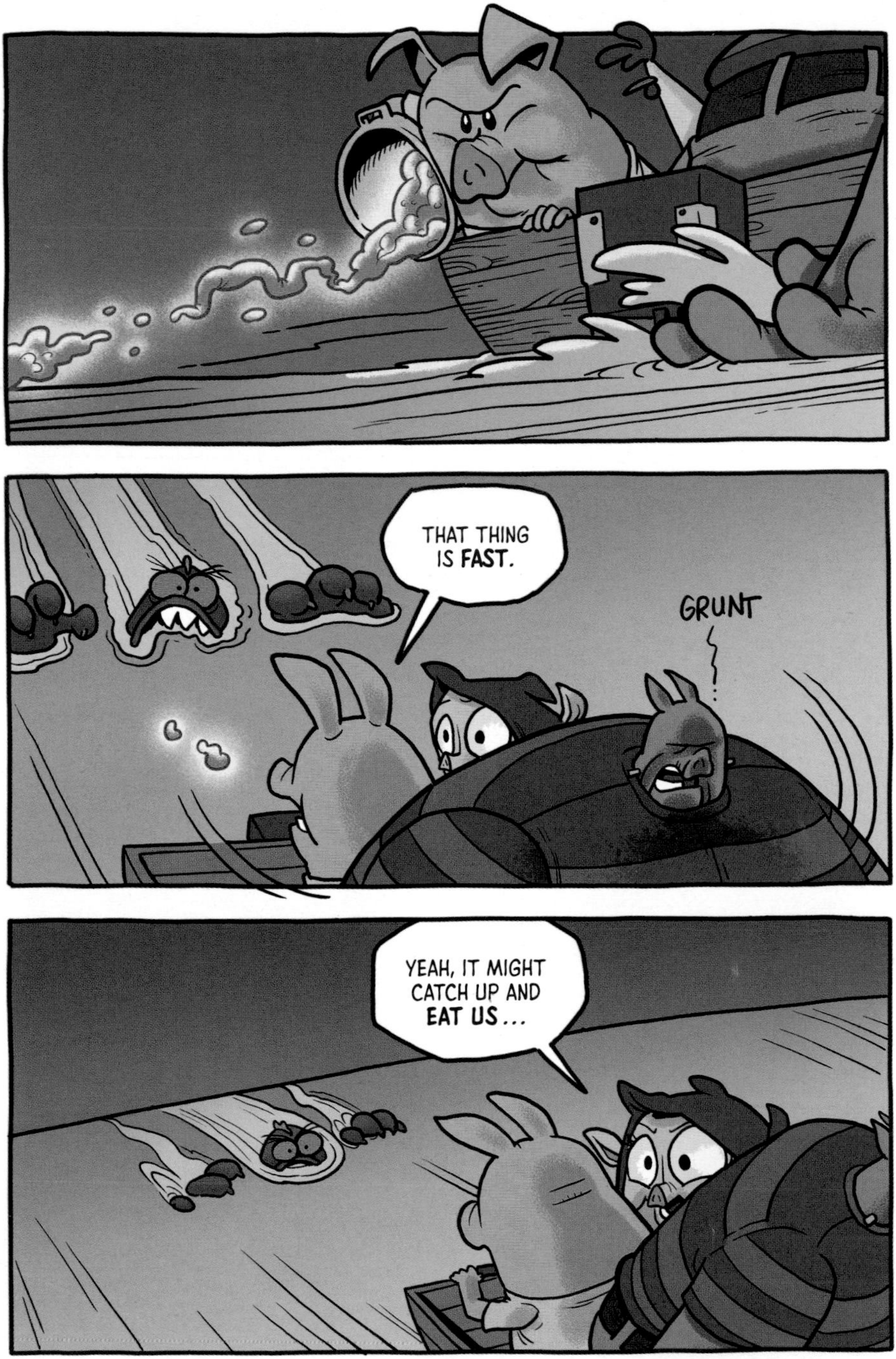
THAT THING IS **FAST**.
GRUNT
YEAH, IT MIGHT CATCH UP AND **EAT US**...

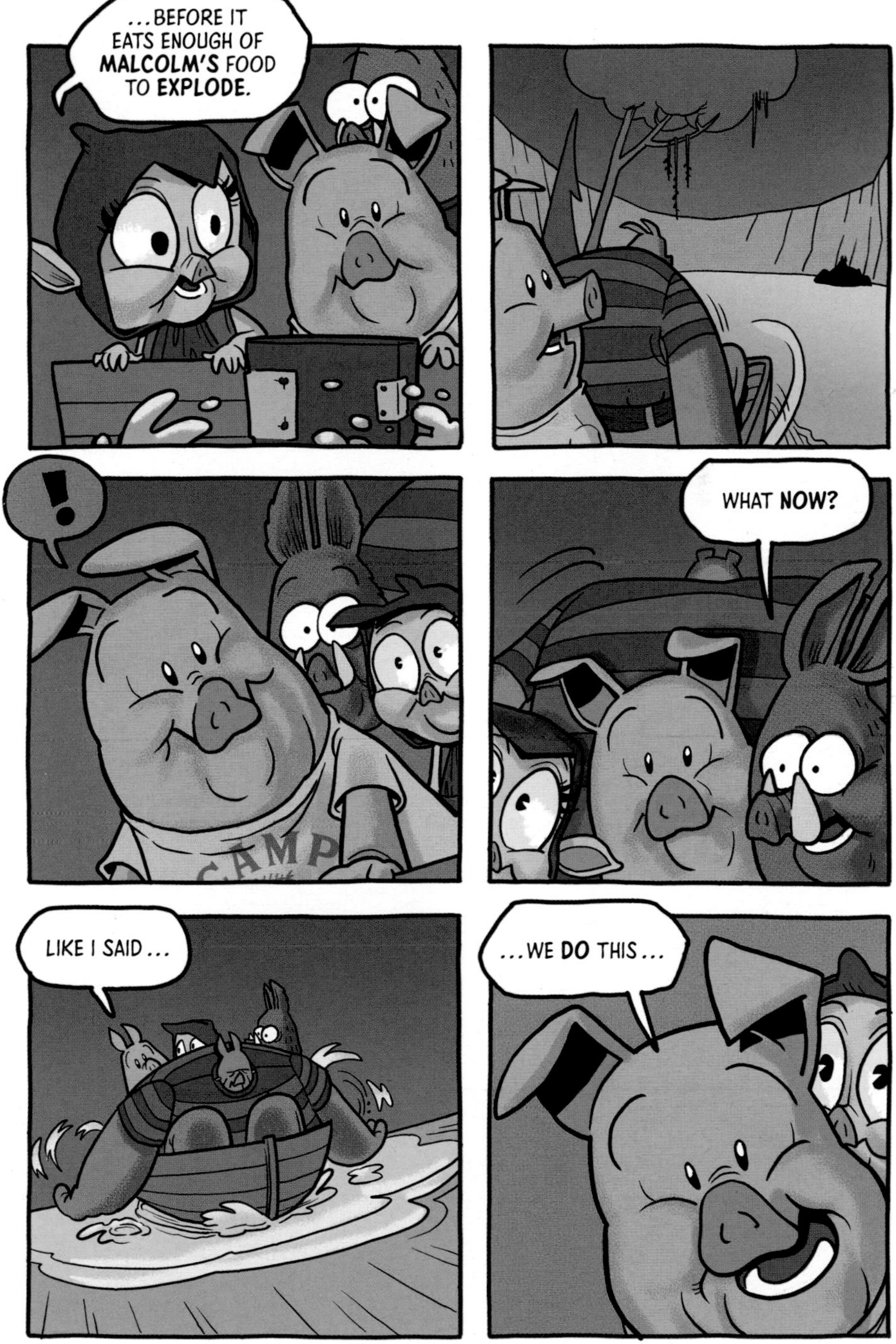

...BEFORE IT EATS ENOUGH OF MALCOLM'S FOOD TO EXPLODE.
!
WHAT NOW?
LIKE I SAID...
...WE DO THIS...

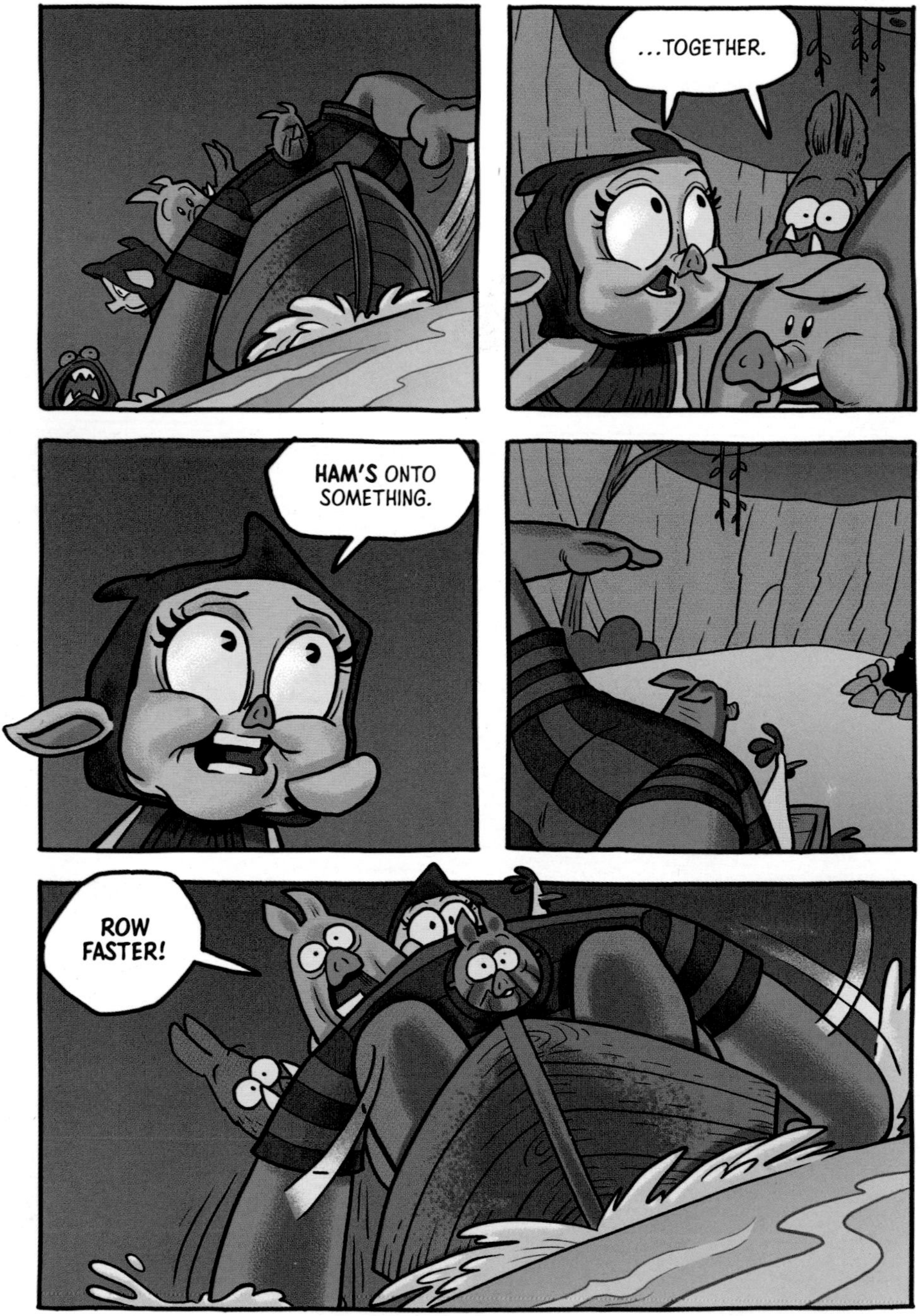
...TOGETHER.
HAM'S ONTO SOMETHING.
ROW FASTER!

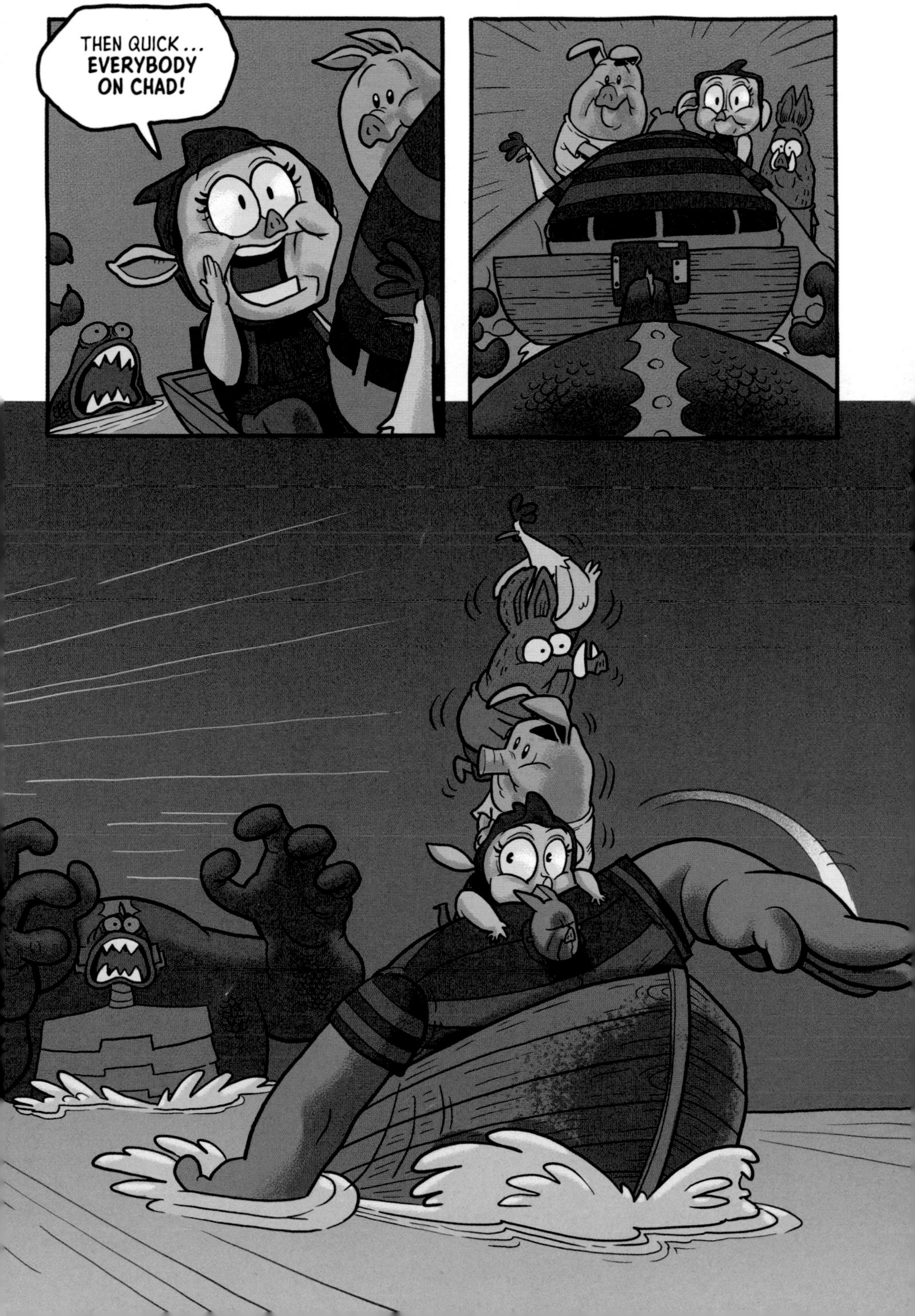
THEN QUICK...
EVERYBODY
ON CHAD!

CHAPTER TWELVE

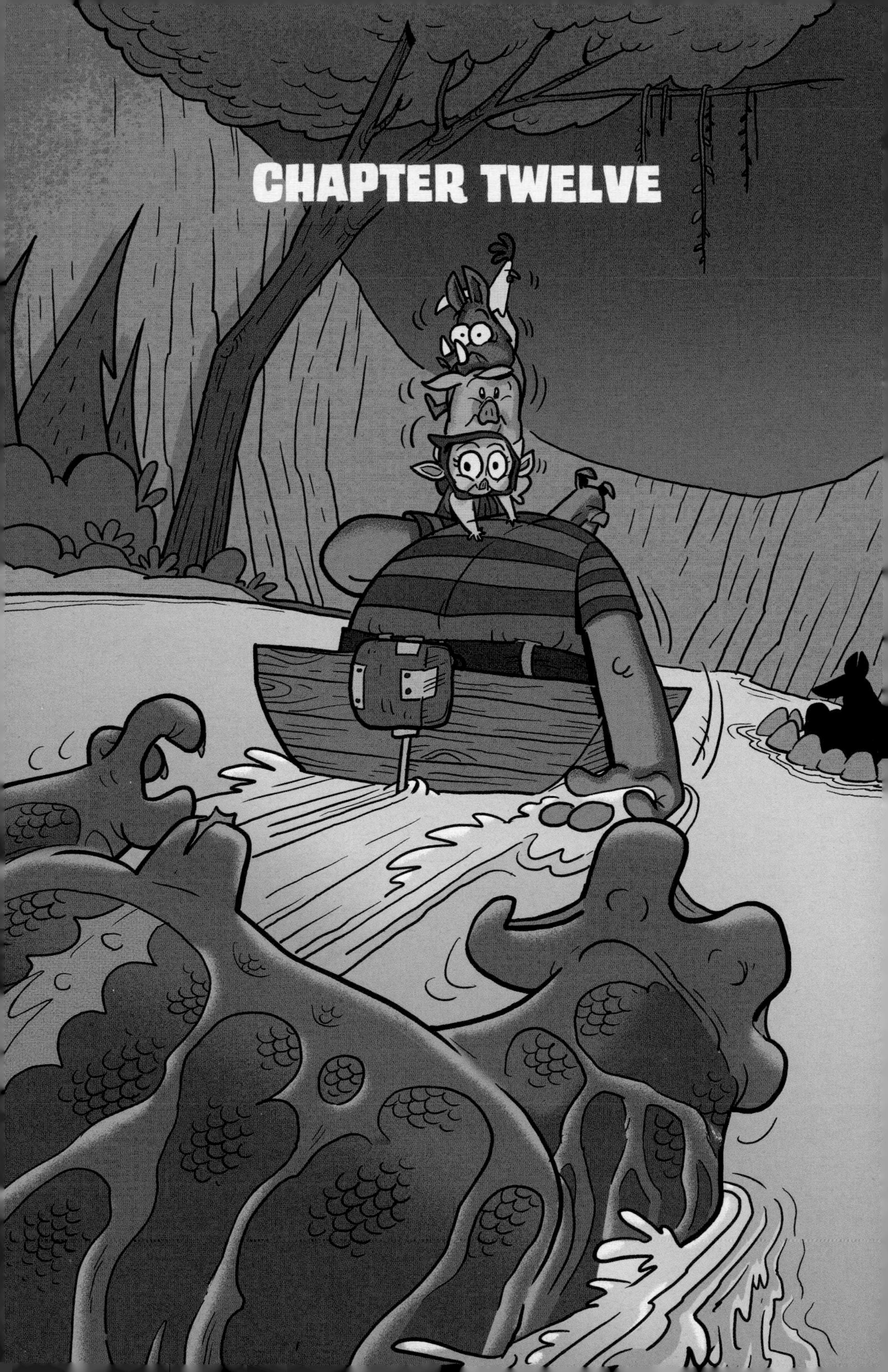

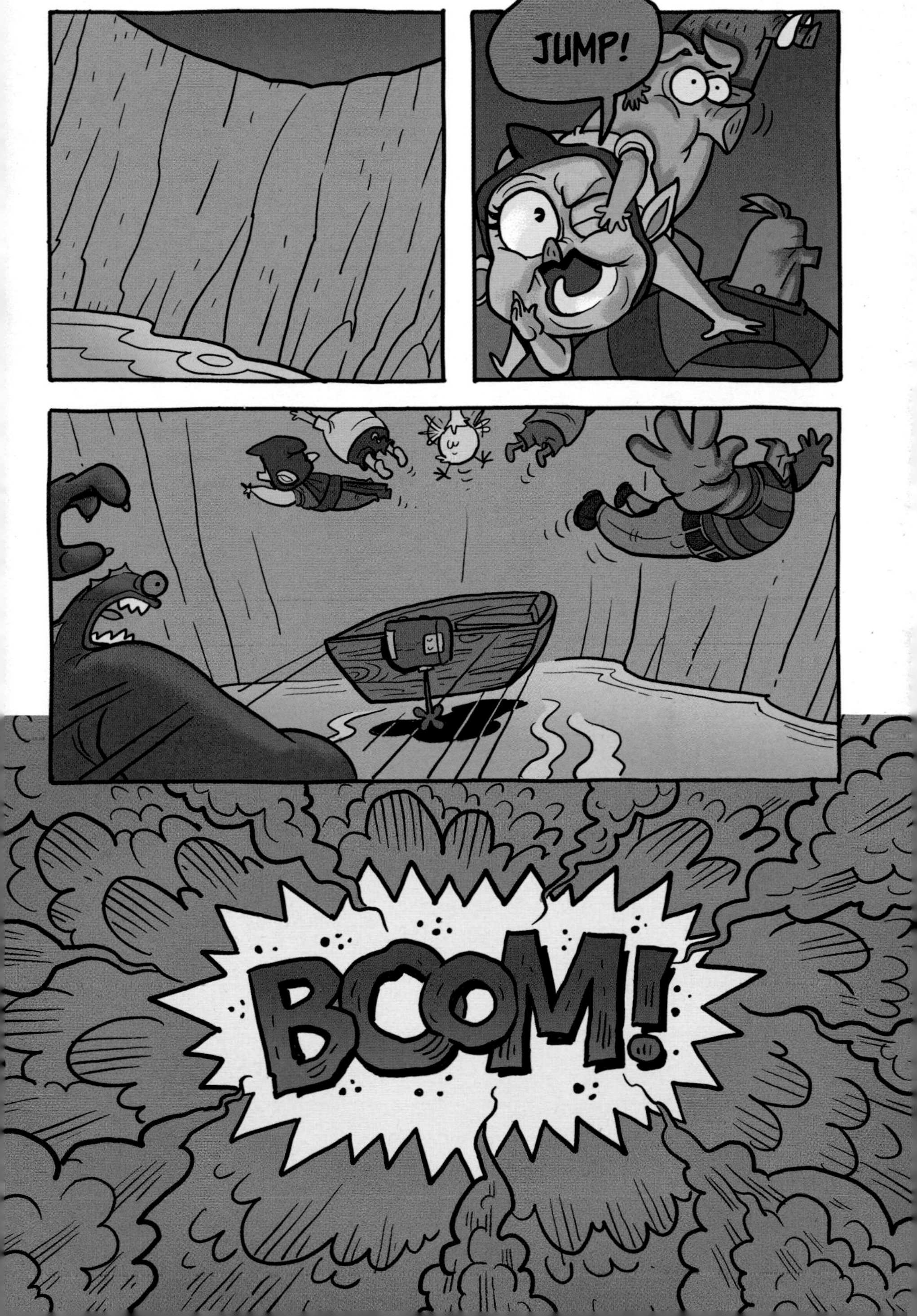
JUMP!
BOOM!

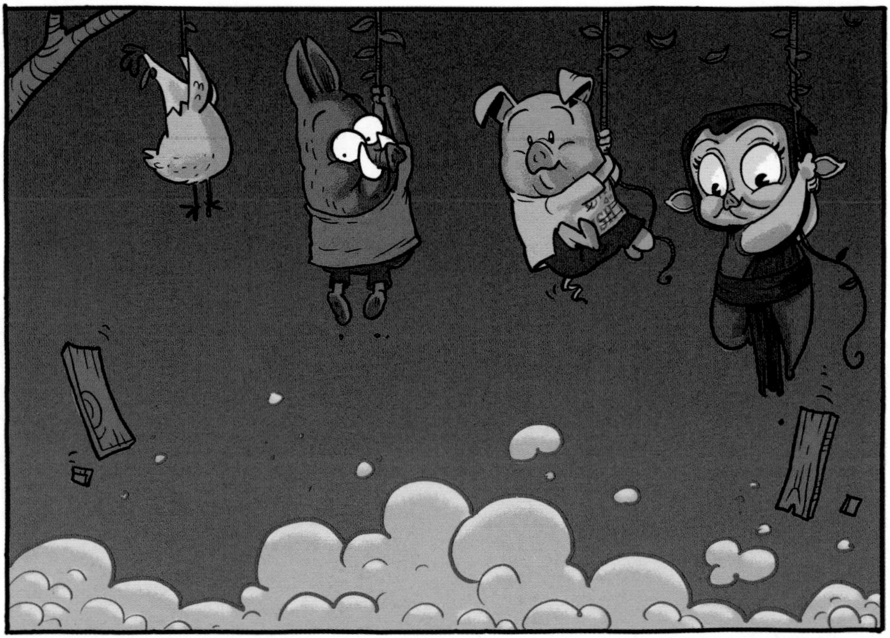

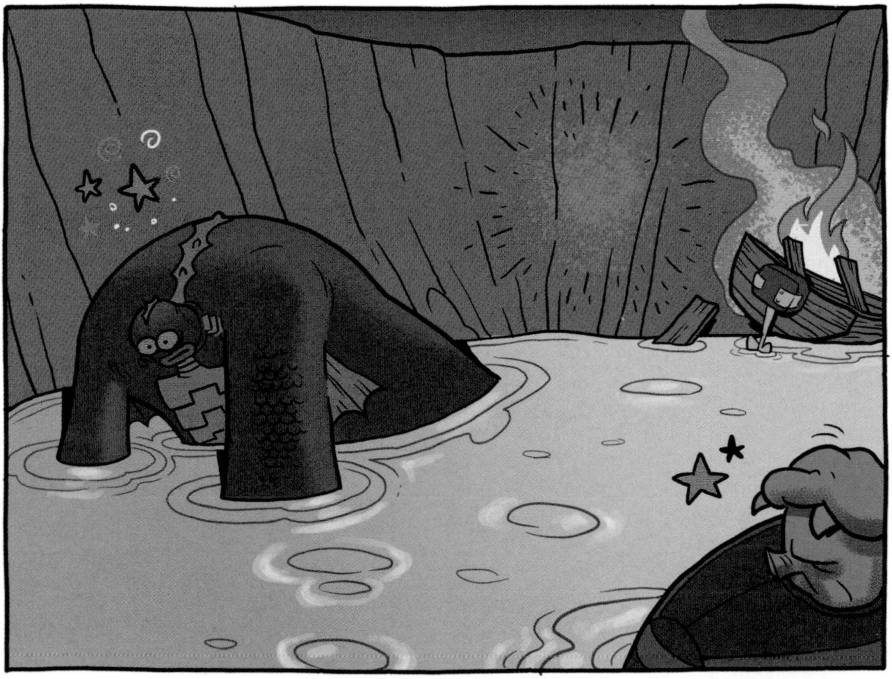

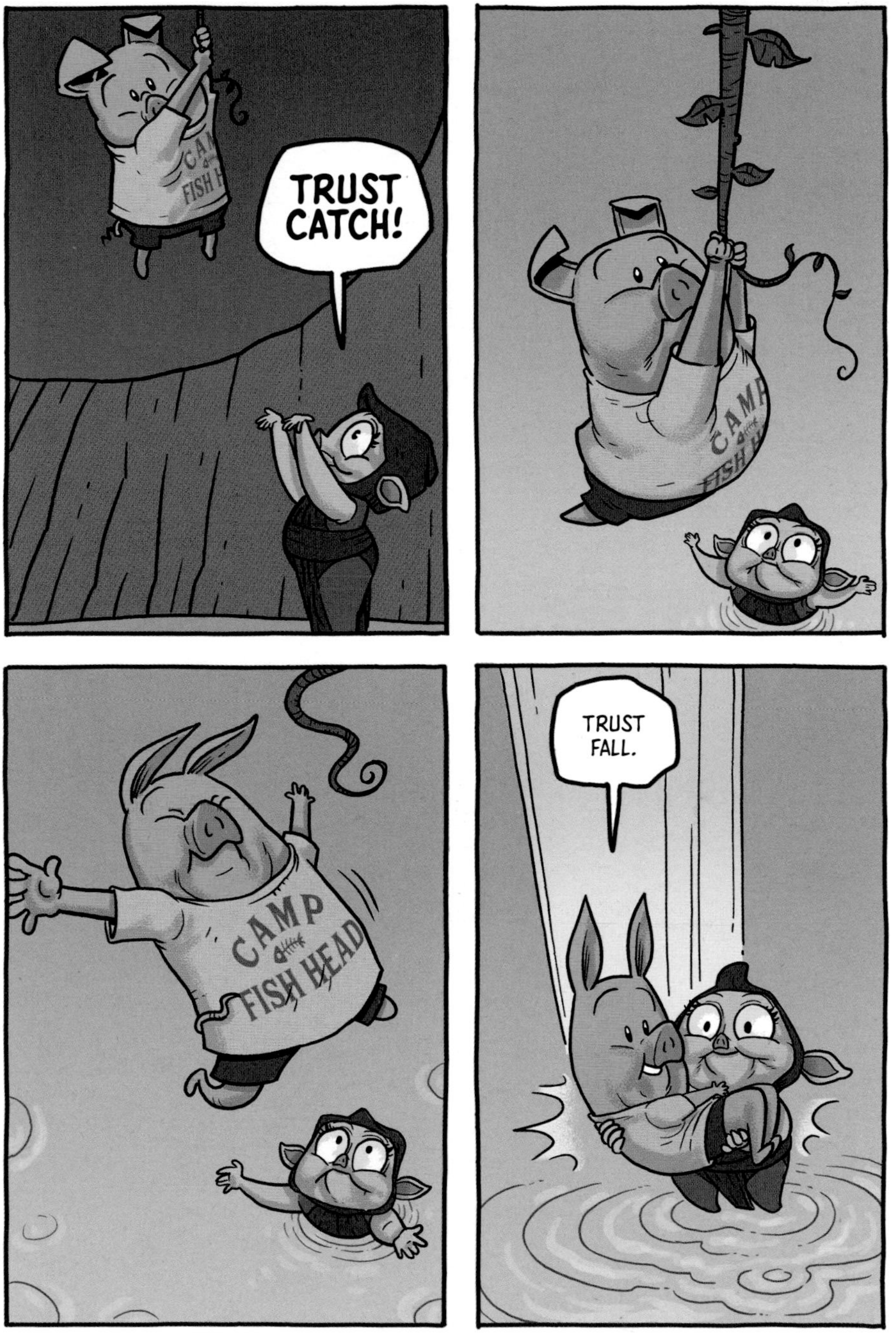

TRUST CATCH!
CAMP FISH HEAD
TRUST FALL.

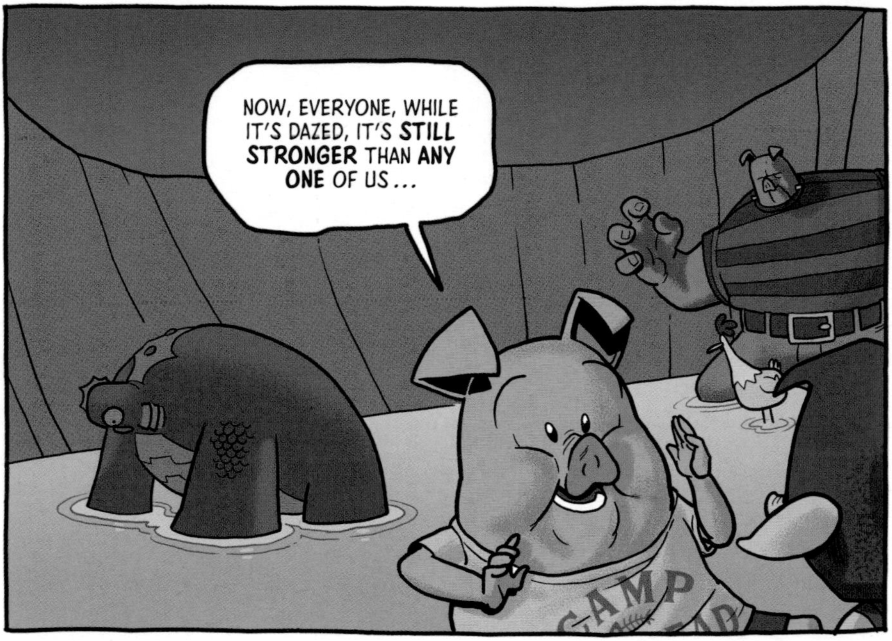
NOW, EVERYONE, WHILE IT'S DAZED, IT'S **STILL STRONGER** THAN **ANY ONE** OF US...

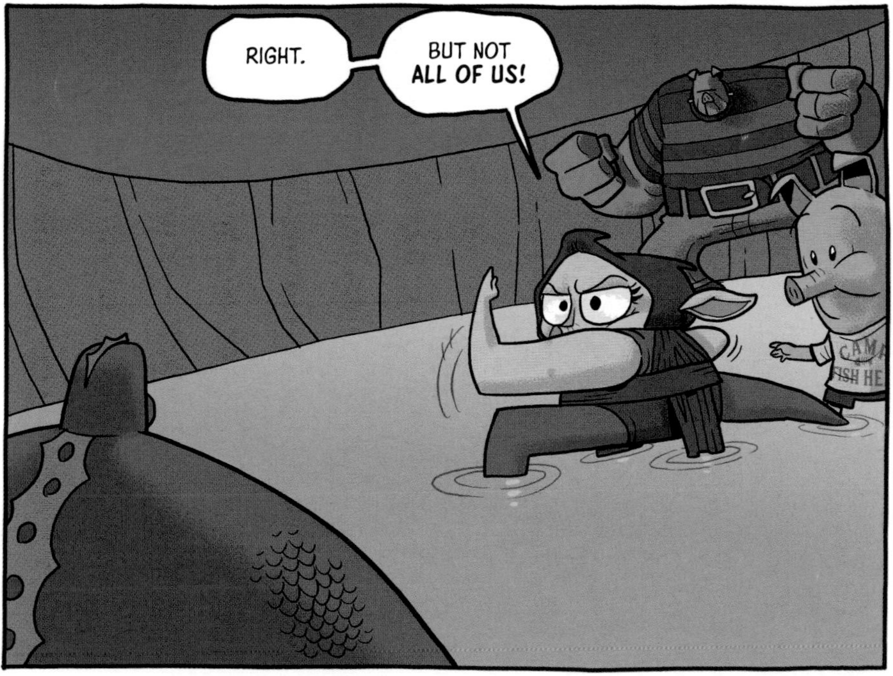
RIGHT.
BUT NOT **ALL OF US!**

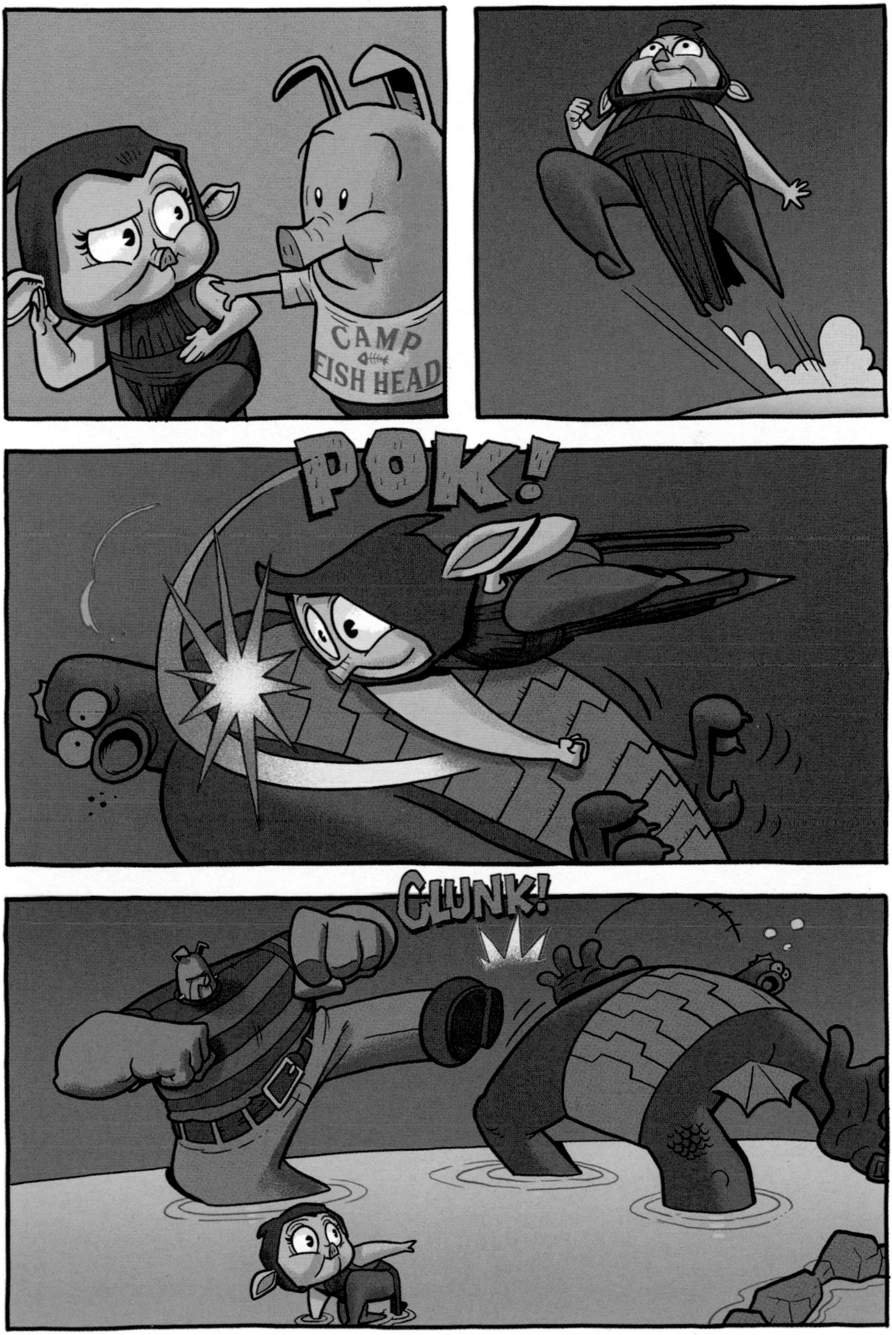
CAMP
FISH HEAD
POK!
CLUNK!

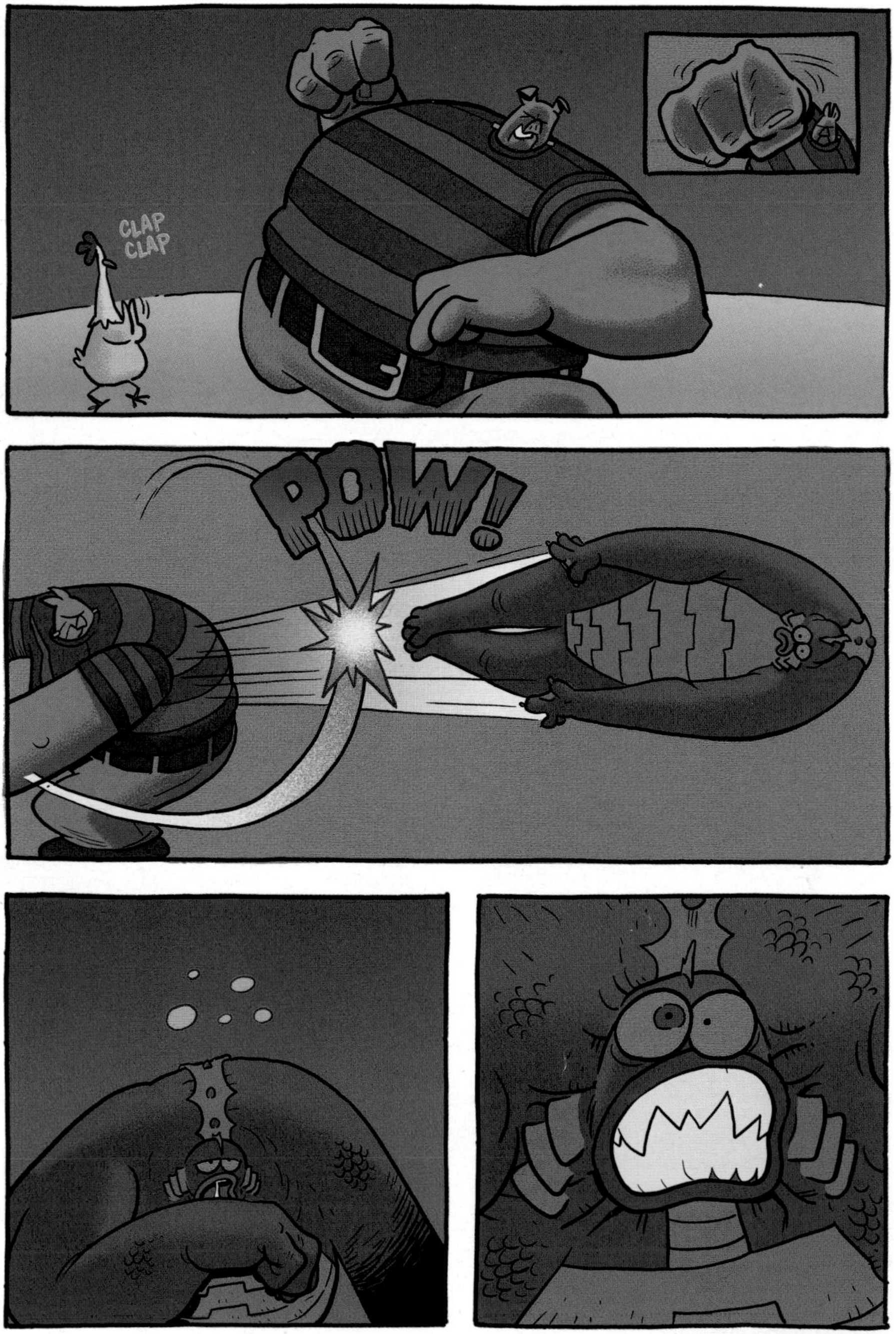
CLAP
CLAP
POW!

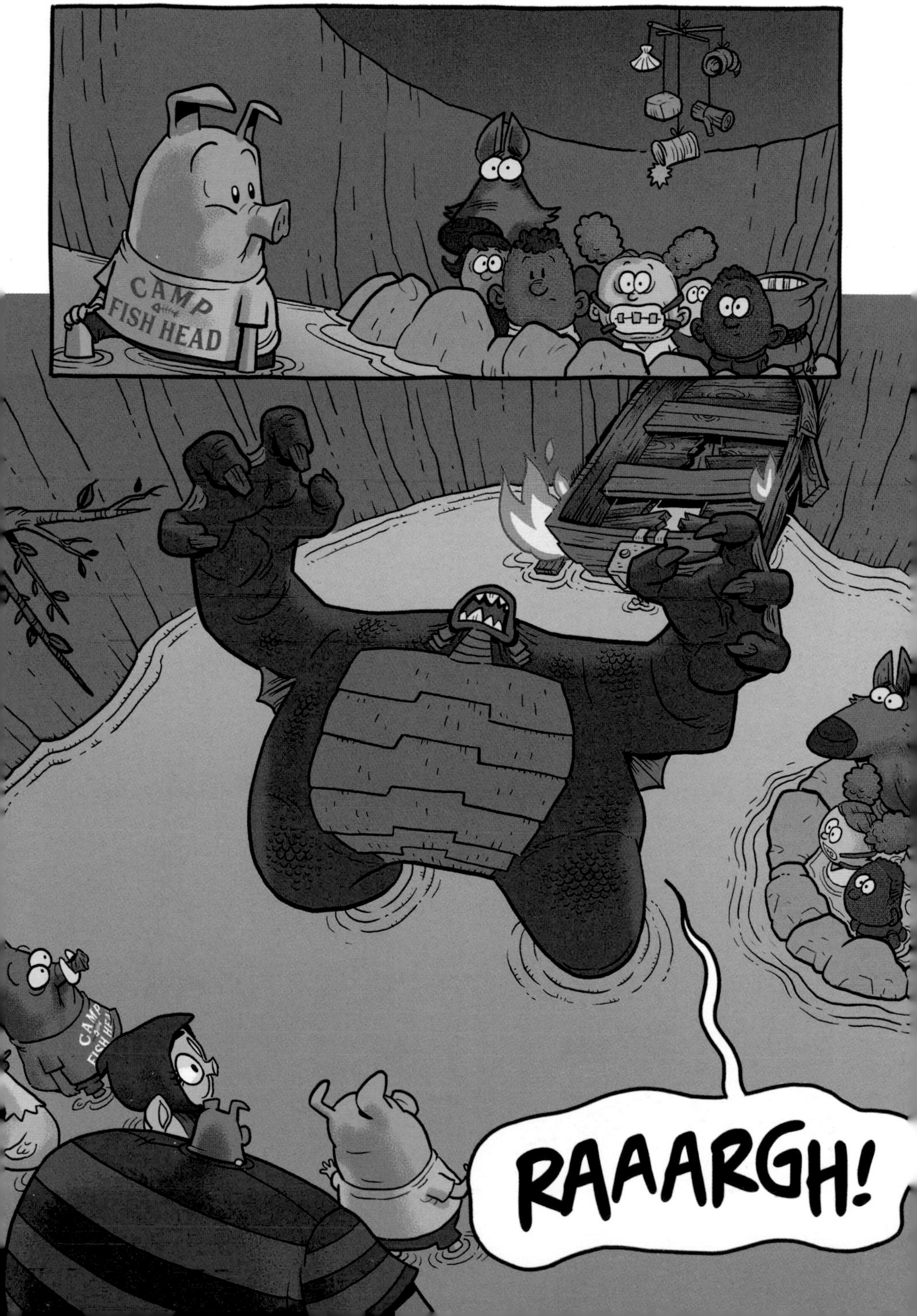
CAMP FISH HEAD
RAAARGH!
CAMP FISH HEAD

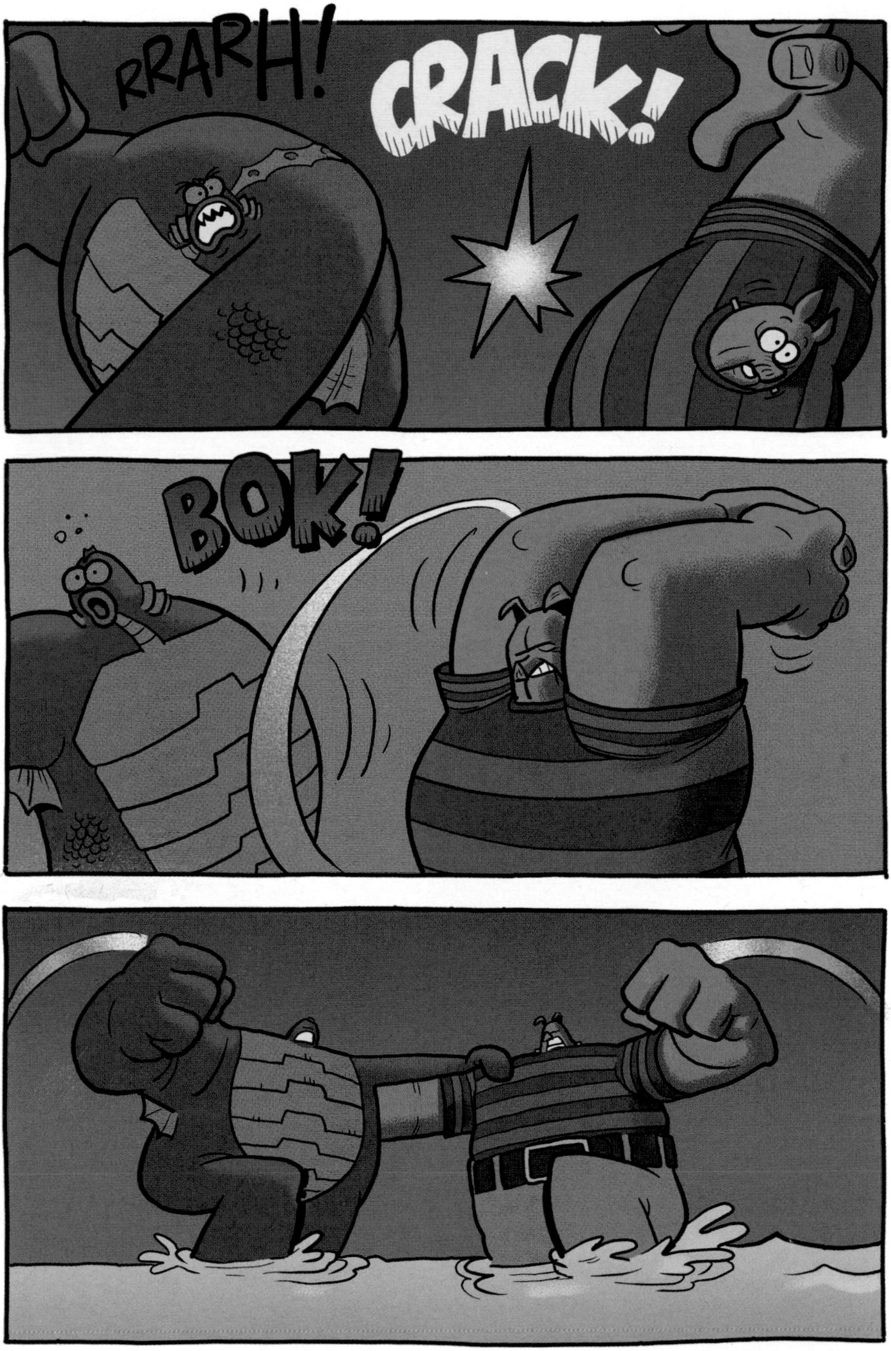
RRARH!
CRACK!
BOK!

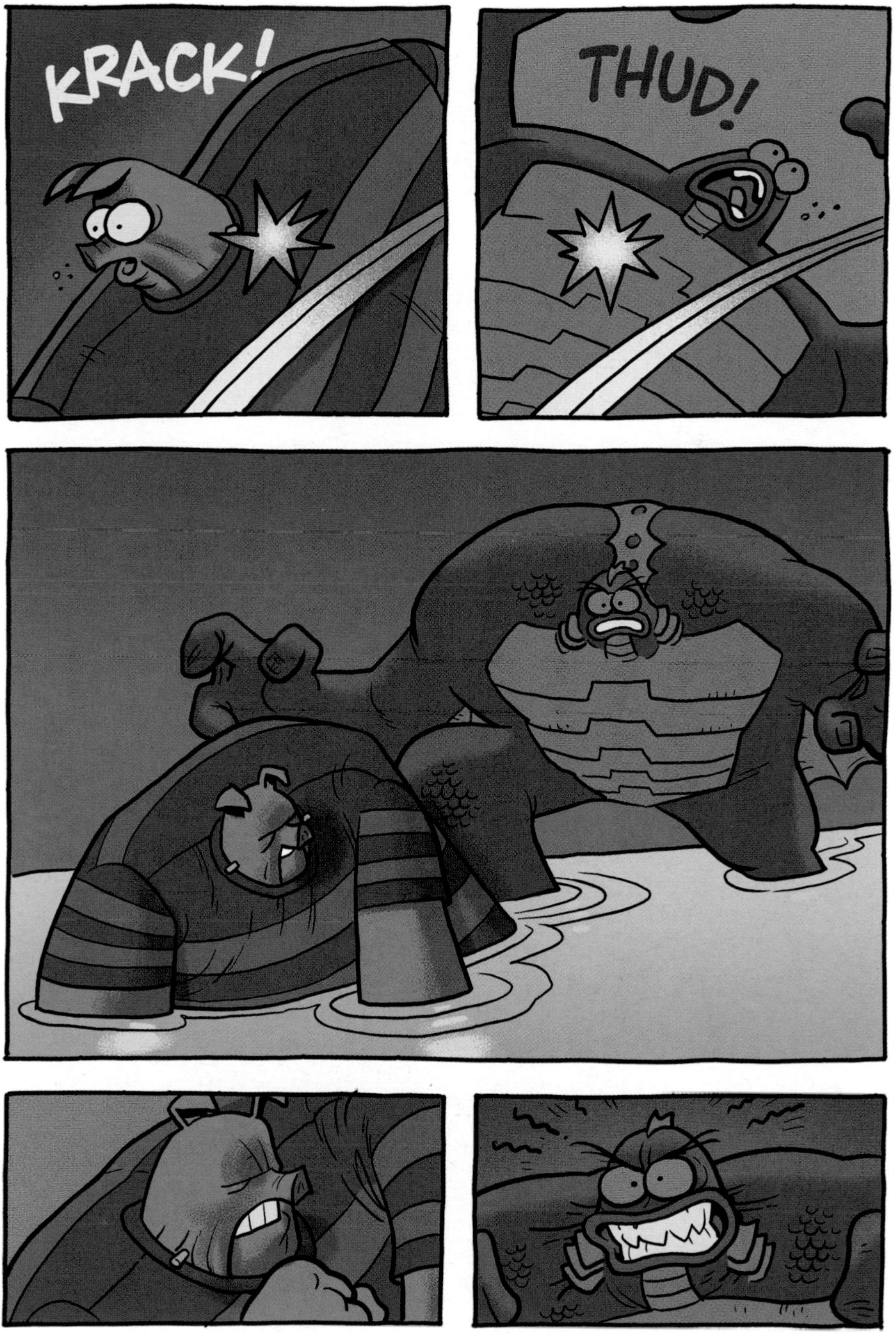
KRACK!
THUD!

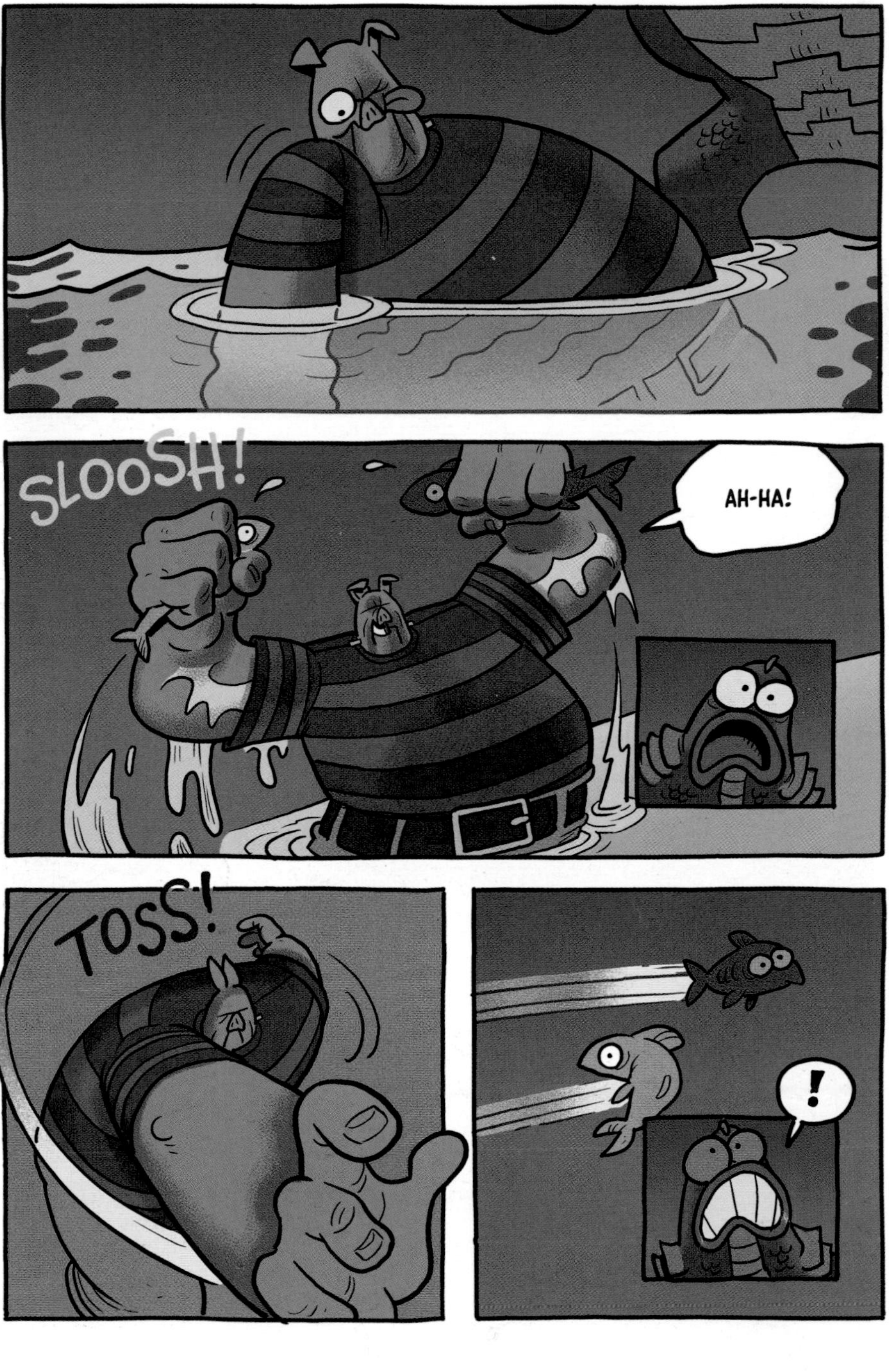
SLOOSH!
AH-HA!
TOSS!
!

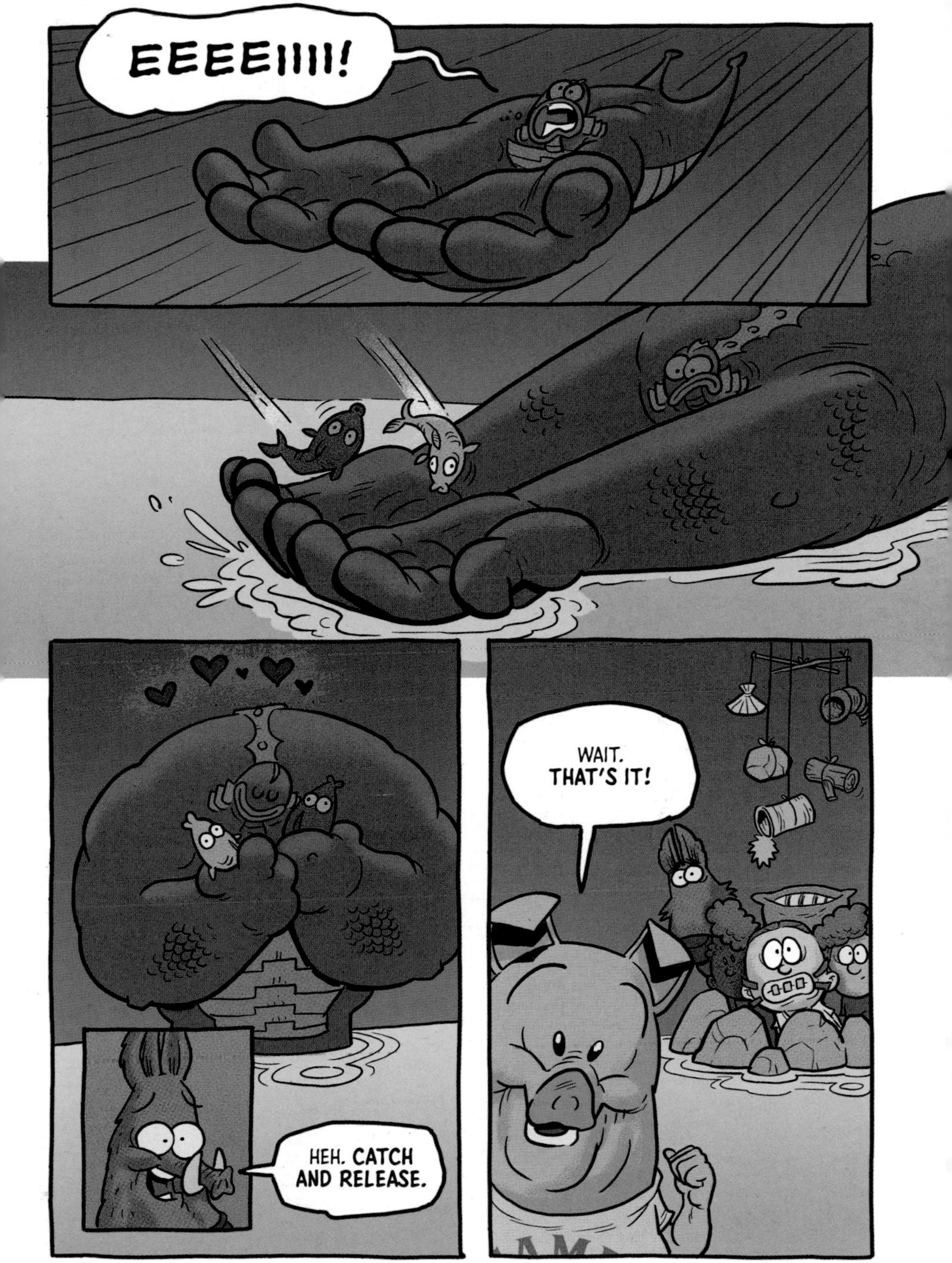
EEEEIIIII!
HEH. CATCH AND RELEASE.
WAIT. THAT'S IT!

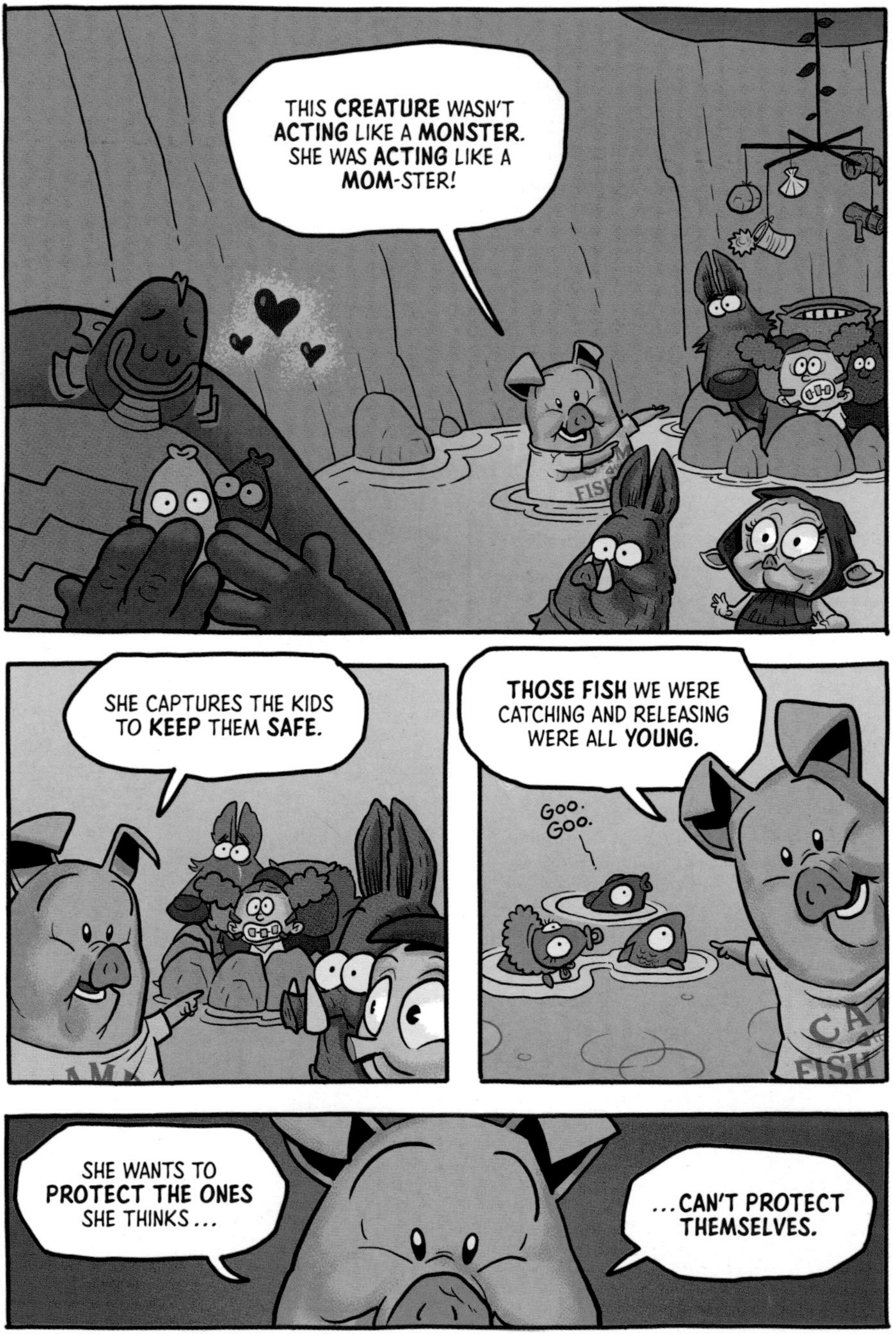
THIS CREATURE WASN'T ACTING LIKE A MONSTER. SHE WAS ACTING LIKE A MOM-STER!
SHE CAPTURES THE KIDS TO KEEP THEM SAFE.
THOSE FISH WE WERE CATCHING AND RELEASING WERE ALL YOUNG.
GOO. GOO.
SHE WANTS TO PROTECT THE ONES SHE THINKS...
...CAN'T PROTECT THEMSELVES.

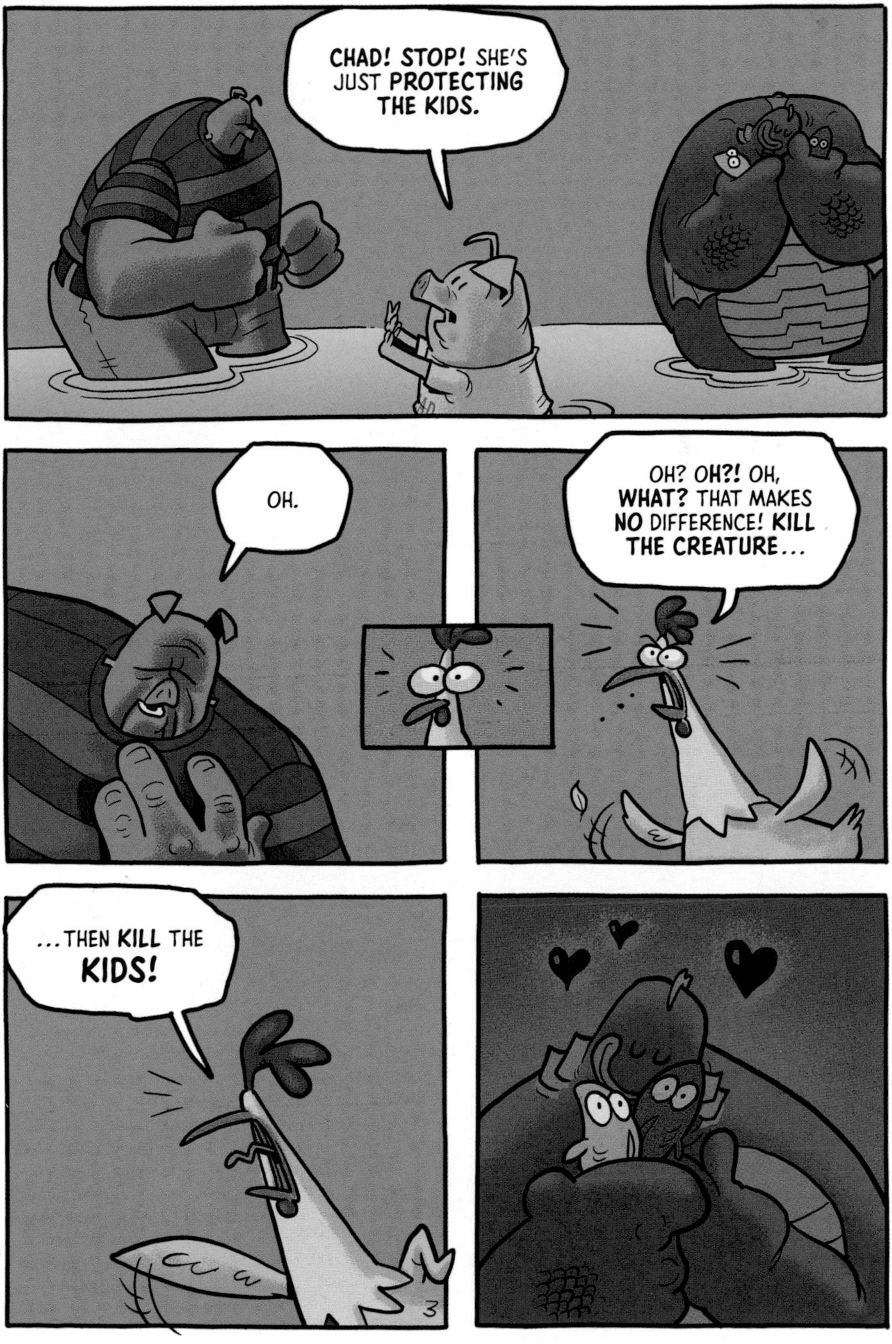
CHAD! STOP! SHE'S JUST PROTECTING THE KIDS.
OH.
OH? OH?! OH, WHAT? THAT MAKES NO DIFFERENCE! KILL THE CREATURE...
...THEN KILL THE KIDS!

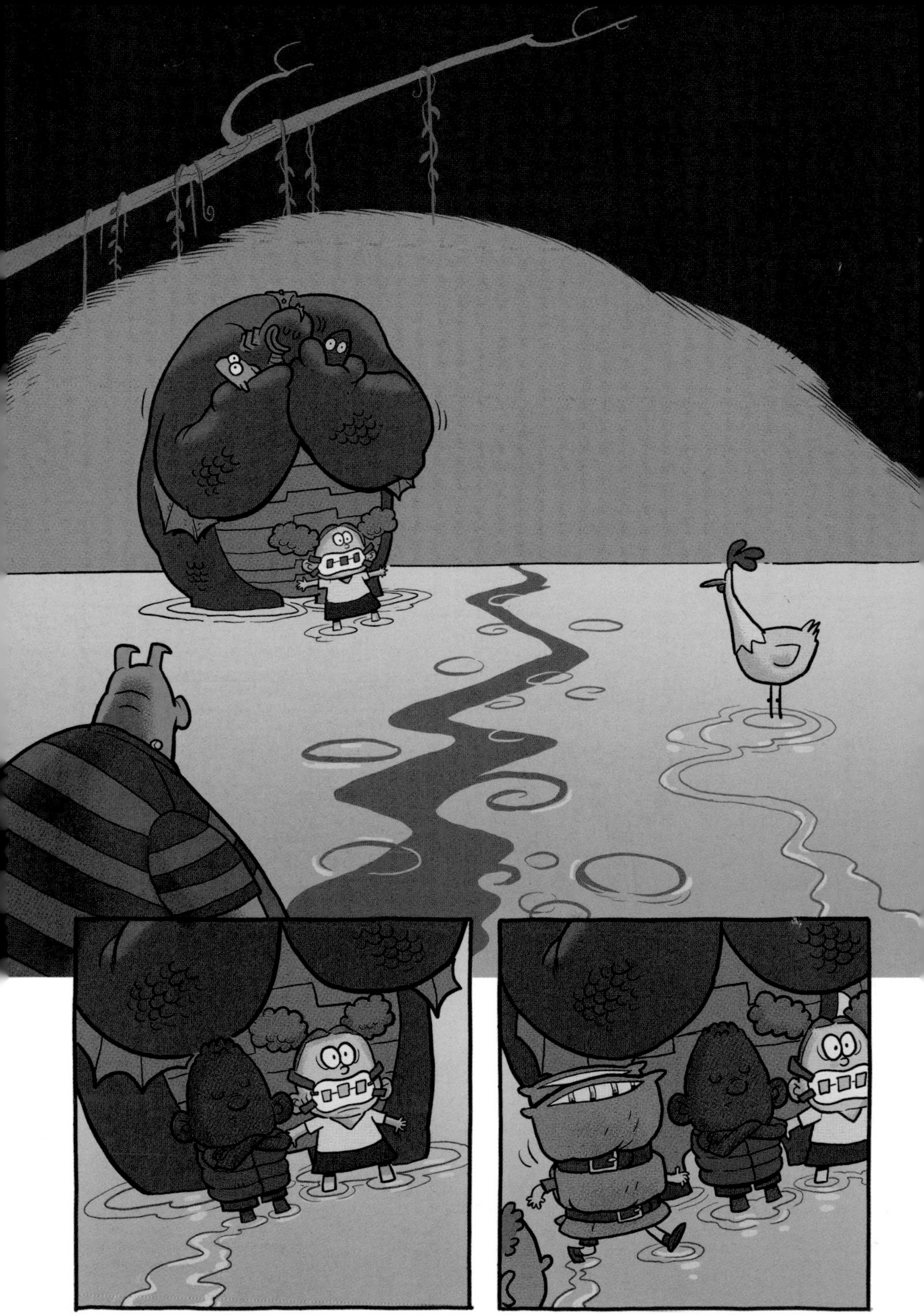

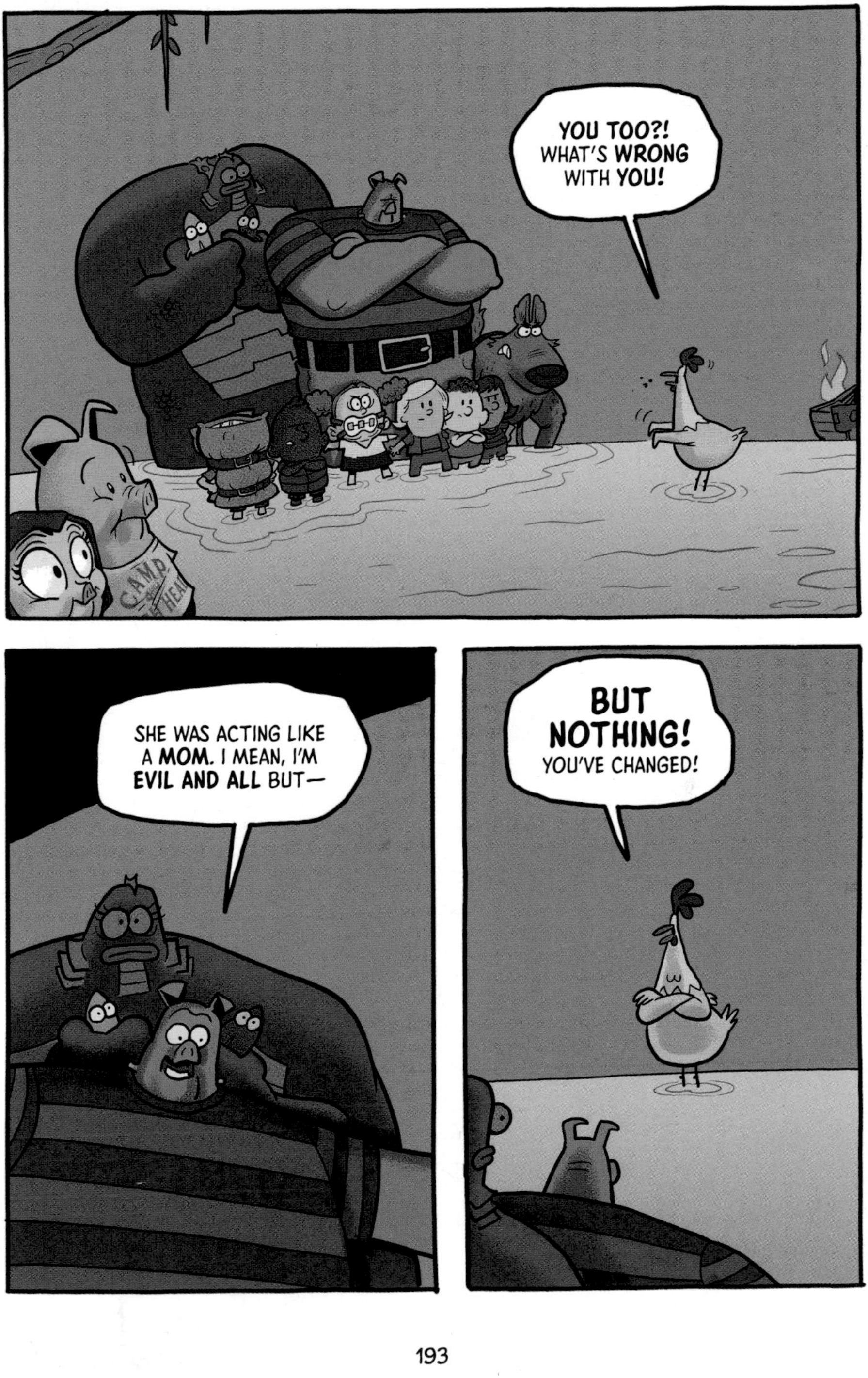
YOU TOO?! WHAT'S WRONG WITH YOU!
SHE WAS ACTING LIKE A MOM. I MEAN, I'M EVIL AND ALL BUT—
BUT NOTHING! YOU'VE CHANGED!

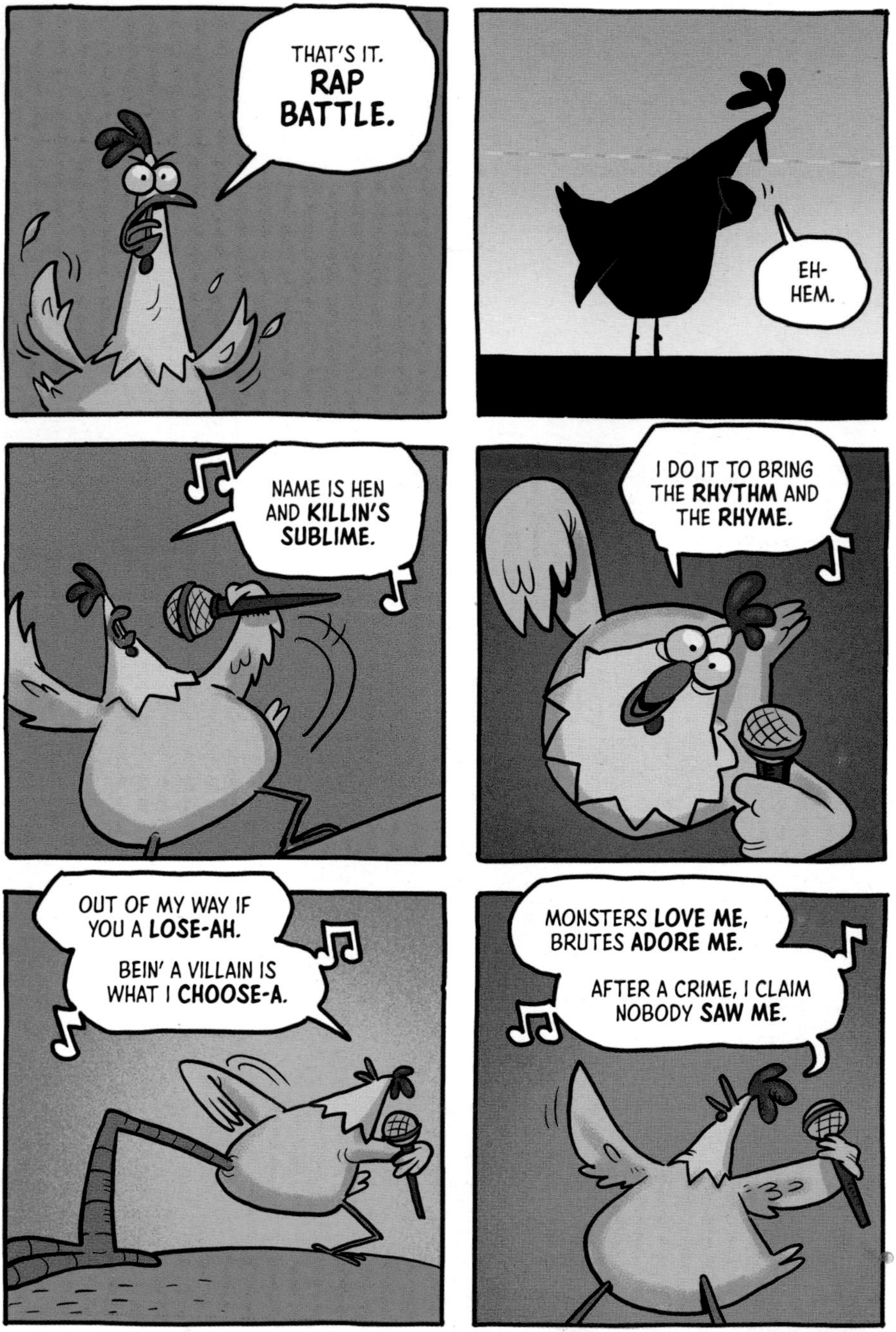
THAT'S IT. **RAP BATTLE.**
EH-HEM.
NAME IS HEN AND **KILLIN'S SUBLIME.**
I DO IT TO BRING THE **RHYTHM** AND THE **RHYME.**
OUT OF MY WAY IF YOU A **LOSE-AH.**
BEIN' A VILLAIN IS WHAT I **CHOOSE-A.**
MONSTERS **LOVE ME,** BRUTES **ADORE ME.**
AFTER A CRIME, I CLAIM NOBODY **SAW ME.**

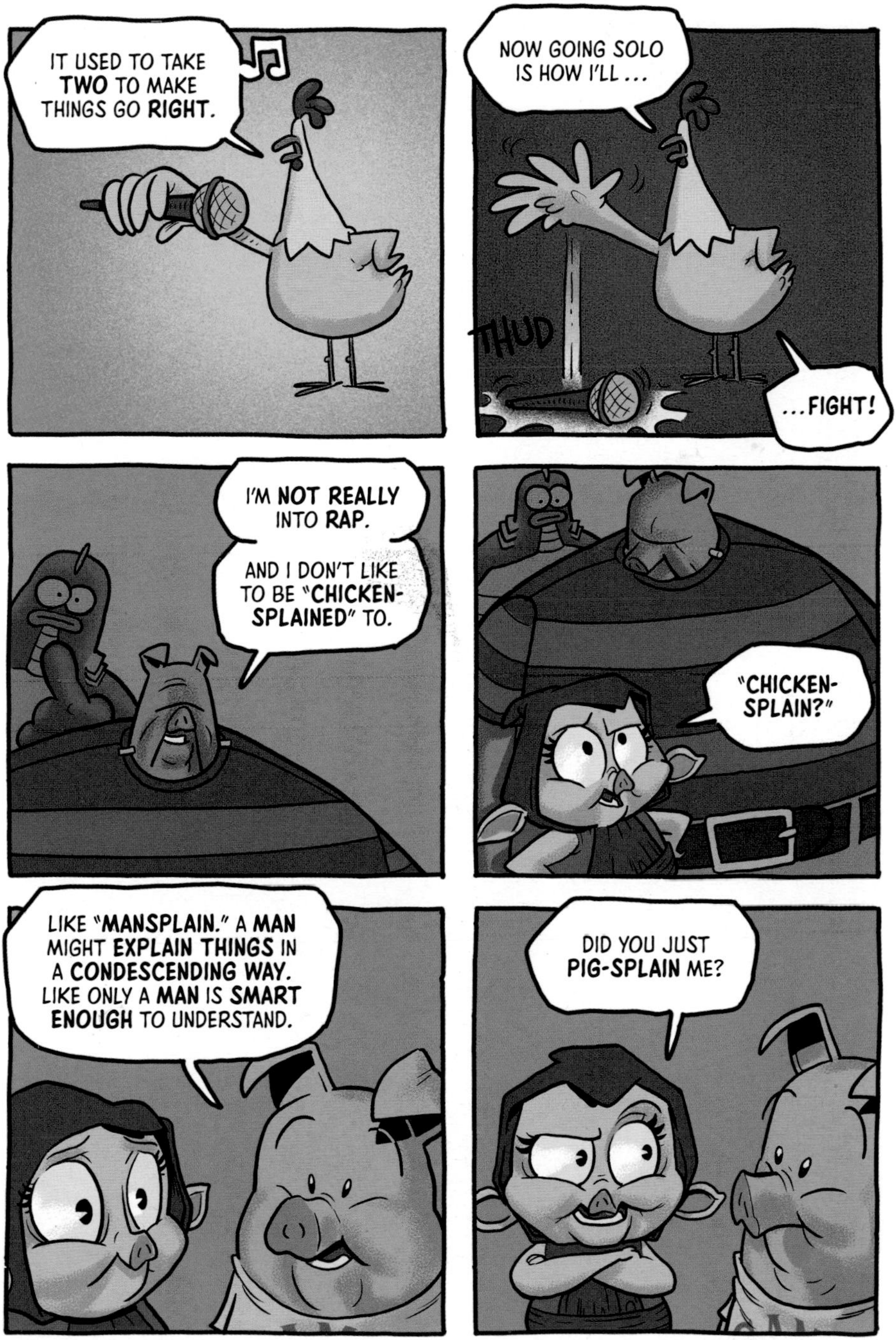
IT USED TO TAKE TWO TO MAKE THINGS GO RIGHT.
NOW GOING SOLO IS HOW I'LL . . .
THUD
. . . FIGHT!
I'M NOT REALLY INTO RAP.
AND I DON'T LIKE TO BE "CHICKEN-SPLAINED" TO.
"CHICKEN-SPLAIN?"
LIKE "MANSPLAIN." A MAN MIGHT EXPLAIN THINGS IN A CONDESCENDING WAY. LIKE ONLY A MAN IS SMART ENOUGH TO UNDERSTAND.
DID YOU JUST PIG-SPLAIN ME?

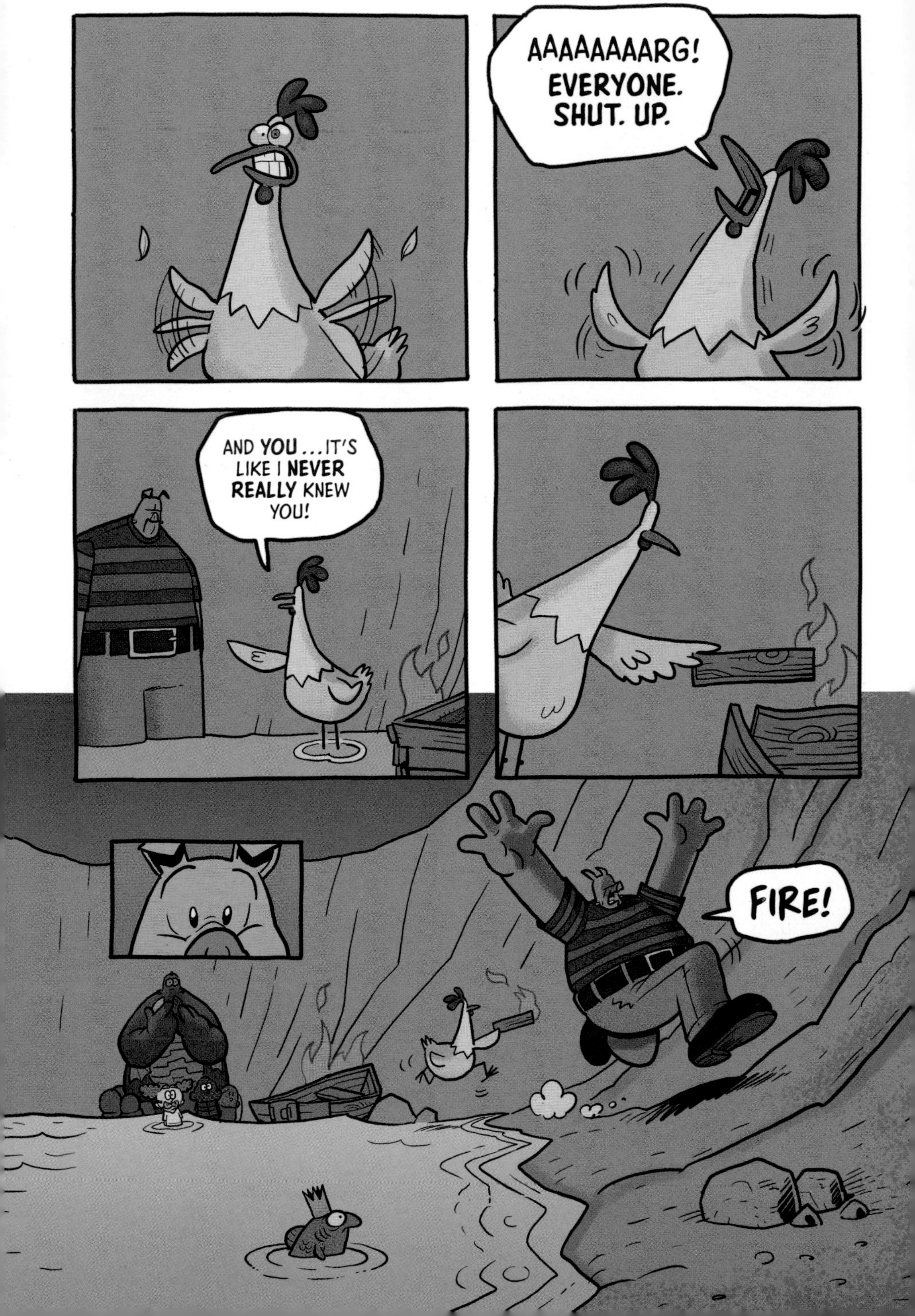
AAAAAAAARG! EVERYONE. SHUT. UP.
AND YOU...IT'S LIKE I NEVER REALLY KNEW YOU!
FIRE!

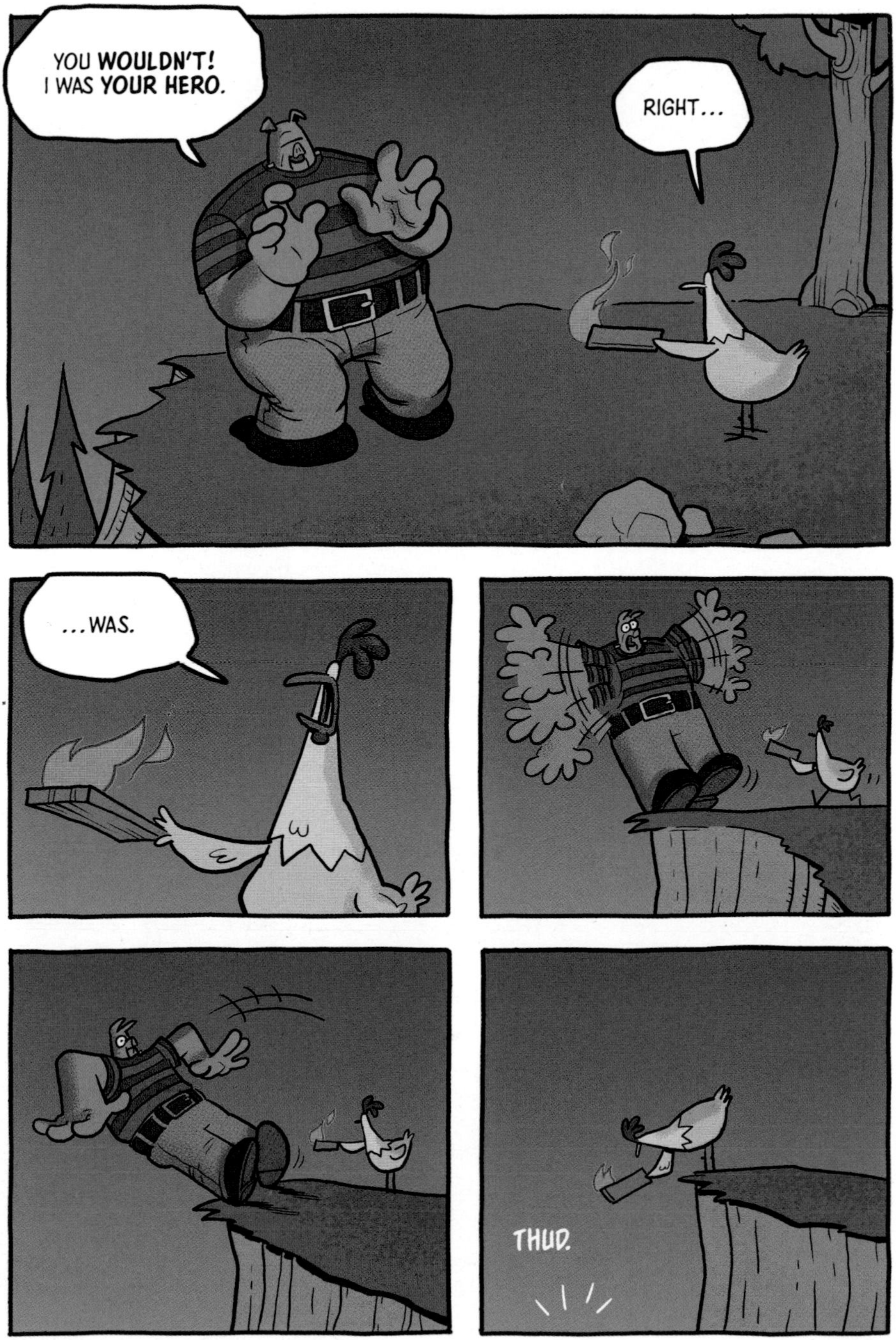

YOU **WOULDN'T!** I WAS **YOUR HERO.**
RIGHT...
...WAS.
THUD.

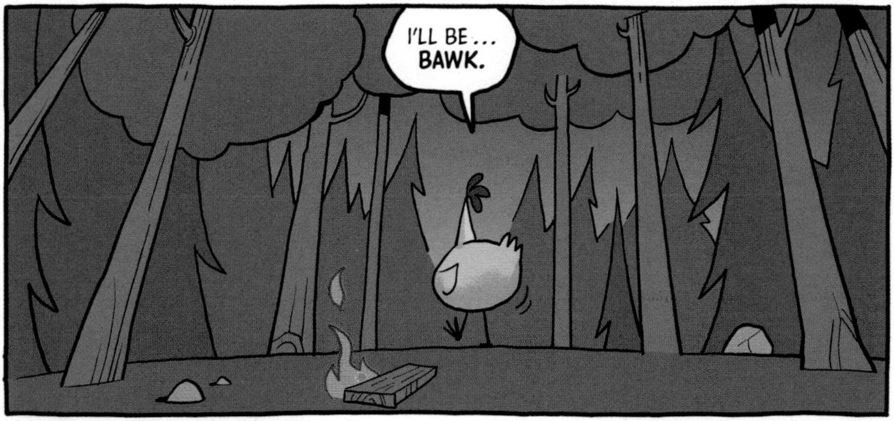
I'LL BE... **BAWK.**

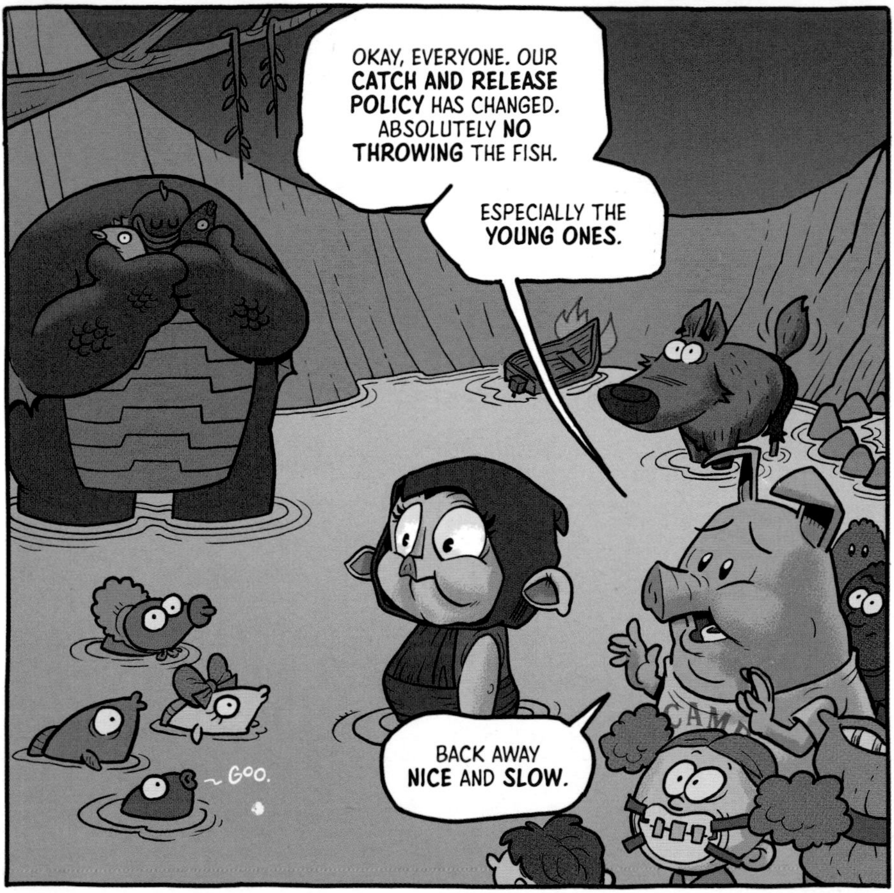
OKAY, EVERYONE. OUR **CATCH AND RELEASE POLICY** HAS CHANGED. ABSOLUTELY **NO THROWING** THE FISH.
ESPECIALLY THE **YOUNG ONES.**
BACK AWAY **NICE** AND **SLOW.**
GOO.

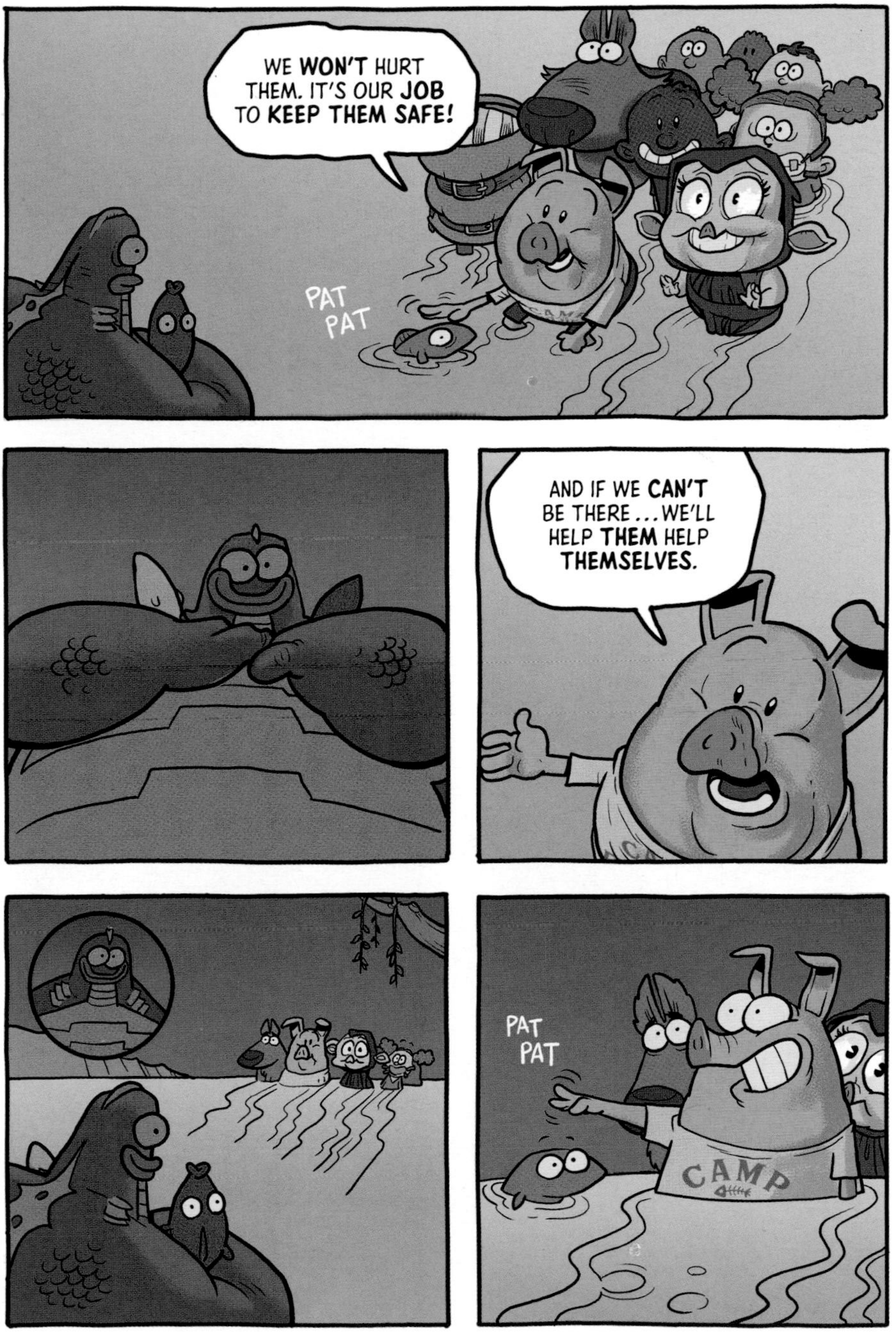
WE WON'T HURT THEM. IT'S OUR JOB TO KEEP THEM SAFE!
PAT PAT
AND IF WE CAN'T BE THERE . . . WE'LL HELP THEM HELP THEMSELVES.
PAT PAT
CAMP

CHAPTER THIRTEEN

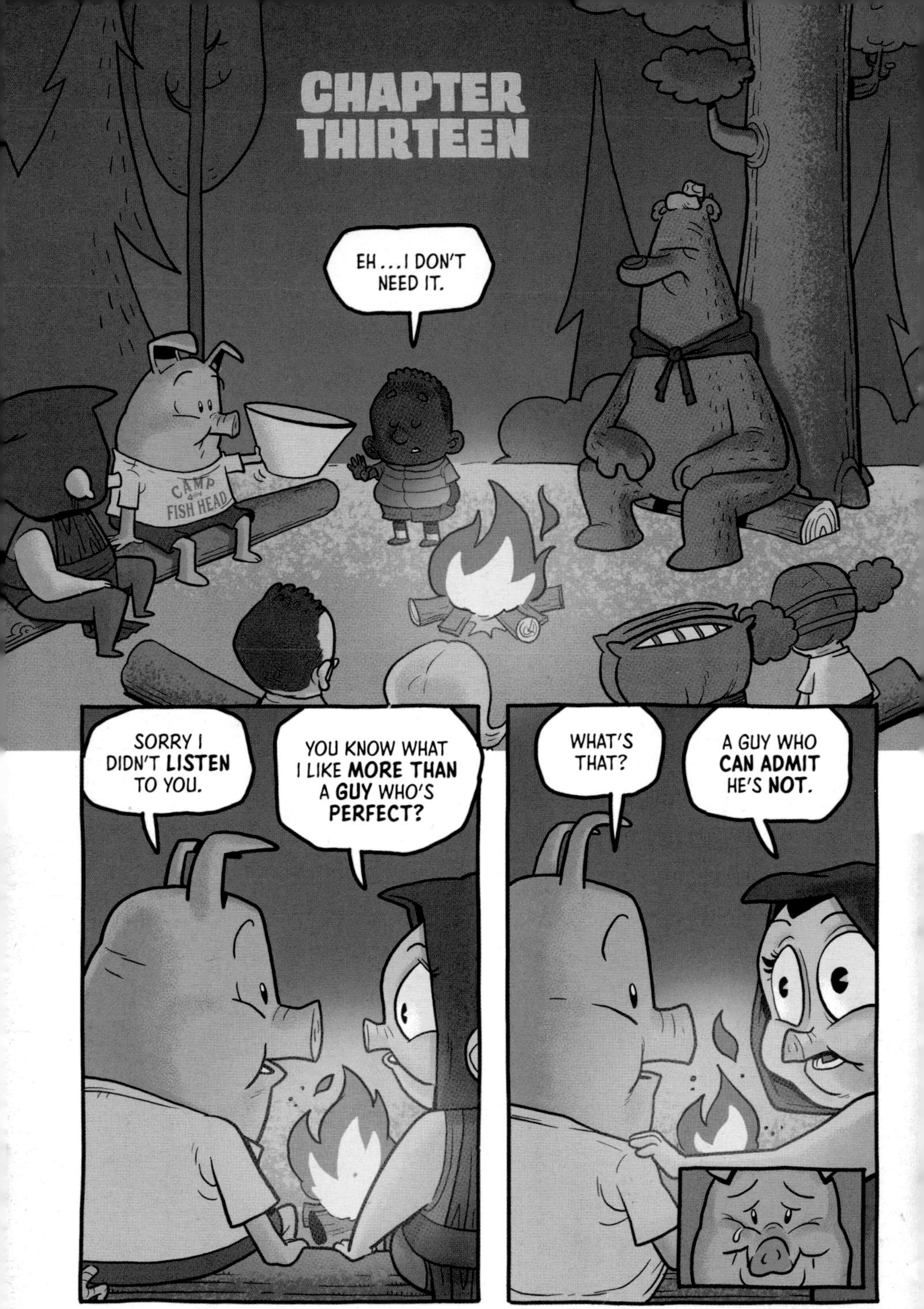

EH . . . I DON'T NEED IT.
CAMP FISH HEAD
SORRY I DIDN'T **LISTEN** TO YOU.
YOU KNOW WHAT I LIKE **MORE THAN** A **GUY** WHO'S **PERFECT?**
WHAT'S THAT?
A GUY WHO **CAN ADMIT** HE'S **NOT.**

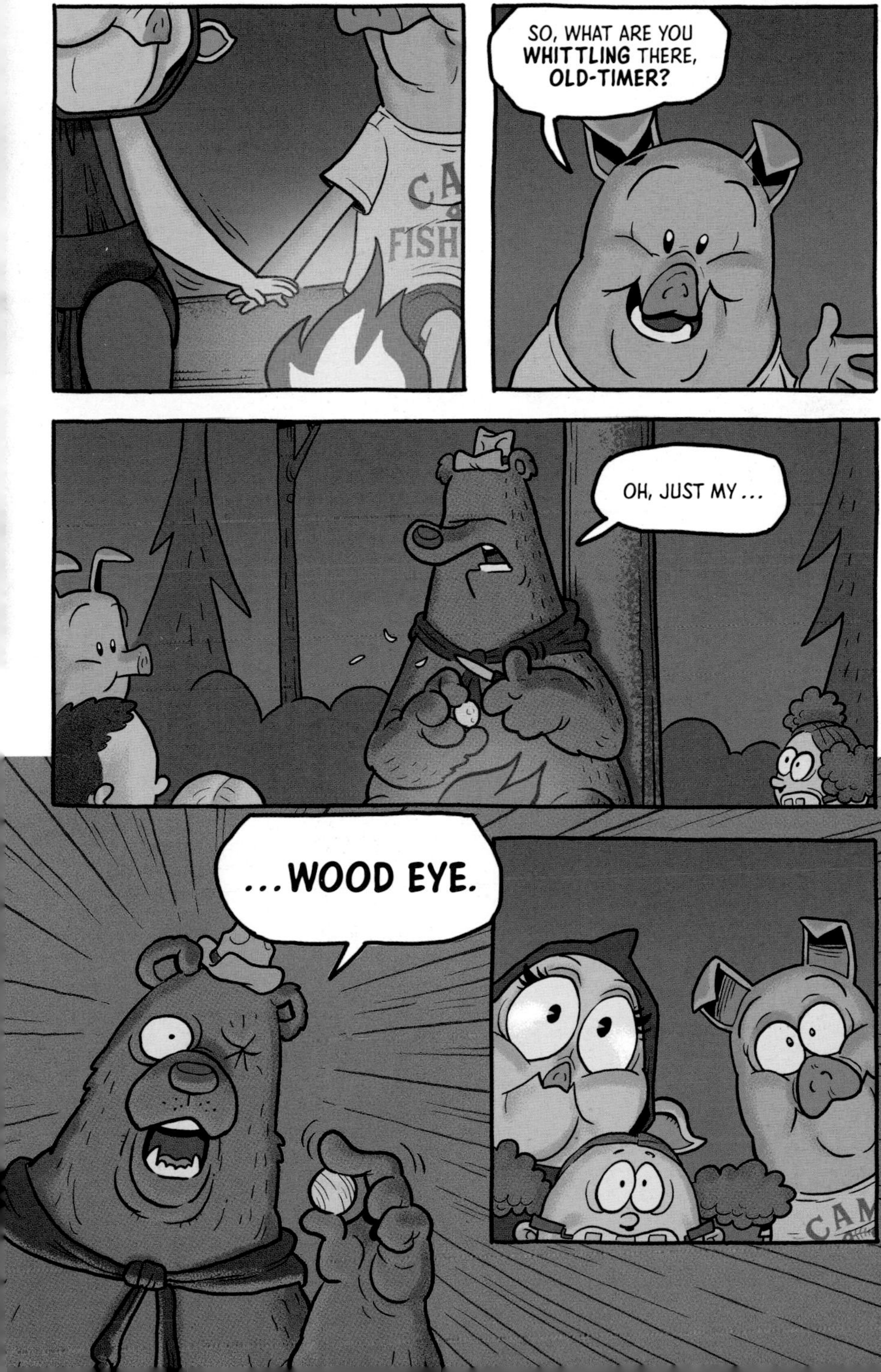
SO, WHAT ARE YOU WHITTLING THERE, OLD-TIMER?
OH, JUST MY ...
...WOOD EYE.

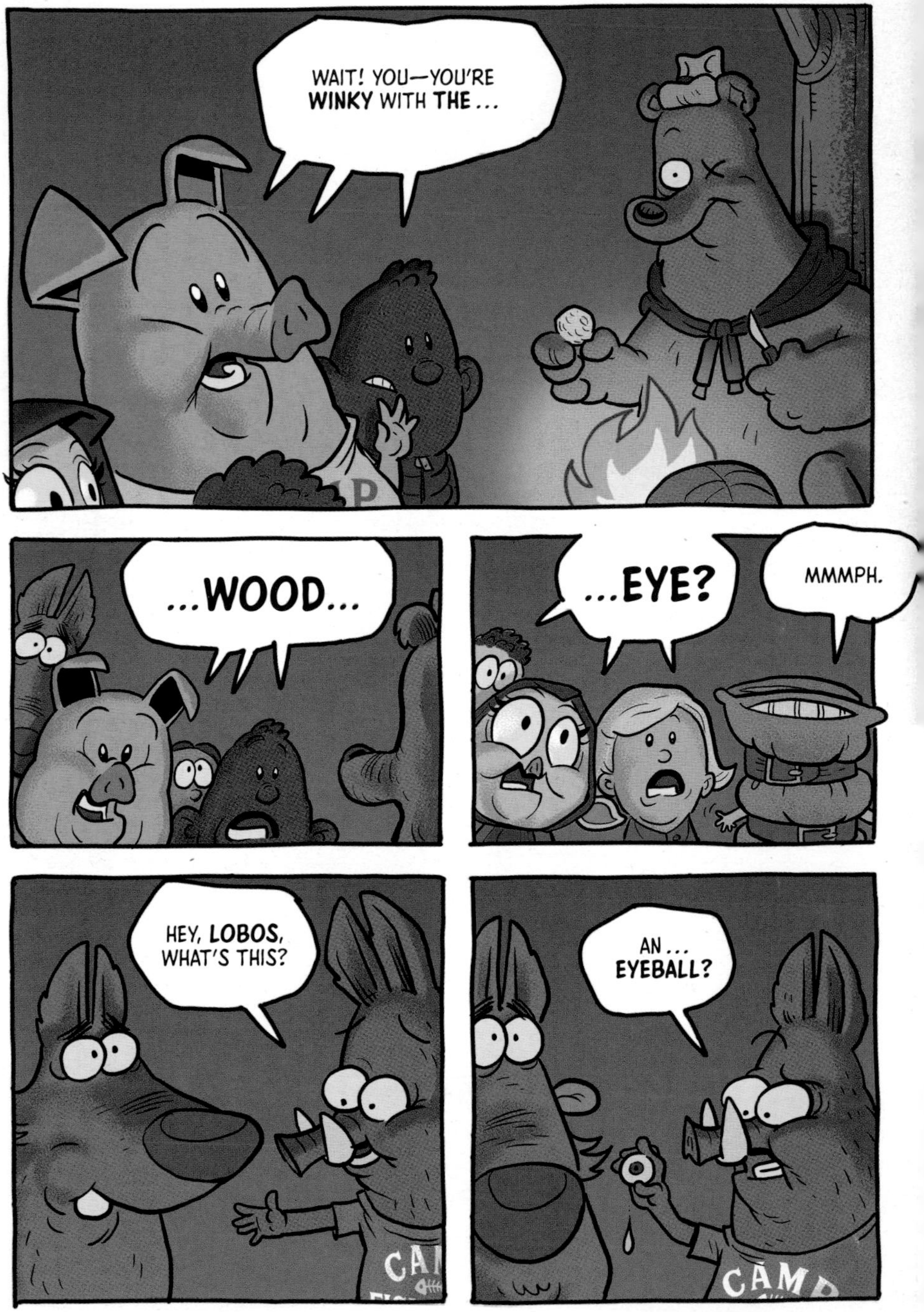
WAIT! YOU—YOU'RE **WINKY** WITH **THE**...
...WOOD...
...EYE?
MMMPH.
HEY, **LOBOS**, WHAT'S THIS?
AN... **EYEBALL?**

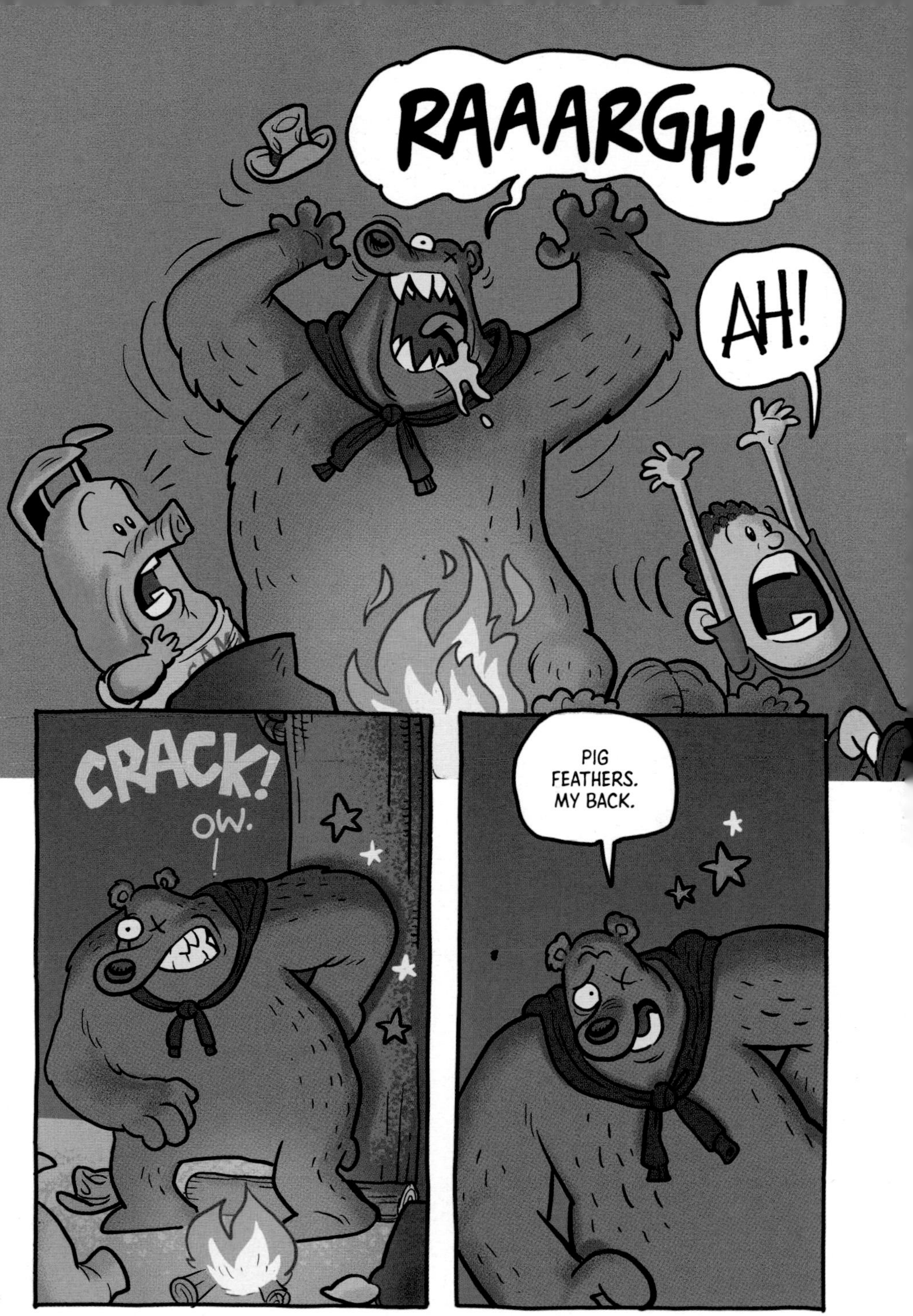
RAAARGH!
AH!
CRACK!
OW.
PIG FEATHERS. MY BACK.

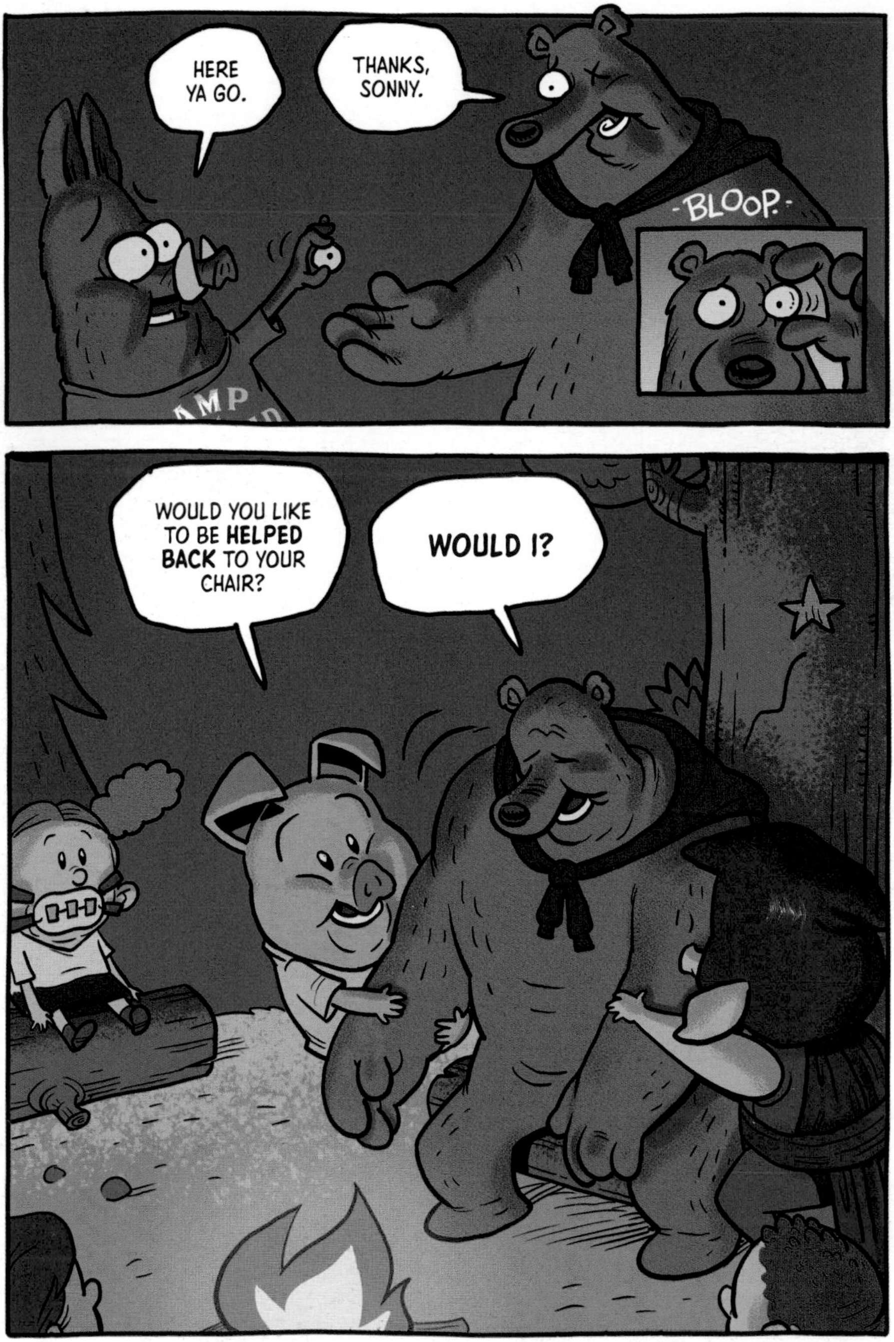
HERE YA GO.
THANKS, SONNY.
-BLOOP.-
WOULD YOU LIKE TO BE **HELPED BACK** TO YOUR CHAIR?
WOULD I?

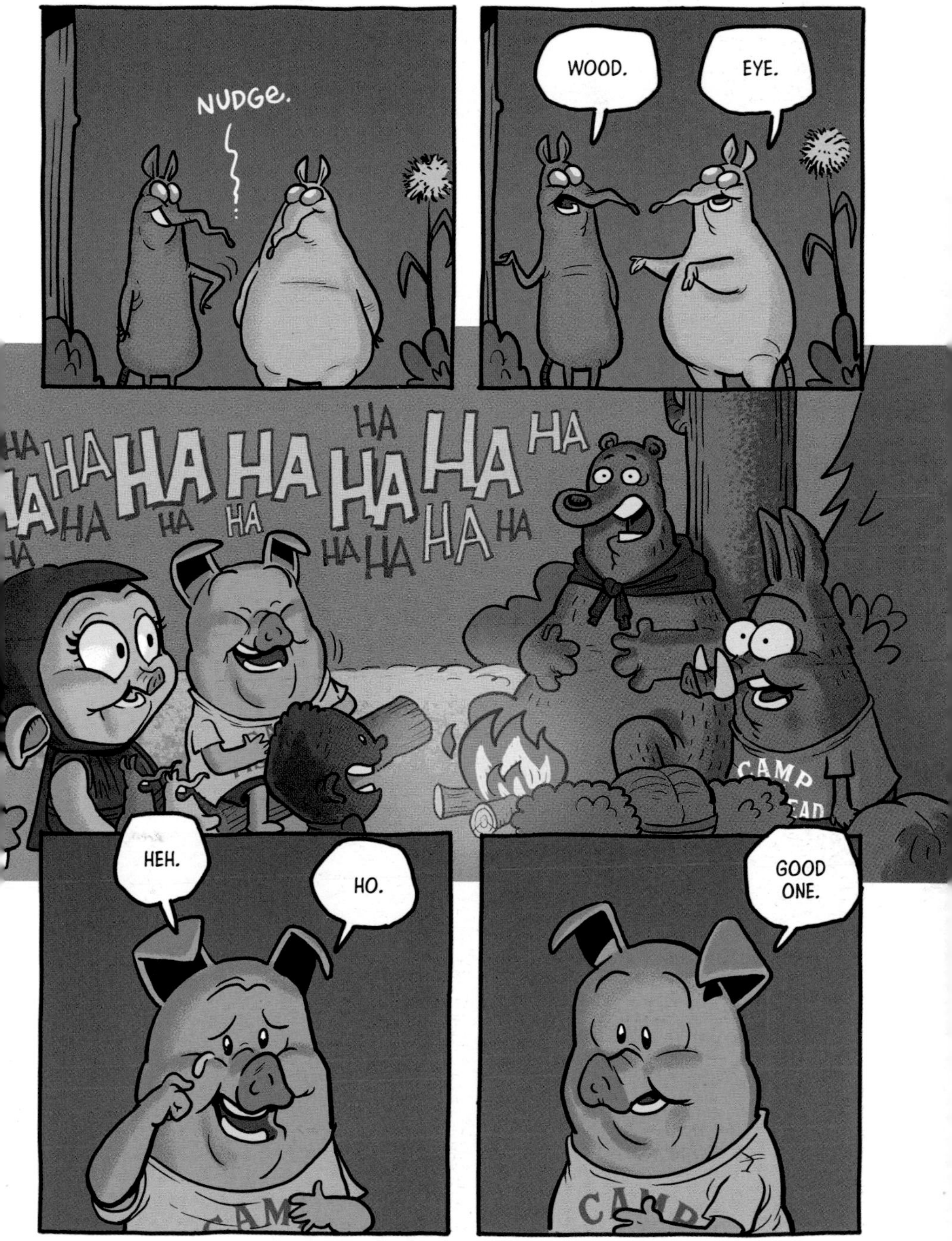
NUDGE.
WOOD.
EYE.
HA HA HA HA HA HA HA HA HA HA HA HA HA HA HA HA HA HA HA
CAMP
HEH.
HO.
GOOD ONE.
CAMP
CAMP

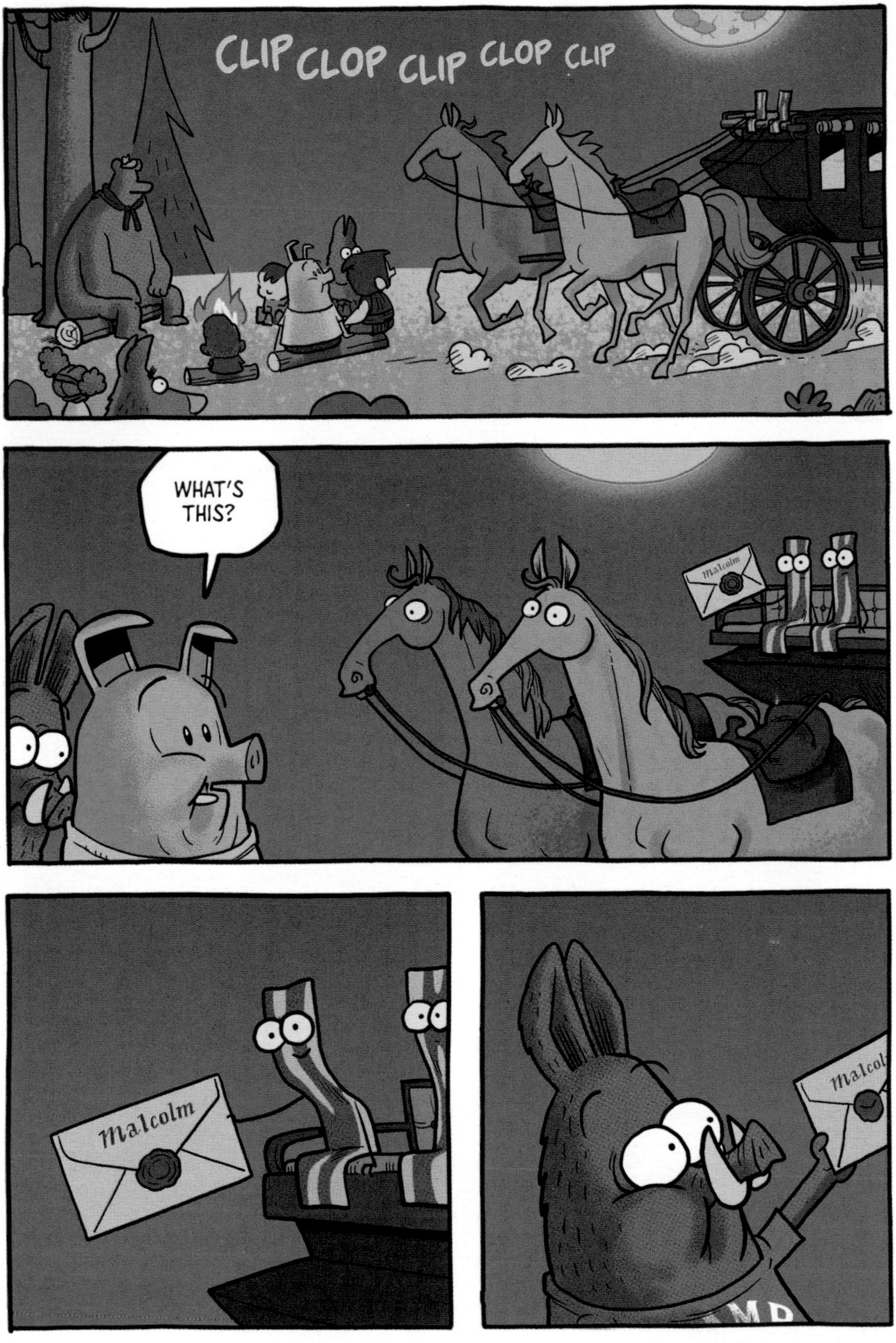
CLIP CLOP CLIP CLOP CLIP
WHAT'S THIS?
Malcolm
Malcolm
Malcolm

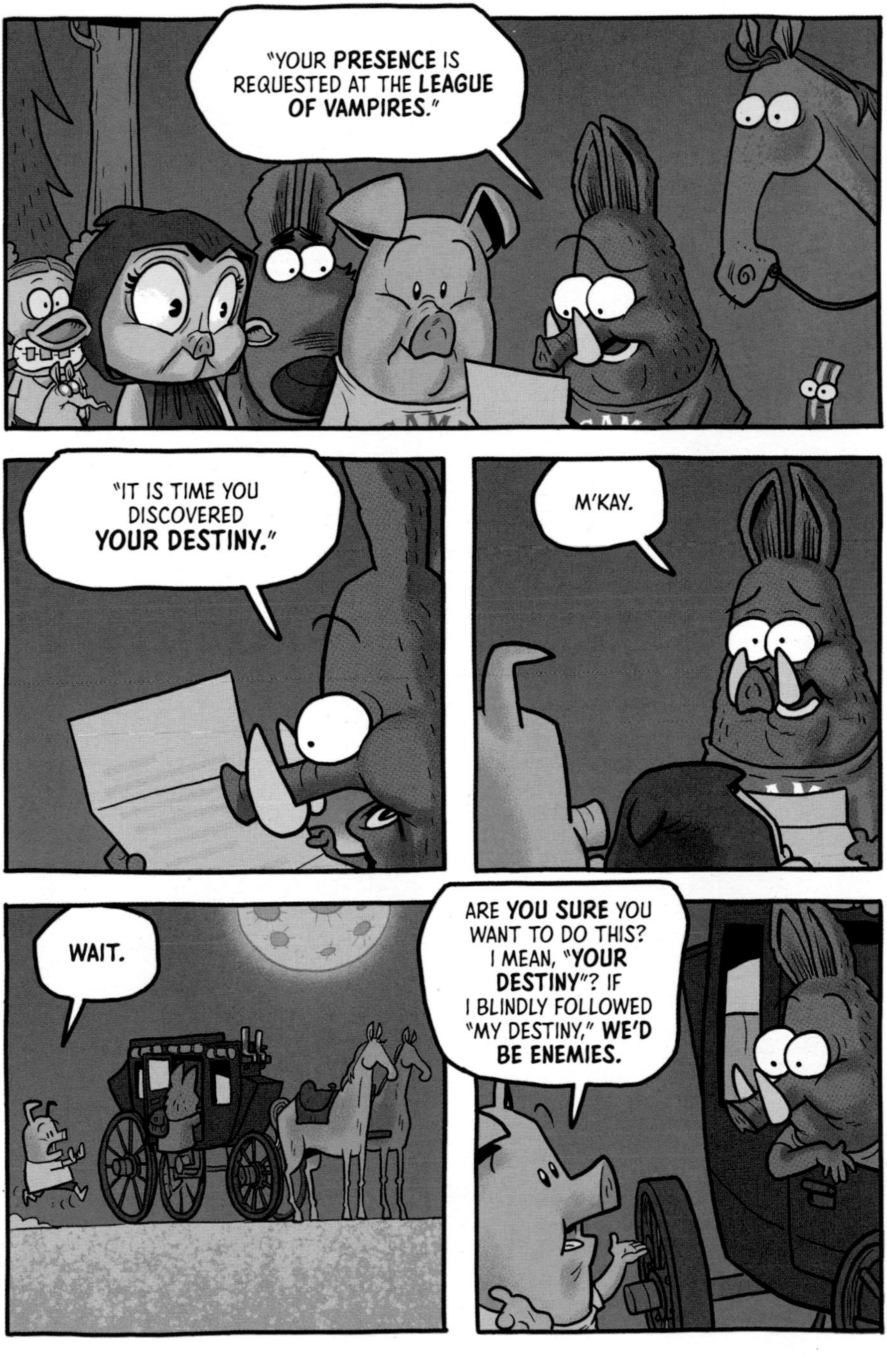
"YOUR PRESENCE IS REQUESTED AT THE LEAGUE OF VAMPIRES."
"IT IS TIME YOU DISCOVERED YOUR DESTINY."
M'KAY.
WAIT.
ARE YOU SURE YOU WANT TO DO THIS? I MEAN, "YOUR DESTINY"? IF I BLINDLY FOLLOWED "MY DESTINY," WE'D BE ENEMIES.

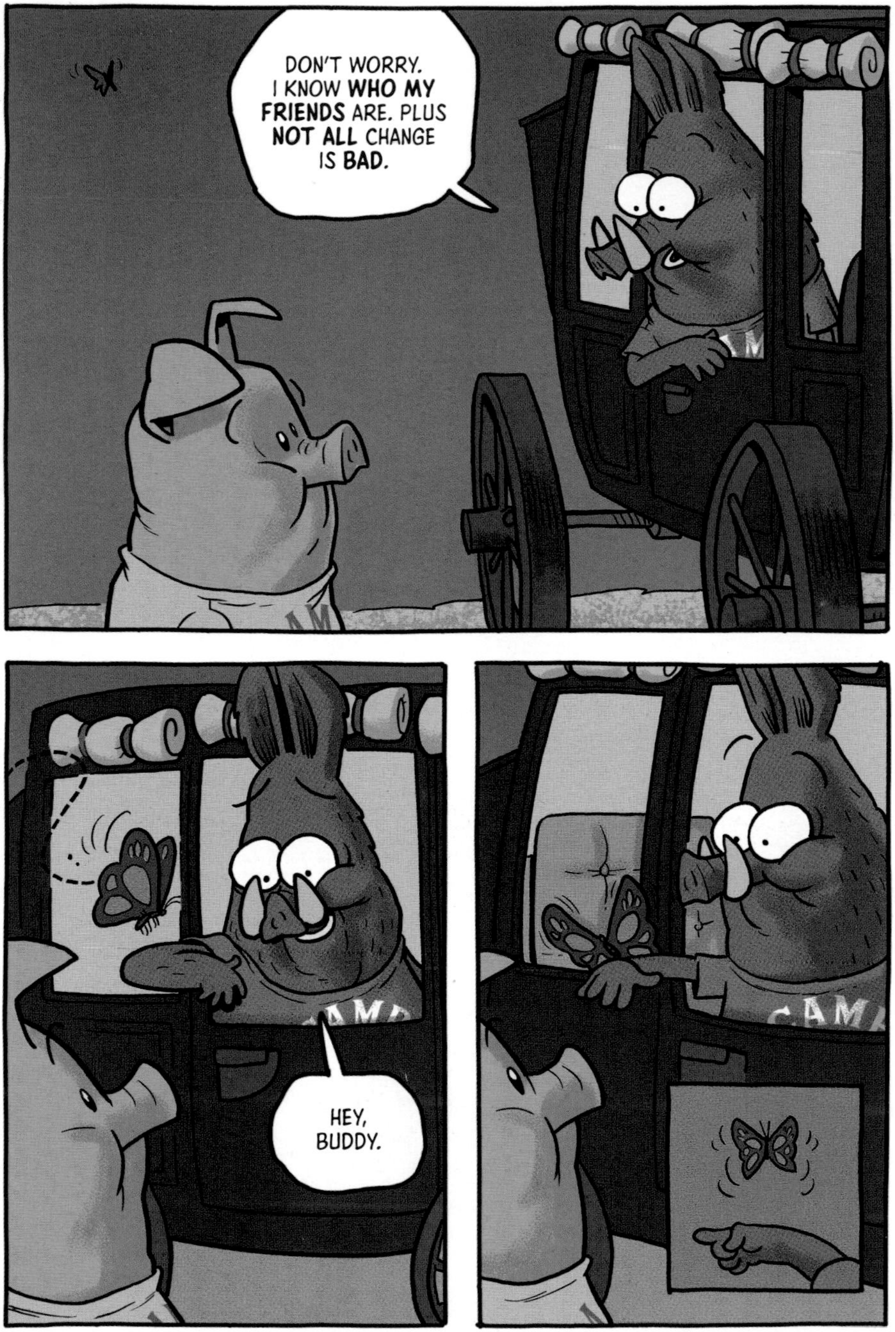
DON'T WORRY. I KNOW **WHO MY FRIENDS** ARE. PLUS **NOT ALL** CHANGE IS **BAD.**
HEY, BUDDY.

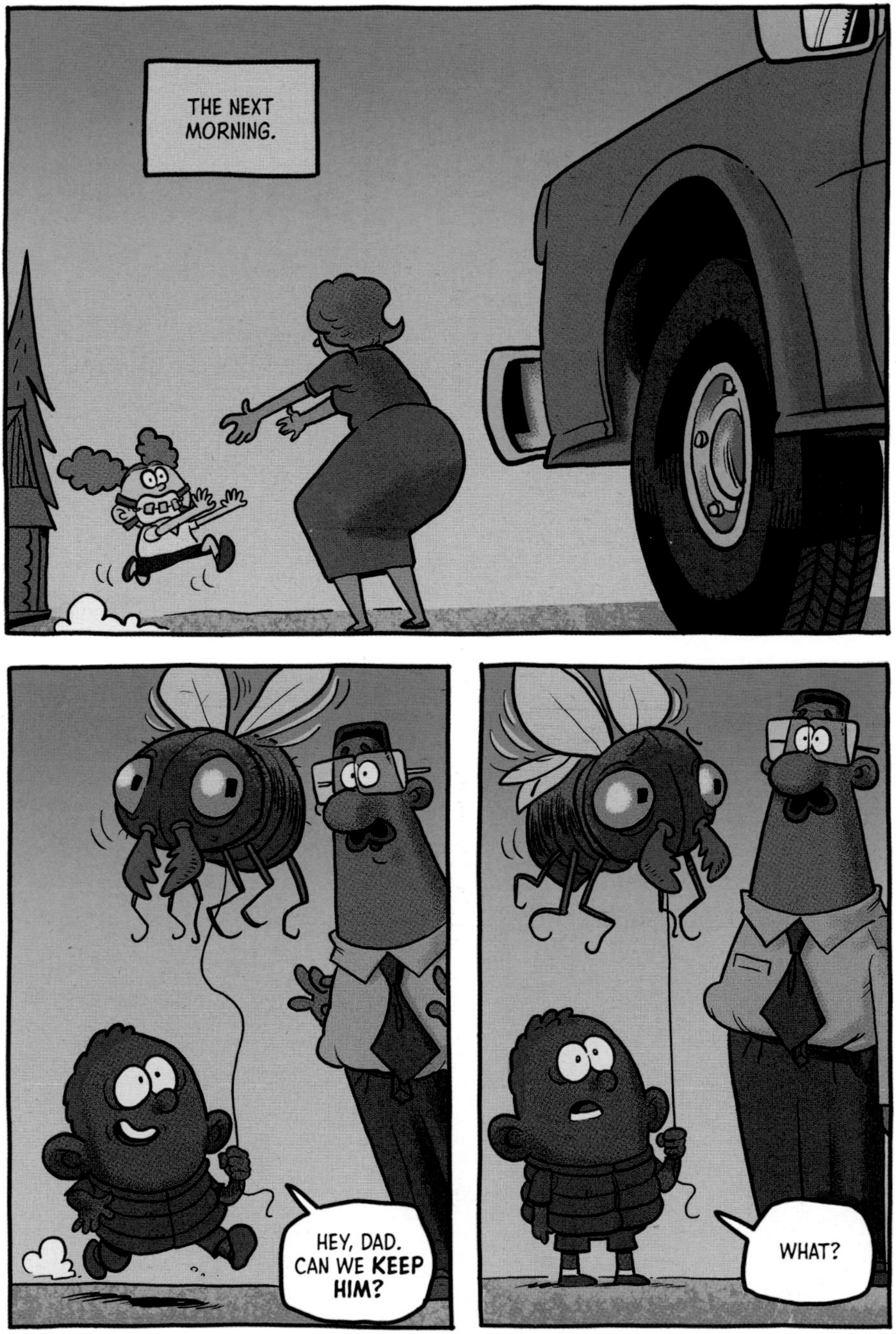
THE NEXT MORNING.
HEY, DAD. CAN WE KEEP HIM?
WHAT?

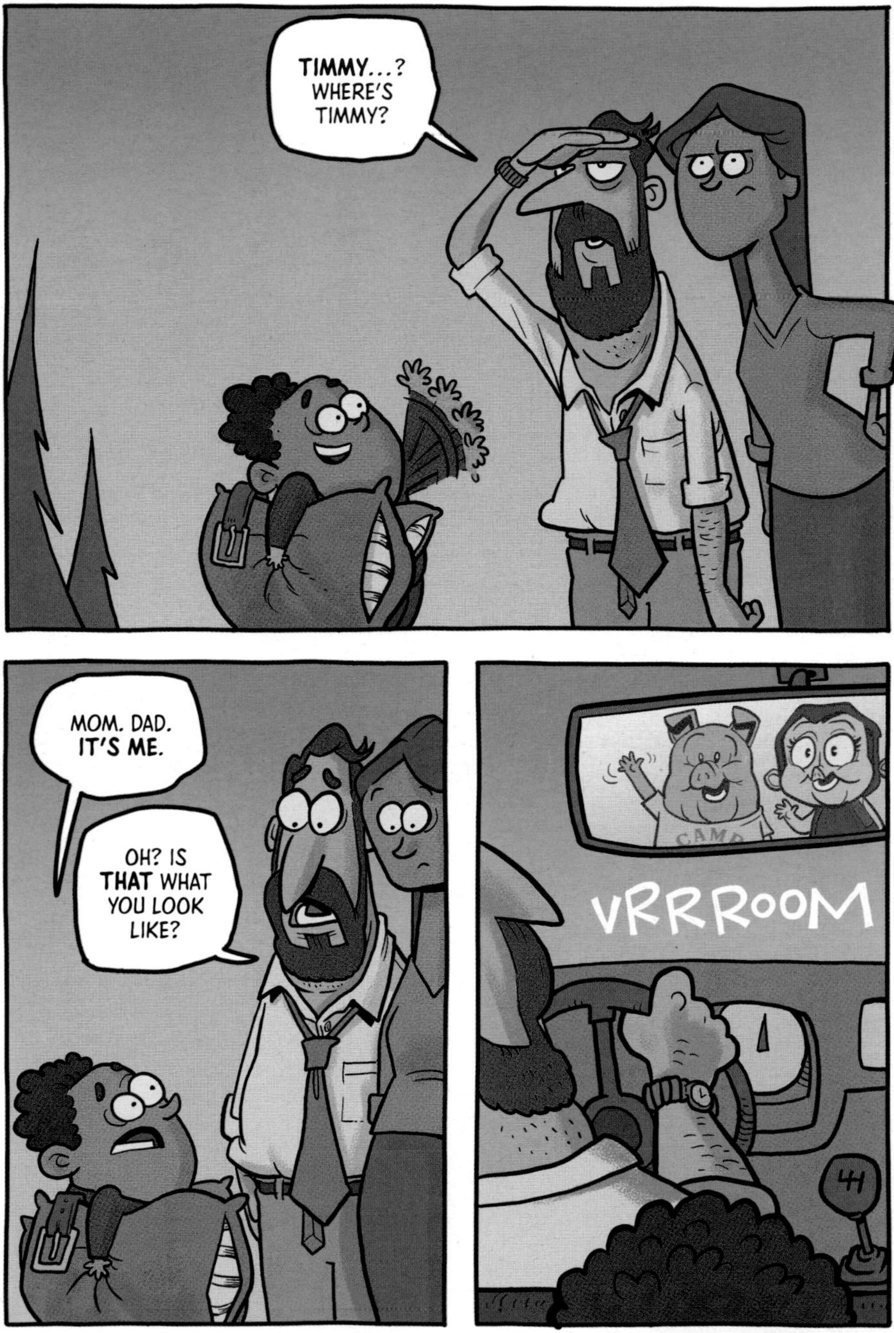
TIMMY...? WHERE'S TIMMY?
MOM. DAD. IT'S ME.
OH? IS THAT WHAT YOU LOOK LIKE?
CAMP
VRRROOM

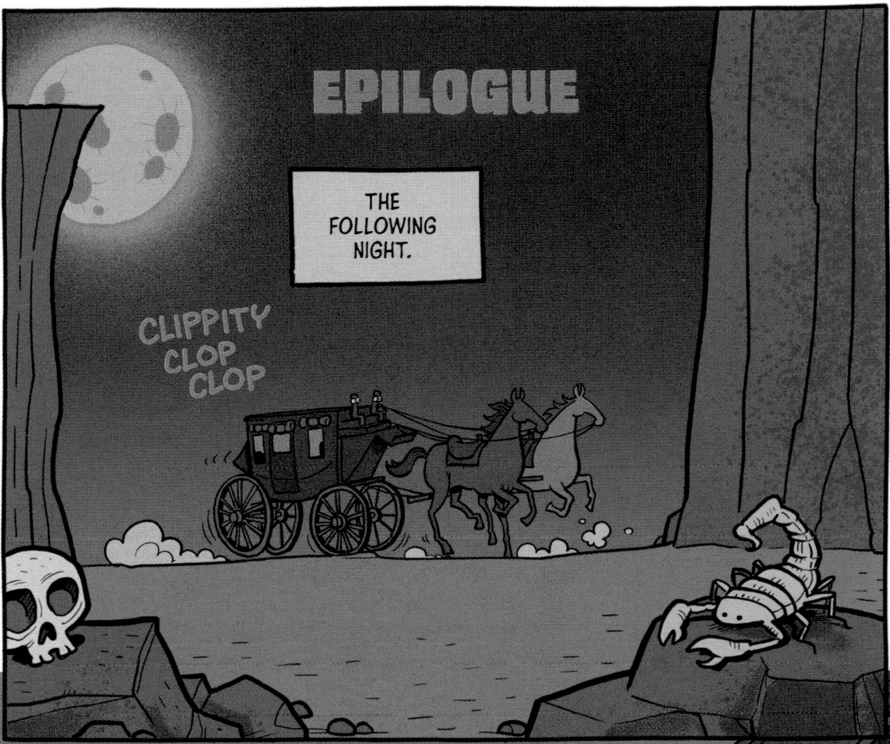
EPILOGUE
THE FOLLOWING NIGHT.
CLIPPITY CLOP CLOP
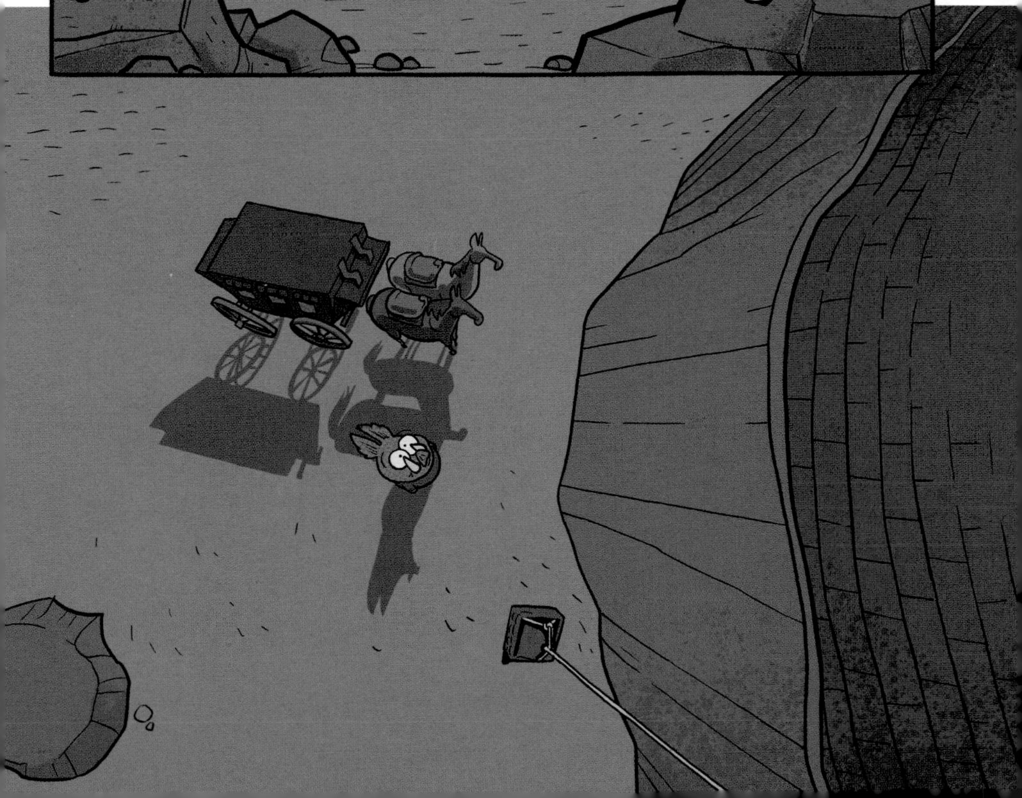

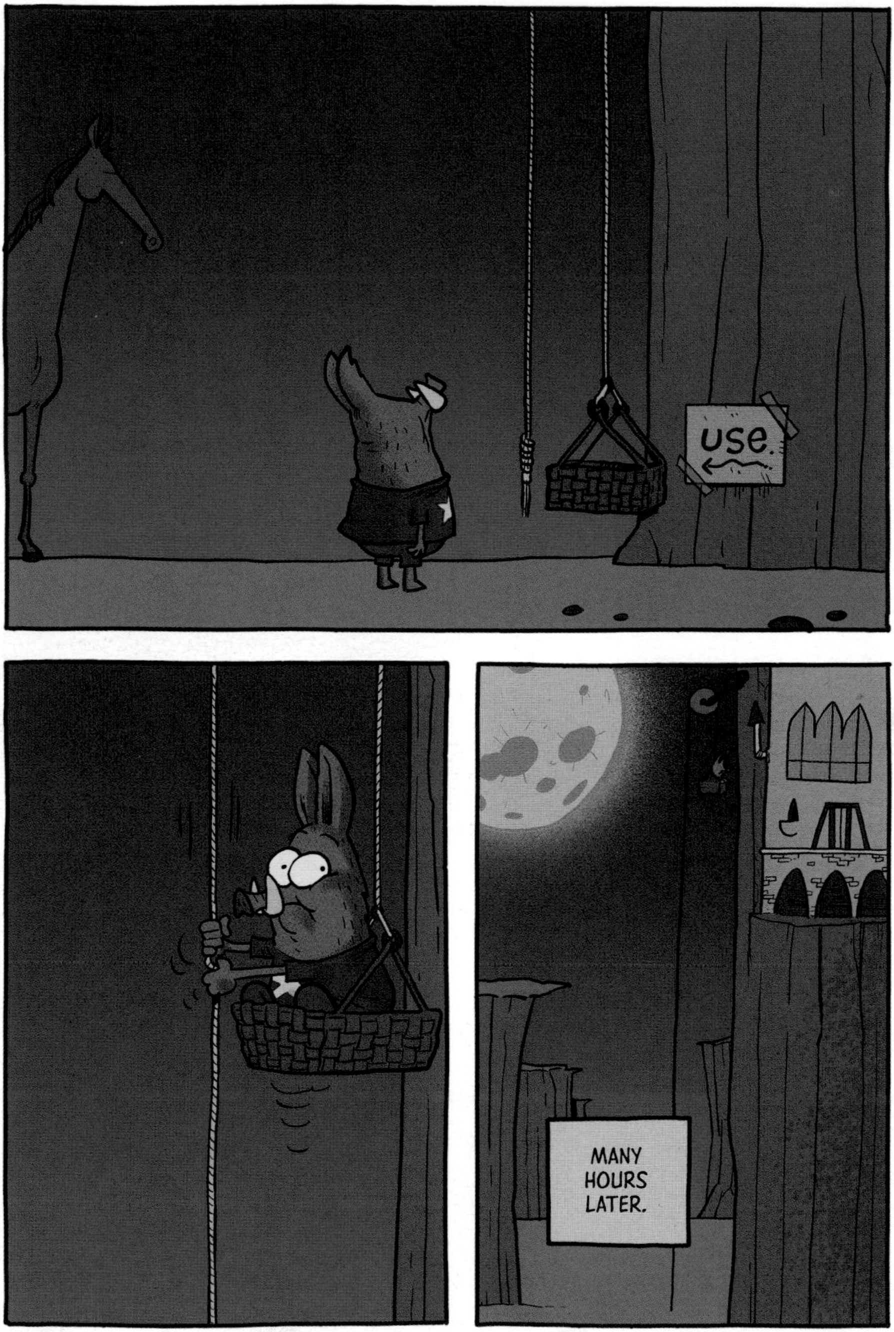
USE.
MANY HOURS LATER.

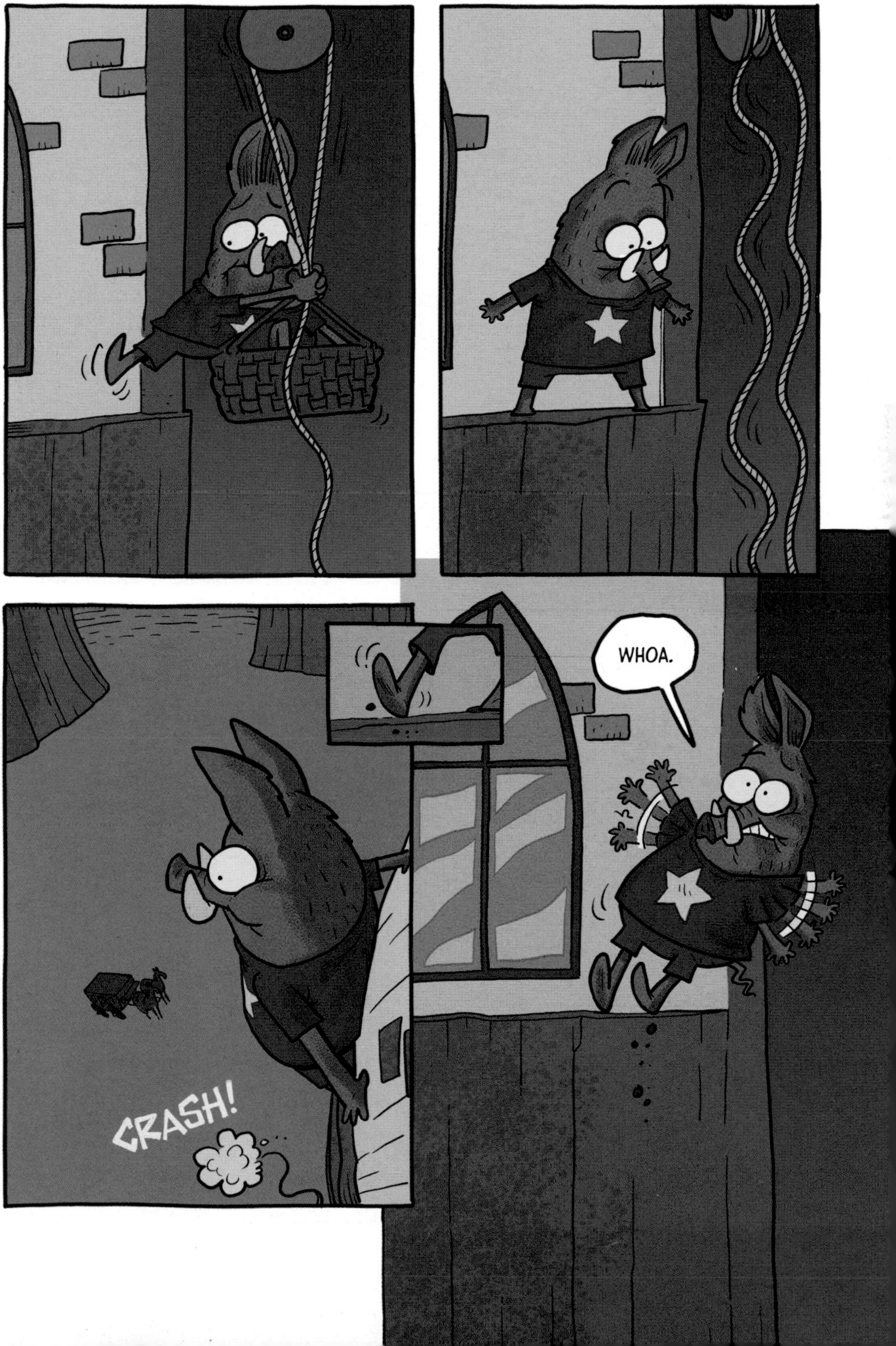
WHOA.
CRASH!

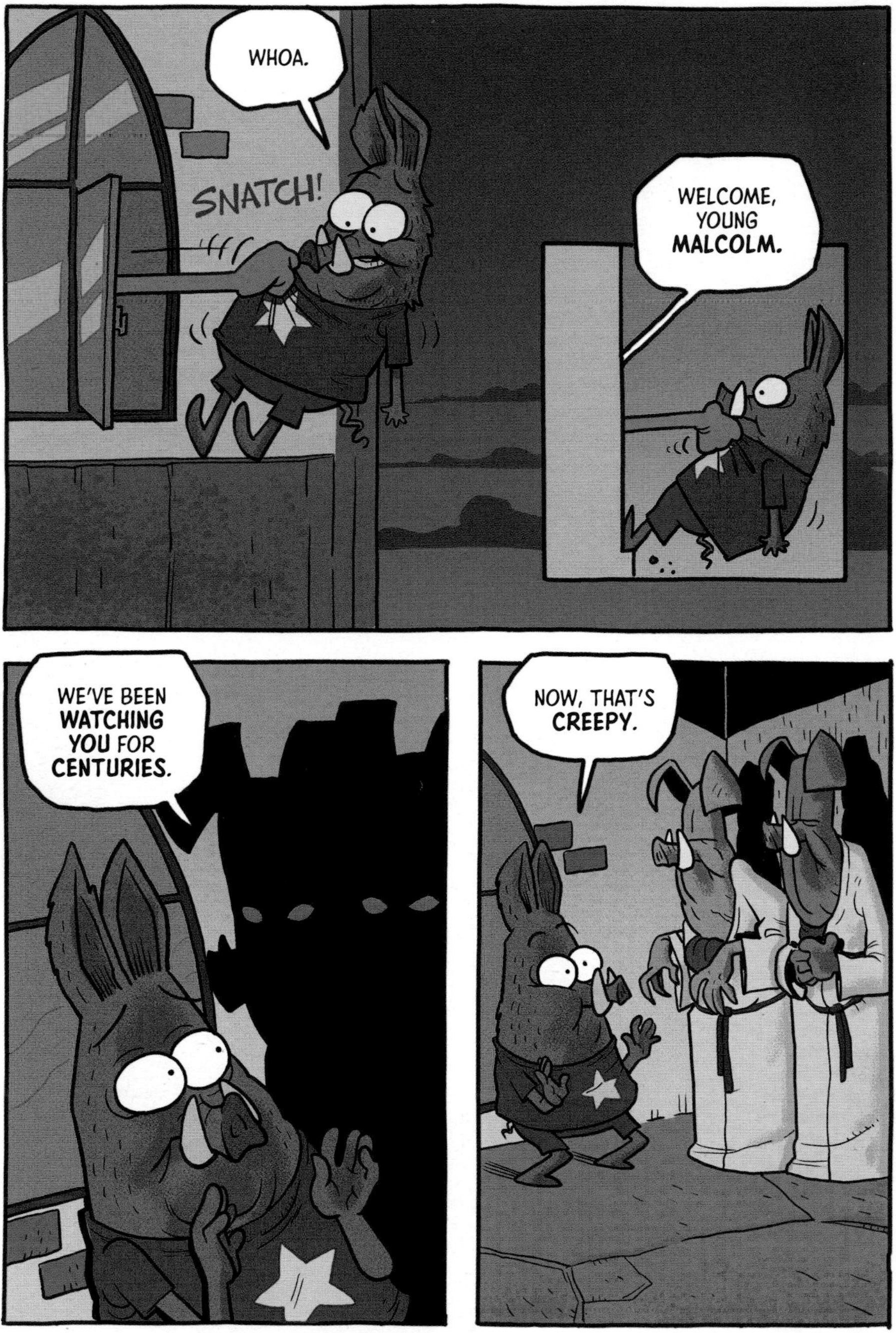
WHOA.
SNATCH!
WELCOME, YOUNG MALCOLM.
WE'VE BEEN WATCHING YOU FOR CENTURIES.
NOW, THAT'S CREEPY.

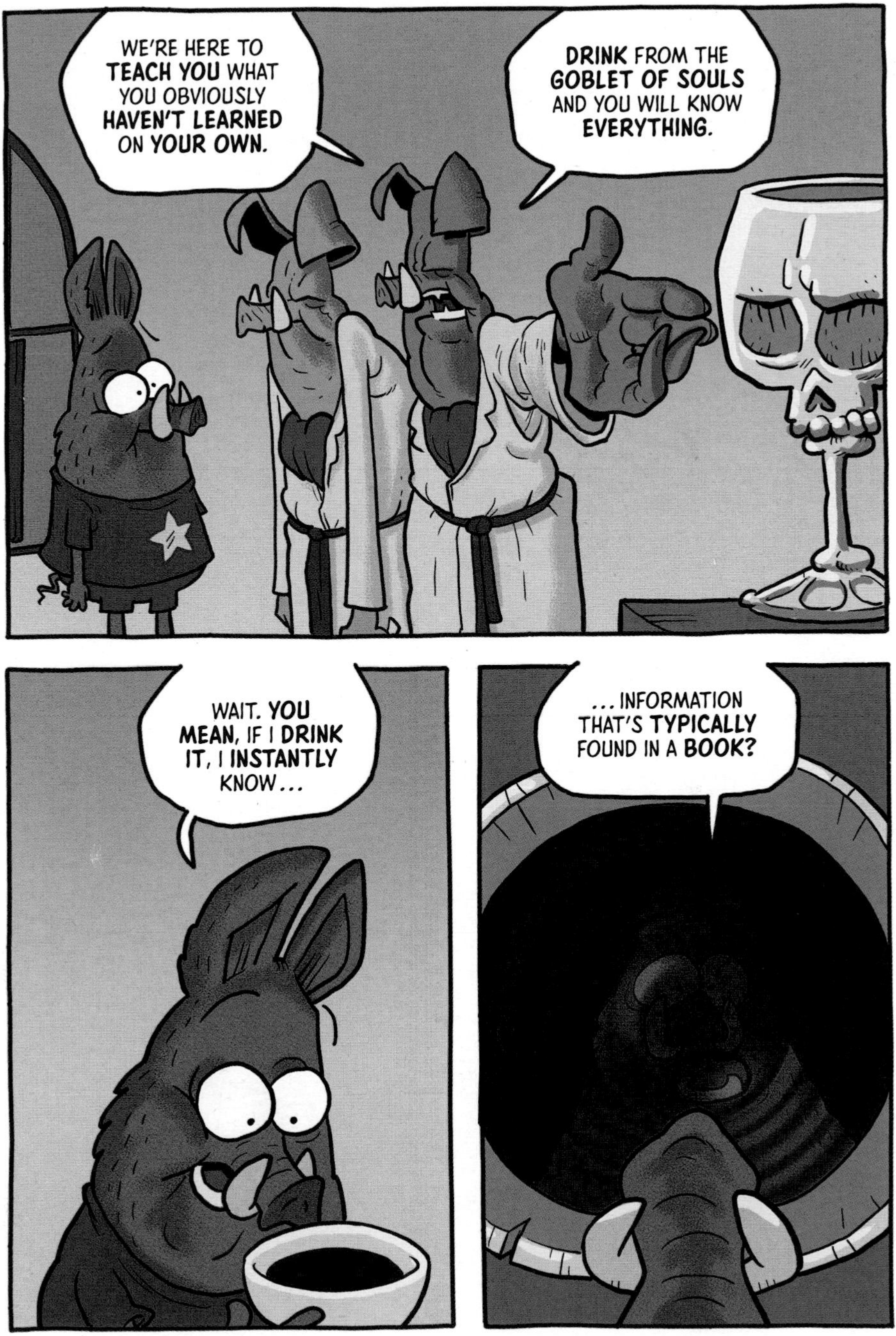
WE'RE HERE TO TEACH YOU WHAT YOU OBVIOUSLY HAVEN'T LEARNED ON YOUR OWN.
DRINK FROM THE GOBLET OF SOULS AND YOU WILL KNOW EVERYTHING.
WAIT. YOU MEAN, IF I DRINK IT, I INSTANTLY KNOW...
...INFORMATION THAT'S TYPICALLY FOUND IN A BOOK?

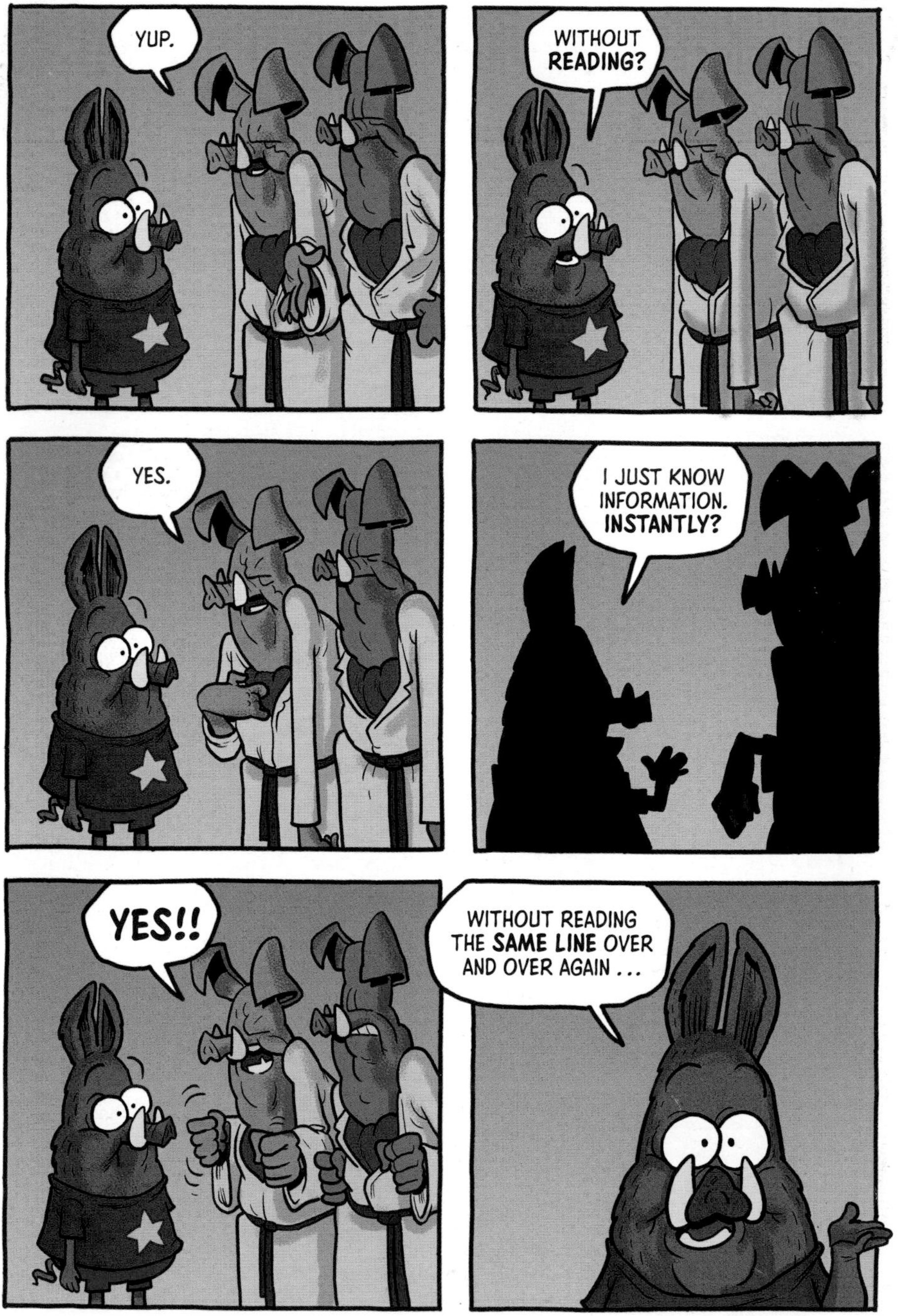
YUP.
WITHOUT **READING?**
YES.
I JUST KNOW INFORMATION. **INSTANTLY?**
YES!!
WITHOUT READING THE **SAME LINE** OVER AND OVER AGAIN . . .

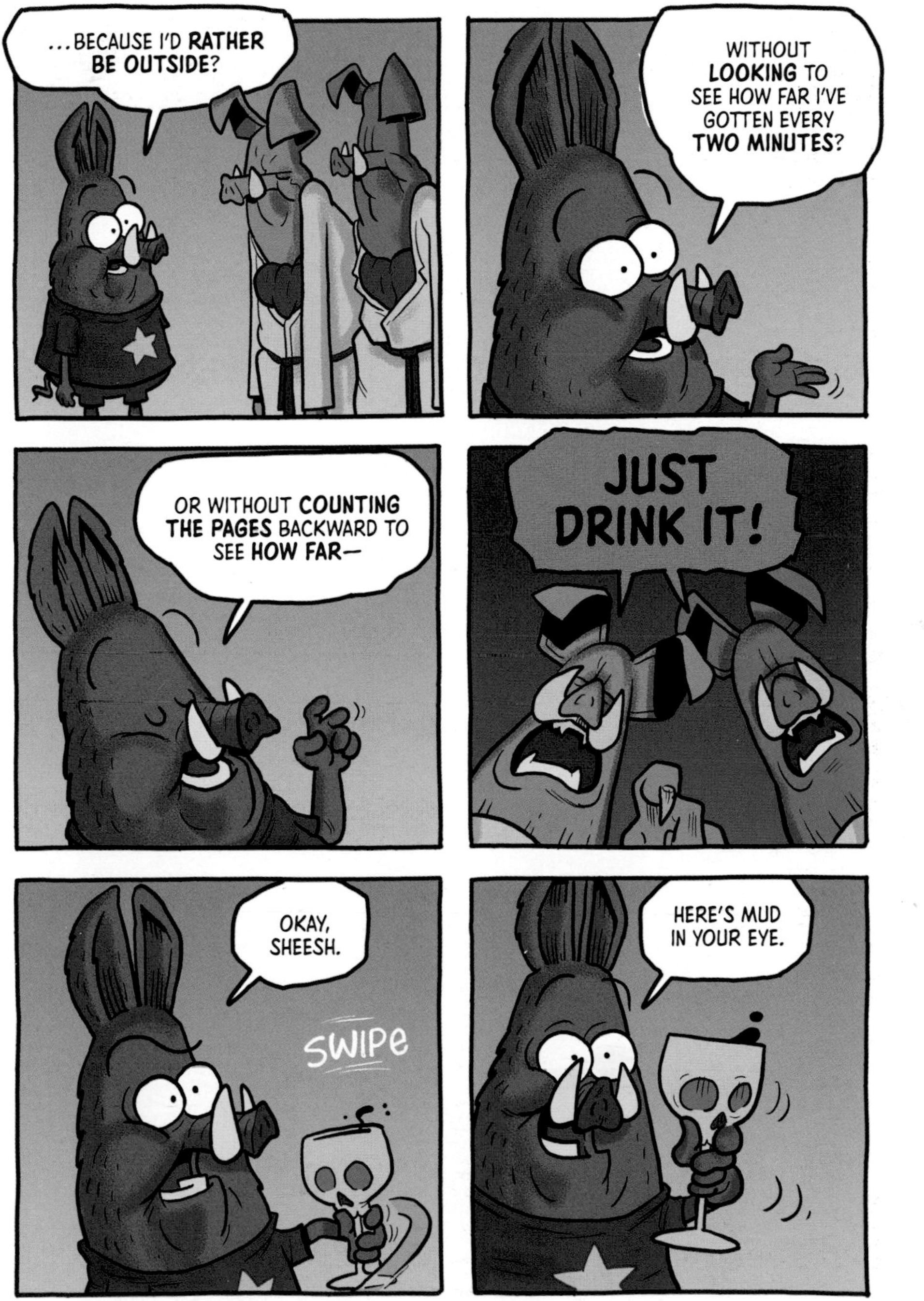
...BECAUSE I'D RATHER BE OUTSIDE?
WITHOUT LOOKING TO SEE HOW FAR I'VE GOTTEN EVERY TWO MINUTES?
OR WITHOUT COUNTING THE PAGES BACKWARD TO SEE HOW FAR—
JUST DRINK IT!
OKAY, SHEESH.
SWIPE
HERE'S MUD IN YOUR EYE.

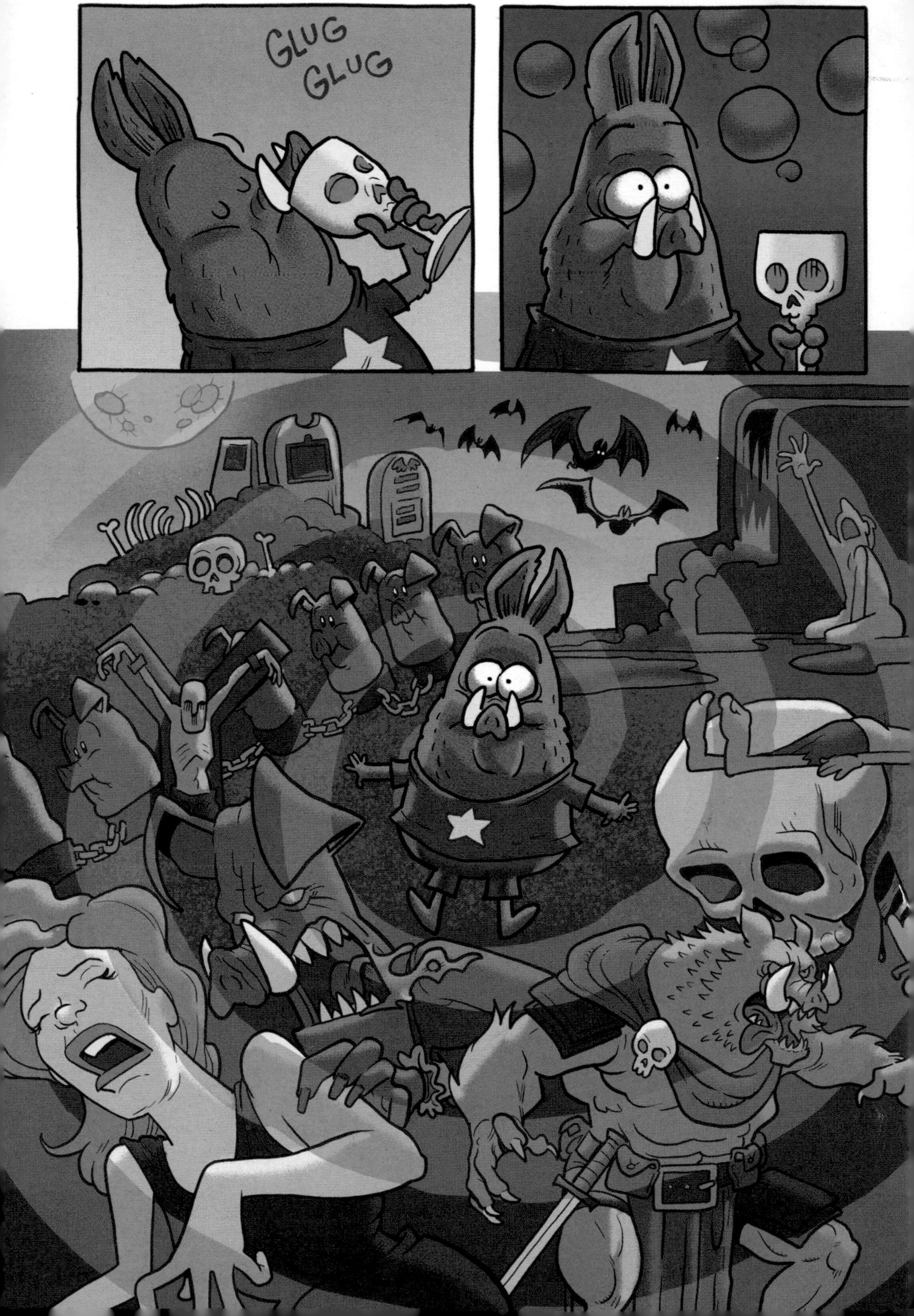
GLUG
GLUG

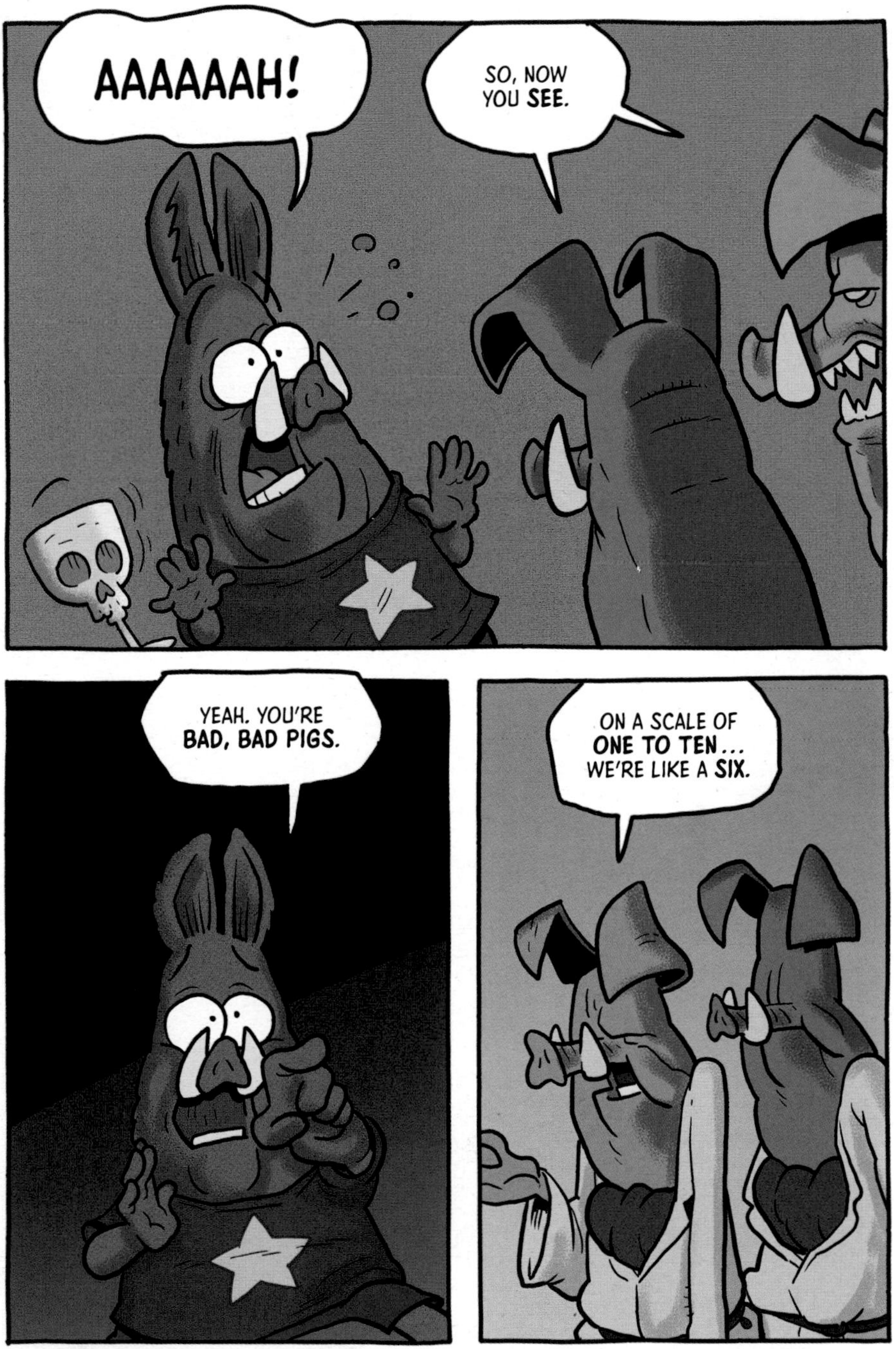
AAAAAAH!
SO, NOW YOU **SEE**.
YEAH. YOU'RE **BAD, BAD PIGS.**
ON A SCALE OF **ONE TO TEN...** WE'RE LIKE A **SIX**.

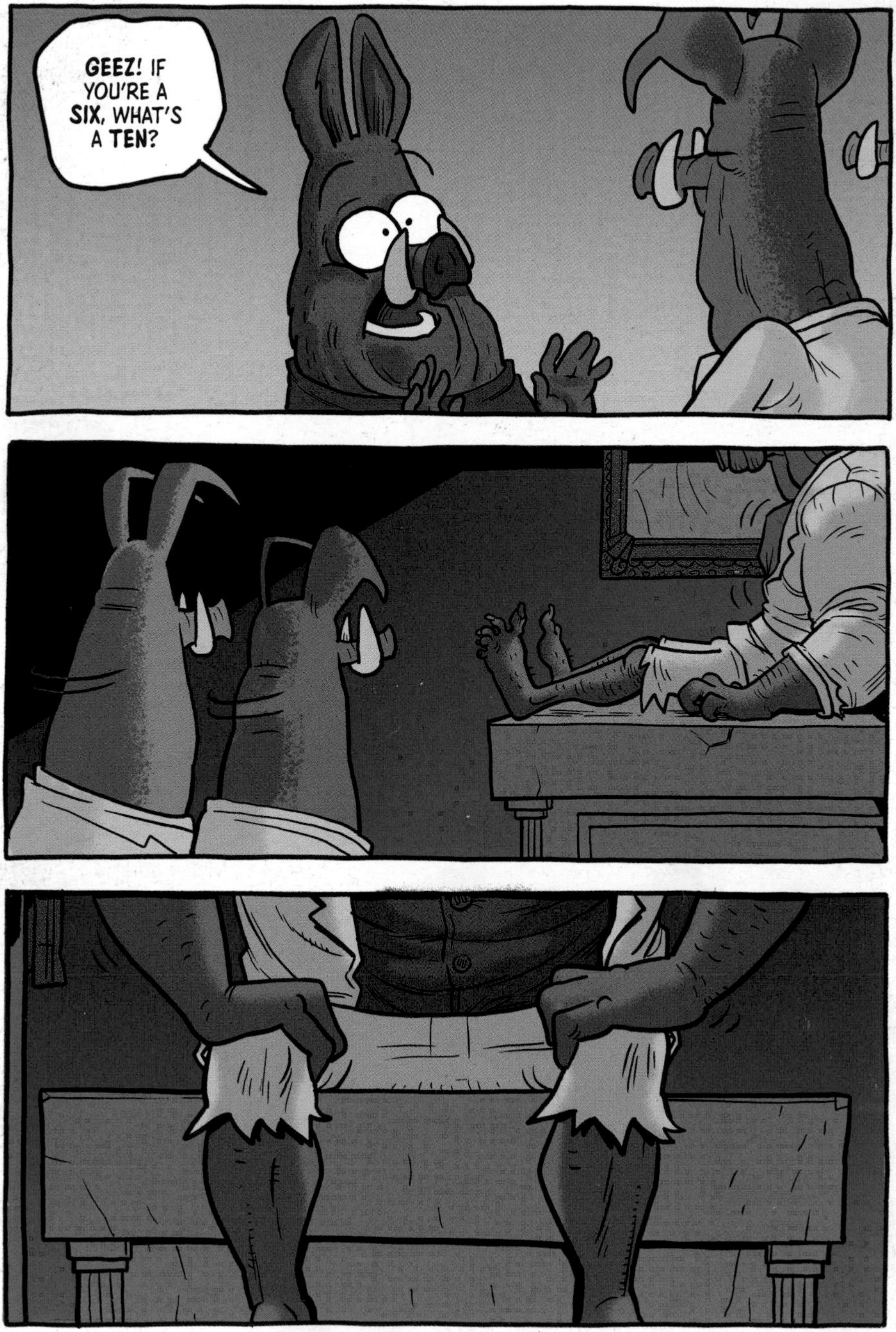
GEEZ! IF YOU'RE A SIX, WHAT'S A TEN?

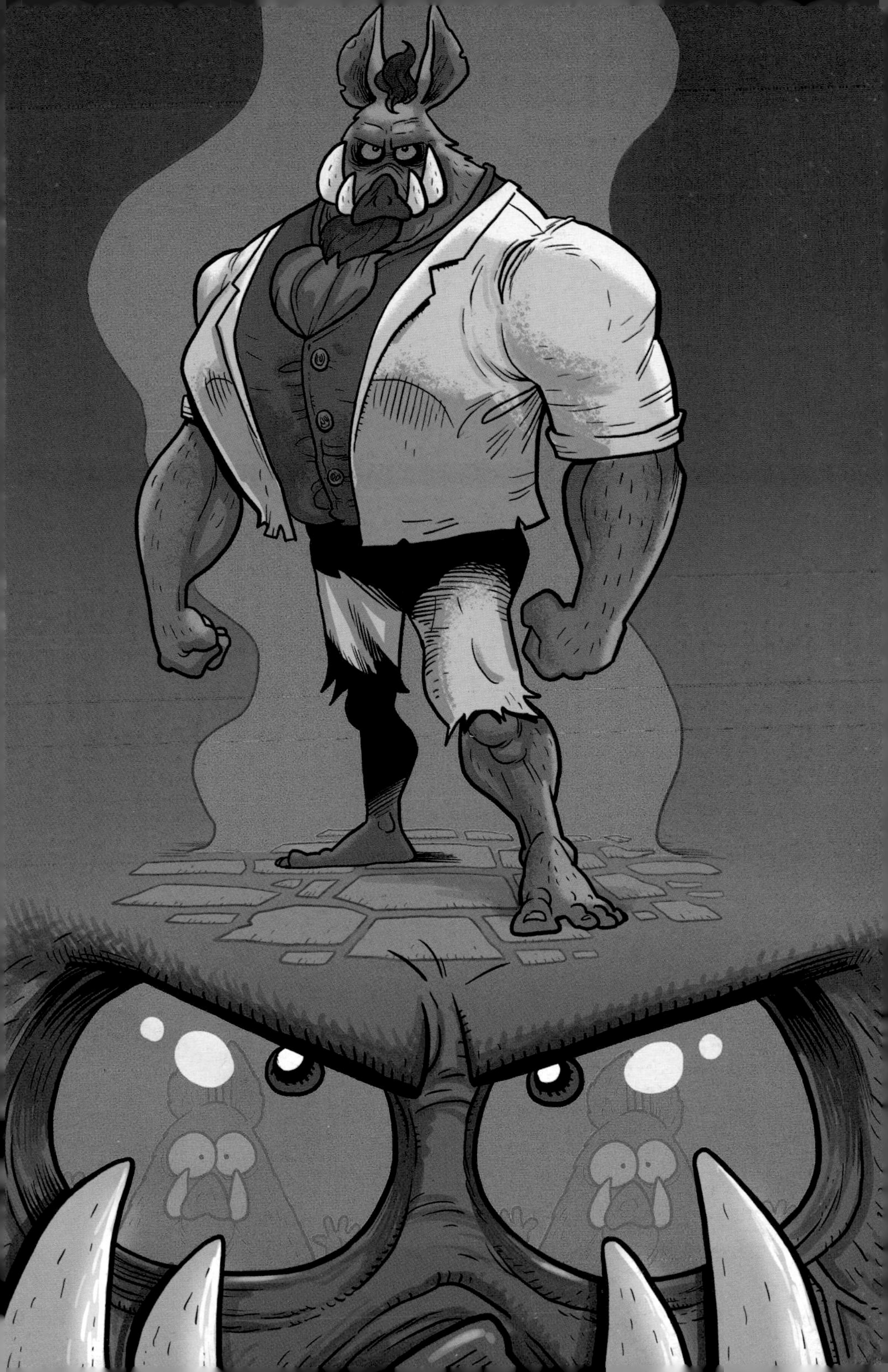

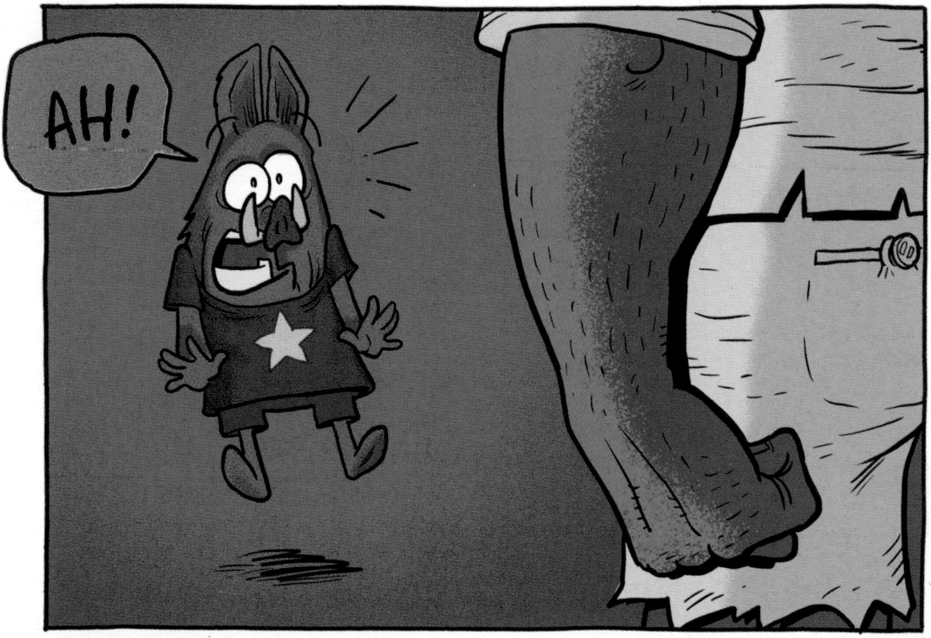
AH!

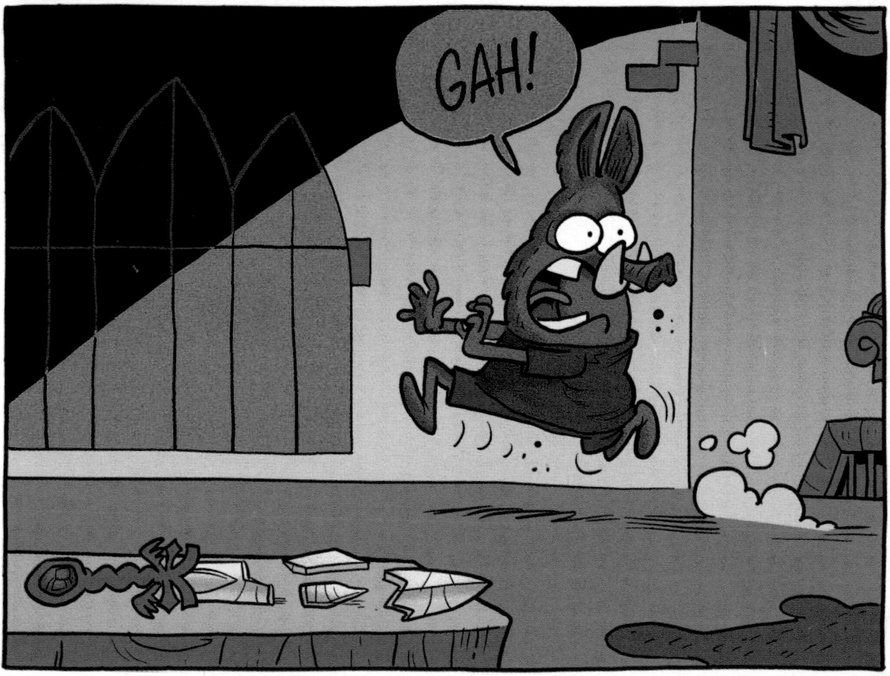
GAH!

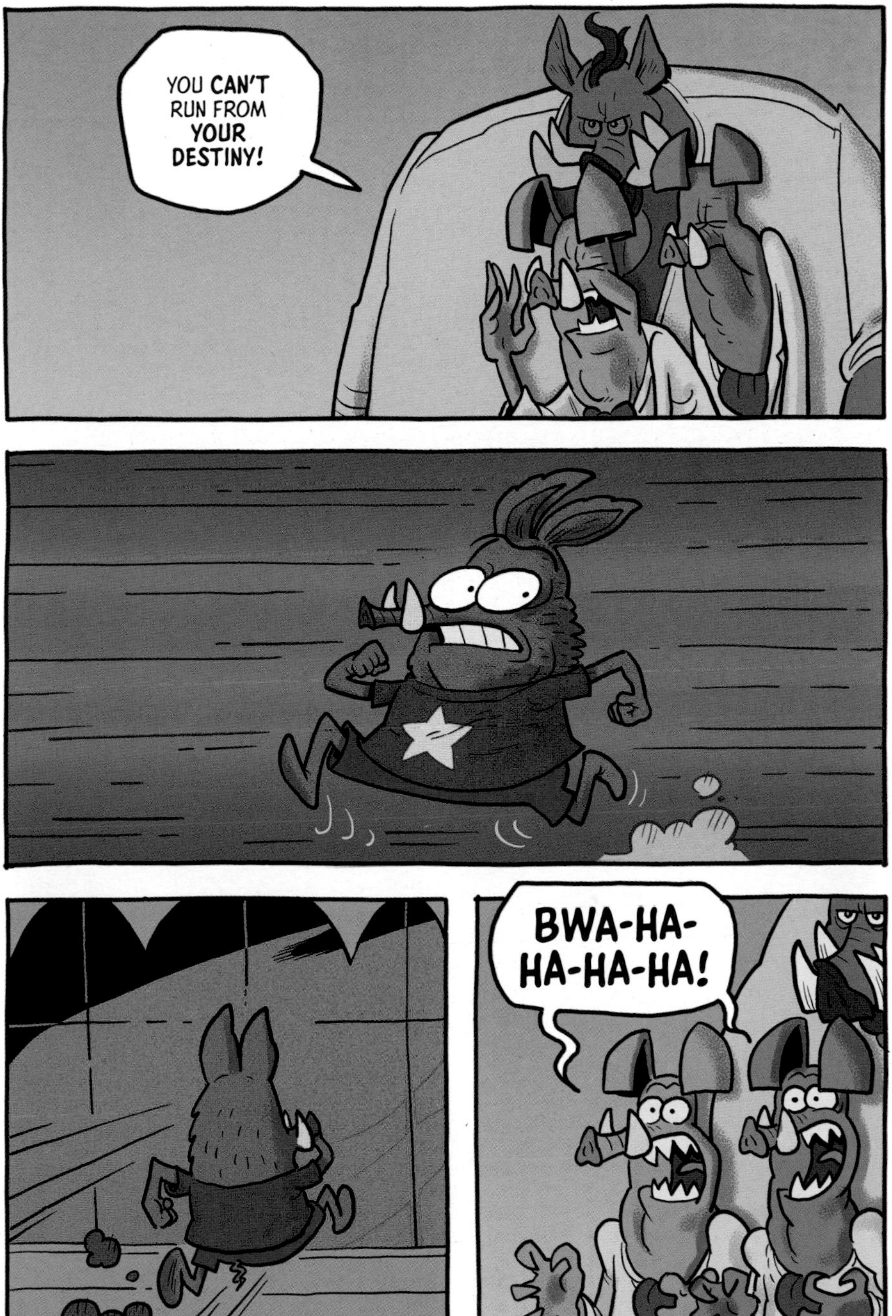
YOU CAN'T RUN FROM YOUR DESTINY!
BWA-HA-HA-HA-HA!

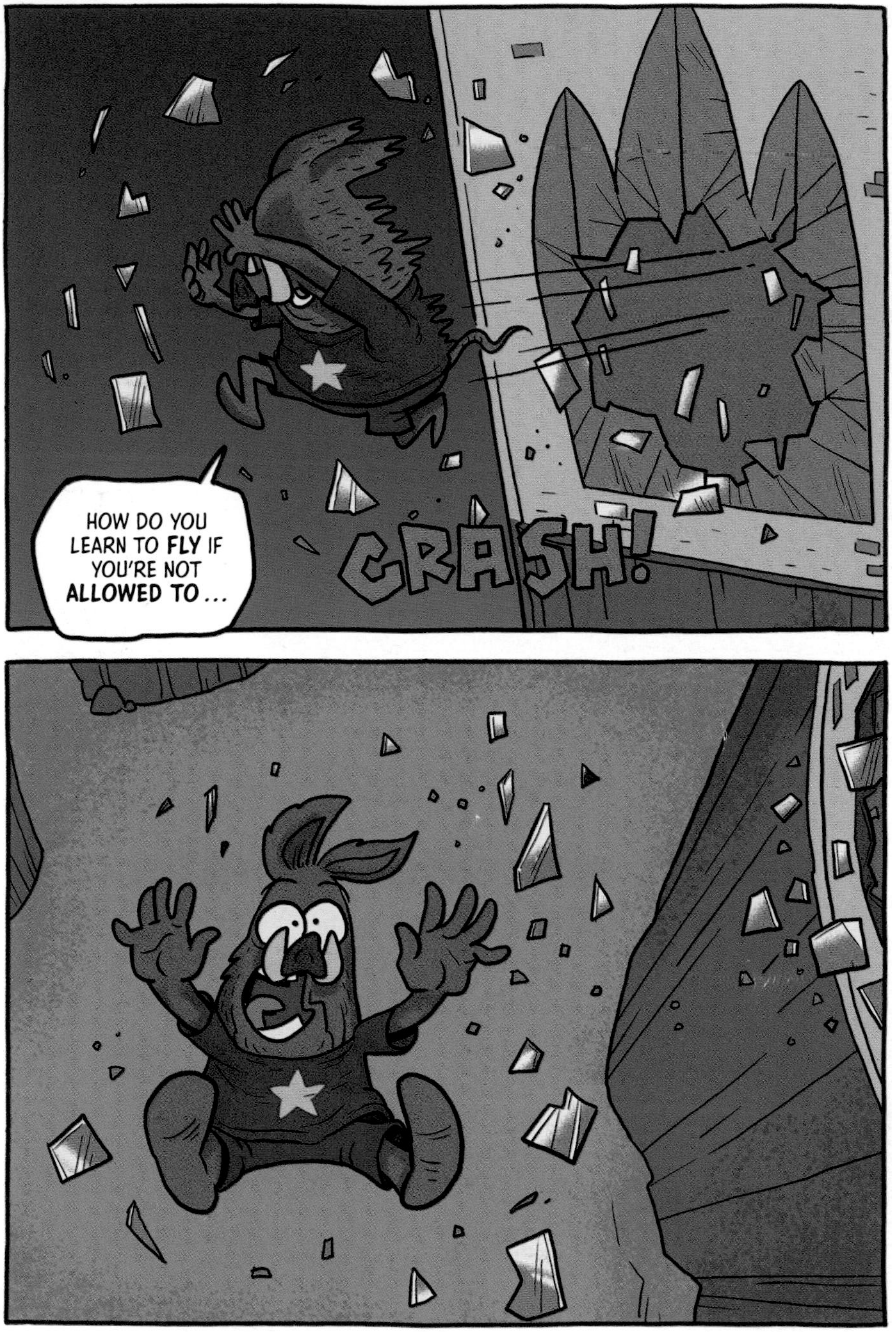
HOW DO YOU LEARN TO **FLY** IF YOU'RE NOT **ALLOWED TO . . .**
CRASH!

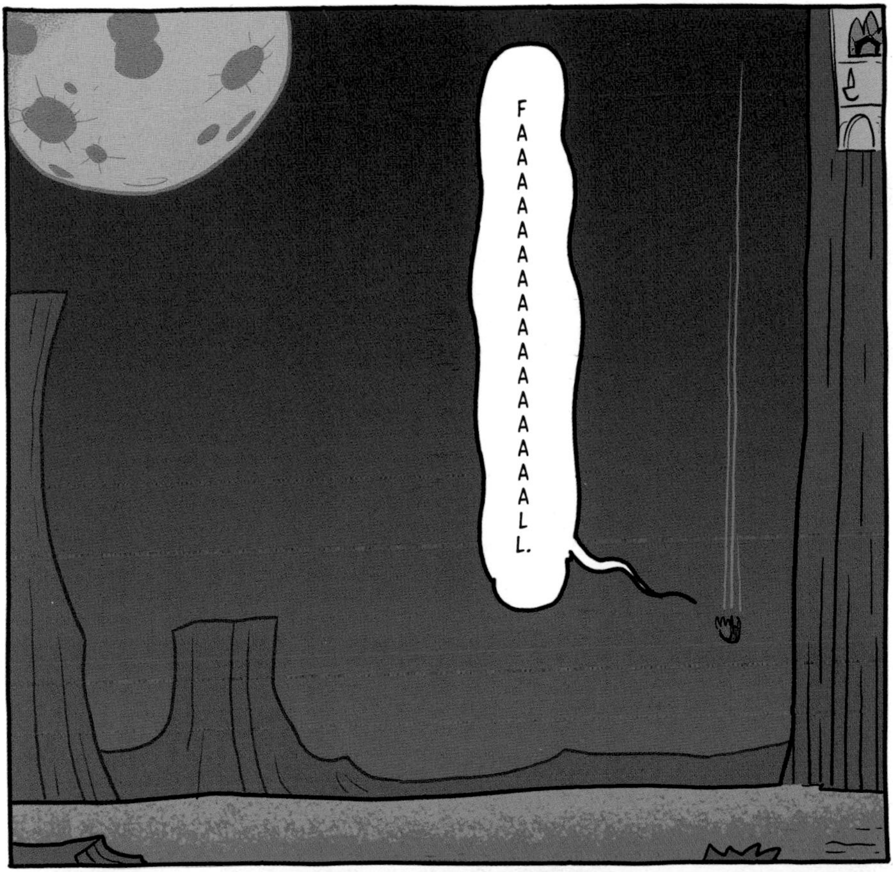
FAAAAAAAAAAAAAAAAAAALL.

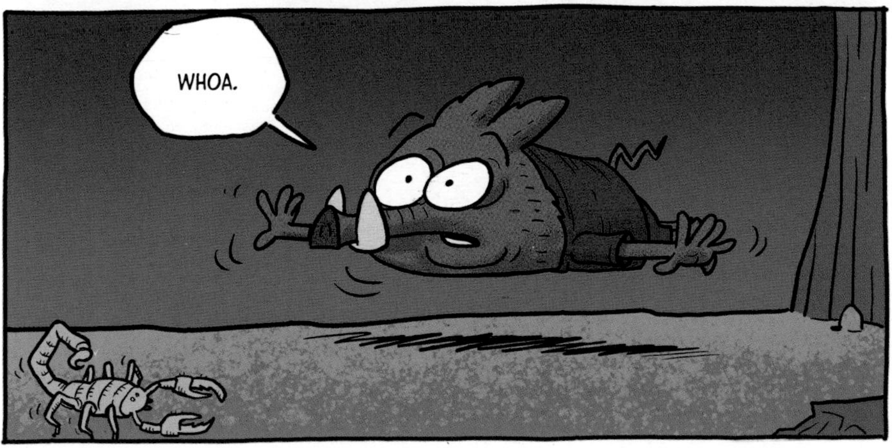
WHOA.

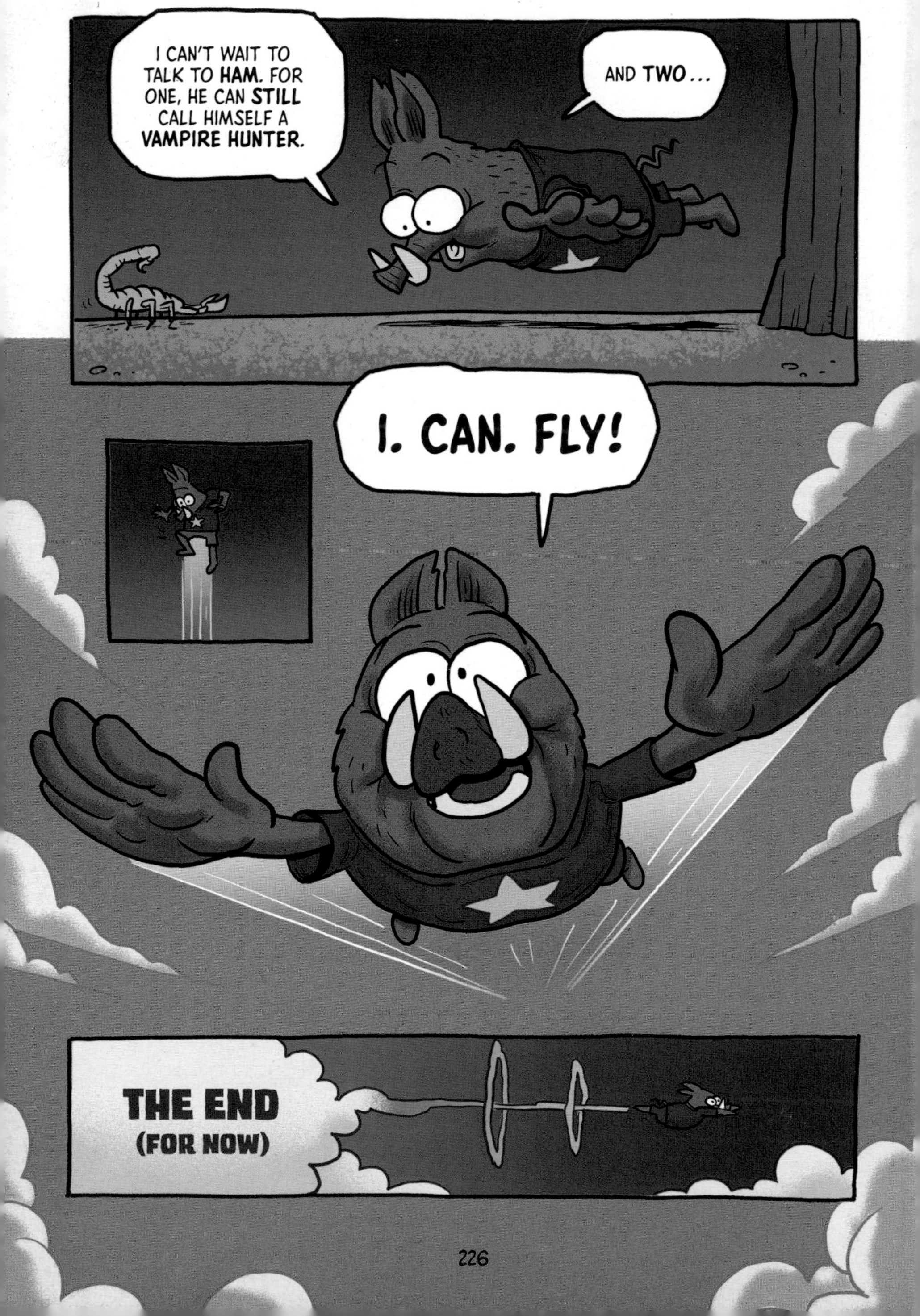
I CAN'T WAIT TO TALK TO HAM. FOR ONE, HE CAN STILL CALL HIMSELF A VAMPIRE HUNTER.
AND TWO...
I. CAN. FLY!
THE END (FOR NOW)

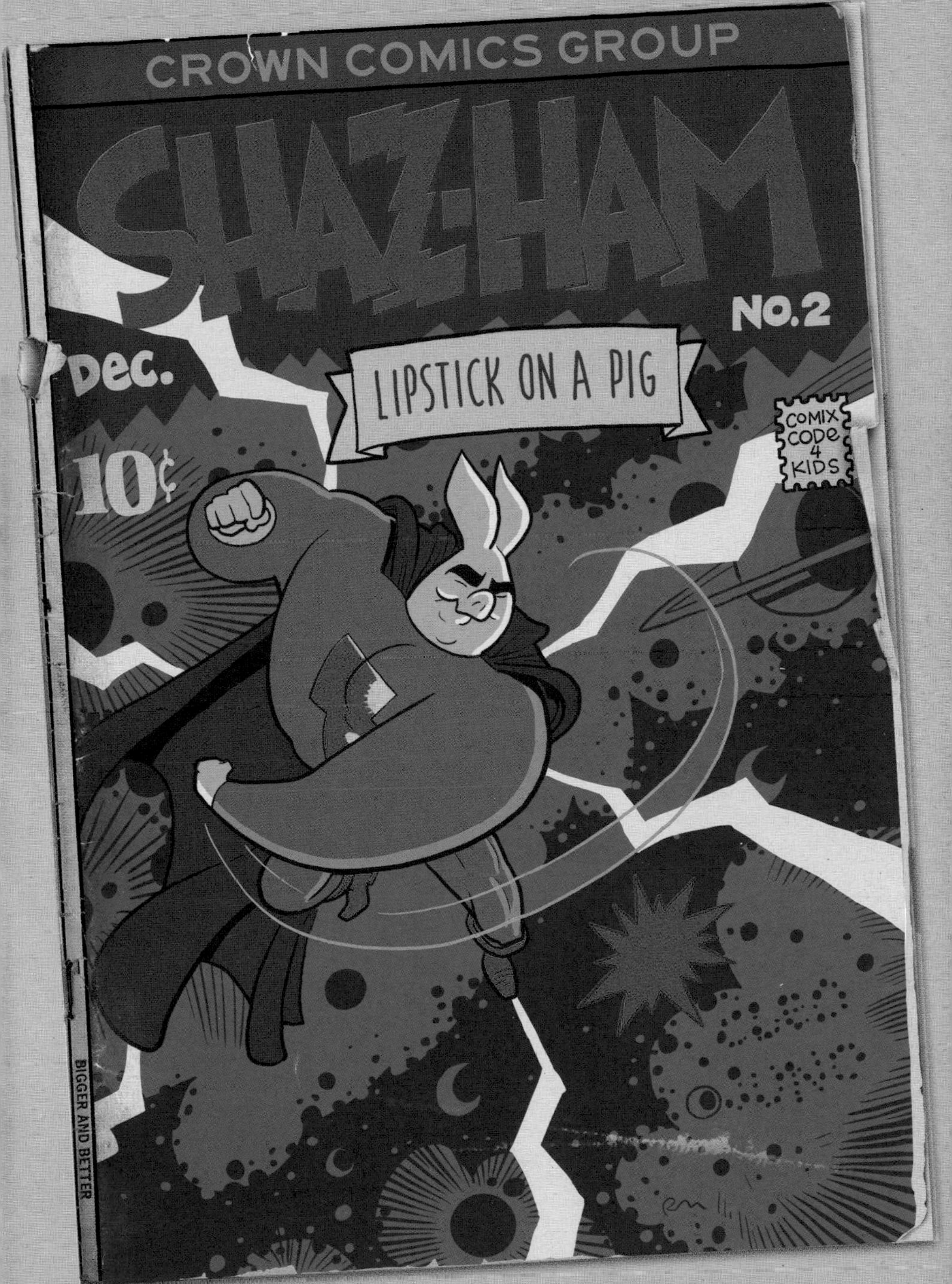
CROWN COMICS GROUP
SHAZ-HAM
NO. 2
DEC.
LIPSTICK ON A PIG
10¢
COMIX CODE 4 KIDS
BIGGER AND BETTER

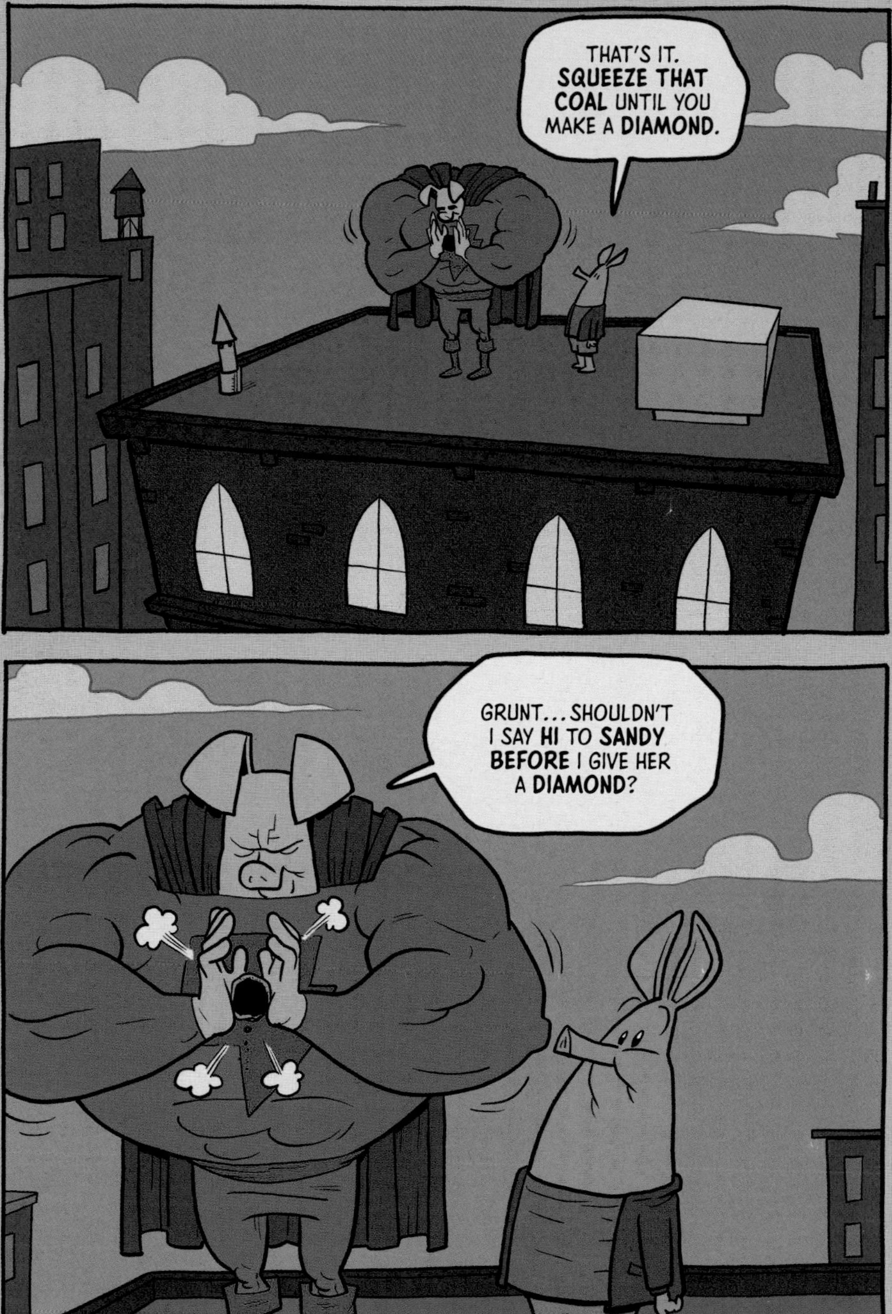
THAT'S IT. SQUEEZE THAT COAL UNTIL YOU MAKE A DIAMOND.
GRUNT... SHOULDN'T I SAY HI TO SANDY BEFORE I GIVE HER A DIAMOND?

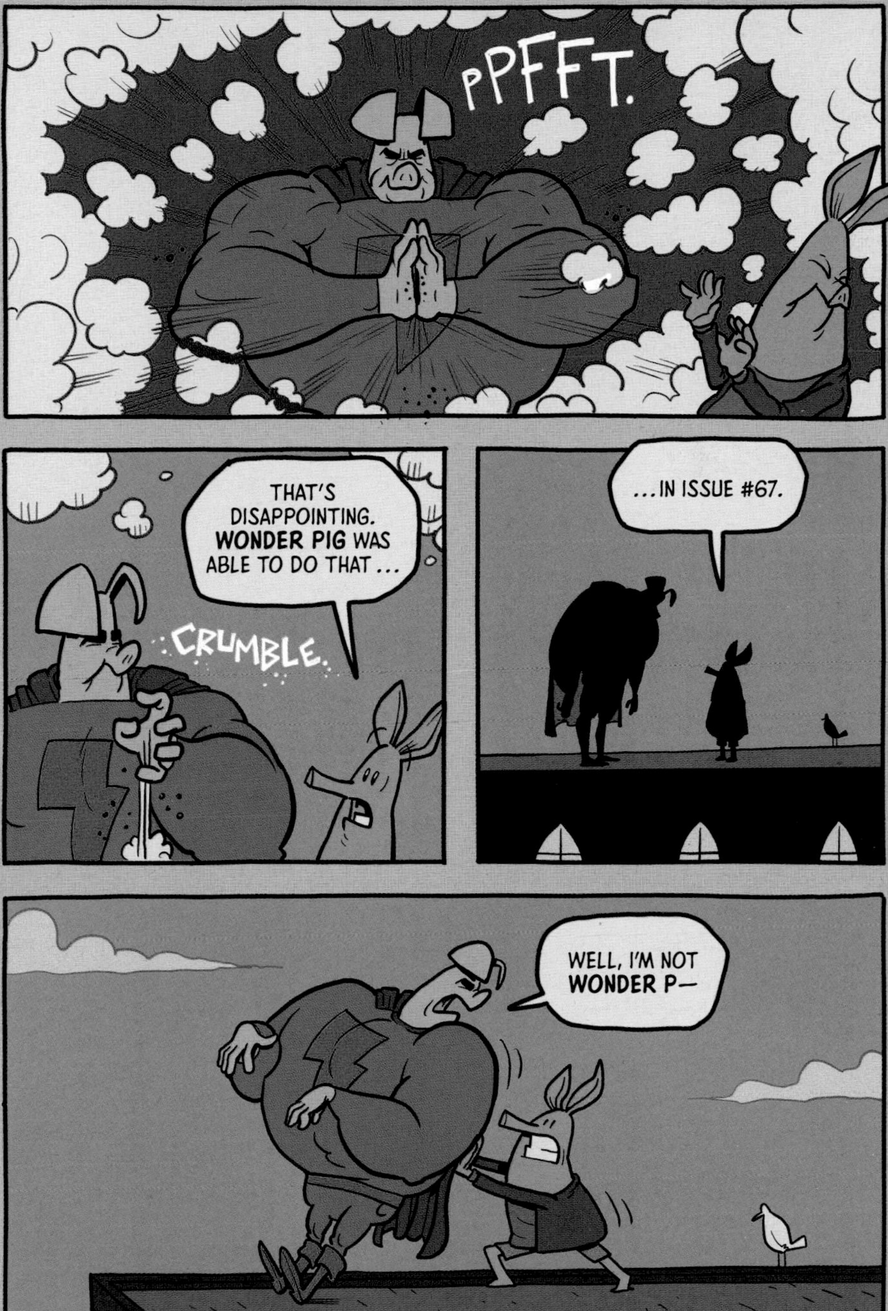
PPFFT.
THAT'S DISAPPOINTING. **WONDER PIG** WAS ABLE TO DO THAT ...
CRUMBLE.
...IN ISSUE #67.
WELL, I'M NOT **WONDER P—**

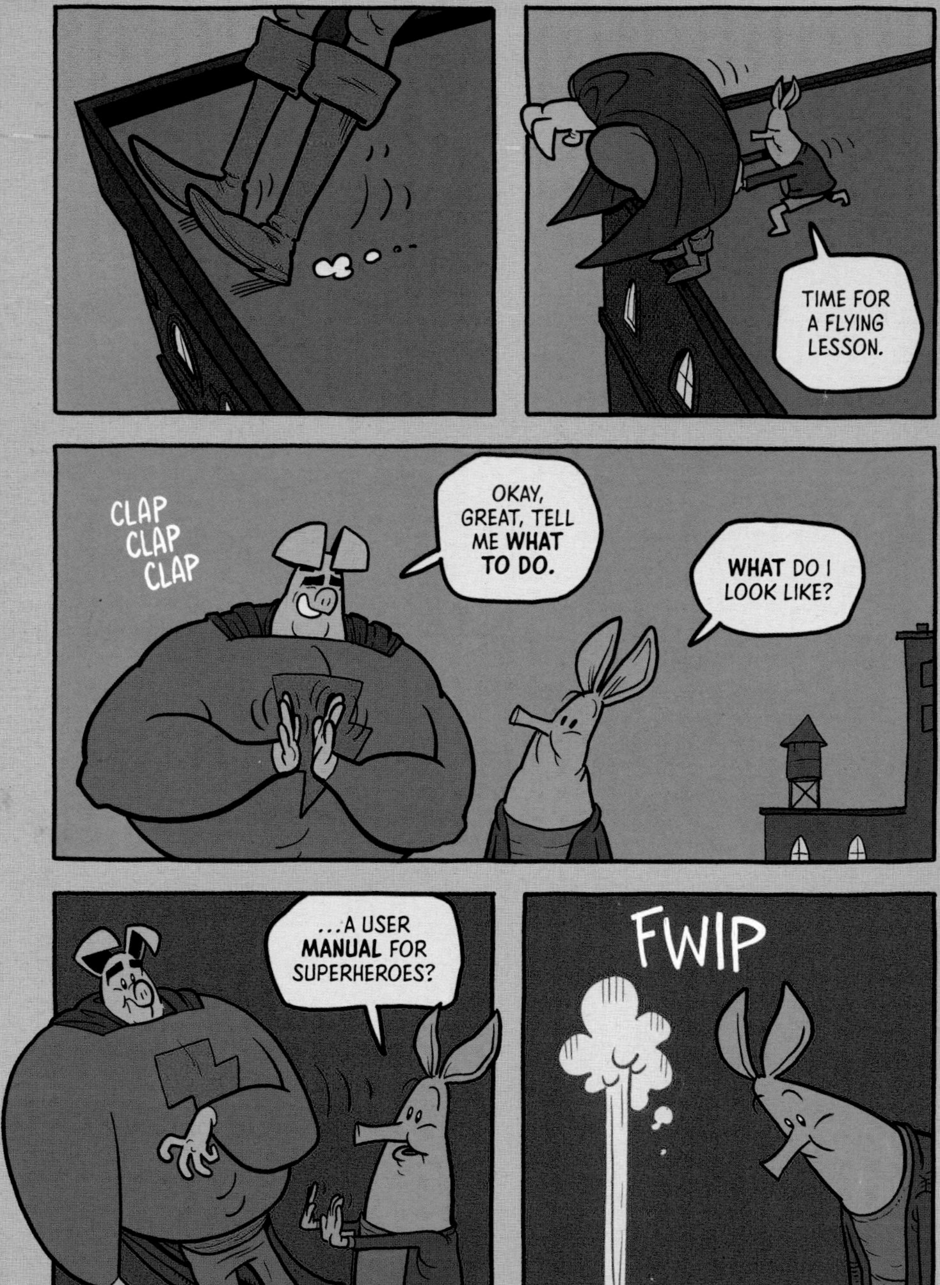
TIME FOR A FLYING LESSON.
CLAP CLAP CLAP
OKAY, GREAT, TELL ME WHAT TO DO.
WHAT DO I LOOK LIKE?
...A USER MANUAL FOR SUPERHEROES?
FWIP

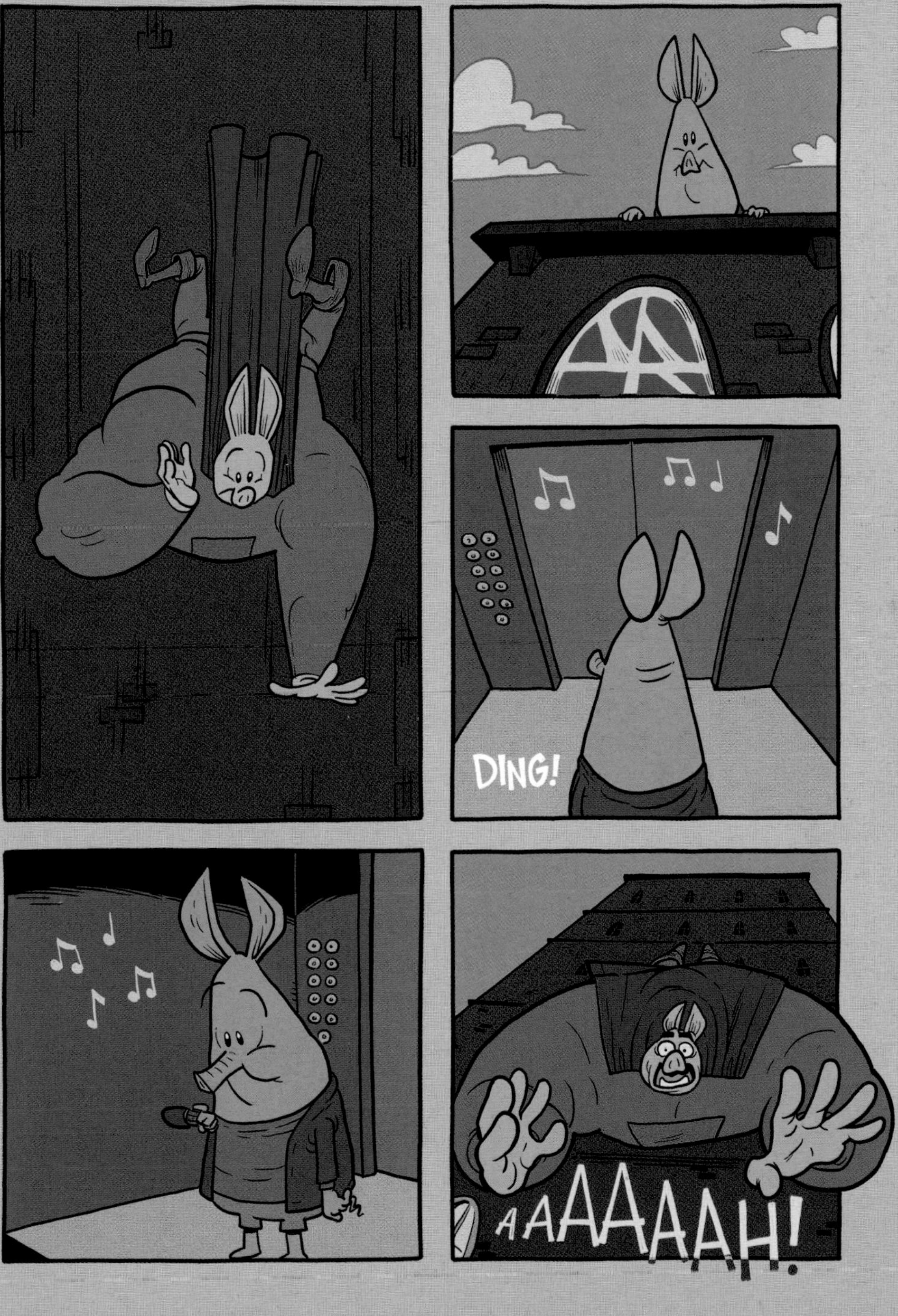
DING!
AAAAAAH!

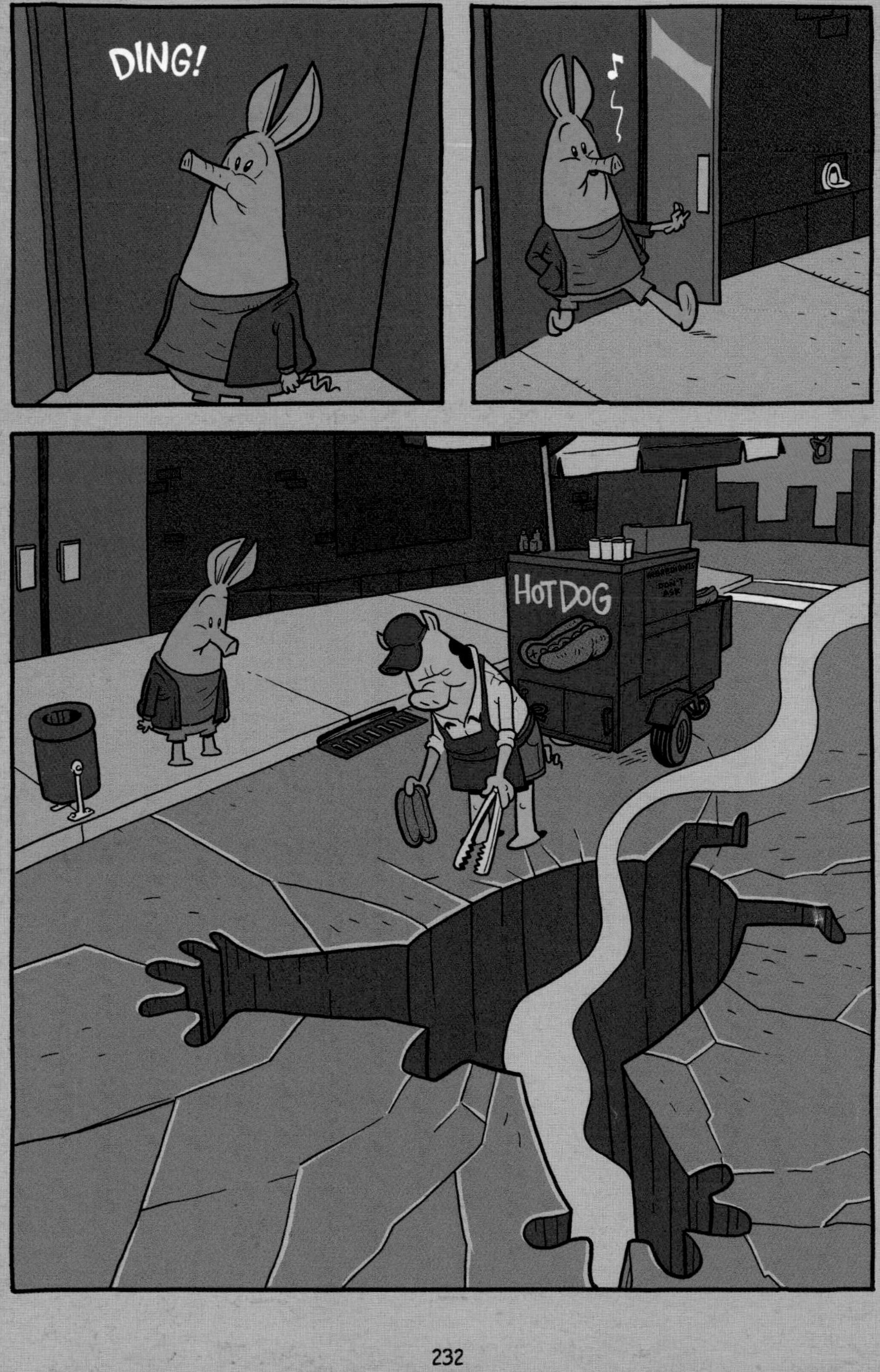
DING!
HOT DOG
DON'T ASK

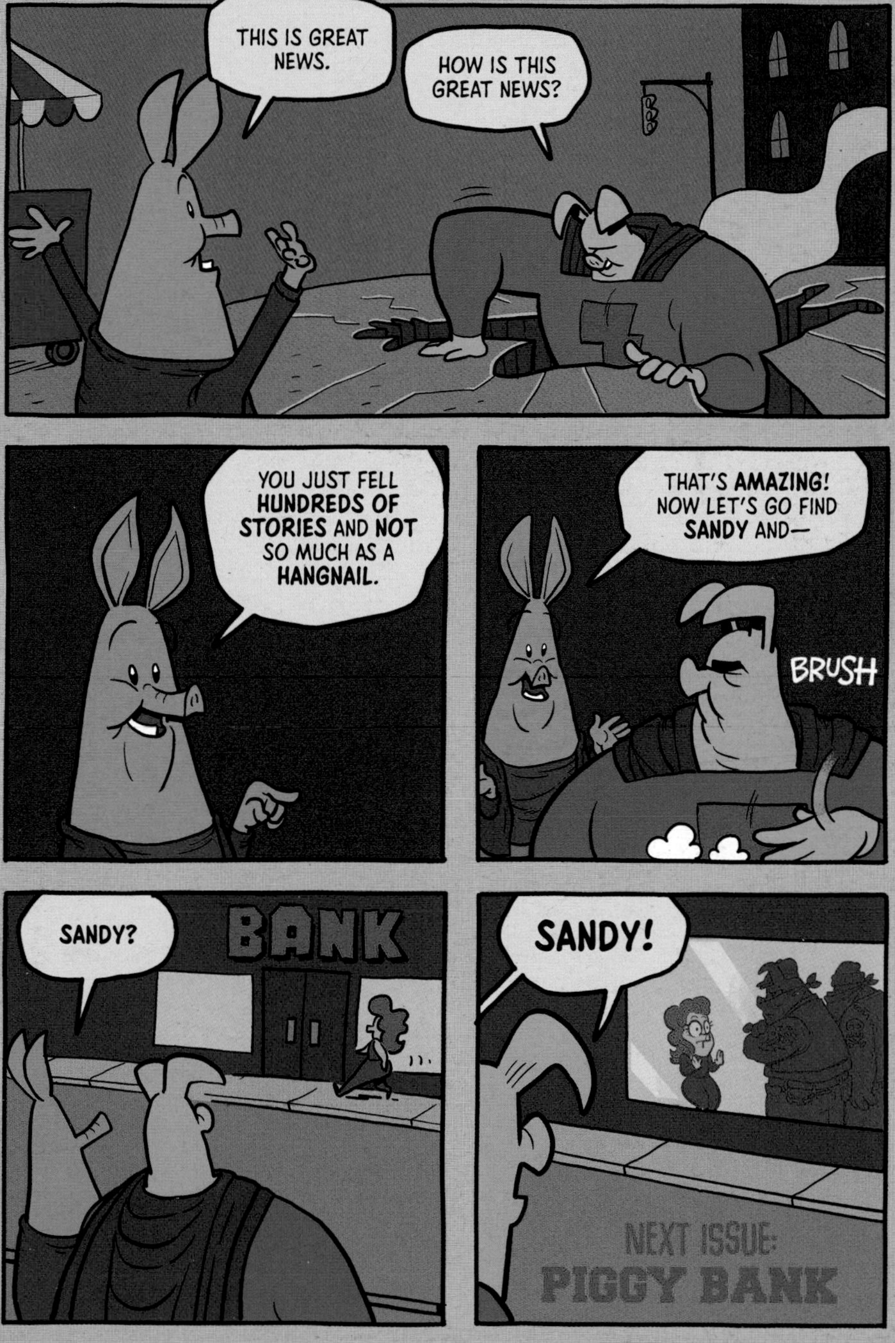
THIS IS GREAT NEWS.
HOW IS THIS GREAT NEWS?
YOU JUST FELL HUNDREDS OF STORIES AND NOT SO MUCH AS A HANGNAIL.
THAT'S AMAZING! NOW LET'S GO FIND SANDY AND—
BRUSH
SANDY?
BANK
SANDY!
NEXT ISSUE:
PIGGY BANK

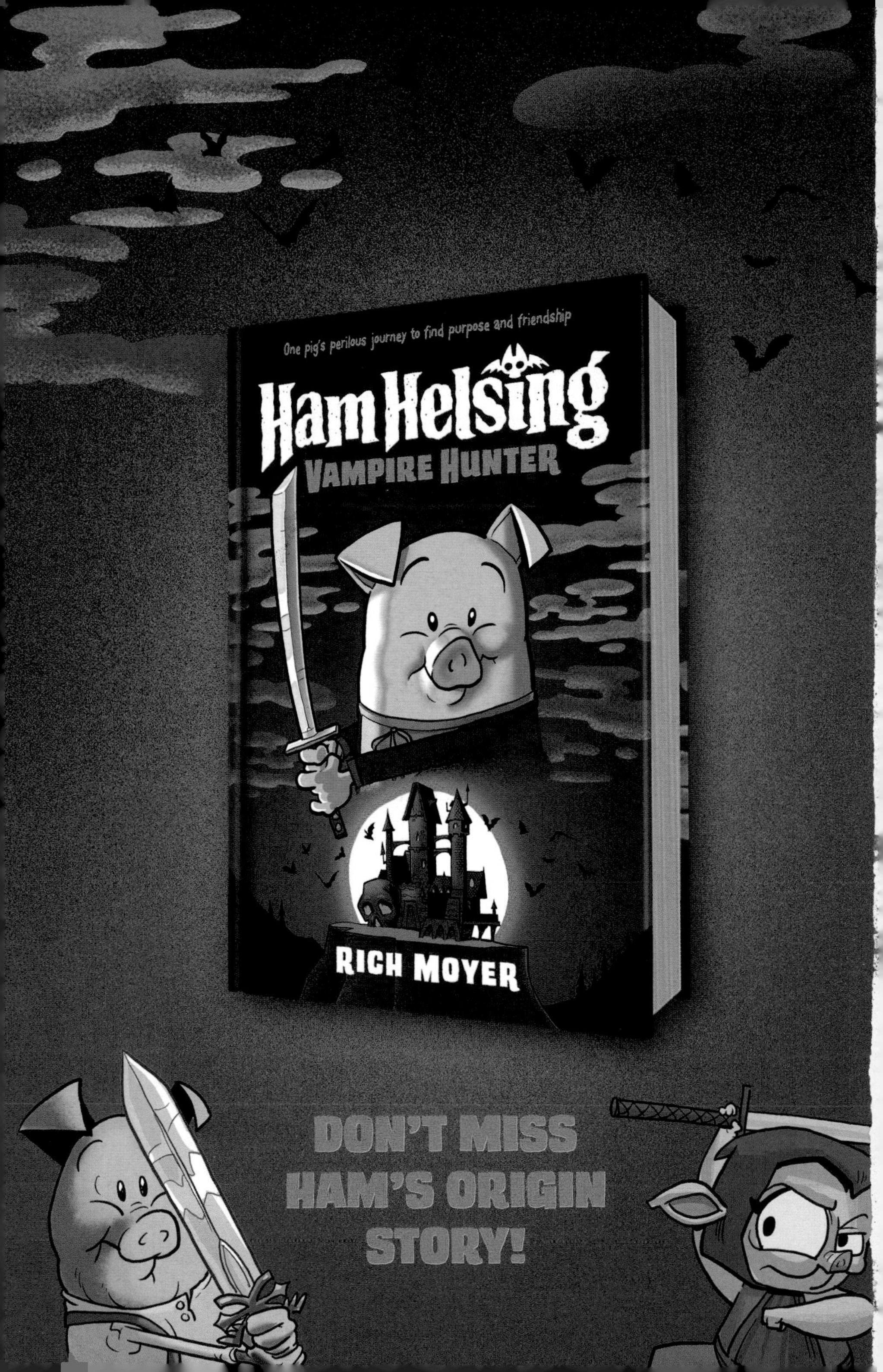

One pig's perilous journey to find purpose and friendship
Ham Helsing
Vampire Hunter
Rich Moyer
DON'T MISS HAM'S ORIGIN STORY!